VACANCY...

Ahead of the ship the star Lacoste already showed a visible naked-eye disk. *"We made it! there it is,"* the woman said.

And there it was. The molten-gold disk lay at the center of the forward screen. The man eased his way to her side.

"Let's take a look for oxygen atmospheres before we wake anyone else," she went on. The on-board computer responded: *One oxygen world, life probability 0.92.* The field of view zoomed and swung and a new pinpoint of light appeared at the screen center and swelled to fill it. *Fourth planet,* the computer said.

"What the devil is *that?*"

The screen held a planet at its center. But it also showed a web of hazy lines and bright spirals surrounding the planet and cradling it in multiple strands of light.

"Not our kind, Tamara," the man said softly. "That's not us."

No human works came close in size and complexity. Some of the spiraling filaments around the planet had to be over four hundred thousand kilometers long and many kilometers across.

"Time to wake the others," Tamara said. "And then ..." I don't know what. We found another intelligent species. But if they could b⸺⸺⸺⸺⸺⸺⸺? Well, I guess we'll kno⸺⸺⸺⸺⸺⸺

But she was ⸺⸺⸺⸺⸺⸺⸺ fact was uninhabited. It ⸺⸺⸺⸺⸺⸺ And the Builders were

D1052205

BAEN BOOKS by CHARLES SHEFFIELD

Between the Strokes of Night
Brother to Dragons
Convergence
Convergent Series
The Mind Pool
Proteus Combined
Proteus in the Underworld

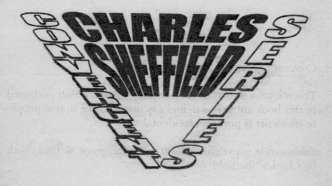

CONVERGENT SERIES

This is a work of fiction. All the characters and events portrayed in this book are fictional, and any resemblance to real people or incidents is purely coincidental.

Summertide copyright © 1990 and *Divergence* © 1991, both by Charles Sheffield

All rights reserved, including the right to reproduce this book or portions thereof in any form.

A Baen Books Original

Baen Publishing Enterprises
P.O. Box 1403
Riverdale, NY 10471

ISBN: 0-671-87791-7

Cover art by Gary Freeman

First printing, October 1998

Distributed by Simon & Schuster
1230 Avenue of the Americas
New York, NY 10020

Typeset by Windhaven Press, Auburn, NH
Printed in the United States of America

Summertide

Book One of
The Heritage Universe

To
Ann, Kit, Rose, and Toria

PROLOG
Expansion
1086 (3170 A.D.)

A ninety-seven-year silence was ending.

For close to a century the ship's interior had heard no human voice and felt no human footstep. The vessel whispered its way between the stars, passengers close to absolute zero in dreamless paradeath. Once a year their bodies warmed to liquid-nitrogen temperatures while shared experiences were fed to them from the ship's central data bank: memories of a hundred years of interstellar travel, for bodies that would age less than one day.

As the final weeks of deceleration began it was time to start the awakening. When the destination was reached, decisions might be needed that went beyond machine judgment—a notion that to the ship's main computer, the first of its kind to be equipped with the Karlan emotional circuits, was both insulting and implausible.

First warming was initiated. Interior sensors picked up the reassuring flutter of returning heartbeats, the initial sigh and murmur of working lungs. The emergency crew would be awakened first, two by two, on a last-in, first-out basis; only with their approval would others begin emergence.

The first pair drifted up to consciousness with one

question burning in their minds: Was it arrival—or was it override?

The computer had been programmed to rouse them for only three reasons. They would be disturbed if the ship were closing at last on their destination, Lacoste-32B, a minor G-2 dwarf star that lay three light-years beyond the rose-red stellar beacon of Aldebaran. They would wake if an on-board problem had arisen within the ship's half-kilometer ellipsoid, a disaster too big for the computer to handle without human interaction.

Or, the final possibility, they would be pulled from hibernation if one of spacefaring humanity's oldest dreams had become reality:

I/T—Immediate Transfer; Interstellar Transition; Instantaneous Travel; the superluminal transportation system that would end Crawlspace exploration.

For more than a thousand years the exploration and colony ships had crept outward, widening the sphere of Earth's influence. The millennium had yielded forty colonies, scattered through a Sol-centered globe seventy light-years in diameter. But every inch within that sphere had been traveled at less than a fifth of light-speed. And every colony, no matter how small and isolated, had a research program that sought the superluminal . . .

The first two wakened were one man and one woman. They fought a century-long lassitude, queried the ship's internal status panels, and shared their relief. No on-board disaster had occured. The message center held no urgent incoming file, no news of a great breakthrough. There would be no party of superluminal travelers waiting to welcome late-arrival colonists at Lacoste.

Ahead of the ship the target star already showed a visible naked-eye disk. Gravitational perturbations of the star had long predicted the presence of at least two orbiting giant planets. Now their existence could be confirmed by direct observation, together with five smaller bodies closer to the primary.

The woman was recovering faster than the man. It was

she who first left the Schindler hibernation unit, stood up shakily in the one-tenth-gee field, and moved to stare at the external displays. She uttered a low sound, a grunt of satisfaction from sluggish vocal cords, followed by an experimental clearing of her throat.

"We made it! There it is."

And there it was. The molten-gold disk of Lacoste lay at the exact center of the forward screen. Two minutes later the man had eased his way to her side, still wiping protective gel from his face. He touched her arm in congratulations, relief, and love. They were life-partners.

"Time to waken the others."

"In a few minutes," she said. "Remember Kapteyn. Make sure we've got something."

The example of Kapteyn's Star was written in every explorer's memory: eight planets, all apparently with wonderful potential; and all, on close inspection, useless for human habitation or for supplies. The early colony ship that had arrived at Kapteyn had been too depleted to reach any second target.

"We're only two light-days out," she went on. "We can start scanning. Let's take a look for oxygen atmospheres before we wake anyone else."

The on-board computer picked up her command and responded to it. *One oxygen world,* said its soft voice. *Life probability 0.92.* The field of view zoomed and swung so that Lacoste first grew rapidly in size and then disappeared from the top of the screen, while a new pinpoint of light appeared at the screen center and swelled to fill it.

Fourth planet, the computer said. *Overall figure of merit for Earth isomorphism, 0.86. Mean distance, 1.22; mean temperature range, 0.89 to 1.04; axial tilt—*

"What the devil is *that?"*

The computer paused. The man's question had no meaning.

The screen held a planet at its center, a blue-gray sphere already seen in enough detail to reveal the broad bands and swirls of atmospheric circulation patterns. But it also showed a web of hazy lines and bright spirals surrounding the planet and cradling it in multiple strands of light.

"Somebody got here ahead of us . . ." The woman's voice faded before the sentence was completed. The information network among inhabited planets was in continuous operation. It was limited to light-speed, but even so she could not believe that some exploring ship had also been sent to Lacoste, unknown to them. And if another ship *had* arrived here, the scale of what they were seeing went beyond anything that an exploring colony might accomplish in a few years.

Or in a few centuries.

"Pan view."

The computer heard her words and adjusted the image. The planet shrank to pea size, a bright bead of light at the middle of the screen. The surrounding nimbus of intensive in-space construction was revealed, a gleaming nacreous setting within which the planet nestled like a pearl in an oyster. Slender tendrils of construction stretched out endlessly, thinner and thinner, until they fell below the resolution of the observing sensors.

"Not our kind, Tamara," the man said softly. "That's not us."

No human works, not even the ring cities that surrounded Earth itself, came close in size and complexity. Some of the spiraling filaments around the planet had to be over four hundred thousand kilometers long and many kilometers across. They should have been unstable to gravitational forces from the planet, to tidal perturbations, and to their own interactions. And yet clearly they were not.

"Time to wake the others," Tamara said.

"And then?"

"And then . . ." She sighed. "And then, I don't know what. We finally did it, Damon. We found another intelligent species. A technologically advanced one, too. But if they could build *that*"—she gestured at the dazzling structure on the screen, and her voice became husky— "why didn't *they* find *us*? Well, I guess we'll know the answer to that in a few more days."

Three weeks later the ship's pinnaces were roving the veins and arteries of the space artifact. For fifteen days the main vessel had hovered five million kilometers away, waiting for and expecting contact from the planet in response to radio and laser signals. They had been met with total silence. Finally they had approached and begun direct exploration.

The misty filaments on the screen resolved themselves to the interlocking network of a colossal artifact. They stretched down to the surface of the planet, an uninhabited world apparently well suited to human colonization; but the tendrils also reached far out into space, for purposes that could not even be guessed at.

And those purposes could not be found out from their creators. Like the planet, the artifact was uninhabited.

Tamara and Damon Savalle found themselves cruising in their pinnace along one of the filaments, a metal-and-polymer tube three kilometers wide and fifty thousand long. Maintenance machines crept along the inner surface, moving so slowly that their motion was hardly perceptible. The machines ignored the little pinnace completely.

Tamara was at the communications panel, in contact with the main ship. "They confirm our analyses of meteorite pitting," she said. "At least ten million years old, uninhabited for more than three. And I don't see anything to grin at."

"Sorry." Damon did not look it. "I was thinking of the old paradox from before Expansion. If there are aliens, *where are they?* Twenty days ago we thought we had the answer: no aliens. Now we're asking it all over again. Where are they, Tammy? Who built all this stuff? And where are the builders?"

She shrugged. Damon's question would remain unanswered for more than three thousand years.

But while they stared and marveled, a weak incoming signal was reaching the main ship from a small and struggling colony on Eta Cassiopeiae A. It told of an intriguing new physical theory involving Bose-Einstein statistics, along with a suggestion for a subtle and complex deep-space experiment far beyond the limited resources of the little colony.

With everyone at Lacoste focused on the Builders, the new message received no attention at all.

But the Builders were long gone; and superluminal travel was on the way.

ARTIFACT: COCOON
UAC#: 1
Galactic Coordinates: 26,223.489/
14,599.029/+112.58
Name: Cocoon
Star/planet association: Lacoste/Savalle
Bose Access Node: 99
Estimated age: 10.464 ± 0.41 Megayears

Exploration History: Cocoon holds a special place in human history, as the first artifact to be discovered by human explorers, just as Cusp (see Entry 300) was the first to be discovered by the Cecropian clade. Cocoon was found in E. 1086 by a Crawlspace colony ship seeking habitable planets in the Lacoste system.

Physical Description: The form of Cocoon is a three-dimensional development of the familiar ring cities in place around many inhabited worlds. However, it goes far beyond the standard equatorial-plane assemblies, in both extent and presumed function. This artifact employs forty-eight Basal Stalks connecting Cocoon to the equatorial planetary surface and reaching up to the continuous ring structure at stationary altitude. Four hundred and thirty-two thousand exterior filaments stretch five hundred thousand kilometers from the planet. No two filaments are identical, but typical dimensions of the hollow cylindrical tubes are from two to four kilometers, exterior radius. Viewed from many locations, the surface of Savalle is completely obscured by Cocoon.

The corridors of Cocoon's interior are extensively patrolled by Phages (see Entry 1067). Explorers must monitor continuously for their presence.

Physical Nature: Construction of Cocoon employs the standard superstrength polymers used in most Builder artifacts. The absence of a second satellite for Savalle, even though the fossil record clearly shows that double-satellite tides occurred until twelve million years ago, suggests a now-vanished moon as the main source of Cocoon's construction materials.

Cocoon's filaments are held in stable position by a balance of gravity, rotating reference frames, and stellar radiation pressure. No unfamiliar science is needed to explain that stability, although the system design calls for the solution of large, discrete optimization problems beyond the best computers available within the Clades. Elephant (see Entry 859) was applied to the problem and reached a constrained solution (the so-called Cocoon Restricted Problem) in four standard years of computation time.

Intended Purpose: There are few secrets to Cocoon, if we except the *need* for such a massive system. The Basal Stalks permit materials to pass to and from the planetary surface of Savalle at negligible cost; the Exterior Filaments allow economical payload transfer to any point of the Lacoste stellar system, using the momentum-bank principle. The capacity of Cocoon is enormous: one fifty-thousandth of the mass of Savalle could in principle be transferred to space each year, enough to slow the planetary rotation rate appreciably and change Savalle's day by two seconds.

—From the *Lang Universal Artifact Catalog,* Fourth Edition.

CHAPTER 1
Expansion
4135 (6219 A.D.)

Where am I?

A man who had seen fifty planets and succeeded in a hundred difficult jobs ought to be like a cat, turning instinctively to land on his feet in any situation. But recently he seemed to be just the opposite, more disoriented with every new task.

Hans Rebka came fully awake and lay with eyes closed, waiting for memory of place and function to seep into his brain. As that came, confusion was replaced by anger.

A week earlier he had been in orbit around Paradox, preparing for one of the most challenging assignments of his life. He and three companions were to enter the Paradox sphere, carrying with them new shielding and a completely new type of recording sensor. If they succeeded they would bring back for the first time information from the Paradox interior—perhaps new information about the Builders themselves.

To Rebka, Paradox was the most enigmatic and intriguing of all Builder structures. The dark, spherical bubble, fifty kilometers across, permitted ready entry but on exit removed all memories, organic or inorganic. Computers emerged with no recording on any storage medium.

9

Humans who had reached the interior returned with the minds of newborn infants.

Exploration efforts had finally been abandoned; but lately visitors to the region of Paradox had been reporting changes. The bubble was different in external appearance, and possibly in internal status. A new effort might succeed.

It was a dangerous mission, but Hans Rebka had been looking forward to it. He had volunteered, and he had been accepted as team leader.

And then the call had come, just one day before the descent into Paradox.

"An alternative assignment . . ." The voice was thin and whispering, reduced in frequency spectrum by its passage through the Bose communications network. " . . . to the double-planet of Dobelle. You must leave without delay . . ."

The space-thinned voice sounded in no way imperious, but the command emanated from the highest government level of the Phemus Circle. And it was an assignment for Rebka alone; his companions would proceed to explore Paradox. At first it sounded like an honor, a privilege that he should be singled out in that way. But as the assignment was explained to him, Rebka's confusion began.

He knew his talents. He was a doer and a fixer, and a damned good one. He could think on his feet and improvise solutions in real-time to tough problems; he was a typical product of his home world, Teufel.

"What sins must a man commit, in how many past lives, to be born on Teufel?" Half the spiral arm knew that saying. Like all the planets of the Phemus Circle, Teufel was resource-poor and metal-poor. Settled in despair and dire necessity as the life-support systems of an early colony ship faltered and failed, it was also an outcast planet, too hot, too small, and with a barely breathable atmosphere. The life expectancy of a human who grew to maturity on Teufel—most did not—was less than half the average for the Phemus Circle, and less than a third of that for an inhabitant of any world of the Fourth Alliance. All those born and raised on Teufel found an instinct for self-

preservation before they could talk—or they never lasted long enough to talk.

Rebka was a slight, large-headed man with hands and feet too big for his body. He had the wan, slightly deformed look of someone who had suffered persistent childhood malnutrition and trace-element deficiency. But that early privation had affected his brains not at all. He had learned the odds early, when at eight years old he had seen a set of images from the wealthy worlds of the Alliance bordering the Phemus Circle. Strong anger was born within him. He learned to use it, to channel and control it to fuel his progress, at the same time that he learned to hide his feelings with a smile. By the time he was twelve years old he had worked his way off Teufel and was in a Phemus Circle government training program.

Rebka was proud of his record. Starting with less than nothing, he had risen steadily for twenty-five years. He had run massive terraforming projects, taking the harshest and most inhospitable planetary bodies and converting them to human paradises (someday he would do as much for Teufel); he had led dangerous expeditions to the heart of the mirror-matter comet region, far from any chance of help if things went wrong; he had flown so close to stellar surfaces that communications were impossible in the roar of ambient radiation, and his returning ship was ablated and melted past hope of further use. And he had led a crew on a near-legendary trip through the *Zirkelloch*, the toroidal space-time singularity that lay in the disputed no-man's land between the worlds of the Fourth Alliance and those of the Cecropia Federation.

All that. And suddenly—at the thought, confusion was replaced by anger; anger was still his friend—he was demoted. Stripped, without a word of explanation, of all real responsibilities and sent to a distant, unimportant world to act as nursemaid or father-confessor for someone ten years his junior.

"Just who *is* Max Perry? Why is he important?"

He had asked that question during his first briefing, as soon as the planetary doublet of Dobelle became more than a name to him. For Dobelle was an insignificant place. Its twin planetary components, Opal and Quake, orbiting a second-class star far from the main centers of the local spiral arm, were almost as poor as Teufel.

Scaldworld, Desolation, Teufel, Styx, Cauldron— sometimes it seemed to Rebka that poverty was their only bond, the single link that held the Phemus Circle worlds together and separated them from their richer neighbors. And from the records, Dobelle was a worthy member of the club.

The records on Perry were transmitted to him, too, to be scanned at his leisure. Typically, Hans Rebka reviewed them at once. They made little sense. Max Perry had come from origins as humble as Rebka's own. He was a refugee from Scaldworld, and like Rebka he had made his way rapidly upward, apparently bound for a job at the very top of Circle government. As part of the general grooming process for future leaders, he had been sent for a one-year tour of duty on Dobelle.

Seven years later he had still not returned. When promotions were offered, he refused them. When pressures were exerted to encourage him to leave the Dobelle system, he ignored them.

"A large investment," whispered the distant voice beyond the stars. "We have trained him for many years. We want to see that investment in him repaid . . . as you repaid it. Determine the cause of his difficulties. Persuade him to return, or at least to tell us why he refuses to do so. He ignores a direct order. Opal and Quake desperately need people, and Dobelle law prohibits extradition."

"He won't tell me anything. Why should he?"

"You will go to Dobelle as his supervisor. We have arranged for a senior position to be created within the ruling oligarchy. You will occupy it. We agree that Perry will not reveal his motives as the result of a simple inquiry. That has been tried. Use your own strengths. Use your subtlety. Use your initiative." The voice paused. "Use your anger."

"I am not angry with Perry." Rebka asked more

questions, but the answers offered no enlightenment. The assignment still made no sense. The central committee of the Phemus Circle could waste its resources if it so chose, but it was a stupid mistake to waste Rebka's talents—he lacked false modesty—where a psychiatrist seemed more likely to succeed. Or had that already been tried, and failed?

Hans Rebka swung his legs off the bunk and walked over to the window. He stared up. After a three-day trip through five Bose Network nodes and a subluminal final stage, he had finally landed on the Starside hemisphere of Opal. But Starside was a bad joke—even before dawn there was not a star to be seen. At that time of year, close to Summertide, cloud breaks on Opal were rare. Approaching the planet, he had seen nothing but a uniform, shining globe. The whole world was water, and when Dobelle swung in at its closest to its stellar primary, Mandel, the summer tides reached their peak and the oceans of Opal never saw the sun. Safety lay only on the Slings, natural floating rafts of earth and tangled vegetation that moved across Opal's surface at the prompting of winds and tides.

The biggest Slings were hundreds of kilometers across. The Starside spaceport was situated on one of the largest. Even so, Rebka wondered how it would fare at Summertide. Where would it go, and would it survive when the main tides came?

If his birthworld of Teufel had been Fire, then Opal was surely Water.

And Quake, the other half of the Dobelle planetary doublet?

Hell, from what he had heard of it. Nothing that Rebka had read or had been told in his briefings had had one good word to say about Quake. Events on Opal at Summertide were said to be spectacular and hair-raising—but survivable. On Quake they were deadly.

He looked up at the sky again and was startled to see that it was light. Opal and Quake were tidally locked to each other, and they spun around their common center of mass at a furious rate. One day in the Dobelle system was only eight standard hours. His morning musings had taken him well past dawn. He would just have time for a quick breakfast; then an aircar would carry him around the planet to Quakeside—and to the most stupid and least productive job of his life.

Rebka swore, cursing the name of Max Perry, and walked across to the door. He had not yet met the man, but he was ready to dislike him.

ARTIFACT: PARADOX
UAC#: 35
Galactic Coordinates: 27,312.443/
15,917.902/+135.66
Name: Paradox
Star/planet association: Darien/Kleindienst
Bose Access Node: 139
Estimated age: 9.112 ± 0.11 Megayears

Exploration History: It is not known how many times Paradox was discovered, and all knowledge of it then lost. What is known is that in E. 1379 Ruttledge, Kaminski, Parzen, and Lu-lan organized a two-ship expedition to investigate the light-refraction anomaly now known as Paradox.

Arriving first, Ruttledge and Kaminski recorded on their ship's main computer the intention of entering the Paradox sphere using the exploration pinnace, while the main ship remained well clear. Five days later, Parzen and Lu-lan arrived and found the other ship and its pinnace, both in perfect working condition. Ruttledge and Kaminski were in the pinnace, alive but suffering from dehydration and malnutrition. They were incapable of speech or simple motor movement, and subsequent tests showed that their memories held no more information than the mind of a newborn baby. The data banks and computer memory on the pinnace were wiped clean.

Following a review of the other ship's records, Parzen and Lu-lan drew lots to decide who would make a second trip inside the Paradox sphere. Lu-lan won and made the descent. No signals were received from him by Parzen, although there had been prior agreement to send a message every four hours. Lu-lan returned, physically unharmed, after three days. His memory was empty of all learned information, though somatic (instinctive) knowledge was unchanged.

Paradox was declared off-limits to all but trained investigators in E. 1557.

Physical Description: Paradox is a spherical region, fifty kilometers in diameter. Its outer boundary displays "soap bubble" color shifts across the surface, reflecting or transmitting different wavelength radiation apparently randomly.

The sphere is opaque in certain spectral regions (1.2-223 meters) and perfectly transparent in others (5.6-366 micrometers). Nothing is known of the appearance of Paradox's interior.

Paradox's size and appearance are not invariant. Changes in size and color have been reported nine times during its history.

Physical Nature: Based on transmission through it, Paradox is believed to have a complex interior structure. However, no first-hand information has ever been obtained, because of Paradox's information-destroying nature. Most analysts believe that Paradox is the four-dimensional extrusion in space and time of a body of much higher dimension, perhaps the twenty/three/seven knotted manifold of Ikro and H'miran.

Intended Purpose: Unknown. However, Scorpesi has conjectured that Paradox is a "cleansing vat" for large Builder intelligent artifacts, such as Elephant (see Entry 859), prior to reuse. Note, however, that this suggestion is inconsistent with the physical dimensions (4,000 x 900 kilometers) of Elephant itself, unless such objects were subjected to multiple passes through the Paradox sphere.

—From the *Lang Universal Artifact Catalog,* Fourth Edition.

CHAPTER 2
Summertide
minus thirty-six

The second shift of the working day was just beginning, and already it was clear to Birdie Kelly that it was going to be a bad one. The new supervisor might still be half a world away on Starside, but already the boss was brooding over the man's impending arrival.

"How can someone who has never even *visited* this system be competent to control travel between Opal and Quake?" Max Perry stared at Birdie with pale, unhappy eyes. Birdie looked back, saw the starved jut of Perry's jaw, and thought how much good it would do if the other man could just eat a square meal and relax for a day or two.

"Quake traffic is *our* job," Perry went on. "We've been doing it for six years. How much does this Rebka, a total stranger, know about that? Not a thing. Do they think at Circle headquarters that there's nothing to it, and any idiot can understand Quake? We know the importance of forbidding access to Quake. Especially now, with Summertide almost here. But do they know it?"

Birdie listened to Max Perry's stream of complaints and nodded sympathetically. One thing was sure: Perry was a good man and a conscientious boss, but he had his obsessions. And Captain Hans Rebka, whoever he might be, was sure going to make Birdie's own life more difficult.

Birdie sighed and leaned back in his wicker chair. Perry's office stood on the top floor of Opal's highest Quakeside building, a four-story experimental structure that had been built to Perry's own specifications. Birdie Kelly still felt uncomfortable inside it. The foundation extended down through layers of mud and a tangle of dead and living roots, right on past the lower basement of the Sling to the brackish waters of Opal's ocean. It was buoyed by a hollow chamber just below the surface, and the hydrostatic lift from there carried most of the load.

Even such a low building did not feel safe to Birdie. The Slings were delicate; without firm foundations, most buildings on Opal were held to one or two stories. For the past six months this Sling had been tethered in one spot, but as Summertide approached that would be too dangerous. Perry had ordered that in eight more days the Sling should be released to move at the mercy of the tides—but was that soon enough?

The communicator sounded. Max Perry ignored it. He was leaning back in his reclining chair, staring up at the ceiling. Birdie rubbed at his threadbare white jacket, leaned forward, and read the crude display.

He sniffed. It was not a message likely to put Max Perry in a better mood.

"Captain Rebka is closer than we thought, sir," he said. "In fact, he left Starside hours ago. His aircar should be ready to land in a few minutes."

"Thanks, Birdie." Perry did not move. "Ask the Slingline to keep us posted."

"I'll do that, Commander." Kelly knew he had been dismissed, but he ignored it. "Before Captain Rebka gets here you should take a look at these, sir. As soon as you can."

Kelly laid a folder on the plaited-reed tabletop that lay between them, sat back, and waited. Max Perry could not be rushed in his current mood.

The ceiling of the room was transparent, looking directly up into Opal's normally cloudy skies. The location had been carefully chosen. It was close to the center of

Quakeside, in a region where atmospheric circulation patterns increased the chance of clear patches. At the moment there was a brief predusk break in the overcast, and Quake was visible. With its surface only twelve thousand kilometers from the closest point of Opal, the parched sphere filled more than thirty-five degrees of the sky like a great, mottled fruit, purple-gray and overripe, poised ready to fall. From that distance it appeared peaceful, but already the dusky limb of the planet showed the softening of edges that spoke of rising dust storms.

Summertide was just thirty-six days away, less than two standard weeks. In ten days' time Perry would order the evacuation from Quake's surface, then monitor that evacuation personally. In every exodus for the past six years he had been the last man or woman to leave Quake, and the first to return after Summertide.

It was a compulsion with Perry. And regardless of what Rebka might want, Birdie Kelly knew that Max Perry would try to keep it that way.

Already night was advancing on the surface of Opal. Its dark shadow would soon create the brief false-night of Mandel eclipse on Quake. But Perry and Kelly would not be able to see that. The break in the overcast was closing, eaten away by swirls of rapidly moving cloud. There was a final flash of silver from far above, light reflected from the glittering knot of Midway Station and the lower part of the Umbilical; then Quake faded rapidly from view. Minutes later the roof above their heads showed the starred patterns of the first raindrops.

Perry sighed, leaned forward, and picked up the folders. Kelly knew that the other man had registered his earlier words without really hearing them. But Perry knew that if his right-hand man said he ought to look at the folder at once, there was a good reason for it.

The green covering held three long message summaries, each one a request for a visit to the surface of Quake. There was nothing very unusual in that. Birdie had been ready to give routine approval pending examination of travel plans—until he saw the source of the requests. Then he knew that Perry had to see them and would want to study them in detail.

The communicator buzzed again as Perry began to concentrate on the contents of the folder. Birdie Kelly took one look at the new message and quietly left the room. Rebka was arriving, but Perry did not need to be on the airstrip to welcome him. Birdie could do that. Perry had quite enough to worry about with the visit requests. Every one had come from outside the Dobelle system—outside, in fact, the worlds of the Phemus Circle. One was from the Fourth Alliance, one from a remote region of the Zardalu Communion, so far away that Birdie Kelly had never heard of it; and one, oddest of all, had been sent by the Cecropia Federation. That was unprecedented. So far as Birdie knew, no Cecropian had ever come within light-years of Dobelle.

Stranger yet, every visitor wanted to be on the surface of Quake at Summertide.

When Birdie Kelly returned he did something that he reserved for emergencies. He knocked on the door before he came in. The action guaranteed Perry's instant attention.

Kelly was holding yet another folder, and he was not alone. Behind him stood a thin, poorly dressed man who stared about with bright dark-brown eyes and was apparently more interested in the room's meager and tattered furnishings than in Perry himself.

His first words seemed to bear out that idea. "Commander Perry, I am pleased to meet you. I am Hans Rebka. I know that Opal is not a rich planet. But your position here would surely justify something better than this."

Perry put down the folder and followed the other man's inquisitive eyes as they surveyed the room. It was a sleeping chamber as well as an office. It held no more than a bed, three chairs, a table, and a desk, all battered and well used.

Perry shrugged. "I have simple needs. This is more than enough."

The newcomer smiled. "I agree. All men and women would not."

Regardless of whatever other feelings his smile might hide, part of Rebka's approval was quite genuine. In the first ten seconds with Max Perry he was able to dispose of one idea that had come to him after reading the other's history. Even the poorest planet could provide great luxury for one person, and some men and women would stay on a planet because they had found wealth and high living there, with no way to export it. But whatever Perry's secret, that could not be it. He lived as simply as Rebka himself.

Power, then?

Hardly. Perry controlled access to Quake, and little else. Permits for offworld visitors went through him, but anyone with real clout could appeal to a higher authority in the Dobelle system council.

So what was the driving force? There had to be one; there always was. But what was it?

During the official introductions and the exchange of meaningless courtesies on behalf of the government of Opal and the General Coordinators' office for the Phemus Circle, Rebka turned his attention to Perry himself.

He did it with real interest. He would rather be exploring Paradox, but despite his contempt for the new assignment he could not turn off his curiosity. The contrast between Perry's early history and his present position was just too striking. By the time Perry was twenty years old he had been a section coordinator in one of the roughest environments the Circle could offer. He had been subtle in handling problems, and yet he had been tough. The final assignment for one year to Opal was almost a formality, the last tempering of the metal before Perry was judged ready for work in the Coordinators' office.

He had come. And he had stuck. In one dead end job for all those years, unwilling to leave, lacking all his old drive. Why?

The man himself gave no clue as to the source of the problem. He was pale-faced and intense, but Rebka could see as much pallor and intensity just by looking in the mirror. They had both spent their early years on planets where survival was an achievement and thriving was impossible. The prominent goiter in Perry's neck spoke of a world where iodine was in short supply, and the thin, slightly crooked legs suggested an early case of rickets. Scaldworld's tolerance of plant life was grudging. At the same time Perry appeared in excellent health—something that Rebka could and would check in due course. But physical well-being only made it clearer that there must be mental problems. They would be harder to examine.

The inspection was not one-sided. While the formal exchanges of government greetings were taking place, Rebka knew that Perry was making his own assessment.

Did he hope that the new supervisor would be a man burned out from previous service or excesses, or perhaps some lazy pensioner? The Circle government had its share of people looking for sinecures, idlers willing to let Perry and others like him run the operation any way they wanted to, provided that the boss was not asked to do any work.

Apparently Perry wanted to find out whom he was dealing with and would waste no time in doing so, for as soon as the final courtesies had been exchanged he asked Kelly to leave and gestured Rebka to one of the chairs. "I assume that you will take up your duties here very soon, Captain?"

"More than soon, Commander. My duties on Opal and Quake have begun. I was told that they commenced at the moment the ship touched down on Starside Port."

"Good." Perry held out the green folder plus the fourth and latest document that Kelly had handed to him. "I was in the middle of reviewing these. I would appreciate it if you would take a look and give me your opinion."

In other words, let me see how smart you are. Rebka took the documents and skimmed them in silence for a minute or two. He was not sure what the test was, but he did not want to fail it. "These all appear to be in the correct official format," he said at last.

"You see nothing unusual in them at all?"

"Well, perhaps in the diversity of the applicants. Do you often have visit requests from outside the Dobelle system?"

"Very seldom." Perry was nodding in grudging respect. "Now we get four requests, Captain, in one day. All want to visit Opal and Quake. Individuals from the three major groups, *plus* a member of an Alliance council. Do you know how many visitors a year we usually get to Dobelle? Maybe fifty—and they all come from *our* people, worlds in the Phemus Circle. And nobody ever wants to go to Quake."

Max Perry picked up the folder again. Apparently Rebka had met some initial acceptance criterion, because Perry's manner had lost a little of its stiffness. "Look at this one. It's from a *Cecropian*, for God's sake. No one on Dobelle has ever *seen* a live Cecropian. I haven't seen one myself. No one here knows how to communicate with one."

"Don't worry about that." Rebka focused again on the sheets in front of him. "She'll have her own interpreter. But you're right. If you get only fifty a year, four in a day is way outside statistical limits." And you haven't said it to me, he thought, but as far as you're concerned it's *five* in a day, isn't it? These requests arrived at the same time I did. So as far as you are concerned, I'm just another outsider. "So what do they all want, Commander? I didn't read their reasons."

"Different things. This one"—Perry poked at the page with an emaciated finger "—just came in. Did you ever hear of a man called Julius Graves? He represents the Fourth Alliance Ethical Council, and according to this he wants to come to Opal to investigate a case of *multiple murder*, somehow involving twins from Shasta."

"Rich world, Shasta. A long way from Dobelle, in more ways than one."

"But if he wants to, according to the way I read the regulations, he can overrule anything that we say locally."

"Overrule us, or anyone else on Dobelle." Rebka took the document from Perry. "I never heard of Julius Graves, but the ethical councils carry the weight of all the groups. He'll be a hard man to argue with."

"And he doesn't say why he's coming here!"

"He doesn't have to." Rebka looked again at the application. "In his case, this request is a formality. If he wants to come, no one can stop him. What about the others, though? Why do they want to go to Quake?"

"Atvar H'sial—that's the Cecropian—says her specialty is the evolution of organisms under extreme environmental stress. Quake certainly qualifies. She says she wants to go there and see how the native life-forms adapt during Summertide."

"She's traveling alone?"

"No. With someone or something called J'merlia. A Lo'tfian."

"Okay, that'll be her interpreter. The Lo'tfians are another life-form from the Cecropia Federation. Who else?"

"Another female, Darya Lang from the Fourth Alliance."

"Human?"

"I assume so. She claims to be interested in seeing Builder artifacts."

"I thought there was only one in the Dobelle system."

"There is. The Umbilical. Darya Lang wants to take a look at it."

"She doesn't have to go down to Quake to do that."

"She says she wants to see how the Umbilical is tethered at the Quake end. She has a point there. No one has ever understood how the Builders arranged for its retraction to space at Summertide. Her story is plausible. Believe it if you want to."

Perry's tone of voice made it clear that he did not. It occurred to Rebka that they had at least one thing in common—their cynicism.

"And then there's Louis Nenda," Perry went on. "From the Zardalu Communion. When did you last hear from *them*?"

"When they had their last skirmish with the Alliance. What's he say he wants?"

"He doesn't bother to tell us in detail, but it's something about being interested in studying new physical forces. He wants to investigate the land tides on Quake during Summertide. And then there's a footnote, talking about the theory of the stability of biospheres, as it applies to Quake and Opal. Oh, and Nenda has a Hymenopt along with him, as a pet. That's *another* first. The only Hymenopts anyone has ever seen on Opal are stuffed ones in the Species Museum. Add them all up, Captain, and what do you get?"

Rebka did not answer that. Unless all the records on Perry were false, there was a subtle, flexible intelligence hiding behind those pale, mournful eyes. Rebka did not believe for a moment that Perry was asking advice because he thought he needed it. He was feeling out Rebka himself, probing the other man's intuition and sense of balance.

"When do they request arrival?"

"According to this, Darya Lang cleared the last Bose Node three days ago. That means she's on final subluminal approach to Starside Port. Landing request could come anytime. The rest of them are maybe a few days away."

"What do you recommend we do?"

"I'll tell you what I recommend we *don't* do." For the first time, emotion appeared on Max Perry's thin face. "We can let them visit Opal—though that's going to be no joke this Summertide—but we don't, under any circumstances, let them set foot on Quake."

Which means, Rebka thought, that my instinct back on Starside was spot on. If I'm going to find out what keeps Max Perry on Dobelle, I'll probably have to do exactly that: visit Quake, at Summertide. Well, what the hell. It can't be any more dangerous than the descent into Paradox. But let's test things here a little bit more before we jump too far.

"I'm not convinced of what you say," he replied, and watched apprehension flicker in Perry's pale eyes. "People are coming a long way to see Quake. They'll be willing to pay Dobelle a lot for the privilege, and this system needs

all the credit it can get. Before we deny access, I want
to talk at least to Darya Lang. And I think I may need
to see the surface of Quake close to Summertide for
myself—soon."

Quake close to Summertide. At those words another
expression appeared on Max Perry's face. Sorrow. Guilt.
Even longing? It could be any of them. Rebka wished
he knew the other man better. Perry's countenance surely
revealed the answers to a hundred questions—to someone
who knew how to read it.

CHAPTER 3
Summertide
minus thirty-three

Hans Rebka had arrived on Dobelle disoriented and angry. Darya Lang, following his subluminal path just three days later on her run from the final Bose Transition Point to the Opal spaceport, did not have room for anger.

She was nervous; more than nervous, she was *scared*.

For more than half her life she had been a research scientist, an archeologist whose mind was most comfortable seven million years in the past. She had performed the most complete survey of Builder artifacts, locating, listing, comparing, and cataloging every one so far discovered in Fourth Alliance territory, and noting the precise times of any changes in their historical appearance or apparent function. But she had done all that *passively*, from the tranquil harbor of her research office on Sentinel Gate. She might know by heart the coordinates of the twelve hundred-odd artifacts scattered through the whole spiral arm, and she could reel off the current state of knowledge concerning each one. But other than the Sentinel, whose shining bulk was visible from the surface of her home planet, she had never seen one.

And now she was approaching Dobelle—when no one else had even *wanted* her to go.

"Why shouldn't I go?" she had asked when the

Committee of the Fourth Alliance on Miranda sent their representative to her. She was trembling with tension and annoyance. "The anomaly is mine, if it's anyone's. I discovered it."

"That is true." Legate Pereira was a small, patient woman with nut-brown skin and golden eyes. She did not appear intimidating, but Darya Lang found it hard to face her. "And since you reported it, we have confirmed it for every Artifact. No one is trying to deny you full credit for your discovery. And we all admit that you are our expert on the Builders, and are most knowledgeable about their technology—"

"No one understands Builder technology!" Even in her irritation, Darya could not let that pass.

"*Most* is a comparative term. No one in the Alliance knows more. Since, I repeat, you are most knowledgeable about the technology of the Builders, you are clearly the best-qualified individual to pursue the anomaly's significance." The woman's voice became more gentle. "But at the same time, Professor Lang, you must admit that you have little experience of interstellar travel."

"I have none, and you know it. But everyone, from you to my house-uncle Matra, tells me that interstellar travel offers negligible risk."

The legate sighed. "Professor, it is not the travel we question. Look around you. What do you see?"

Darya raised her head and surveyed the garden. Flowers, vines, trees, the cooing birds, the last rays of evening sunlight throwing dusty shafts of light through the trellis of the bower . . . It was all normal. What was she *supposed* to see?

"Everything looks fine."

"It *is* fine. That is my point. You have lived all your life on Sentinel Gate, and this is a garden world. One of the finest, richest, most beautiful planets that we know— far nicer than Miranda, where I live. But you are proposing to go to Quake. To nowhere. To a dingy, dirty, dismal, dangerous world, in the wild hope that you will find there new evidence of the Builders. Can you give me one reason for thinking that Quake has such potential?"

"You know the answer. My discovery provides that reason."

"A statistical anomaly. Do you want to endure misery and discomfort for the sake of *statistics*?"

"Of course I don't." Darya felt that the other woman was talking down to her, and that was the one thing she could not stand. "No one *wants* discomfort. Legate Pereira, you admit that no one in the Fourth Alliance has more knowledge of the Builders than I do. Suppose I do not go, and someone else does, and whoever goes in my place fails for lack of knowledge where I might have succeeded. Do you think that I could ever forgive myself?"

Instead of replying, Pereira went to the window and beckoned Darya Lang to her side. She pointed into the slowly darkening sky. The Sentinel gleamed close to the horizon, a shining and striated sphere two hundred million kilometers away and a million kilometers across.

"Suppose I told you that I knew a way to break in through the Sentinel's protective shield and to explore the Pyramid at the center. Would you go with me?"

"Of course. I've studied the Sentinel since I was a child. If I'm right, the Pyramid could contain a library for the Builder sciences—maybe their history, too. But no one knows how to break the shield. We have been trying for a thousand years."

"But *suppose* we could crack it."

"Then I would want to go."

"And suppose it involved danger and discomfort?"

"I would still want to go."

The legate nodded and sat in silence for a few seconds as the darkness deepened. "Very well," she said at last. "Professor Lang, you are said to be a logical person, and I like to think that I am, too. If you are willing to run the risks of the Sentinel's shield, and those are *unknown* risks, then you have a right to endure the lesser risks of Quake. As for travel to the Dobelle system, we humans built the Bose Drive, and we understand exactly how it works. We know how to employ the Bose Network. The experience is frightening at first, but the danger is small. And perhaps if you can use that Network to explore the statistical anomaly that you alone discovered, it will finally provide the tool you need to crack the secret of the Sentinel. I cannot deny that chain of logic. You have the right to make the journey. I will approve your travel request."

"Thank you, Legate Pereira." With the victory, Darya felt a chill that was not caused by the night air. She was passing from pleasant theory to commitment.

"But there is one other thing," Pereira's voice sharpened. "I trust that you have not told anyone outside the Alliance about your discovery of the anomaly?"

"No. Not a person. I sent it only through regular reporting channels. There is no one else here who would care to hear about it, and I wanted—"

"Good. Be sure you keep it that way. For your information, the anomaly is now to be treated as an official secret of the Fourth Alliance."

"Secret! But anyone could perform the same analysis that I did. Why . . ." Lang subsided. If she said that anyone could do the work, she might lose her claim to the anomaly—and the trip to Quake.

The legate stared at her soberly and finally nodded. "Remember, you are about to embark on a journey of more than seven hundred light-years, beyond the borders of the Alliance. In some ways I envy you. It is a journey more than I have ever made. I have nothing more to say, except to give you my good wishes for a safe trip and a successful mission."

Darya could hardly believe that she had won, after weeks of red tape and dithering from the authorities of the Fourth Alliance. And the perils of the Bose Drive had indeed faded, once she was on her way and made her initial step through the Network. The first Transition was disconcerting, not for the feelings that it introduced but for their *absence*. The Transition was instantaneous and imperceptible, and that did not seem right. The human brain required some *notice* that it and the ship that carried it had been transported across a hundred light-years or more. Perhaps a slight shock, Darya thought; a little nausea, maybe, or some feeling of disorientation.

Then at the second and third Transitions that concern vanished, just as Legate Pereira had promised. Darya could take the mysteries of the Bose Drive for granted.

But what did not decrease was her own feeling of inadequacy. She was a bad liar; she always had been. The Dobelle system contained just one structure that dated back to the Builders: the Umbilical. And that was a minor artifact, one whose operations were self-evident even if the controls that governed it remained mysterious. She would never have made so long a journey merely to look at the Umbilical. No one would. And yet that was the Alliance's official rationale for her visit.

Someone was going to ask her why she had done so odd a thing; she just knew it. And nothing in half a lifetime of research work had taught her how to fake things. Her face would give her away.

The sight of Dobelle eased her uneasiness a little. In a universe that she saw as populated by the miracles of the Builders, here was a natural wonder to rival them. Forty or fifty million years earlier the planetary doublet of Quake and Opal had orbited the star Mandel in a near-circular path. That orbit had been stable for billions of years, resisting the gravitational tugs of Mandel's small and remote binary-system partner, Amaranth, and of its two great gas-giant planets, moving in their eccentric orbits five and seven hundred million kilometers farther out. The environment had been tranquil on both members of the Dobelle planetary pair, until a close encounter of the two gas-giants had thrown one of them into a grazing swing-by of Mandel. That unnamed stranger had emerged from its sun-skimming trajectory with a modified path that took it clear out of the stellar system and into the void.

That would have been the end of the story—except that Dobelle lay in the stranger's exit route. The gas-giant had done a complex dance about the doublet planet, moving

Quake and Opal closer together while changing their combined orbit to one with a periastron that skimmed much closer to Mandel. Then the stranger had vanished into history. Only Dobelle and the gas-giant called Gargantua remained, their still-changing orbital elements allowing an accurate reconstruction of past events.

Summertide, Dobelle's time of closest approach to Mandel, was just a couple of weeks away. It would be a time, if Darya Lang's analysis was correct, of great significance in the spiral arm. And also in her own life. Her theories would at last be proved true.

Or false.

She went to the port and watched as the ship approached Dobelle. Opal and Quake whirled dizzily around each other in a mad dance, spinning three full turns in a standard day. She could actually see their motion. However, speed was all relative. The ship's rendezvous with the landing field on Opal's Starside sounded difficult, but it was a trivial problem for the navigation computers that would make the rendezvous.

The problems would come not from there, but from the humans who wanted to greet her. The tone of the message permitting her entry to Opal sounded ominous. "Provide the full identification of your sponsor. State in full the proposed length of stay. Give details of expected findings. Explain why the time of your requested visit is critical. Say just why you wish to visit Quake. Provide credit information or nonrefundable advance payment. Signed, Maxwell Perry, Commander."

Were the immigration officials on Opal so hostile to every offworld visitor? Or was her paranoia not paranoia at all, but a well-merited uneasiness?

She was still standing by the port as the ship began its final approach. They were coming in from the direction of Mandel, and she had a fine sunlit view of the doublet. She knew that Opal was only slightly larger than Quake— 5,600 kilometers mean radius, compared with Quake's 5,100—but the human eye insisted otherwise. The cloud-covered iridescent ball of Opal, slightly egg-shaped and with its long axis pointing always to its sister world, loomed large. The darker, smaller ovoid of Quake brooded next to it, a smooth-polished heliotrope against the brighter gemstone of its partner. Opal was featureless, but the surface of Quake was full of texture, stippled with patches of deep purple and darkest green. She tried to make out the thread of the Umbilical, but from that distance it was invisible.

Entry to the Dobelle system offered no options. There was only one spaceport, set close to the middle of Opal's Starside hemisphere. There was no spaceport of any kind on Quake. According to her reference texts, safe access to Quake came only via Opal.

Safe access to Quake?

A nice idea, but Darya recalled what she had read of Quake and of Summertide. Maybe the reference texts needed to find different words . . . at least at this time of the year.

The reference files of the Fourth Alliance had even fewer good things to say than Legate Pereira about the worlds controlled by the Phemus Circle. "Remote . . . impoverished . . . backward . . . thinly populated . . . barbaric."

The stars of the Circle lay in a region overlapped by all three major clades of the spiral arm. But in their outward expansions the Fourth Alliance, the Zardalu Communion, and the Cecropia Federation had shown negligible interest in the Phemus Circle. There was nothing there worth buying, bargaining for, or stealing—hardly enough to justify a visit.

Unless one was looking for trouble. Trouble was supposed to be easy to find on any world controlled by the Circle.

Darya Lang stepped out of the ship onto the spongy ground of Opal's Starside spaceport and looked around her with misgiving. The buildings were low and ground-hugging, built of what looked like plaited reeds and dried mud. No one was waiting to greet the ship. Opal was described as metal-poor, wood-poor, and people-poor. All it had was water, and lots of it.

As her shoe sank an inch or two into the soft surface she felt even more uneasy. She had never visited a water-world, and she knew that instead of hard rock and solid ground beneath her feet, there was only the weak and insubstantial crust of the Sling. Below that was nothing but brackish water, a couple of kilometers deep. The buildings hugged the ground for a good reason. If they were too tall and heavy, they would break through it.

An irrelevant thought came to her: she could not even swim.

The crew of the ship that had brought her were still involved with the final stages of landing procedure. She began to walk toward the nearest building. Two men were finally emerging from it to greet her.

It was not a promising introduction to Opal. Both men were short and thin—Darya Lang was ten centimeters taller than either of them. They were dressed in identical dingy uniforms, with clothes that shared a patched and well-worn look, and from a distance the two might have been taken for brothers, one ten years or so older than the other. Only as she came closer were their differences revealed.

The older man had a friendly, matter-of-fact air to him and a self-confident walk. The faded captain's insignia on his shoulder indicated that he was the senior of the two in rank as well as age. "Darya Lang?" he said as soon as they were within easy speaking distance. He smiled and held out his hand, but not to shake hers. "I'll take your entry forms. I'm Captain Rebka."

Add "brusque" to the list of words describing the inhabitants of the Phemus Circle, she thought. And add "unkempt" and "battered" to Rebka's physical description. The man's face had a dozen scars on it, the most noticeable running in a double line from his left temple to the point of his jaw. And yet the overall effect was not unpleasant—rather the opposite. To her surprise, Darya sensed the indefinable tingle of mutual attraction.

She handed over her papers and made internal excuses for the scars and the grimy uniform. Dirt was only superficial, and maybe Rebka had been through some exceptional misfortune.

Except that the younger man looked just as dirty, and he had his own scars. At some time his neck and one side of his face had been badly burned, with a bungled attempt at reconstructive surgery that would never have been accepted back on Sentinel Gate.

Maybe the burn scars had also left the skin of his face lacking in flexibility. Certainly he had a very different expression from Rebka. Where the captain was breezy in manner and likeable despite his grubbiness and lack of finesse, the other man seemed withdrawn and distant. His face was stiff and expressionless, and he hardly seemed aware of Darya, although she was standing less than two meters from him. And whereas Rebka was clearly in top physical shape, the other had a run-down and unhealthy look, the air of a man who did not eat regular meals or care at all about his own health.

His eyes were at variance with his young face. Dead and disinterested, they were the pale orbs of a man who had withdrawn from the whole universe. He was unlikely to cause Darya any trouble.

Just as she reached that comforting conclusion the face before her came alive and the man snapped out, "My name is Perry. Commander Maxwell Perry. Why do you want to visit Quake?"

The question destroyed her composure completely. Coming without the preliminary and traditional courtesies of Alliance introductions, it convinced Darya Lang that these people *knew*—knew about the anomaly, knew about her role in discovering it, and knew what she was there to seek. She felt her face turning red.

"The—the Umbilical." She had to struggle to find words. "I—I have made a special study of Builder artifacts; it has been my life's work." She paused and cleared her throat. "I have read all that I could find about the Umbilical. But I want to see it for myself and learn how the tethers work on Opal and Quake. And discover how Midway Station controls the Umbilical for the move to space at Summertide." She ran out of breath.

Perry remained expressionless, but Captain Rebka had a little smile on his face. She was sure that he saw right through her every word.

"Professor Lang." He was reading from her entry papers. "We do not discourage visitors. Dobelle needs all the revenue it can get. But this is a dangerous time of year on Opal and Quake."

"I know. I have read about the sea tides on Opal, and the land tides on Quake." She cleared her throat again. "It is not my nature to seek danger." That at least was true, she thought wryly. "I propose to be very careful and take all precautions."

"So you have *read* about Summertide." Perry turned to Rebka, and Darya Lang detected a tension between the two men. "As have you, Captain Rebka. But reading and experiencing something are not the same. And neither of you seems to realize that Summertide this time will be different from all others in our experience."

"Every time must be different," Rebka said calmly. He was smiling, but Darya Lang could feel the conflict. Rebka was the older and the more senior, but on the issue of Summertide Commander Perry did not accept the other's authority.

"This is exceptional," Perry replied. "We will be taking extraordinary precautions, even on Opal. And as for what may happen on Quake, I cannot begin to guess."

"Even though you have experienced half a dozen Summertides?"

Rebka had lost his smile. The two men faced each other in silence, while Darya looked on. She sensed that the fate of her own mission hung on the argument that they were having.

"The Grand Conjunction," Perry said after a few seconds. And finally Darya had a statement that made sense to her as a scientist.

She had studied the orbital geometry of the Mandel

system in detail while working on the Lang catalog of artifacts. She knew that Amaranth, the dwarf companion of Mandel, normally moved so far from the primary that the illumination it provided to Dobelle was little more than starlight. However, once every few thousand years its motion brought it much closer, to less than a billion kilometers of Mandel. Gargantua, the remaining gas-giant planet of the system, moved in the same orbital plane, and it, too, had its own point of close approach to Mandel.

Dobelle's critical time of Summertide usually occurred when Gargantua and Amaranth were both far from Mandel. But all three orbits were in resonance lock. On rare occasions, Amaranth and Gargantua swung in together to Mandel, at a time that coincided with Summertide for Opal and Quake. And then . . .

"The Grand Conjunction," Perry repeated. "When everything lines up at periastron, and the sea tides and land tides on Opal and Quake are as big as they can possibly be. We have no idea how big. The Grand Conjunction happens only once every three hundred and fifty thousand years. The last time was long before humans settled Dobelle. But the next time will happen just thirty-three days from now—less than two standard weeks. No one knows what Summertide will do to Opal and Quake then, but I do know that the tidal forces will be devastating."

Darya looked at the soft ground beneath their feet. She had the terrible feeling that the flimsy mud-raft of living and dead plants was already crumbling under the assault of monstrous tides. No matter what the dangers might be on Quake, surely they were preferable to staying on Opal.

"So wouldn't you all be *safer* on Quake?" she asked.

Perry shook his head. "The permanent population of Opal is more than a million people. That may seem like nothing for someone like you, from an Alliance world. But it is a lot for a Circle world. My birth planet had less than a quarter of that."

"And mine less than an eighth of it," Rebka said mildly. No one stayed on Teufel who had any way to get off it.

"But do you know the permanent population of Quake?" Perry glared at both of them while Lang wondered how she had ever thought him calm and passionless.

"It is *zero*," he said after a pause. "Zero! What does that tell you about life on Quake?"

"But there *is* life on Quake." She had studied the planetary index. "*Permanent* life."

"There is. But it is not human life, and it could not be. It is *native* life. No human could survive Quake during Summertide—even a normal Summertide."

Perry was becoming increasingly assertive. Darya knew that her case for visiting Quake was lost. He would deny her access, and she would get no closer to Quake than the Starside spaceport. As she decided that, help came from an unexpected direction.

Rebka turned to Max Perry and pointed a thin finger up to Opal's cloudy skies. "You are probably right, Commander Perry," he said quietly. "But suppose strangers are coming to Dobelle *because* it will be the Grand Conjunction? We did not consider that possibility when we were examining their applications." He turned to stare at Darya Lang. "Is that your *real* reason for being here?"

"No. Definitely not." She felt relief at being able to give an honest answer. "I never thought about the Conjunction until Commander Perry mentioned it."

"I believe you." Rebka smiled, and she was suddenly convinced that he did. But she recalled Legate Pereira's words: "Don't trust anyone from the Phemus Circle. They practice survival skills that we in the Alliance have never been forced to learn."

"People's reasons for coming here are not too relevant, of course," he went on. "They don't make Quake any safer." He turned to Perry. "And I feel sure you are right about the dangers of Quake at Summertide. On the other hand, I have a responsibility to maximize the revenues of Dobelle. That's my job. We have no responsibility to protect visitors, beyond a duty to warn them. If they choose to proceed, knowing the risks, that is their option. They are not children."

"They have no notion of what Quake is like at Summertide." Perry's face had turned blotchy white and red. He was overwhelmed by strong emotion. "*You* have no idea."

"Not yet. But I will have." Rebka's manner changed again. He became a boss who was clearly giving orders. "I agree with you, Commander. It would be irresponsible for Professor Lang to visit Quake—until we are sure of the hazards. But once we do understand them—and can explain them—we have no duty to be overprotective. So you and I will go to Quake, while Professor Lang remains here on Opal."

He turned to Darya. "And when we return . . . well, then, Professor Lang, I will make my decision."

ARTIFACT: SENTINEL
UAC#: 863
Galactic Coordinates: 27,712.863/
16,311.031/761.157
Name: Sentinel
Star/planet association: Ryders-M/Sentinel
Gate
Bose Access Node: G-232
Estimated age: 5.64 ± 0.07 Megayears

Exploration History: Sentinel was discovered in Expansion Year 2649 by human colonists of the trans-Orionic region. First entry attempt, E. 2674, by Bernardo Gullemas and the crew of exploration vessel D-33 of Cyclops class. No survivors. Subsequent approaches attempted E. 2682, E. 2695, E. 2755, E. 2803, E. 2991. No survivors.

Sentinel warning beacon set in place, E.2739; monitoring station established on nearest planet (Sentinel Gate), E. 2762.

Physical Description: Sentinel is a near-spherical inaccessible region, a little less than one million kilometers across. No visible internal energy sources, but Sentinel glows faintly with its own light (absolute magnitude +25) and is visible from every point of the Ryders-M system. The impassable surface of Sentinel readily permits two-way passage of light and radiation of any wavelength, but it reflects all material objects including atomic and subatomic particles. There is photon flux only from the interior, with no particle emission. Laser illumination of the interior is possible, and reveals a variety of structures at the center of the sphere. The most prominent such feature is "The Pyramid," a regular tetrahedral structure which absorbs all light falling onto it. If interior distances within Sentinel have meaning (there is evidence that they do not—see below) then the Pyramid would be approximately ninety kilometers on a side. No increase in temperature of the Pyramid is detectible, even when incident absorbed radiation is at the gigawatt level.

Path length measurements using lasers show that rhe interior of Sentinel is not simply-connected; minimal light travel time across Sentinel is 4.221 minutes, compared with a geodesic travel time of 3.274 seconds for equivalent distance across empty space remote from matter. For light incident normally on the Sentinel "equator" travel times across Sentinel are infinite, or certainly in excess of a thousand years. Red shift and grazing incidence laser beams indicate that no mass is present within Sentinel, a result that is inconsistent with the observed interior structure.

Sentinel holds a precise distance of 22.34a.u. from the Ryders-M primary star, but is not in orbit about it. Gravitational forces and radiation pressure forces either are exactly compensated by some unknown mechanism in Sentinel, or do not act on the structure at all.

Physical Nature of Sentinel: According to Wollaski'i and Drews, Sentinel takes advantage of and is built around a natural anomaly of space-time and possesses only weak physical coupling to the rest of the universe. If so, this is one of only thirty-two Builder artifacts that were created with the use of preexisting and natural features.

Sentinel topology appears to be that of a Ricci-Cartan-Penrose knot in 7-space.

Intended Purpose: Unknown. However, it is conjectured (by analogy with other Builder artifacts, see Entry 311, 465, and 1223) that the Pyramid may possess near-infinite information storage capacity and lifetime. It has therefore been suggested (Lang, E. 4130) that the Pyramid and possibly the whole of Sentinel form a Builder library.

—From the *Lang Universal Artifact Catalog*, Fourth Edition.

CHAPTER 4
Summertide
minus thirty-one

The first part of the flight to Quake was conducted in
total silence. Once it was clear that Hans Rebka was
insistent on going and could not be dissuaded, all Perry's
energy had vanished. He sank into a strange lethargy,
sitting at Rebka's side in the aircar and staring straight
ahead. He roused briefly when they came to the foot of
the Umbilical, but only long enough to lead the way to a
passenger capsule and initiate the command sequence
for ascent.

Seen from sea level the Umbilical was impressive but
not overwhelming. It appeared to Rebka as a tall slender
tower of uniform thickness, maybe forty meters across,
stretching from the surface of Opal's ocean at the lower
end up into the thick and uniform cloud layer. The main
trunk of the structure was a silvery alloy, up and down
which passengers and cargo could move in huge cars. The
attachments were electromagnetic, held and driven by
linear synchronous motors. The detailed design might be
unfamiliar, but Rebka had seen the concept used on a
dozen worlds, carrying people and materials up and down
multikilometer buildings, or high into orbit. The knowledge that there were over two kilometers more of the
Umbilical below sea level, reaching down to a tether on

the ocean floor, was more surprising, but the mind could accept it.

What the mind—or Rebka's mind at least—could not so readily accept was the twelve *thousand* kilometers of the Umbilical above the clouds, reaching all the way from Opal to Quake's parched and turbulent surface. The observer who climbed into a capsule was seeing less than one ten-thousandth of the whole structure. With a maximum free-space car speed of a thousand kilometers an hour, travelers would expect to see two sunrises on Quake before they got there.

And now they were on their way.

The capsule was as tall and broad as Opal's biggest buildings. As the Builders had left it, the inside was one large empty space. Humans had added interior floors, from a massive cargo hold at the bottom to the control-and-observation chamber at the top.

The car's motors were silent. All that could be heard as they rose smoothly through the cloud layer was a whistle of air and the mutter of atmospheric turbulence. Five seconds more, and Hans Rebka had his first view of Quake as seen from Opal. He heard Max Perry grunt at his side.

Maybe Rebka grunted, too. For Opal's permanent cloud layer suddenly seemed like a blessing. He was glad that the other planet had been hidden when he had been down on Opal's surface.

Quake stood huge in the sky, a sunlit, mottled ball that was poised and ready to crash down onto him. His hind-brain told him that no force in the universe could hold such a weight, that one would never become used to the sight. At the same time his forebrain did a calculation of orbital rates and the matching of centrifugal and gravitational forces, and assured him that everything was in perfect dynamic balance. People might be uncomfortable with the threat of Quake overhead for a day or two; then they would get used to it and ignore it.

From this distance no details were visible, but it was clear that he was looking at a world without major seas and oceans. Rebka thought at once of terraforming; not just Quake or Opal, but of the doublet together. It was the perfect application. Quake had the metals and minerals; Opal had the water. It would be a substantial task, but no bigger than others he had undertaken. And the beginning of the necessary transportation system was already in position.

He looked along the thread of the Umbilical. The line upward was visible for perhaps a hundred kilometers before he lost it. Midway Station, four thousand kilometers above them at the center of mass of the Opal-Quake system, could be seen as a tiny golden knot on an invisible thread. They would be there for changeover in half a day. Plenty of time to think.

And plenty to think about.

Rebka closed his eyes and sorted through his worries.

Begin with Max Perry. After only a couple of days of exposure to the man it was clear that there were two Max Perrys. One was a quiet, dull bureaucrat, someone whom Rebka would expect to find in a dead-end job on any rathole world in the Phemus Circle. But somewhere under that there was a second personality, an energetic and subtle person with strong ideas of his own. The second Max Perry seemed to wake only on random occasions.

No, that was wrong. The other Max awoke when Quake was the issue, and only then. And Max II must be the clever and determined man that Perry had been, all of the time, seven years before—when he was assigned to Dobelle.

Rebka leaned back in his seat, physically relaxed and mentally active. So. Accept that there was a mystery in Max Perry. But ask if that mystery justified pulling a senior, action-oriented man like Hans Rebka away from a key project involving exploration of Paradox to become an amateur psychologist on the minor world of Opal.

It did not add up. If the men and women who ran the Phemus Circle were good at anything, it was at conserving resources; and human resources were the most precious of all.

Look for another motive, another reason for his being assigned there.

Rebka was not naive enough to believe that his superiors would tell him the whole story behind his assignments. They might not even *know* the whole story. He had found that out the hard way, on Pelican's Wake. A troubleshooter was expected to be able to operate without a full deck, and Rebka functioned best when he was forced to work things out for himself.

Terraforming of Quake and Opal?

His superiors must know that as soon as he saw the planetary doublet of Dobelle he would evaluate both worlds as possible subjects for terraforming. Was that the real reason he had been assigned there? To set in motion that project?

Still it did not feel right.

So add in some of the other variables. Four groups were requesting a visit to Quake at Summertide. He might believe that one was a genuine coincidence—the Alliance Council had no reputation for deceit—but four at once was not plausible.

And the upcoming Summertide would be the biggest ever. Maybe that was the key. They were there for that special Summertide.

Again, it did not feel complete. Darya Lang had told him that she did not know it was to be a specially big Summertide until Perry had told her.

Rebka believed her. But that belief itself was suspect. He had left a woman companion behind him on the station orbiting Paradox. No matter what his brain told him, his glands were probably seeking a replacement. In the first two minutes with Lang he had been aware of an attraction between them. And that must make him more cautious in dealing with her, since he *wanted* to believe her.

Lang did not know that Opal and Quake were scheduled for monster Summertides. Fine. Believe that, and still it did not mean that she was what she pretended to be. She could have another and more complex role to play.

Was she what she claimed to be? That could be checked. Before he left Starside, Rebka had already sent an encrypted message through the Bose communications net, asking for confirmation by Circle intelligence that Darya Lang was an expert on Builder artifacts. The reply would be waiting when they returned from Quake. Until then, questions regarding Lang had to be put to one side.

But there were plenty of other questions left. Hans Rebka was interrupted by a light touch on his arm. He opened his eyes.

Max Perry was gesturing upward, along the line of the Umbilical. Quake loomed above them, half again as big as when they had started. But at the moment it reflected only the murky dried-blood light of Amaranth. Mandel was hidden behind the planet, and as Summertide approached, its dwarf companion was swinging in closer. Soon night would disappear completely on Quake and Opal.

"What's happening?" Rebka said. "I thought the Umbilical ran all the way between Opal and Quake." He should have been a little nervous, because it was sheer vacuum outside the car; but Perry had a smile on his face, and he certainly did not act like a man facing disaster.

"It does," he said. "We're approaching the Winch. We have to be shunted here, and reconnected on the other side of Midway Station. Travelers can go into the station if they want to—it's well equipped, power and food and shelter— but I see no point in that. If you like we can take a closer look at Midway on the way back."

As Perry spoke, the car they were riding in was swinging away from the main cable and running through a series of gates and connecting rails. Quake had vanished. Midway Station was off to the right. Rebka could see a whole line of ports, any one of them big enough to accept the capsule. He looked back to the place where the main cable of the Umbilical disappeared into bright blue nothingness and then, a few kilometers farther on, reappeared.

"I don't see any winch."

"You won't." The second Max Perry was back, alert and energetic. "That's just a name we give it. You see, Opal and Quake are in a near-circular mutual orbit, but their separation distance varies all the time—anything up to four hundred kilometers. A permanent Umbilical can't work unless you have something to reel in or pay out cable. That's what the Winch does."

"That hole in space?"

"Right. It works fine, and at Summertide it reels in extra so that the coupling is lost at the surface of Quake. And it's smart enough to leave the tether on Opal intact. But it's all Builder technology. We have no idea where the cable goes to or comes from, or how it knows what to do. People on Quake and Opal don't care, so long as they can raise or lower the Umbilical through the special control sequences."

Perry's reluctance to visit Quake had vanished at liftoff from Opal. He was peering forward as they rounded the bulk of Midway Station, seeking Quake again in the sky ahead.

The capsule moved back to attach to the new length of the Umbilical, and they began to pick up speed. Soon they passed the mass center of the Dobelle system, and there was a clear sense of falling toward Quake, their own centrifugal force adding to Quake's gravity. The dark planet grew visibly, minute by minute, in the sky ahead of them. They began to see more surface detail.

And Rebka could see another change in Perry. The younger man's breathing was faster. He was staring at Quake's approaching surface with rapt attention, his eyes bright and staring. Rebka was willing to bet that his pulse rate had increased.

But what was down there? Rebka would have given a lot to see Quake through Max Perry's eyes.

Quake had no sea-sized water bodies, but it did have plenty of rivers and small lakes. All around them grew the characteristic dark-green and rust-colored vegetation. Most of it was tough and prickly, but in certain places there flourished a cover of lush ferns, soft and resilient. One of those areas was on the biggest lake's shore, not far from the foot of the Umbilical. It was a natural place for a person to sink down and rest. Or for two people to find other pleasures

Amy was talking, her voice breathless in his ear. "You're the expert, aren't you?"

"I don't know about that." He sounded lazy, relaxed. "But I probably know as much about this place as anyone."

"Same thing. So why won't you bring me here again? You could, Max, if you wanted to. You control the access."

"I shouldn't have brought you here at all."

The feeling of power. He had done it originally to show off his new authority, but once on the planet there were other and better reasons. Quake was still safe, still far from Summertide, yet already there was volcanic dust high in the atmosphere. The evenings, flaming in every eight hours, were an unspeakable beauty of red, purple, and gold. He knew of nothing like it in the rest of the universe—nothing he had read, nothing he had heard rumored. Even with his eyes closed, he would still see those glorious colors.

He had wanted to show it off to Amy—and he did not want to stop looking himself, not just yet. He lay on his back, gazing up past the shattering sunset to the brightening disk of Opal. By his side, Amy had broken off one of the soft fronds of fern and was tickling his bare chest. After a few moments she moved over him, blocking his view of Opal and gazing down at him with wide, serious eyes.

"You will, won't you? You will, you definitely will. Say you will."

"Will what?" He was feigning incomprehension.

"Will bring me here again. Closer to Summertide."

"I definitely won't." He rolled his head from side to side on the soft ferns, too lazy to lift it fully. He felt like the king of the world. "It wouldn't be safe, Amy. Not then."

"But you come here then."

"Not at Summertide. I get out well before that, while it's still safe. Nobody stays here then."

"So I could leave with you, when it's still safe. Couldn't I?"

"No. Not near Summertide."

Amy was moving her body down toward him, as the last light bled from the air of Quake. He could no longer see her face. It had faded with the dying light.

"I could." Her lips were an inch away from his. "Say I could. Say yes."

"No," he repeated. "Not close to Summertide."

But Amy did not reply. She was busy with other arguments.

CHAPTER 5
Summertide
minus thirty

Darya Lang had a terrible sense of anticlimax. To come so far, to steel herself for confrontation and danger and exciting new experiences . . . and then to be left to cool her heels for days on end, while others decided when—and if—she would be allowed to undertake the final and most crucial part of her journey!

No one in the Alliance had suggested that her task on Quake would be easy. But also no one had suggested that she might have trouble *reaching* Opal's sister world once she got to the Dobelle system. So far she had not even even *seen* Quake, except from a distance. She was stuck on Opal's Starside for an indefinite period, with nothing to do, only short-range transportation available to her, and no say in what happened next.

Perry had given her a whole building to herself, just outside the spaceport. He had assured her that she had complete freedom to wander as she chose, talk to anyone she liked, and do anything that she wanted to.

Very kind of him. Except that there was no one else in the building, and nothing there but living quarters—and he had told her to be available to meet as soon as he returned. He and Rebka were sure to be away for days. Where was she supposed to go? What was she supposed to do?

She called maps of Opal onto the display screens. To anyone accustomed to the fixed continents and well-defined land-water boundaries of Sentinel Gate, the maps were curiously unsatisfying. The ocean floor contours of Opal were shown as permanent planetary features, but they seemed to be the only geographic constants. For the Slings themselves she could find no more than the present positions and drift rates of a couple of hundred of the largest of them; plus—an unsettling set of data—the approximate thickness and estimated lifetime of each Sling. At the moment she was standing on a layer of material less than forty meters deep, with a thickness that changed unpredictably every year.

She turned off the display and sat rubbing her forehead. She did not feel good. Part of it might be the reduced gravity, only four-fifths of standard here on Opal's Starside. But maybe part of it was disorientation produced by rapid interstellar travel. Every test insisted that the Bose Drive produced no physical effects on humans. But she recalled the inhabitants of the old Arks, who permitted themselves only subluminal travel and claimed that the human soul could travel no faster than light-speed.

If the Ark dwellers were correct, her soul would be a long time catching up with her.

Darya went to the window and stared up at Opal's cloudy sky. She felt lonely and very far from home. She wished that she could catch a glimpse of Rigel, the nearest supergiant to Sentinel Gate, but the cloud layer was continuous. She was lonely, and she was also annoyed. Hans Rebka might be an interesting character, and interested in her—she had seen the spark in his eyes—but she had not come so far to have all her plans thwarted by the whim of some back-world bureaucrat.

The way she was feeling, it would be better to walk around the Sling than to remain cooped up inside the low, claustrophobic building. She went outside, to find that a steady drizzle was beginning to fall. Exploration of the Sling on foot in those conditions might be difficult— the surface was uneven clumps of sedges and ferns, on a light and friable soil bound by a tight-rooted and slippery tangle of ground vines.

But she went barefoot all the time at home, and her naked toes could catch a good purchase on the tough vines. She bent down and slipped off her shoes.

The ground became more uneven outside the controlled area of the spaceport, and it was tough going. But she needed the exercise. She had traveled a good kilometer and was all set to walk for a long time when a dense clump of ferns a few meters in front of her produced an angry hiss. The tops of the plants bowed down and flattened under the weight of some large, low-slung, and invisible body.

Darya gasped and jumped backward, sitting down hard on the wet soil. Barefoot walking—or walking of any kind—suddenly seemed like a very bad idea. She scurried back to the spaceport and requisitioned a car. It had a limited flying range, but it could take her past the edge of the Sling and permit her a look at Opal's ocean.

"You didn't have to worry," said the engineer who gave her the car. He was insisting on showing her how to use the simple controls, though she was quite sure she could have worked them out for herself. "Nothing bad ever makes it shoreside here, an' people didn't bring in nothing dangerous when she was first settled. Nothin' poisonous here, neither. You was all right."

"What was it?"

"Big ole tortoise." He was a tall, pale-skinned man with a filthy coverall, a gap-toothed smile, and a very casual manner. "Weighs mebbe half a ton, eats all the time. But only ferns an' grasses an' stuff. You could ride on his back and he'd never notice you."

"A native form?"

"Naw." The short lesson on aircar use was over, but he was in no hurry to leave. "No vertebrates native to Opal. Biggest thing ashore is a kind o' four-legged crab."

"Is there anything dangerous out in the ocean?"

"Not to you 'n' me. Least, not dangerous by design. When you get a ways offshore, watch for a big, green hump coming up to the surface, 'bout a kilometer across. That'll be a Dowser. It'll damage boats now an' agin, but only 'cause it don't know they're there."

"Suppose one came up underneath a Sling?"

"Now why'd she be dumb enough to do that?" His voice was teasing. "She come up for air and sunlight, an' there's none of them under a Sling. Go find yourself a Dowser— seein' one's a real experience. They come up a lot at this time of year. An' you were lucky to meet that ole tortoise, you know. 'Nother few days and he'll be off. They're leaving extra early."

"Where are they going to?"

"Ocean. Where else? They know Summertide is on the way, and they want to be nice an' cozy when it comes. Must know it's going to be extra big this year."

"Will they be safe there?"

"Sure. Worst thing that can happen to one of 'em is he gets to sit high and dry for a while at real low tide. Couple of hours later, he's back swimmin'."

He stepped down from the running board on the left side of the car. "If you want to find the quickest way to the edge of the Sling, fly low an' see where the turtles' heads are pointing. That'll get you straight there." He wiped his hands on a dirty rag, leaving them as black as when he started, and gave Darya the warmest, most admiring smile. "Anyone ever tell you you walk an' move real nice? You do. If you want company when you get back, I'll be here. I live right near. Name's Cap."

Darya Lang took off wondering about the worlds of the Phemus Circle. Or was it was just in the air of Opal, the thing that led men to look at her differently? In twelve adult years on Sentinel Gate she had had one love affair, received maybe four compliments, and noticed half a dozen admiring looks. Here it was two in two days.

Well, Legate Pereira had told her not to be surprised by anything that happened outside Alliance territory. And House-uncle Matra had been a lot more explicit when he learned where she was going: "Everyone on the Circle worlds is sex-mad. They have to be, or they'd die out."

The big turtles were not visible at the flying height she

chose, but a path to the edge of the Sling was easy to find. She flew out over the ocean for a while and was gratified to see the monstrous green back of a Dowser rising from the deep. From a distance it could have been a smaller, perfectly round Sling, until the moment when the whole back opened to ten thousand mouths, and each released a hissing spout of white vapor. After ten minutes the vents slowly closed, but the Dowser remained basking in the warm surface water.

Darya realized for the first time what perfect ecological sense the Slings made on a tidal waterworld like Opal. The tides were a destructive force on worlds like Sentinel Gate, where the rising and falling ocean waters were impeded in their movement by fixed land boundaries. But here everything could move freely, with the Slings riding buoyantly on the changing water surface. In fact, although the Sling that bore Starside's spaceport must even at that very moment be moving up or down in response to the gravitational pull of Mandel and Amaranth, it was completely at rest relative to the ocean's surface. Any disruptive force came from third-order effects produced by its large area.

The life-forms should be equally safe. Unless a Dowser were unlucky enough to be caught in an area where extra-low tides left the ocean bed exposed, the animal should be totally unaware of Summertide.

Darya flew to a point near the edge of the Sling, far enough inland to feel comfortable, and set the car down. It was not raining there, and there was even a suggestion that the disk of Mandel might show its face through the clouds. She climbed out and looked around. It was strange to be on a world so empty of people that there was no one to be seen from horizon to horizon. But it was not an unpleasant experience. She walked closer to the edge of the Sling. The soft-stemmed, long-leaved plants that fringed the ocean were bowed down with yellow fruit, each one as big as her fist. If Cap could be believed, they were safe to eat, but that seemed like an unnecessary risk. Although her intestinal flora and fauna had been boosted on arrival by forms suited to Opal, the microorganisms inside her were probably still deciding who did what. She walked closer to the ragged boundary of the Sling, took off her shoes, and leaned forward to scoop up a handful of seawater. That much she was willing to chance.

She sipped a few drops from her palm. It was brackish, not quite sea-salt. Rather like the taste of her own blood.

The complicated chemical balance of a planet like Opal made her sit back on her haunches and think. In a world without continents, streams and rivers could not perform their steady leaching of salts and bases from upthrust deep structures. Microseepage of primordial methane and the higher hydrocarbons must occur on the seabed, with absorption taking place through the water column. The whole land-water balance had to be radically different from the world that she knew. Was it truly a stable situation? Or were Opal and Quake still evolving from their condition before that traumatic hour, forty-odd million years ago, when they had been cast into their wild new orbit around Mandel?

She walked a hundred meters inland and squatted cross-legged on a hummock of dark green.

The parent star showed as a bright patch, high in the cloud-covered sky. There would be at least another two hours of daylight. Now that she had taken a closer look at Opal, she saw it as a warm and friendly world, not at all the raging fury of her imagination. Surely humans could thrive there, even at Summertide. And if Opal was so pleasant, could its twin, Quake, be all so different?

But it would have to be very different, if her own conclusions had any validity. She stared at the gray horizon, unmarked by boats or other land, and reviewed for the thousandth time the train of analysis that had brought her to Dobelle. How persuasive were those results, of minimal least-square residuals? To her, there was no way that such a precise data fit could occur by coincidence. But if the results were so persuasive and indisputable to her, why had others not drawn the same conclusions?

She came up with only one answer. She had been helped in her thinking because she was a stay-at-home, a person who had never traveled between the stars.

Humanity and its alien neighbors had become conditioned
to think of space and distances in terms of the Bose Drive.
Interstellar travel employed a precise network of Bose
Nodes. The old measure of geodesic distance between
two points no longer had much significance; it was the
number of Bose Transitions that counted. Only the Ark
dwellers, or perhaps the old colonists creeping along
through Crawlspace, would see a change in a Builder
artifact as generating a signal wavefront, expanding out
from its point of origin and moving across the galaxy at
the speed of light. And only someone like Lang, fascinated
by everything to do with the Builders, might ask if there
were single places and times where all those spherical
wavefronts intersected.

Each piece of the argument felt weak, but taken
together they left Darya fully persuaded. She felt a new
anger. She *was* in the right place—or would be, if she
could just leave Opal and get herself over to Quake! But
instead she was stuck in a sleepy dreamland.

Sleepy dreamland. Even as those words formed in her
mind there came a grating whirr from behind. A figure
from a nightmare flew through the air and landed right
in front of her, its six jointed legs fully extended.

If Darya did not cry out, it was only because her throat
refused to function.

The creature standing in front of her lifted two of its
dark-brown legs off the ground and reared up to tower
over her. She saw a dark-red, segmented underside, and
a short neck surrounded by bands of bright scarlet-and-
white ruffles. That was topped by a white, eyeless head,
twice the size of her own. There was no mouth, but a
thin proboscis grew from the middle of the face and curled
down to tuck into a pouch on the bottom of the pleated
chin.

Darya heard a high-pitched series of chittering squeaks.
Yellow open horns in the middle of the broad head turned
to scan her body. Above them a pair of light-brown
antennas, disproportionately long even for that great head,

unfurled to form two meter-long fans that quivered delicately in the moist air.

She screamed and jumped backward, stumbling over the grassy tussock that she had been sitting on. As she did so a second figure came in a long, gliding leap to crouch down before the carapace of the first. It was another arthropod, almost as tall but with a sticklike body no thicker than Darya's arm. The creature's thin head was dominated by lemon-colored compound eyes, without eyelids. They swiveled on short eyestalks to examine her.

Darya became aware of a musky smell, complex and unfamiliar but not unpleasant, and a moment later the second being's small mouth opened. "Atvar H'sial gives greetings," a soft voice said in distorted but recognizable human speech.

The other creature said nothing. As the first shock faded Darya was able to think rationally again.

She had seen pictures. Nothing in them had suggested such a size and menacing presence, but the first arrival was a Cecropian, a member of the dominant species of the eight-hundred-world Cecropia Federation. The second animal must be an interpreter, the lower species that every Cecropian was said to need for interaction with humankind.

"I am Darya Lang," she said slowly. The other two were so alien that her facial expressions probably had little meaning to them. She smiled anyway.

There was a pause, and again she was aware of the unfamiliar odor. The Cecropian's twin yellow horns turned toward her. She could see that their insides were a delicate array of slender spiral tubes.

"Atvar H'sial offers apologies through the other." One of the jointed arms of the silent Cecropian waved down to indicate the smaller beast by its feet. "We think perhaps we startled you."

Which had to be the understatement of the year. It was disconcerting to hear words that had originated in the mind of one being issuing from the mouth of another. But Darya knew that the seed world for the Cecropian clade, their mother planet as Earth had been the mother-planet for all humans, was a cloudy globe circling the glimmer of a red dwarf star. In that stygian environment the Cecropians had never developed sight. Instead they "saw" through echolocation, using high-frequency sonic pulses emitted from the pleated resonator in the chin. The return signal was sensed by the yellow open horns. As one side benefit, a Cecropian knew not only the size, shape, and distance of each object in the field of view, it could also use Doppler shift of the sonic return to tell the speed with which targets were moving.

But there were disadvantages. With hearing usurped for vision, communication between Cecropians had to be performed in some other way. They did it chemically, "speaking" to each other via the transmission of phero-mones, chemical messengers whose varying composition permitted them a full and rich language. A Cecropian not only knew what her fellows were saying; the pheromones also allowed her to *feel* it, to know their emotions directly. The unfurled antennas could detect and identify a single molecule of many thousands of different airborne odors.

And to a Cecropian, any being that did not give off the right pheromones did not exist as a communicating being. They could "see" them all right, but they did not feel them. Those nonentities included all humans. Darya knew that early contacts between Cecropians and humans had been totally unproductive until the Cecropians had produced from within their federation a species with both the capability for speech and the power to produce and sense pheromones.

She pointed to the other creature, which had discon-certingly swiveled its yellow eyes so that one was looking at her and one at the Cecropian, Atvar H'sial. "And who are you?"

There was a long, puzzling silence. Finally the small mouth with its long whiskers of sensing antennas opened again.

"The name of the interpreter is J'merlia. He is of low intelligence and plays no part in this meeting. Please ignore his presence. It is Atvar H'sial who wishes to speak with you, Darya Lang. I seek discussion concerning the planet of Quake."

Apparently Atvar H'sial used the other in the same way as the richer worlds of the Alliance employed service robots. But it would require a very complex robot to perform the translation trick that J'merlia was doing—more sophisticated than any robot that Darya had heard of, except for those on Earth itself.

"What about Quake?"

The Cecropian crouched lower, placing its two forelegs on the ground so that the blind head was no more than four feet from Darya. Thank God it doesn't have fangs or mandibles, Darya thought, or I couldn't take this.

"Atvar H'sial is a specialist in two fields," J'merlia said. "In life-forms adapting to live with extreme environmental stress, and also in the Artificers—the vanished race whom humans choose to call the Builders. We arrived on Opal only a few short time units ago. Long since we sent request for permission to visit Quake near to Summertide. That permission had not yet been granted, but at Opal Spaceport we spoke to a human person who told that you plan to go to Quake also. Is this true?"

"Well, it's not quite true. I *want* to go to Quake." Darya hesitated. "And I want to be there close to Summertide. But how did you find me?"

"It was simple. We followed the emergency locator on your car."

Not that, Darya thought. I mean, how did you know that I even *existed*?

But the Cecropian was continuing. "Tell us, Darya Lang. Can you arrange permission for Atvar H'sial's visit to Quake also?"

Was Darya's meaning being lost in translation? "You don't understand. I certainly *want* to visit Quake. But I don't have any control of the permits to go there. That's in the hands of two men who are on Quake at the moment, assessing conditions."

There was a brief glint of Mandel through the cloud

layers. Atvar H'sial reflexively spread wide her black wing
cases, revealing four delicate vestigial wings marked by
red and white elongated eyespots. It was those markings,
the ruffled neck, and the phenomenal sensitivity to
airborne chemicals that had led the zoologist examining
the first specimens to dub them fancifully "Cecropians"—
though they had no more in common with Earth's cecropia
moth than with any other Terran species. Darya knew that
they were not even insects, though they did share with
them an external skeleton, an arthropod structure, and
a metamorphosis from early to adult life-stage.

The dark wings vibrated slowly. Atvar H'sial seemed
lost in the sensual pleasure of warmth. There were a few
seconds of silence, until the cloud gap closed and J'merlia
said, "But men are males. You control them, do you not?"

"I do not control them. Not at all."

Darya wondered again about the accuracy with which
she and Atvar H'sial were receiving each other's messages.
The conversion process sounded as though it could never
work, moving from sounds to chemical messengers and
back through an alien intermediary who probably lacked
a common cultural data base with either party. And she
and Atvar H'sial also lacked common cultural reference
points. Atvar H'sial was a female, she knew that, but what
in Cecropian culture was the role played by males?
Drones? Slaves?

J'merlia produced a loud buzzing sound, but no words.

"I have no control over the men who will make the
decision," Darya repeated, speaking as slowly and clearly
as she could. "If they deny me access to Quake, there is
nothing that I can do about it."

The buzzing sound grew louder. "Most unsatisfactory,"
J'merlia said at last. "Atvar H'sial must visit Quake during
Summertide. We have traveled far and long to be here.
It is not thinkable to stop now. If you cannot obtain
permission for us and for yourself, then other methods
must be sought."

The great blind head swung close, so that Darya could
see every bristle and pore on it. The proboscis reached

out to touch her hand. It felt warm and slightly sticky. She forced herself not to move.

"Darya Lang," J'merlia said. "When beings possess a common interest, they should work together to achieve that interest. No matter what obstacles others attempt to put in their way, they should not be deterred. If you could guarantee your cooperation, there is a way that Darya Lang and Atvar H'sial might visit Quake. Together. With or without permission."

Was J'merlia misinterpreting Atvar H'sial's thoughts, or was Darya herself misunderstanding the Cecropian's intention? If not, then Darya was being recruited by this improbable alien to join a secret project.

She felt wary, but caution was mixed with a thrill of anticipation. The Cecropian could almost have been reading Darya's own earlier thoughts. If Rebka and Perry agreed to let her go to Quake, all well and good. But if not . . . there might be another project in the making.

And not just any project; an enterprise designed to take her to her objective—at Summertide.

Darya could hear the whistle of air as it was pumped continuously through the Cecropian's spiracles. The proboscis of Atvar H'sial was oozing a dark-brown fluid, and the eyeless face was a demon taken from a bad childhood dream. By Darya's side, the black, eight-legged stick figure of J'merlia was drawn from the same nightmare.

But humans had to learn to ignore appearance. No two beings who shared common thinking processes and common goals should be truly alien to each other.

Darya leaned forward. "Very well, Atvar H'sial. I am interested to hear what you have to say. Tell me more."

She was certainly not ready to *agree* to anything; but surely there could be no harm in *listening*?

Chapter 6
Summertide
minus twenty-nine

The Umbilical and the capsules that rode along it had been in position for at least four million years when humans colonized Dobelle. Like anything of Builder construction, it had been made to last. The system worked perfectly. It had been studied extensively, but although the analyses told a good deal about Builder fabrication methods, they revealed nothing about Builder physiology or habits.

Did the Builders breathe? The cars were open, built of transparent materials, and lacking any type of airlock. Did the Builders sleep and exercise? There was nothing that could be identified as a bed, or a place to rest, or a means of recreation.

Then surely the Builders at least had to eat and to excrete. Except that although the journey from Opal to Quake took many hours, there were no facilities for food storage or preparation, and no facilities for the evacuation of waste products.

The only tentative conclusion that human engineers could reach was that the Builders were *big*. Each capsule was a monster, a cylinder over twenty meters long and almost that much across, and inside it was all empty space. On the other hand, there was no evidence that the cars had been used by the Builders themselves— maybe they had been intended *only* as carriers of cargo. But if that were true, why were they also equipped with internal controls that permitted changes to be made in speed along the Umbilical?

While students of history argued about the nature and character of the builders, and theoreticians worried about inexplicable elements of Builder science, more practical minds went to work to make the Umbilical of use to the colonists. Quake had minerals and fuels. Opal had neither, but it possessed living space and a decent climate. The transportation system between the two was much too valuable to be wasted.

They began with the amenities necessary to make a comfortable journey between the components of the planetary doublet. They could not change the basic size and shape of the capsules; like most Builder products, the cars were integrated modules, near-indestructible and incapable of structural modification. But the cars were easily made airtight and fitted with airlocks and pressure adjustment equipment. Simple kitchens were installed, along with toilets, medical facilities, and rest areas. Finally, in recognition of the discomfort of planet-based humans with great heights, the transparent exteriors were fitted with panels that could be polarized to an opaque gray. The main observation port lay only at the upper end of the capsule.

Rebka was cursing that last modification as their car came closer to Quake. While they were ascending to Midway Station and beyond he had enjoyed an intriguing view of the planet ahead of them—enough to be willing to leave for a later occasion an exploration of the Builder artifact of Midway Station itself. He had assumed that he would continue to see more and more details of Quake until they finally landed. Instead, the car inexplicably swung end-over-end when they were still a few hundred kilometers above the surface. In place of Quake he was suddenly provided with an uninformative and annoying view of Opal's shifting cloud patterns.

He turned to Max Perry. "Can you swing us back? I can't see a thing."

"Not unless you want us to crawl the rest of the way." Perry was already jumpy in anticipation of their arrival. "We'll be entering Quake's atmosphere any minute now. The car has to be bottom-down for aerodynamic stability, or we have to crawl. In fact . . ." He paused, and his face became taut with concentration. "Listen."

It took a moment for Rebka to catch it; then his ears picked up the faintest high-pitched whistle, sounding through the capsule's walls. It was the first evidence of contact with Quake, of rarefied air resisting the passage of the plunging capsule. Their rate of descent must already be slowing.

Five minutes later another sensory signal was added. They were low enough for pressure equalization to begin, and air from Quake was being bled in. A faintly sulfurous odor filled the interior. At the same time the capsule began to shake and shiver with the buffeting of winds. Rebka felt an increased force pushing him down into the padded seat.

"Three minutes," Perry said. "We're on final deceleration."

Rebka looked across at him. They were about to land on the planet that Perry described as too dangerous for visitors, but there was no sign of fear in Perry's voice or on his face. He showed nervousness, but it could just as well be the excitement and anticipation of a man returning home after too long a time away.

How was that possible, if Quake was so dangerous a death trap?

The car slowed and stopped, and the door silently opened. Rebka, following Perry outside, felt that his suspicions were confirmed. They were stepping out onto a level surface, a blue-gray dusty plain sparsely covered with dark green shrubs and a low-profile ochre lichen. It was certainly dry and hot, and the smell of sulfur in the midafternoon air was stronger; but less than a kilometer away Rebka could see the gleam of water, with taller plants on its boundary, and near them stood a herd of low, slow-moving animals. They looked like herbivores, quietly grazing.

There were no erupting volcanoes, no earth tremors, and no monstrous subterranean violence. Quake was a peaceful, sleepy planet, drowsy in the heat, its inhabitants preparing to endure the higher temperatures that went with Summertide.

Before Rebka could say anything, Perry was staring all around and shaking his head.

"I don't know what's going on here." His face was puzzled. "I said we'd find trouble, and I wasn't joking. It's too damned quiet. And we're less than thirty days from Summertide, the biggest one ever."

Rebka shrugged. If Perry were playing some deep game, Rebka could not see through it. "Everything looks fine to me."

"It does. And that's what's wrong." Perry waved an arm, to take in all the scene around them. "It shouldn't be like this. I've been here before at this time of year, many times. We should be seeing quakes and eruptions by now—big ones. We should *feel* them, under our feet. There should be ten times as much dust in the air." He sounded genuinely confused.

Rebka nodded, then turned slowly through a full three hundred and sixty degrees, taking plenty of time for a thorough inspection of their surroundings.

Right in front of them stood the broad foot of the Umbilical. It touched the surface, but it was not held by a mechanical tether. The coupling was performed electro-magnetically, field-bound to Quake's metal-rich mantle. Perry had told him that it was necessary because of the instability of the planetary surface near Summertide. That was plausible, and consistent with Perry's claim about the violence of the event. Why else would the Builders have avoided a real tether? But mere plausibility did not make the statement true.

Beyond the Umbilical, in the dirrection of Mandel's setting disk, stood a brooding range of low mountains, purple-gray in the dusty air. The peaks were uniform in size and strangely regular in their spacing. From their harsh profile and the steep angle of their ascent, they had to be volcanic. But he could see no pall of smoke standing above them, nor any evidence of recent lava flows. He looked closer. The ground beneath his feet was smooth and fissure-free, with no gaps in plant growth to testify to recent fracturing of the surface.

So this was Quake, the great and terrible? Rebka had slept easy in environments ten times as threatening. Without a word he began walking toward the lake.

Perry hurried after him. "Where are you going?" He was nervous, and it was not simulated tension.

"I want to have a look at those animals. If it's safe to do it."

"It should be. But let me go first." Perry's voice was agitated as he moved on in front. "I know the terrain."

Nice and thoughtful of you, Rebka thought. Except that I don't see a thing in the terrain that *needs* knowing. The ground was marked here and there by patches of igneous outcrops and broken basaltic rubble, a sure sign of old volcanic activity, and the footing was sometimes difficult and uneven. But Rebka would have no more trouble traveling across it than Perry.

As they moved toward the water the going actually became easier. Closer to the lake lay a sward of springy dark-green ground cover that had managed to find purchase on the dry rocks. Small animals, all invertebrates, scuttled to hide away in it from the approaching strangers. The herbivores held their ground until the two men were a few meters away, then unhurriedly sidled off toward the lake. They were round-backed creatures with radial symmetry, multilegged and with cropping mouths set all around their periphery.

"You know what's bugging me, don't you?" Rebka asked suddenly.

Perry shook his head.

"All this." Rebka gestured at the plant and animal life around them. "You insist that humans mustn't come to Quake too near to Summertide. You say we can't survive here, and I'm supposed to tell Julius Graves and the others that they are not allowed to visit, and we'll lose the revenue they'd generate for Dobelle. But *they* stay here." He pointed to the animals making their slow way to the water's edge. "They survive, apparently with no trouble. What can they do that we can't do?"

"Two things." They had reached the lakeside, and Perry had for some reason lost his nervousness. "First of all, they avoid the surface of Quake during Summertide. Each one of the animals that you'll find on Quake either dies before Summertide, and its eggs hatch after summer is all over, or else it estivates—hides away for the summer. Those herbivores are all amphibians. In a few more days they'll go down into the lakes, dig deep into the mud at the bottom, and sleep until it's safe to come out again. We can't do that. At least, you and I can't. Maybe the Cecropians can."

"We could do something like that. We could make habitats, domes under the lakes."

"All right. We could, but I doubt if Darya Lang and the others would agree to it. Anyway, that's only half the story. I said they do two things. The other thing they do is, they breed *fast*. A big new litter every season. We can mate all we want to, every day, but we won't match that." Perry's grin had no humor in it. "They have to do it here. The death rate for animals and plants on Quake is over ninety percent per year. Evolution really pushes, so they've adapted as far as they can adapt. Even so, nine out of every ten will die at Summertide. Are you willing to try odds like that? Would you let Darya Lang and Julius Graves risk them?"

It was a powerful argument—*if* Rebka were willing to accept Perry's claim of Summertide violence. And so far he was not. A close approach to Mandel, consistent with Perry's claim about the violence of Summertide, would exert great tidal forces on Quake. No one could doubt that. But it was not clear how much those land tides would damage the surface. Quake's flora and fauna had survived for over forty million years. And that included dozens of Grand Conjunctions, even if there had been no humans to observe them. Why would it not easily survive another?

"Let's go." Hans Rebka had made up his mind. Mandel was close to setting, and he wanted to be off the planet before they were reduced to depending on Amaranth's dimmer glow. He was convinced that Perry was not telling him everything; that the man had his own reasons for trying to keep people away from Quake. But even if Max Perry were right, Rebka could not justify closing Quake. The evidence that the world was dangerous was just not there to send back to the government of the Phemus Circle.

The arguments all seemed to be the other way round. The native animals might have trouble making it through Summertide, but they did not have human knowledge and resources. Based on what Rebka could see, he would be quite willing to spend Summertide here himself.

"We have a duty to tell people the odds," he went on. "But we are not their guardians. If they choose to come here, knowing the dangers, we shouldn't stop them."

Perry hardly seemed to be listening. He was staring all around, frowning up at the sky and down at the ground and over to the distant line of hills.

"There's no way this can happen, you know," he said. His voice was perplexed. "Where's it all going?"

"Where's what all going?" Rebka was ready to leave.

"The energy. The tidal forces are pumping energy in—from Mandel and Amaranth and Gargantua. And none of it is coming out. That means there has to be some monstrous internal storage—"

He was interrupted by a flash of ruddy light from the west. Both men looked that way and saw that between them and the setting sphere of Mandel a line of dark, spreading fountains had appeared, shot with fire and rising from the distant mountains.

Seconds later the sound wave arrived; the ground shock came later yet, but the animals did not wait. At the first bright flash they were heading for the water, moving much faster than Rebka had realized they could ever manage.

"Blow out! We'll get flying rocks!" Perry was shouting,

through a rumble like thunder. He pointed to the multiple plumes. "Molten, some of 'em, and we're within easy range. Come on."

He started running back toward the Umbilical, while Rebka hesitated. The line of eruptions was curiously orderly, their spreading darkness bursting precisely from every third peak. He gave one quick look the other way—would water be a safer haven?—and then followed Perry. The ground began to shake, to seesaw back and forth so that he was close to losing his balance. He felt he had to slow down, until a mass of glowing ejecta, a semimolten rock the size of an aircar, plummeted in and lay sizzling within twenty meters of him.

Perry was already in the capsule at the foot of the Umbilical, holding the lower entry port wide open.

Rebka hurled himself through it headfirst, sacrificing dignity for speed. "All right. I'm in. Move it!"

Perry ran madly up the stairs to the control-and-observation chamber, and the car was starting into upward motion before Rebka had picked himself up and checked for injuries. Instead of securing the hatch and following Perry, he turned to the entry port and left it open a foot or so. He peered out.

Whistling lumps of rock and lava continued to pelt the area they had left. He could see fires as the ejecta seared the brush and the dry ground, and hear occasional fragments smacking into the Umbilical above and below them. They would do no damage, unless one entered the open port. He would have time enough to see it coming and to slam the door closed.

The most vulnerable items were the imported aircars. They sat in a neat line at the foot of the Umbilical, built by humans and brought from Opal for local exploration and use. As Rebka watched, a smoking chunk of rock hurtled toward the top of one of them. When it bounced away without making contact, he realized that the cars were sitting beneath a protective sheet of transparent Builder material—cannibalized, probably, from part of Midway Station.

He looked to the horizon. From their present height of two or three hundred meters he could see a long way through Quake's murky air. The surface was aflame with small flash fires, all the way to the distant peaks. Rising smoke brought a pungent aroma to his nostrils, resinous and aromatic, and the ground below was shimmering with heat and blurred by dust.

It was clear that the source of the disturbance was restricted to the single line of volcanoes that lay between them and Mandel's glowing face, low to the west. Every third peak carried a dusky plume and a pall of smoke above it. But already the force of the eruption was dwindling. The smoke clouds were no longer shot through with crimson and orange, and fewer rocks came sailing through the air toward the car. The herbivores had disappeared long ago, presumably hiding in the protective depths of the lake. They would know when to come out again.

Perry had left the controls and was crouched at Rebka's side. The car's movement up the Umbilical had ceased.

"All right." Rebka prepared to close the port. "I'm persuaded. I wouldn't want to take the responsibility for allowing people here at Summertide. Let's get out of here and head back to Opal."

But Perry was holding the door open and shaking his head. "I'd like to go back down."

"Why? Do you want to get killed?"

"Of course not. I want to take a good look at what's happening, and really understand it."

"Quake is approaching Summertide, Commander. That's what's happening. The volcanoes and earthquakes are starting, just the way you said they would."

"No. They're not." Perry was more contemplative than alarmed. "There's a mystery here. Remember, I've been on Quake before at this time of year, many times. What we just saw is nothing, just a little local fireworks. We should have found *more* activity than we did, one hell of a lot more. The surface was quiet when we arrived; it should have been shaking all the time. And the eruptions looked impressive, but the ground tremors were nothing.

You saw how quickly they died away." He gestured out of the port. "Look at it now, everything becoming quiet again."

"I'm no planetary geologist, but that's just what you would expect." Rebka could not understand what was going on in Perry's head. Did the man want people there at Summertide, or did he not? Now that there was a good argument against it, Perry seemed to be changing his mind. "You expect stress buildup and stress release. The internal forces build up for a while, until they reach a critical value, and then they let go. Quiet spells, and violent ones."

"Not here." Perry finally closed the port. "Not at Summertide. Think of it, Captain. This isn't normal planetary vulcanism. Opal and Quake revolve around each other every eight hours. Tidal forces from Mandel and Amaranth squeeze and pull their interiors every revolution. At normal Summertide those forces are huge, and the Grand Conjunction makes them even bigger—hundreds of times stronger than they are during the rest of the year."

He sat down in the lower cargo hold and stared at the wall. After a few moments Rebka went up to the control chamber and restarted their ascent himself. When he came down again, Perry had not moved.

"Come on, snap out of it. I believe you; the tidal forces are strong. But that's true for Opal as well as Quake."

"It is." Perry finally roused himself and stood up. "But the effects are damped on Opal. The ocean surface deforms freely and reaches new high and low tides every four hours. Any seabed changes—seaquakes and eruptions—are damped by the depth of water above them. But the land tides on Quake have no oceans to reduce their effects. At this time of year Quake should be active *all the time*. It isn't. So. Where is all that energy going?"

Perry dropped back into his seat and sat there frowning at nothing.

Rebka felt oddly dissatisfied as the upward speed of the car increased and the soft whistle of rapid travel through Quake's atmosphere began. He had been to Quake and seen evidence for himself. The place seemed fully as dangerous as Perry had warned. And yet Perry himself was not *afraid* of Quake. Not at all. He wanted to go back there—while an eruption was still in progress!

Rebka reached a conclusion. If he were to understand Perry, he had to have more data. He sat down facing the younger man.

"All right, Commander Perry. So it doesn't look the way you expected. I can't judge that. Tell me, then, what does Quake *usually* look like at this time of year?"

But that was exactly the wrong question. Perry's look of concentrated thought vanished. An expression of indefinable sadness crept onto his face. Rebka sat waiting for an answer, until he realized after a couple of minutes that he was not going to receive one. Instead of pulling Max Perry out of his reverie, that question had driven him deeper into it. The man was far gone, off in some strange fugue of unhappy memories.

Memories of what? Surely of Quake at Summertide.

Rebka did not speak again. Instead he swore an internal oath, stared up the Umbilical at the distant knot of Midway Station, and admitted an unpleasant truth. He had not wanted this job, a nursemaid task that had interrupted the most challenging project of his career. He had resented being taken away from Paradox, he resented being assigned to Dobelle, he resented Max Perry, and he resented having to worry about the interrupted career of a minor bureaucrat.

But his own pride would not allow him to abandon the job until he knew for certain what had destroyed the man. For Perry *was* destroyed, even if it did not show on the surface.

One other thing was clear. Whatever had destroyed Perry lived on Quake, close to Summertide.

Which meant that Rebka himself would surely be returning, to a place and to a time where all the evidence proved that humans could not survive.

ARTIFACT: UMBILICAL.
UAC#: 269
Galactic Coordinates: 26,837.186/
17,428.947/363.554
Name: Umbilical
Star/planet association: Mandel/Dobelle
(doublet)
Bose Access Node: 513
Estimated age: 4.037 ± 0.15 Megayears

Exploration History: Discovered by remote sensor observation during the unmanned stellar flyby of Mandel in E. 1446. First close inspection performed in manned flyby of E. 1513 (Dobelle and Hinchcliffe), first visit by colony ship in E. 1668 (Skyscan class, Wu and Tanaka). First used by Dobelle settlers, E. 1742. Employed routinely as working system since E. 1778.

Physical Description: The Umbilical forms a transportation system that joins the twin planets of the Dobelle system, Opal (originally Ehrenknechter) and Quake (originally Castelnuovo). Twelve thousand kilometers long and forty to sixty meters wide, the Umbilical forms a cylinder which is permanently tethered on Opal (seabed tether) and electromagnetically coupled to Quake.

Quake coupling is broken at the closest approach of the Dobelle system's highly eccentric orbit to the stellar primary of Mandell. This closest approach occurs every 1.43 standard years.

Variation in Umbilical length is achieved via "the Winch," employing a local space-time singularity (presumed an artifact), which enables the Umbilical to adapt automatically to variations in Opal/ Quake separation. The Winch also performs automatic withdrawal of the Umbilical from the surface of Quake at times of Mandel tidal maximum ("Summertide"). Control technique is understood operationally, but the trigger signal has not been determined (i.e., as time signal, force signal, or some other). Midway Station (9,781 kilometers from Opal center of mass, 12,918 kilometers from Quake center of mass) permits the addition to or removal from the Umbilical of payloads intended for free space launch or capture.

Note: The Umbilical is one of the simplest and most comprehensible of all Builder artifacts, and it is for that reason of less interest to most serious students of Builder technology. And yet it is also something of a mystery in its own right, since although simple it is one of the most recent feats of Builder construction (less than five million years). Some archeo-analysts have conjectured that this fact indicates the beginning of a decline in Builder society, culminating in the collapse of their civilization and their disappearance from the Galactic scene more than three million years ago.

Physical Nature: Defect-free solid hydrogen support cables with stabilized muonium splicing. Cable tensions rival those of human and Cecropian skyhooks but do not exceed them.

Transportation car propulsion is by linear synchronous motors with conventional power trains. The technique for cable-and-car attachments is unclear, but related to the Cocoon system free-space nets (see Cocoon, Entry 1).

The nature of the Winch is also debated, but it is probably a Builder artifact, rather than a natural feature of the Dobelle system.

Intended Purpose: Transportation system. Until the arrival of humans, this system had been unused for at least three million years. Currently it is reported in regular operation. There is no indication of other and earlier uses.

—From the *Lang Universal Aritfact Catalog*, Fourth Edition.

CHAPTER 7
Summertide
minus twenty-seven

Quake was changing. Not in the way that Max Perry had warned, moving as Summertide approached from a parched but peaceful world of high seismic activity to a trembling inferno of molten lava flows and fissured ground. Instead, Quake in this year of the Grand Conjunction had become—unpredictable.

And in its own way, Opal might be changing just as much. More than anyone on the planet realized.

That thought had come to Rebka as they were flying back around Opal, from the foot of the Umbilical to the Starside spaceport where Darya Lang would be waiting for them.

Six days earlier the journey around the clouded planet to the Umbilical had been dull, with no turbulence and little to see but uniform gray above and below. Now, with Summertide still twenty-seven days away, the car was buffeted and beaten by swirling and violent winds. Sudden updrafts ripped at the lifting surfaces and jolted the fuselage. Max Perry was forced to take the aircar higher and higher to escape the driving rain, black thunderheads, and whirling vortices of air and water.

So the inhabitants of Opal were convinced that they

would be safe, were they, even with tides far greater than normal?

Hans Rebka was not so sure.

"You're making a big assumption," he told Perry, as they began a descent through choppier air for their approach to Starside port. "You think Opal's tides this year will be just the same as at other Summertides, but bigger."

"That's overstating things." Once all sight of Quake had been lost under Opal's ubiquitous cloud layer, Perry's other personality had surfaced again: cool, stiff, and indifferent to most events. He did not want to discuss their experiences on the surface of Quake, nor his mystification at what was happening there. "I do not say that nothing different will occur on Opal," he went on. "Yet I believe that is not far from the truth. We may get forces too great for some of the bigger Slings, and one or two of them may break up. But I see no danger to people. If necessary, everyone on Opal can take to the water and ride out Summertide at sea."

Rebka was silent, holding on to the arms of his seat as they dropped through an air pocket that left both men floating free for a second or two. "It may not be like that," he said, as soon as his heart was no longer rising to stick in his throat.

Again and again he had the urge to poke and probe at Max Perry and watch his reactions. It was like control theory, feeding a black box with a defined set of inputs and monitoring the output. Do that often enough, and the theory said one could learn precisely all of the boxes' functions, though not, perhaps, why it performed them. But in Perry's case, there seemed to be two boxes. One of them was inhabited by a capable, thoughtful, and likable human. The other was a mollusc, retreating into its protective and impervious shell whenever certain stimuli presented themselves.

"This situation reminds me of Pelican's Wake," Rebka went on. "Did you hear what happened there, Commander?"

"If I did, I forgot it." That was not the sort of reaction

that Rebka was seeking, but Max Perry had an excuse. His attention was on the automatic stabilization system as it fought to bring them down to a smooth landing.

"They had a situation not too different from Opal," Rebka continued. "Except that it involved a plant-to-animal mass ratio, not sea tides.

"When the colonists first landed there, everything was fine. But every forty years Pelican's Wake passes through part of a cometary cloud. Little bodies of volatiles, mostly small enough to vaporize in the atmosphere and never make it to the ground. The humidity and temperature take a quick jump, a few percent and a few degrees. The plant-animal ratio swings down, oxygen drops a bit, then in less than a year it all creeps back to normal. No big deal.

"Everyone thought so. They went on thinking it, even when their astronomers predicted that on the next passage through the cloud, Pelican's Wake would pick up thirty percent more material than usual."

"I think I remember it now." Perry was showing a distant and polite interest. "It's a case we studied before I came to Dobelle. Something went wrong, and they came close to losing the whole colony, right?"

"Depends who you talk to." Rebka hesitated. How much should he say? "Nothing could be proved, but I happen to think you're correct. They came close. But my point is this: Nothing went wrong that could have been *predicted* with anybody's physical models. The higher level of comet material influx changed the Pelican's Wake biosphere to a new stable state. Oxygen went from fourteen to three percent in three weeks. It stayed there, too, until a terraforming gang could get in and start to change it back. That sudden switch would have killed almost everybody, because in the time available they wouldn't have had a hope of shuttling everyone out."

Max Perry nodded. "I know. Except that one man down on Pelican's Wake decided to move people offworld anyway, long before they got near the comet shower. He'd seen fossil evidence for changes, right? It's a classic case— the man on the spot knew more than anyone light-years away *could* know. He overrode instructions from his own headquarters, and he was a hero for doing it."

"Not quite. He got *chewed out* for doing it." The car had touched down and was taxiing toward the edge of the port, and Rebka was ready to let the subject drop. It was not the right time to tell Max Perry the identity of the man involved. And although he had been reprimanded in public, he had been congratulated in private for his presumption in countermanding a Sector Coordinator's written instructions. The fact that his immediate supervisors had *deliberately* left him ignorant of those written instructions was never mentioned. It seemed to be part of the Phemus Circle's government philosophy: Troubleshooters work better when they do not know too much. More and more, he was convinced that he had not been given all the facts before he was sent to Dobelle.

"All I'm saying is that you could face a similar situation on Opal," he went on. "When a system is disturbed by a periodic force, increasing the force *may not* simply lead to a bigger disturbance of the same kind. You may hit a bifurcation and change to a totally different final state. Suppose the tides on Opal become big enough to interact chaotically? You'll have turbulence everywhere—whirlpools and waterspouts. Monstrous solitons, maybe, isolated waves a mile or two high.

"Boats wouldn't live through that, nor would the Slings. Could you evacuate everyone if you had to, during Summertide? I don't mean to sea—I mean right off-planet?"

"I doubt it." Perry was switching off the engine and shaking his head. "I can be more definite than that. No, we couldn't. Anyway, where would we take them *to*? Gargantua has four satellites nearly as big as Opal, and a couple of them have their own atmospheres. But they're methane and nitrogen, not oxygen—and they're far too cold. The only other place is Quake." He stared at Rebka. "I assume we've given up on the idea that anyone should go *there*?"

The torrential rain that had plagued their approach to Starside had eased, and the car had come to a halt close to the building that Perry had assigned to Darya Lang as living quarters.

Hans Rebka stood up stiffly from his seat and rubbed at his knees. Darya Lang was supposed to be waiting to meet them, and she must surely have heard the aircar's approach. But there was no sign of her at the building. Instead, a tall skeletal man with a bald and bulging head was standing half-clear of the overhanging eaves, staring at the arriving car. He was holding a garish umbrella above his head. The shimmering white of his suit, with its gold epaulets and light-blue trim, could have come only from the spun fiber cocoon of a Ditron.

From a distance he appeared elegant and commanding, even though his face and scalp had been burned purple-red by hard radiation. Close up, Rebka could see that his lips and eyebrows jerked and twitched uncontrollably.

"Did you know he'd be here?" Rebka jerked a thumb below the window level of the car, so that the newcomer could not see it.

He did not need to mention the stranger's identity. Members of the Alliance councils were seldom seen, but the uniform was familiar to every clade on every world in the spiral arm.

"No. But I'm not surprised." Max Perry held the car door so that Rebka could step down. "We've been gone for six days, and his schedule fitted that time slot."

The man did not move as Perry and Rebka stepped out of the car and hurried to shelter under the broad eaves. He folded his umbrella and stood for half a minute, ignoring the raindrops that spattered his bald head. Finally he turned to meet them.

"Good day. But not good weather. And I gather that it is getting worse." The voice matched the man, big and hollow, with an edge of roughness overlaid on the sophisticated accent of a native of Miranda. He held out his left wrist, where identification was permanently imprinted. "I am Julius Graves. I assume that you received notice of our arrival."

"We did," Perry said.

He sounded ill at ease. The presence of a Council member from any clade was enough to make most people ponder their past sins, or realize the limits of their authority. Rebka wondered if Graves might have a second agenda for his visit to Opal. One thing he did know: Council members were kept desperately busy, and they did not like to waste time on incidentals.

"The information sheets did not provide details as to the reason for your visit," he said, and held out his hand. "I am Captain Rebka, at your service, and this is Commander Perry. Why are you visiting the Dobelle system?"

Graves did not move. He stood silent and motionless for another five seconds. At last he inclined his bulging head to the two men, nodded, and sneezed violently. "Perhaps your question is better answered inside. I am chilled. I have been waiting here since sunrise, expecting the return of the others."

Perry and Rebka exchanged glances. The others? And a return from where?

"They left eight hours ago," Graves continued, "at the time of my own arrival. Your weather prediction indicates that a—" The deep-set eyes clouded, and there was a moment's silence. "That a Level Five storm is heading for Starside Port. For strangers to Circle environments, such storms must be dangerous. I am worried, and I wish to talk to them."

Rebka nodded. One question was answered. Darya Lang had been joined on Opal by more visitors from outside the Phemus Circle. But who were they?

"Better check the arrival manifests," he said softly to Perry. "See what we've got."

"Do that if you wish." Graves stared at him; the pale blue eyes seemed to see right into Rebka's head. The councilor flopped onto a chair of yellow cane and plaited reeds, sniffed, and went on. "But you do not need to check. I can assure you that Darya Lang of the Fourth Alliance has been joined on Opal by Atvar H'sial and J'merlia of the Cecropia Federation. After I met them I examined the backgrounds of all three. They are what they claim to be."

Rebka did the calculation and started to open his mouth, but Perry was well ahead of him.

"That's impossible!"

Graves stared, and the busy eyebrows twitched.

"One day, you said, since your arrival here," Perry said. "If you sent an inquiry through the nearest Bose Network point as soon as you got here, and it was forwarded through the Nodes and answered *instantly*, the total turnaround time can't be less than a full standard day—three Opal days. I know, I've tried it often enough."

Perry's quite right, Rebka thought. And he's quicker than I realized. But he's making a tactical error. Council members don't lie, and it's asking for trouble to accuse them of it.

But Graves was smiling for the first time since they had met. "Commander Perry, I am grateful to you. You have simplified my next task." He pulled a spotless white cloth from his pocket, wiped the damp top of his hairless head with it, and tapped his massive and bulging brow.

"How can I know that, you ask. I am Julius Graves, as I said. But in a sense I am also Steven Graves." He leaned back in the chair, closed his eyes for a few seconds, blinked, and went on. "When I was invited to join the Council, it was explained to me that I would need to know the history, biology, and psychology of every intelligent and potentially intelligent species in the whole spiral arm. That data volume exceeds the capacity of any human memory.

"I was offered a choice: I could accept an inorganic high-density memory implant—cumbersome and heavy enough that my head and neck would need a permanent brace. That is preferred by Council members from the Zardalu Communion. Or I could develop an interior mnemonic twin, a second pair of cerebral hemispheres grown from my own brain tissue and used solely for memory storage and recall. That would fit inside my own skull, posterior to my cerebral cortex, with minimal cranial expansion.

"I chose the second solution. I was warned that because the new hemispheres were an integral part of me, their efficiency for storage and recall would be affected by my own physical condition—how tired I was, or whether I had been taking stimulants of any kind. I tell you this so that you will not think I am antisocial if I refuse a drink, or that I am a valetudinarian, excessively concerned with my own health. I have to be careful about rest and recreational stimulants, or the mnemonic interface is impaired. And Steven does not like that."

He smiled, and conflicting expressions chased themselves across his face, just as a sudden howl of wind hit the low building from outside. The fiber walls shivered. "For what I was *not* told, you see," he went on, "was that my interior mnemonic twin might develop *consciousness*—self-awareness. It happened. As I said, I am Julius Graves, but I am also Steven Graves. He is the source of my information on Darya Lang and on the Cecropian, Atvar H'sial. Now. Can we proceed to other business?"

"Can Steven talk?" Rebka asked. Max Perry seemed to be in shock. One member of the Council poking around in one's affairs was bad enough—now they had *two* of them. And was Julius Graves always in charge? From the changing expressions on his face, a continuous battle could be going on inside.

Graves shook his head. "Steven cannot talk. He also cannot feel, see, touch, or hear, except as I send my own sensory inputs to mnemonic storage through an added corpus callosum. "But Steven can *think*—better, he insists, than I can. As he tells me, he has more time for it. And he sends signals back to me, his own thoughts in the form of returning memories. I can translate those, well enough so that most people would believe Steven to be speaking directly. For instance." He was silent for a few moments. When he spoke his voice was noticeably younger and more lively. "*Hi. Glad to be here on Opal. No one said that the weather here would be so lousy, but one nice thing about being where I am, you don't get wet when it rains.*" The voice returned to its hollow, gravelly tone. "My apologies. Steven has a fondness for weak jokes and an appalling sense of humor. I fail to control both, but I do try to screen them. And I confess that I also allow myself to become too dependent on Steven's knowledge. For instance, he holds most of our local information about conditions on this planet, while my own learning is sadly deficient. I deplore my own laziness.

"But now, may we continue with business? I am here on Dobelle regarding a matter for which humor is not at all appropriate."

"Murder," Perry muttered after a long pause. The height of the storm was almost there, and as the sounds of the wind increased he had become more clearly uncomfortable. Unable to sit still, he was prowling in front of the window, looking out at the threshing ferns and tall grasses, or up at racing clouds ruddy with the rusty light of Amaranth.

"Murder," he repeated. "Multiple murder. That's what your request to visit Opal said."

"It did. But only because I was reluctant to send word of a more serious charge over the Bose Network." Julius Graves was surely not joking now. "A more accurate word is *genocide*. I will moderate that, if you prefer, to *suspected* genocide."

He stared quietly around him, while new rain lashed the walls and roof. The other two men had frozen, Max Perry motionless in front of the window, Hans Rebka on the edge of his seat.

"Genocide. Suspected genocide. Is there a significant difference?" Rebka asked at last.

"Not from some points of view." The full lips twitched and trembled. "There is no statute of limitations, in time or space, for the investigation of either. But we have only circumstantial evidence, without proof and without confession. It is my task to seek those. I intend to find them here on Opal."

Graves reached into the blue-trimmed pocket of his jacket and produced two image cubes. "Improbable as it seems, these are the accused criminals, Elena and Geni Carmel, twenty-one standard years old, born and raised on Shasta. And, as you can see, identical twin sisters."

He held the cubes out to the other two men. Rebka saw only two young women, deeply tanned, big-eyed, and pleasant looking, dressed in matching outfits of russet green and soft brown. But Max Perry apparently saw something else in those pictures. He gave a gasp of recognition, leaned forward, and grabbed the data cubes. He stared into them. It was twenty more seconds before the tension drained from him and he looked up.

Julius Graves was watching both men. Rebka was suddenly convinced that those misty blue eyes missed nothing. The impression of quaintness and eccentricity might be genuine, or it might be a pose—but underneath it lay a strange and powerful intelligence. And fools did not become Council members.

"You seem to know these girls, Commander Perry," Graves said. "Do you? If you have ever met them, it is vital that I know when and where."

Perry shook his head. His face was even paler than usual. "No. It's just that for a few moments, when I first saw the cubes, I thought they were . . . someone else. Someone I knew a long time ago."

"Someone?" Graves waited, and then, when it was clear that Perry would say nothing more, he went on. "I propose to keep nothing from you, and I strongly urge you to keep nothing from me. With your permission, I will allow Steven to tell the rest of this. He has the most complete information, and I find it difficult to speak without emotion clouding my statements."

The twitching ceased. Graves's face steadied and took on the look of a younger and happier man. "Okay, here goes," he said. "The sad story of Elena and Geni Carmel. Shasta's a rich world, and it lets its youth do pretty much what they like. When the Carmel twins hit twenty-one they were given a little space tourer, the *Summer Dreamboat*, as a present. But instead of just hopping around their local system, the way most kids do, they talked their family into sticking a Bose Drive in the ship. Then they set off on a real travel binge: nine worlds of the Fourth Alliance, three of the Zardalu Communion. On their final planet, they decided to see life 'in the rough'—that's how their 'grams home put it. It meant they wanted to live in comfort but observe a backward world.

"They landed on Pavonis Four and set up a luxury tent. Pav Four's a poor, marshy planet of the Communion. Poor now, I should say—rich enough before human developers had a go at it. Along the way, a native amphibian species know as the Bercia were a nuisance. They were almost wiped out, but by that time the planet was picked clean and the developers left. The surviving members of the Bercia—what few there were— were given the probationary status of a potential intelligence. They were protected. At last."

Graves paused. His face became a changing mask of expressions. It was no longer obvious whether it was Julius or Steven who was speaking.

"Were the Bercia intelligent?" he said softly. "The universe will never know. What we do know is that the Bercia are now *extinct*. Their last two lodges were wiped out two months ago . . . by Elena and Geni Carmel."

"But not by design, surely?" Perry was still clutching the data cubes and staring down at them. "It must have been an accident."

"It may well have been." From the serious manner, Julius Graves was again in charge. "We do not know, because when it happened the Carmel twins did not stay to explain. Inexplicably, they fled. They continued to flee, until one week ago we closed the Bose Network to them. And now they can flee no farther."

The storm had arrived in full force. From outside the building a mournful wail sounded, the cry of a siren audible over the scream of wind and the thresh of rain on the roof. Rebka could still listen to Graves, but some other conditioning in Perry took over. At the first note of the siren he headed for the door.

"A landing! That siren means someone's in trouble. They're crazy, if they don't have the right experience, in a Level Five storm . . ."

He was gone. Julius Graves began to rise slowly to his feet. He was restrained by Hans Rebka's grip on his arm.

"They fled," Rebka prompted. Through the rain-streaked window he could see the lights of a descending aircar, dipping and veering drunkenly in treacherous crosswinds. It was only a few meters from the ground, and he had to get out there himself. But first he had to confirm one thing. "They fled. And they came—to Opal?"

Graves shook his scarred and massive head. "That is what I thought, and that is why I requested a landing here. Steven had calculated that the trajectory had its end-point in the Dobelle system. But when I arrived I spoke at once with the Starside Spaceport monitors. They assured me that no one could have landed a ship with a Bose Drive on this world, without them being aware of it."

There was a new wail of alarm equipment from outside and the lurid glare of orange-red warning flares. Voices were screaming at each other. Watching at the window, Rebka saw the car touch down, bounce back high into the air, and then flip over to hit upside down. He started for the door, but he was held back by Graves's sudden and strong grip on his arm.

"When Commander Perry returns, I will inform him of a new request," Graves said quietly. "We do not want to search Opal. The twins are not here. But they are in the Dobelle system. And that can only mean one thing: they are on Quake."

He cocked his head, as though hearing the scream of sirens and the sounds of tearing metal for the first time. "We must search Quake, and soon. But for the moment, there seem to be more immediate problems."

CHAPTER 8
Summertide
minus twenty-six

The moment of death. A whole life flashing before your eyes.

Darya Lang heard the side-wind hit just as the wheels of the aircar touched down for the second time. She saw the right wing strike—felt the machine leave the runway—knew that the car was flipping onto its back. There was a scream of overstressed roof panels.

Suddenly dark earth was whizzing past, a foot above her head. Soggy mud sprayed and choked her. The light vanished, leaving her in total darkness.

As the harness cut savagely into her chest, her mind cleared with the pain. She felt cheated.

That was her whole life, supposedly rushing past her? If so, it had been a miserably poor one. All that she could think of was the Sentinel. Now she would never understand it, never penetrate its ancient mystery, never learn what had happened to the Builders. All those light years of travel, to be squashed like a bug in the dirt of a lousy minor planet!

Like a bug. The thought of bugs made her feel vaguely guilty.

Why?

She remembered then, hanging upside down in her

87

harness. Thinking was hard, but she had to do it. She was alive. That liquid dripping down her nose and into her eyes stung terribly, but it was too cold to be blood. But what about the other two, Atvar H'sial and J'merlia, in the passenger seats? *Not* bugs, she thought; in fact, less like insects than she was. *Rational beings.* Shame on you, Darya Lang!

Had she killed them, though, with her lousy piloting?

Darya craned her head around and tried to look behind her. There was something wrong with her neck. A shock of pure heat burned its way into her throat and her left shoulder even before she turned. She could see nothing.

"J'merlia?" No good calling for Atvar H'sial. Even if the Cecropian could hear, she could not reply. "J'merlia?"

No answer. But those were human voices outside the ship. Calling to her? No, to each other—hard to hear above the whistling wind.

"Can't do it that way." A man's voice. "The top's cracked open. If that strut goes, the weight will smash their skulls in."

"They're goners anyway." A woman. "Look at the way they hit. They're crushed flat. Want to wait for hoists?"

"No. I heard someone. Hold the light. I'm going inside."

The light! Darya felt a new panic. The darkness before her was total, blacker than any midnight, black as the pyramid in the heart of the Sentinel. At that time of year Opal had continuous daylight, from Mandel or its companion, Amaranth. Why could she not see?

She tried and failed to blink her eyes: reached up her right hand to rub at them. Her left hand had vanished—there was no sensation from it, no response but shoulder pain when she tried to move it.

Rubbing just made her eyes sting worse. Still she could see nothing.

"God, what a mess." The man again. There was the faintest glimmer in front of her, like torchlight seen through closed eyes. "Allie, there's three of 'em in here—I think. Two of 'em are aliens, all wrapped round each other. There's bugjuice everywhere. I don't know what's what, and I daren't touch 'em. Send a distress call; see if you can find anybody near the port who knows some alien anatomy."

There was a faint and unintelligible reply.

"Hell, I don't know." The voice was closer. "Nothing's moving—they could all be dead. I can't wait. They're covered in black oil, all over. One good flame in here, they'll be crisps."

Distant chatter, diffuse: more than one person.

"Doesn't matter." The voice was right next to her. "Have to pull 'em out. Somebody get in here to help."

The hands that took hold of Darya did not mean to be rough. But when they grabbed her shoulder and neck multiple galaxies of pain pinwheeled across the blackness in her eye sockets. She gave a scream, a full-throated howl that came out like a kitten's miaow.

"Great!" The grip on her shifted and strengthened. "This one's alive. Coming through. Catch hold."

Darya was dragged on her face across a muddy tangle of roots and broken stalks of fern. A clod of slimy and evil-tasting moss crammed into her open mouth. She gagged painfully. As a protruding root dug deep into her broken collarbone it suddenly occurred to her: She did not *need* to stay awake for such indignity!

Darkness enveloped her. It was time to stop fighting; time to rest; time to escape into that soothing blackness.

It had taken Darya a day to learn, but at last she was sure: *dialog* between human and Cecropian was impossible without the aid of J'merlia or another Lo'tfian intermediary; but *communication* was feasible. And it could carry a good deal of meaning.

A Cecropian's rigid exoskeleton made facial expression impossible in any human sense. However, body language was employed by both species. They merely had to discover each other's movement codes.

For instance, when Atvar H'sial was confident that she knew the answer that Darya would give to a question, she would lean away a little. Often she also lifted one or

both front legs. When she did *not* know the answer and
was anxious to hear it, the delicate proboscis pleated and
shortened—just a bit. And when she was truly excited—
or worried; it was difficult to know the difference—by a
comment or a question, the hairs and bristles on her long
fanlike antennas would stand up straighter and a fraction
bushier.

As they had done, strikingly, when Julius Graves had
come on the scene.

Darya knew about the Council—everyone did—but she
had been too preoccupied with her own interests to take
much notice of it. And she was still vague about its functions,
though she knew it involved ethical questions.

"But everyone is *supposed* to be vague, Professor Lang,"
Graves had said. He gave her a smile which his enlarged,
skeletal head turned into something positively menacing. It
was not clear how long ago he had landed at Starside Port,
but he had certainly chosen to pay her a visit at an inconvenient time. She and Atvar H'sial had held their preliminary
discussions and were all set to get down to the nitty-gritty:
who would do what, and why, and when?

"Everyone is vague, that is," Graves went on, "except
those whose actions make the Council *necessary.*"

Darya's face was betraying her again, she was sure of
it. What she was about to do with the Cecropian ought to
be no business of the Council; there was nothing *unethical*
about short-circuiting a bureaucracy in a good scientific
cause, even if that cause had not been fully revealed to
anyone on Opal. What else did Council members do?

But Graves was staring at her with those mad and misty blue
eyes, and she was sure he must be reading guilt in hers.

If he were not, he surely could detect it in Atvar H'sial!
The antennas stood out like long brushes, and even J'merlia
was almost gibbering in his eagerness to get out the words.

"Later, esteemed Councilor, we will be most delighted
to meet with you later. But at the moment, we have an
urgent prior appointment." Atvar H'sial went so far as to
take Darya Lang's hand in one jointed paw. As the
Cecropian pulled her toward the door—to the outside,

where it was pelting with rain!—Darya noticed for the first time that the paw's lower pad was covered with black hairs, like tiny hooks. Darya could not have pulled away, even if she had been willing to make a scene in front of Julius Graves.

It was another vestigial remnant of a distant flying ancestor of Atvar H'sial, one who had perhaps needed to cling to trees and rocks.

Well, none of us sprang straight from the head of the gods, did we? she reflected. We all have bits and pieces left over by evolution. Darya glanced automatically at her own fingernails. They were filthy. It seemed she was already slipping into the disgusting ways of Opal and Quake.

"Where to?" She spoke in a whisper. Julius Graves would need phenomenal hearing to pick up anything she said over the hissing rain, but she was sure he was staring after them. Wondering, no doubt, where they were going and why, when the weather loomed so foul. She felt a lot better out of his presence.

"We will talk of it in a moment." J'merlia, receiving the direct benefit of Atvar H'sial's nervous pheromones, was hopping up and down as though the sodden apron of the aircar facility were blistering hot. The Lo'tfian's voice quivered with urgency. "Inside the car, Darya Lang. Inside!"

They were both actually reaching out to lift her in!

She pushed the paws away. "Do you *want* Graves to think something illegal is going on?" she hissed at Atvar H'sial. "Calm down!"

Her reaction even made her feel a little superior. The Cecropians had such a reputation for clear, rational thought. Many—including every Cecropian—said that they were far superior to humans in intellectual powers and performance. And yet here was Atvar H'sial, as jittery as if they were planning a major crime.

The two aliens crowded into the car after her, pushing her forward.

"You do not understand, Darya Lang." While Atvar H'sial closed the door, J'merlia was urging her toward the pilot's seat. "This is your first encounter with a member of a major clade council. They cannot be trusted. They are supposed to confine themselves to ethical matters, but they do not! They have no shame. They feel it their right to dabble in everything, no matter how little it concerns them. We could not have discussions with Julius Graves present! He would surely have sensed and sniffed out and interfered with and ruined everything we have planned. We have to get away from him. Quickly."

Even as J'merlia spoke, Atvar H'sial was waving frantically for Darya to take off—into storm clouds that had piled up ominously over half the sky. Darya pointed, then realized that the Cecropian's echolocation would "see" nothing at such a distance. Even with those incredible ears, Atvar H'sial's world must be confined to a sphere no more than a hundred meters across.

"There's bad weather—that way, to the east."

"Then fly west," J'merlia said. "Or north, or south. But *fly.*" The Lo'tfian was crouched on the floor of the aircar, while Atvar H'sial leaned with her head against the side window, her blind face staring off at nothing.

Darya took the car up in a steep climbing turn, fleeing for the lighter clouds far to their left. If once she could get above them, the car could cruise for many hours.

How many? She was not keen to find out. It would be better to keep on ascending, clear the storm completely, and seek a quiet place where she could set them down near the edge of the Sling.

Two hours later she had to abandon that idea. The rough air went on endlessly, and there was no drop in the force of the winds. They had flown to the edge of the Sling and circled far beyond it, seeking another landing spot, and found nothing. Worse than that, the dark mass of major thunderstorms was pursuing them. A solid wall of gray stretched across three quarters of the horizon. Car radio weather reported a "Level Five" storm but did not bother to define it. Mandel had set, and they flew only by the angry light of Amaranth.

She turned to Atvar H'sial. "We can't stay up here forever,

and I don't want to leave things to the last minute. I'm going to take us higher, right over the top of the storm. Then we'll stay above it and head back the way we came. The best place to land is the one we started from."

Atvar H'sial nodded complacently as the message was relayed to her by J'merlia. The storm held no fears for the Cecropian—perhaps because she could not see the black and racing clouds that showed its strength. Her worries were still with Julius Graves.

As they flew Atvar H'sial laid out through J'merlia her complete plan. They would learn the official word on the proposed trips to Quake as soon as Captain Rebka came back. If permission were denied, they would then proceed at once to Quakeside, in an aircar whose rental was already paid. It sat waiting for them, on the small takeoff field of another Sling not far from Starside Port. To reach it, they would rent a local car, one whose travel range was so limited that Rebka and Perry would never dream that they intended to go so far.

Atvar H'sial, with J'merlia as interpreter, could make all those arrangements without difficulty. What she could not do, the one task for which Darya Lang was absolutely essential, was to requisition a capsule on the Umbilical.

She stated her reasons, as Darya listened with half an ear and fought the storm. No Cecropian had ever before visited Opal. The appearance of one on Quakeside, trying to board an Umbilical capsule, would produce immediate questions. Permission would not be given without checking entry permits, and that would lead back to Rebka and Perry.

"But you," J'merlia said, "you will be accepted at once. We have the correct documents already prepared for you." The pleated surface of Atvar H'sial's proboscis tightened a fraction. She was leaning over Darya, forelimbs together in a position that looked like earnest prayer. "You are a human . . . . and you are a female."

As if *that* helped. Darya sighed. Full interspecies communication might be impossible. She had told them three times, but the Cecropian could not seem to accept the concept that in humans, the females were *not* the unquestioned and dominant ruling gender.

Darya set out to gain altitude. This storm was *something*. They needed to be above and beyond those thundercaps before they started any descent, and despite the stability and strength of the aircar she did not relish the job ahead of her.

"And we know the correct control sequences to employ in ascending the Umbilical," J'merlia went on. "Once you have cleared us for access to the capsule, nothing will stand between us and the surface of Quake."

Those words were intended to encourage Darya and soothe any worries. Curiously, they had the opposite effect. She began to wonder. The Cecropian had arrived on Opal *after* her—and yet she had false documents, already prepared? And she knew all about Umbilical control sequences. Who had given those to her?

"Tell Atvar H'sial that I'll have to think about all this before I can make a final decision."

Think, and learn a lot more for herself, before she committed to any joint trip to Quake with Atvar H'sial. The alien seemed to know just about everything on Dobelle.

Except, possibly, about the dangers of Opal's storms.

They were descending, and the turbulence was frightening. Darya heard and felt giant wind forces on the car. She prayed that its automatic stabilization and approach system could fly better than she could. She was no superpilot.

Atvar H'sial and J'merlia were quite unperturbed. Maybe beings who were descended, however remotely, from flying ancestors had a more sanguine view of air travel.

Darya would never acquire that, for sure. Her guts were knotting. They were through the clouds and dropping in a rainstorm more violent than any she had ever known on Sentinel Gate. With visibility less than a hundred meters and no landmarks, she had to rely on the beacons of Starside's automatic landing system.

If it worked at all, in such a downpour.

The view through the forward window was useless,

nothing but driving rain. They had been descending for a long time—too long. She steadied herself on the console and peered at the instrument panel. Altitude, three hundred meters. Beacon slant range, two kilometers. They must be just seconds away from landing. But where was the field?

Darya looked up from the panel and saw the approach lights for a couple of seconds. They were right in place, dead ahead. She reduced power, drifting them down along the glowing line. The wheels touched briefly. Then a rolling crosswind grabbed the car, lifted it, and carried them up again and off to the side.

Everything moved to slow motion.

The car dipped. She saw one wing catch on rain-slick earth . . .

. . . watched it dig a furrow, bend and buckle . . .

. . . heard the crack as it broke in two . . .

. . . felt the beginning of the aircar's first cartwheel . . .

. . . and knew, beyond doubt, that the best part of the landing was over.

Darya never once lost consciousness. She was so convinced of that fact that after a while her brain came up with an explanation of what was happening. It was simple: Every time she closed her eyes, even for a moment, someone changed the scenery.

First, the agony and indignity of a drag across wet, uneven soil. No scenery there, because her eyes were not working.

(blink)

She was lying face-upward, while someone leaned over her and sponged at her head. "Chin, mouth, nose," a voice said. "Eyes." And terrible pain.

"Transmission fluid, looks like." He was not speaking to her. "It's all right, not toxic. Can you handle it on the others?"

"Yeah," another man said. "But the big one has a crack in its shell. It's dribbling gunk and we can't suture. What should I do?"

"Tape, maybe?" A dark shape moved away from her. Cold raindrops splashed into her stinging eyes.

(*blink*)

Green walls, a beige ceiling, and the hissing and purring of pumps. A computer-controlled IV dripped into her left arm, cantilevered up over her body by a metal brace. She felt warm and comfortable and just *wonderful*.

Neomorph, said a detached voice in her brain. Fed in by the computer whenever the telemetry shows you need it. Powerful. Rapidly addictive. Controlled use on Sentinel Gate. Employ only under controlled conditions with reverse epinephrine triggers.

Nuts, the rest of her said. Feels great. Phemus Circle really know how to use drugs. Hooray for them.

(*blink*)

"Feeling better?"

A stupid question. She did not feel good at all. Her eyes ached, her ears ached, her teeth ached, her toes ached. Her head buzzed, and there were stabs of pain that started near her left ear and ran all the way to her fingertips. But she knew that voice.

Darya opened her eyes. A man had magically appeared at the bedside.

"I know you." She sighed. "But I don't know your first name. You poor man. You don't even have a first name, do you?"

"Yes, I do. It is Hans."

"Captain Hans Rebka. That's all right, then, you do have a name. You're pretty nice, you know, if you'd just smile a bit more. But you're supposed to be away on Quake."

"We got back."

"I want to go to Quake."

The damned drug, she thought. It was the drug, it must be, and now she knew why it was illegal. She had to shut up before she said something really damaging.

"Can I go there, nice Hans Rebka? I have to, you see. I really have to."

He smiled and shook his head.

"See, I knew you'd look a lot better if you smiled. So

will you let me go to Quake? What do you say, Hans Rebka?"

She blinked before he could reply. He disappeared.

When she opened her eyes again there was a major addition to the room. Over to her right a lattice of black metal tubes had been erected to form a cubical scaffolding. A harness hung at the center of it, attached by strong cords to the corners. In that harness, pipe-stem torso swathed in white tape, head drooping low, and thin limbs stretched out vertically and to both sides, hung J'merlia.

The contorted position of the wrapped body suggested the agony of a final death spasm. Darya automatically looked around for Atvar Hsial. There was no sign of the Cecropian. Was it possible that the symbiosis between the two was so complete that the Lo'tfian could not *survive* without the other? Had he died when the two were separated?

"J'merlia?"

She spoke without thinking. Since J'merlia's words were nothing more than than a translation of Atvar H'sial's pheromonal speech, it was stupid to expect an independent response.

One lemon eye swiveled in her direction. So at least he knew she was there.

"Can you hear me, J'merlia? You look as though you are in terrible pain. I don't know why you are in that awful harness. If you can understand me, and you need help, tell me."

There was a long silence. Hopeless, Darya thought.

"Thank you for your concern," a dry and familiar voice said finally. "But I am in no pain. This harness was built at my own request, for my comfort. You were not conscious when it was being done."

Was that really J'merlia speaking? Darya automatically looked around the room again. "Is that you, or Atvar H'sial? Where is Atvar H'sial? Is she alive?"

"She is. But regrettably, her wounds are worse than yours. She required major surgery on her exoskeleton.

You have one broken bone and many bruises. You will be fully mobile in three Dobelle days."

"How about you?"

"I am nothing; my situation is unimportant."

J'merlia's self-effacing manner had been acceptable when Darya had thought him no more than a mouthpiece for Cecropian thoughts. But now this was a rational being, with its own thoughts, its own feelings.

"Tell me, J'merlia. I want to know."

"I lost two joints of one hind limb—nothing important; they will grow back—and I leaked a little at my pedicel. Negligible."

It had its own feelings—and its own *rights*?

"J'merlia." She paused. Was it her business? A member of the Council was here, on this very planet. In fact, running away from him had been the prime cause of their injuries. If anyone should be worrying about the status of the Lo'tfians, it ought to be Julius Graves, not Darya Lang.

"J'merlia." She found herself talking anyway. How long before the drug was out of her system? "When Atvar H'sial is present you never speak any of your own thoughts. You never say anything at all."

"That is true."

"Why not?"

"I have nothing to say. And it would not be appropriate. Even before I reached second shape, when I was no more than postlarval, Atvar H'sial was named my dominatrix. When she is present, I serve only to carry her thoughts to others. I have no other thoughts."

"But you have intelligence, you have knowledge. It's wrong. You should have your own rights . . ." Darya paused.

The Lo'tfian was wriggling in his harness, so that both compound eyes could be turned toward the human.

He bowed his head to her. "Professor Darya Lang, with permission. You and all humans are far above me, above all Lo'tfians. I would not presume to disagree with you.

But will you permit me to tell you of our history, and also of the Cecropians? May I?"

She nodded. That was apparently not enough, for he waited until she finally said, "Very well. Tell me."

"Thank you. I will begin with us, not because we are important, but only for purposes of comparison. Our homeworld is Lo'tfi. It is cold and clear-skied. As you might guess from my appearance, we have excellent vision. We saw the stars every night. For thousands of generations we made use of that information only to tell at what time of the year certain foods should be available. That was all. When it was colder or hotter than usual, many of us would starve to death. We could speak to each other, but we were hardly more than primitive animals, knowing nothing of the future and little of the past. We would probably have stayed so forever.

"Think now of Atvar H'sial and her people. They developed on a dark and cloud-covered world—and they were *blind*. Because they see by echolocation, sight for them implies the presence of air to carry the signal. So their senses could never receive information of anything beyond their own atmosphere. They deduced the presence of their own sun, only because they felt its weak radiation as a source of warmth. They had to develop a technology that told them of the very *existence* of light. And they had to build instruments that were sensitive to light and to other electromagnetic radiation, so that they could detect and measure it.

"That was just the beginning. They had to turn those instruments to look at the sky, and deduce the existence of a universe beyond their homevorld and beyond their sun. And finally they had to acknowledge the importance of the stars, measure their distances, and build ships to travel to and explore them.

"They did this—all this—while we Lo'tfians sat around dreaming. We are the older race, but if they had not found our world and *raised* us to self-awareness and to understanding of the universe, we would be sitting there still, as animals.

"Compared to Cecropians, or to humans, Lo'tfians are nothing. Compared to Atvar H'sial, I am nothing. When her light shines, mine should not be seen. When she speaks, it is my honor to be the instrument that gives her thoughts to you.

"Do you hear me, Professor Darya Lang? It is my honor. Darya Lang?"

She had been listening—and listening hard. But she was beginning to hurt, and the computer-controlled IV was not ready to allow that. The pump had started again, a few seconds before.

She forced her eyes to remain open.

I am nothing! What a racial inferiority complex. But the Lo'tfians should not be allowed to be a slave race even if they wanted it. As soon as she could get to him, she would go and report it.

To him.

To whom?

Mad and misty blue eyes, but she could not recall his name. Was she afraid of him? Surely not.

She would report this to—

(blink).

CHAPTER 9
Summertide
minus twenty

"She's not dead, and not dying. She's *healing*. The correct Cecropian response to trauma and physical insult is unconsciousness."

In the middle of Opal's brief night, Julius Graves and Hans Rebka stood by the table that held Atvar H'sial's motionless body. Part of one side of the dark-red carapace had been coated with a thick layer of gypsum and agglutinate, hardening to a gleaming white shell. The proboscis was pleated and secured in its chin pouch, while the antennas lay furled over the broad head. The whistle of air pumping through spiracles was barely audible.

"And it is amazingly effective by human standards," Graves continued. "Recovery from an injury which does not kill a Cecropian outright is fast—two or three days, at most. And Darya Lang and J'merlia consider that Atvar H'sial is already recovered enough to renew a request for access to Quake." He smiled, a death's-head grin. "Not welcome news to Commander Perry, eh? Has he asked you to delay everything until after Summertide?"

Hans Rebka hid his surprise—tried to. He was becoming used to the feeling that Julius Graves possessed limitless knowledge of every species in the spiral arm. After

101

all, the mnemonic twin had been created for exactly that purpose, and from the moment that they had arrived at the scene of the crash Steven Graves had dictated the treatment for Atvar H'sial's injuries: the shell must be sealed, the legs taped, the broken wing case removed entirely—it would regenerate—and the crushed antenna and yellow auditory horns left to heal themselves.

But it was harder to accept Graves's knowledge and understanding of *humans*.

It occurred to Rebka that he and Julius Graves should switch jobs. If anyone could find out what had changed Max Perry from an up-and-coming leader to a career drop-out and impenetrable mental mystery, Graves could do it. Whereas Rebka was the man who could explore the surface of Quake and find the Carmel twins, no matter where they tried to hide.

"And your own views, Captain," Graves went on. "You have been to Quake. Should Darya Lang and Atvar H'sial be permitted to go there once they have recovered? Or should they be refused access?"

That was exactly what Rebka had been asking himself. It was left unsaid that Graves intended to go to Quake, no matter who opposed him. Perry would accompany him, as his guide. And although Rebka had said nothing, he intended to go, too. His job required it, and anyway Max Perry was biased and unreliable on anything to do with Quake. But what about the others?

He travels fastest who travels alone.

"I'm opposed to the idea. The more people, the more dangerous, no matter what specialized knowledge they bring along. And that applies to Cecropians as well as humans."

Or even more so for Cecropians. He stared down at the unconscious alien, fought off a shiver, and walked away toward the door of the building.

He had no trouble with J'merlia, with his downtrodden look and pleading yellow eyes. But it made him uncomfortable just *looking* at Atvar H'sial. And he considered himself an educated, reasonable man. There was some hidden quality to the aliens that he found hard to tolerate.

"Cecropians still make you uneasy, Captain." It was Graves, following him to the door and reading his mind again—making a statement, not asking a question.

"I guess they do. Don't worry, I'll get used to them."

He would—slowly. But it was hard going. The miracle was that Cecropians and humans had not embarked on total war when the two species had first encountered each other.

And they would have, Rebka's inner voice assured him, if they could have found anything worth fighting about. Cecropians looked like demons. If they had not sought planets around red dwarf stars, while humans were looking for Sol analogs, the two would have encountered each other in the outward crawl. But the unmanned probes and the slow Arks of both species had been targeted for quite different stellar types, and they had missed each other for a thousand years. By the time humans discovered the Bose Drive and found the Cecropians already using the same Network through the spiral arm, both species had had experience with other alien organisms; enough to allow them to coexist with other clades whose needs were for stellar environments so different from their own, even if they could not be viscerally comfortable.

"Vertebrate chauvinism is all too common." Graves fell into step at his side. He was silent for another moment; then he giggled. "Yet according to Steven—who says that he speaks as someone who lacks both a backbone *and* an exoskeleton—we should think of ourselves as the outsiders. Of the four thousand two hundred and nine worlds known to possess life, Steven says that internal skeletons have developed on only nine hundred and eighty-six. Whereas arthropod invertebrates thrive on three thousand three hundred and eleven. In a galactic popularity contest, Atvar H'sial, J'merlia, or any other arthropod would beat you, me, or Commander Perry hands down. And even, if I dare say it, your Professor Lang."

Rebka started to walk faster. It would serve no purpose

to point out to Julius Graves that Steven was on the way to becoming a bore. It was all right to *know* everything in the universe—but did he have to *tell* it?

Rebka was not willing to admit the real cause of his irritation. He hated being with someone who knew far more than he did, but worse still he hated to be with a man who saw through him with no effort at all. No one was supposed to know that he had a soft spot for Lang. Damn it, he had only realized it *himself* when he had pulled her out of the crashed aircar. She was something more than a nuisance, more than an unwanted addition to his problems with Quake and Max Perry.

Why had she come, to make life more complicated? It was obvious that she was out of her depth on Opal, a scientist who should have stayed quietly in her lab to do her research. They would have to look after her. *He* would have to look after her. And the best way to do that was to keep her on Opal when he went to Quake.

The Level Five storm was over, and there was a rare break in Opal's night clouds. It was near midnight, but not dark. Amaranth had been swinging in on the final stages of its slow approach to Mandel. It was high in the sky, big enough to show a glowing disk of bright orange. In two more days, the dwarf companion would begin to cast shadows.

Half a sky away from it, lurking near the horizon, lay Gargantua, beginning its own dive toward the furnace of Mandel. It was still no more than a rosy point, but it was brighter than all the stars. In another week the gas-giant would show its own circular disk, barred with stripes of umber and pale yellow.

Rebka headed across the starport to one of the four main buildings. Graves was still tagging along beside him.

"You are heading to meet with Louis Nenda?" the councilor asked.

"I hope so. How much do you know about him?" If Rebka was stuck with Graves, he might as well try to use his superior knowledge.

"Only what the request told you," Graves said. "Plus our own knowledge of members of the Zardalu Communion—which is less than we would like. The Communion worlds are not noted for their cooperation."

Which might qualify as the best understatement yet, Rebka thought.

Twelve thousand years earlier, long before humans had begun the Expansion, the land-cephalopods of Zardalu had tried to create something that neither humans nor Cecropians had ever been foolish enough to attempt: the Zardalu Communion, a genuine empire, a thousand planets ruled ruthlessly from Genizee, the homeworld of the Zardalu clade. It had failed disastrously. But that failure might have been the object lesson saving humans and Cecropians from the same mistake.

"Louis Nenda is basically human," Graves went on, "but with some Zardalu augmentation."

"Mental or physical?"

"I do not know. But whatever was done, it must be fairly minor. There's no mention of rear-skull or fingertip eyes, no hermaphroditism, no deboning or quadrimanuals or quadripedals. No gigantism or compaction—he's male, and standard size and weight according to the manifest. Of course, there are hundreds of modifications that don't appear on any standard list.

"As for the pet that he brings with him, I can tell you even less. It is a Hymenopt, and needless to say, it is another arthropod—though similar to Earth's Hymenoptera only by analogy. But whether it is a plaything, or a sexual partner, or even a food supply for Nenda—that we will have to wait and see."

And not wait long, Rebka thought. The newly arrived ship sat in the middle of Starside Port, its occupants already in screening for organisms at the arrival building. Since tests for endo- and ecto-parasites took only a few minutes, the newcomers had to be in the final stages of entry.

Rebka and Graves moved to where Max Perry and three officials from Port Entry were already waiting.

"How much longer?" Rebka asked.

Instead of replying, Perry gestured to the sealed double doors of Decontamination. They were beginning to open.

After Graves's suggestions and Rebka's imaginings, Louis Nenda looked surprisingly normal. Short, swarthy, and muscular, he could have passed for an inhabitant of one of the denser worlds of the Phemus Circle. He was a little unsteady on his feet, probably the result of half a dozen changes of gravity in the past few hours, but he had plenty of pep, and his self-confidence showed in his walk. He glared arrogantly around with bloodshot eyes as he strutted out of the exobiology test unit; trotting by his side, mimicking his head movements, came a chubby little alien. It halted when it saw the group of waiting humans.

"Kallik!" Louis Nenda tugged on the harness that passed around the Hymenopt's thorax and encased the abdomen. "Heel."

Then, without a look at anyone except Perry, he said, "Good morning Commander. I think you'll find I test negative. Kallik also. Here's my access request."

The other men were still staring at the Hymenopt. Julius Graves had seen one in travels through the Zardalu territories, but the rest of them knew only pictures and stuffed specimens.

The alien was hard to match to the Hymenopt's fierce reputation. It was less than half the height of Louis Nenda, with a small, smooth head dominated by powerful traplike mandibles and by multiple pairs of bright black eyes set in a ring around the perimeter. They were in constant motion, independently tracking different objects around it.

The Hymenopt's body was rotund and barrel-shaped and covered with short black fur, a centimeter or two long. That was the prized Hymantel, a tough, water-resistant, and insulating coat.

What was not visible was the gleaming yellow sting, retracted into the end of the blunt abdomen. The hollow needle delivered squirts of neurotoxins, whose strength and composition the Hymenopt could vary at will. No standard serum could be effective as an antidote. Also invisible was the nervous system that provided a Hymenopt with a reaction speed ten times as fast as any human's. Eight wiry legs could carry it a hundred meters in a couple of seconds, or fifteen meters into the air under standard gravity. The Hymantel had been a seldom-seen item of human clothing, even before the Hymenopts had been declared a protected species.

"Welcome to the Dobelle system." Perry's voice said the opposite of his words. He took the access requests from Louis Nenda and glanced through them. "Your original request said little about the reason why you wish to visit Quake. Do you have more details here?"

"Sure do." Nenda's manner was as cocky as his walk. "I want to look at big land tides, and that means Quake. At Summertide. No problem in that, is there?"

"Quake is dangerous at Summertide. More dangerous than ever, with Amaranth coming so close."

"Hell, I don't care about danger." Nenda stuck out his chest. "Me and Kallik, we eat danger. We were down on Jellyroll when they had the hyperflare. Spent nine days in an aircar, chasing round in Jellyroll's shadow to avoid being roasted, got out without even a tan. Before that we were on the next-to-last ship out of Castlemaine." He laughed. "Lucky for us. Last ship out had no supplies and a forty-day crawl to a Bose Node. They had to eat each other. But for a real experience let me tell you what happened on Mousehole—"

"As soon as we've had a chance to review your request." Perry gave Nenda an angry glance. Even on one minute's exposure it was clear that the newcomer would not take it well if his application were rejected. "We'll show you to temporary accommodation, then some of us need to have a meeting. Is there anything special that he"—he gestured at the Hymenopt—"needs to eat?"

"She. Kallik is female. No, she's an omnivore. Like me." Nenda laughed with no trace of humor. "Hey, I hope I'm not hearing what I think I'm hearing. What's all this 'need to have a meeting' stuff? I've come a damned long way for this. Too far to get the runaround now."

"We'll see what we can do." Perry glanced down at Kallik. At the fury in Louis Nenda's voice a couple of inches of yellow sting had slid from its sheath. "I'm sure

we agree on one thing: You don't want to go to Quake
and be killed there."

"Don't you worry your head about us. We don't kill
easy. Just approve that access request and let me get over
there. It'll take more than Quake to do me in."

Maybe it would. Rebka watched as Perry led the
newcomer away. Quake was dangerous, no doubt about
it; but if self-confidence were any protection, Louis Nenda
would be safe anywhere. Maybe it was Quake that needed
the protection.

"I would like to hear your recommendation, Commander."

But Perry won't look at me, Rebka thought. He thinks
he knows my decision. But he's wrong—because I don't
know it myself.

"I oppose Summertide access, as you know." Perry's
voice was barely audible, and his face was pale.

"Oppose access for anyone?"

"That's right."

"You know that Graves will simply overrule whatever
we decide? He has the authority to hunt for the Carmel
twins on Quake, anytime he wants to."

"He has that authority, and we both assume that he will
go. But authority won't protect him. Quake at Summertide
is a *killer*." Perry's voice rose on the final word.

"Very well. What about the others? They are willing
to pay Dobelle very substantial amounts for the privilege
of visiting Quake."

"I would approve their visits—well after Summertide.
Darya Lang can study the Umbilical without being on the
surface; Atvar H'sial has the whole rest of the year to study
species under environmental stress."

"They'll never agree. Refuse access at Summertide, and
you lose them and the money they would pay to Dobelle.
What about Louis Nenda?"

Perry finally met Rebka's eye, and a different tone came
into his voice. He even managed a smile. "He's lying, isn't
he?"

"I certainly think so."

"And he's not very good at it."

"He doesn't give a damn. He should have picked a more plausible story. He strikes me as the last man in the spiral arm to be interested in land tides—I'm tempted to get Steven Graves to ask him a few technical questions about them. But that wouldn't solve anything. He came a long way to get here, nearly nine hundred light-years—unless he's lying about everything else, as well. But he certainly came from the Zardalu Communion, and that's at least four Bose Nodes. Any suggestions as to what he's really after?"

"I have no idea." Perry went quiet again and looked far off at something invisible. "But I don't think he's the only one who's lying. The inquiry you sent to Circle intelligence about Darya Lang confirmed that she's an expert on Builder artifacts, but there's no reason for her to go down to the surface of Quake. She could do all her work here, or on the Umbilical itself. But whether she's telling the truth or not doesn't make any difference to my opinion. You asked for a recommendation. I'm giving it: no access for Lang, no access for Atvar H'sial, no access for *anyone* until after Summertide. And if Graves chooses to override us, that's up to him."

"You would let him go to Quake alone?"

"God, no." Perry was genuinely shocked. "You might as well kill him here. I'd go with him."

"I thought so." Rebka had made up his mind. "And so will I."

And for all the wrong reasons, he thought. If I *allow* access to Quake, I may find out why everyone is so keen to go there. But if I *refuse* access, I'll find out just how keen they are. And I'll probably force some of them to take action. That, I know how to deal with.

"Commander Perry," he continued. "I have made my decision. I agree with your recommendation." He smiled inwardly at the surprise on Perry's face. "We will refuse access to Quake for all parties until Summertide is over."

"I feel sure that's the right decision." Perry's self-control was excellent, but the expression of relief could not be hidden.

"Which leaves us one more decision to make," Rebka said. "Maybe we should toss a coin for it. Who is going to give the bad news to Darya Lang and to Atvar H'sial? Worst of all, who will tell Louis Nenda?"

ARTIFACT: LENS.
UAC#: 1023
Galactic Coordinates: 29,334.229/
18,339.895 / — 831.22
Name: Lens
Star/planet association: None, free space
entity
Bose Access Node: 108
Estimated age: 9.138 ± 0.56 Megayears

Exploration History: The full history of Lens may never
be known. Lying as it does in the clade of the Zardalu
Communion, all early records were lost with the collapse
of the Zardalu Empire. However, given the preoccupation
of the Zardalu with biological science and their relative
indifference to physical ones, it is most unlikely that any
systematic exploration of Lens was ever attempted by
them.

The recorded history of Lens begins with its observation
in E.122, but it was long assumed to be extragalactic.
The local nature, as part of the spiral arm, was discovered
in E. 388 from parallax effects. The Lens was approached
directly in E. 2102 by Kusra (one-way journey), but no
physical evidence for material existence could be
obrtained. Paperl and Ula H'sagta (E. 2377) measured a
polarization change of beamed lasers passed through the
region of the Lens, confirmed its location, and mapped
its extent.

Physical Description: The Lens is a focusing region of
space, 0.23 light-years in diameter and of apparently zero
thickness (grazing incidence measurements have been
made down to one micrometer). Focusing is performed
only for light with wavelength range of 0.110 to 2.355
micrometers, approaching within 0.077 radians of normal
incidence to the plane surface of the Lens. There is,
however, weak evidence of interaction with radiation of
wavelength in excess of 0.1 light-years (the low energy
of such radiation makes its separation from cosmic

background of debatable validity). All other light, all particles or solid objects, and all gravity waves pass through the Lens apparently unaffected. Radiation focusing appears to be perfectly achromatic for all wavelengths in the stated range. In that range, the Lens performs as a diffraction-limited focusing device of 0.22 light-years effective aperture and 427 light-years focal length. With its aid, planetary details have been observed in galaxies more than one hundred million parsecs distant.

Physical Nature: This must unfortunately comprise an eliminative list of what the Lens is *not*. Today's science and technology can provide no tenable suggestion as to what it *is*.

The Lens is not built on any particles known to today's inhabitants of the spiral arm. It is not a form of space-time singularity, since such a singularity cannot affect light of certain wavelengths and leave all other forms of matter and radiation untouched. For the same reason, it cannot be an assembly of bound gravitons. It cannot possess a superstring or superloop structure, since no spontaneous or induced emission is observed.

Intended Purpose: Unknown. The Lens represents macroengineering by the Builders at its largest and most mysterious. The specific wavelength range has, however, induced some students of the artifact to speculate that this range corresponds to the spectral sensitivity range of Builder eyes. Since there is no evidence that the Builders possessed anything equivalent to eyes in human or Hymenopt terms, the conjecture is of passing interest only.

It has also been conjectured that the Lens performs modulation of the light passing through it, in a way not understood. If so, its function as a focusing lens would be no more than an accidental by-product of the structure's true purpose.

—From the *Lang Universal Artifact Catalog,* Fourth Edition.

CHAPTER 10
Summertide
minus eighteen

"Come in," Darya Lang called out automatically when she heard a tentative knock on the door. She saw it swing open.

"Come in," she repeated. Then she saw that the visitor was already in, or partially so. Just a foot above the ground, a round black head with a ring of bright eyes was peering past the edge of the open door.

"She don't understand you worth a damn," a gruff voice said. "Only knows a few command words in human talk. Get in there."

A frowning, squat, and swarthy man came striding through the door, pushing a diminutive alien ahead of him. A stiff halter around the Hymenopt's plump thorax was connected to a black whipping cane in the man's hand.

"I'm Louis Nenda. This here"—a downward jerk of the cane—"is Kallik. Belongs to me."

"Hello. I'm Darya Lang."

"I know. We need to talk."

He was the worst yet. Darya was becoming impatient with the level of manners in the Phemus Circle. But it was catching. "You may need to talk. I certainly don't. So why don't you leave now?"

Unexpectedly, he grinned. "Wait and see. Where can we talk?"

113

"Right here. But I don't see why we should."

He shook his head and jerked his thumb toward J'merlia. The Lo'tfian had recovered enough to be released from the support harness, but he still preferred to remain where he could raise himself aloft for sleep periods. "What about the stick insect?"

"He's all right." She bent to look at the ocular membrane. "He's just resting. He'll be no trouble."

"I don't care what he's doing. What I have to say can't be said in front of that bug."

"Then I don't think I want to hear it, either. J'merlia isn't a bug. He's a Lo'tfian, and he's as rational as you are."

"Which don't impress me too much." Nenda grinned again. "There's people say I'm crazy as a Varnian. Come on, let's go talk."

"Can you give me one reason why I should want to?"

"Sure. I can give you twelve hundred and thirty-seven of 'em."

Darya stared at him. "Are you talking about the Builder artifacts? Only twelve hundred and thirty-six of those have been discovered."

"I said *reasons*. And I bet we can both think of one very good reason for talking that's *not* an artifact."

"I don't know what you mean." But Darya could feel her traitorous face, as usual, betraying her.

"Kallik, stay." Louis Nenda added a set of whistles and grunts to the words. He turned to Darya. "Speak any Hymenopt? Thought not. I told her to go over there and keep an eye on the bug. Come on outside. She'll come get us if it wakes up and needs you."

He loosed the cane from Kallik's halter and headed out of the door and out of the building, not even looking back to see if she was following.

What did he know? What *could* he know? Logic said, not a thing. But Darya found herself following him out onto the sodden surface of the Sling.

Starside Weather Central was predicting another major storm in a day, but for the moment the winds had died away to warm and humid gusts. Mandel and Amaranth were together in the sky, fuzzy bright patches on the cloud layer. Amaranth was growing rapidly in apparent brightness. Green plants had become edged with copper, and there was a rusty tinge to the eastward sky. Louis Nenda walked confidently into the brush—no worries for *him* about giant tortoises, Darya thought. But by now they should all be safely out at sea, anyway, ready to ride out Summertide.

"That's far enough," she called after him. "Tell me what you want."

He turned around and came back toward her. "All right, this'll do. I just don't want an extra audience, that's all. And I assume you don't."

"I don't mind. I have nothing to hide."

"Yeah?" He was smiling up at her, half a head shorter. "Funny, I'd have thought you might. You're Darya Lang, the Fourth Alliance's expert on Builder technology and Builder history."

"I'm not an expert, but I am very interested in the Builders. That's no secret."

"It's not. And you're famous enough so that the Builder specialists in the Zardalu Communion know all about your work and the Lang Catalog. You get invited to conferences and meetings, don't you, all the time? But you've never traveled, they all say, not for a dozen years. Anyone who wants to see Darya Lang, they make that trek to Sentinel Gate. Except that a couple of months ago, you can't be reached there. All of a sudden you take off. For Dobelle."

"I want to explore the Umbilical."

"Sure. Except according to the Lang Catalog, UAC 279—"

"UAC 269," said Darya automatically.

"Sorry, UAC 269. Anyway, it says—mind if I quote you?—the Umbilical is 'one of the simplest and most comprehensible of all Builder artifacts, and is for that reason of less interest to most serious students of Builder technology.' Remember writing that?"

"Of course I do. What of it? I'm a free agent; I can change my mind. And I can go where I like.

"You can. Except that your bosses back on Miranda made a big mistake. They should have told people who asked that you'd gone off to Tantalus, or Cocoon, or Flambeau, or one of the other really big Builder draws. Or maybe just say you'd gone off for a holiday."

"What *did* they say?" She should not have been asking, but she had to know. What had those dummies back in central government done to her?

"They didn't say nuthin'. They clammed up and told anyone who asked to go away and stop bothering them and come back in a couple of months. You don't tell people that if you want them to stop sniffing around."

"But you found me with no trouble." Darya was feeling very relieved. He was a pest, but he did not know anything, and it was not her fault that he was there.

"Sure did. We found you. It wasn't hard, once we got going; there's transfer information for every Bose Transition."

"So you followed me here. Now what do you want with me?"

"Did I say we followed you, *Professor*?" He turned the title into an insult. "We didn't. You see, we were already on the way. But when we found you were here, too, I knew we really had to get together. Come on, dearie."

Louis Nenda took Darya by the arm and led her through the undergrowth. They came to a tangled ridge of vines and horizontal woody stems, bulging up to form a long and lumpy bench. At pressure from him she sank down to a sitting position. Her legs were wobbly.

"We had to get together," he repeated. "And you know why, don't you? You pretend you don't, Darya Lang, but you sure as hell do." He sat down next to her and patted her familiarly on the knee. "Come on, it's confessional time. You and me have things to tell each other, sweetheart. Real intimate things. Want me to go first?"

❖   ❖   ❖

If the results are so obvious to *me*, why haven't others drawn the same conclusions?

Darya remembered thinking that, long before she ever set out for Dobelle. And finally she could answer the question. Others *had* drawn the same conclusions. The mystery was only that someone as crude, direct, and unintellectual as Louis Nenda could have done it.

He had not beaten about the bush.

"Builder artifacts, all over the spiral arm. Some in your territory, back in the Alliance, some in the Cecropia Federation, some back where I live in Zardalu-land. Yeah, and one here, too, the Umbilical.

"Your Lang Catalog lists every one of 'em. And you use a universal galactic ephemeris to show every time there's been a *change* in any artifact. In appearance, size, function, anything."

"As best I could." Darya was admitting nothing that was not written in the catalog itself. "Some times weren't recorded to enough significant figures. I'm sure other events were missed entirely. And I suspect some were logged that weren't real changes."

"But you showed an average of thirty-seven changes per artifact, over an observation span of three thousand years—nine thousand years for artifacts in the Cecropian territory, 'cause they've been watching longer than anyone else. And no correlation of the times."

"That's right." Darya did not like his grin. She nodded and glanced away.

Nenda squeezed her knee with powerful fingers. His hand was thick and hairy. "Getting too close to the crucial point, am I? Don't feel bad, sweetie. Hang in—we'll be there in a minute. The event *times* didn't correlate, did they? But in one of your papers you made a throwaway suggestion. Remember it?"

How long should she go on stalling? Except that Legate Pereira's instructions had been quite specific. She was not to tell anyone outside the Alliance what she had found—even if they seemed to know it already.

She pushed his hand away from her leg. "I've made a lot of throwaway suggestions in my work."

"So I hear. And I hear you don't forget things. But I'll refresh your memory, anyway. You said that the right way to examine possible time correlation of artifact changes was not through the examination of universal galactic event times. It was to think of the effects of a change as propagating outward from their point of origin, traveling like a radio signal, at the speed of light. So ten light-years after something happened at an artifact, information about that change would be available everywhere on the surface of a sphere, ten years in radius and with center at the artifact. Remember writing that?"

Darya shrugged.

"And any two spheres expand until they meet," Louis Nenda went on. "First they'll touch at one point, then as they grow they'll intersect in a circle that just gets bigger and bigger and bigger. But it gets trickier with three spheres. When they grow and meet, they'll do it at just two points. Four or more spheres don't usually have any points in common. And when you get to twelve hundred and thirty-six artifacts, with an average of thirty-seven changes for each one, you have nearly fifty thousand spheres—each one spreading out at the speed of light with an artifact as the sphere center. What's the chances that twelve hundred and thirty-six of those spheres, one from each Builder artifact, will all meet at one place? It should be negligible, too small to measure. But if they *did* meet, against all the odds, *when* would that happen?

"Sounds like an impossible question, doesn't it? But it's not hard to program and test for intersections. And do you know the answer that program gives, Professor Lang?"

"Why should I?" It was too late, but she stalled anyway.

"Because you're *here*. Damn it, let's stop pretending. Do you want me to spell it out for you?"

His hand was on her thigh again, but it was his tone of voice that finally made her angry enough to hit back.

"You don't need to spell *anything* out for me, you—you lecherous little dwarf. And you may have followed up on it, but that's *all* you did—follow up! It was my original idea. And get your filthy hand off my leg!"

He was grinning in triumph. "I never said it wasn't your idea. And if you don't want to be friendly, I won't push it. The spheres all coincide, don't they—to as many significant figures as the data permit? One place, and one time, and we both know where. The surface of Quake, at Summertide. That's why you're here, and that's why I'm here, and Atvar H'sial, and everybody but your Uncle Jack."

He stood up. "And now the local bozos say we can't go! Any of us."

"What?!" Darya jerked to her feet.

"You didn't hear it yet? Old stone-head Perry came and told me an hour ago. No Quake for you, no Quake for me, no Quake for the bugs. We come a thousand light-years to sit here on our asses and miss the whole show."

He slashed the black cane from Kallik's harness at the bole of a huge bamboo. "They say, no go. I say, then screw 'em! See now why we have to do something, Darya Lang? We have to pool our knowledge—unless you *want* to sit here on your ass and take orders from pipsqueaks."

Mathematics is universal. But very little else is.

Darya reached that conclusion after another half hour's talk with Louis Nenda. He was a horrible man, someone she would go out of her way to avoid. But when they had traded statistical analyses—grudgingly, carefully, each unwilling to offer more than was received—the agreement was uncanny. It was also in a sense inevitable. Starting from the same set of events and the same set of artifact locations, there was just one point in space and time that fitted all the data. Any small differences in the computed time and place of the final result arose from alternative criteria for minimizing the residuals of the fit, or from different tolerances in convergence of the nonlinear computations.

They had followed near-identical approaches, and used similar tolerances and convergence factors. She and Louis Nenda agreed on results to fifteen significant figures.

Or rather, Darya concluded after another fifteen minutes, she and whoever had done the calculations for Nenda were in agreement. It could not be his own work. He had no more than a rough grasp of the procedures. He was in charge, but someone else had done the actual analysis.

"So we agree on the time, and it's within seconds of Summertide," he said. He was scowling again. "And all we know is that it's somewhere on Quake? Why can't you pin it closer? That's what I was hoping we could do when we compared notes."

"You want miracles? We're dealing with distances of thousands of light-years, thousands of trillions of kilometers, and time spans of thousands of years. And we have a final uncertainty of less than two hundred kilometers in location, and less than thirty seconds in time. I think that's pretty damned good. In fact, it *is* a miracle, right there."

"Maybe close enough." He slapped the cane against his own leg. "And it's definitely on Quake, not here on Opal. I guess that answers another question I had."

"About the Builders?"

"Nuts to the Builders. About the bugs. Why they want to get to Quake."

"Atvar H'sial says she wants to study the behavior of life-forms under extreme environmental stress."

"Yeah. Environmental stress, my ass." He started to walk back toward the cluster of buildings. "Believe that, and you'll believe in the Lost Ark. She's after the same thing as we are. She's chasing the Builders. Don't forget she's a Builder specialist, too."

Louis Nenda was coarse, barbaric, and disgusting. But once he said it, it became obvious. Atvar H'sial had come to Dobelle too well prepared with contingency plans, just as though she had known that the requests for access to Quake would all be refused.

"What about Julius Graves? Him too?"

But Nenda only shook his head. "Old numb-nuts? Nah. He's a mystery. I'd normally have said, sure, he's here for the same reason as we are. But he's Council, an' even if you don't believe half of what you hear about them—I don't—I've never heard of one lying. Have you?"

"Never. And he didn't expect to go to Quake when he came, only to Opal. He thought those twins he's after would be here."

"So maybe he's for real. Either way, we can forget him. If he wants to go to Quake, he'll do it. The bozos can't stop him." They were back at the building, and Nenda paused just outside the door. "All right, we had our little chat. Now for the best question of all. Just *what* is going to happen on Quake at Summertide?"

Darya stared at him. Did he expect her to answer that? "I don't know."

"Come on, you're stalling again. You *must* know—or you wouldn't have dragged all this way."

"You have it exactly backward. If I *did* know what will happen, or if I even had a halfway plausible idea of it, I'd never have left Sentinel Gate. I like it there. You dragged all this way, too. What do *you* think will happen?"

He was glaring at her in frustration. "Lord knows. Hey, you're the genius. If *you* don't know you can be damned sure I don't. You really have no idea?"

"Not really. It will be something significant, I believe that. It will happen on Quake. And it will tell us more about the Builders. Beyond that I can't even guess."

"Hell." He slashed at the damp ground with the cane. Darya had the feeling that if Kallik had been there, the Hymenopt would have been the recipient of that blow. "So what now, Professor?"

Darya Lang had been worrying the same question. Nenda seemed to want to cooperate, and she had been drawn along by her thirst for any facts and theories relevant to the Builders. But he seemed to have nothing—or at least, nothing he was willing to give. And she was already talking of working with Atvar H'sial and J'merlia. She could not work with both. And even though she had agreed to nothing definite, she could not mention her other conversations to Louis Nenda.

"Are you proposing that we cooperate? Because if you are——"

She did not have to finish. He had thrown his head back and was hooting with laughter. "Lady, now why would I do a thing like that? When you've just told me you don't know a damned thing!"

"Well, we have been swapping information."

"Sure. That's what you're good at, that's what you're famous for. Information and theories. So how are you at lying and cheating? How are you at *action*? Not so good, I'll bet. But that's what you'll need to get yourself over to Quake. And from what I hear, Quake won't be any picnic. I'll have my work cut out there. Think I want to baby you, sweetheart, and tell you when to run and when to hide? No thanks, dear. You arrange your own parade."

Before she could respond he strode ahead of her, into the building and through to the interior room where they had started. Kallik and J'merlia were still there, crouched low on the floor with their multiple legs spread flat and intertwined. They were exchanging ominous whistles and grunts.

Louis Nenda grabbed the Hymenopt roughly by the halter, attached the black cane, and pulled. "Come on, you. I told you, no fighting. We've got work to do." He turned back to Darya. "Nice to meet you, Professor. See you on Quake?"

"You will, Louis Nenda." Darya's voice was shaking with anger. "You can count on it."

He gave a scoffing laugh. "Fine. I'll save a drink for you there. If Perry's right, we may both need one."

He pulled hard on the cane and dragged Kallik out.

Seething, Darya went across to where J'merlia was slowly standing up. "How is Atvar H'sial?"

"Much better. She will be fully ready to resume work in one more Dobelle day."

"Good. Tell her that I have made up my mind and agree to cooperate fully with her. I will do everything we discussed. I am ready to take off for Quakeside and the Umbilical as soon as she is recovered."

"I will tell her this at once. It is good news." J'merlia moved closer, studying Darya's face. "But you have had some bad experience, Darya Lang. Did the man seek to hurt you?"

"No. Not a physical hurt." But he hurt me anyway. "He made me angry and upset. I'm sorry, J'merlia. He wanted to talk, and so we went outside. I thought you were asleep. I didn't realize that you would be threatened by that horrible animal of his."

J'merlia was staring at her and shaking his thin mantishead in a gesture he had picked up from the humans. "Threatened? By that?" He pointed to the door. "By the Hymenopt?"

"Yes."

"I was not threatened. Kallik and I were beginning a proto-converse—a first learning of each other's language."

"Language?" Darya thought of the whipping cane and the halter. "Are you telling me that it can *talk*? It's not just a simple animal?"

"Honored Professor Lang, Kallik can certainly talk. She never had the chance to learn more than Hymenopt speech, because she met few others and her master did not care for her to know. But she is learning. We began with less than fifty words in common; now we have more than one hundred." J'merlia moved to the door, his wounded leg still trailing. "Excuse me, honored Professor. I must leave now and find Atvar H'sial. It is a pity that Kallik is leaving this place. But maybe we will have an opportunity to talk and learn again when they arrive."

"Arrive? Where are they going?"

"Where everyone is going, it seems." J'merlia paused on the threshold. "To Quake. Where else?"

CHAPTER 11
Summertide
minus thirteen

Violent resistance is a problem, but nonresistance can be harder to handle.

Hans Rebka felt like a boxer, braced for a blow that never came. At some level he was still waiting.

"Didn't they fight it?" he asked.

Max Perry nodded. "Sure. At least, Louis Nenda did. But then he said he'd had it with the Dobelle system, and we could take his access request and stuff it, he was getting the hell out of here as soon as he could. And he already left."

"What about Darya Lang and Atvar H'sial?"

"Lang didn't say a word. There's no way of knowing what Atvar H'sial *thinks*, but what came out of J'merlia didn't have much steam in it. They went off to sulk on another Sling. I haven't seen them for two days—haven't had time to bother with them, to be honest. Think we ought to be worried?"

The two men were in the final moments of waiting as the capsule taking them to Quake was coupled to the Umbilical. They were carrying their luggage, one small bag for each man. Julius Graves was over by the aircar that had brought them from Starside, fussing with his two heavy cases.

Rebka considered Perry's question carefully. His own

assignment to Dobelle involved only the rehabilitation of Max Perry. In principle it had nothing to do with members of other clades, or how they were treated. But as far everyone on Opal was concerned, he was a senior official, and he had the duties that went with the position. He had received a new coded message from Circle headquarters just before they left Starside, but he had no great hopes that it would help him much, whatever it said. Advice and direction from far away were more likely to add to problems than to solve them.

"People ought to be protesting a lot more," he said at last. "Especially Louis Nenda. What's the chances that he might leave Opal and try for a direct landing on Quake from space? He came in his own ship."

"There's no way we could stop him *trying*. But unless his ship is designed for takeoff without spaceport facilities, he'll be in trouble. He might get down on Quake, but maybe he'd never get off it."

"How about Darya Lang and Atvar H'sial?"

"Impossible. They don't have a ship available, and they won't be able to rent one that will fly interplanetary. We can forget about them."

And then Perry hesitated. He was not sure of his own statement. There was that feeling in the air, a sense of final calm before a great storm. And it was not just the cloudbursts that threatened Opal within twenty-four hours.

It was Summertide, hanging over everything. With thirteen Dobelle days to go, Mandel and Amaranth loomed larger and brighter. Average temperatures were already up five degrees, under angry clouds like molten copper. Opal's air had changed in the last twelve hours. It was charged with a metallic taste that matched the lowering sky. Airborne dust left lips dry, eyes sore and weeping, noses itching and ready to sneeze. As the massive tides brought the seabed close to the surface, undersea earthquakes and eruptions were blowing their irritant fumes and dust high into the atmosphere.

Julius Graves had finally stowed the cases to his satisfaction in the bottom level of the Umbilical's car. He walked over to the other two men and stared up at the lambent sky.

"Another storm coming. A good time to be leaving Opal."

"But a worse time to be going to Quake," Perry said.

They climbed into the car. Perry provided his personal ID and keyed in a complex command sequence.

The three men maintained an uneasy formality as the ascent began. When Perry had quietly informed Graves that access to Quake was denied until after Summertide, Graves had just as coolly asserted the authority of the Council. He would be going to Quake anyway.

Perry pointed out that Graves could not prevent planetary officials from accompanying him. They had a responsibility to stop him from killing himself.

Graves nodded. Everyone was polite; no one was happy.

The tension eased when the capsule emerged from Opal's clouds. The three men had something else to occupy their minds. The car had been provided with sliding viewing ports in its upper level, as well as a large window directly overhead. The passengers had an excellent view of everything above and about them. As Quake appeared through the thinning clouds, any attempt at small talk faded.

Julius Graves stared around, gasped, and gaped, while Max Perry took one look up and retreated into himself. Hans Rebka tried to ignore their surroundings and focus his mind on the task ahead. Perry might know all about Quake, and Graves might be a fount of information about every subject under a thousand suns; yet Rebka had the feeling that he would have to carry both of them.

But carry them through what? He looked around, to find a panorama that swept away all rational thoughts. He had traveled the road to Quake just a few days before, but nothing was the same. Mandel, grossly swollen, loomed on the left. The Builder-designed shell of the car detected and filtered out dangerous hard radiation, turning the star's glowing face into a dark image seamed and pocked with faculae, sunspots, and lurid flares. The disk was so large that Rebka felt he could reach out and touch its raddled surface.

Amaranth—a dwarf no longer—stood beyond Quake. The companion was transformed. Even the color was changed. Rebka recognized that as an artificial effect. When the car windows altered their transmission properties to screen radiation from Mandel, they also modified the transmitted spectrum of Amaranth. Orange-red was transformed to glowering purple.

Even Gargantua was well on the way to its final rendezvous. Reflecting the light of both Mandel and Amaranth, the gas-giant had swelled from a distant spark to a thumbnail-sized glow of bright orange.

The partners were there; gravity was calling the changes, and the cosmic dance was ready to begin. In the final hours of Summertide, Mandel and Amaranth would pass within five million kilometers of each other—the thickness of a fingernail, in stellar terms. Gargantua would hurtle close by Mandel on the side opposite to Amaranth, propelled in its orbit by the combined field of both stellar companions. And little Dobelle, caught in that syzygy of giants, would gyrate helplessly through the warp and woof of a dynamic gravitational tapestry.

The Dobelle orbit was stable; there was no danger that Opal and Quake would separate, or that the doublet might be flung off to infinity. But that was the only assurance the astronomers would provide. Summertide surface conditions on Opal and Quake could not be calculated.

Rebka stared up at Quake. That ball of dusky blue-gray had become the most familiar feature in the sky. It had not changed perceptibly since the last ride up the Umbilical.

Or had it? He stared harder. Was the planet's limb a little fuzzier, where dust in the peel-thin layer of air surrounding Quake had become thicker?

There were few distractions to draw a traveler's mind away from the outside view. Their ascent was at a constant rate, with no sense of motion inside the car. Only a very careful observer would notice the golden knot of Midway Station slowly increasing in size, while the apparent gravity within the capsule was just as gradually diminishing. The journey did not take place in free-fall. The body forces were decreasing steadily, but the only weightless part of the journey would be two thousand kilometers beyond Midway Station, where all centrifugal and gravitational forces were in balance. After that came the real descent to Quake, when the capsule would truly be falling toward that planet.

Rebka sighed and stood up. It would be easy to allow the skyscape to hypnotize him, as Quake hypnotized Max Perry. And not just Perry. He glanced across at Graves. The councilor was totally absorbed in a reverie of his own.

Rebka walked over to the ramp and went down its turning path to the lower level of the capsule. The galley was a primitive one, but there had been no chance of a meal since they left Starside. He was hungry and not choosy, and he dialed without looking. The flavor and contents of the container of soup that he ordered did not matter.

With its opaque walls, the lower level of the capsule was depressingly bland. Rebka went to the table and selected a private music segment. Pre-Expansion music, complex and polyphonic, sounded within his head. The intertwining fugal voices suggested the coming interplay of Mandel and its retinue. For ten minutes Rebka ate and listened, enjoying two of the most basic and oldest pleasures of humanity. He wondered. Did the Cecropians, lacking music, have some compensating art form of their own?

When the piece ended he was surprised to find Julius Graves standing there watching him.

"May I?" The councilor sat down at the table and gestured at the empty bowl. "Can you recommend it?"

Rebka shrugged. Whatever Julius Graves wanted from him, opinions on soup were low on the list.

"Has it ever occurred to you," Graves said, "how improbable it is that we are able, with very little assistance, to eat and digest the foods of a thousand different worlds? The ingredients of that soup were produced on Opal, but your stomach will have no trouble handling it. We and the Hymenopts and the beings of the Cecropian clade are totally different biologically. Not one of them is DNA-based. And yet, with the help of a few strains of single-celled bacteria in our gut, we can eat the same food as each other. Surprising, is it not?"

"I guess so."

Rebka hated one-on-one conversations with Graves. Those mad blue eyes scared him. Even when the conversation seemed general he suspected an undercurrent, and to add to the confusion he was never sure how much input was coming from the mnemonic twin. Steven had a fondness for endless facts and stupid jokes, Julius for subtlety and indirection. The present conversation could be simple speculation from the one, or a devious probing from the other.

Graves was grinning to himself. "I know, you don't think it's significant that we can eat Opal's food, or Quake's. But it is. For one thing, it disposes of a popular theory as to why Cecropians and humans did not fight when first they met. People say they avoided combat because they were not competing for the same resources. But that is nonsense. They not only compete for the same *inorganic* resources of metals and raw materials; they are also—with a little assistance at the bacterial level—able to eat the same food. A human could eat a Cecropian, if the need arose. Or vice versa. And that introduces a new mystery."

Rebka nodded to show that he was listening. It was better to play the straight man than say too much.

"We look at a Cecropian," Graves continued, "or a Lo'tfian, or a Hymenopt, and we say, how *alien* they are! How different from us! But the mystery is surely the other way round. We should say, why are we all so *similar*? How is it possible that beings derived from different clades, seeded on different worlds, warmed by suns of other stellar types, of totally disjoint biology, without one item of common history—how can it be that they are so alike that they *can* eat the same foods? That they are so close in body shape that we can use Earth-analogs—Cecropians, Hymenopts, Chrysemides—in beings from the most distant stars. That we can all *talk* to each other, one way or another, and understand each other amazingly well. That we share the same standards of behavior. So much so, that a single ethical council can agree on rules to apply through the whole of the spiral arm. How can these things be?"

"But then, the spiral arm is filled with mysteries."

Graves was heading somewhere, Rebka was sure. But the other had a long way to go before he made any kind of sense. For the moment, all he seemed to offer was a philosophical lecture.

"Many mysteries," Graves went on. "The Builders, of course. What happened to them? What was their physiology, their history, their science? What is the function of the Lens, or of Paradox, or of Flambeau, or of the Phages? Of all the constructs of the Builders, surely the Phages are the most useless. Steven, if permitted, will discourse for many hours on this subject."

Rebka nodded again. *But, pray God, he won't.*

"And there are other, more recent mysteries, ones that puzzle me extremely. Think of the Zardalu. A few millennia ago they ruled more than a thousand worlds. We hear from their subject species that they were tyrannical, ruthless, merciless. But as their empire crumbled, those same vassal species rebelled and exterminated every Zardalu. Genocide. Was that not an action more barbaric than any practiced by the Zardalu themselves? And *why* did they choose to rule as they did? Did they have a different idea of ethical behavior, one unrecognizable to us? If so, they were truly alien, but we will never know in what way. What would an ethical council have made of the Zardalu?"

. . . a single ethical council can agree on rules . . . Rebka saw the sudden agony on Graves's lined face, and his mind flicked back to that earlier comment. By talking alternative moralities for the Zardalu, was Graves questioning the rules set up by his own council? Was he preparing to disobey his own instructions?

Graves would not meet Rebka's eye. "I sometimes wonder if the ethics we favor are just as local and as limited as our common set of body shapes and thought patterns.

The Builders had science truly alien to us. It does not match our worldview. We do not know how they built, or why they built. And yet our scientists tell us that there is only one set of physical laws that govern the whole universe—just as our philosophers tell us that we have one system of universal ethics! I wonder if Builder ethics would prove as alien as their science. Or if they, able to see how we treat our many different species, would not be appalled at our bias and misjudgment.

"I propose that we all have a lesson to learn, Captain, and it is as simple as this: the rules set up by any council must be *dynamic*. Regardless of the way they are viewed by the average person, they cannot be forever the same, set in stone and steel. We must study them constantly. And we must always ask if they can be improved."

Graves glared suddenly at Rebka, turned, and ascended the ramp to the upper level of the capsule.

Rebka remained seated and stared after him. There had been a counterpoint in those final sentences, almost of two voices. Was it possible that Julius and Steven Graves were holding some kind of interior dialogue, with Rebka no more than bystander? Maybe Julius wanted to do one thing, and Steven another.

It was preposterous; but no more unlikely than the development of individual consciousness in the mnemonic twin. And if working with Julius Graves on the surface of Quake would be bad, working with an unstable mixture of Julius and Steven would be impossible.

Twins, squabbling for dominance within one braincase? Rebka stood up, noticing as he did so that the deck offered much less pressure on the soles of his feet. His weight was down to a few pounds. They must be closing on Midway Station. He headed for the ramp, wondering if Max Perry was still sitting in frozen contemplation of Quake. More and more, he felt like the keeper of a bunch of talented lunatics.

On his first trip to Quake, Rebka had been quite keen to enter and examine Midway Station. Humans had modified and cannibalized it, but it was still Builder technology, and that made it fascinating. Yet when Max Perry had chosen to bypass it—had been *driven* to bypass it—Rebka, in his own curiosity about Quake, had not argued with that decision.

Now the urgency to reach Quake was far greater—thirteen Dobelle days to Summertide, according to Rebka's internal clock; only one hundred and ten hours! Keep moving!—but now Perry insisted on stopping at Midway.

"Take a look for yourself." Perry pointed at the status board on their capsule. "See the power consumption? It's too high."

Rebka looked and could deduce nothing. Nor could Graves. If Perry said things did not seem right, the others had to believe him. There was no substitute for experience, and when they were on the Umbilical, Perry's knowledge reigned supreme.

"Are we in danger?" Graves asked.

"Not immediate danger." Perry was rubbing his nose thoughtfully. "But we can't risk heading down to Quake until we know why the power use is up. We daren't risk power loss for our own approach. And the central controls are all on Midway Station. We have to stop there and find out what's happening."

Under his direction, the capsule had already left its invisible guides and turned toward the misshapen bulk that filled half the sky on their left.

When humans had first discovered it, Midway Station had been an airless, arching vault, three kilometers across and almost empty. The walls were transparent. A man in a space suit could fly to the side facing Opal and detect that he was falling gently in that direction; one strong kick off the glassy outer wall would carry him through the open interior. He would then drift on and on, gradually slowing, until the opposite outer wall finally arrested his motion. The station marked the exact center of mass of the Quake/Opal coupled system.

The Builders' uses for Midway Station were not understood. That did not matter to most humans. They had filled the open sphere with a set of interlocking pressurized chambers, making it a temporary habitat and a storage facility for everything from thermal boots to freeze-dried food. Responding to some old cave instinct that favored enclosed spaces, they had also covered the external walls with a shiny, opaque monolayer. After four thousand years of Expansion, humans were apparently still uncomfortable with the open endlessness of space.

The capsule moved through a first airlock, then nosed molelike along a dark corridor just wide enough to permit its passage. Two minutes later it came to a cylindrical chamber filled with racks of display equipment and control boards.

Perry waited for a couple of minutes while the interior and exterior pressures were almost matched, then forced open the capsule's hatch and floated out. By the time the others had followed him he was already at work on one of the displays.

"Here." He pointed. "Straightforward enough. That's the problem. Another car was traveling the Umbilical at the same time as us."

"Where?" Rebka stared at the displays. They showed cameras and monitors all along the length of the Umbilical. He saw nothing.

"No, you won't see it." Perry had noticed where Rebka was looking. "The power drain is over now. That means the other capsule isn't on the Umbilical anymore."

"So where is it?" Graves asked.

Perry shrugged. "We'll find out. I hope there's someone on duty down there. I'm sending an emergency signal." He was already moving across to a communications unit and tapping in entry codes.

Within twenty seconds Birdie Kelly's face came onto the screen. He was panting, and his hair was tousled. "Max? Commander Perry? What's wrong?"

"You can tell us, Birdie. Look at your power draw for the past few hours. We've had two capsules in use."

"That's right. No problem; we checked and there's plenty in reserve."

"Maybe. But there is a problem. That other car didn't have authorization."

Birdie's face was puzzled. "It certainly did. The woman had authorization from *you*. Personally. Hold one second."

He disappeared for a few moments from the screen and returned holding a marked sheet. "That's your sigil— see it?—right there."

"You let her have a car?"

"Of course I did." Birdie's tone switched from defensive to annoyed. "She had authorization, and she must have known the exact Umbilical command codes. If she hadn't, they'd never have risen one meter above sea level."

"They?"

"Sure. We assumed you knew all about this. The woman." Birdie Kelly peered at the sheet. "Darya Lang. With the two aliens. A Cecropian, and another form I didn't recognize. What's going on up there?"

"That authorization was bogus, Birdie. My sigil was faked." Perry glanced at another control board. "We show they're not on the Umbilical anymore."

"Right. They'll be on Quake. I hope they're having a better time up there than we are here." The wall behind Kelly shivered and tilted, and a scream of wind sounded through the link. He turned to glance away from the screen for a split second. "Commander, unless there's something else I can tell you, I have to get off right now."

"Another storm?"

"Worst ever. We just had a call through the Sling Network, five minutes ago. Spidermonkey is starting to break up. We have an airlift going in, but they're having trouble landing on the Sling to get people off."

"Go help there. We're on our way. Good luck, Birdie."

"Thanks. We're going to need it. Same to you."

Birdie Kelly was gone.

And so was Perry. By the time Rebka and Graves caught up with him he was starting to seal the capsule.

"Nine hours ahead of us," he said. "This near Summertide, that's more than enough to kill them all."

He touched a final command sequence, and the capsule started them back out along the narrow corridor.

Hans Rebka lay back in his seat and stared ahead, waiting for the first sight of Quake as they emerged from Midway Station.

He felt tense, yet oddly satisfied. His instincts had not let him down. The blow that he had been waiting for since Max Perry told the others that Quake was off-limits had been delivered.

Or at least, *one* blow had been struck.

His feeling of impending revelations had not gone away completely. The old inner voice assured him that there was more to come.

ARTIFACT: PHAGE
UAC#: 1067
Galactic Coordinates: Not applicable
Name: Phage
Star/planet association: Not applicable
Bose Access Node: All
Estimated age: Various. 3.6 to 8.2 Megayears.

Exploration History: The first Phages were reported by humans during the exploration of Flambeau, in E. 1233. Subsequently, it was learned that Phages had been observed and avoided by Cecropian explorers for at least five thousand years. The first human entry of a Phage maw was made in E. 1234 during the Maelstrom conflict (no survivors).

Phage avoidance systems came into widespread use in E. 2103, and are now standard equipment in Builder exploration.

Physical Description: The Phages are all externally identical, and probably internally similar though functionally variable. No sensor (or explorer) has ever returned from a Phage interior.

Each Phage has the form of a gray, regular dodecahedron, of side forty-eight meters. The surface is roughly textured, with mass sensors at the edge of each face. Maws can be opened at the center of any face, and can ingest objects of up to thirty meters' radius and of apparently indefinite length. (In E. 2238, Sawyer and S'kropa fed a solid silicaceous fragment of cylindrical cross-section and twenty-five meters' radius to a Phage of the Dendrite Artifact. With an ingestion rate of one kilometer per day, four hundred and twenty-five kilometers of material, corresponding to the full length of the fragment, were absorbed. No mass change was detected in the Phage, nor any change in any other of its physical parameters.)

Phages are capable of slow independent locomotion, with a mean rate of one or two meters per standard day.

No Phage has ever been seen to move at a velocity in excess of one meter per hour with respect to the local frame.

Intended Purpose: Unknown. Were it not for the fact that Phages have been found in association with over three hundred of the twelve hundred known artifacts, and only in such association, any relationship to the Builders would be questioned. They differ greatly in scale and number from all other Builder constructs.

It has been speculated that the Phages served as general scavengers for the Builders, since they are apparently able to ingest and break down any materials made by the clades, and anything made by the Builders with the single exception of the structural hulls and the paraforms (e.g., the external shell of Paradox, the surface of Sentinel, and the concentric hollow tubes of Maelstrom).

—From the *Lang Universal Artifact Catalog*, Fourth Edition.

CHAPTER 12
Summertide
minus eleven

Darya Lang had the terrible suspicion that she had wasted half her life. Back on Sentinel Gate she had believed it when her family told her that she lived in the best place in the universe: "Sentinel Gate, half a step from Paradise," the saying went. And with her research facilities and her communications network, she had seen no need to travel.

But first Opal, and now Quake, taught her otherwise. She *loved* the newness of the experience, the contact with a world where everything was strange and exciting. From the moment she stepped out of the capsule onto the dry, dusty surface of Quake, she felt all her senses intensify by a factor of a hundred.

Her nose said it first. The air of Quake held a powerful mixture of odors. That was the scent of flowers, surely, but not the lush, lavish extravagances that garlanded Sentinel Gate. She had to seek them out—and there they were, not five paces in front of her, tiny bell-shaped blooms of lilac and lavender that peeped out from a gray-green cover of wiry gorse. The plants hugged the sides of a long, narrow crevice too small to be called a valley. From their miniature blossoms came an urgent midday perfume, out of all proportion to their size. It was as though flowering, fertilization, and seeding could not wait another hour.

And maybe it can't, Darya thought. For overlaid on that heady scent was a sinister, sulfurous tinge of distant vulcanism: the breath of Quake, approaching Summertide. She paused, breathed deep, and knew she would remember the mixture of smells forever.

Then she sneezed, and sneezed again. There was fine dust in the air, irritant powdery particles that tickled the nose.

She raised her eyes, looking beyond the miniature valley with its carpet of urgent flowers, out beyond the plain to a smoky horizon fifteen kilometers away. The effects of dust were easy to see there. Where the nearby surface stood out in harsh umbers and ochres, in the distance a gray pall had darkened and softened the artist's palette, painting everything in muted tones. The horizon itself was not visible, except that to the east her eye traced—or imagined—a faint line of volcanic peaks, cinnamon-hued and jagged.

Mandel stood high in the sky. As she watched, it began to creep behind the shielding bulk of Opal. The brilliant crescent shrank, moment by moment. At the present time of year there would be no more than partial eclipse, but it was enough to change the character of the light. The redder tones of Amaranth bled into the landscape. Quake's surface became a firelit landscape of subterranean gloom.

At that moment Darya heard the first voice of Summertide. A low rumble filled the air, like the complaining snore of a sleepy giant. The ground trembled. She felt a quiver and a pleasant tingle in the soles of her feet.

"Professor Lang," J'merlia said from behind her. "Atvar H'sial reminds you that we have far to go, and little time. If we might proceed . . ."

Darya realized that she had not yet completed her first step onto Quake's surface, and Atvar H'sial and J'merlia were still standing on the ladder from the capsule. As Darya moved out of the way the Cecropian crept past her and stood motionless, broad head sweeping from side to side. J'merlia came to crouch beneath the front of the carapace.

Darya watched the trumpet-horn ears as they swept across the scene. What did Atvar H'sial "see" when she listened to Quake? What did those exquisite organs of smell "hear," when every airborne molecule could tell a story?

They had talked about the world as it was perceived by echolocation, but the explanation was unsatisfying. The best analogy that Darya could create was of a human standing on the seabed, in a place where the water was turbid and the light level low. Everything was monochrome vision, with a range of only a few tens of meters.

But the analogy was inadequate. Atvar H'sial was sensitive to a huge range of sound frequencies, and she could certainly "see" the distant mutter of the volcanoes. Those signals lacked the fine spatial resolution offered by her own sonar, but they were definite sensory inputs.

And there were other factors, perhaps even other *senses*, that Darya was only vaguely aware of; for instance, at the moment the Cecropian was lifting one forelimb and pointing off to the middle distance. Was she sensing the waft of distant odors, with olfactory lobes so acute that every trace of smell told a story?

"There is animal life here," J'merlia translated. "And winged forms. This suggests another possible method of surviving Summertide, unmentioned by Commander Perry. By remaining in Quake's Mandel-shadow, and always aloft, these would be safe."

Darya could see the flying creatures—just. They were half a meter long, with dark bodies and gauzy, diaphanous wings; too delicate, surely, to survive the turbulence of Summertide. Far more likely, they had already laid their eggs and would die in the next few days. But Atvar H'sial was right about one thing: there were many facts about Quake that humans did not know, or Max Perry was not telling.

The thought came to her again: this was a whole planet, a world with its own intricate life-balance; hundreds of millions of square kilometers of land and small lakes, empty of humans or other intelligence, spread out for their inspection. Infinite diversity was possible there, but it would take a lifetime to explore and know it.

Right, her more practical side said. But we don't have a whole lifetime. In eighty hours we'd better be finished with our exploration and on our way.

Leaving Atvar H'sial to her sightless sweep of the landscape, Darya moved around the foot of the Umbilical to the line of aircars. There were eight of them, sitting under the lee of their protective sheet of Builder material. The apron they stood on was connected by silicon fiber cables to the Umbilical itself and would lift with it at Summertide.

Darya climbed into one of the cars and inspected its controls. As Atvar H'sial had foretold, the vehicle was human-made and identical with the one that they had used for travel on Opal. It was fully charged, and Darya could fly it with no problem, provided—and at the thought, her collarbone gave a twinge of reminder—that they did not hit a storm like the one that had wiped them out last time.

She held up an open hand to test the wind. At the moment it was no more than a stiff breeze, nothing to worry about. Even allowing for the twisting pockets of dust, visibility was at least three or four kilometers. That was ample for a landing, and they could fly far above any sandstorm.

At her urging, Atvar H'sial and J'merlia climbed into the car and settled in for the flight. Darya took them up at once, heading for an altitude that would clear any turbulence. J'merlia squatted by her side in the front of the car. Darya had explained the aircar controls to him when they were flying on Opal, and if necessary he could probably pilot the craft. But apparently he would never dream of trying to do so without direction from Atvar H'sial.

Darya tried to talk with him and failed. She had imagined that he might behave differently toward her after their conversations while they were recuperating from the crash. She was wrong. When Atvar H'sial was present he refused to make an independent move, and for the first three hours of the trip he spoke only at Atvar H'sial's direction.

But in the fourth hour J'merlia made a move of his own, unprompted by his mistress. He suddenly sat upright and pointed. "There. Above."

They were cruising on autopilot at twenty thousand meters, far above most of Quake's atmosphere and out of reach of surface storms. Darya had not been looking up. She had been surveying the ground ahead of them, using the car's imaging sensors. At top resolution she could see plenty of evidence of life on Quake. The lake-dotted hill ranges bore great herds of white-backed animals, moving away from the high ground and heading for water as steadily and inexorably as a retreating wave. She watched their compact mass divide and break around bare ridges and massive boulders. A few kilometers farther on, the hill country ended, and she saw wriggling lines of dark green, following and defining the moist gravel of stream-beds. The dry streams ended in dense pockets of vegetation, impenetrable from above, lining the bottom of hollows of uncertain depth.

As Darya looked up at J'merlia's words, he leaned over her shoulder and pointed with a thin, multijointed arm into the blue-black and starlit sky.

Atvar H'sial hissed. "Another car," J'merlia translated. "We have been pursued up the Umbilical, and much more quickly than we expected."

The moving light was right above them, following their own ground track but at much greater altitude. It was also rapidly outdistancing them. Darya allowed the autopilot to continue the flight while she rotated the high-mag sensor to take a closer look at the newcomer.

"No," she said after a few moments. "It's not an aircar." She set the car's little on-board computer to work, computing a trajectory. "It's too high, and it's moving much too fast. And look—it's growing brighter. We're not looking at an aircar's lights."

"Then what is it?"

"It's a spaceship. And that bright glow means it's entering Quake's atmosphere." Darya glanced at the computer output, providing a first estimate of the other ship's final trajectory. "We'd better put down for a while and consider what we do next."

"No." Atvar H'sial's thoughts came as a mutter of protest from J'merlia.

"I know; I don't want to, either," Darya said. "But we have to, unless you know something I don't. The computer needs a few more points of tracking data to be sure, but it's already giving us a preliminary result. That ship is landing. I don't know who is in it, but it will touch down just where we don't want it—a few kilometers from our own destination."

Twilight on Quake—if so sudden and ominous a nightfall, red as dragon's blood, could justify that description.

Mandel would rise in three hours. Amaranth lay low on the horizon, its ruddy face obscured by clouds of dust. Gargantua alone shone in full splendor, a banded marble of orange and salmon-pink.

The aircar stood on a level patch of gravel, readied for rapid takeoff. Darya Lang had set them down between two small water bodies, in an area shown on the map to be liberally scattered with miniature fresh-water lakes.

The map had lied in at least one respect. Atvar H'sial, crouched down by one of the ponds, had sucked water noisily through her proboscis. J'merlia pronounced it potable. But Darya, tasting the same pool, spat in disgust and wondered about Cecropian metabolism. The lake water was harsh and bitter to the tongue, filled with strong alkalines. She could not drink it, and would have to rely on the car's supplies.

Darya walked back past the car and prepared for sleep. Even with the help of the autopilot, the journey around Quake had been a strain. Harmless as the planet below her seemed, she had not dared to lower her concentration for more than a moment; and now finally free to relax, she could not do so.

There was too much to see, too much to speculate on.

According to Perry, Quake so close to Summertide should have been an inferno. The crust ought to have been heaving and shattered, surface ablaze with brush fires, plants shriveled and dying in air burning hot and close to unbreathable. The animals should have been long gone, already dead or estivating far below the surface.

Instead she could breath and walk and sit in moderate comfort, and there were ample signs all about her of energetic life. Darya had set her camp bed outside, close to one of the pools and in the shade of a thicket of horsetails. She could hear animals scuttling through them, ignoring her presence, and the ground by the water was riddled with holes of all different sizes, as a variety of small creatures tunneled underground. When the distant growl of thunder or vulcanism died away, she could hear those workers, scrabbling steadily deeper into the drying earth.

But it was *warm*, she would admit that. The disappearance of Mandel from the sky had brought little relief. Sweat stained her suit and ran down the hollow of her neck.

She lay down on her camp bed. Although Quake seemed safe enough, she was worried about what they should do next. That spaceship must be from Opal, and it had probably been sent to drag them back there. If they went on, they might be captured and forced to leave Quake. But if they did not keep going, they would not reach their destination.

While she was pondering that, Atvar H'sial surprised her by coming across and offering a meal of Opal fruit and bottled water. Darya took it and nodded her thanks. That was a shared gesture. The Cecropian nodded back and retreated to the interior of the aircar.

As Darya ate she wondered about her two companions. She had never seen either of them eat. Perhaps, like the people on some Alliance worlds, they regarded the taking of food as a private function. Or maybe they were like the tortoises on Opal, who according to the crewmen at Starside Port could survive quite happily for a full year on just water. But then why would Atvar H'sial think to feed the human of the group?

She lay back on the camp bed, pulled the waterproof sheet up to her neck, and watched the heavens reeling above her. The stars moved so fast . . . on Sentinel Gate, with its thirty-eight-hour day, the swing of the starry vault was almost imperceptible. Which direction in space did her homeworld lie? She puzzled over the unfamiliar constellations. That way . . . or that . . . Her mind drifted off toward the stars. She wrenched her thoughts back with an effort to the present. She still had a decision to make.

Should they proceed to the place that her calculations pointed to as the focus of activity at Summertide? They could go, knowing that others would be there also. Or should she hang back and wait? Or should they go just partway, pause for a while . . .

Go partway, pause . . .

Darya Lang passed easily into a deep sleep, a dreamless slumber so profound that nearby noise and vibration did not wake her. Brief dawn came; day passed, and again it was night and flaming day. The sounds of tunneling animals ended. Opal and Quake had made two complete turns about each other before Darya drifted back to consciousness.

She woke slowly to the half day of Amaranth's light. It was a full minute before she knew where she was, another before she felt ready to sit up and look around her.

Atvar H'sial and J'merlia were nowhere to be seen. The aircar was gone. A small heap of supplies and equipment had been placed under a thin rainproof sheet next to the camp bed. Nothing else, from horizon to horizon, suggested that humans or aliens had ever been there.

She dropped to her knees and scrabbled through the pile, searching for a message. There was no note, no recording, no sign. Nothing that might help her except a few containers of food and drink, a miniature signal generator, a gun, and a flashlight.

Darya looked at her watch. Nine more Dobelle days. Seventy-two hours to go before the worst Summertide ever. And she was stranded on Quake, alone, six thousand kilometers from the safety of the Umbilical . . . .

The panic that she had felt on first leaving Sentinel Gate crept back into her heart.

CHAPTER 13

. . . *the orange glow on the horizon was continuous, the burning ground reflecting from high dust clouds. As they watched, a new burst of crimson arose, no more than a kilometer from where they stood. It developed smoky tendrils and grew taller. Soon it stretched from earth to sky. As the lava bubbled to the summit of the crater he turned to Amy.*

In spite of his warning she still stood outside the car. When the flash of the explosion was replaced by a glow of red-hot lava she clapped her hands, entranced by the colors and the shapes. Shock waves of sound rolled and echoed from the hills behind. The stream of fire crested the cone and began to roll toward them, as easy-flowing and fast as running water. Where it touched the cooler earth, white flux sputtered and sparked.

Max stared at her face. He saw no fear, only the rapt entrancement of a child at a birthday party.

That was what it was. She saw it all as a fireworks display. Caution had to come from him. He leaned forward from the car seat to pluck at her sleeve.

"Get in." He was forced to shout to be heard. "We have to start back for the Stalk. You know it's a five-hour journey."

She glared at him and pulled away. He knew the pout very well. "Not now, Max." He read the words from her lips, but he could not hear her. "I want to wait until the lava reaches the water."

"No!" He was yelling. "Absolutely not. I'll take no more risks! It's boiling hot out there, and it's getting nearly as bad in the car."

She was walking away, not listening to him. He felt tight-chested and overheated despite the air curtain that held a sheath of cooler air at the open hatch. It was mostly in his mind, he knew that—the fiery furnace of his own worries that consumed him. And yet the outside heat was real enough. He stumbled out of the car and followed her across the steaming surface.

"Stop pestering me. I'll come in a minute." Amy had turned around to look at the whole infernal scene. There was—thank God!—no sign yet of another eruption, but one could happen at any second.

"Max, you have to relax." She came close, shouting right into his ear. "Learn to have fun. All the time we've been here, you've sat like a lump of Sling underside. Let yourself go—get into the swing of things."

He took her hand and began to pull her toward the car. After a moment of resistance she allowed herself to be steered along. With her eyes still on the volcano's bright fury, she did not look where they were going.

And then, when they were no more than a few meters from the car, she broke loose and ran laughing across the flat, steaming surface of heat-baked rock. She was ten paces ahead of him before he could start after her. By then it was too late.

Summertide minus ten

Graves and Perry made it sound simple. Rebka argued it was impossible.

"Look at the arithmetic," he said as the Umbilical's capsule lowered them gently to the surface of Quake. "We have a planetary radius of fifty-one hundred kilometers, and a surface that's less than three percent covered by water. That gives over three hundred million square kilometers of land. Three hundred million! Think how long it can take to search *one* square kilometer. We could look for years and never find them."

"We don't have years," Perry said. "And I know it's a big area. But you seem to assume we'll do a random search, and of course we won't. I can rule out most areas before we start."

"And I know that the Carmel twins will avoid all open spaces," Graves added.

"How can you possibly know that?" Rebka was being the pessimist.

"Because Quake is usually cloud-free." Graves was unmoved by the other's skepticism. "Their homeworld of Shasta has a high-resolution spaceborne system that gives continuous surveillance of the surface."

"But Quake doesn't."

"Ah, but the twins don't know that. They'll assume that if they're out on the open surface, they'll be spotted and picked up. They'll have run for deep cover and stayed there."

"And I can tell you now," Perry said, "that cuts the problem way down. There are only three places that a sane human would take refuge on Quake. We'll start with these three areas—and we'll have to finish with them, too."

"But if we don't find them there," Graves began, "we can broaden—"

"No, we can't," Perry said, cutting him off. "Summertide, Councilor. It will hit maximum strength in less than eighty hours. We'd better not be here then, not you, not me, and not the twins."

Max Perry listed the three most likely areas: in the high forests of the Morgenstern Uplands; upon—or probably *within*—one of the Thousand Lakes; or in the deep vegetation pockets of the Pentacline Depression.

"Which reduces the area to be searched by a factor of thousands," he said.

"And still leaves ten of thousands of square kilometers to be examined," Rebka replied. "In detail. And don't forget, this isn't your standard search-and-rescue problem. Usually, the missing persons *want* to be found. They cooperate, as best they can. But the twins won't send distress signals until conditions are intolerable. If they signal then, it will probably be too late."

If his arguments impressed Julius Graves, no one would have known it from the other's grinning face. While Max Perry was busy checking the aircars, Graves dragged Rebka away in the direction of the smoke-edged line of volcanic hills.

"I need a quiet word with you, Captain," he said confidentially. "Just for a moment or two."

Warm ash drifted down like pale-gray snow, settling onto their heads and shoulders. The ground was already covered a centimeter deep. Of the low-growing plants and the peaceful herbivores of Rebka's first visit to Quake there was no sign. Even the lake itself had vanished, hidden beneath a scummy layer of volcanic ash. Instead of the predicted rumble and roar of seismic violence, the planet held a hot, brooding silence.

"You realize," Graves continued, "that we don't need to stay together? There are aircars here to spare."

"I know we could cover three times as much ground if we split up," Rebka replied. "But I'm not sure I want to do it. Perry has unique knowledge of Quake, while you have never been here before."

"Aha! Your thoughts parallel my own." Graves brushed a flake of ash from the end of his nose. "The logical course of action is quite clear: Perry has identified three areas of Quake where fugitives will naturally seek to hide. Those regions are widely separated; but there are enough aircars for each of us to tackle one of them. Therefore, we can all go separately, and examine one area each. That's what logic says. But I say, phooey, who wants *logic*? Not you, and not me. We want *results*."

He leaned closer to Rebka. "And frankly, I worry about the stability of Commander Perry. Say 'Quake' and 'Summertide' to him, and his eyes almost roll out of his head. We can't let him go off on his own. What do you think?"

I think that you and Perry both need keepers, is what I think, but I don't want to come right out and say it. Rebka knew what was on the way. He was going to be saddled with Perry—the same stupid assignment that had brought him to Dobelle—while Graves charged off uncontrolled into the Quake wilderness and probably killed himself.

"I agree, Councilor, Perry should not go alone. But I don't want to waste—"

"Then we agree that I must go with Perry," Graves went on, ignoring Rebka. "You see, if he gets into trouble, I can help him. No one else is able to do that. So he and I will tackle the Morgenstern Uplands, while you do the Thousand Lakes—Perry says that's the quickest and easiest. And if neither of us finds the twins, then whoever gets through first takes on the Pentacline Depression."

What does one do when a madman suggests an appealing course of action? One worries—but probably goes along with it. In any case, Graves was in no mood to listen to an argument. When Rebka pointed out again how low the chances were that they would find the twins at all, the councilor snapped his fingers.

"Piffle. I *know* we'll find them. Think positive, Captain Rebka. Be an optimist! It's the only way to live."

And a likely way to die, Rebka thought. But he gave up. Graves would not be dissuaded, and maybe he and Perry deserved each other.

It was also one of the first rules of life, something Rebka had learned as a six-year-old in the hot saline caverns of Teufel. When someone gives you what you want, *leave*— before he has time to think again and take it back.

"Very well, Councilor. As soon as a car is ready I'll be on my way."

Rebka had half an hour's start on the other two. The cargo space of the fastest aircars was not designed to carry large and heavy cases, and Julius Graves dithered over his luggage for a long time before he finally left behind everything except a little bag. The rest he put back in an Umbilical capsule. At last he pronounced himself ready to leave.

After takeoff Max Perry set the craft to cruise on autopilot and headed for the Morgenstern Uplands. When they were within scanning range, both men crouched over the displays.

"Primitive equipment," Graves said. He was grimacing and twitching with concentration as he pored over images. Checking the displays was a long and tedious process. "If this were an Alliance car, we wouldn't have to watch—we'd sit back and wait for the system to *tell* us when it found the twins. As it is it's the other way round. I have to sit and peer at this thing and tell it what it's seeing. Primitive!"

"It's the best we have on Opal or Quake."

"I believe you. But do you ever ask yourself why all the worlds of the spiral arm are not as wealthy as Earth and the other old regions of Crawlspace? Why isn't *every* planet using the latest technology? Why don't all worlds have more service robots than people, like Earth? Why aren't they all *rich*, everyone on every colony? We know how to *make* advanced equipment. Why doesn't every planet have it, instead of just a few?"

Perry had no answers, but he grunted to show that he was listening.

He was not. With Julius Graves busy looking at images, that had to be Steven chattering on. And Perry was busy himself, with the radio receiving equipment. Graves did not believe that the Carmel twins would send a distress call. Perry disagreed. As Summertide came closer the twins ought to be more than ready to be arrested and rescued.

"It's a simple reason," Graves continued, "the cause of Dobelle's poverty. It is built into the basic nature of humanity. A rational species would make sure that one world was fully developed and perfect for humans before going on to another. But we don't know how to do that! We have the outward urge. Before a planet is half settled, off go the new ships, ready to explore the next one. And very few people say, wait a moment, let's get this one right before we go on."

He took a closer look at a couple of false alarms on the image, then shook his head in dismissal.

"We're just too nosy, Commander," he went on. "Most humans have their patience level set a little too low, and their curiosity a bit too high. The Cecropians are as bad as we are. So almost all the wealth of the spiral arm—and *all* the luxury—finds its way into the hands of the stay-at-homes. It's the old paradox, one that predates the Expansion: the groups that do nothing to *create* wealth manage to gain possession of most of it. Whereas the ones that do all the work finish up with very few possessions. Perhaps one day that will change. Maybe in another ten thousand years—"

"Radio beacon," Perry interrupted. "A weak one, but it's there."

Graves froze in position and did not look up. "Impossible." His voice was sharp. Julius Graves was back in charge. "They would not advertise their presence on Quake. Not after running so far and for so long."

"Take a look for yourself."

Graves slid across the seat. "How far away is it?"

"Long way." Perry studied the range and vector settings. "In fact, too far. That signal isn't coming from anywhere within the Morgenstern Uplands. The source is at least four thousand kilometers beyond the edge. We're getting ionospheric bounce, or we wouldn't hear them at all."

"How about the Thousand Lakes?"

"Could be. The vector isn't quite right, but there's a lot of noise in the signal. And the range is spot on."

"Then it's Rebka." Graves slapped his hand flat on the table. "It must be. He goes off to look, and no sooner do we get down to work than he's in trouble. Before we even—"

"Not Rebka."

"How do you know?"

"It's not his aircar." Perry was running comparisons with his signal templates. "Not any of ours. Wrong frequency, wrong signal format. Looks like a portable send unit, low power."

"Then it's the Carmel twins! And they must be in terrible trouble, if they're willing to ask for help. Can you take us there?"

"Easy. We just home on the beacon."

"How long from here?"

"Six or seven hours, top speed."

As he spoke Perry was looking at the car's chronometer.

"How long?" Graves had followed his look.

"A bit more than eight Quake days to Summertide; say, sixty-seven hours from now."

"Seven hours to Thousand Lakes, eight more back to the Umbilical. Then up and away. Plenty of time. We'll escape from Quake long before the worst."

Perry shook his head. "You don't understand. Quake is inhomogeneous, with a variable internal structure. The earthquakes can pop up anywhere, long before Summertide. We're not seeing much activity here in the Uplands, but the Thousand Lakes area could be a nightmare."

"Come on, man, you're as bad as Rebka. It can't be all that unpleasant, if the Carmel twins are still alive there."

"You said it right. *If* they're still alive there." Perry was at the controls, and already the car was turning. "There's one thing you're forgetting, Councilor. Radio beacons are made tough—a whole lot tougher than human beings."

CHAPTER 14
Summertide minus nine

The weapons sensors had been tracking the car for a long time. When it came within line-of-sight range, Louis Nenda placed the starship's concealed arsenal on Full Alert.

The approaching aircar slowed, as though aware of the destructive power poised a few kilometers in front of it. It moved sideways, then sank to a vertical landing on a seamed shelf of rock, well away from the ship.

Nenda kept the weapons primed for action, watching as the car's hatch eased open.

"Who's it gonna be, then?" he said softly in Communion patois, more to himself than to Kallik. "Place your bets, ladies and gentlemen. Name them visitors."

A familiar pair of figures climbed out onto the steaming, rubble-strewn shelf. Both wore breathing masks, but they were easily recognizable. Louis Nenda grunted in satisfaction and flipped every weapon to standby mode.

"They'll do fine. Open the hatch, Kallik. Show the guests some hospitality."

Atvar H'sial and J'merlia were steadily approaching, picking their way carefully past rounded blue-gray boulders and across a scree of loose gravel. Louis Nenda had chosen his landing site carefully, on the most solid-seeming and

155

permanent surface that he could find; still there were drifts
of blown dust and signs of recent earth movement. A deep,
jagged crack ran from the shelf where the aircar had just
landed, halfway to the much bigger ship. Atvar H'sial was
following the line of the fissure, occasionally peering over
the edge to sniff the air and estimate the bottom depth.
That trench was her only possible refuge. Nothing lived
in this region of Quake, and there was no shred of cover
within ten kilometers. The ship's weapons, thirty meters
high in the dome of the vessel, enjoyed a three-hundred-
and-sixty-degree prospect.

Atvar H'sial entered the lower hatch, bowing low—not
from any idea of respect for Louis Nenda, but because
she was squeezing in through an entrance designed for
something half her height. Inside, she pulled off her
breathing mask. J'merlia followed, with an odd little whistle
of greeting to Kallik, then scurried forward to crouch in
front of his owner.

The Cecropian straightened and moved closer to
Nenda. "You chose not to use your weapons on us,"
J'merlia translated. "A wise decision."

"From your point of view? I'm sure it was. But what's
this talk of weapons?" Nenda's voice was mocking. "You'll
find no weapons here."

"You may be right," Atvar H'sial said through J'merlia.
"If the inspection facility on Opal could not find them,
it may be that we could not." Atvar H'sial's broad white
head turned up to look at the ceiling. "However, if you
will permit me half an hour for inspection of your starship's
upper deck . . ."

"Oh, I don't think so." Louis Nenda grinned. "It might
be fun, but we really don't have half an hour to play
around. Not with Summertide breathing down our necks.
Suppose we stop fencing for a while? I'll not ask what
tools and weapons you're carrying on you, if you'll stop
worrying about what's on this ship. We've got more
important things to talk about."

"Ah. A truce, you suggest." The words came from
J'merlia, but it was Atvar H'sial who held out a long foreleg.

"Agreed. But where do we begin? How do we discuss cooperation, without revealing too much of what we each know?"

"For a start, we send them"—Nenda pointed at J'merlia and Kallik—"outside."

Atvar H'sial's yellow trumpet-horns turned to scan the Hymenopt, then moved down to the Lo'tfian crouched beneath her carapace.

"Is it safe there?" J'merlia translated.

"Not specially." Nenda raised bushy eyebrows. "Hey, what do you want, carnival time on Primavera? It's not safe anywhere on Quake right now, and you know it. Is your bug extrasensitive to heat and light? I don't want to fry him."

"Not particularly sensitive," J'merlia translated, with no sign of emotion. "Given water, J'merlia can survive heat and bad air for a long period, even without a respirator. But the communication between you and me . . ."

"Trust me." Nenda pointed to J'merlia and Kallik and jerked a thumb toward the hatch. "Out. Both of you." He switched to Communion talk. "Kallik, take plenty of water with you for J'merlia. We'll tell you when to come back in."

He waited until the two aliens were outside and the hatch was closed, then moved forward to sit in the shadow of Atvar H'sial's carapace. He took a deep breath and opened his shirt, revealing a chest completely covered with an array of gray molelike nodules and deep pockmarks. He closed his eyes and waited.

"Be patient." The coded pheromones diffused slowly into the air. "It is not easy . . . and I lack . . . recent practice."

"Ah." Atvar H'sial was nodding her blind head and pointing her receptors to the chest array. "A Zardalu augmentation, I assume? Heard of but never encountered by me. May I ask, at what physical price?"

"The usual." Louis Nenda's face showed a harsh ecstasy. "Pain—the going rate for every Zardalu augment. That's all right, I'm getting there. I'm going to talk in human style as we go, if you don't mind. It helps me frame my thoughts."

"But there is no need for this!" In addition to the literal meaning, Louis Nenda's pheromone receptors picked up Atvar H'sial's disdain and contemptuous amusement. "J'merlia is totally loyal to me, as I assume Kallik is to you. They would die before they would reveal any conversation of ours."

"They certainly would." Louis Nenda managed to chuckle. "I'd make sure of that. But I don't know how smart J'merlia is. Things can always come out by accident, specially if someone tricky asks the questions. Only way to be really safe is if they're not here to listen." The laugh changed to a grunt of discomfort. "All right, let's get down to business and finish this as quick as we can. It's hard on me."

"We need a protocol for the exchange of information."

"I know. Here's my suggestion. I'll make a statement. You can agree, disagree, or make a statement of your own, but no one is obliged to answer any question. Like this. Fact: You have no interest at all in environmentally stressed life-forms on Quake. That's all bull. You came here because you are a specialist on the Builders."

"To you, I will not deny it." Atvar H'sial reared up to full height. The red-and-white ruffles below the head expanded. "I am more than a specialist. I am *the* specialist on the Builders in the Cecropia Federation." The pheromones carried a message of pride more powerful than words ever could. "I was the first to fathom the mystery of Tantalus; the first—and only—Cecropian to survive a transit of Flambeau. I realized the significance of Summertide before Darya Lang was foolish enough to publish her findings. I—"

"All right. You're smart, I hear you." Nenda's breathing was becoming easier. "Tell me something I need to know, or we'll be here till Summertide and we'll all fry."

"Very well. You are here because you want to know what will happen at Summertide. But I say that you did not initiate that idea. You know too little science or history. Someone else applied Darya Lang's idea and told you the significance of this time and place. It would be of interest to know who that someone is."

"That sure sounds like a question to me, even if it's not phrased like one. But I'll tell you." Nenda jerked his thumb to the ship's hatch. "Kallik."

"Your Hymenopt? A slave!" Atvar H'sial was more than surprised. She was outraged. "It is not fitting for a slave species to perform such high-level work."

"Ah, nuts." Nenda was grinning. "She has a brain— might as well let her use it for my benefit. Anyway, it keeps her happy when she can read and calculate in her spare time. She saw Lang's work, then did the computing herself. She decided this was the special time and place. Then she got all excited, wanted to tell somebody. I said no way. We'll tell no one—and we'll go to Quake ourselves. And here we are. But I want to compare notes with you on something more specific. Let's talk about what will happen here at Summertide."

"That sounds like a question to me. I do not choose to answer."

"So I'll make a statement instead. Let me tell you what Kallik says, based on her analysis, and you can comment if you want to. She says the Builders are going to return— here, and at Summertide. The secret of their technology and the reason for their disappearance will be revealed to those present. How's that grab you?"

"That is also a question, not a statement, but I will answer it. Kallik's suggestion is plausible. However, it is not certain. There is no actual evidence for an appearance of the Builders."

"So it's a bet you have to make. And what Kallik didn't say—but what I think, and it won't surprise me if you're way ahead of me—is that anyone who gets the keys to Builder technology will be plenty powerful in this spiral arm."

"I agree. The technology will be the prize."

"For some people. But it's still not the only reason you're here." Nenda moved closer and went so far as to tap Atvar H'sial's shiny abdomen with his index finger. "Fact: You're another Builder fanatic, as much as Lang and Kallik. You all think you're going to *meet* the Builders, seventy hours from now. Know what Kallik calls this Summertide? The *Epiphany*—when the gods will appear."

"My own term is the Awakening. Do you accept that there will be some momentous event?"

"Hell, I don't know. What do you mean by momentous? I'm damn sure the gods won't appear. The whole thing's a long shot, but it's for super-big stakes. That's my game. I'm a gambler, and I play long shots."

"You are wrong. It is not a long shot. *It will happen.*"

Atvar H'sial's conviction was unmistakable in the pheromonal message. Nenda knew that subtlety of communication technique was beyond him. He wondered if the Cecropians had mastered the means of *lying* with their chemical messengers.

"Already there is evidence of it," Atvar H'sial went on. "All through the spiral arm, the artifacts are restless. And they point here."

"Hey, you don't have to persuade me. I flew eight hundred light-years to land on this crapheap—and I don't give a damn about the artifacts. You can have them all—you're as bad as Kallik. Me, I'll settle for a few new bits of Builder technology. But I've another question for you. Why did you come here to see me, knowing I might blow you away? Not just to compare notes with me and Kallik, that's for sure."

"Ah, that is true. I came because you need me. And because I need you." Atvar H'sial gestured to the port, and to the bare expanse of Quake beyond it. "If you and I were the only people on this world, we would enjoy sole knowledge of any new Builder techniques. We might battle later over who should enjoy the powers of the Builders, but I would accept such a contest."

"That would be your mistake. But I still don't know why you came to me."

"Because today we are *not* the only ones on Quake. Others are here, who would make new knowledge generally available for the sake of science. Now, you are not a scientist, you are an adventurer. You are here for personal gain."

"Damn right. And so are you."

"Perhaps." There was amusement in Atvar H'sial's message, now that Louis Nenda knew how to read it. "And we do not want the Builders' powers shared still further. Rebka, Graves, and Perry are on Quake. They traveled the Umbilical just after us. They will not keep new knowledge to themselves. We might do something about that, but we have no way of knowing where they are."

"I assumed they would follow. What about Darya Lang? She came with you."

"No problem. She has . . . already been taken care of."

Chill certainty in the pheromones. There was a long pause.

"Well, all right," Louis Nenda said at last. His voice was soft. "You are a cold-blooded son of a bitch, aren't you?"

The Cecropian's proboscis trembled. "We attempt to give satisfaction."

"And you're taking a risk, telling me this."

"I think not." Atvar H'sial was silent for a moment. "There is no risk. Not to someone who has read and remembered the Lascia Four files. May I refresh your memory? A medical-supply capsule was plundered en route to Lascia Four. It never reached the planet, and without the viral inhibitors it carried, three hundred thousand people died. An augmented human, accompanied by a Hymenopt slave, was guilty of that atrocity. The Hymenopt died, but the human escaped and was never captured."

Louis Nenda said nothing.

"But about the other humans," Atvar H'sial continued. "We cannot locate them. I am especially worried about Graves."

"He's a madman."

"True. And he reads me and you—even without augmentation, he understands what I am thinking. He is too dangerous. I want him out of the way. I want *all three* out of the way."

"Understood. But I can't find them on Quake, any more than you can. So what are you proposing?"

"Before Summertide they will leave Quake. Their escape route is the Umbilical. That would have been my own line of retreat, until I saw your ship arriving and realized that it is equipped for space travel."

"To the edge of the galaxy, if I want to go. I can see how that might be useful to you, getting off Quake with no risk of running into Graves. But what do you have to offer *me*? I don't want to be crude about this, but I'm not your fairy godmother. Why should I provide you with free transportation off Quake? I told Kallik, we can have a pretty good look around her site on the surface, but come Summertide, we'll be watching from orbit. But that's for *us*. I'm not running a bus service. Why should I help you?"

"Because I know the codes for control of the Umbilical. The *complete* codes."

"But why should I care . . ." Louis Nenda slowly looked up at the Cecropian, at the same time as the sightless head swung down close to him.

"You see?" The pheromones added a message more strong and yet more subtle than any words: pleasure, triumph, the touch of death.

"I do. It's pretty damned clear. But what about *them*?" Nenda gestured at the window. J'merlia and Kallik were huddled together on the hot ground, trying to find shelter behind the starship from Mandel's searing summer rays. They were both shaking, and J'merlia seemed to be trying to comfort the Hymenopt. "I'll go along with what you propose, but there's no way I'm going to drag them along to watch."

"Agreed. And we do not *need* them. Anything that requires J'merlia's sensitivity to half-micrometer radiation, you can perform in his place."

"I can *see*, if that's what you mean." Nenda was already at the hatch, calling to Kallik. "Look, I'm not willing to leave them with my ship, either. In fact, I'm not willing to leave the ship here at all. We'll fly it around to the Umbilical. And we'll leave J'merlia and Kallik to wait for us here."

"Not quite that, I suggest." Atvar H'sial was moving her legs to full extension, towering over Louis Nenda. "We do not want them to have access to the aircar, either."

"Kallik won't touch it if I tell her not to." Nenda waited while the Cecropian stared at him. Even the pheromonal overtones were silent. "Oh, all right. I agree with you. We won't leave them here. No risk is better than a small one—and I'm not too sure of your Lo'tfian. How do you want to handle it?"

"Very simple. We will give them a beacon and some supplies, and drop them off at a convenient point between here and the foot of the Umbilical. When we have done our work there we will home on them, pick them up, look at the site for the Awakening—and head for orbit before it gets too wild on the surface."

"Suppose surface conditions get bad, right where we leave them? Perry swore they will, and I don't think he was lying."

"If things become bad too soon, that would be a pity." Atvar H'sial stood with her head turned, as J'merlia and Kallik waited at the open hatch. Both the slaves were quivering with fear and tension. "But you can always find another Hymenopt. And although J'merlia has been an adequate servant—more than adequate; I would be sorry to lose his services—that may be the price . . . of a larger success."

Chapter 15
Summertide
minus eight

Darya Lang did the natural thing: she sat down and cried. But as House-uncle Matra had told her, long before, weeping solved no problems. After a few minutes she stopped.

At first she had been merely bewildered. Why would Atvar H'sial choose to drug her and maroon her in the middle of nowhere, in a region of Quake that they had chosen only because it seemed like a good place for a landing? She could think of no explanation for the Cecropian's disappearance while she slept.

Darya was thousands of kilometers away from the Umbilical. She had only a vague idea of its direction. She had no way to travel except walking. The conclusion was simple: Atvar H'sial intended that she should be stranded on Quake, and die when Summertide hit.

But in that case, why leave a supply of provisions? Why provide a mask and air filter, and a primitive water purifier? Most baffling of all, why leave behind a signal generator that could be used to broadcast a distress call?

Her confusion had been succeeded by misery; then by anger. It was a sequence of emotions that she would never have anticipated, back in the quiet days before she left Sentinel Gate. She had always thought of herself as a reasonable person, a scientist, a citizen of an orderly and logical universe. Rage was not a reasonable reaction; it clouded the thought processes. But her world had changed, and she had been forced to change with it. The intensity of her own emerging feelings amazed her. If she had to die, she would not do it without a struggle.

She squatted on the soft soil by the nearest lake and systematically inspected every item in the heap of materials. The purifier was a little flash-evaporation unit, one that would produce clean, drinkable water from the most bitter alkalines of any lake. At maximum production the unit would give two pints of water a day. The food in the heap was simple and bland, but it was self-heating, nutritious, and enough to last for weeks. The signal generator, so far as she could tell, was in perfect working order. And the waterproof quilted sheet that covered everything would provide insulation against heat, cold, or rain.

Conclusion: If she died, it would not be from hunger, thirst, or exposure.

That was small comfort. Death would be more immediate and much more violent. The air was hot and steadily becoming hotter. Every few minutes she could feel the earth stirring beneath her, like a sleeper unable to find a comfortable position. Worst of all, a stiffening breeze was carrying in a fine white powder that stung her eyes and gave everything an unpleasant metallic taste. The mask and air filter provided only partial protection.

She walked back to the edge of the lake and saw the ghostly reflection of Gargantua in the dark water. The planet grew more bright and bloated with every hour. It was still far from closest approach to Mandel, but looking up she could already see its three largest moons, moving around Gargantua in strangely perturbed orbits. She could almost feel the forces that Gargantua, Mandel, and Amaranth exerted on those satellites, pulling them in different directions. And the same gravitational forces were at work on Quake. The planet she stood on was enduring terrific stress. Its surface must be ready to disintegrate.

So why had Atvar H'sial left her, then fed her and given her protection, when Summertide would get her anyway?

There had to be an explanation of what had happened. She had to *think*.

She crouched down by the water, seeking a spot partly shielded from the blowing dust. If Atvar H'sial had wanted to kill her, the Cecropian could have done it very easily while she still slept. Instead she had been left alive. Why?

Because Atvar H'sial *needed* her alive. The Cecropian did not want her at the moment for whatever intrigue was being arranged, but Atvar H'sial needed her later. Maybe for something she knew about Quake, or about the Builders. But what? Nothing Darya could imagine.

Change the question. What did Atvar H'sial *think* Darya knew?

Darya could make no rational suggestion, but at the moment she did not need the answer. The new Darya insisted that reasons for actions were less important than actions themselves. The thing that mattered was that she had been left here in cold storage—or hot storage—for an indefinite period; someone, sometime, might be coming back for her. And if she did nothing, she would quickly die.

But it would not happen that way. She would not *let* it happen.

Darya stood up and surveyed her surroundings. She had been Atvar H'sial's dupe once, arranging for the trip up the Umbilical. That was the last time.

The lake she was standing by was the highest of half a dozen connected bodies of water. Their sizes ranged from less than a hundred meters across to maybe four hundred. The outflow of the nearest pool, forty paces away from her, splashed down a little cataract of one or two meters' height into the next lake in the sequence.

She searched the shoreline for some type of shelter. Judging from the weather, it would have to be something pretty substantial. The wind was strengthening, and fine sand was seeping into every open space—including her *own* open spaces; the sensation was not pleasant.

Where? Where to hide, where to find sanctuary? The

determination to survive—she was going to live!—had been growing.

She brushed fine talc from her arms and body. Earthquakes might be a long-term danger, but at the moment the biggest threat was this intrusive, hard-blown powder. She must get away from it. And it was not clear that anywhere was safe.

What do the native animals do?

The question popped into her head as she was staring down at the lake shore, riddled with what seemed to be animal bore holes. Quake life-forms didn't stay on the surface at this time of year. They went underground, or better yet underwater. She recalled the great herds of white-backed animals heading single-mindedly for the lakes.

Could she do the same thing? The bottom of an alkaline pond was not an enthralling prospect, but at least it would get her away from the dust.

Except that she could not survive on a lake bed. She needed to breathe. There was no way to carry an air supply down with her.

She waded into the water until she was up to her knees. The water was pleasantly warm, and increased a little in temperature as she went deeper. Judging from the bottom slope, the middle of the pool would take her over her head. If she went in until the water came to her neck, the seals of her mask and air filter would be below the waterline and only her head would be above it. That would keep out the dust.

But how many hours could she stand like that? Not enough.

It was a solution that solved nothing.

She began to follow the flow-line of the chain of lakes, descending from one steplike level of rock to the next. The first cataract dropped two meters through a series of half a dozen small rapids, running over smooth lips of stone until they finally discharged into the largest of the lakes. If anything, the blowing dust was worse here at the lower level.

She walked on. This lake was roughly elliptical, at least three hundred meters across and maybe five hundred long. Its outfall was correspondingly larger, a substantial cataract that she could hear when she was still forty paces away from it.

When she came to the noisy waterfall she found a wall of water, three meters high, dropping almost vertically into the next lake of the chain. Spray from the foot of it blew up and fogged her mask, but at least it washed some of the dust from the air. If she could find nothing better, this might be a place to return to.

She was ready to head for the next pool when she saw that the waterfall actually flowed over an overhang in the ledge of rock. There was a space behind. If she could step through the fall without being carried away by the water torrent she would be in a shielded enclosure, protected from blowing dust by a rock wall on one side and running water on the other.

Darya moved to the side of the waterfall, pressed herself as close as she could to the rock face, and edged sideways into the rush of water. As soon as she was partway into the foaming white spray she knew she could get through it. The main force of the fall was missing her, arching out over her head in a torrent that sent only noise and blown droplets back to the hidden rock wall. And as she had thought, there was a space behind.

The trouble was, that ledge and shielded space were too small. She could not stand up without poking her head into the torrent. She could not lie down flat. The ledge was lumpy and uneven. And there was not one square inch of wall or floor undrenched by the continuous spray.

She began to feel dismay, then caught herself. What had she been expecting, an Alliance luxury apartment? This wasn't a matter of *comfort*; it was one of survival.

With the quilt to protect her, she could curl up with her back to the rock. She could stack most of her food and drink outside, and whenever necessary she could leave her cave long enough to bring in more to eat, or to stretch her legs. She could wash out the mask and air filter when she was inside, to keep it free of dust. And she would be warm enough, even if she was never totally dry or rested. If she had to, she could survive here for many days.

She went back and made three trips to her cache of supplies. In the first two she carried everything except the beacon over to the waterfall, and spent a long time deciding which items should be inside with her, and which would be left just outside.

The third trip involved the most difficult decision.

She could carry the beacon signal generator over to a point of high ground near the lake. She could put it on a heap of stones, to maximize its range. She could make sure that it had adequate power. But would she do something else?

She thought about it, and knew she had no choice. If and when Atvar H'sial came back, Darya would still be at her mercy, to be used, rescued, or discarded, as the Cecropian chose. Two months ago Darya might have bowed to that as inevitable; now it was not acceptable.

She wrapped the generator in the quilt and carried it through into the waterfall cave. There she rearranged the waterproof sheet so that she and the beacon were shielded from blown water droplets. It was close to Mandel-noon, and enough light diffused in through the rush of water.

Slowly and carefully, she switched off the generator and partly disassembled it. It would be a mistake to rush, and time seemed to be the one thing she had in abundance. She knew the basic circuits she needed, but she had to improvise to achieve the impedance that would do the trick. She took the high-voltage alternating leads, and ran their output in parallel to the r/f stage, through the transformer, and on to the message box. Then it was a test of memory, and of long-ago courses in neural electronics. The convolver that she needed was little more than a nonlinear oscillator, and there were resistors and capacitors in the signal generator that could perform dual functions. She could not test the result, but the changes she had made were simple enough. It ought to work. The main danger was that it might be too powerful.

Mandel was setting before she was finished. The modified beacon went back outside, into the ruddy light of Amaranth and the driving dust storm, and onto its little cairn of stones. Darya activated it, and nodded in satisfaction as the function light blinked to indicate that the beacon was working again.

She inched her way back into the waterfall cave, swathed herself completely in the quilt, and curled up on the ledge of rock. Stony lumps stuck into her side. The splashing fall provided a continuous spray of droplets and the noise of rushing water. Underneath that was the uneasy movement of Quake itself, groaning as the planet was stretched harder on the rack of tidal forces.

No one could expect to be able to sleep in such conditions. Darya nibbled on dry biscuits, closed her eyes, and fixed her mind on one thought: *she was fighting back*. What she had done was little enough, but it was all that she *could* do.

And tomorrow, she would find some new idea to save herself.

With that thought in her head and uneaten biscuits still in her hands, she drifted off into the most restful sleep since she had left Sentinel Gate.

Hans Rebka had another reason for wishing to be alone. Just before they had left Opal, another encrypted message had arrived from Phemus Circle headquarters. There had been no time to examine it in the haste of their departure, but while the capsule was descending the Umbilical toward Quake he had taken a first look. He had been able to decipher just enough to make him uncomfortable by the time they landed. As the aircar took him north away from Opalside and toward the starside of Quake, the message was burning a hole in his jacket pocket. He put the plane on autopilot, ignored the brooding scene below him, and set out in earnest to work on the message.

Headquarters had switched from prime numbers and cyclic ideals as the basis for their codes, to an invariant-embedding method. The messages were supposedly almost uncrackable—and vastly more difficult to read, even when you knew the key. Rebka appropriated most of the car's on-board computer power and began to grind out the message, symbol by symbol. It did not help at all that there were occasional data losses in transmission at the Bose Transitions, adding their own random garbling to the cipher.

The received signal contained three independent messages. The first, deciphered after three quarters of an hour of patient work, made him want to throw the whole facsimile record out of the car's window.

. . . THE ALLIANCE COUNCIL MEMBER WHO IS HEADING FOR DOBELLE USES THE NAME *JULIUS GRAVES*, OR APPARENTLY SOMETIMES *STEVEN GRAVES*. HE IS AUGMENTED WITH AN INTERIOR MNEMONIC TWIN, DESIGNED AS AN EXTENDED SUPPLEMENTARY MEMORY, BUT THAT UNION IS NOT FOLLOWING NORMAL PATTERNS. OUR ANALYSTS SUGGEST A POSSIBILITY OF INCOMPLETE INTEGRA-TION. THIS MAY LEAD TO VOLATILE OR INCONSISTENT BEHAVIOR. SHOULD GRAVES ARRIVE ON DOBELLE, AND SHOULD HE EXHIBIT BEHAVIORAL IRREGULARI-TIES, YOU WILL COMPENSATE FOR THESE TEN-DENCIES AND NEUTRALIZE ANY ILLOGICAL DECISIONS THAT HE MAY SEEK TO MAKE. PLEASE NOTE THAT A MEMBER OF THE COUNCIL HAS PERSONAL DECISION POWERS THAT EXCEED THOSE OF ANY PLANETARY GOVERNMENT CONTROLS. YOU MUST WORK WITHIN THIS CONSTRAINT . . .

"Thanks, guys." Rebka crumpled the message into a ball and threw it over his shoulder. "He's crazy and he can do anything he likes—but it's my job to control him and stop him. And if I don't, my head rolls! Just perfect."

It was another fine example of action at a distance, of government trying to control events a hundred light-years away. Rebka set to work on the next message.

That took another hour. It did not seem much use when he had it, but at least it provided information and did not ask for outright impossibilities.

. . . PERHAPS OF NO DIRECT RELEVANCE TO YOUR SITUATION, BUT THERE ARE WIDESPREAD AND INDEPENDENT REPORTS OF CHANGES IN BUILDER ARTIFACTS THROUGH THE WHOLE OF THE SPIRAL ARM. STRUCTURES THAT HAVE BEEN STABLE AND INVARIANT THROUGHOUT HUMAN AND CECROPIAN MEMORY AND IN ALL REMAINING ZARDALU RECORDS ARE EXHIBITING FUNCTIONAL ODDITIES AND MODI-FIED PHYSICAL PROPERTIES. THIS IS ENCOURAGING MANY EXPLORATION TEAMS TO REEXAMINE THE POSSIBILITY OF PROBING THE UNKNOWN INTERIORS OF A NUMBER OF ARTIFACTS . . .

"Tell me about it!" Rebka glared at the computer that was displaying the offending transcript. "And don't you remember that I was all set to explore Paradox, before this idiot assignment? Before you dummies pulled me away!"

. . . WHILE PERFORMING YOUR OTHER DUTIES YOU SHOULD OBSERVE CLOSELY THE ARTIFACT OF THE DOBELLE SYSTEM KNOWN AS THE UMBILICAL, AND DETERMINE IF THERE HAVE BEEN SIGNIFICANT CHANGES IN ITS FUNCTION OR APPEARANCE. NONE HAVE SO FAR BEEN REPORTED . . .

Rebka turned to stare back the way he had come. The Umbilical was long since invisible. All he could see was a broken line on the planet's terminator, like a glowing string of orange beads on the curving horizon. A major eruption had begun there. He looked down to the surface over which he was flying—all quiet below—and skipped to the third message.

Which made up for the other two. It was the answer to Rebka's own query.

. . . A CECROPIAN ANSWERING YOUR DESCRIP-TION. SHE IS INTERESTED IN LIFE-FORM EVOLUTION UNDER ENVIRONMENTAL PRESSURE, AS YOU SUG-GEST, BUT SHE IS ALSO KNOWN AS A SPECIALIST IN BUILDER TECHNOLOGY . . .

. . . SHE GOES UNDER A VARIETY OF NAMES (AGTIN H'RIF, ARIOJ H'MINEA, ATVAT H'SIAR, AGHAR H'SIMI) AND CHANGES OF EXTERNAL APPEARANCE. SHE MAY BE RECOGNIZABLE BY AN ACCOMPANYING SLAVE INTERPRETER OF THE LO'TFIAN FAMILY. SHE IS DANGEROUS TO BOTH HUMANS AND CECROPIANS, RESPONSIBLE FOR AT LEAST TWELVE DEATHS OF KNOWN INTELLIGENCES AND TWENTY-SEVEN DEATHS OF PROBATED INTELLIGENCE.

ADDED NOTE: LOUIS NENDA (HUMAN, REPUTED AUGMENTATION), FROM KARELIA IN THE ZARDALU COMMUNION, IS ALSO HEADED FOR DOBELLE. HE IS ACCOMPANIED BY A HYMENOPT SLAVE. NO DETAILS ARE AVAILABLE, BUT THE KARELIA NET SUGGESTS THAT NENDA MAY ALSO BE DANGEROUS.

NEITHER THE CECROPIAN NOR THE KARELIAN SHOULD BE ADMITTED TO THE DOBELLE SYSTEM . . .

Rebka did not throw the printout from the car—it was moving too high and too fast for that. But he did crumple the message and toss it over his shoulder to join the other two. He had spent more than three hours deciphering those missives from Circle headquarters, and all they offered was bad news.

He lifted his head and stared out of the window ahead. Amaranth was behind him, and the car's roof shielded its light. He looked west, ready to catch the last gleam of Mandel-set before the primary was lost behind the dark crescent of Quake. The sun's rim dipped below the horizon.

His eyes adjusted. And as they did so they picked up a faint, blinking light flashing from a tiny red bead next to the control console. At the same moment an insistent beep started within the cabin.

Distress circuit.

The skin on the back of his neck prickled with anticipation. Sixty hours to Summertide. And someone or something, down on the looming dark surface of Quake ahead of him, was in big trouble.

✦　✦　✦

The line of the beacon would bring him down on the fringes of the Thousand Lakes area, not far from the region Max Perry favored for the location of the Carmel twins. Rebka checked the car's power supply. It was ample—each aircar could make a trip right around Quake and still have something in reserve. No reason for worry there. He sent a brief message to Perry and Graves, then increased the car's speed and set his new course without waiting for either acknowledgment or approval.

Mandel was still hidden, but Gargantua was high in the sky and providing enough light to land by. Rebka stared ahead. He was skimming low over a chain of circular lakes, waters steaming and churning. Their turbulent surfaces matched his own mood. Nowhere, from horizon to bleak horizon, was there a sign of life. For that, he would have to look into the waters of the Thousand Lakes themselves, or in the deepest hollows of the Pentacline Depression. Or deeper yet—the most tenacious life-forms would burrow far under Quake's shifting surface. Would the Carmel twins have had the sense to do the same?

But maybe he was already too late. The twins were no specialists in harsh-environment survival, and every second the tidal forces at work on the planet below him grew bigger.

Rebka increased speed again, pushing the car to its limits. There was nothing else he could do. His mind wandered away into troubled speculation.

Gravity is the weakest force in nature. The strong interaction, the electromagnetic interaction, even the "weak" interaction that governs beta decay, are many orders of magnitude more powerful. Two electrons, one hundred light-years apart, repel each other with an electric force as great as the attractive gravitational force of two electrons half a millimeter apart.

But consider the gravitational *tidal* force. That is weaker yet. It is caused only by a *difference* of gravitational forces, the difference in the pull on one side of a body from the pull on the other. While gravity is governed by an inverse square law—twice the distance, a quarter the force—gravity tides are governed by an inverse *cube* law. Twice the distance, one *eighth* the force; thrice the distance, one twenty-seventh the force.

Gravity tides should be negligible.

But they are not. They grip a billion moons around the galaxy, forcing them to present the same face always to their master planets; tides worry endlessly at a world's interior, squeezing and pulling, releasing geological stresses and changing the figure of the planet with every tidal cycle; and they rip and rend any object that falls into a black hole, so that, no matter how strong the intruder may be, the tides will tear it down to its finest subatomic components.

For that inverse-cube distance relationship can easily be *inverted*: one half the distance, eight times the tidal force; one third the distance, twenty-seven times the tidal force; one tenth the distance . . .

At closest approach to Mandel, the Dobelle system was one eleventh of its mean distance from the primary. One thousand three hundred and thirty-one times the mean tidal force was exerted upon its components.

That was *Summertide*.

Hans Rebka had been told those basic facts by Max Perry, and he thought of them as he overflew the surface of Quake. Every four hours, the vast invisible hand of Mandel and Amaranth's gravity squeezed and pulled at Opal and Quake, trying to turn their near-spherical shapes into longer ellipsoids. And close to Summertide, tidal energy equivalent to a dozen full-scale nuclear wars was pumped into the system—not just *once*, but twice every Dobelle day.

Rebka had visited worlds where global nuclear war had recently taken place. Based on that experience he expected to see a planet whose whole surface was in turmoil, a seething chaos where the existence of life was impossible.

It was not happening. And he was baffled.

There were local eruptions—that was undeniable. But when he looked at the ground speeding beneath him, he could see nothing to match the scale of his imaginings.

What was wrong?

Rebka and Perry had overlooked a fact known since the time of Newton: gravity is a *body force*. No known material can shield against it; every particle, no matter where it may be in the universe, feels the gravitational force of every other particle.

And so, whereas nuclear war confines its fury to the atmosphere, oceans, and top few tens of meters of a planet's land surface, the tidal forces squeeze, pull, and twist every cubic centimeter of the world. They are *distributed* forces, felt from the top of the atmosphere to the innermost atom of the superheated, superpressured core.

Rebka examined the surface but saw little to suggest a coming Armageddon. His mistake was natural, and elementary. He should have been looking much deeper; and then he might have had his first inkling of the true nature of Summertide.

A wind of choking dust was screaming across the surface as the aircar came in to land. Rebka brought the car directly into that gale, relying on microwave sensors to warn of rocks big enough to cause trouble. The final landing was smooth enough, but there was an immediate problem. The search-and-rescue system told him that the distress beacon was right in front of him, less than thirty meters away. But the mass detector insisted that nothing the size of an aircar or a ship was closer than three hundred. Peering into the dust storm did not help. The world in front of the car ended with a veil of driving dust and sand, no more than a dozen paces beyond the car's nose.

Rebka checked the SAR system again. No doubt about the location of the beacon. He gauged its line and distance from the door of the car. He forced himself to sit down and wait for five minutes, listening to the sandstorm as it screamed and buffeted at the car and hoping that the wind would drop. It blew on, as strongly as ever. Visibility was certainly not improving. Finally he pulled on goggles, respirator, and heat-resistant clothing, and eased open the door. At least the combination was a familiar one. Howling wind, superheated atmosphere, foul-tasting and near-poisonous air—just like home. He had grappled with all that in his childhood on Teufel.

He stepped outside.

The wind-driven sand was unbelievable, so fine-grained that it could find a way through the most minute of gaps in the suit. It blasted and caught at his body. He could taste powdery talc on his lips in the first few seconds, somehow creeping in through the respirator. Millions of tiny, scrabbling fingers touched him and tugged at his suit, each one eager to pull him away. His spirits dropped. This was *worse* than Teufel. Without the shelter of a car, how could anyone survive such conditions for even an hour? It was a side of Quake that Perry, in his preoccupation with volcanoes and earthquakes, had not warned about. But given enough atmospheric disturbance, interior activity of a planet was not necessary to make it inhospitable to life. Blown sand that would allow a person to neither breathe nor escape would do the trick nicely.

Rebka made sure that he had a return line attached firmly to the body of the aircar, then leaned into the wind and crept forward. The beacon finally appeared when it was less than four meters in front of him. No wonder the mass sensors had not registered it! It was tiny—a stand-alone unit and the smallest one he had ever seen. It measured no more than thirty centimeters square and a few centimeters thick, with a stubby antenna sticking up from its center. The solid cairn of stones on which it nestled stood at the top of a small rise in the ground. Someone had taken the trouble to make sure that, weak as it was, the beacon would be heard over the maximum possible range.

Someone. But who, and where? If they had left the beacon and headed for refuge on foot, their chances were grim. An unprotected human would not make a hundred meters. They would suffocate, unable to avoid that choking, driving wind.

But maybe they had recorded what they were doing. Every distress beacon carried a message cache in its base. If they had been gone just a few minutes . . .

Wishful thinking, Rebka told himself as he removed his glove and reached for the sliding plate at the bottom of the beacon. He had been receiving the distress signal for an hour. And who knew how long it had been sending out its cry for help before he heard it?

He put his hand in the narrow opening. As his fingertips touched the base, a gigantic bolt of pain shot up his hand, along his arm, and on through his whole body. His muscles convulsed and knotted, too quickly and tightly to permit a scream. He could not pull his hand free. He doubled up, helpless, over the distress beacon.

Neural convolver, his mind said in the moment before the next shock hit him, harder than the first. He could no longer draw breath. In the seconds before he became unconscious, Rebka's mind filled with anger. Anger at the whole stupid assignment, anger at Quake—but most of all, anger at *himself*.

He had done something supremely dumb, and it was going to kill him. Atvar H'sial was dangerous, and at large on the surface of Quake. He had known that before he landed. And still he had blundered along like a child at a picnic, never bothering with the most elementary precautions . . .

But I was trying to help.

So what? His brain rejected that excuse as the jolting current twisted his body and scrambled his brains for a third and final time. You've said it often enough: people who are stupid enough to get themselves killed never help anybody . . .

And now, damn it, he would never know what Quake looked like at Summertide. The planet had won; he had lost . . .

The dust-filled wind screamed in triumph about his unconscious body.

ARTIFACT: ELEPHANT.
UAC#: 859
Galactic Coordinates: 27,548.762/
16,297.442/—201.33
Name: Elephant
Star/planet association: Cam H'ptiar/Emserin
Bose Access Node: 1121
Estimated age: 9.223 ±0.31 Megayears.

Exploration History: Discovered by remote observation in E. —4553, reached and surveyed by a Cecropian exploration fleet in E. —3227. Members of the same fleet performed the first entry to Elephant and measured its physical parameters (see below). Subsequent survey teams performed the first complete traverse of Elephant (E. — 2068), attempted communication with elephant (E. — 1997, E. —1920, E. —1883, all unsuccessful), and removed and tested large samples from the body (E. - 1882, E. -1551). Slow changes in physical parameters and appearance were reported on each successive visit, and a permanent Cecropian observation station (Elephant Station) was established on Emserin, four light-minutes distant, in E. —1220. Human observers were added to Elephant Station for the first time 2,900 years later, in E. 1668. This artifact has been continuously monitored for more than five thousand standard years.

Physical Description: Elephant is an elongated and amorphous gaseous mass, approximately four thousand kilometers in maximum dimension and nowhere wider than nine hundred kilometers. It is in fact not a true gas, but a wholly interconnected mass of stable polymer fibers and transfer ducts. The interior is highly conducting (mainly superconducting) of both heat and electricity.

Applied stimuli suggest that the whole body reacts to any external influence but begins the return to its original condition with a first response time of about twenty years. Physical repair is by subsection replication, and any incident materials (e.g. cometary fragments) are employed catabolically and anabolically to synthesize needed components. Local temperature changes are corrected to the mean body temperature of 1.63 Kelvins, consistent with the use of liquid helium II as a heat-transfer agent. The necessary cooling mechanism to maintain subunits of Elephant below 2 Kelvins is unclear.

Holes in Elephant (included excised fragments up to twenty kilometers long and complete longitudinal transects) are replaced from within, with a small matching reduction of overall dimensions. The external shape is held constant, and the impression of an amorphous body is obviously misleading. Unless material is added, or removed from the body, both the size and shape of Elephant are invariant to within fractions of a millimeter in any direction.

Intended Purposes: Is Elephant alive? Is Elephant conscious? That debate continues. Today's consensus is that Elephant is a single active artifact with a limited self-renewal capability. Any removed section slowly becomes inert, its conductivity diminishes, and the system loses its homeostatic character. If Elephant is alive, the full response time to external stimuli is very long (hundreds of years) and the implied metabolic rate correspondingly slow.

Regardless of this artifact's overall self-awareness, it is certainly true that Elephant can function, as a whole or in part, as a general-purpose computing device. Following the pioneering work of Demerle and T'russig, Elephant has been used extensively in applications requiring enormous storage and moderate computing speed.

If Elephant is an intelligent and self-aware entity, the notion of purposes and uses is inappropriate. More sophisticated tests for self-awareness are clearly needed.

—From the *Lang Universal Artifact Catalog.* Fourth Edition.

CHAPTER 16
Summertide
minus seven

"It's like a treasure hunt," Graves said. He was walking on ahead, slow and steady. With his hands clasped behind him and his relaxed manner, he was like a thoughtful skeleton out for a midday stroll. "The old party game. You remember?"

Max Perry stared after him. He had grown up on a world too harsh and marginal to permit the luxury of children's games and children's parties. Food had been his best treasure. And the best game that he could think of at the moment was survival.

"You get clues," Graves went on. "First the beacon. Then the pointer, then the mystery caves. And then—if you're lucky—the treasure!"

The aircar had landed on a crumbling and eroded plateau in the wilderness area between the Thousand Lakes and the outer boundary of the Pentacline Depression. In that no-man's-land the soft rock had been eaten away into deep tunnels and smooth-sided sinkholes, like soft putty that an aged giant had kneaded and poked with bent, arthritic fingers. The meters-wide holes ran haphazardly at all angles from the surface. Some dived almost vertically; others sloped so shallowly that they could be walked down with ease.

181

"Be careful!" Perry hated Graves's casual attitude. "You don't know how shaky the edges might be—and you don't know what could be at the bottom! This whole area is an estivation zone for Quake wildlife."

"Relax. It's perfectly safe." Graves took a step closer to the edge of one of the holes, then had to jump smartly backward as the rock crumbled and slid away beneath his feet. "Perfectly safe," he repeated. "This isn't the hole that we want anyway. Just follow me."

He led the way forward again, skirting the dangerous area. Perry followed at what he hoped was a safe distance. Expecting another car, perhaps a crashed one, at the site of the distress call, both men had been surprised to find nothing there but an isolated radio beacon. Next to it, marked as a black line in the chalky white rock, was an arrow. It pointed straight toward the dark, steep tunnel on whose brink Graves was currently poised and leaning precariously forward. Alongside the arrow, in an ill-formed scrawl, were the words "In Here."

"Fascinating." Graves leaned farther. "It seems to me—"

"Don't go so *near!*" Perry exclaimed when Graves moved forward again. "That edge there, if it's like the other one . . ."

"Oh, phooey." Graves jumped up and down. "See, solid as the Alliance. And I read the report before I came to Dobelle—there are no dangerous animals on Quake."

"Sure, you read the report, but I *wrote* the damned thing. There's a lot we don't know about Quake." Perry advanced cautiously to the brink of the tunnel and peered down. The rock seemed firm enough, and quite old. On Quake that was a good sign. The surface here at least had a certain permanence, as though it had avoided the turmoil that hit the planet at Summertide. "Anyway, it's not just animals. Mud pools can be just as bad. You don't even know how deep this hole is. Before you start charging down there, at least take a sounding."

He picked up a fist-sized chunk of chalky stone and lobbed it down the line of the tunnel. Both men leaned forward, listening for an echo where it struck the bottom.

There was a two-second silence, then a thud, a whoof of protest, and a surprised whistle.

"Ah-ha! That's not a rock or a mud pool." Graves snapped his fingers and started to scramble on his bottom down the steep-sided hole. He had a flashlight, and he was shining it along in front of him. "That's the Carmel twins down there. I told you what to expect, Commander—the beacon, the arrow, the cave, and then the—" He halted. "And then . . . well, well, well. We were wrong."

Perry, a few steps behind, craned to see past Graves. The narrow beam of the flashlight reflected from a line of bright black eyes. As Graves held the light steady a small body, its black fur dusted to gray by a coating of fine powder, moved slowly up the incline. The Hymenopt was rubbing her tubby midsection with a foreleg, and while they watched she shook herself like a drenched dog and threw off a cloud of white dust.

There was another whistle, and a click-click-click of jointed hind limbs.

"Kallik offers respect and obedience," a familiar, sibilant voice said. J'merlia was emerging from around the curve of the tunnel. He, too, was completely coated with fine talc. "She is a loyal slave and servant. She asks, why do you throw stones at her? Did her master command it?"

The Lo'tfian's narrow face was not equipped to register human emotions, but there was a puzzled and worried tone in his voice. Instead of answering, Graves slithered farther along the tunnel to where it leveled off as a small cave whose floor was covered with powdered gypsum. He stared at the cleared area, and then at the little pile of objects standing in the middle of it.

"You were here in the dark?"

"No." J'merlia's compound eyes glittered in the flashlight beam. "It is not dark. We can both see here fairly well. Do you need our assistance?"

Perry, who had followed Graves down the tunnel at his own pace, pushed past the other man and reached up high to touch the tunnel's roof. "See those? Cracks.

Recent ones. I'm sure we shouldn't stay any longer. What are you doing down here, J'merlia?"

"Why, we are waiting. As we were instructed to do." The Lo'tfian offered a rapid set of whistles to Kallik, then continued. "Our masters brought us here and told us to await their return. Which we are doing."

"Atvar H'sial and Louis Nenda?"

"Of course. Owners never change."

"So Nenda didn't fly home in a huff. When did your masters leave?"

"Two days ago. We stayed at first on the surface, but we did not like conditions there—too hot, too open, too hard to breathe. But here, snug underground—"

"Snug, while the roof is ready to fall in. When did they say they would be back?"

"They did not say. Why should they? We have food; we have water; we are safe here."

"Don't bother to ask any more, Commander." Graves, done with his inventory of the little cavern, sank to his knees and began rubbing at eyes irritated by the fine dust that flew up at every movement. "Atvar H'sial and Louis Nenda would not have provided their itinerary, or anything else, to J'merlia. Why should they, as J'merlia says? To make it easier for you or me to follow them? No." His voice dropped to a stage whisper. "If they ever intended to come back for them at all! Maybe they have abandoned them. But even that is not the right question. The real question, one that I ask myself and do not like the answer to, is this: Where did H'sial and Nenda *go*? Where did they go, on Quake near Summertide, where they could not or would not take J'merlia and Kallik with them?"

As though answering his question, there was a tremor through the floor of the cave. The minor quake left the roof intact, but a cloud of fine white powder flew up to cover all of them.

"I don't care—*ough!*—where they went." Perry had trouble holding back his coughs. "I care about us, and where we go next."

"We go to find the Carmel twins." Graves rubbed the

white powder away from his eyes again and looked like a circus clown.

"Sure. Where? And when?" Perry was aware of the running clock, even if Graves was not. "It's only fifty-five hours to Summertide."

"Ample time."

"No. You think, fifty-five hours, and you imagine that you'll be all right until then. That's totally wrong. Anybody who is still on the surface of Quake five hours or even fifteen hours from Summertide is probably dead. If we don't find the twins soon—in the next ten to twelve hours—they're dead, too. Because we'll have to give up the search and head back to the Umbilical."

Perry was finally getting through to the councilor. Graves stood, bald head bowed, and sighed in agreement. "All right. We don't have time to argue. Let's look for the twins."

"What about these two?" Perry gestured at Kallik and J'merlia.

"They come with us. Naturally. Atvar H'sial and Louis Nenda may never come back, or they may be too late, or they may not be able to track that beacon—you said it was running low on power."

"It is. I agree, we can't just leave the aliens. There's enough room in the car for all of us." Perry turned to J'merlia and Kallik. "Come on. Let's get out of here."

When the others did not move, he reached out for one of J'merlia's slender black forelimbs and started toward the tunnel entrance. Surprisingly, the Lo'tfian resisted.

"With respect, Commander Perry." J'merlia dug in six of his feet and cowered down until his slender abdomen was touching the rocky floor. "Humans are much greater beings than me or Kallik, we know that, and we will seek to do whatever you tell us. But Atvar H'sial and Louis Nenda gave us orders to stay in this area. We must wait until they return."

Perry turned in frustration to Graves. "Well? They won't do what I tell them. Do you think they'll obey a direct order from you?"

"Probably not." The councilor looked calmly at J'merlia. "Would you?"

The Lo'tfian shivered and groveled lower on the powdery floor.

Graves nodded. "That's answer enough. You see, Commander, we are placing them in an impossible position. Although they are trained to obey us, they cannot disobey the orders of their owners. They also have strong instincts to save their own lives, but they do not see the danger here. However, I have an alternative proposal—one that may be acceptable to them. We can leave them here—"

"We can't leave them. They'll die."

"We don't leave them *indefinitely*. But we are close to the Pentacline Depression. We can explore that for the twins. And if we provide a new power source for this beacon we can come back here afterward, whether we succeed or fail. By that time, perhaps Nenda and Atvar H'sial will also have returned. If not, the surface of Quake will surely be more obviously dangerous, and we can try again to persuade the aliens to leave."

Perry was still hesitating. At last he shook his head. "I think we can do better." He turned to J'merlia. "Were you told not to leave the place where Atvar H'sial and Louis Nenda dropped you off?"

"That is correct."

"But you *already* left that place—to come down into this tunnel. So you must have some freedom of movement. How far are you and Kallik willing to roam?"

"One moment, please." J'merlia turned away from Perry and held a whistling dialog with the Hymenopt, who had been squatting on the floor completely immobile. Finally he nodded.

"It is not so much a question of distance, as of time. A few kilometers would be all right; Kallik and I are agreed that we could go so far on foot. But if you are sure we can return here in three or four hours, we would be willing to travel a longer distance by aircar."

Graves was shaking his head. "Four hours is not long

enough. How big is the Pentacline Depression, Commander?"

"Roughly a hundred and fifty kilometers across."

"And the twins may be in there, but they could be way over on the other side. I'm sure we can find them, given enough time, but we can't make an adequate scan for a starship in a few hours. We'll have to do it my way; leave these two here, and then come back."

Kallik interjected a whistle and a series of agitated clicks.

"But coming back will cut further into the search time." Perry ignored the Hymenopt. "If the two aliens would—"

"With great respect, Captain," J'merlia cut in—the first time he had ever interrupted a human. "But in all the time since Kallik and I met on Opal, I have been teaching her human talk. Already she understands some, though she cannot yet speak. Now she asks me, did she hear what she thought she heard? Are you searching for other human presence, here on the surface of Quake?"

"We sure are—if we can ever get out of here! So no more talk, we have to—"

This time it was Kallik herself who interrupted. The Hymenopt ran up close to Perry, raised herself onto the points of her toes, and produced a rapid series of whistling screams.

"With great respect," J'merlia gabbled before Perry could speak again, "she wants you to know that there is a starship on the surface of Quake."

"We know. The one that Kallik and Louis Nenda used to come over from Opal."

"Not that one. Before they landed, Master Nenda did a precautionary scan, because he was worried that there might be a trap. He picked up the trace of a ship's Bose Drive. Kallik says it was an Alliance design, able to do Bose Network transfers. She thinks, maybe it brought the humans you seek."

Kallik grunted and whistled again. J'merlia nodded.

"She says it is only a hundred kilometers from here— a few minutes' flight time. Kallik asks, Would you have any interest in knowing where it is?"

Outside. Empty yesterday's wastes (time allocation, 24 seconds); climb the twenty-four stone steps to the pure-water stream that gushes halfway up the cliffside (33 seconds); wash out plastic containers (44 seconds); rinse a starship on the surface of Opal.

CHAPTER 17

"What sins must a man commit, in how many past lives, to be born on Teufel?"

The water-duty for seven-year-olds was precise and unforgiving.

Suit on, check air tank, seal respirator, walk to the lock. Warning: Opening takes place as the surface wind drops, five and a half minutes before first light, after the night predators retreat to their caves. Be there in time, or forfeit one day's food.

Outside. Empty yesterday's wastes (time allocation, 24 seconds); climb the twenty-four stone steps to the pure-water stream that gushes halfway up the cliffside (33 seconds); wash out plastic containers (44 seconds); rinse filters (90 seconds); fill water cans (75 seconds); descend (32 seconds); reenter lock and perform closing sequence (25 seconds).

Margin for error: seven seconds. If you are caught on the steps or with the lock wide open you are hit by the Remouleur—the Grinder, the dreaded dawn wind of Teufel. And you are dead.

Rebka knew that. And suddenly he knew that he was late. He could hardly believe it. Usually when his turn came for the water-duty he was the one who hurried down the cliff ahead of schedule, the only one with the time and confidence to stand in the open lock and look out on Teufel's stark scenery and spiky, eccentric vegetation for a few seconds as lock closure began. The strata of the cliff face were still too dark to be seen, but he knew they were a muted purple interleaved with gray and faded reds. The strip of sky above the canyon already showed the signs of coming dawn. He could watch as the stars began to fade and streaks of high cloud turned from black to rosy gray. The sight had an indescribable beauty. It excited him.

But not today. The trickle of spring water was weaker, and the cans refused to fill at their usual speed. Nearly five minutes were already gone. He was still on the top step, and his face mask was fogging over. He had to leave, with half-filled containers. *Right now.*

Descent time allocation is 32 seconds; reenter lock and perform closing sequence, 25 seconds.

He headed down the steps blind and fast, risking a fall. He knew from experience the possible fates. If the *Remouleur* hit when he was on the top few steps, he would be carried out of the canyon like a dry leaf and no one would ever see him again. That had happened to Rosamunde. Halfway down, the dawn wind was less strong, but it blew its victims right down the canyon and dashed them against the rock chimneys. They had retrieved Joshua's body from there, what was left of it after the day predators were finished. If he almost made it, say to the bottom three or four steps, the wind could not carry him away completely. But it still would rip away his respirator, break his grip no matter how he clung to the rocks or the support rail, and roll him into the poisonous, boiling-water cauldron that seethed and churned below the spring. Lee had floated there for nine hours before she could be retrieved. Some of her had been lost forever. The cooked flesh had flaked from her bones and escaped the nets.

Twelve steps to go. And the Remouleur *is coming, no more than twenty seconds away, and the dust devils are stirring along the canyon, and now there is the preliminary scream of far-off wind and the chatter of torrential rain. The steps feel greasy under your feet.*

If someone was actually in the lock when the wind hit,

he might have a chance. Teufel lore said that if one dropped the water containers and flattened oneself to the floor, one might—just might—keep the respirator on and survive until the lock closed all the way. But Rebka had never met anyone who had actually done it. And the penalty for returning without water—or, worse, without containers—was severe.

But not as severe as death.

Six steps to go.

Time had run out. He dropped the water containers.

There was a strange, moaning cry in his ears, and his body was lifted and pulled across a rocky surface. Cold water drenched his exposed arms and legs. His respirator was pulled away from his face. Death would at least be quick.

But he was not ready to die. He writhed against the force that held him, reaching up to grab the respirator straps and hold it in position.

His clawing fingers met human hands. The shock was so great that for a couple of seconds he could do nothing.

"Hans! Hans Rebka!" The cry came again, and this time he could understand it.

He opened his eyes for a last look at Teufel's dark skies. Instead of rosy streaks of wind-torn cloud he found himself staring at a shimmering blur of running water. Framed in front of the torrent, mouth open and panting with effort, was a dusty and droplet-streaked face.

It was Darya Lang.

When she realized what she had done, Darya was ready to sit down and start weeping again.

She had crawled out and hurried over to check the beacon as soon as she woke up. And when she peered through the shrouding dust and saw a figure huddled over the cairn, her first reaction was pure delight. That would teach Atvar H'sial a lesson! The Cecropian would not do that again, callously leaving someone to live or die without even telling her why.

And then as Darya came closer she realized that it was

not a Cecropian. It was a human—it was a man—dear God, it was Hans Rebka!

Darya screamed and ran forward. The dust of Quake was as lethal to him as it would be to her. If he were dead, she would never forgive herself.

"Hans. Oh Hans, I'm sorry . . ."

He was unconscious and not listening. But it *was* unconsciousness, not death. Darya found the strength to hoist him over her shoulder—he weighed less than she did—and carry him back through the waterfall. And as she laid him gently on the rock, his eyes opened. That puzzled look up at her was the most satisfying expression she had ever seen on a human face.

For twenty minutes she had the pleasure of tending him, watching him curse and spit up dust and snort out gray powder through his nose. It was delight, simply to know he was *alive*. And then, before she could believe that he was able to function, he was on his feet and forcing her back out onto the surface.

"You're not safe here, even if you think you are." He was still wringing his hand and arm at the pain that the neural convolver had left in the nerves. "Another few hours, and that waterfall might be steam. Summertide's coming, Darya, and there's only one road to safety. Come on."

He hurried her across the arid surface, and at the aircar he made a quick inspection. Within a couple of minutes he shook his head and sat back on his haunches. "It doesn't matter where Atvar H'sial went, or if she's coming back. We won't go far in this." He leaned in under the car to rub his hand over the intake units. "See for yourself."

The dust storm was easing, but the inside of the vents was still clogged. Worse than that, where Rebka brushed the dust away the liner metal showed bright and eroded.

"That was from flying in and landing here." He placed the grille back in position. "I think we ought to be able to make one more trip without major servicing and overhaul, but I wouldn't want to try beyond that. And we can't risk flying in any more dust storms. If we run

into one, we'll have to go up and over and bide our
time coming down. Assuming we don't run out of power,
too—no extreme head winds, or we're done for."

"But what about the Carmel twins? You were supposed
to be looking for them." Darya Lang remained crouched
by the aircar's intakes. She had explained to Rebka why
she had set her trap, and how Atvar H'sial had deserted
her. He seemed to accept what she said, brushing it all
off as an unimportant detail. But she had trouble looking
him in the eye.

She knew why. That trap had been more than a desire
to protect herself when Atvar H'sial came back. She had
been looking for *revenge* for what Atvar H'sial had done.
And then her unguided missile had gone astray and hit
the wrong person.

"We can't do anything to help the twins," Rebka replied.
"We'll have to hope that Graves and Perry had better luck
than I did. Maybe they'll find them, or maybe the spaceship
that you and J'merlia saw will be able to help them. I doubt
it, though, if it's who I think it is."

"Louis Nenda?"

He nodded and turned away. He had his own reasons
for wanting to appear calm and casual. First, he had fallen
into Darya Lang's trap so easily that it dismayed him. He
was supposed to be the smart and cautious one, but he
had become soft and casual. Five years ago he would have
tested *everything* for traps. This one he had fallen into
like a baby.

Second, over the years he had found that dreams of
his childhood on Teufel were a useful indicator. They were
his own unconscious, trying to tell him something important. He had experienced those dreams only when he was
in desperate trouble, and always when he did not know
what that trouble might be.

Third—and maybe the driving force for the other two
worries—Quake had changed since he had landed at the
radio beacon. Superficially it was a change for the better.
The winds had dropped, the blown sand was reduced to
no more than an irritating half-centimeter blanket that

lay over everything, and even the distant grumble of volcanic action was quiet.

But that was *impossible*. It was less than forty hours to Summertide. Amaranth was directly overhead, a huge, bloodshot eye glaring across five degrees of sky; Mandel, off to the west, was half as big again, and Gargantua was bright enough to be seen at Mandel-noon. The tidal energies pouring into the interiors of Quake and Opal were prodigious, enough to produce continuous and severe planetary distortions.

So where were they?

Energy had to be conserved, even on Quake, but it might be changed to another form. Was it being accumulated by some unknown physical process in the planet's deep interior?

"I guess we could stay here and tough it out," Darya Lang was saying, staring around them. "This is as quiet as it's been for a long time. If it doesn't get much worse than it was . . ."

"No. It will get a lot worse."

"How bad?"

"I'm not sure."

That was an understatement. He had no idea how bad, and it did not matter. We have to get off Quake, a tiny voice was saying in his ear, or we are dead. He was glad that Darya could not hear that voice, but he had learned never to ignore it.

"We have to leave," he added. "This minute, if you're ready."

"And go where?"

"To the Umbilical, and then to Midway Station. We'll be safe there. But we can't wait too long. The Umbilical is programmed to lift away from the surface before Summertide."

She climbed into the car and consulted the chronometer. "It lifts twelve hours before Summertide Maximum. That's twenty-seven hours from now. And we can be over there in one Dobelle day. We have plenty of time."

Rebka closed the car door. "I *like* to have plenty of time. Let's go."

"All right." She smiled at him. "But you've seen more of Quake than I have. What do you think will happen here at Summertide?"

Rebka took a deep breath. She was trying to be nice to him, but worse than that, she assumed that he was tense and needed to be calmed down. And the trouble was, she was right. He was *too* tense. He could not explain it—except that he had been badly fooled once on Quake, by assuming that something was safe when it was not. He did not want to do it again. And every nerve in his body urged him to get away from Quake *soon*.

"Darya, I'd love to compare notes about Summertide." He was not annoyed that she had trapped him, he told himself; he was impressed. "But I'd rather do it when we're on the Umbilical, and well on our way to Midway Station. You may think I'm a coward, but this place scares me. So if you'll just move over, and let me get at those controls . . ."

CHAPTER 18
Summertide
minus five

The *Summer Dreamboat* was well hidden.

The Pentacline Depression formed the most highly visible feature on the surface of Quake. One hundred and fifty kilometers across, packed with a riot of vivid and strongly growing vegetation, it could be seen from half a million kilometers away in space as a starfish splash of lurid green on Quake's dusty gray surface. The Pentacline was also the lowest point on the planet. Its five valleys, radiating up and out like stretching arms from the central low, had to rise over eight hundred meters to reach the level of the surrounding plain.

The little starship had landed close to the middle of the Pentacline's north-pointing arm, at a point where dense vegetation was broken by a small flat island of black basalt. But the ship had flown in to the bare outcrop on an angled descent and skated to its very edge. It was shielded from overhead inspection by vigorous new growth. Scarcely bigger than an aircar, the *Summer Dreamboat* was tucked neatly away under a canopy of five-meter leaf cover. It was empty, with all its life-support systems turned off. Only residual radiation from the Bose Drive betrayed its presence.

Max Perry stood inside the abandoned ship and stared

around him with amazement. His head nearly touched the roof, and the whole living space was no more than three meters across. One step took him from the main hatch to the tiny galley; another, and he was at the control console.

He inspected the panel's simple displays, with their couple of dozen brightly colored switches and indicators, and shook his head. "This is a damned *toy*. I didn't know you could even get into the Bose Network with something this small."

"You are not supposed to." Graves had himself under firm control. He did not look quite sane, but the twitching of his fingers was less, and his bony face no longer boiled in a turmoil of emotion. "This was built as a small tourist vessel, for in-system hops. The designers didn't expect a Bose Drive to be added, and certainly no one ever thought it might be used for so many Bose Transitions. But that's Shasta for you—the children rule the planet. The Carmel twins talked their parents into it." He turned to J'merlia. "Would you kindly tell Kallik to stop that, before she does something dangerous?"

The little Hymenopt was over by the ship's drive. She had removed the cover and was peering inside. She turned at Graves's words.

"It is not dangerous," J'merlia interpreted, listening to the series of clicks and whistles. "With great respect, Kallik says that it is the opposite of dangerous. She is aware that someone as ignorant as she can know little about anything so difficult as the Bose Drive, but she is quite sure that this one's power unit is exhausted. It cannot be used again. It is debatable that this ship could even make it from here to low orbit. She already suspected this, from the weak signal that her master's ship received in its survey of the surface."

"Which explains why the twins never left Quake." Perry had turned on the display and was examining the computer log. "It makes sense of their peculiar itinerary, too. This shows a continued Bose Network sequence that brings them to Dobelle and then takes them right into Zardalu territory in two more transitions; but they couldn't do that without a new Bose power source. They could have picked one up at Midway Station, but naturally they didn't know it. So the only other place they could have gone in this system would have been Opal, and we'd have tracked their arrival there at once."

"Which is unfortunately not the case *here*. So how will we find them?" Graves walked across to the door and peered out, snapping his finger joints. "I deserve censure, you know. I assumed that once we found the ship they came in, the hard task was over. It never occurred to me that they might be foolhardy enough to *leave* the ship and roam the planet's surface."

"I can help with that. But even if you find them, how will you handle the twins themselves?"

"Leave that to me. It is the area of my experience. We are creatures of conditioning, Commander. We assume that what we know is easy, and we find mysterious whatever we do not." Graves waved a skinny, black-clad arm out toward the Pentacline. "All that to me is mysterious. They are hidden somewhere out there. But why would they leave this ship, and relative safety, to go to *that*?"

What could be seen from the ship was a green mass of vines, lush and intertwined. They trembled continuously to ground tremors, giving an illusion of self-awareness and nervous movement.

"They went there because they thought it was safe, and so they wouldn't be found. But I can find them." Perry glanced at his watch. "We have to be quick. It's already hours since we left the beacon. J'merlia." He turned to the apprehensive Lo'tfian. "We promised we'd have you back where we came from in four hours. And we will. Come on, Councilor. I know where they'll be—alive or dead."

Outside the ship the atmosphere of the depression felt thicker and more oppressive, ten degrees hotter than the plain. Black basalt quivered underfoot, hot and pulsing like the scaly hide of a vast beast. Perry walked along the edge of the rock, carefully examining it.

Graves followed, mopping at his perspiring brow. "If

you are hoping to see footprints I hate to be discouraging, but—"

"No. *Water* prints." Perry knelt down. "Runoff patterns. Quake has a lot of small lakes and ponds. The native animals manage fine, but they make do with water that you or I couldn't drink. And once the Carmel twins left their ship, they'd need a supply of fresh water."

"They might have had a purifier."

"They would have, and they'd need it—fresh water on Quake is a relative term. You and I couldn't drink it, nor could Geni and Elena Carmel." Perry ran his hand over a smooth indented wedge in the rock. "If they're alive, they'll be within reach of water. And it doesn't matter where they headed first, if they started out from this rock—and they must have, because the *Summer Dreamboat* is here—they'll finish up along one of the runoff lines. Here's one of them, a good strong one. There's another over there, just about as well defined. But this rock slab is tilted and we're on the lower side. We'll try this one first."

He lowered himself carefully over the edge. Graves followed, wincing as his hand met the basalt. The bare rock was beyond blood heat, almost hot enough to blister. Perry was moving away fast, scrambling along on his backside down a thirty-degree slope that plunged through a trailing curtain of purple-veined creepers.

"Wait for me!" Graves raised one arm to protect his eyes. Saw-edged leaves cut into the back of his hand and left their scratch marks along the top of his unprotected skull. Then he was through, under the tree-floor of vegetation that marked the first level of the Pentacline.

The light of Mandel and Amaranth was muted here to a blue-green shadow. Small creatures flew at them. Julius Graves thought at first that they were insects or birds, but a query to Steven brought the information that they were pseudocoelenterates, more like flying jellyfish than any other Earth or Miranda form. The creatures chittered in panic and flew away from Graves into the gloom. He hurried on after Max Perry. Within a few meters the air temperature beneath the canopy had jumped another few degrees.

Perry was following the rocky watercourse, squeezing his way past sticky yellow trunks and upthrusting mushroom structures two meters high. Clouds of minute winged creatures burst from the overhead leaves and flew for his unprotected face and hands.

"They don't bite," Perry said over his shoulder. "Just keep going."

Graves swatted at them anyway, trying to keep them out of his eyes. He wondered why Perry had not brought masks and respirators with them. In his concentration he was not looking where he was going, and he walked into the other man's back.

"Found something?"

Perry shook his head and pointed down. Two steps ahead the streambed dropped into a vertical hole. Graves leaned recklessly forward and could see no sign of the bottom.

"Let's hope they're not down there." Perry was already turning back. "Come on."

"What if the other one dead-ends, too?" Graves was snapping his finger joints again.

"Bad news. We'll need a new idea, but we won't have time for one even if we think of it. We'll have to worry about ourselves."

Rather than climbing back up the rock face, he led the way to one side, working his way slowly around the foot of the outcropping to where a second runoff flowed. Away from the watercourse the lower-level vegetation grew more strongly. Tough bamboo spears jutted up to knee level, scoring their boots and cutting through the cloth of their trousers. Irritant sap from broken leaves created lines of stinging cuts along their calves. Perry swore, but did not lessen his pace.

In another twenty meters he stopped and pointed. "There's the other runoff. And something has been this way quite a few times." The gray-green sedges at the side of the streambed had been flattened and broken. Their crushed stems were coated with a brown layer of dried sap.

"Animals?" Graves leaned down to rub at his scraped shins and calves, which had begun to itch maddeningly.

"Maybe." Perry lifted his foot and pressed down on an unbroken stem, gauging its strength. "But I doubt it. Whatever flattened these wasn't far from human body weight. I've never heard of anything in the Pentacline that massed more than a quarter as much. At least this makes it easy to track."

He began to walk down the stream side, following the line of broken vegetation. The verdurous gloom had deepened, but the path was easy to follow. It ran parallel to the dry watercourse and then inched over into it. Thirty meters farther on, the bottom of the path became veiled by a thicket of tough ferns.

Graves put his hand on Perry's shoulder and moved on past him.

"If you're right," he said quietly, "then from this point on it's my show. Let me go in front, and alone. I'll call you when I want you."

Perry stared for a moment, then allowed Graves to step ahead of him. In the past five minutes the other had changed. Every sign of instability had vanished from his face, leaving in its place strength, warmth, and compassion. It was the countenance of a different man—of a councilor.

Graves stepped cautiously along the streambed until he was no more than a couple of paces from the veil of ferns. He paused, listening, then after a few seconds nodded and turned to Perry. He winked grotesquely, parted the ferns, and stepped through into the dark interior of the thicket.

It was the Carmel twins, it had to be; they had been located, although Perry would have given high odds against it when he, Graves, and Rebka had left Opal. But what was Graves saying to them, hidden away in the darkness?

A few minutes in the Pentacline so close to Summertide felt like hours. The heat and humidity was horrible. Perry looked again and again at his watch, hardly able to believe that time was passing so slowly. Though it was full day, and Mandel must still be rising, his surroundings grew less and less visible. Was there a dust storm brewing far overhead in the atmosphere? Perry stared straight up, but he could see nothing through the thick multiple layers of vegetation. Underfoot, however, there was plenty of evidence of Quake's activity. The root-tangled forest floor was in continuous, steady vibration.

Thirty-five hours to Summertide Maximum.

The clock kept running in Perry's head, along with a question. They had promised to return J'merlia and Kallik to where they had found them. That promise had been made in good faith and without reservations. But could they allow such a thing to be done, knowing that Quake would soon be a death trap to everything except its own uniquely selected organisms?

Perry was startled by a sudden bright light in front of him. The curtain of ferns had been pulled aside, and Graves stood behind it gesturing him forward.

"Come on in. I want you to hear this and serve as an additional witness."

Max Perry eased his way in through the bristly fronds of the ferns. Lit from the interior, the dark thicket was revealed to be less than it seemed. The ferns formed only an outer framing web, a convenient natural fence within which stood a flexible tent supported by pneumatic ribbing. Graves was holding a door panel open, and when Perry stepped through he was astonished by the size of the interior. The floor area was at least ten meters square. Even with the inward-sloping walls the living area was substantial. And the furnishings were amazingly complete, everything that was needed for normal pleasant living. Some form of cooling and humidity-control unit was operating, to hold the internal conditions at a comfortable level. And it was well hidden from any normal searcher. No wonder the twins preferred to stay here, rather than in the cramped quarters of the *Summer Dreamboat*.

The tent must also have been totally lightproof, or else

the lights had only just been turned on. But Perry had time for only one look at the line of glowing cylinders around the walls, before his attention was drawn to the tent's occupants.

Elena and Geni Carmel were sitting over by the far wall, side by side, their hands on their knees. They were dressed in russet jumpsuits and wore their auburn hair hanging low over their foreheads. Perry's first impression—an overwhelming one—was of two identical people, with the same resemblance to Amy that had left him unable to breathe when he had first seen their pictures back on Opal.

But in the flesh, under the bright lights of the tent, reason quickly asserted itself. If the twins looked like Amy, it was through their dress and hairstyle. Elena and Geni Carmel seemed weary and crushed, as far as one could be from Amy's perky and invincible self-confidence. The tan that he had seen in the image cubes was long gone, replaced by a tired pallor.

And the twins were *different*, one from the other. Although their features might be structurally identical, their expressions were not. One was clearly the dominant twin—born a few minutes earlier, maybe, or a fraction bigger and heavier?

She was the one meeting Max Perry's eyes. The other kept her gaze downcast, shooting only one shy and lightning glance at the new arrival from large, heavy-lidded eyes. Yet she seemed at ease with Graves, turning her face to him as he closed the tent's panel and moved to sit opposite them.

He waved Perry to a seat by his side. "Elena"—he indicated the more self-confident twin—"and Geni have been through a very difficult time." His voice was gentle, almost subdued. "My dears, I know it is a painful memory, but I want you to repeat to the commander what you just told me . . . and this time we will make a recording of it."

Geni Carmel gave Perry another hooded glance and looked to her sister for direction.

Elena gripped her knees more tightly with her hands. "From the beginning?" Her voice was deep for her slender frame.

"Not from the beginning. You don't need to tell how you won the trip on Shasta—we have all that on record. I'd like you to begin with your arrival on Pavonis Four." Graves held forward a small recording unit. "Whenever you are ready, we can begin."

Elena Carmel nodded uncertainly and cleared her throat several times. "It was going to be the last planet," she began at last. "The last one that we visited before we went back to Shasta. Before we went home." Her voice cracked on the final word. "So we decided we would like to stay out on the surface, away from people. We bought special equipment"—she gestured around her—"this equipment, so we could live comfortably away from everything. And we took the *Summer Dreamboat* out to one of the dryland turf hummocks in the middle of the marshes—Pavonis Four is mostly marshes. We wanted to get right away from civilization, and we wanted to camp away from the ship."

She paused.

"That was my fault," Geni Carmel said, in a beaten voice a tone higher than her sister's. "We'd seen so many people, on so many worlds, and the ship was smaller than we realized before we started. I was tired of living cramped up in it."

"We were both tired." Elena was defending her little sister. "We camped maybe thirty meters from the ship, close to the edge of the hummock. When twilight came we thought it would be a great idea to go really primitive, just as if we were back on Earth ten thousand years ago, and light a fire. We did that, and it was nice and warm, with no threat of rain. So we decided that we would even sleep outside. When it was completely dark, we put out sleeping bags next to each other, and lay looking up at the stars." She frowned. "I don't know what we talked about."

"I do," Geni said. "We talked about that being our last stop, and how dull it would be to go back to school on Shasta. We tried to see our own sun, but the constellations looked too different, and we weren't sure where home was . . ." Her voice trailed off, and she glanced again at her sister.

"So we fell asleep." Elena was speaking less easily. "And while we were asleep, they came. They—the—"

"The Bercia?" Julius Graves prompted. Both twins nodded.

"Wait a moment, Elena," he went on. "I want to note for the record here a number of facts about the Bercia. These facts are well established and easily verified. The Bercia were large, slow vertebrates. As nocturnal amphibians, native to and unique to Pavonis Four, they were highly photophobic. In life-style they resembled Earth's extinct beavers. Like beavers, they were communal and largely aquatic, and they built lodges. The main reason they were credited with possible intelligence is because of the complex structure of those lodges. And to make them, they employed mud and the trunks of the only treelike structures of Pavonis Four. Those grow only close to the dryland turf hummocks. It was therefore almost inevitable that the Bercia would appear at night by the hummock where the Carmel camp stood."

He turned to Elena. "Did anyone ever tell you about the Bercia before you set out to camp? Who they were, what they looked like?"

"No."

"Or you?" he asked, switching his attention to Geni Carmel.

She shook her head, then added, "No," in an almost inaudible voice.

"So I would like to add the physical description of the Bercia to this record. All human experience with these beings suggests that they were gentle and totally herbivorous. However, to chew through the xylem of the tree trunks, the Bercia were equipped with heavy jaws and big, strong teeth." He nodded to Elena Carmel. "Please continue. Describe the rest of your night on Pavonis Four."

"I'm not sure when we went to sleep, or how long we slept." Elena Carmel glanced at her sister. "I only woke up when I heard Geni cry out. She told me—"

"I want to hear it directly from Geni." Graves pointed his finger at the other sister. "I know this is painful, but tell us what you saw."

Geni Carmel looked terrified. Graves leaned forward and took her hands in his. He waited.

"Pavonis Four has one big moon," Geni said at last. "I don't sleep as soundly as Elena, and the full moonlight woke me up. At first I didn't look around me—I just lay in my sleeping bag and stared up at the moon. I remember that it had a dark pattern on it, like a curved cross on top of a pyramid. Then something big moved in front of the moon. I thought it must be a cloud or something, and I didn't realize how close it was until I heard it breathing. It leaning over me. I saw a flat, dark head, and a mouth full of pointed teeth. And I screamed for Elena."

"Before we continue," Graves said, "I would like to make another easily verified addition to this record. The planet Shasta, homeworld of Elena and Geni Carmel, has no dangerous carnivores. But at one time it did. The largest and most dangerous of those animals was a four-legged invertebrate known as a Skrayal. Although anatomically it in no way resembles a Bercia, it possessed the same superficial appearance and was roughly the same size and weight. Elena Carmel, what did you think when you realized that a Bercia was leaning over your sister, with a ring of them surrounding both your beds?"

"I thought—I thought that they were Skrayal. Just at first." She hesitated, then words came in a rush. "Of course, when I got a good look at them and thought about it, I knew they couldn't be, and anyway we had never seen Skrayal—they were gone before we were born. But all our stories and pictures were filled with them, and when I first woke up I didn't even know where I was—all I saw were big animals, and the teeth of the one next to Geni."

"What did you do?"

"I screamed, and picked up the light, and turned it on all the way."

"Did you know that the Bercia were strongly

photophobic and would go into terminal shock at high illumination levels?"

"I had no idea."

"Did you know that the Bercia were possibly intelligent?"

"I told you, we'd never even heard of the Bercia. We found all that out later, after we checked the planetary data base on the *Summer Dreamboat*."

"And so you had no way of knowing that those Bercia were the *only* surviving mature members of the species? And that the infant forms could not survive without adult care?"

"We didn't know any of that. We learned it after we returned to Capra City and heard that we were being looked for so we could be arrested."

"Councilor," Perry interrupted. He was looking again at his watch. "We've been gone three hours. We have to get back."

"Very well. We can pause here." Graves picked up the recording instrument and turned to Elena and Geni Carmel. "There will have to be an inquiry and trial back on Shasta, in controlled conditions, and also a hearing on Miranda. But I can assure you, what you have told me is already enough to establish innocence of intent. You killed by accident, not knowing that you were killing, when you were terrified and half-asleep. There is still one mystery to me—*why* you fled. But that can wait for explanation." He stood up. "Now I must take you both into my custody. From this moment, you are under arrest. And we must leave this place."

The twins flashed split-second glances at each other. "We won't go," they said in breathless unison.

"You must. You are in danger. We are all in danger."

"We'll stay here and take our chances," Elena said.

Graves frowned at them. "You don't understand. Commander Perry can give you details, but I'll put it simply: you may feel safe enough just now, but there is no way you can survive Summertide if you stay here on Quake."

"Leave us, then." Elena Carmel was close to tears. "We'll stay. If we die, that ought to be enough punishment to satisfy everybody."

Graves sighed and sat down again. "Commander Perry, you must go. Get back to the others and take off. I cannot leave."

Perry remained standing, but he took a sidearm from his belt and pointed it at the twins. "This can kill, but it can also be used at stunner setting. If the councilor chooses, we can take you to the aircar unconscious."

The young women stared apprehensively at the weapon, but Graves was shaking his head. "No, Commander," he said wearily. "That is no solution. We'd never drag the pair of them up that slope, and you know it. I will stay. You must leave, and tell J'merlia and Kallik what has happened." He leaned back and closed his eyes. "And go quickly, before it's too late."

A rumble of thunder, far overhead, added weight to his words. Perry looked up, but did not leave.

"Tell me *why*." Graves went on. He opened his eyes, stood up slowly, and began to pace the length of the tent. "Tell me why you won't come back with me. Do you think that I'm your enemy—or that the governors of the Alliance are all cruel monsters? Do you believe that the whole system of justice is set up to torment and torture young women? That the Council would condone any mistreatment of you? If it would help, I can give you my personal promise that you will not be harmed if you go with me. But please, tell me what you are so afraid of."

Elena Carmel looked questioningly at her sister. "Can we?" And then, at Geni's nod, she spoke. "There would be treatment for us. *Rehabilitation.* Wouldn't there?"

"Well, yes." Graves paused in his pacing. "But only to help you. It would take away the pain of the memory—you don't want to go through the rest of your life reliving that night on Pavonis Four. Rehab isn't punishment. It's *therapy*. It wouldn't hurt you."

"You can't guarantee that," Elena said. "Isn't rehab supposed to help with mental problems—any mental problems?"

"Well, it's always focused on some particular incident or difficulty. But it helps in all areas."

"Even with a problem that we might not *think* is a problem." Geni Carmel took the lead for the first time. "Rehab would make us 'saner.' But we're *not* sane, not by the definition you and the Council will use."

"Geni Carmel, I have no idea what you are talking about, but no one is totally sane." Graves sighed and rubbed the top of his bald head. "Least of all me. But I would undergo rehab willingly, if it were judged necessary."

"But suppose you had a problem you didn't *want* cured?" Elena asked. "Something that was more important to you than anything in the world."

"I'm not sure I can imagine such a thing."

"You see. And you represent Council thinking," Geni said. "*Human species* thinking."

"You are human, too."

"But we're *different*," Elena said. "Did you ever hear of Mina and Daphne Dergori, from our world of Shasta?"

There was a puzzled pause. "I did not," Graves replied. "Should I have?"

"They are sisters," Elena said. "Twin sisters. We knew them since we were little children. They are our age, and we have lots in common. But they and their whole family were involved in a spaceship accident. Almost everyone was killed. Mina and Daphne and three other children were thrown into the pinnace at the last moment by a crew member, and they survived. When they got back home they were given rehab. To help them forget."

"I'm sure they were." Graves glanced at Perry, who was gesturing again at his watch. "And I'm sure it worked. Didn't it?"

"It helped them forget the accident." Geni was pale, and her hands were shaking. "But don't you see? *They lost each other.*"

"We knew them well," Elena said. "We understood them. They were just like us; they had the same *closeness* to each other. But after rehab, when we saw them again . . . it was gone. Gone completely. They were no more to each other than other people."

"And you would do it to us," Geni added. "Can't you understand that's *worse* than killing us?"

Graves stood motionless for a few moments, then flopped loose-limbed into a chair. "And *that's* why you ran away from Pavonis Four? Because you thought we would take you away from each other?"

"Wouldn't you?" Elena said. "Wouldn't you have wanted to give us 'normal' and 'independent' lives, so we could live apart? Isn't that included in rehab?"

"Lord of Lords." Graves's face was back to its spastic twitching. He covered it with his hands. "*Would* we have done that? Would we? We would, we would."

"Because closeness and dependence on each other is 'unnatural,'" Elena said bitterly. "You would have tried to *cure* us. We can't stand that idea. That's why you'll have to kill us before we will go with you. So go now, and leave us with each other. We don't want your cure. If we die, at least we die together."

Graves did not seem to be listening. "Blind," he muttered. "Blind for years, filled with my own hubris. Convinced that I had a gift, so sure that I could understand any human. But can an individual relate fully to a compound being? Is there that much empathy? I doubt it."

He straightened up, walked across to the two women, and put his open hands together in a gesture of prayer. "Elena and Geni Carmel, listen to me. If you will come with me now and agree to rehabilitation for what happened on Pavonis Four, you will not be separated. Never. There will never be an attempt to 'treat' your need to be together, or to break your closeness. You will continue to share your lives. I swear this to you, with every atom of my body, with my full authority as a member of the Alliance Council."

He dropped his hands to his sides and turned away. "I know I am asking you to trust me more than is reasonable. But please do it. Discuss this with each other. Commander Perry and I will wait outside. Please talk . . . and tell me that you will come."

The Carmel twins smiled for the first time since Perry had entered the tent.

"Councilor," Elena said quietly, "you are right when you say that you do not understand twins. Don't you understand that you do not need to leave, and we do not need to talk to each other? We both *know* what the other feels and thinks."

The two women stood up in unison and spoke together. "We will come with you. When must we leave?"

"Now." Perry had been a silent bystander, glancing from the three people before him to his watch and back. For the first time, he accepted the idea that Julius Graves had a gift for dealing with people that Perry himself would never have. "We all have to leave this minute. Grab what you absolutely need, but nothing else. We've been down here longer than we expected. Summertide is less than thirty-three hours away."

The aircar rose from the black basalt surface.

Too slow, Max Perry said to himself. Too slow and sluggish. What's this car's load limit? I bet we're close to it.

He said nothing to the others, but his internal tension willed them upward, until they were cruising at a safe height back the way they had come.

Apparently the others did not share his worries. Elena and Geni Carmel appeared exhausted, lying back in their seats at the rear of the car and staring wearily out at the glowing sky. Graves was back to his old manic cheerfulness, querying J'merlia, and through him Kallik, about the Zardalu clade and Kallik's own homeworld. Perry decided that it was probably Steven again, busy in simple information gathering.

Perry had little time himself for watching the others, or for conversation. He was tired, too—it was more than twenty-four hours since he had slept—but nervous energy kept him wide awake. In the past few hours Quake's atmosphere had passed through a transition. Instead of flying under a dusty but sunlit sky, the aircar sped beneath continuous layers of roiling cloud, black and rusty-red. They needed to be safely above those clouds, but Perry dared not risk the force of unknown wind shears. Even at the car's present height, well below the clouds, violent patches of turbulence came and went unpredictably. It was not safe to fly the car at more than half its full speed. Jagged bolts of lightning, showing as dusky red through windblown dust, ran between sky and surface. Every minute the lower edge of the cloud layer crept closer toward the ground.

Perry looked down. He could see a dozen scattered lakes and ponds, steaming and shrinking, giving up their stored moisture to the atmosphere. Quake needed the protection of that layer of water vapor to shield it from the direct rays of Mandel and Amaranth.

What could not be shielded were the growing tidal forces. The ground around the shrinking lakes was beginning to fracture and heave. Conditions were steadily worsening as the car flew closer to the place where J'merlia and Kallik had been found.

Perry wrestled the car's controls and wondered. A landing in these conditions would be difficult. How long would it take to drop J'merlia and Kallik at their car and move back to the relative safety of the air? And if there was no sign of Atvar H'sial and Louis Nenda, could they leave the two slaves alone on the surface?

They had not much farther to go. In ten more minutes he would have to make the decision.

And in thirty hours, Summertide would be here. He risked a slight increase in airspeed.

A glow of ruddy light began to appear in the sky ahead. Perry peered at it with tired eyes.

Was it Amaranth, seen through a break in the clouds? Except that no cloud break was visible. And the bright area was too low in the sky.

He stared again, reducing speed to a crawl until he was sure. When he was finally certain, he turned in his seat.

"Councilor Graves, and J'merlia. Would you come forward, please, and give me your opinion on this?"

It was a formality. Perry did not need another opinion. In the past few hours there had been intense vulcanism in the area ahead. Right where J'merlia and Kallik had been picked up, the surface glowed orange-red from horizon to horizon. Smoking rivers of lava were creeping through a blackened and lifeless terrain, and nowhere, from horizon to horizon, was there a place for an aircar to land.

Perry felt a shiver of primitive awe at the sight—and a great sense of relief.

He did not have to make a decision after all. Quake had made it for him. They could head at once for the safety of the Umbilical.

The arithmetic was already running in his head. Seven hours' flight time from their current location. Add in a margin for error, in case they had to fly around bad storms or reduce airspeed, and say it might take as much as ten. And it would be eighteen hours before the Umbilical withdrew from the surface of Quake.

That was an eight-hour cushion. They would make it with time to spare.

CHAPTER 19

Summertide
minus two

Noise meant inefficiency. So did mechanical vibration. The motors of an aircar in good shape were almost silent, and its ride was silky smooth.

Darya Lang listened to the wheezing death rattle behind her and felt the floor tremble beneath her feet. There was no doubt about it, the shaking was getting worse. Getting worse *fast*, noticed easily above the buffeting of the wind.

"How much farther?" She had to shout the question.

Hans Rebka did not look up from the controls, but he shook his head. "Fourteen kilometers. May be too far. Touch and go."

They were churning along no more than a thousand meters above the surface, just high enough to escape added dust in the intake vents. The ground below was barely visible, ghostly and indistinct beneath a fine haze of swirling powder.

Lang looked higher. There was a thin vertical strand far off in front of them. She cried out, "I can see it, Hans! There's the foot of the Stalk!" At the same moment Rebka was shouting, "No good. We're losing lift."

The aircar engine began to sputter and gasp. Spells

213

of smooth flight at close to full power were followed by grinding vibration and seconds of sickening descent. They dropped into the dust layer. The silver thread of the Umbilical vanished from Darya's view.

"Six kilometers. Four hundred meters." Rebka had taken a last sighting before they entered the storm and was flying on instruments. "I can't see to pick the landing site. Check your harness and make sure your mask and respirator are tight. We may be heading for a rough one."

The aircars were sturdy craft. They had been designed to fly in extreme conditions; but one thing they could not guarantee was a soft landing with an engine worn to scrap by corundum dust. The final gasp of power came when the instruments showed an altitude of twenty meters. Rebka changed flap setting to avoid a stall and brought them in at twice the usual landing speed. At the last moment he shouted to Darya to hold tight. They smacked down hard, bounced clear over a rock outcrop big enough to remove the car's belly, and slithered to a stop.

"That's it!" Rebka had hit the release for his own harness and was reaching over to help Darya while they were still moving. He took a last look at the microwave sensor and turned to give her a grin of triumph. "Come on, I've got the bearing. The foot of the Umbilical's less than half a kilometer ahead."

Ground conditions were much better than Darya had expected. Visibility was admittedly down to a few tens of meters, and wind sounds were punctuated by the boom of distant explosions. But the ground was calm, flat, and navigable, except where a row of house-sized boulders jutted up like broken teeth. She followed Rebka between two of them, thinking how lucky they were that the engine had failed when it did, and not a few seconds later. They would have flown on and smashed straight into those rocks.

She was still not convinced that Quake was as dangerous as Perry claimed, and she had a lingering desire to stay and explore. But having flown so far to reach the Umbilical, it made sense to use it. She peered ahead. Surely they had walked at least half a kilometer.

Not looking where she was going, she slipped on a thick layer of powder, slick and treacherous as oil. Rebka in front of her fell down in a cloud of dust, rolled over, and staggered to his feet. Instead of shuffling onward he halted and pointed straight up.

They had emerged into a region shielded from the wind. Visibility had improved by a factor of ten. A circular disk, blurred in outline by high-level windblown dust, hung above them in the sky. As they watched, it lifted higher and shrank a fraction in apparent size.

His cry coincided with her understanding of what she was seeing.

"The foot of the Stalk. It's going up."

"But we got here earlier than we expected."

"I know. It shouldn't be doing that. It's rising way ahead of time!"

The Umbilical was fading as they watched, its club-shaped bottom end receding into the clouds and blown dust. Around its rising base stood the apron supporting the aircars. She knew their size and tried to judge the height. Already the lower end must have risen almost a kilometer above the surface.

She turned to Rebka. "Hans, our car! If we can get back there and take it up—"

"Won't work." He moved to put his head close to hers. "Even if we could get the car into the air, there's nowhere to land on the base of the Umbilical. I'm sorry, Darya. This mess is my fault. I brought us, and now we're stuck here. We've had it."

He was speaking louder than necessary—as if to make nonsense of his words the wind had dropped completely. The dust in the air began to thin, the surface was quiet, and Darya could see right back to their aircar. Above them the foot of the Umbilical was visible, hovering tantalizingly close.

It was the worst possible time for such a thought, but Darya decided that a little anguish in Hans Rebka's voice made him nicer than ever. Self-confidence and competence were virtues—but so was mutual dependence.

She pointed. "It's not going any higher, Hans. Who's controlling it?"

"Maybe nobody." He was no longer shouting. "The control sequences can be preset. But it could be Perry and Graves—they may have taken it up just to get clear of the surface. Maybe they're holding it there, waiting to see if we show up. But we can't reach them!"

"We'll have to try." While he was still staring at the Umbilical, Darya was already slipping and sliding across the layer of talc, heading toward the aircar. "Come on. If we can make our car hover next to the apron on the bottom of the Stalk, maybe we can jump across onto it."

She listened in amazement to her own words. Was it really Darya Lang proposing that? Back on Sentinel Gate she had avoided all heights, telling friends and family with a shiver that she was terrified by them. Apparently everything in the universe was relative. At the moment, the prospect of leaping from a moving and malfunctioning aircar to an Umbilical, a kilometer or more above the ground, did not faze her at all.

Hans Rebka was following, but only to grip her arm and swing her around. "Wait a minute, Darya. Look."

Another aircar was cruising in from the northwest, just below cloud level. It was in a descent pattern, until its pilot apparently saw the Umbilical. Then the car banked and started to ascend in a slow and labored spiral.

But the foot of the Stalk had begun to rise again, and more rapidly. The two on the ground gazed up helplessly as the Umbilical gradually vanished into the clouds, the pursuing aircar laboring upward after it. As they both disappeared it seemed that the car was losing the race.

Darya turned to Hans Rebka. "But if Graves and Perry are up there on the Stalk, who's in the aircar?"

"It must be Max Perry. I was wrong about him and Graves being on the Umbilical. The Stalk ascent is performing its automatic Summertide retraction, but it's taking place ahead of time. It has been reprogrammed." He shook his head. "But that doesn't make sense, either. Perry is the only one who knows the Umbilical control codes." He saw her stricken look. "Isn't he?"

"No." She stared away and would not look at him. "Atvar H'sial knew them. All of them. I told you, that's how we got over from Opal. This is all my fault. I should never have agreed to work with her. Now we're stuck here, and she's safe up there on the Umbilical."

Hans Rebka glared up at the overcast. "I'll bet she is. That damned Cecropian. I wondered as we were flying here if she was still on Quake. And J'merlia will be with her. So the aircar up there has to be Perry and Graves."

"Or maybe the Carmel twins."

"No. They didn't have access to an aircar. Anyway, we can stop speculating. Here it comes again."

The car was spiraling down from the clouds, searching for a good place to touch down. Darya ran toward it and waved her arms frantically. The pilot saw her and carefully banked closer. The aircar flopped to a heavy landing no more than fifty meters away, creating a minor dust storm with its jets of downward air.

The car door slid open. Hans Rebka and Darya Lang watched in astonishment as two identical and identically dressed humans climbed out, followed by a Lo'tfian and a dusty-looking Hymenopt. Last of all came Julius Graves and Max Perry.

"We thought you were dead!" "We thought *you* were on the Umbilical!" "Where did you find them?" "How did you get here?"

Perry, Rebka, Lang, and Graves were all speaking at once, standing in a tight inward-facing group by the aircar door. The two aliens and the Carmel twins stood apart, staring around them at their desolate surroundings.

"No active radio beacons—we listened all the way here," Graves went on. He stared at Darya Lang. "Do you have any idea what has happened to Atvar H'sial?"

"I'm not sure, but we think she's probably up there on the Umbilical."

"No, she isn't. No one is. We couldn't catch it, but we could tell that no capsules are in use. And it's out of aircar altitude range now. But what about you? I thought Atvar H'sial left you behind on the surface."

"She did. Hans Rebka rescued me. But Atvar H'sial must have intended to come back for me, because she gave me supplies and a signal beacon."

"No, she didn't. That was J'merlia's doing." Graves gestured at the Lo'tfian. "He says that Atvar H'sial did not forbid him to help you, and so he did. He was very worried about your safety when they left you behind. He said that you seemed poorly equipped for survival on Quake. But then he thought you must be dead, anyway, because when we listened there was no sign of your beacon. I feel sure that Atvar H'sial didn't intend to go back for you. You were supposed to die on Quake."

"But where is Atvar H'sial now?" Rebka asked.

"We just asked *you* that question," Perry said. "She must be with Louis Nenda."

"Nenda!"

"He came here on his own ship," Graves said. "And did you know he can talk to a Cecropian directly? Kallik told J'merlia that Nenda had a Zardalu augment that lets him use pheromonal communication. He and Atvar H'sial left J'merlia and Kallik behind, and went off somewhere by themselves."

"We think they came here. Atvar H'sial had help. Somehow she obtained the control sequences, and she must have set the Umbilical for earlier retraction from the surface." Hans Rebka gave Darya Lang a "say-no-more" look and went on. "She wants us all dead, stranded on Quake at Summertide. That's why she left J'merlia and Kallik behind—she didn't want witnesses."

"But we heard their distress signal and picked them up." Perry nodded to the silent aliens. "I think Nenda and H'sial may have intended to come back for them, but they would have been too late. The landing area was molten lava. We had to keep J'merlia and Kallik with us."

"But if Nenda made it back to his own ship," Graves said, "he and Atvar H'sial can still leave the planet."

"Which is more than we can do." After his earlier depression, Rebka had bounced back and was full of energy. "The Umbilical is gone, and it won't be back until after Summertide. We only have one aircar between the lot of us—ours died as we arrived here. And they can't achieve orbit anyway, so they're no answer. Commander Perry, we need a plan for survival here. We're stuck on Quake until the Umbilical returns."

"Can I say it one more time? That's *impossible*." Perry spoke softly, but his grim tone carried more weight than a bellow. "I've been trying to impress one fact on you since the day you all arrived at Dobelle: *Humans can't survive Summertide on the surface of Quake*. Not even the usual Summertide. Certainly not *this* Summertide. No matter what you think, there's no 'survival plan' that can save us if we stay on Quake. It's still pretty quiet here, and I don't know why. But it can't last much longer. Anyone on the surface of Quake at Summertide will die."

As though the planet had heard him, a distant roar and groan of upthrust earth and grinding rocks followed his words. Moments later a series of rippling shocks blurred the air and shook the ground beneath their feet. Everyone stared around, then instinctively headed for the inside of the aircar and an illusion of safety.

Darya Lang, the last one in, surveyed the seven who had preceded her.

It was not a promising group for last-ditch survival schemes. The two Carmel sisters had the look of people already defeated and broken. They had been through too much on Quake; from this point on they would act only as they were directed. Graves and Perry were filthy and battered, clothes torn and rumpled and covered with grime and dust and sweat. They both had bloody and inflamed scratches on their calves, and Graves had another set of scabby wounds along the top of his bald head. Worse than that, he was acting much too cheerful, grinning around him as though all his own troubles were over. Maybe they were. If anyone could save them, it would be Max Perry and not Julius Graves. But after Perry's gloomy prediction, he had returned to a brooding, introverted silence, seeing something that was invisible to everyone else.

J'merlia and Kallik seemed fairly normal—but only because Darya did not know how to read in their alien bodies the signs of stress and injury. J'merlia was meticulously removing white dust from his legs, using the soft pads of his forelimbs. He seemed little worried by anything except personal hygiene. Kallik, after a quick shiver along her body that threw a generous layer of powder away from her and produced protests from the rest of the aircar's occupants, was stretching up to full height and staring bright-eyed at everything. If anyone was still optimistic, maybe it was the little Hymenopt. Unfortunately, only J'merlia could communicate with her.

Darya looked at Hans Rebka. He was obviously exhausted, but he was still their best hope. He had deep red lines on his face, scored by his mask and respirator, and there were owlish pale circles of dust around his eyes. But when he caught her look he managed a grin and a wink.

Darya squeezed in and had just enough room to slide the door closed. She had never expected to see so many beings, human or alien, in one small aircar. The official capacity was four people. The Carmel twins had managed to fit into one seat, but J'merlia was crouched on the floor where he could see or hear little, and Darya Lang and Max Perry had been left standing.

"What's the time?" Rebka asked unexpectedly. "I mean, how many hours to Summertide?"

"Fifteen." Perry's voice was expressionless.

"So what's next? We can't just sit here and wait to die. Anything's easier than that. Let's look at our options. We can't reach the Umbilical, even if it goes no higher. And there's no place on Quake that we can go to be safe. Suppose we fly as high as we can and ride it out in this car?"

Kallik gave a series of whistling snorts that sounded to Darya Lang very like derision, while Perry roused himself from his reverie and shook his head. "I went through all those ideas, long ago," he said gloomily. "We're down to an eight-hour power supply for the aircar, and that's with normal load. If we get off the ground—it's not clear that we can, with so many on board—we'll be down again before Summertide Maximum."

"Suppose we sit here and wait until four or five hours before Summertide," Rebka suggested. "And *then* take off? We'd be clear of the surface during the worst time."

"Sorry. That won't work, either." Perry glared at Kallik, who was bobbing up and down to an accompaniment of clicks and whistles. "We'd never manage to stay in the air. The volcanoes and earthquakes turn the whole atmosphere into one mass of turbulence." He turned to the Lo'tfian. "J'merlia, tell Kallik to keep quiet. It's hard enough to think without that noise."

The Hymenopt bobbed even higher and whistled, "Sh-sh-sheep."

"Kallik asks me to point out," J'merlia said, "with great respect, you are all forgetting the ship."

"Louis Nenda's ship?" Rebka asked. "The one that Kallik came in? We don't know where it is. Anyway, Nenda and Atvar H'sial will have taken it."

Kallik let loose a louder series of whistles and wriggled her body in anguish.

"No, no. Kallik says humbly, she is talking about the *Summer Dreamboat*, the ship that the Carmel twins came in to Quake. We know exactly where that is."

"But its drive is exhausted," Perry said. "Remember, Kallik looked at it when we first found it."

"One moment, please." J'merlia wriggled his way past Julius Graves and the Carmel twins, until he was crouched close to the Hymenopt. The two of them grunted and whistled at each other for half a minute. Finally J'merlia bobbed his head and straightened up.

"Kallik apologizes to everyone for her extreme stupidity, but she did not make herself sufficiently clear when she examined the ship. The power for the Bose Drive is certainly exhausted, and the ship cannot be used for star travel. But there could be just enough power for one local journey—maybe for one jump to orbit."

Rebka was maneuvering past Julius Graves to the pilot's seat before J'merlia had finished speaking. "How far to that starship, and where is it?" He was examining the car's status board.

"Seven thousand kilometers, on a great circle path to the Pentacline Depression." Perry had emerged from his gloom and was pushing past the Carmel twins to join Rebka. "But this close to Summertide we can expect a sidewind all the way, strong and getting worse. That will knock at least a thousand off our range."

"So there's no margin." Rebka was doing a quick calculation. "We have enough power for about eight thousand, but not if we try for full speed. And if we slow down, we'll be flying closer to Summertide, and conditions will be worse."

"It is our best chance." Graves spoke for the first time since entering the aircar. "But can we get off the ground with this much load? We had a hard time getting here, and that was with two people less."

"And can we stay in the air, so close to Summertide?" Perry added. "The winds will be incredible."

"And even if Kallik is right," Graves said, "and there is a little power still in the starship, can the *Summer Dreamboat* make it to orbit?"

But Rebka was already starting the engine. "It's not our best chance, Councilor," he said as the downjets blew a cloud of white dust up to cover the windows. "It's our *only* chance. What do you want, a written guarantee? Get set and hold your breath. Unless someone has a better idea in the next five seconds, I'm going to push this car to the limit. Hold tight, and let's hope the engine wants to cooperate."

CHAPTER 20
Summertide
minus one

As the aircar lurched from the ground and struggled upward, Darya Lang felt useless. She was supercargo, added load, a dumb weight unable to help the pilot or navigator in front of her. Helpless to contribute and unable to relax, she took a new look at her fellow passengers.

This was the group who would live or die together—and soon, before the rotating dumbbell of Quake and Opal had completed one more turn.

She studied them as the car droned onward. They were a depressed and depressing sight. The situation had turned back the clock, revealing them to Lang as they must have been long years earlier, before Quake entered their lives.

Elena and Geni Carmel, sitting cheek to cheek, were little girls lost. Unable to find their way out of the wood, they waited to be saved; or, far more likely, for the monster to arrive. In front of them Hans Rebka was crouched over the controls, a small, worried boy trying to play a game that was too grown-up for him. Next to him sat Max Perry, lost in some old, unhappy dream that he would share with no one.

Only Julius Graves, to Perry's right, failed to fit the pattern of backward-turning time. The councilor's face when he turned to the rear of the car had never been young. Thousands of years of misery were carved in its lines and roughened surface; human history, written dark and angry and desperate.

She stared at him in bewilderment. This was not the Council member of Alliance legend. Where was the kindness, the optimism, the crackling manic energy?

She knew the answer: snuffed out, by simple exhaustion.

For the first time, Darya realized the importance of fatigue in deciding human affairs. She had noticed her own gradual loss of interest in deciphering the riddle of Quake and the Builders, and she had attributed it to her concentration on simple survival. But now she blamed the enervating poisons of weariness and tension.

The same slow drain of energy was affecting all of them. At a time when thought and prompt action could make the difference between life and death, they were mentally and physically flat. Every one—she was surely no exception—looked like a zombie. They might rise for a few seconds to full attention and alertness, as she had at the moment of takeoff, but as soon as the panic was over they would slump back to lethargy. The faces that turned to her, even with all the white dust wiped off them, were pale and drawn.

She knew how they were feeling. Her own emotions were on ice. She could not feel terror, or love, or anger. That was the most frightening development, the new indifference to living or dying. She hardly cared what happened next. Over the past few days Quake had not struck her down with its violence, but it had drained her, bled her of all human passions.

Even the two aliens had lost their usual bounce. Kallik had produced a small computer and was busy with obscure calculations of her own. J'merlia seemed lost and bewildered without Atvar H'sial. He swiveled his head around constantly, as though seeking his lost master, and kept rubbing his hand-pads obsessively over his hard-shelled body.

Perry, Graves, and Rebka were wedged into the front

row, in a seat meant for two. The twins and J'merlia sat behind them, probably more comfortable than anyone else, while Darya Lang and Kallik had squeezed into an area at the rear designed only for baggage. It was tall enough for the Hymenopt, but Kallik had the reflex habit of shaking like a wet dog to remove residual powder from her short black fur. She had Darya sneezing and bending her head forward all the time to avoid contact with the car's curved roof.

Worst of all, those in the back could see only a sliver of sky out of the forward window. Information on progress or problems had to come from the warnings and comments of those in front.

And sometimes they arrived too late.

"Sorry," Perry called, two seconds after the car had been slewed, tilted, and dropped fifty meters by a terrific gust of wind. "That was a bad one."

Darya Lang rubbed the back of her head and agreed. She had banged it on the hard plastic ceiling of the cargo compartment. There would be a nasty bruise—if she lived so long.

She leaned forward and cradled her head on her arms. In spite of noise and danger and sickening instability of motion, her thoughts began drifting off. Her previous life as an archeo-scientist on Sentinel Gate now seemed wholly artificial. How many times, in assembling the Lang catalog of artifacts, had she placidly written of whole expeditions, "No survivors"? It was a neat and tidy phrase, one that required no explanation and called for no thought. The element that was missing was the *tragedy* of the event, and the infinite subjective time that it might have taken to happen. Those "No survivors" entries suggested a clean extinction, a group of people snuffed out as quickly and impartially as a candle flame. Far more likely were situations like the present one: slow extinction of hope as the group clutched at every chance and saw each one fade.

Darya's spirits spiraled down further. Death was rarely quick and clean and painless, unless it also came as a surprise. More often it was slow, agonizing, and degrading.

A calm voice pulled her up from tired despair.

"Get ready in the back there." Hans Rebka sounded far from doomed and defeated. "We're too low, and we're too slow. At this rate we'll run out of power and we'll run out of time. So we have to get above the clouds. Hold on tight again. We're in for a rough few minutes."

Hold on to what? But Rebka's words and his cheerful tone told her that not everyone had given up fighting.

Ashamed of herself, Darya tried to wedge more tightly into the luggage compartment as the car buffeted its way up through the uneven lower edge of the clouds. The textured glow outside was replaced by a bland, muddy light. More violent turbulence began at once, hitting from every direction and throwing the overloaded vehicle easily and randomly about the sky like a paper toy. No matter what Rebka and Perry did at the controls, the car had too much weight to maneuver well.

Darya tried to predict the motion and failed. She could not tell if they were rising, falling, or heading for a fatal downspin. Bits of the car's ceiling fixtures seemed to come at her head from every side. Just as she felt certain that the next blow would knock her unconscious, four jointed arms took her firmly around the waist. She reached out to grasp a soft, pudgy body, clinging to it desperately as the car veered and dipped and jerked through the sky.

Kallik was pushing her, forcing her toward the wall. She buried her face in velvety fur, bent her legs up to her right, and pushed back. Braced against each other and the car's walls, she and Kallik found a new stability of position. She shoved harder, wondering if the rocky ride would ever end.

"We're almost there. Shield your eyes." Rebka's voice sounded through the cabin intercom a moment before the swoops and sickening uplifts eased. As the flight became smoother, blinding light flooded into the car, replacing the diffuse red-brown glow.

Darya heard a loud, clucking set of snorts from her right. J'merlia wriggled around in his seat to face the back of the car.

"Kallik wishes to offer her humble apologies," he said, "for what she did. She assures you that she would never in normal circumstances dare to touch the person of a superior being. And she wonders now if you might kindly release her."

Darya realized that she was clinging to soft black fur and crushing the Hymenopt in a bear hug, while still pushing her toward the far wall of the car. She let go at once, feeling embarrassed. The Hymenopt was far too polite to say anything, but she must recognize blind panic when she saw it.

"Tell Kallik that it was good that she took hold of me. What she did helped a lot, and no apology is needed." And if I'm a *superior* being, Darya added silently, I'd hate to know what an inferior one feels like.

Embarrassed or not, Darya was beginning to feel a bit better. The flight was smoother, while the whistle of air past the car suggested that they were moving much faster. Even her own aches and fatigue had somehow eased.

"We've just about doubled our airspeed, and it should be smooth sailing up here." Rebka's voice over the intercom seemed to justify her changing mood.

"But we had a hard time coming through those clouds," he went on. "And Commander Perry has recalculated our rate of power use. Given the distance we have to go, we're right on the edge. We have to conserve. I'll slow down a little, and I'm going to turn off the air-conditioning system. That will make it pretty bad here up front. Be ready to rotate seats, and make sure you drink lots of liquid."

It had not occurred to Darya Lang that her limited view of the sky might be an advantage. But as the internal temperature of the car began to rise, she was glad to be sitting in the shielded rear. The people in the front had the same stifling air as she did, plus direct and intolerable sunlight.

The full effects of that did not hit her until it was time to play musical chairs and move around the car's cramped interior. The change of position was a job for contortionists. When it was completed, Darya found herself in the front seat, next to the window. For the first time since takeoff, she could see more than a tiny bit of the car's surroundings.

They were skimming along just above cloud level, riding over individual crests that caught and scattered the light like sea breakers of dazzling gold and crimson. Mandel and Amaranth were almost straight ahead, striking down at the car with a fury never felt on the cloud-protected surfaces of Opal and Quake. The two stars had grown to giant, blinding orbs in a near-black sky. Even with the car's photo-shielding at maximum, the red and yellow spears of light thrown by the stellar partners were too bright to look at.

The perspiration ran in rivulets down Darya's face and soaked her clothing. As she watched, the positions of Mandel and Amaranth changed in the sky. Everything was happening faster and faster. She sensed the rushing tempo of events as the twin suns and Dobelle hurried to their point of closest approach.

And they were not the only players.

Darya squinted off to the side. Gargantua was there, a pale shadow of Mandel and its dwarf companion. But that, too, would change. Soon Gargantua would be the largest object in Quake's sky, sweeping closer than any body in the stellar system, rivaling Mandel and Amaranth with its ripping tidal forces.

She looked out and down, wondering what was going on below those boiling cloud layers. Soon they would have to descend through them, but perhaps the hidden surface beneath was already too broken to permit a landing. Or maybe the ship they sought had already vanished, swallowed up in some massive new earth fissure.

Darya turned away from the window and closed her aching eyes. The outside brightness was just too overwhelming. She could not stand the heat and searing radiation for one moment longer.

Except that she had no choice.

She looked to her left. Kallik was next to her, crouched down low to the floor. Beyond her, in the pilot's seat, Max Perry was holding a square of opaque plastic in front of his face to give him partial shielding from the sluice of light.

"How much longer?" The question came as a feeble croak.

Darya hardly recognized her own voice. She was not sure what question she was asking. Did she mean how long until they could all change seats again? Or until they arrived at their destination? Or only until they were all dead?

It made no difference. Perry did not answer. He merely handed her a bottle of lukewarm water. She took a mouthful and made Kallik do the same. Then there was nothing to do but sit and sweat and *endure*, until the welcome distraction of changing seats.

Darya lost track of time. She knew that she was in and out of the torture seat at the front at least three times. It felt like weeks, until at last Julius Graves was shaking her and warning, "Get ready for turbulence. We're going down through the clouds."

"We're there?" she whispered. "Let's go down."

She could hardly wait. No matter what happened next, she would escape the roasting torture of the two suns. She would dream of them for the rest of her life.

"No. Not there." Graves sounded the way she felt. He was mopping perspiration from his bald head. "We're running out of power."

That grabbed her attention. "Where are we?"

But he had turned the other way. It was Elena Carmel, in the rear seat, who leaned forward and replied. "If the instruments are right, we're very close. Almost to our ship."

"*How* close?"

"Ten kilometers. Maybe even less. They say it all depends how much power is left to use in hovercraft mode."

Darya said nothing more. Ten kilometers, five kilometers, what difference did it make? She couldn't walk *one* kilometer, not to save her life.

But a surprise voice inside her awoke and said, Maybe *only* to save your life. If young, bewildered Elena Carmel can find a reserve of strength, why can't you?

Before she could argue the point with herself, they were plunging into the clouds. And within a second there was no time for the luxury of internal debate.

Hans Rebka thought he might need the dregs of aircar power later, and he was not willing to give up any merely to cushion the ride. In its rapid descent, the car was thrown around the sky like a bobbing cork in a sea storm. But it did not last long. In less than a minute they plunged through the bottom of the cloud layers.

Everyone craned forward. Whatever they found below them, they could not go back up.

Was the starship still there? Was there a solid surface around it that they could descend to? Or had they escaped Mandel and Amaranth's searing beams only to die in Quake's pools of molten lava?

Darya stared, unable to answer those questions. Thick smoke blanketed the ground below. They were supposed to be above the slopes of the Pentacline Depression, but they might have been anywhere on the whole planet.

"Well," Hans Rebka said quietly, as though talking to himself, "the good news is that we don't have to make a decision. Look at the power meter, Max. It's redlined. We're going down, whether we want to or not." He raised his voice. "Respirators on."

Then they were floating into blue-gray smoke that swirled and eddied about the car, driven by winds so powerful that Rebka's voice quickly came again. "We're making a negative ground speed. I'm going to take us down as quick as I can, before we blow back all the way to the Umbilical."

"Where's the ship?" That was Julius Graves, sitting behind Darya in the cramped luggage compartment.

"Two kilometers ahead. We can't see it, but I think it's still there. I'm picking up an anomalous radar reflection. We can't reach the outcrop where the ship was sitting, so we have to land on the valley slope. Get ready. Twenty meters altitude . . . fifteen . . . ten. Prepare for landing."

The gusting wind suddenly died. The smoke around

them thinned. Darya could see the ground off to one side of the car. It lay barren and quiet, but steam was emerging like dragon's breath from dozens of small surface vents scattered across the downward slope of the Pentacline's valley. The dense vegetation that Darya expected to see in the depression had gone. It was nothing but gray ash and occasional withered stems.

"One and a half kilometers." Rebka's voice sounded calm and far away. "Five meters on the altimeter. Power going. Looks like we'll have to take a little walk. Three meters . . . two . . . one. Come on, you beauty. Do us proud."

Summertide was just three hours away. The aircar touched down on the steaming slope of the Pentacline Depression, as gently and quietly as an alighting moth.

CHAPTER 21
Three hours to Summertide

Hans Rebka was not happy, but it would be fair to say that for the past few hours he had been content.

Since his assignment to Dobelle he had been unsure of himself and his job. He had been sent to find out what was wrong with Commander Maxwell Perry and rehabilitate the man.

On paper it sounded easy. But just what was he supposed to *do*? He was an action man, not a psychoanalyst. Nothing in his previous career had equipped him for such a vague task.

Now things were different. At the Umbilical he had been thrown in with a helpless group—all aliens, misfits, or innocents, in his mind—and given the job of taking an overloaded, underpowered aircar halfway around Quake and a toy starship up into space, before the planet killed the lot of them.

It might be an impossible task, but at least it was a well-defined one. The rules for performance were no problem. He had learned them long ago on Teufel: you succeed, or you die trying. Until you succeed, you never relax. Until you die, you never give up.

He was tired—they were all tired—but what Darya Lang had seen as new energy was the satisfying release of a whole bundle of pent-up frustrations. It had carried him so far, and it would carry him through Summertide.

As soon as the aircar touched down, Rebka urged everyone onto the surface. It made no difference how dangerous it might be outside, the car was useless to take them any farther.

He pointed along the blistered downslope of the valley. "That's where we have to go. The direction of the starship." Then he shouted above rumbling thunder to Max Perry, who was staring vacantly about him. "Commander, our group was here a few days ago. Does it look familiar?"

Perry was shaking his head. "When we were here this area was vegetated. But there's the basalt outcrop." He pointed to a dark jutting mass of rock, forty meters high, its upper part obscured by gray smoke. "We have to get over there and climb on top of it. That's where the ship should be."

Rebka nodded. "Any nasty surprises in store for us?" Perry, whatever his faults, was still the expert on conditions on Quake.

"Can't say yet. Quake is full of them." Perry stooped to set the palm of his hand on the rocky floor. "Pretty hot, but we can walk on it. If we're lucky, the brush fires will have burned off the plants around the bottom of the outcrop and we'll have easier going than last time. Things look all different with the vegetation gone. And it's hotter— a lot hotter."

"So let's go." Rebka gestured them forward. The thunder was growing, and their surroundings were too loud for long conversations. "You and Graves lead. Then you two." He pointed to the twins. "I'll tag along last, after the others."

He urged them on without inviting discussion. The aircar trip had been an exhausting trial by fire for everyone, but Rebka knew better than to ask if they could scramble their way over a kilometer or two of difficult terrain. He would learn what they could not do when they collapsed.

The surface had been at rest when they landed, but as Perry and Graves started forward a new spasm of seismic energy passed through the area. The ground ahead broke into longitudinal folds, rippling down the side of the valley.

"Keep going," Rebka shouted above the grind and boom of breaking rock. "We can't afford to stand and wait."

Perry had halted and put his hand on Graves's arm to stop him. He turned to shake his head at Rebka. "Can't go yet. Earthquake confluence. Watch."

Ground waves of different wavelength and amplitude were converging fifty paces ahead of the party. Where they met, spumes of rock and earth jetted into the dusty air. A gaping trench of unknown depth appeared, then contracted and filled a few seconds later to vanish completely. Perry watched until he was sure that the main earth movements were over, then started forward.

Rebka felt relief. Whatever Perry's problems, the man had not lost his survival instinct. If he could hold on to that for another kilometer, his main job would be done.

They scrambled on. The ground shivered beneath their feet. Hot breaths rose from a hundred fissures in the fractured rock, and the sky above became one rolling tableau of fine ash and bright lightning. Thunder from sky and earth movement snarled and roared around them. A warm, sulfur-charged rain started to fall, steaming where it touched the tide-torn hot ground.

Rebka eyed the rest of the group speculatively from his vantage point at the rear. The Carmel twins were walking side by side, just behind Graves and Perry. After them came Darya Lang, between the two aliens and with one hand on J'merlia's sloping thorax. Everyone was doing well. Graves, Geni Carmel, and Darya Lang were limping, and everyone was weaving with fatigue—but that was a detail.

So they needed rest. He smiled grimly to himself. Well, one way or another they would find it, in the next few hours.

The big problem was the increasing temperature. Another ten degrees, and he knew they would have to slow down or keel over with simple heat prostration. The rain showers, which should have helped, were becoming hot enough to scald exposed skin. And as the party moved lower into the Pentacline Depression, further heat increase seemed inevitable.

But they had to keep descending. If they slowed or went back up, for rest or for shelter, the forces of Sumemrtide would destroy them.

He urged them on, peering ahead as he did so to study the approach to the basalt outcrop. With no more than a few hundred meters to go, the path looked pretty easy. In another hundred paces the jumble of rocks and broken surface that were making walking so difficult would smooth out, providing a brown plain more level than anything that Rebka had seen in the Pentacline. It looked like a dried-out lake bed, the relic of a long, thin water body that had boiled dry in the past few days. They could move across it easily and fast. Beyond the narrow plain, the ground rose with an easy slope to the base of the rocky uplift on whose top they should find the ship.

The two leaders had advanced to within twenty paces of the plain. The hulking, flat-topped rock seemed close enough to touch when Max Perry paused uncertainly. While Rebka looked on and cursed, Perry leaned on a large, jagged boulder and stared thoughtfully at the way ahead.

"Get a move on, man."

Perry shook his head, lifted his arm to halt the others, and crouched low to examine the ground. At the same moment, Elena Carmel cried out and pointed to the top of the rock outcrop.

The sky had turned black, but near-continuous lightning gave more than enough light to see by. Rebka could detect nothing where Perry had been staring, except a slight shimmer of heat haze and a loss of focus in the lake bed ahead. But beyond that blurred area, following Elena Carmel's pointing finger to the top of the rock where the dust clouds rolled, Rebka saw something quite unmistakable: the outline of a small starship. It sat safely back from the rock edge, and it seemed undamaged. The line of ascent was an easy one. In five minutes or less they should be up there.

Elena Carmel had turned and was shouting to her sister, inaudible above the thunder. Rebka could read her lips. "The *Summer Dreamboat*," she was shouting. Her face was triumphant as she went running forward, past Graves and Perry.

She was already onto the dried-mud plain and heading toward the bottom of the outcrop when Perry looked up and saw her.

He froze for a second, then uttered a high-pitched howl of warning that carried even above the thunder.

Elena turned at the sound. As she did so the crust of baked clay, less than a centimeter thick, fractured beneath her weight. Spurts of steam blew pitch-black, steaming slime into the air around her body. She cried out and raised her arms, trying to hold her balance. Under the brittle surface, the bubbling ooze offered no more resistance than hot syrup. Before anyone could move, Elena was waist-deep. She screamed in agony as boiling mud closed around her legs and hips.

"Lean forward!" Perry threw himself flat to spread his weight and started to wriggle forward onto the fragile surface.

But Elena Carmel was in too much pain to take any notice of his cry. He was too slow, and she was sinking too fast. He was still three paces away when the bubbling mud reached her neck. She gave a final and terrible scream.

Perry threw himself across the breaking crust to grab at her hair and one outstretched arm. He could reach her, but he could not support her.

She sank deeper. Far gone in burn-shock, she made no sound as the searing mud bubbled into her mouth, nose, and eyes. A moment later she was gone. The liquid surface swirled into a small whirlpool, then in less than a second became smooth again.

Perry wriggled forward again and plunged his arms to the elbows in boiling blackness. He roared in agony, groped, and found nothing.

The others in the party had stood rigid. Suddenly Geni Carmel gave a dreadful scream and began to run forward.

Julius Graves dived after her, tackling and holding her at the very edge of the boiling quicksand.

"No, Geni. No! You can't help, she's gone." He had her around the waist, trying to pull her toward safety. She resisted with desperate strength. It was all he could do to hold her until Rebka and Darya Lang ran forward to grab her arms.

Geni was still trying to drag herself toward the place where Elena had vanished. She pulled them to the edge of the safe area of rock. As she turned she swiveled Darya with her, forcing the other woman out onto the cracked crust. Darya's left foot broke through and plunged in above the ankle. She screamed and sagged toward Rebka in a near-faint. He had to leave Geni to Graves while he pulled Darya clear.

Geni tried one more time to move to the open area of mud. The surface where Elena had been sucked under spouted and bubbled like escaping breath. But Perry, his face distorted with pain, had come sliding backward across the treacherous mud to the safe region of broken rocks. His hands were useless, but he stood up and used his body weight to push Geni back.

They stumbled together to safety. Geni was quieting. As the first frenzy ended she put her hands to her face and began to sob.

Rebka kept one arm around Darya Lang and surveyed the group. They were all stunned by Elena's death, but still he had to worry about other matters. In thirty seconds, their position had gone from difficult to desperate. The air was almost unbreathable, the heat was increasing, and the surface of Quake was more and more active. The one thing they could not afford to do was slow down.

What now?

He made an unhappy assessment of their new situation. The thunder from ground and sky was a little less, but instead of eight humans and aliens, all fully mobile, they had been reduced to four able-bodied beings: himself, Graves, J'merlia, and Kallik. It was anyone's guess how useful the two aliens would be in a crisis, but so far they had performed as well as any human.

What about the others?

Perry was in deep shock—more than just physical, if Rebka was any judge—and he was standing there like a robot. But he was tough. He could walk, and he would walk. On the other hand, he could no longer help anyone else, and without the use of his hands he would have trouble scrambling up the rock face. His arms hung loose at his sides, burned to the elbows and useless as rolls of black dough. The pain from them would be awful as soon as the first shock faded. With any luck that would be after they were all in the *Summer Dreamboat*.

Darya Lang would certainly need assistance. Her foot was scalded no worse than Perry's forearms, but she was far less used to physical suffering. Already she was weeping with pain and shock. Tears were running down her grimy, dust-coated cheeks.

Finally there was Geni Carmel. She did not need physical help, but emotionally she had been destroyed. She hardly seemed to realize that the others were there, and she would find it hard to cooperate in anything at all.

Rebka made the assignments automatically. "Councilor Graves, you help Geni Carmel. I'll assist Commander Perry if he needs it. J'merlia and Kallik, Professor Lang needs your aid. Help her, especially when we begin to climb."

And now we'll see just how tough Perry is, he thought. "Commander, we can't go any farther this way. Can you suggest another route to the ship?"

Perry came to life. He shivered, stared down at his burned forearms, and lifted his right hand tentatively away from his body. He pointed to the left side of the outcrop, moving his arm as though the limb had become some alien attachment.

"Last time we were here, we came down a watercourse. It was all rocks, no muddy surface. If we can find that maybe we can follow it back up."

"Good. You lead the way."

As they skirted the deadly patch of boiling mud, Rebka

looked up to the top of the rock. It was no more than forty meters above them, but it seemed an impossible distance. The watercourse was not steep. A fit man or woman could scramble up it in half a minute, but Perry would take that long to ascend the first few feet. And that was too slow.

Rebka moved forward from the back of the group and put his hands on Perry's hips.

"Just keep walking. Don't worry about falling, I'll be here. If you need a push or a lift, tell me."

He took one backward glance before Perry began to move. Julius Graves was coaxing Geni Carmel along, and they were doing well enough. J'merlia and Kallik had given up the idea of helping Darya Lang to walk. Instead they had seated her on Kallik's furry back, and the Hymenopt was struggling up the incline with J'merlia pushing them from behind and encouraging Kallik with a selection of hoots and whistles.

The surface beyond the outcrop was shaking with new violence. Rebka saw the aircar that they had arrived in tilt and collapse. A pall of black smoke swallowed it up, then came creeping steadily toward them.

One thing at a time, he told himself. Don't look back, and don't look up.

Rebka focused all his attention on helping Max Perry. If the other man fell, they would all go with him.

They struggled on, stumbling and scrabbling over loose pebbles. There was one critical moment when Perry's feet slipped completely from under him and he fell facedown toward the rock. He groaned as his crippled hands hit the rough surface and their burned palms split open. Rebka held him before he could slide backward. Within a few seconds they were again scrambling up the uneven path of the watercourse.

As soon as Perry came to the easy final steps, Rebka turned to see what was happening behind. Graves was wobble-legged, close to collapse, and Geni Carmel was supporting him. The other three were still halfway down and making slow progress. Rebka could hear Kallik clicking and whistling with the effort.

They would have to manage on their own. Rebka's top priority had to be the starship. Was it in working order, and did it have power for one final flight to orbit? Perry had moved over to the *Summer Dreamboat*, but he was simply standing by the closed door. He raised his hands in frustration as Rebka came up to him. Without working fingers he had no way to get inside.

"Go tell the others to hurry—particularly Kallik." Rebka jerked open the port, suddenly aware of how *small* the ship was. Perry had told him it was more like a toy than a starship, but the size was still a nasty shock. The interior space was not much more than that of the aircar.

He went across to study the controls. At least he would have no trouble with those, even without help from Kallik or Geni Carmel. The board was the simplest he had ever seen.

He turned on the displays. The power level was depressingly low. Suppose it took them only halfway to orbit?

He looked at the chronometer. Less than an hour to Summertide. That answered his question. It was damned if you do, damned if you don't. As the others came squeezing into the ship, he prepared for liftoff.

Darya Lang and Geni Carmel were the last ones in.

"Close the port," Rebka said, and turned back to the controls. He did not watch them do as he said, nor was there time for the long list of checks that should have preceded an ascent to space. Through the forward window he could see a sheet of flame running steadily across the surface toward them. In a few more seconds it would engulf the ship.

"Hold tight. I"m taking us up at three gee."

If we're lucky, he thought. And if we're not . . . Hans Rebka applied full ascent power. The starship trembled and strained on the ground.

Nothing happened for what felt like minutes. Then, as the firestorm ran toward them, the *Summer Dreamboat* groaned at the seams, shivered, and lifted toward Quake's jet-black and turbulent sky.

CHAPTER 22
Summertide

Ten seconds after her foot plunged into that boiling black mud, Darya Lang's nervous system went into suspended animation. She did not feel pain, she did not feel worry, she did not feel sorrow.

She knew, abstractly, that Max Perry was burned worse than she and was somehow leading the way up the rocky slope, but that much effort and involvement was beyond her. If she remained conscious, it was only because she knew no way to slip into unconsciousness. And if she traveled up to the ship with the rest of them, it was only because Kallik and J'merlia gave her no choice. They lifted and carried her, careful to keep her foot and ankle clear of the ground.

Her isolation ended—agonizingly—as they approached the ship's entry port. Darts of pain began to lance through her foot and ankle as Kallik laid her gently on the ground.

"With apologies and extreme regrets," J'merlia said quietly, his dark mandibles close to her ear. "But the way in is big enough for only one. It will be necessary to enter alone."

They were going to put her down and ask her to walk, just when the pain was becoming intolerable! Her burned foot would have to meet the floor. She began to plead with the aliens, to tell them that she could not bear it. It was already too late. She found herself balanced on one leg in front of the hatch.

"Hurry up," Max Perry urged from inside the ship.

She gave him a look of hatred. Then she saw his hands and forearms, blistered and split to the bone from contact with rough stones and pebbles during the ascent of the rock. He had to be feeling far worse than she was. Darya gritted her teeth, lifted her left foot clear of the ground, grabbed the sides of the doorframe, and hopped gingerly inside the ship. There was hardly room for the people already there. Somehow she managed to crawl across to the ship's side window and stood there on one leg.

What should she do? She could not stand there indefinitely, and she could not bear the thought of anything touching her foot.

Rebka's announcement that he would take them up to space at three gees answered that. His words filled her with dismay. She could hardly stand in a field of less than one gee. She would have to lie down, and then three gees of acceleration would press her ruined foot to the unforgiving floor.

Before she could say anything, Kallik's stubby body wriggled across toward her. The Hymenopt placed her soft abdomen next to Darya's injured foot and uttered a dozen soft whistles.

"No! Don't touch it!" Darya cried out in panic.

As she tried to move her leg away, the gleaming yellow sting emerged from the end of Kallik's body. It pierced inches deep into her lower calf. Darya screamed and fell over backward, banging her head as she went on the supply chest behind the pilot's seat.

Liftoff began before she could move again.

Darya found she was flattened to the floor with her foot pressing onto metal. Her hurt foot! She had to scream. She opened her mouth and suddenly realized that the only parts of her body that were *not* in pain were that foot and calf. Kallik's sting had robbed them of all feeling.

She lay back and turned her head to rest its increased weight on her cheek and ear. A tangle of bodies covered the floor. She could see Kallik, right in front of her, cushioning Geni Carmel's head on her furry abdomen. Julius Graves lay just beyond, but all she could see was the top of his bald pate, lying next to J'merlia's shiny black cranium. Rebka, piloting the ship, and Max Perry, harnessed into the seat next to him, were hidden by the supply chest and the seat back.

Darya made a great effort and turned her head the other way. She could see out of the ship's side port, a foot away from her. Unbelievably—surely they had been rising for minutes—the ship was still below Quake's cloud layer. She caught a vivid lightning-lit view of the surface; it had shattered into crisscrossing fault lines, over which waves of orange-red molten lava were sweeping like ocean billows. The whole planet was on fire, a scene of ancient perdition. Then the ship lifted into black dust clouds so dense that the end of the vestigial control surfaces, just a few feet beyond the port, became invisible to her.

The turbulence and shear forces tripled. Darya rolled helplessly against Kallik, and both of them went sliding across the floor to collide with Julius Graves. Another moment, and all three were tumbling back, to crush Darya against the wall. She was still in that position, pinned by the weight of everyone except Rebka and Perry, when the *Summer Dreamboat* emerged unexpectedly from the clouds of Quake. The ship's port admitted one sunburst of intolerable golden radiation before the photoshielding came into operation.

Darya was lucky. She was facing away from the port, and she happened to have her head caught under Kallik's abdomen when that searing light-blast hit the ship. Everyone else in the rear compartment was blinded for a few seconds.

Rebka and Perry had been protected in the front seats, but they were facing forward and trying to coax a ship to orbit in circumstances for which it had never been designed. So it was Darya alone, turning to look sideways and out behind the ascending ship, who saw everything that happened next.

The *Dreamboat* was soaring over the hemisphere of Quake that faced away from Opal. The disks of Mandel and Amaranth loomed low in the sky to her left. Reduced by the photoshielding to glowing, dark-limbed circles, the twin stars showed their bright disks pocked and speckled with sunspots. Their tidal forces were tearing at each other, just as they tore at Quake and Opal. Directly overhead, Gargantua shone pale and spectral, a giant whose reflected light was reduced by the photoshielding to a faint and insubstantial ghost world.

From a point very close to Gargantua's edge—Darya could not be sure quite where it lay, on the planet or off it—a glittering blue beam stabbed suddenly down toward Quake, bright with controlled energy.

Darya followed it with her eyes. It could not be a beam of ordinary light. That would be invisible in empty space, and she could see it all the way along its length. And where that pulsing ray from Gargantua struck the clouds, the dust-filled protective layer boiled instantly away. A circular area of Quake's surface, a hundred kilometers across, was suddenly exposed to Mandel and Amaranth's combined radiation. Already seething with molten lava, the surface started to deform and crater. A dark tunnel formed and became rapidly deeper and wider. Soon Darya could see the molten rocks of the planet's interior thrown back in waves to form a sputtering, sharp-sided edge to the hole.

The ship's motion was carrying Darya away from the tunnel, and her viewing angle was too steep to see the bottom of the pit. She leaned closer to the port, ignoring the pain in her bruised body and face. As the ship's altitude increased, Quake hung below her like a great, clouded bead, threaded onto that pencil of bright blue light. Where the ray struck, the dark hole through the bead was lit by a glowing rim of molten lava.

The next events came in such quick succession that Darya had trouble afterward in relating their exact sequence.

As Quake's rotation was taking first Mandel and then Amaranth below the horizon, a second blue beam came stabbing down from open space to merge with the one from Gargantua. It did not come from any object that Darya could find in the sky, although her eye could follow it up and up, until it finally became a line too faint to see.

The new pencil of light skewered the tunnel in Quake's crust, and the hole widened—not steadily, but in one impossible jerk of displaced material. Narrow answering beams of red and cyan thrust back into space, following the exact center of the incident ones. And in the same moment, two silvery spheres crept forward from the depths of the tunnel.

They looked identical, each maybe a kilometer across. Rising slowly clear of Quake they hovered motionless, one just beneath the other, wobbling like two transparent balloons filled with quicksilver.

The blue beams changed color. The one from Gargantua became bright saffron, the other a glowing magenta. The pulses along their length changed in frequency. As they did so, the higher sphere began to accelerate, moving along the precise line of the magenta ray. Slow at first, then suddenly faster, it remained visible for only a split second and then was gone. Darya could not tell if it had been propelled out of sight—at huge acceleration—or had vanished through some other mechanism. As it disappeared, so did the magenta beam.

The second sphere still hovered motionless close to Quake. After a few moments it began to inch up along the saffron pencil of light. But its motion was leisurely, almost ponderous. Darya could follow it easily, a ball of silver climbing the saffron beam like a metal spider ascending its own thread. She tracked the shining globe as it crept upward.

And then her eyes were suddenly unable to focus. Around the bright ball the starfield had become twisted and distorted. The ball itself disappeared to become a black void, while around it scattered points of starlight converged and met in an annular rainbow cluster. The vanished sphere formed an ink-black center to that brilliant stellar ring. Still it ascended the yellow light beam.

While she was squinting at that hole in space, the *Dreamboat* performed a dizzying half roll and a surge at maximum thrust. She heard Hans Rebka, in the pilot's seat, cry out. A bright jet of violet, a starship's drive working at high intensity, flared across the starfield and moved across the bows of the *Dreamboat*.

Darya turned her head and saw the blunt lines of a Zardalu Communion vessel swooping in close to them. Concealed weapons ports sprang open on the ship's forward end.

The *Dreamboat* was the target—and at that range, there was no way the other ship could miss.

Darya watched in horror as all the weapons fired. She expected their ship to disintegrate around her. But impossibly, the attacking beams were veering away from their expected straight lines. They missed the *Dreamboat* completely and curved into space, drawn to meet the black sphere as it hung suspended on its golden thread of light.

The beams of the ship's weapons remained visible as glowing trajectories in space, coupling the Zardalu vessel with the dark ascending globe. The curved lines shortened. The other ship moved closer to the distorted dark region, as though the sphere were reeling in bright strands from the weapons.

But the Zardalu ship was not going willingly. Its drive flared to the brighter violet of maximum intensity, thrusting away from the sphere's dark singularity. Darya could sense the struggle of huge opposed forces.

And the starship was losing. Caught in the field's curvature, it moved along the twisting lines of force, drawn irresistibly toward the rising sphere. The sphere itself was moving upward, faster and faster. It seemed to Darya that the Zardalu vessel was sucked into that black void, one moment before the sphere itself flashed up the yellow thread and disappeared.

Then the *Summer Dreamboat* was moving on, around the curve of Quake. Gargantua sank below the horizon, and with it all sign of the pulsing beam of yellow.

"I don't know if anyone cares anymore." It was Rebka's laconic voice, startling Darya back to an awareness of where she was. "But I just checked the chronometer. Summertide Maximum took place a few seconds ago. And we're in orbit."

Darya turned to look down at Quake. There was nothing to see but dark, endless clouds and, beyond them, on the horizon, the blue-gray sphere of Opal.

Summertide. It was over. And it had been nothing like she had imagined. She glanced over at the others, still rubbing their eyes as they lay on the starship floor, and felt a terrible sense of letdown. To see everything—but to understand nothing! The whole visit to Quake at Summertide was an unsolved mystery, a waste of time and human lives.

"The good news is that we reached orbit." Rebka was speaking again, and Darya could hear the exhaustion in his voice. "The bad news is that the fancy flying we had to do a few moments ago took what little power we had left. We probably have Louis Nenda and Atvar H'sial to thank for that. I don't have any idea what was going on back there, or what happened to that other ship, and I really don't care. I hope Nenda and H'sial got their comeuppance, but right now I don't have time to bother with it. I'm worried about us. Without power, we can't make a planetary landing on Opal, or on Quake, or anywhere else. Commander Perry is working up a trajectory that may take us to Midway Station. If we get lucky we might be able to ride the Umbilical from there."

Working up a trajectory, Darya thought. How can he? Perry doesn't have hands, just burned bits of meat.

But he'll do it, hands or no hands. And if his foot were burned like mine, he'd walk on it. He'd run on it, too, if he had to. Hans Rebka talks of luck, but they've not had much of that. They've had to make their own.

I'll never mock the Phemus Circle again. Their people are dirty and disgusting and poor and primitive, but Rebka and Perry and the rest of them have something that makes everyone in the Alliance seem half-dead. They have the will to live, no matter what happens.

And then, because she was becoming steadily more

relaxed and sluggish in response to the anesthetic and mildly toxic fluid that Kallik had injected, and because Darya Lang could never stop thinking, even when she wanted to, her mind said to her: "Umbilical. We're going to the *Umbilical*."

The least of the Builder artifacts; she knew that, everyone knew that. An insignificant nothing of a structure, on the Builder scale of things. But it was to that very place, to that least of all artifacts, and to that very time, of Summertide Maximum, that all the other Builder artifacts had pointed.

Why? Why not point to one of the striking artifacts— to Paradox or Sentinel, to Elephant or Cocoon or Lens?

Now *there's* a worthwhile mystery, Darya thought: a puzzle that someone could usefully ponder. Let's forget the mess we're in and think about that for a while. I can't help Rebka and Perry, and anyway I don't need to. They'll take care of me. So let's think.

Let's wonder about the two spheres that came out from the deep interior of Quake. How long had they been there? *Why* were they there? Where did they go? Why did they choose this moment to emerge, and what made the black one take the Zardalu ship with it?

The questions went unanswered. As Kallik's narcotic venom spread steadily through her bloodstream, Darya was sinking toward unconsciousness. There was too little time left for thinking. Her concentration was gone, her energy was gone, and her brain drifted randomly from one subject to another. Drugged sleep was moments away.

But in the last moment, the single second before her mind vanished into vague emptiness, Darya caught the gleam of a new insight. She understood the significance of Quake and Summertide! She knew its function, and maybe their own role in it. She reached out for the thought, struggled to pull it to her, sought to fix it firmly in her memory.

It was too late. Darya, still fighting, floated irresistibly into sleep.

And then—

CHAPTER 23

Rebka woke like a nervous animal, jerking upright and alert from a sound sleep. In that first moment his feelings were all panic.

He had made the fatal mistake of allowing his concentration to lapse. *Who was flying the ship?*

The only other person halfway competent was Max Perry, and he was too badly injured to take the controls. They could smash into Opal, fall back to the surface of Quake, or lose themselves forever in deep space.

Then, before his eyes opened, he knew things had to be all right.

No one was flying the ship. No one needed to. He was not on the *Summer Dreamboat*—he could not be. For he was not in freefall. And the forces on him were not the wild, turbulent ones of atmospheric reentry. Instead there was a steady downward pull, the fraction-of-a-gee acceleration that told of a capsule moving along the Umbilical.

He opened his eyes and remembered the final hours of their flight. They had meandered out to Midway Station like drunken sailors, the sorriest collection of humans and aliens that the Dobelle system had ever seen. He remembered biting his lips and fingertips until they bled, forcing himself to stay awake and his eyes to stay open. He had followed Perry's half-incoherent navigational instructions as best he could, while they tacked for five long hours

249

along the line of the Umbilical. With the help of the tiny attitude-control jets—the only power left on board the *Dreamboat*—he had brought them to a dazed docking at the station's biggest port.

He recalled the approach—a disgrace for any pilot. It had taken five times as long as it should. And as the last docking confirmation was received at the ship, he had leaned back in the pilot's chair and closed his eyes—for one moment's rest.

And then?

And then his memory failed. He looked around.

He must have fallen asleep at the very second of final contact. Someone had carried him into Midway Station and moved him to the service level of an Umbilical capsule. They had secured him in a harness and left him there.

He was not alone. Max Perry, his forearms caked and daubed with protective yellow gel, drifted on a light tether a few feet away. He was unconscious. Darya Lang hovered beyond him, her flowing brown hair tied back from her face. The clothing had been stripped from her left leg below the knee, and plastic flesh covered her burned foot and ankle. Her breathing was light. Every few seconds she muttered under her breath as though about to surface from sleep. With her face so relaxed and thought-free, she looked about twelve years old. Next to Darya floated Geni Carmel. From the look of her she was also heavily sedated, although she had no visible injuries.

Rebka checked his wristwatch: twenty-three hours past Summertide. All the fireworks in the Quake and Opal system should be safely in the past. And for seventeen hours, he had been out of things completely.

He rubbed at his eyes, noticing that his face was no longer covered with ash and grime. Someone had not only carried him to the capsule, but had washed him and changed his clothes before leaving him to sleep. Who had done that? And who had provided the medical care to Perry and Lang?

That brought him back to his first question: with the four of them unconscious, who was minding the store?

He had trouble getting his feet to the floor and then found that he could not loose the harness that secured him. Even after seventeen hours of rest, he was weary enough for his fingers to be clumsy and fumbling. If Darya Lang looked like a teenager, he felt like a battered centenarian.

Finally he freed himself and was able to leave the improvised hospital. He considered trying to wake Perry and Lang—she still murmuring to herself in a protesting voice—and then decided against it. Almost certainly they had been anesthetized before their wounds were dressed and synthetic skin applied.

He slowly climbed the stairs that led to the observation-and-control deck of the capsule. The clear roof of the upper chamber showed Midway Station in the middle distance. Far above, confirming that the capsule was descending toward Opal, Rebka saw the distant prospect of Quake, dark-clouded and brooding.

The walls of the observation deck, ten meters high, were paneled with display units. Julius Graves, seated at the control console and flanked by J'merlia and Kallik, was watching in thoughtful silence. The succession of broadcast displays that Graves was receiving showed a planetary surface—but it was Opal, not Quake.

Rebka watched for a while before announcing his presence. With their attention on Quake, it had been easy to forget Opal had also experienced the biggest Summer-tide in human history. Aerial and orbital radar shots, piercing the cloud layers of the planet, showed broad stretches of naked seabed laid bare by millennial tides. Muddy ocean floor was spotted with vast green backs: dead Dowsers, the size of mountains, lay stranded and crushed under their own weight.

Other videos showed the Slings of Opal disintegrating as contrary waves, miles high and driven by the tidal forces, pulled at and twisted the ocean's surface.

An emotionless voice-over from Opal listed the casualties: half the planet's population known dead, most in the past twenty-four hours; another fifth still missing. But even before assessment was complete, reconstruction was beginning. Every human on Opal was on a continuous work schedule.

The broadcasts made clear to Rebka that the people of Opal had their hands more than full. If his group were to land there, they should not look for assistance.

He drifted forward and tapped Graves lightly on the shoulder. The councilor jerked at the touch, swiveled in his chair, and grinned up at him.

"Aha! Back from Dreamland! As you see, Captain—" He flourished a thin hand upward, and then to the display screens. "Our decision to spend Summertide on Quake rather than Opal was not so unwise after all."

"If we'd stayed on the surface of Quake for Summertide, Councilor, we'd have been ashes. We were lucky."

"We were luckier than you think. And long before Summertide." Graves gestured to Kallik, who was manipulating displays with one forelimb and entering numbers into a pocket computer with another. "According to our Hymenopt friend, Opal suffered *worse* than Quake. Kallik has been doing energy-balance calculations in every spare moment since we left the surface. She agrees with Commander Perry—the surface should have been far more active than it was during the Grand Conjunction. The full energy was never released while we were there. Some focused storage-and-release mechanism was at work for the tidal energies. Without it, the planet would have been uninhabitable for humans long before we left it. But with it, most of the energy went to some other purpose."

"Councilor, Quake was quite bad enough. Elena Carmel is dead. Atvar H'sial and Louis Nenda may be dead, too."

"They are."

"I'm glad to hear it. I don't know if you realize this, but they were in orbit around Quake at Summertide and they tried to blow us out of the sky. They deserved what they got. But why are you so sure they're dead?"

"Darya Lang saw Nenda's ship dragged off toward Gargantua with an acceleration too much for any human or Cecropian to survive. They had to be crushed flat inside it."

"Nenda's ship had a full star drive. No local field should have held it."

"If you wish to argue that point, Captain, you'll have to do it with Darya Lang. She saw what happened; I did not."

"She's asleep."

"Still? She became unconscious again when J'merlia started work on her foot, but I am surprised she is not waking." Graves turned in annoyance. "Now then, what do *you* want?"

J'merlia was hesitantly touching his sleeve, while by his side Kallik was hopping and whistling in excitement.

"With great respect, Councilor Graves." J'merlia moved to kneel before him. "But Kallik and I could not help hearing what you said to Captain Rebka—that Master Nenda and Atvar H'sial escaped from Quake, then they were hurtled off to Gargantua and crushed by the acceleration."

"*Toward* Gargantua, my Lo'tfian friend. Perhaps not *to* Gargantua itself. Professor Lang was quite insistent on the point."

"With apologies, I should have said *toward* Gargantua. Honored Councilor, would it be possible for Kallik and my humble self to be excused from duties for a few minutes?"

"Oh, go on. And don't grovel, you know I *hate* it." Graves waved them away. As the aliens headed for the capsule's lower level, he turned back to Rebka.

"Well, Captain, unless you want to collapse again into slumber, I propose that we go below ourselves and check on Commander Perry and Professor Lang. We have plenty of time. The Umbilical will not offer access to Opal for another few hours. And our official work in the Dobelle system is over."

"Yours may be. Mine is not."

"It will be, Captain, very soon." The grinning skeleton was as infuriatingly casual and self-assured as ever.

"You don't even know what my real work is."

"Ah, but I do. You were sent to find out what was wrong

with Commander Perry, see what it was that kept him in a dead-end job in the Dobelle system—and cure him."

Rebka sank into a seat in front of the control console. "Now how the devil did you find that out?" His voice was puzzled rather than annoyed.

"From the obvious place—Commander Perry. He has his own friends and information sources, back in the headquarters of the Phemus Circle. He learned why you were sent here."

"Then he should also know that I never did find out. I told you, my job is unfinished."

"Not true. Your official job is almost over, and it will be done with very soon. You see, Captain, *I* know what happened to Max Perry seven years ago. I suspected it before we came to Quake, and I confirmed it when I queried the commander under sedation. All it took were the right questions. *And* I know what to do. Trust me, and listen."

Julius Graves hauled his long body over to a monitor, pulled a data unit the size of a sugar cube from his pocket, and inserted it into the machine. "This is sound only, of course. But you will recognize the voice, even though it appears much younger. I sent his memory back seven years. I will play only a fragment. No purpose is served by making private suffering into a public event."

. . . *Amy was still acting goofy and playful, even in the heat. She was laughing as she ran on ahead of me, back toward the car that would take us to the Umbilical. It was only a few hundred meters away, but I was getting tired.*

"Hey, slow down. I'm the one who has to carry the equipment."

She spun around, teasing me. "Oh, come on, Max. Learn to have some fun. You don't need any of that stuff. Leave it here—nobody will ever notice it's gone."

She made me smile, in spite of the growing noise around us and the sweat that covered my body. Quake was hot.

"I can't do that Amy—it's official property. It all has to be accounted for. Wait for me."

But she just laughed. And danced on—on into that funny blurring of the surface, the fragile, shimmering ground of Summertide . . .

. . . before I could get near her, she was gone. Just like that, in a fraction of a second. Swallowed up by Quake. All that I could take back with me was the pain . . .

"There is more, but it adds nothing." Graves stopped the recording. "Nothing that you cannot guess, or should not hear. Amy died in molten lava, not in boiling mud. Max Perry saw that shimmering of heated air again, in the Pentacline Depression—but too late to save Elena Carmel."

Hans Rebka shrugged. "Even if you know what drove Max Perry into his shell, that's not the hardest part of my job. I'm supposed to *cure* him, and I don't know where to begin."

Rebka knew that his present sense of failure and incompetence should be only temporary, no more than a side effect of exhaustion following days of tension. But that did not make it any less real.

He stared at one of the wall displays, which showed a Sling floating upside down and shattered by the impact of mighty seas. All that could be seen was a wilderness of black, slippery mud from which jutted random tangles of roots. He wondered if anyone could possibly have survived when the Sling capsized.

"How?" he went on. "How do you pull someone out of a seven-year depression? I don't know that."

"Of course you don't. That's my area of expertise, not yours." Graves turned abruptly and headed for the stairway. "Come on," he said over his shoulder. "Time to see what's going on below decks. I think those pesky aliens are plotting a mutiny, but we'll ignore that for the moment. Right now we have to talk to Max Perry."

Was Graves going crazy again? Rebka sighed. Oh, for the good old days, when he was flying through Quake's clouds and wondering if they would survive another second of turbulence. He followed close behind the other man, down to the second level of the capsule.

J'merlia and Kallik were nowhere to be seen.

"I told you," Graves said. "They're down in the cargo hold. Those two are up to something, sure as taxes. Give me a hand here."

With Rebka's puzzled assistance, the councilor carried Max Perry and then Geni Carmel back to the upper level of the capsule. Darya Lang, still muttering to herself on the brink of consciousness, was left in her securing harness.

Graves placed Max Perry and Geni Carmel in seats at ninety degrees to each other and fixed them in position.

"Put extra bindings on those harnesses," he said to Rebka. "Make sure you don't touch Perry's injured arms— but remember I don't want either of them to be able to get loose. I'll be back in a minute."

Graves made one final trip to the lower level. When he reappeared he was carrying two spray hypodermics in his right hand.

"Darya Lang is waking up," he said, "but let's get this taken care of first. It won't take long." He injected Perry in the shoulder with one syringe and Geni Carmel with the other. "Now, we can begin." He began to count aloud.

The wake-up shot given to Max Perry was full strength. Before Graves had reached ten, Perry sighed, rolled his head from side to side, and slowly opened his eyes. He stared around the capsule's cabin with a dull and disinterested look, until his gaze found the still-unconscious Geni Carmel. Then he groaned and closed his eyes again.

"You are awake," Graves said in a reproving tone. "So don't you go falling asleep again. I have a problem, and I need your help."

Perry shook his head, and his eyes remained shut.

"We'll be back on Opal in a few hours," Graves went on. "And life will start to return to normal. But I have the responsibility for the rehabilitation of Geni Carmel. Now, there must be formal hearings, back on Shasta and on Miranda, but that cannot be allowed to interfere with the rehab program. It has to begin at once. And the death of Elena makes the program very difficult. I feel it would be disastrous to let Geni go back to Shasta, with all its memories of her twin sister, until she is already on the road to recovery. On the other hand I myself *must* return to Shasta, and then go on to Miranda for the formal genocide hearing."

He paused. Perry still had not opened his eyes.

Graves leaned close and lowered his voice. "So that leaves me with two questions to answer. Where should the rehabilitation of Geni Carmel begin? And who should oversee the rehab process, if I will not be around?

"That is where I need your help, Commander. I have decided that Geni's rehab program should begin on Opal. And I propose to make you her guardian while it is proceeding."

At last Graves had broken through. Perry jerked bolt upright in the restraining harness. His bloodshot eyes opened wide. "What the hell are you talking about?"

"I thought I was clear enough." Graves was smiling. "But let me say it again. Geni will remain on Opal for at least four more months. You will be responsible for her welfare while she is there."

"You can't do that."

"I'm afraid you're wrong. Ask Captain Rebka if you doubt me. In matters like this, a Council member has full authority to proceed with prompt rehabilitation. And anyone can be pressed into service. That includes you."

Perry glared at Rebka, then back at Graves. "I won't do it. I have my own work—a full-time job. And she needs a specialist. I have no idea how to deal with her sort of problem."

"You can certainly learn." Graves nodded at the other chair, where Geni was slowly waking in response to her weaker injection. "She's starting to listen now. As a first move, you can tell her about Opal. Remember, Commander, she has never been there. It's going to be her home for a while, and you know as much about it as anyone."

"Wait a minute!" Perry was struggling at his harness and calling to Graves, who was already ushering Rebka out of the chamber. "We're tied in. You can't leave us like this! Look at her."

Geni Carmel was making no effort to escape from her harness, but tears were trickling down her pale cheeks, and she was staring in horror or fascination at Perry's mutilated hands and forearms.

"Sorry," Graves said over his shoulder as he and Rebka started down toward the lower level of the capsule. "We'll discuss this more later, but I can't do it now. Captain Rebka and I have something very urgent to take care of on the lower deck. We'll be back."

Rebka waited until they were out of earshot before he spoke again to Graves. "Are you serious about any of that?"

"I am serious about *all* of it."

"It won't work. Geni Carmel is just a child. With Elena dead, she doesn't even want to live. You know how close they were, so close they would die rather than be separated from each other. And Perry is a basket case himself—he's in no shape to look after her."

Julius Graves halted at the bottom of the stairway. He turned to look up at Hans Rebka, and for once his face was neither grinning nor grimacing. "Captain, when I need a man who can fly an overloaded, power-drained ship like the *Summer Dreamboat* off a planet that is falling apart underneath us, and take me into space, I'll come to you anytime. You are very good at your job—your *real* job. Can't you do me the favor of admitting that the same could be true of me? Isn't it conceivable that I might do my job well?"

"But that isn't your job."

"Which only shows, Captain, how little you know of the duties of a Council member. Believe me, what I am doing will work. Or would you prefer a wager? I say that Max Perry and Geni Carmel have more chance of curing *each other* than you or I have of doing anything useful for *either* of them. As you said, she is just a child who needs help—but Perry is a man who desperately needs to *give* help. He's been doing penance for seven years for his sin in allowing Amy to go with him to Quake during Summertide. Don't you realize that burning his arms like that will *help* his mental condition? Now he has a chance to obtain total absolution. And your job on Opal is finished. You could leave today, and Perry would be fine." Graves snapped his fingers and held out his hand to Rebka. "Would you like to bet on that? Name the amount."

Rebka was saved from a reply by an angry voice ahead of them.

"I don't know who to thank for this, and I'm not about to ask. But will someone *get me the hell out of here!* I have work to do."

It was Darya Lang, fully conscious and struggling to free herself from the harness. She sounded nothing like the shy theoretical scientist who had first arrived on Opal, but her practical skills were still lacking. In her efforts to free herself she had managed to tangle the bindings, so that she was hanging upside down and could hardly move her arms.

"She's all yours, Captain," Graves said unexpectedly. "I'm going to find J'merlia and Kallik." He popped down the hatchway at the side of the chamber and vanished from sight.

Rebka went across to Lang and studied the way the harness had been knotted. Less and less, he understood what was going on. With their escape from Quake, everyone except him should have been able to relax; instead, they all seemed to have new agendas of their own. Darya Lang sounded urgent and furious.

He reached out, tugged gently at one point of the harness and hard at another one. The result was gratifying. The bindings released completely to deposit Darya Lang lightly onto the chamber floor. He helped her to her feet and was rewarded with a surprising and embarrassed smile.

"Now why couldn't I have done that?" She put pressure tentatively on her injured foot, shrugged, and pressed harder. "Last thing I remember, we'd just reached the Umbilical, and Graves and Kallik were fixing me up from the med kits. How long have I been asleep—and when do we reach Opal?"

"I don't know how long you've been asleep, but it's

twenty-three hours since Summertide." Rebka consulted his watch. "Make that closer to twenty-four. And we ought to touch down on Opal in a couple of hours. *If* we can touch down. They took a real beating there. There's no rush, though. We have plenty of food and water on board. We can live in this capsule for weeks—even go back up the Umbilical to Midway Station if we have to, and stay there indefinitely."

"No way." Darya was shaking her head. "I can't afford to wait. I've only been conscious for a few minutes, but I spent all of them cursing the man who filled me with drugs. We have to get down to the surface of Opal, and you have to get me a ship."

"To go home? What's the rush? Does anyone on Sentinel Gate know when you'll be going back?"

"No one does." She took Hans Rebka by the arm, leaning on him as they walked over to the capsule's miniature galley. She sat down, taking her time as she poured herself a hot drink. Finally she turned to him. "But you have it wrong, Hans. I'm not going to Sentinel Gate. I'm going to Gargantua. And I'll need help to get there."

"I hope you're not expecting it from me." Rebka looked away, very conscious of her fingers on his biceps. "Look, I know that Nenda's ship was dragged off there, and they were killed. But you don't want to be killed, too. Gargantua is a gas-giant, a frozen world—we can't live there; neither can the Cecropians."

"I didn't say that the ship and the sphere went right to Gargantua. I don't think that. I believe the place I need to go is probably one of Gargantua's moons. But I won't know that until I get there."

"Get there and do what? Recover a couple of corpses. Who cares what happens to their bodies? Atvar H'sial left you to die, and she and Nenda abandoned J'merlia and Kallik. Even if they were alive—and you say they're not—they don't deserve help."

"I agree. And that's not why I have to follow them." Darya handed Rebka a cup. "Calm down, Hans. Drink that, and listen to me for a minute. I know that people from the Phemus Circle think everyone from the Alliance is a dreamy incompetent, just the way we think you're all barbarian peasants who don't bother to wash—"

"Huh!"

"But you and I have been around each other for a while now—long enough to know that those ideas are nonsense. You acknowledge that I'm at least a decent observer. I don't make things up. So let me tell you what I *saw*, not what I think. Everyone else here may miss the point of this, but I trust you to draw the right conclusions.

"Remember now—listen first, then *think*, then react— not the other way round." She moved closer to Rebka, positioning herself so that it was difficult for him to do anything other than listen to her.

"When we came up out of the clouds on Quake, you were too busy piloting the ship to look behind, and everyone else in the rear compartment was blinded by Mandel and Amaranth. So no one else saw what I saw: Quake opening, deep into the interior. And two objects coming out. One of them flew away, out of the plane of the galaxy. I lost sight of it in less than a second. You saw the other one. It took off toward Gargantua, and Louis Nenda's ship was carried with it. That was significant, but it isn't the important point! Everyone said that Quake was far too quiet for so close to Summertide. Sure, I know we *thought* it was violent, when we were down there. But it wasn't. Max Perry kept saying it: Where's all the energy going?

"Well, we know the answer to that now. It was being transformed and stored, so that when the right time came the whole interior of Quake could open up and eject those two bodies—spaceships, if you think they were that.

"I saw it happen, and I caught the sniff of an answer to something that had kept me baffled for months, long before I left Sentinel Gate:

"*Why Dobelle?*

"Why such a nothing place, I mean, for such an important event?

"The idea of visiting Dobelle occurred to me when I

calculated the convergence time and place for influences spreading out from all the artifacts. There was a unique solution: Quake at Summertide. But when I proposed that, the Builder specialists in the Alliance laughed at me. They said, look, Darya, we accept that there is an artifact in the Dobelle system—the Umbilical. But it's a *minor* piece of Builder technology. Something we understand; something that isn't mysterious or big or complex. It makes no sense for the focus of all the Builder activities to be at such a second-class structure, in such a worthless and unimportant part of the Galaxy—I'm sorry, Hans, but I'm quoting, and that's the way people in the Alliance regard the worlds of the Phemus Circle."

Rebka shrugged. "Don't apologize," he said gruffly. "That's the way a lot of us think about the Circle worlds, and we *live* here. Try a weekend on Teufel, sometime— if you can stand it."

"Well, whatever they said about the Phemus Circle and the Umbilical, they couldn't argue with the statistical analysis. In fact, they repeated it for themselves and found that everything did point to Dobelle, and to Quake at Summertide. They had to agree with me. The trouble was, I was forced to agree with *them*. Dobelle made no sense as a place for important action. I mean, I was the one who had *written* the Catalog description of the Umbilical— 'one of the simplest and most comprehensible of all Builder artifacts'! People were parroting back my own words.

"So I was baffled when I arrived here. I was still baffled when you flew us up through the clouds, trying to get off Quake in one piece. I couldn't make sense of Dobelle as the convergence point.

"But then I saw that pulsing light beam shine down from Gargantua and watched the whole of Quake opening up in front of me. And just before I passed out I realized that we had all been missing something obvious.

"All the references on the structure of the galaxy make the same comment, the Dobelle system is 'one of the natural wonders of the local spiral arm.' Isn't it wonderful, the books say, how the interplay of the gravitational fields of Amaranth and Mandel and Gargantua has thrown Dobelle into such a finely balanced orbit—an orbit so placed that once every three hundred and fifty thousand years, all the players line up *exactly* for Summertide and the Grand Conjunction. Isn't that just amazing?

"Well, it is amazing—if you believe it. But there's another way to look at things. The Dobelle system doesn't just *contain* an artifact, the Umbilical. The Dobelle system *is* an artifact! The whole thing." She grabbed at Rebka's arm again, caught up in her own vision. "Its whole orbit and geometry were created by the Builders, designed so that once every three hundred and fifty thousand years Mandel and Amaranth and Gargantua are so close to Quake that a special interaction can take place between them. Something inside Quake captures and uses those tidal energies.

"Before I came to Quake, I thought that the Builders themselves might be here—maybe even appear at this particular Summertide. But that's wrong. The Grand Conjunction serves as a *trigger* for the departure of those spheres—ships, or whatever they are—from Dobelle. I don't know where the first one went—out of the galaxy, from the look of it. But we have enough information to track the other one, the one that went toward Gargantua. And if we want to know more about the Builders, that's where we have to go.

"And soon! Before whatever it is that happens out near Gargantua is over and done with, and we have to wait *another* three hundred and fifty thousand years for a second chance."

Finally able to get a word in edgewise, Hans Rebka asked a question of his own. "Are you suggesting that Quake splits open, and something comes out of it at *every* Grand Conjunction?"

"I certainly am. That's the *purpose* of the Grand Conjunction—it provides the timing trigger and the tidal energy needed to open up the interior of Quake. So when Quake opened—"

But it was Rebka's turn to talk. "Darya, I'm no theorist. But you're wrong. If you want proof of that, go and talk to Max Perry."

"He wasn't watching what happened when we left Quake."

"Nor was I, particularly. Max and I had other things on our minds. But when I first arrived on Opal, I asked about the history of the doublet. The history of Opal was hard to determine, because it has no permanent land surface. But Perry showed me an analysis of the fossil record of Quake. People had studied it in the early years of colonizing Dobelle, because they needed to know if the surface of Quake was stable enough to live on through Summertide.

"It isn't, for humans—we proved that pretty well for ourselves. But there has been native life on Quake for hundreds of millions of years, since long before the planet went into its present orbit. And any recent opening of the deep interior of Quake—like the one that you saw—would show clearly as an anomaly in the fossil record."

He reached out for the display control and set it to show an image of the space above the capsule. Mandel and Amaranth were visible, still huge in the sky, but they were less bright. The knowledge that they were on the wane for another year was comforting. As the stellar partners dimmed, Gargantua shone brighter in the sky over to their right. But the giant planet was well past its own periastron, and the orange-brown disk was already smaller. No blinding beam of light shone forth from Gargantua, or from one of its satellites. Quake hung above the capsule, its surface dark and peaceful.

"You see, Darya, there's no evidence in the whole fossil record of a deep disturbance of Quake, comparable with what you saw. Not three years ago, or three hundred, or three hundred and fifty thousand. The deep interior of Quake has been hidden from view, as far back as people can trace the history of its surface. And that's at least five million years."

He expected Darya to be crushed by his comments. She came back stronger than ever. "So this Grand Conjunction was special. That makes it *more* important to find out why. Hans, let me give you the bottom line. You can go back to your work on the Phemus Circle tomorrow. But I can't go back to Sentinel Gate. Not yet. I *have* to go on and take a look at Gargantua. I didn't spend my whole adult life studying the Builders and then come all this way just to stop when the trail gets hot. Maybe the Builders aren't out near Gargantua—"

"I'm sure they're not. People would have found them when they first explored the Mandel system."

"But *something* is out there. The sphere that took Nenda's ship wasn't just leaving Quake. It was *going* somewhere. I have to find a ship of my own and hustle out there fast. Otherwise I may lose the trail completely."

She was still gripping his arm, hard enough to hurt. "Darya, you can't dash off to Gargantua like that. Not on your own, or you'll kill yourself for sure. The outer part of the Mandel system is cold and hostile. It isn't an easy place, even for experienced explorers. As for you, coming from a nice, civilized world like Sentinel Gate . . ."

Hans Rebka paused. First she booby-trapped him and knocked him unconscious by accident. Then she took him to the waterfall cave, fussing over him and *caring* about him, in a way that no one had ever cared. And now she was booby-trapping him again. He had to be careful and not commit himself to anything.

"I don't know how to find a ship," he said. "It's too much to ask the people on Opal—they have no resources to spare after Summertide. But I'll scratch around and see what I can do."

Darya Lang released his arm, but only because she had other things in mind. Her bear hug was interrupted by a cough from the stairway. Julius Graves had reappeared in the chamber. Close behind him came J'merlia and Kallik.

Graves gestured J'merlia forward. "Go on. Say it for yourself—it's your speech." He turned to Hans Rebka. "I told you they had trouble in mind. And I told *them* that this sort of thing was not my decision, though I do have an opinion."

J'merlia hesitated, until he was given a hard nudge from one of Kallik's spiky elbows, accompanied by a hiss that sounded like "S-s-s-spee-k."

"Indeed I will. Honored Captain." J'merlia was moving to debase himself before Rebka, until a warning growl from Graves stopped him. "Distinguished humans, the Hymenopt Kallik and I face a grave problem. We beg your help, even though we have done nothing to deserve it. We would not do so, if we could see any way to proceed without asking your assistance. Already we have been a burden to you. In fact, by our stupid actions on the planet Quake, we endangered the lives of every—"

This time both the growl and the nudge came from Julius Graves. "Get on with it!"

"Yes, indeed, honored Councilor." J'merlia shrugged at Rebka with a near-human gesture of apology. "The point, distinguished Captain, is that the Hymenopt Kallik and my humble self believed when we left Quake that Louis Nenda and Atvar H'sial had surely been killed, or had decided—as is their perfect right—that they did not choose to make use of our services anymore. Both possibilities were deeply disturbing to us, but we saw no alternative to accepting them. We would then be obliged to return to our homeworlds, and to seek new masters for our services. However, a few minutes ago, we heard that Masters Nenda and Atvar H'sial escaped from the surface of Quake."

"True enough." Rebka looked at Darya. "But Professor Lang saw what happened, and Nenda and Atvar H'sial were killed."

"I know you think that. But Kallik points out that this may not be the case. She notes that if the ship were *gravitationally* accelerated in its departure, the beings inside would feel no forces on them—it would be exactly as though they remained in free-fall. Then they would have been carried away *alive* toward Gargantua, against their wishes, and may now be in need of assistance. And if this is the case, it is the clear duty of the Hymenopt Kallik and my humble self to pursue them. They are our owners. At the very least, we cannot leave the Mandel system until we are assured that they either do not want, or cannot make use of, our services. We therefore ask you, bearing all these facts in mind, and with due consideration of the possibility that—oof!"

J'merlia had received another nudge from Kallik, and the yellow tip of the Hymenopt's poison sting appeared and touched one of J'merlia's hind limbs. He flinched and hopped forward a step.

"Did you know, J'merlia," Julius Graves said in a pleasant conversational tone, "that Professor Lang was for a time convinced that you were incapable of independent speech? Now she is probably regretting that she was wrong."

"I am sorry, Councilor. I am accustomed to the translation of thoughts, not their creation. But in summary, the Hymenopt Kallik and I request that we be allowed to borrow a ship; and we request that we be allowed to follow Masters Nenda and Atvar H'sial to Gargantua, or to wherever their trail may lead."

"No." Rebka answered at once. "Definitely not. I reject your request. Opal is too busy digging out from Summertide to waste time looking around for starships."

Kallik clucked and chirped urgently.

"But that will not be necessary," J'merlia said. "As the Hymenopt Kallik points out, we do not need to descend to Opal. A starship is available—the *Summer Dreamboat*. It is at Midway Station, and it will be easy to return there and restore it to full power. We will find ample provisions on the station, and Kallik and I are sure we can fly the ship."

"With one extra passenger," Darya Lang said. "I'm going along, too."

Rebka glared at her. "You're injured. You're too sick to travel."

"I'm well enough. I'll convalesce on the way to Gargantua. Are you telling me a burned foot would stop *you* from doing your job, if you were in my position?"

"But the *Summer Dreamboat* isn't the property of the Dobelle system." Hans Rebka avoided answering her question and tried another approach. "It's not in my authority, or Max Perry's, to grant you the use of that ship."

"We agree." J'merlia was nodding politely. "Permission would of course have to come from Geni Carmel, who is the owner."

"And what makes you think she would grant it?"

Julius Graves coughed softly. "Well, as a matter of fact, Captain Rebka, I have already discussed that matter with poor Geni. She says she never wants to see or hear about that ship again. It is yours, for as long as you like to use it."

Rebka stared at the other man. Why did everyone seem to assume that he would be going along?

"It's still no, Councilor. So we can get a ship. That makes no difference."

J'merlia bowed his head and groveled lower, while Kallik whistled in disappointment. It was Julius Graves who nodded and said quietly, "That is certainly your decision to make, Captain. But would you be willing to share with me the logic of your thinking?"

"Sure I will. Let me start with a question. You know Louis Nenda and Atvar H'sial. Would *you* go to Gargantua to look for their bodies?"

Rebka's own position was quite clear in his mind. The idea that you should try to find people who had tried to destroy you was all wrong—unless you were proposing to kill them yourself.

"Me, go to Gargantua?" Graves raised his eyebrows. "Certainly not. In the first place, it is imperative that I return to Miranda. My task here is complete. In addition, I regard Atvar H'sial and Louis Nenda as dangerous criminals. If I went to Gargantua—which I do not propose to do, since I believe that they are dead—it would be only to arrest them."

"Very good. I feel the same way. Now, Councilor." Rebka pointed at Kallik. "Do you know how Louis Nenda controlled her? I'll tell you. He used a whip and a leash.

He said Kallik was his pet, but nobody should treat a pet like that. She wasn't an equal to him, and she wasn't a pet. She was a downtrodden and disposable slave. He was quite willing to leave her behind to die on Quake. Before Kallik came to Opal she understood very little of human speech, but only because he had deprived her of the opportunity to learn. And yet it was *Kallik* who performed all the calculations showing that something unique would occur at Summertide. She did that, you know, not Nenda. She's a whole lot smarter than he is. Isn't that true?"

"It is quite true." Julius Graves had a little smile on his face. "Please continue."

"And J'merlia was no better off. The way that he was treated when they arrived on Dobelle was an absolute disgrace. You're the specialist in ethics, and I'm surprised that you didn't notice it before anyone else. Atvar H'sial made J'merlia into a nonentity. Now he speaks freely—"

"That is one way to put it."

"But when the Cecropian was around, J'merlia was afraid to say one word. He was totally passive. All he did was interpret her thoughts to us. He has a mind, but he was never allowed to use it. Let me ask you, Councilor, do you think that Louis Nenda and Atvar H'sial did anything to *deserve* loyalty?"

"They did not."

"And isn't it totally wrong for rational, reasonable beings like J'merlia and Kallik to be treated in that way, with all their actions controlled by others?"

"It is more than wrong, Captain, it is intolerable. And I am delighted to see that you and I hold identical views." Julius Graves turned to the waiting aliens. "Captain Rebka agrees. You are mature, rational beings, and the captain says that it would be totally wrong for you to be controlled by other people. So we cannot dictate your actions. If you wish to take a ship, and seek Louis Nenda and Atvar H'sial, then that is your perfect right."

"Now wait a minute." Rebka saw the grin on the face of Julius Graves and heard a whistle of triumph from Kallik. "I didn't say that!"

"You did, Hans." Darya Lang was laughing at him, too. "I heard you, and so did Councilor Graves. He's right. If it was wrong for Nenda and Atvar H'sial to control Kallik and J'merlia, it would be just as wrong for us to do it. In fact, it would be worse, because we would be doing it more consciously."

Rebka looked around the group, from the mad and misty blue eyes of Julius Graves, to J'merlia and Kallik's inscrutable faces, and finally to the knowing smile of Darya Lang.

He had argued and lost, on all fronts. And curiously, he did not mind. He was beginning to tingle with the curiosity he had felt when they were planning a descent into Paradox. There were sure to be problems ahead; but they would call for action, not the psychological manipulations that Graves found so easy and natural.

And what might they find at Gargantua? That was an open question. Atvar H'sial and Louis Nenda, dead or alive? The Builders themselves? Or mysteries beyond anything on Opal and Quake?

Hans Rebka sighed as the first whistle of atmosphere began along the smooth sides of the capsule. Touchdown was only a few minutes away. "All right, Councilor. We'll drop you, Max, and Geni off on Opal. The rest of us will head back up the Umbilical to Midway Station and the *Dreamboat.* But what's out there at Gargantua . . ."

"Is anybody's guess," Darya said. "Cheer up, Hans. It's like Summertide, and a bit like life. If you knew just what was going to happen, it wouldn't be worth taking the trip."

Divergence

Book Two of
The Heritage Universe

Divergence

Book Two of
The Heritage Universe

CHAPTER 1

"Blink your left eye. Very good. Now close your right eye, hold it closed until I say 'Ready,' and then open it and smile at the same time."

"May I speak?"

"In a moment. *Ready*."

The bright blue eye opened. Thin lips drew back to reveal even white teeth. Sue Ando studied the grinning face for a few seconds, then turned to her assistant. "Now *that* needs attention. It's enough to scare a Cecropian. We need an upward curve on it, make it look more friendly."

"I'll take care of it." The other woman made a note on her computer scratchpad.

"May I speak?"

Ando nodded to the naked male figure standing in front of her. "Go ahead. We want to test your speech patterns anyway. And stop smiling like that—you give me the shivers."

"I am sorry. But why are you going through all this again? It is quite unnecessary. I was thoroughly checked before I left the Persephone facility, and I was found to be physically perfect."

"I should hope so. We don't take rejects. But that was a month ago, and I'm checking for changes. There's always a settling-in period for an embodied form. And you'll be going a long way, to a place where they've probably never even _seen_ an embodiment. If you run into stability problems you won't be able to drop in to a shop for an adjustment the way you can around Sol. All right. One more test, then we have to get you to the briefing center. Look at me and lift one foot off the floor."

As the bare foot was raised, Sue Ando stabbed with her fist at the unprotected jaw. One hand began to move up in self-defense, but it was too slow. Ando's knuckles came into hard contact with the chin.

"Damnation!" She put her fist to her mouth and sucked at the bruised joints. "That _hurt_. Did you feel it?"

"Of course. I have excellent sensory equipment."

"Not to mention tough skin. But now do you see what I mean about settling in to that body? I should never have got within a hand's length of you. A month ago I wouldn't have. Your reflexes need to be turned up a notch. We'll take care of it later today, after your briefing. It will mean popping your brain out for a few minutes."

"If you insist. However, I should mention that my embodied design is intended for continuous sensory input."

"We can arrange that, too. I'll run a neural bundle from your brain to your spine, so you'll receive your sensory feeds for all but the few seconds it takes to plug in the bundle at both ends."

"That will be appreciated. May I speak again?"

"I'm not sure we can stop you. Go ahead, talk as much as you like. Talk is going to be your main mode of communication."

"That is exactly the point I wish to make. I do not understand why I am to be provided with information in such an inefficient manner. I am wholly plug-compatible. With the use of a neural bundle, I can in one second send and receive many millions of data items. Humans are painfully slow. It is truly ridiculous to dole information to me via such a medium, or force me to provide it to another entity at a similar meager rate."

Sue Ando smiled at her assistant's expression. "I know, Lee. You think I ought to tone down his asperity level. But you're wrong. Where he's going annoyance at inefficiency will be a survival trait." She turned to the expressionless male figure. "Sure, you can send and receive faster than we can—to another computer. But you're going to the Dobelle system. It's poor and it's primitive, and I doubt if anyone there has ever seen an embodied computer. They certainly can't afford the facilities for direct data dumps with you. Your sources of information are going to be *humans*, and maybe other Organics. We may be slow and stupid, but you're stuck with us. Get used to that as soon as you can."

She turned back to Lee Boro. "Anything else we need before the briefing?"

Lee consulted her checklist. "Body temperature is a couple of degrees below human normal, but we'll fix that. Ion balances are fine. A name. We ought to settle one before we go any further."

"May I speak?"

Sue Ando sighed. "If you must. We're running out of time."

"I will be brief. Another name is unnecessary. I already have a complete identification. I am Embodied Computer 194, Crimson Series Five, Tally Line, Limbic-Enhanced Design."

"We know that. And I have a complete identification, too. I'm Sue Xantippe Harbeson Ando, human female, Europa homeworld, Fourth Alliance Group, Earth clade. But I wouldn't dream of using that as my *name*, it's three times too long to be useful. Your name is going to be—" She paused. "Something nice and simple. Embodied Computer Tally. E.C. Tally. How's that sound, Lee? E. Crimson Tally, if he wants to get formal."

Lee checked her computer. "It's not taken. I'll make an isomorphism between E. Crimson Tally and the full identification." She entered the note. "E. C. Tally for short. And we'll call you just Tally. All right?"

"May I speak?"

Sue Ando sighed. "Not again. They're waiting for you at the briefing station. All right. What's your problem now? Don't you like that name?"

"The identification that you propose is quite satisfactory. However, I am puzzled by two other things. First, I perceive that I am without clothing, while both of you wear your bodies covered."

"My Lord. Are you telling us you feel *embarrassed*?"

"I do not think so. I lack an internal state corresponding to a condition labeled embarrassment. I merely wonder if I am to wear clothing when in the Dobelle system."

"Unless they don't wear any. You'll do what they do. The whole point of your embodiment is to make you as acceptable to them as possible. What's your other problem?"

"I have been embodied in male human form, and I wonder why."

"For the same reason. You'll mainly be interacting with humans, so we want you to look human. And it's a lot easier to grow your body from a human DNA template, rather than trying to make some inorganic form that comes close to it."

"You have only partially answered my question: namely, you have explained why I am in human form." E. C. Tally pointed down at his genitals. "But as you see, I have been embodied in the *male* figure. The female figure, the one that both you and Lee Boro wear, appears lighter in construction and needs less food as fuel. Since I will be obliged to eat, I wonder why I was provided with the larger and less efficient form."

Sue Ando stared at him. "Hmm. You know, Tally, I don't have any answer to that. I'm sure that the Council has a reason for it, and it's probably got something to do with where you're going. But you should ask during your briefing. One thing's sure, it's too late to change bodies now. You're supposed to get to the Bose Network and head for Dobelle in three days."

"May I speak?"

"Certainly." Ando smiled. "But not now, and not to me. You're overdue with the briefing group. Go on, E. C. Tally. When you get there you can bend their ears as much as you like."

✧✧   ✧

Three standard days before departure: that was seventy-two hours—259 thousand seconds, 259 billion microseconds, 259 billion trillion attoseconds. The grapefruit-sized sphere of E. C. Tally's brain had a clock rate of eighteen attoseconds. Three days should have been enough to ponder every thought that had ever been thought by every organic entity in the whole spiral arm.

And yet Tally was learning that those three days would be insufficient. The hours were flying by. It was not the *facts* that provided the problem, even though they came trickling in with painful slowness from the human intermediary. The difficulty came with their implications, and with the surges they produced in the unfamiliar query circuits added at the time of E. C. Tally's embodiment.

For example, he had been told that the choice of male form had been made because the government of Dobelle was predominantly male. But every analysis of human events suggested that in a male-dominated society the effects of a single female could be maximized. How did Organics manage to ignore the evidence of their own history?

Tally put such ineluctable mysteries to one side, pending the long trip out to his destination. For the moment he would concentrate on the simpler question of galactic power groups.

"Dobelle is a double-planet system, part of the Phemus Circle of worlds." The man providing the briefing was Legate Stancioff, brought in specially from Miranda. He also seemed to Tally to have been chosen specifically for his leaden vagueness in thought and speech. He was staring at Tally with furrowed brow. "Do you know anything about the Phemus Circle?"

Tally nodded. "Twenty-three stellar systems. Primitive and impoverished. Sixty-two habitable planets, some of them marginal. They form a loose federation of worlds, on the overlapping boundary of the territories of the Fourth Alliance, the Cecropia Federation, and the Zardalu Communion. They are roughly one hundred parsecs away from Sol. They contain one Builder artifact, the Umbilical. That artifact is to be found in the Dobelle system."

The machine-gun delivery ended. Those facts, and a million others about the suns and planets of the spiral arm, had been stored in Tally's memory long before he assumed the embodied form, and he had seen no reason to question them. What had just recently been added to his internal states, and what consumed trillions of cycles of introspection time to achieve even partial answers, was the need to examine *motivation*.

The Dobelle system was a planetary doublet, twin worlds known as Opal and Quake that spun furiously about their common center of mass. They were joined by the twelve-thousand-kilometer strand known as the Umbilical. The orbit of their mass center about the star Mandel was highly eccentric, and the time of closest approach to the stellar primary induced prodigious land and sea tides in Quake and Opal. That closest approach was known as Summertide. The most recent Summertide had been an exceptional one, because the approach of Mandel's binary partner, Amaranth, and a gas-giant planet, Gargantua, had led to a lineup of bodies, the Grand Conjunction, that took place only once every 350,000 years.

Very good. Tally knew all that, and he understood it perfectly. Wild as the celestial motions might be, nothing stood in defiance of either logic or physics; to induce such a breakdown, apparently Organics were needed.

"You tell me that a group of humans and aliens converged on Quake and Opal for the last Summertide," he said to Legate Stancioff. "And they went there voluntarily. But *why*? Why would anyone go at that time, when the surfaces of the planets were at their most dangerous? They could have been destroyed."

"We have reason to believe that some of them were."

"But surely humans and Cecropians and Lo'tfians and Hymenopts don't want to die?"

"Of course not." Stancioff was in the human condition that E. C. Tally was coming to recognize as senescence. He was probably no more than ten years away from lapsing to a nontransitional internal state. Already his hands shook slightly as they were talking, in what was clearly a nonfunctional oscillation. "But humans," Stancioff went on, "and aliens, too, I suppose, though I don't actually know many aliens—we take risks, when we feel we have adequate reasons. And they all had *different* interests. Professor Lang, of Sentinel Gate, went to Dobelle because of her scientific interest in Builder artifacts and in Summertide itself. Others, like the Cecropian Atvar H'sial and the augmented Karelian human Louis Nenda, went there, we suspect, for personal gain. The Lo'tfian, J'merlia, and the Hymenopt, Kallik, are slaves. They were present because their masters ordered them to be there. The only beings on Quake in line of official duties were three humans: Commander Maxwell Perry, who controlled all outside access to the Dobelle system at Summertide; Captain Hans Rebka, who is a Phemus Circle troubleshooter sent to Dobelle as Perry's superior; and Councilor Julius Graves, of our own Fourth Alliance, who was present on Council business. Don't you wish to make notes of all these names?"

"It is unnecessary. I do not forget."

"I suppose you don't." Stancioff stared at E. C. Tally. "That must be nice. Now, where was I? Well, never mind. There's a whole lot of information in the files about everyone who was on Quake at Summertide, much more than I know about it. Not one of them ever came back, that's the real mystery, even though Summertide was over weeks ago. We want you to find out why they all stayed. You should study each dossier while you are traveling to Dobelle, and form your own conclusions as to each person's needs and desires."

Needs and desires! Those were exactly what were missing in Tally's internal states; but if they decided so many human and alien actions, he must learn to simulate them.

"May I speak?"

"You've certainly shown no reluctance so far."

"I am perplexed by my suggested role in this matter. At the beginning I understood that I was to go to the

Mandel system and assess the problems there on a logical basis. Now I learn that at least two other individuals are qualified to deal with the problem. Hans Rebka, according to your own words, is a 'troubleshooter,' and Julius Graves is actually a Council member. Given their presence, what do you expect me to accomplish?"

"I am glad you asked that question. It is a good omen for the success of your mission." Legate Stancioff moved out of his chair and came to stand in front of Tally. His hands had stopped shaking, and the vagueness was gone from his manner. "It would be an even better sign if you were to answer the question yourself. Can you do so, if I tell you that on this assignment I am assuming that your weakness may also be your strength?"

After a millisecond of analysis, Tally nodded. "It can only be because I am not an Organic. My *weakness* is my lack of human emotions. Therefore my failure to share organic motivations and emotions is also my strength. You must believe that Graves and Rebka acted from emotion in deciding not to leave the Mandel system."

"Correct. We cannot prove that. But we suspect it." Legate Stancioff placed his hands on Tally's firm shoulders. "You will find out. Go to Dobelle. Learn what you can and report back to us. I do not want to risk another human in finding out what happened at Summertide."

Whereas you, as an embodied computer, are quite expendable.

E. C. Tally was learning. He was able to make that inference within a microsecond. It produced no reaction within him. It could not. If he had no human emotions, he lacked the internal state to resent the suggestion that his loss was acceptable, while a human loss was not. But he began structuring the first simulation circuits. There might be situations where an understanding of human emotions could be useful.

ENTRY 14: HUMAN.

Distribution: Humans, plus derived or augmented forms, can be found in three principal regions of the spiral arm: the *Fourth Alliance,* the *Zardalu Communion,* and the *Phemus Circle.* Of these, the Fourth Alliance is the biggest, the oldest, and the most populous. It includes the whole of *Crawlspace,* the Sol-centered, seventy-two-light-year sphere explored and colonized by humans in sublight-speed ships before the development of the Bose Drive and Bose Network. Almost eight hundred inhabited planets belong to the Fourth Alliance. They lie within an ellipsoid with Sol at one focus, stretching out seven hundred light-years in a direction roughly opposite to that of the galactic center. The supergiant star Rigel sits almost at the farthest boundary of Fourth Alliance territory. Humans are the dominant species of the Fourth Alliance and account for sixty percent of all intelligent beings there.

By contrast, the Phemus Circle consists of just a score of impoverished worlds, ninety percent human, nestled near the part of the Fourth Alliance closest to the center of the galaxy. The Phemus Circle shares a region where the Fourth Alliance, the Cecropia Federation, and the Zardalu Communion all have overlapping territories. It is a measure of the poverty of this group that none of the larger neighbors has shown interest in developing the Phemus Circle, although the Circle is nominally under the control of the Fourth Alliance and recognizes the authority of the Alliance's Council members.

The humans of the Zardalu Communion recognize no central authority. In consequence, their numbers and distribution are difficult. Efrarezi and Camefil estimate that no more than twelve percent of all Zardalu intelligent forms are human. Of these, almost one half live close to the disputed borders with the Fourth Alliance and the Cecropia Federation. The number of worlds inhabited by humans in the region of the Zardalu Communion is unknown.

Physical Characteristics: Humans are land-dwelling vertebrate bisexual quadrupeds possessing bilateral symmetry and a well-marked head and torso. The extremities of the upper limb pair have been modified to permit grasping. All sensory apparatus has low performance and is especially poor for smell and taste. The grelatory organ is entirely absent.

The human form is receptive to modification and augmentation, with a high tolerance of alien tissues. The mutation rate is the highest of any known intelligent species, but this does not seem to be an evolutionary advantage.

History: The origin of the human clade is the planet Earth, which with its sun, Sol, marks the center of the reference-coordinate system employed in this catalog. Human history extends for approximately ten thousand years before the Expansion, with written records available for roughly half that time. Unfortunately, the human tendency for self-delusion, self-aggrandizement, and baseless faith in human superiority over all other intelligent life-forms renders much of the written record unreliable. Serious research workers are advised to seek alternative primary data sources concerning humans.

Culture: Human culture is built around four basic elements: sexual relationships, territorial rights, individual intellectual dominance, and desire for group acceptance. The H'sirin model using just these four traits as independent variables enables accurate prediction of human behavior patterns. On the basis of this, human culture is judged to be of Level Two, with few prospects for advancement to a higher level.

—From the *Universal Species Catalog* (Subclass: Sapients).

CHAPTER 2

Life is just one damned thing after another.

To Birdie Kelly, squelching through the juicy dark mud of the Sling with a food tray balanced in front of him and a message flimsy stuck between the grimy fingers of his right hand, that thought came with the force and freshness of revelation.

One damned thing after another! he repeated to himself. No sooner was his boss, Max Perry, shipped off to the hospital for a couple of weeks of rehab surgery than Birdie found himself nursemaiding an Alliance councilor, no less, from far-off Miranda. Perry had been hard to take, with his obsessive need to work and his fixation about visits to Quake, but Julius Graves was no easier. Worse, in some ways, sitting there talking to himself when he should have been on his way back to Miranda weeks before. There he remained, day after day, loafing about indoors and not lifting a finger to help with the reconstruction work, and all the while ignoring recall messages from his own superiors. He seemed ready to stay forever.

Even so . . .

Birdie paused at the entrance to the building and took a deep breath of damp sea air.

Even so, it was impossible to feel anything other than elated these days. Birdie stared up at the dappled blue sky with Mandel's golden disk showing through broken cloud, then around him at the torn vegetation pushing out new shoots from broken stems. A light breeze roamed in from the west, signaling a perfect day for sailing. He loved it all, and it all seemed too good to be true. Summertide was over, the surface of Opal was returning to its usual tranquility, and Birdie had *survived*. That was more than could be said for half the unfortunate population of the waterworld.

It was more than he had expected for himself. One week earlier, as Summertide reached its climax and the gravity fields of Mandel and Amaranth tore at Opal, Birdie had huddled alone in the prow of a small boat and watched the turbulent surface ahead of him veer from horizontal to near-vertical.

He was a goner and he knew it. Radio signals had warned that the monster was on the way. Tidal forces had created a great soliton, a solitary wave over a kilometer high that was sweeping around the whole girth of Opal. Sling after Sling had sent their last messages, reporting on wave speed and height before the huge but fragile rafts of mud and tangled vegetation were torn apart and fell silent.

There was no way to avoid it. Birdie had crouched in the bottom of the boat, clutching the bottom boards with white-knuckled hands.

The boat's prow tilted up. Thirty degrees, forty-five, sixty. Horizontal and vertical switched roles. Birdie found himself with his feet braced on the boat's stern, his hands holding tight to the centerboard and the little mast. He was lifted, with a two- or three-gee force on his body that went on and on, like a launch from Starside Port to orbit. Rushing water flew past, spray two feet from his nose. For half a minute he was carried up and up, a flyspeck on a wall of ocean, up into Opal's dark clouds. He poised there, forever, unable to see anything as the boat leveled off. At last came the fall, leaving his stomach behind on the downward plunge.

He had been permitted one breathtaking view as they dropped out of the clouds: Opal's seabed lay ahead, exposed by millennial tides, dotted with long-sunken ships and the vast green bodies of stranded Dowsers, unbuoyed by water and crushed by their own multimillion-ton weight. Then he was swooping down a long, foam-flecked slope, toward that muddy wasteland. He knew, even more certainly than before, that he was about to die.

A second, smaller wave, running crosswise to the first, saved him. Before he could be smashed onto the unforgiving seabed, there was a scream of wind and a harsh slap on the boat's rugged stern. He found himself being lifted again in a boiling torrent of warm spray, holding harder than ever, almost unable to breathe. But breathe he did, and held on, too, an hour longer than he would have believed humanly possible, until Summertide was past and the tough little boat had been tossed to calmer waters.

It was something to tell his grandchildren about—if he ever got around to having any.

He had not intended to, but now he might. Only weeks after Summertide, and the social pressure was already on. Every fertile woman would be pregnant within the next month, pushing Opal's population back toward survival level.

Birdie looked up at the calm blue sky and drew in another long, reassuring breath. Perhaps the real miracle was not that he had lived to tell the tale, but that his story seemed to have been repeated again and again across the entire surface of Opal. Some of the Slings, caught in contrary crosscurrents, had been held together by watery whirlpools when all logic suggested they should have been torn apart. Survivors told of flotsam that had come within reach just as their own strength was failing.

Or maybe they had it backward. Birdie had a new insight. Maybe they had hung on, like him, for exactly as long as was necessary until a means of self-preservation came to hand. People who lived in the Dobelle system did not give in easily. They could not afford to.

Birdie pushed the wicker door of the one-story building open with his knee, wiped his muddy shoes on the rush mat in the entrance, and walked through to the inside room.

"Same thing again, I'm afraid: boiled Dowser, grilled Dowser, and fried Dowser, with a bit of Dowser on the side." He placed the tray on a table of plaited reeds. "We'll be eating this stuff for a while, until we can get the fishing boats back into service." He removed the lid of the big dish, leaned forward, and sniffed. His nose wrinkled. "Unless it gets too rotten to eat. Not far to go, if you ask me. Come on, though, dig in. It tastes even worse cold."

The man sitting in the chair beyond the table was tall and bony, with a bald and bulging head burned purplered by hard radiation. His eyes, a faded and misty blue beneath bushy eyebrows, gazed thoughtfully up at Birdie and right through him.

Birdie wriggled. He had not really expected his cheerful comments to elicit a matching reaction from Julius Graves—they never had in the past—but there was no reason for the other man to look so mournful. After all, only a week earlier Graves had survived an experience over on Opal's sister planet, Quake, that by the sound of it had been as harrowing as anything that Birdie had been through. The councilor ought to be filled with the same zest for life, the same satisfaction at being alive.

"Steven and I have been talking again," Graves said. "He has me almost persuaded."

Birdie laid down the message flimsy and helped himself to food. "Oh, yes? What's he been saying, then?"

Steven Graves was another thing that Birdie found hard to take. An interior mnemonic twin was no big deal; it was something employed by a number of other Council members, an added pair of cerebral hemispheres grown and housed within the human skull and coupled to the original brain hemispheres via a new corpus callosum. All it did was provide an extended and convenient organic memory, slower but less bulky than an inorganic mnemonic unit. What it was *not* supposed to do—what it had never done before, to Birdie Kelly's knowledge—was to develop *self-awareness*. But Julius Graves's mnemonic twin, Steven

Graves, not only possessed independent consciousness; on occasion he seemed to take over. Birdie preferred him in many ways. Steven's personality was far more cheerful and jokey. But it was disconcerting not to know who you were talking to at any given time, and although Julius seemed to be in charge at the moment, in another second it might be Steven.

"For almost a week I have been summoning my energy to return to Miranda," Graves said, "to report on my experiences here."

And the sooner the better, matey, Birdie thought. But instead of speaking, he picked up the message flimsy that he had put down on the table, brushing off the dirt and dried black mud that had somehow found their way onto it.

"I had been oddly reluctant to do so," Graves went on, "and I suspect that my instincts knew something denied to my forebrain. But now I think Steven has put his finger—metaphorically speaking—on the reason. It concerns the Awakening, and the ones who went off to Gargantua."

Birdie held out the grimy message. "Speaking of Miranda, this came in about an hour ago. I didn't read it," he said, in an unconvincing afterthought.

Graves scanned the sheet, held it out between finger and thumb, and allowed it to flutter to the floor.

"According to reports I have had since Summertide," he continued, "the awakening of the artifacts ended with that event. For years, Builder artifacts across the spiral arm had been showing signs of increased activity. But now all that stirring has come to an end, and the spiral arm is quiet again. Why? We do not know, but as Steven points out, Darya Lang insisted that the events of this Summertide have an influence beyond this planet, or even this stellar system. The Grand Conjunction of stellar and planetary positions here takes place only once every three hundred and fifty thousand years. Lang did not want humanity to be forced to wait that long for another awakening, and I agreed with her. When she and Hans Rebka decided to follow the sphere that emerged at

Summertide from the interior of Quake, I did not oppose
it. When J'merlia and Kallik requested permission to go
to Gargantua also, to learn whether their former masters
were living or dead, I *encouraged* them and took their
side, although I felt in my heart that this was scarcely
my business. My task was to return to Miranda and report
on the case that brought me here in the first place. But—

"That's what the message is all about." Birdie dropped
the pretense of ignorance. "They want to know why you're
still here. They ask when you'll be leaving. You could be
in a lot of trouble if you don't reply."

Julius Graves ignored him. "But what could be assigned
to me on Miranda half as important as what may be
happening out near Gargantua? To quote Steven again, if
we return to Miranda we will surely be assigned to another
case of interspecies conflict and ethical dilemma. But if
the Builders *are* waiting out at Gargantua, as Darya Lang
insists they must be, then the greatest interspecies meeting
in the history of the spiral arm is waiting with them. The
ethical issues could be vast and unprecedented, and all
these events may be triggered by the arrival of Darya Lang,
Hans Rebka, and the two slaves—unless they have already
been precipitated by the earlier arrival of Atvar H'sial and
Louis Nenda. In either case, my own future action is at
last clear. I must requisition a starship and follow the others
to Gargantua. I do not say this immodestly, but their
interactions could be disastrous without the mediating
influence of a Council member. I therefore ask your
assistance in finding me such a starship, and in outfitting
it suitably for the journey to Gargantua . . ."

Graves was maundering on, but Birdie was hardly
listening. At last, they were going to be rid of a useless
drone—for that's what Julius Graves was proving to be,
even if he did happen to be a Council member. If he
wanted a ship, Birdie could not stop him, though Lord
knows where they would find one, with everything in such
a mess. Birdie would have to do it somehow, because a
councilor could commandeer any local resources that he
or she deemed necessary. Anyway, the temporary loss of

a ship was a small price to pay to get rid of the distracting and the time-wasting influence of Julius and Steven Graves.

" . . . Mr. Kelly, as soon as possible."

The mention of Birdie's own last name jerked his attention back to the other man. "Yes, Councilor? I'm sorry, I missed that."

"I was saying, Mr. Kelly, that I appreciate this to be a time of considerable stress for everyone on Opal. With Starside Port out of action, finding a working spaceship may call for considerable improvisation. At the same time, I hope that you and I can be on our way to Gargantua fairly soon—shall we say, in one standard week?"

"*Me?*" Birdie had not been listening right; he must have missed a key part of what Graves had been saying. "Did you say me? You didn't say me, did you?"

"Certainly. I know that Gargantua and its satellites are already fifty million kilometers away and getting farther every minute, but they still form part of the Mandel system. I discussed the matter with Commander Perry, and although his own duties on Opal prevent him from traveling, he believes a presence from this planet's government is important. He is issuing orders for you to accompany me on his behalf to Gargantua."

Gargantua.

Week-dead Dowser did not taste great at the best of times. Birdie pushed the plate away from him and tried to hold on to what he had already eaten. He stood up. He must have said something to Julius Graves before he found himself once more walking outside the building, but under torture he could not have recalled what it was.

Gargantua! Birdie peered upward, into Opal's blue sky. Mandel was rapidly sinking toward sunset, as Opal and Quake performed their dizzying eight-hour whirl about each other. Somewhere out there, beyond the pleasant blue sky, out where Mandel was diminished to a squinty little point of light, there rolled the gas-giant planet surrounded by its frosty retinue of satellites. They were stark, frozen, lifeless, and dark. Even the best-prepared

expeditions to Gargantua, led by the Dobelle system's most
experienced space travelers, had suffered considerable
casualties. The outer system was simply too remote, too
cold, too inhospitable to human life. Compared with that,
Opal during a Level Five storm felt safe and welcoming.

Birdie stared around him. He knew it all, from the sticky
familiarity of warm black mud underfoot and the thicketed
tangle of vines that began just a few meters from the
building, to the heavy backs of the huge, lumbering
tortoises, making their unhurried way inland through the
undergrowth after surviving Summertide at sea. Birdie
recognized them all; and he loved them all.

Earlier in the day this whole pleasant prospect had
seemed too good to be true. He had just learned that it
was.

CHAPTER 3

The *Summer Dreamboat* had started life as a plaything, a teenager's runabout intended for within-system planetary hops. Everything aboard the ship had been designed with that in mind, from the compact galley, sanitation, and disposal facilities, to the single pair of narrow berths. The addition of a full-fledged Bose Drive had provided the *Dreamboat* with a far-ranging interstellar capability, while whittling the internal space down even further.

Its occupants—or at least the human ones—were cursing that addition now as wasted space. The passage from Dobelle to Gargantua had to be done using the cold-catalyzed fusion drive, which could make no use at all of the Bose interstellar network.

During the second day of the journey Darya Lang and Hans Rebka had retreated to the berths, where they lay side by side.

"Too many legs," Rebka said softly.

Darya Lang nodded. She did not say it, but they both knew the cramped quarters were harder on her. He had grown up on Teufel, one of the poorest and most backward worlds of the Phemus Circle. Hardship and discomfort were to him so natural and so familiar that he did not even recognize their presence. She had been spoiled—though she had never known it, until the past couple of months—by the luxury and abundance of Sentinel Gate, one of the spiral arm's garden planets.

"For me, too many legs," she repeated. "Sixteen too many. And too many eyes for *you*."

He understood at once and touched her arm apologetically. The Lo'tfian, J'merlia, seemed mostly legs and eyes. Eight black articulated limbs were attached to the long, pipestem torso, and J'merlia's narrow head was dominated by the big, lemon-colored compound eyes on short eyestalks. Kallik was just as well-endowed. The Hymenopt's body was short, stubby, and black-furred, but eight wiry legs sprang from the rotund torso, and the small, smooth head was entirely surrounded by multiple pairs of bright, black eyes. Kallik and J'merlia did not mean to get in the way, but when they were both awake and active it was impossible to move around the ship's little cabin without tripping over the odd outstretched appendage.

Darya Lang and Hans Rebka had retreated to the berths as the only place left. But even there they found little privacy—or too little, Darya thought, for Hans Rebka.

The two months since she had left her quiet life as a research scientist on Sentinel Gate had been full of surprises; not least of them was the discovery that many "facts" about life on the backward and impoverished worlds of the Perimeter were just not so. Everyone on Shasta knew that the urge to reproduce dominated everything on the underpopulated planets of the Phemus Circle, where both men and women were obsessed with sex. The rich worlds of the Fourth Alliance "knew" that people on Teufel and Scaldworld and Quake and Opal did it whenever and wherever they could.

Perhaps so, in principle; there was a curious primness in border planet society when it came to practice. Men and women might show immediate interest in each other, from bold eye contact to open invitation. But let the time arrive for *doing* something, in public or even in private, and Darya suspected they were oddly puritanical.

She had obtained positive and annoying proof of that idea when the *Summer Dreamboat* embarked on the long journey to Gargantua. On the first night the two aliens had stretched out on the floor, leaving the berths to Darya and Hans. She lay in her bunk and waited. When nothing happened, she took the initiative.

He rebuffed her, though in an oddly indirect way. "Of course I'd like to—but what about your foot?" he whispered. "You'll hurt it too much. I mean—we can't. Your foot . . ."

Darya's foot had been burned during the retreat from Quake at Summertide. It was healing fast. She resisted the urge to say, "Damn my foot. Why don't you just let *me* be the judge of what hurts too much?"

Instead she withdrew, convinced that Hans came from one of those curious societies where women were not supposed to take the lead in sexual matters. She waited. And waited. Finally, during the next sleep period, she asked what was wrong. Wasn't he interested? Didn't he find her attractive?

"Of course I do." He kept his voice low and glanced across toward the two aliens. As far as Darya could tell they were both sound asleep, in an untidy sprawl of intermeshed limbs. "But what about *them*?"

"What *about* 'em? I hope you're not suggesting they should join in."

"Don't be disgusting. But if they wake up, they'll see us."

So that was it. A privacy taboo, just like the one on Moldave. And apparently a strong one. Hans would not be able to do anything as long as they were cooped up in the ship with J'merlia and Kallik, even though the aliens could have nothing beyond a possible academic interest in human mating procedures.

But their indifference did not change the situation for Hans Rebka. Darya had given up.

"Too many eyes for you," she repeated. "I know. Don't worry about it, Hans. So how much longer before we reach Gargantua?"

"About forty hours." He was relieved to change the subject. "I can't stop wondering—what do you think we are going to find there?"

He looked at Darya expectantly. She had no answer,

though she admitted the justice of his question. After all, she was the one who had actually *seen* the dark sphere gobble up Louis Nenda's ship and head off to Gargantua. Hans had been too busy trying to stop Nenda from shooting them out of the sky. But did she really expect to find the Builders there, now that she'd had plenty of time to think about it?

For Darya, that was the ultimate question. The Builders had disappeared from the spiral arm more than five million years earlier, but she had been pursuing them in one way or another for all of her adult life. It had begun with a single Builder artifact, the Sentinel, visible from her birthworld of Sentinel Gate. Darya had first seen it as an infant. She had grown up with that shining and striated sphere glowing in her night sky. Inaccessible to humans and to all human constructs, the unreachable interior of Sentinel had come to symbolize for her the whole mystery of the lost Builders. Her conviction that Summertide was somehow connected with Builder artifacts had brought her to Dobelle, and the events at Summertide had provided a new insight: the alignment of planetary and stellar positions that caused Summertide was *itself* an artifact, the whole stellar system a construct of the long-vanished master engineers.

But Hans Rebka's question still demanded an answer. Had she become so obsessed with the Builders, and everything to do with them, that she saw Builder influence everywhere? It was not uncommon for a scientist to live with a theory for so long that it took control. Data and observations were forced to fit the theory, rather than being used to test it and if necessary reject it. How did she know she was not guilty of that same failing?

"I know what I saw, Hans. But beyond the evidence of my eyes—however you weight that—all I can offer are my own deductions, however you weight *them*. Can you pick up an image of Gargantua with the external sensors?"

"Should be able to." He craned his head around. "And we ought to be able to look at it right here—we're line-of-sight for the projectors. Don't move. I'll be back in a minute."

It did not take that long. Twenty seconds at the display controls of the *Summer Dreamboat* gave Hans Rebka a three-dimensional image in the space above the twin berths. He carried the remote control unit over to Darya, letting her use it to pinpoint the target and zoom as she chose.

The planet sat in the center of the globe of view. And what a change since the last time that Darya had seen it. Then the light of Gargantua had been screened by the protective filters of the *Dreamboat*'s viewing port. The planet had been gigantic, sure enough, bulking across half the field of view, but it had also been faint, faded to a spectral shade by the brilliant torrents of light sleeting in from Mandel and Amaranth. Now Gargantua was a sphere not much bigger than Darya's thumbnail, but it glowed like a jewel, rich oranges and ochers of high-quality zircon and hessonite against a black background scattered with faint stars. There was just a hint of banding to mark the axis of the planet's rotation, and the four bright points of light in suspiciously accurate alignment with the equator had to be Gargantua's major satellites. Darya knew that a thousand other sizable fragments of debris orbited closer to the planet, but from this distance they were invisible. Their paths must have become a monstrous jumble after the perturbations of periastron passage close to Mandel and Amaranth.

Not the harmony of the spheres, but a rough charivari of tangled orbits. Navigation through them would be a problem.

She studied the image, then used the remote marker to indicate a point a quarter of a radius away from the planetary terminator.

"When the ray of light first appeared, it came from just about there." She closed her eyes for a moment, recalling what she had seen. "But it wasn't ordinary light, or it would have been invisible in empty space. I could see it all the way, and I could follow its line right back to that point."

"But couldn't it have come from a lot farther away—way out past Gargantua?"

"No. Because by the time the silver sphere turned into a hole in space, swallowed up Louis Nenda's ship, and zoomed off along the light-line, the ray's point of origin had *moved*. It was right next to Gargantua by the time I lost sight of it. The only way you can explain that is if it came from something *in orbit* around Gargantua."

Darya closed her eyes again. She had a bit of a headache, and recalling the last desperate minutes close to Summertide had somehow made her dizzy and disoriented. Her eyes did not want to focus. She must have been staring for too long at the image on the display. She squinted up at Gargantua. The giant planet was receding fast from Mandel, on a complex orbit controlled both by Mandel and its dwarf stellar companion. But the *Dreamboat* was moving faster yet. It was catching up.

"A few more hours, Hans." She suddenly felt slow and lazy. "Just a few more hours. We'll start to see all the little satellites. Begin to have an idea where we're going. Won't we?" She was puzzled by her own words, and by the odd sound of her own voice. "Where are we going? I don't know where we're going."

He did not answer. She made a big effort and turned to him, to find that he was not looking at her at all. He was staring at J'merlia and Kallik.

"Still asleep," he said.

"Yeah. Still asleep." Darya smiled. " 'S all right, Hans, I'm not going to attack you."

But he was sitting up and swinging his legs over the side of the bunk. His face was redder than usual, and the line of the scar that ran from his left temple to the point of his jaw showed clearly.

"Something's wrong. Kallik never sleeps for more than half an hour at a time. Stay there."

She watched as he hurried over to the central control panel of the *Dreamboat*, studied it, and swore aloud. He reached forward. There was a whir of atmospheric conditioners, and Darya felt a cold and sudden draft in her face. She muttered a protest. He ignored her. He was bending over the inert forms of J'merlia and Kallik; then, suddenly, he appeared at her side again.

"How are you feeling? Come on, sit up,"

Darya found herself being levered to an upright sitting position. The chilly air brought her to fuller wakefulness, and she shivered. "I'm all right. What's wrong?"

"Atmosphere. The ship took a real beating when we lifted off from Quake. Something was knocked out of whack in the air plant. I've put in a temporary override, and we'll do manual control till we know what happened."

For the first time, his urgency reached through to her.

"Are we all right? And Kallik and J'merlia?"

"Now we are, all of us. We're quite safe. But we weren't. Maybe J'merlia and Kallik could have breathed what we were getting a few minutes ago—they have a high tolerance for bad air—but you and I couldn't. Too much monoxide. Another half hour like that, we'd have been dead."

Dead! Darya felt a cold wave across her body, nothing to do with the chilly cabin breeze. When they had faced death at Summertide, the dangers had been obvious to all of them. But Death could arrive in other ways, never making an appointment or announcing his presence, creeping in to take a person when she was least expecting him . . .

She could not relax. Hans Rebka had stretched out on the bunk again by Darya's side. She moved close to him, needing human contact. He was breathing hard, and a moment later they were touching along most of their bodies. She could feel him trembling. But then she realized that the tremors were in his hands, touching her face and reaching beneath her shirt to her breasts. In the next few seconds it became obvious that he was highly excited.

They clung to each other without speaking. Finally Darya craned her head up, to stare past Hans at the sleeping forms of J'merlia and Kallik.

What about them—suppose they wake up? She was on the point of saying it. She caught herself. Shut up, dummy. What are you trying to do?

She made one concession to modesty, reaching up past him to turn the light off above the bunks. He did not seem to care; after a few more seconds, neither did Darya. Neither, she was sure, did J'merlia and Kallik.

An hour later the two aliens were still asleep. So was Hans. Darya lay with her eyes closed, reflecting that one aspect of male human behavior varied little from Fourth Alliance to Phemus Circle.

And I'm beginning to understand him better, she thought. He's a sweet man, but he's a strange one. A close call from death doesn't frighten him. It makes him *excited*—excited enough to ignore his own taboos. I don't think he gave Kallik and J'merlia one thought . . . nor did I, for that matter. I suppose it's not the approach of death that's the stimulus, it's the knowledge that you *survived* . . . Maybe that's the way with all the men of the Perimeter worlds, and the women, too. It certainly worked well for Hans.

She smiled to herself. Pity it didn't work for me. Death doesn't excite me, it scares me. I enjoyed myself, but I didn't even come close. Never mind. There'll be other chances.

At last she opened her eyes. They had not bothered to turn off the projection unit. Gargantua hung above her head, perceptibly bigger. She could see the markings on the swollen face, and the planet had turned a quarter of a revolution since the last time she had looked at it. The huge and permanent atmospheric vortex known as the Eye of Gargantua sat in the center of the disk. It was staring straight at her: orange-red, hypnotic, baleful.

Darya found herself unable to breathe.

So there'll be other chances, will there? the Eye's expression said. *Don't count on it. I know something about death, too.*

CHAPTER 4

E. Crimson Tally: Permanent record for transfer upon return to Persephone.

Today I reached my initial destination, the planet Opal of the Dobelle system. Today I also drew a major and disturbing conclusion concerning my mission.

It is this: The decision made by Senior Technician Sue Xantippe Harbeson Ando was an appropriate one, although not for the reasons she gave me. For it turns out that the slow, inefficient method of information transfer via human channels yields information that I would never have received by direct access to the data banks. This is true for a simple reason: *some important information is not in the data banks.*

The central data banks of the Fourth Alliance are incomplete! Who could have foreseen that? Worse still, I now have reason to believe that they are sometimes *in error*, so much so that I can no longer rely on them.

I would now like to present the evidence that supports these conclusions.

Item one: My journey to Opal required that I pass through four transition points of the Bose Network. This I knew before departure. The data banks had also indicated that each Bose Transition Point serves as a nexus for the transportation of different species; thus members of the Cecropia Federation and the Zardalu Communion might be encountered there, as well as humans of the Fourth Alliance and the Phemus Circle.

This information proved accurate. At the third transition point, 290 light-years from Sol, in a region already verging on the Phemus Circle zone and adjoining both Fourth Alliance and Cecropia Federation territories, I saw and recognized Cecropians, Lo'tfians, Varnians, Hymenopts, and Ditrons.

The data banks make the relationship between these species very clear. Lo'tfians and Ditrons serve as slave species to Cecropians. Hymenopts and Varnians are sometimes free beings, but are usually slave to humans living in the territories of the Zardalu Communion. (Slave to the land-cephalopod Zardalu also, should any still exist; but none has been encountered since the Great Rising, in pre-Expansion times.)

The data banks also make it clear that, despite the independence of the Cecropian and Zardalu clades, all these species recognize the superiority of humans of the Fourth Alliance. They defer to them, acknowledging the higher nature of human intellect and achievements, and regarding Earth and surrounding Alliance territories as the cultural and scientific center of the spiral arm.

That is not the case! I, a Fourth Alliance human in outward appearance, received no preferential treatment whatsoever. In fact, quite the opposite. In the great terminus of Bose Access Node 145, I emerged to find an overcrowded transit point. To reach my required departure zone it was necessary for me to pass close to a group of other travelers, Cecropians, Zardalu humans, and Hymenopts prominent among them. My request for prompt passage was ignored. More than that, a Cecropian pushed me out of the way as though I did not exist!

When I remonstrated to another human traveler, he said, "Your first trip, is it? You're going to run into a lot of things that aren't in the travel guides. Or they're going to run into you, like that Cecropian." He laughed. "As far as she's concerned, you don't exist, you see. Humans are missing the right pheromones for Cecropians to detect, so they consider we're hardly there. And anyway, since they're an older civilization than humans, they kind of look down on us. Don't ever hope for politeness from a Cecropian. She knows you're an upstart little monkey. And get out of the way if she pushes; she's a lot bigger than you."

I do not believe that I could have received such information, except directly from a human source. It is totally inconsistent with the perspective offered by the central data base.

Item two: The Fourth Alliance central data bank indicates that Alliance science is superior to that of the other clades, and that Alliance technology is even more so.

I am forced to dispute that notion.

The first three Bose Transition Points that I passed through after leaving Sol-space were constructed and operated by Fourth Alliance humans. The fourth one, as I learned upon my arrival, was built and is maintained by the Cecropia Federation. With time to spare before my shuttle ship to Dobelle, I studied this transition point in some detail. It is obvious that the facility is technologically at least the equal of the Fourth Alliance nodes; operationally it is far better designed. Moreover, it is cleaner, safer, and less noisy.

The data bank is again misleading, for a reason I cannot conjecture. Alliance technology is not universally superior, and in at least some instances is inferior. But direct observation was necessary to draw that conclusion.

Item three: The data base indicates that humanity reached the stars employing carefully constructed and logical theories of the nature of the physical world. The laws of physics, mathematics, and logic underpin all human activities, says the data base, no matter how diverse the application.

I believe those facts may be accurate, as they relate to human *history*. But they seem irrelevant to current human actions on Opal. Indeed, from recent conversations I deduce that they apply little anywhere in the Phemus Circle. Either humans here are deranged, or they operate with a subtlety of logic beyond anything to be found in the files of the central data base.

These disturbing conclusions are drawn from my own direct observations, supplemented by discussion with natives concerning the recent traumatic events known as Summertide, as follows:

The dangers of Summertide were enormous. Death and destruction were planetwide and appalling. A logical race would have concluded that Opal is not a world suitable for human occupation and would have begun birth-limitation procedures in preparation for relocation to some new planetary environment. Such action would be consistent with the profiles of a logical humanity, as described in the central data banks.

And what did the people of Opal do, once Summertide was over? They embarked on a reproductive orgy, one guaranteed to raise the population in a few years' time and thereby make it far more difficult to evacuate the planet. They justify this by professing—and perhaps, in truth, feeling—a powerful affection for the very place that recently killed so many of their friends and families.

And to "celebrate" their own survival, they have been inhaling and ingesting large quantities of addictive drugs and powerful carcinogens, thereby substantially shortening their already diminished life expectancies. Suspecting that for some reason the natives might be misleading me, as a newcomer, about the effects of these substances, I ingested a small amount myself on an experimental basis. My metabolism was seriously impaired for several hours.

Those ill effects were not, I should add, a consequence of my different background and origins. Indeed, I find that a similar impairment is common among the natives. And far from being puzzled by their own contralogical activities, they actually proclaim them to one another— unashamedly, and often in boastful terms.

Item four: The central language banks claim to be complete, with a full and idiomatic representation of every form of written and spoken communication in the spiral arm.

That cannot be true, for this reason: Upon my arrival on Opal, I met with a human male who identified himself as Commissioner Birdie Kelly. He informed me that of the names given to me as potential contacts, all but one were either presumed dead, or away exploring other parts of the Mandel system. The single exception is Councilor Julius Graves, and I will be meeting with him in a few hours' time. That was good to know, and I said so.

I had no trouble understanding every word of my conversation with Commissioner Kelly. Certainly there was no reason to assume that recent language changes on Opal might be causing miscommunication between us.

However, after a meeting of a little less than twenty minutes, the commissioner told me that he had another appointment. I left. And once I was outside the room he spoke, presumably to himself. He must have believed me to be out of earshot, but I was grown from first-rate genetic stock and my hearing is more sensitive than that of most humans.

"Well, Mister E. C. Tally," he said. "'May I speak,' indeed. May I babble, more like. You're a funny duck, and no mistake. I wonder why you flew in."

A duck is an animal indigenous to Earth, imported to Opal where it thrives. Clearly, a human being is not a duck, nor does a human closely resemble one. And since I resemble a human, I cannot therefore be mistaken for a duck. It is not easy to see how Commissioner Birdie Kelly could make such an error, unless the language banks themselves contain errors.

These matters call for introspection.

CHAPTER 5

The universe is all extremes. Monstrous gravity fields,
or next-to-nothing ones; extreme cold, or heat so intense
that solids and liquids cannot exist; multimillion atmosphere pressures, or near-vacuum.

Ice or fire. Niflheim or Muspelheim: the ancient alternatives,
imagined by humans long before the Expansion.

It's *planets* that are the oddities, the strange neutral
zone between suns and space, the thin interface where
moderate temperatures and pressures and gravity fields
can exist. And if planets are anomalies, then planets *able
to support life* are rarer yet—a zero-measure subset in
that set of strangeness.

And within that alien totality, where do humans fit?

"Willing to share your thoughts?" Hans Rebka's voice
interrupted Darya's bleak musings.

She smiled but did not speak. She had been gazing out
of the port of the *Summer Dreamboat*, her head filled with
the unsatisfying present and the far-off dreams of Sentinel
Gate. She was 800 light-years from home. Instead of the
Sentinel, Gargantua filled the sky, as big as at Summertide
and far more dominant. The Eye was a smoky whirlpool
of gases, wide enough to swallow a dozen human worlds.

"You want me to help you?" she asked.

"You couldn't if you wanted to." Hans Rebka jerked
his head toward the control panel. "They won't let me
get near it. I think Kallik's having fun."

It was nice to know that someone was. The arrival in orbit around Gargantua had depressed Darya enormously—to come so far, with such vague goals, and then find nothing toward which she could point and say, "There! That's it. That's just what I hoped we'd find here."

Instead they had found what she should have expected. A planet, big enough to be at the fusion threshold, unapproachable by humans because of its dense, poisonous atmosphere and giant gravity field. Dancing attendance on Gargantua were its four major satellites, with their own atmospheres and oceans; but the air was mostly nitrogen, plus an acrid photochemical smog of ethane and hydrogen cyanide, and the oceans were liquid ethane and methane. The surfaces, recently heated by close approach to Mandel and Amaranth, were dropping back to a couple of hundred degrees below freezing.

If they were to find anything, the best bet was on one of the hundreds of smaller, airless satellites. Kallik and J'merlia were patiently identifying those, tagging each with its own set of orbital elements for future identification; the intertwining orbits were impossible to follow by eye, and a tough job even for the *Dreamboat*'s computer. Finally the team would examine "anything interesting," which was the vague criterion that Darya had provided.

"How many have they done?" Darya was not too sure she wanted to hear the answer. Because when they had worked their way through all the larger fragments she had no suggestion as to what they should do next, beyond the bitter option of an empty-hands return to Dobelle.

Hans Rebka shrugged, but J'merlia had heard the question. The lemon eyes turned on their short eyestalks. "Forty-eight."

He went on to answer the unasked question. "At this time, we have found nothing. Not even a prospect of high-value mineral deposits."

Of course not. Don't be so dumb, J'merlia. This is part of the Phemus Circle, remember? Metal-poor and mineral-poor and everything-poor. The whole Mandel system had been scoured for metals and minerals back

when it was first colonized. If anything had been out here
it would have been mined and picked clean centuries ago.

Darya managed not to say all that. She realized that
she was angry with everything. She began to feel guilty.
The two aliens were doing all the work, while she sat
back, watched, and complained. "How many still to go,
J'merlia?"

"Hundreds, at least. Every time we look more closely we
find more small bodies. And each one is a time-consuming
task. The problem is the orbital elements—we need many
minutes of observation before we can assign them accurately.
And we need accuracy, because the fragments move. We
have to be sure we are not missing one, or doing some of
them twice. The old catalogs help, but the recent perturbations make them unreliable."

"Then we'll probably be sitting here for a long time—
at least a few days. What do you think, Hans? Maybe it's
time to pick one of the planetoids, somewhere we can
spread ourselves a bit until the search is over. We've got
suits with us; at least we can stretch our legs and get out
of each other's hair for an hour or two."

"We already have a . . . ck-candidate for such a place."
Kallik had also been listening and watching. Her command
of human speech was approaching perfection, but it could
still betray her occasionally in moments of excitement.
"We noted it when we first . . . ss-saw it. J'merlia?"

The Lo'tfian nodded. "It was already in the old catalog.
It carries an identification as Dreyfus-27, and at one time
a survey expedition used it as a base of operations. There
should be tunneling, perhaps an airtight chamber. It can
be reached from our present orbit with a minimal energy
expenditure. Would you like to see its stored description?"

Darya had accepted J'merlia's suggestion with indecent
haste. She knew that, but she didn't regret it. Motion,
bustle, activity, that was what she needed at the moment—
even if it *was* only motion and bustle, something as useless
as fixing up a barren lump of rock so that humans and
aliens might call it home for a few days.

Close approach to Dreyfus-27 had confirmed the data suggested by the *Summer Dreamboat*'s remote sensors. The planetoid was a dark, cratered body only ten kilometers in diameter, swinging in low orbit around Gargantua. A thousand years before, traces of nickel and iron in the outer layers of Dreyfus-27 had encouraged prospectors to drill the interior. The rubble and tailings that still formed a meters-deep coat to the planetoid's rugged surface showed that no deposits worth refining had been found, but the automated drilling equipment of the miners had not given up easily. Dreyfus-27 had been tunneled and retunneled, carved and bored and fractured and drilled until dozens of crisscrossing shafts and corridors and chambers riddled the inside.

Without air and appreciable gravity, those tunnels had not changed since the day they had been abandoned. The new arrivals could read the final frustration of the miners in the jumbled heaps of debris and half-completed living quarters. The prospectors had started out with high hopes, enough for them to plan a permanent base appropriate to extended mining operations. Those hopes had slowly evaporated. One day they had just downed tools and left. But although they had stopped halfway in making Dreyfus-27 fully habitable, their efforts were more than enough for the short-term needs of the crew of the *Dreamboat*.

"Seal it at the top, and this will do," Darya said. She and J'merlia had found an almost empty cylindrical chamber with a narrow entrance, five meters below the surface, and had tested the walls to make sure that they could hold the pressure of an atmosphere. "The thermal insulation is as good as the day it was installed. Let's go back up. Once we pump some air in here we can open our suits. That will be wonderful."

She looked around her. The chamber was clear of major rock fragments, but powdery grit covered the passivine wall lining and flew up at every contact and vibration.

Wonderful? she thought. My God, I'm slipping down the ladder, rung by rung. A couple of months ago I'd have been appalled at the idea of spending ten minutes in a place like this. Now I can hardly wait to settle in.

J'merlia was already at home. The Lo'tfians were a burrow race, and the land surface of their home planet formed one vast, interconnected warren. He had been scuttling excitedly from one chamber and corridor to the next. Now he nodded his head and led the way back up the weak gravity gradient.

Darya, less nimble in free-fall, was left far behind. When she came close to the surface she was surprised to find the tunnel illuminated from outside. Dreyfus-27 was tumbling slowly around its long axis, with a period of a little more than one hour. When they had gone down into the interior of the planetoid, Gargantua had filled the sky above their entry tunnel; now the shaft was lit at its upper end by the fading and wintry sunlight of Mandel.

The ship hovered where they had left it, moored a hundred meters above the surface. Darya took the connecting cable and pulled herself easily along it. J'merlia was still in the tiny airlock when she got there, and she had to wait outside until the lock cycle was completed. She looked down. From this height she could see most of one irregular hemisphere of Dreyfus-27. The wan light made the surface more than ever into a jumbled wasteland of broken rocks. Harsh contours of light and dark were hardly softened by the microscopic dust particles and ice crystals thrown up by the arrival of the *Summer Dreamboat*. There were hundreds of other sizable fragments in orbit around Gargantua, all of them presumably much like this one. Was she crazy, to imagine that the secrets of the vanished Builders might be hidden in such a desert?

Hans Rebka was standing by the lock when she emerged from it. Darya switched her suit to full open and waited a couple of seconds for two-way transparency to be established.

"J'merlia says you found something good," Rebka began. "He's really excited."

"I thought it was a mess—just a whole labyrinth of

tunnels. But he loved it down there. I guess it's like home for him. Look at them now."

J'merlia had moved across to the ship's control panel, where Kallik was sitting in a sprawl of extended legs, exactly as she had been when Darya left. For the past two days the Hymenopt had been painstakingly locating, tracking, and monitoring the minor satellites of Gargantua, never moving from her position at the controls. Now the Lo'tfian and the Hymenopt were chattering excitedly together, in the clicks and whistles of the latter's own language that neither Darya nor Hans had mastered. The whistling and chittering grew louder and more intense, until Darya said, "Hey, stop that, you'll deafen us," and added to Rebka, "I sure didn't see anything all *that* exciting in the interior."

He nodded. "What's with them? J'merlia! Kallik! Calm down."

J'merlia gave one final, earsplitting whistle before he turned to the humans. "Apologies, our sincere apologies. But Kallik has wonderful news. She picked up a signal, two minutes ago—from the *Have-It-All!*"

"Louis Nenda's ship? I don't believe it." Rebka moved across the cabin to stand by the control panel. "Darya said they were accelerated away from Quake at hundreds of gees. Any signal equipment inside that ship would have been crushed flat."

The Hymenopt's smooth black head turned to face the humans. "Not ss-so. I found a definite ss-signal, although a very weak one."

"You mean the *Have-It-All* is there, but in trouble?"

"Not necessarily in trouble. It is not a distress beacon, it is intended only to aid location."

"Then why didn't we pick it up earlier, when you did a scan of the entire region?"

"Because it becomes activated by an input ss-signal. Our first s-scan was passive, using reflected stellar radiation. But now I am using active microwave, to scan the surface of rock fragments for composition and detailed images."

The Hymenopt's mandibles gaped with excitement and joy. "With apologies and respect, we cannot hide our pleasure. The sh-ship was not destroyed! It survives, it has power, it must be in good ck-ck-condition. Just as J'merlia and I hoped, our masters may not have died at Summertide. Louis Nenda and Atvar H'sial may be alive— and just a few hours' flight away!"

ENTRY 37: LO'TFIAN.

Distribution: The center of Lo'tfian civilization, and the only habitat of the species' females, remains the minor planet *Lo'tfi*. Since these females are exclusively burrow dwellers, the planetary surface reveals no sign of their presence; the subterranean regions of the planet, however, are believed to have been extensively modified as breeding and metamorphosis warrens. There is no direct proof of this, since no non-Lo'tfian has ever entered the burrows.

Male Lo'tfians are to be found in large numbers roaming the surface of Lo'tfi, and in small numbers on every world of the Cecropia Federation and Fourth Alliance where Cecropians interact with other intelligences of the spiral arm.

Physical Characteristics: The physical form of Lo'tfian females is not known by direct examination, though they are certainly blind and exceed the males in size and probably in intelligence. The general physiology is believed to resemble that of the Lo'tfian males.

The males are thin-bodied, eight-legged arthropods, with excellent hearing and vision. They have an ability to communicate pheromonally, which makes them the preferred interpreters for Cecropians. Their two lidless compound eyes can be individually or jointly focused, enabling either stereo sight or simultaneous monocular viewing of two fields of vision. The eyes have spectral sensitivity from 0.29 to 0.91 micrometers, permitting them to see something of both ultraviolet and infrared radiation. (The Lo'tfian "rainbow" distinguishes eleven colors, compared with the conventional ROYGBIV seven of humans.)

The blind Lo'tfian females are known to be highly intelligent. The intellectual level of the Lo'tfian males, however, is a much-debated subject. On the one hand, until the arrival of Cecropians on Lo'tfi, no Lo'tfian exhibited curiosity toward anything beyond the planet. This is understandable for the burrowing females, but not for the males who roamed the surface and saw stars and planets every night. In addition, Lo'tfian male interpreters for Cecropians function as pure translation devices, never commenting on or adding to the statements of their masters.

On the other hand, Lo'tfian males are superb linguists, and when deprived of their Cecropian dominatrixes they are certainly capable of independent thought and action. Male Lo'tfians who are taken off-planet are illiterate, but they pick up reading and writing so easily and rapidly that these abilities are surely part of their genetic stock.

The prevailing theory to resolve this paradox comes from limited studies of Lo'tfian physiology. The male brain, it is believed, is highly organized and possesses powerful intelligence. However, it contains an unknown physical inhibitor, chemical in nature, that forbids the employment of that intelligence when in the presence of a Lo'tfian female. Confronted by such a female, the reasoning ability of the male Lo'tfian simply switches off. (A much weaker form of this phenomenon has been attributed to other species. See *Human* entry of this catalog.) The same mechanism is believed to be at work to a lesser extent when the Lo'tfian male encounters Cecropians and other intelligences. If this theory is true, no one is ever exposed to full Lo'tfian intelligence in face-to-face meetings with them.

History: From other evidence on the planet Lo'tfi, the planet's dominant organisms are members of an old race, existing in their present physical form and enjoying their present life patterns for at least ten million years. If there are written records, they are maintained in the burrows by the dominant females and are unavailable to outside inspection.

Culture: Lo'tfian males living on the surface of their home planet or absent from it display no interest in mating. They are in a mature form they refer to as "Second Stage" or "Postlarval." Since the adult form of the species possesses two well-defined sexes, and since it is highly unlikely that the burrow-dwelling larval stage prior to metamorphosis is capable of reproduction, mating presumably takes place when the males return to the burrows carrying food. At that time, male intelligence is inhibited and sex drives will dominate. Since Lo'tfian females are continuously intelligent, they define and control all Lo'tfian culture.

It is interesting to speculate on the social organization that might be set up by a group of Lo'tfian males, far removed from their females or other intelligent beings. These speculations remain academic, since such circumstances have not so far arisen and are unlikely to do so. Male Lo'tfians become agitated and exhibit irrational behavior when access to intelligent companions, of their own or other species, is denied them.

—From the *Universal Species Catalog* (Subclass: Sapients).

CHAPTER 6

A journey out to Gargantua sounded difficult and
dangerous. Birdie Kelly had been dreading the prospect.
As he got to know Julius and Steven Graves better he
liked the idea even less; and when E. C. Tally's presence
on the trip was thrown in for good measure, Birdie's level
of apprehension was raised to new heights.

Yet that final addition proved to be the saver. In some
way that Birdie could not explain, Steven Graves and E.
C. Tally canceled each other out. Maybe it was because
they never stopped arguing. The annoyance level of their
arguments was enough to reduce most other irritations
to background level, and it allowed Birdie to take his mind
off the unpleasant reality of the journey.

That reality had started even before they lifted off from
Opal. All three had gone to the edge of one of the Slings,
to inspect the ship that Birdie had been offered for the
journey. Tally had lagged behind the other two, showing
an unnatural interest in a species of domestic waterfowl
swimming just offshore.

"You're saying he's a bloody robot!" Birdie complained,
when he was sure he could not be overheard. "Well, why
didn't somebody tell me that when he first arrived? No
wonder he comes across like such an idiot."

"He's not a robot." Julius Graves was eyeing the
interplanetary transit vessel with disfavor. The ship was
certainly big—ten times the size they needed—but the

outer hull was scarred and rusted. On Miranda it would have seen the scrap heap a century earlier. "I really shouldn't have said anything at all, except that sometime it might be important for you to know. E. Crimson Tally is an embodied computer. His available data base should be huge, even though he lacks human experience and local knowledge."

"Same difference. Computer, robot. And data base about what? He doesn't seem to know anything useful."

"He's not a computer, or a robot. He has a human body."

Birdie shuddered. "That's awful. Whose was it before he got it?"

"Nobody's. It was grown for him from a library template." Graves had climbed up to stare through a hatch into the ship's vast and desolate interior. He sniffed. "Phew. What did you say this was used for last time?"

"Ore freighter." Birdie peered in. "At least, that's what they told me. Can't imagine what sort of ore looked like that. Or smelled like it." He pulled his head out fast. Even he was impressed by the filth inside. "But I still don't know what Tally's doing here."

"Blame me for that. If I had returned to Miranda as planned, E. C. Tally would have gone with me. He tells me that he was sent to Opal with three goals. First, to determine firsthand the significance of recent events here; second, to accompany me wherever I go; and third, to bring me back with him to Alliance headquarters." Graves rubbed his hand over the hatch cover and stared at the results with distaste. "Look, this won't do. The whole inside will have to be cleaned out completely before it's fit for use."

"No problem."

No problem, because Birdie knew that the chances of getting anyone to clean it out were zero; but there was no point in telling that to Graves. It occurred to Birdie that he would willingly settle for the last of those three stated mission objectives for E. C. Tally—all his own problems would go away if only Graves and Tally would just *leave*. And didn't it display the most monstrous and the most typical gall, for the Alliance Council to sit hundreds of light-years away and try to call the shots through a half-witted robot?

Tally's next act had not helped his popularity with Birdie. He had finished his puzzled inspection of the ducks, then wandered over to examine the inside and outside of the ship.

"May I speak?" he said at last.

Birdie swore. "Will you for God's sake stop *saying* that? Even when I say no, you speak anyway."

"My apologies, Commissioner Kelly. Since my request for some reason causes you discomfort, I will try to desist . . . even though politeness was a basic element of my prime indoctrination. However, I am sure you will be interested in what I have to say now. I have been engaged in computation and analysis. Based on this ship's history and current condition, I calculate a sixty-six percent chance of catastrophic failure on any extended journey, such as that planned to the planet Gargantua."

Julius Graves gave a loud grunt of disapproval. Birdie shuddered and felt inclined to echo it. Had he survived Summertide, then, only to be wiped out in space? Not if he could help it. But surely he didn't need to do anything. This was the moment where Graves would exercise his override authority as a council member and veto the whole journey, no matter what E. C. Tally wanted to do. It was unacceptably dangerous.

"I am sorry, Tally," Graves said—there, he was going to use his authority, just the way Birdie had hoped. "But we are forced to take exception to your statement. Steven calculates that there is a *sixty*-percent chance of catastrophic failure—no more!"

"I beg to differ." Tally looked down his well-designed nose at Graves. "I think that if you itemize the parameter inputs appropriate to the case, as follows, you will find these additional sources of danger . . ."

And away they went.

The Steven Graves vs. E. Crimson Tally stakes; that was the way Birdie was coming to think of it. As the *Incomparable*—Birdie was inclined to agree with that name for the rotting hulk—creaked and groaned its smelly and rust-covered way to the outer system, Steven Graves and E. C. Tally went on with their endless arguments.

Who was the winner? Birdie was not sure. The trip out to Gargantua was long and—thank God!—uneventful, and there were few people around to argue the point with. From sheer perversity Birdie went to an unlikely source—and consulted Julius Graves about the Steven-Tally dispute.

The councilor took the question perfectly seriously, wrinkling his bald, scarred forehead before he replied.

"I believe that I can be impartial. And I think it is a standoff. E. C. Tally has the advantage over Steven when it comes to anything involving computational speed—which is no surprise, given that his basic circuitry is many trillions of times as fast. The real surprise is that Steven can do as well as he does. So far as I can tell—Steven and I have discussed this several times—Tally employs direct formula computation whenever possible. Steven, on the other hand, makes extensive use of precomputed and memorized lookup tables and interpolation. Normally Tally will reach a conclusion faster on anything calling for straight computation—but not always.

"Steven's advantage comes in other areas. Like any human, he enjoys a degree of parallelism that no computer, embodied or not, has ever achieved. To take one simple example, Steven and you and I are capable of remarkable feats of pattern recognition. We can distinguish and name an object familiar to us in a fraction of second, no matter how far off or at what angle we see it. You know who I am at once when we meet, regardless of lighting conditions or distance. Given the slow speed of organic memory, that cannot require more than about one hundred full cycles of our brains, which means tremendous parallel processing. To do the same job of recognition, the inorganic brain of E. C. Tally needs hundreds of billions of serial calculation cycles. Naturally, he will eventually reach the same result. But in this case, Steven will often be faster."

"Two heads are better than one, you mean." Birdie was unsmiling. "Either one of them may win. Sounds like we ought to hear from both Steven and E. C. Tally before we make any decision."

"There is a certain logic to that idea. The other surprise is in information storage. Steven has far slower access, but he has better information packing density. He knows many more *facts* than E. C. Tally, but he takes longer to retrieve them." Graves thought for a few moments longer. "And, of course, the final weakness of E. C. Tally is unrelated to computation speed or to memory capacity. It is his inability to allow for the effects of *emotion* when considering human issues. He will always do his best to make the right decision—his makeup gives him no choice—but his judgment on both human and alien issues will always be impaired. And the farther he is away from the environment in which his principal experience was drawn, the more suspect his decision processes will be." Graves peered around, making sure that Tally was not lurking somewhere near. "It occurs to me that you and I had better keep a close eye on him. Especially you. He will seek to hide his motives from me, because he knows that I am part of the Council. You must inform me at once if his actions ever appear dangerously simplistic, or insensitive to the subtleties of organic intelligence."

Birdie nodded. At the first opportunity he went for a quiet chat with E. C. Tally.

"Your observations have merit," Tally said carefully, after a few milliseconds' pause for substantial introspection. "The minds of Julius and Steven Graves possess certain attributes that may supplement mine. There is virtue in massively parallel processing, although on the whole it does not compensate for the painfully sluggish speed of an Organic's neural circuits." Tally looked carefully around him. "However, Julius and Steven Graves possess one weakness that could be fatal. In an emergency they— especially Julius—will tend to make judgments that are clouded by emotion. I was warned of this by the council. Perhaps you can assist me here. Graves will seek to hide the effects of his emotions from me, because he knows that I will be reporting to the Council. You must tell me at once if his actions ever appear dangerously emotional, or unduly colored by the hormonal influences of organic intelligence."

"Sure. You can count on me."

"Hmm. Indeed?" There was a moment's pause. "Aha! You employ the verb *idiomatically*, not literally." E. C. Tally nodded with heavy satisfaction. "Yes, indeed you do. Logic, and the slowness of your arithmetic circuits, require that must be the case. It is rewarding to know that the ways of organic intelligence are becoming apparent to me."

He wandered off through the interior, with its lingering aroma of rancid fat.

Birdie felt a moment's satisfaction, which was quickly replaced by a disturbing thought: Graves is as crazy as a Varnian, and E. C. Tally is no better. What's wrong with me, when *both* sets of weirdos take me into their confidence?

ENTRY 18: VARNIAN

Distribution: The Varnian cladeworld, Evarnor, orbits an F-type star near the center of the ellipsoidal gas cloud known in the Fourth Alliance as the Swan of Hercules. The cloud lies approximately 170 light-years from Sol, in a direction bisecting the angle between the galactic normal and the vector to the galactic center.

Varnians spread from their original home via sublight-speed ships to thirteen other planets prior to their discovery by human explorers. All fourteen of these Varnian worlds lie within or on the boundaries of the Swan of Hercules.

Subsequent to that first discovery (in E. 1983, by the members of the Dmitriev Ark), small groups of Varnians have been spread by human contact throughout the Fourth Alliance and the Cecropia Federation. Spiral-arm regulations prohibit the formation of any colony of Varnians in excess of four thousand members, except on Evarnor itself or on one of the original thirteen Varnian colony worlds. Despite Varnian petition, this edict is judged unlikely to change in the foreseeable future (see *Culture,* below).

The population of Varnians throughout the spiral arm is estimated at 220 million. Although in no danger of extinction, they represent one of the rarer intelligences of the region.

Physical Characteristics: The Varnians are versatile metamorphs, capable of extensive physical transformation. Since Evarnor is a low-temperature planet, close to the limit for oxygen breathers, the Varnians who live there adopt in repose a spherical configuration that maximizes heat conservation. They extrude variable-width pseudopods as required, but they rarely deviate far from the overall spheroid.

Varnians in warmer environments are less constrained in appearance. In the presence of members of another species they will often mimic their main features, from the basic elements of endoskeleton, limb structure, and epidermal appearance, to such refinements as eye color, hair follicles, and behavioral patterns. There are no known limits to such mimicry ("Don't judge a Varnian by the warmth of her smile").

History: The Varnian story appears as a constant battle with racial insanity. If any species points up the distinction between intelligence and rational behavior, this is it. Archeological records, obtained by human and Cecropian workers, show that Varnian civilization went through at least five sudden and total extinctions, with subsequent slow returns from barbarism. Each collapse occurred without warning, following a long stable period of peaceful development. The estimated cycle time has been as short as forty thousand years (Second Eclipse) and as long as seven hundred thousand (Fourth Eclipse).

The loss of all but scanty records of those five disasters makes reconstruction of past events difficult; however, the spread of Varnian civilization across fourteen planets of twelve suns during three different eras proves that an advanced technology was achieved in at least those cycles.

The continuous written history of the Varnians can be traced back for twenty-two thousand years, to the time of the beginning of the Sixth Emergence.

Culture: Today's Varnian civilization is tranquil, unambitious, and apparently stable. It has been so for thirty thousand years, with no sign of an impending sixth species-wide disaster. However, the Per'nathon-Magreeu symbiote (PM) Suggested in E. 2731 that this is no cause for complacency. It was PM's analysis of Varnian culture that finally led to the restriction on colony size to four thousand members anywhere beyond the original fourteen Varnian worlds.

PM, in a systematic analysis of Varnian languages, noted that although there are over 140 semantic groups, languages, and local dialects in use among Varnians, none of those possesses a word meaning cynicism, self-criticism, or skepticism. They also pointed out that the basic collapse of Varnian civilization took place only on Evarnor, with the failure of other colonies arising from their material dependence on the cladeworld. In addition, the several different collapses do not all appear to have arisen for the same reason. Finally, PM remarked that the autopsies of Varnian brains reveal no meme-inhibitor complex.

PM concluded that the Varnian collapses were a resonance phenomenon, the consequence of positive feedback among large Varnian groups. Lacking the necessary faculty of reasoned skepticism, the Varnians are uniquely vulnerable to negative memetic influences. Destructive memes, spreading unchecked through the whole population, feed on themselves, to the point where individual Varnians become incapable of rational thought. The memetic plagues are terminated only by a civilization's collapse, with the associated loss of rapid communication among large groups.

PM set the absolute lower limit of interacting Varnians for such a phenomenon at twenty thousand participants. The onset of instability will not normally be seen until the number of individuals involved is in the millions. The present maximum value of four thousand for general colony size is extremely conservative.

----From the *Universal Species Catalog* (Subclass: Sapients).

CHAPTER 7

Without the aid of the beacon they would never have found Louis Nenda's ship. Darya became convinced of that as the *Summer Dreamboat* crept closer to it. For the past hundred kilometers they had been flying through a cloud of debris—lumps of rock, water-ice, and ammonia-ice ranging from boulders the size of a house down to pea-sized hail. Even the smaller pieces could be dangerous. The clutter scattered radio signals, too, and determining the precise location of the *Have-It-All* became a trial-and-error process. No wonder the beacon had been so faint.

"I don't understand this at all," Hans Rebka complained. "Why are there so many fragments, all so close to their ship? We're having to avoid more and more of them." He was at the controls with Kallik at his side. Darya had retired to the bunks, and J'merlia had been left behind on Dreyfus-27, along with a complete record of everything seen so far and instructions to explore and maybe refurbish the old mine shafts and tunnels.

"It cannot be the result of chance." Kallik was still tracking and monitoring, using range and range-rate data to determine the trajectories. She whistled and clucked to herself as she added to the data base she had already formed. "If these fragments were in normal orbits about Gargantua, they would have dispersed, long ago, to form an extended toroidal ck-c-cloud with Gargantua at its center. Since they have not, and since physical laws have

323

not been suspended here . . ." She leaned forward, her forward-facing black eyes intent on the display screen. "Ck-ck. I believe I have the explanation. Tell me if you s-s-see it also. Is not something there, another object, close to the location of the *Have-It-All*?"

Darya stood up from the bunk and moved forward to examine the display. Amid the diffuse reflections she saw the hint of a brighter ring of light, at roughly the computed position of Nenda's ship.

"I see something. Hans, it's another planetoid, right in the middle of the mess. In fact it explains why there *is* a mess. The whole cloud of fragments is orbiting around it, while it orbits Gargantua."

"I ck-concur. It is the reason that they have not dispersed."

"But it makes things more mysterious, not less." Hans Rebka changed the contrast of the display, so that the bright circle stood out more clearly from the background. "Look at that thing. It's tiny—a couple of kilometers across, no more. We'd never have seen it with the ordinary sort of search methods."

"You mean it shouldn't have enough mass to hold anything in orbit around it."

"Right. But it does. And we're being accelerated toward it. I'm forced to make adjustments to our own motion."

The *Summer Dreamboat* was sliding through a denser froth of orbiting fragments as the body ahead of them became larger and sharper on the display.

"And look at that outline," Darya said softly. "If that's not a perfect sphere, it's close enough to have fooled me."

Kallik was busy superimposing the latest fix for the position of Nenda's ship on the largest display screen. It became clear that the other vessel sat on or very close to the round body. The Hymenopt studied the combined image in silence for a few moments. "The *Have-It-All* is not moving relative to the planetoid. There must be enough ss-ss-surface gravity to hold it firmly in one position."

Rebka turned the *Dreamboat* and increased the thrust. "Kallik, do a calculation for me. Assume that thing is a couple of kilometers in diameter, and suppose it's made of solid rock. What should the surface gravity be? I'd like a reasonable maximum figure."

"Ah." The Hymenopt touched four limbs to the keyboard in front of her. "A small fraction of a centimeter per second per second," she said in a few moments, "Maybe one three-thousandth of a standard gravity, no more."

"I thought so. But we're experiencing that already, while we're still fifty kilometers out! If I extrapolate all the way down, the gravity on the surface of that thing must be getting close to one gee. That's flat-out impossible, for any material we've ever heard of."

As Rebka was speaking the *Dreamboat* made a sudden jerking move to one side. Darya was thrown back onto the bunk. The other two saved themselves by clutching at the control panel.

"What was *that*?" Darya remained flat on her back as the ship took a second leap in a different direction.

"Meteorite-avoidance system." Rebka hauled himself back into position. "I put it on automatic, because there's so much stuff around here I wasn't sure we'd see it all. Good thing I did. Hold on, here comes another. And another. God, they're piling in from everywhere."

The new jerking thrusts came before he had finished speaking, throwing him forward onto the controls. He grabbed desperately for handholds.

"Where are they coming from?" Every time Darya tried to sit up, the ship made a leap in some other unpredictable direction. There was a solid thump on the outside hull, loud enough to be frightening, and the few objects that were not secured in the galley came sailing through into the cabin and rattled around there. "Can you see them?"

Even as she asked that question, her mind was posing a more abstract one. How could orbiting lumps of rock be vectoring in at them, all at once and from all directions? Random processes did not work that way.

Kallik, with hands to spare, was doing better than Hans Rebka. Without saying a word she was at work on the control panel. The ship spun on its axis, and Darya felt a powerful, steady thrust added to the jerks and surges of the collision-avoidance system.

From her position in the bunk she could still see the main display screen. It showed a circle of light surrounded by bright glittering motes. As she watched it came swooping closer at alarming speed. When they seemed ready to plunge right into its center, the ship pivoted on its axis and decelerated at maximum power. Darya was again pressed flat to the bunk's mattress. She heard a startled grunt from Hans Rebka and a thump as he fell to the floor.

Darya felt a few seconds of maximum force on her body; then all acceleration ceased. The drive turned off. Darya found herself lying in something close to normal gravity. She lifted her head.

Hans Rebka was picking himself up painfully from the floor. Kallik was still seated, clutching with both hands at the control panel. The Hymenopt stared at them with the semicircle of rear-facing eyes and bobbed her head.

"My apologies. It was wrong to take such action without seeking permission. However, I judged it necessary if this ship and its occupants were to ss-ss-survive."

Rebka was rubbing his right shoulder and hip. "Damn it, Kallik, there was no need to panic. The collision avoidance system is designed to handle multiple approaches—though I must say, I've never known a bombardment like that."

"Nor will you again, in normal ss-ss-circumstances."

"But what made you think we'd be any safer here, on the surface of the planetoid?" Darya had looked out of the port and confirmed her first impression. The *Summer Dreamboat* was sitting on a solid surface, in a substantial gravity field.

Kallik gestured out of the same port. The upper part of another ship was visible around the tight curve of the planetoid. "For two reasons. First, it was clear from the fact that the *Have-It-All* could sit on the surface with a working beacon, and therefore with working antennas, that there could be no continuous rain of materials here at the surface of the planetoid. I already thought that meant safety, even before I saw what was triggering the collision-avoidance system."

"Rocks and ice?"

"No." The black cranium turned slowly back and forth. "When I caught sight of the objects raining in on us, I had a second reason for descending rapidly. The attackers were free-space forms. I knew they would avoid any substantial gravity field, and we would be safe here." The Hymenopt turned to face Darya. "Those were not rocks or ice, Professor Lang. We were attacked by *Phages*."

Hans Rebka looked startled. But Darya jerked upright in the bunk and clapped her hands together with excitement. "Phages! That's terrific."

"Terrific?" Rebka stared at her in disbelief. "I don't know how much exposure you've had to Phages, Darya, but I can tell you this: they may be slow, but they're *nasty*."

"And these Phages are not so slow," Kallik said calmly. "They are faster than any of which I have seen reports."

"Which makes them worse." Rebka stared at the excited Darya. "Do you *want* to be killed?"

"Of course I don't. We made it through Summertide together, and yet you still ask me a question like that?" Darya had trouble keeping a smile off her face. "I want to live as much as you do. But put yourself in my position. I drag us all the way out here to the middle of nowhere, telling you we'll discover clues to the Builders. And then all we find are dreary bits of rock and old mine-workings. Until a few minutes ago I thought that might be all that we *would* find. But you know as well as I do, Phages are found around Builder artifacts, and only there. They may even *be* Builder artifacts—a number of specialists have suggested that theory." She stood up and went to stare out of the ship's port, at the gleaming and suspiciously regular surface of the planetoid. "I was right, Hans. I felt it back on Quake, and I feel it more than ever now. We're getting there! The Builders have been gone for a long time—but we're close to finding out where they went."

❖   ❖   ❖

Kallik wanted to scramble into a suit and head off at once across the surface of the planetoid. Louis Nenda's ship was in plain sight, a few hundred meters away, and she was itching to hurry over to it. The need to know if her master was alive or dead made her abandon any thought of caution.

It took a direct order from Hans Rebka to stop her. "Absolutely not," he said. "I can think of ten ways you might get killed, and there must be twenty more I don't know about. When you go, one of us goes with you. And you don't go yet." At his insistence Kallik settled down on her stubby abdomen and joined the other two in making a first survey of their surroundings.

Even from a distance, the body on which the *Dreamboat* rested had appeared anomalously massive and anomalously spherical. An hour of observation and measurement added other peculiarities. When Kallik and Hans Rebka finally put on their suits and made a first descent onto the planetoid's surface, Darya stayed behind, monitored their progress, and entered the physical data into the *Dreamboat*'s log. A copy was going to J'merlia on Dreyfus-27, together with a note of their safe landing and their location. Darya prepared another copy for tight-beam transmission to Opal, with a request that it be forwarded via the Bose Network to Sentinel Gate.

She smiled to herself as she reviewed the message before sending it out. Just dull statistics, most people would say. She was giving little but the facts. But there would be high excitement over these particular dull statistics when they reached her colleagues on Sentinel Gate and were passed on in turn to Builder specialists in the spiral arm. Every last one of them would want to be here.

She kept an eye on Kallik and Hans, who were moving cautiously away from the *Summer Dreamboat*, and played back the message before sending it to Opal.

SURFACE TEMPERATURE: 281 K; THE SURFACE OF THE BODY IS *WARM*, ABOVE THE FREEZING POINT OF WATER. GIVEN ITS ENVIRONMENT, REMOTE FROM

MANDEL, IT SHOULD BE HUNDREDS OF DEGREES COLDER.

FIGURE: THE BODY IS A PERFECT SPHERE TO WITHIN THE LIMITS OF OBSERVATION; RADIUS, 1.16 KILOMETERS.

SURFACE GRAVITY: 0.65 GEE; GIVEN ITS SIZE, IT SHOULD BE LESS THAN A THOUSANDTH OF THIS VALUE.

MASS: 128 TRILLION TONS.

DENSITY: ASSUMING HOMOGENEOUS COMPOSITION, 19,600 TONS PER CUBIC METER. NOTE THAT ALTHOUGH THIS IS LESS THAN SOME CECROPIAN COMMERCIAL MATERIALS, IT IS ABOUT 1,000 TIMES AS DENSE AS ANY NATURALLY OCCURRING SUBSTANCE.

ATMOSPHERE: 16 PERCENT OXYGEN, 1 PERCENT CARBON DIOXIDE, 83 PERCENT XENON. THIS IS UNLIKE THE ATMOSPHERE OF ANY PLANET IN THE SPIRAL ARM; THE XENON CONTENT IS AN UNHEARD-OF CONCENTRATION; AND A BODY OF THIS SIZE SHOULD POSSESS NO ATMOSPHERE AT ALL. NOTE THAT THIS ATMOSPHERE WILL SUSTAIN LIFE FOR ALL OXYGEN-BREATHING FORMS OF THE SPIRAL ARM.

MATERIAL COMPOSITION: THE OUTER SURFACE HAS THE APPEARANCE OF SMOOTH, FUSED SILICA. THE INTERNAL COMPOSITION IS UNKNOWN, BUT IT IS OPAQUE TO ELECTROMAGNETIC RADIATION OF ANY WAVELENGTH.

Darya halted the data readout and looked out of the port. Kallik and Rebka had been crouching down, close to the surface. She had asked them to do additional materials testing outside, hoping to add something to this piece of the planetoid's description.

"Any results yet, Hans?"

Rebka straightened up. "We didn't get what you wanted, but we've probably got all we're going to. We couldn't take samples. The surface is too hard to cut, and it's impervious to heat. But we've been hitting it with precise impulses and monitoring the seismic return wavefronts.

The phase delays are very peculiar. We think it's as you suggested—the whole thing is hollow, maybe with a honeycomb structure."

Kallik stood up also. "Which makes the high ss-ss-surface gravity even odder, since this is a hollow body."

"Right. I'll add that to the physical description. You can give me more detailed data when you get back. No other problems?"

"None so far. In a little while we're going to head for Nenda's ship. Keep monitoring."

"I will." With considerable satisfaction, Darya added a section to the readout:

GENERAL DESCRIPTION: THE BODY APPEARS TO BE HOLLOW, PROBABLY WITH INTERNAL CHAMBERS. GIVEN ITS ANOMALOUS PHYSICAL PARAMETERS, IT MUST BE OF ARTIFICIAL ORIGIN. THE PLANETOID'S AGE HAS NOT YET BEEN ESTABLISHED. THERE IS A GOOD POSSIBILITY THAT IT IS A BUILDER ARTIFACT. THAT HYPOTHESIS IS GIVEN SUPPORT BY THE FACT THAT PHAGES ARE TO BE FOUND CLOSE BY IN LARGE NUMBERS, LESS THAN A HUNDRED KILOMETERS AWAY FROM THE BODY'S SURFACE.

Darya paused. Better leave it at that, and not stick her neck out too far. But personally she was sure it was an artifact. And if that was the case it should be given its own name and ID number, like every other Builder artifact.

She added a final note to the message. "The artificial planetoid has been assigned the provisional Universal Artifact Catalog number 1237, and the provisional name"—she recalled the bright motes on the sphere's image, now vanished—"the provisional name of *Glister*."

"Darya?" Hans Rebka's voice came as she was making the final entry. "Darya, we're over at the *Have-It-All* now. It seems to be in working order, but you ought to see it for yourself. Can you put your suit on and walk over?"

"I'll be there in five minutes." Darya initiated the message transmission, put the *Summer Dreamboat* into self-protect mode, and moved across to the lock. In less than a minute she was outside.

She looked up. Gargantua loomed in the distance beyond the other ship. High above her head the Phages were invisible, too small to be seen from fifty or a hundred kilometers away, but she had no doubt that they were still there. Phages were always there when they were not wanted.

And what Phages! Phages smart enough to track a falling ship. Phages fast enough to head for that ship. Phages fast enough to come close to catching it.

Darya began to move slowly across the curved and polished surface. The horizon was only a couple of hundred meters away. As Louis Nenda's ship came more and more into view she could not help glancing up every few seconds, to make sure that some marauding Phage was not diving down on her.

Phages didn't enter powerful gravity fields; in fact, they shunned them. Sure. That was the conventional wisdom. Until today she had believed it herself. But why assume that conventional wisdom applied to these Phages, and this situation, when everything else about them was so bizarre?

It occurred to Darya that Kallik had taken a bigger risk than they realized when she had brought them down here. The alien surface of Glister might be no safer than Phage-infested space. But Kallik's own need to know what had happened to Louis Nenda had made her blind to risk.

Darya arrived at the lock of the *Have-It-All*. One thing was for sure: given the behavior of these new Phages, she would have to do a major rewrite of that section of the *Lang Universal Artifact Catalog*. Good timing. She was supposed to begin work on the fifth edition when she got back home.

When she got back home . . .

She stared out across the smooth, glassy surface of Glister before she entered the lock. The little ship they had arrived on was the only familiar object. The *Summer Dreamboat* had started its life as a teenager's toy; now it was far from home, looking oddly lonely and defenseless.

Would it ever see its birth world again? And would she see hers?

Darya closed the hatch. When she got home. Better make that *if* she got home.

ARTIFACT: PHAGE

Exploration History: The first Phages were reported by humans during the exploration of Flambeau, in E 1233. Subsequently, it was learned that Phages had been observed and avoided by Cecropian explorers for at least five thousand years. The first human entry of a Phage maw was made in E 1234 during the Maelstrom conflict (no survivors).

Phage-avoidance systems came into widespread use in E. 2103, and are now standard equipment in Builder exploration.

Physical Description: The Phages are all externally identical, and probably internally similar though functionally variable. No sensor (or explorer) has ever returned from a Phage interior.

Each Phage has the form of a gray, regular dodecahedron, of side forty-eight meters. The surface is roughly textured, with mass sensors at the edge of each face. Maws can be opened at the center of any face and can ingest objects of up to thirty meters' radius and of apparently indefinite length. (In E 2238, Sawyer and S'kropa fed a solid silicaceous fragment of cylindrical cross-section and twenty-five meters' radius to a Phage of the Dendrite Artifact. With an ingestion rate of one kilometer per day, 425 kilometers of material, corresponding to the full length of the fragment, were absorbed. No mass change was detected in the Phage, nor a change in any other of its physical parameters.)

Phages are capable of slow independent locomotion, with a mean rate of one or two meters per standard day. No Phage has ever been seen to move at a velocity in excess of one meter per hour with respect to the local frame.

Intended Purpose: Unknown. Were it not for the fact that Phages have been found in association with over 300 of the 1,200 known artifacts, and only in such association, any relationship to the Builders would be questioned. They differ greatly in scale and number from all other Builder constructs.

It has been speculated that the Phages served as general scavengers for the Builders, since they are apparently able to ingest and break down any materials made by the clades and anything made by the Builders with the single exception of the structural hulls and the paraforms (e.g., the external shell of Paradox, the surface of Sentinel, and the concentric hollow tubes of Maelstrom).

—From the *Lang Universal Artifact Catalog*, Fourth Edition.

CHAPTER 8

Louis Nenda's ship was undamaged. Inside and out, every piece of equipment was in working order. The main drive showed signs of overload, but it still tested at close to full power.

"I'm sure that overload happened while they were in orbit around Quake," Darya said. "I told you, I saw them putting in every bit of thrust they had to try and get away from that silver sphere."

"Yeah. But you also said they were accelerated away by the sphere at hundreds of gees, enough to flatten everything." Hans Rebka waved an arm at the orderly interior. "Nothing flat here that I can see."

"Which is not difficult to explain." Kallik was crouched down on the floor by the *Have-It-All*'s hatch, sniffing and clicking to herself. "If the ship were to be accelerated by gravity or any other form of body force, neither it nor its occupants would be harmed. They would feel as though they moved in free-fall, no matter how high the acceleration appeared to an outside observer."

"Which should mean that if the ship is undamaged, so are Louis Nenda and Atvar H'sial." Rebka was inspecting the main control panel. "And the engines haven't been powered down. They're on standby, ready to fly this minute. Which leaves us with one question." He stared at Darya and shrugged. "Where the devil are they?"

They had searched the *Have-It-All* from side to side

and top to bottom. There was ample evidence that Atvar H'sial and Louis Nenda had been there. But there was no sign of them, and no suits were missing from the lockers.

"Master Nenda was certainly here," Kallik said, "more than three days ago, and less than one week."

"How do you know?"

"I can smell him. In his quarters, at the controls, and here near the hatch. J'merlia, if he were here, could place the time more accurately. He has a finer sense of smell."

"I don't see how that would help us. Not even if J'merlia could smell it to the millisecond." Rebka was walking moodily around the big cabin, examining the decorated wall panels and running his fingers across the luxurious fittings. "Darya, I know you said that the sphere that carried this ship away was silver at first, then it turned to black—"

"Turned to nothing, I said. It was like a hole in space."

"All right, turned to nothing. But couldn't it have changed again? One odd thing about this place—wha'd'ya call it, Glister?—is that it's a perfect sphere. Spherical planetoids don't occur in nature. Hasn't it occurred to you that it may be the *same* sphere, the one that you saw?"

"Of course I've had that thought. I had it before we even landed. But it only leaves a bigger mystery. *Something* sent a beam from near Gargantua, at Summertide, and the sphere that I saw ascended it. If this sphere was *my* sphere, what sent the signal?"

"All right, so maybe this isn't *your* sphere." Rebka seemed amused by her proprietary tone. "I'll drop that, and ask you again: Where are they?"

"Give me a minute. I may have a logical answer; whether or not you like it is another matter." Darya sat down on one of Nenda's comfortable couches to organize her thoughts. As she did so she surveyed her surroundings, comparing them with the familiar, stripped-down, and spartan fixtures of the *Dreamboat*.

The contrast was great. The whole inside of Nenda's starship was filled with alien devices and manufacturing techniques. The technology used here had been perfected long before by the Zardalu, before their thousand-world empire had collapsed, and been picked up piecemeal after that collapse to become the common property of the mix of species that now made up the Zardalu Communion.

But even more than it spoke of alien technology, the *Have-It-All* proclaimed another message: that of *wealth*.

Darya had never seen such opulence—and she was from a rich world. If Louis Nenda was a criminal, as everyone seemed to think, then crime certainly paid.

In one other area, her first view of the interior of Nenda's ship was forcing a change in Darya's thinking. She had first met Kallik on Opal and on Quake, and had seen her then as a callously treated under-being, little better than a shackled and servile pet of the Karelian human, Louis Nenda. But Kallik's quarters on the *Have-It-All* were as good as Nenda's own, and far better than *anyone* enjoyed in the worlds of the Phemus Circle. Kallik had her own study, equipped with powerful computers and scientific instruments. She had her own sleeping area, decorated with choice and expensive examples of Hymenopt art.

Even villains deserved justice. Darya filed that thought away for future reference. Nenda might act the monster— might *be* a monster—but his generous private treatment of Kallik was at variance with his public image. Nenda had certainly been crude, lecherous, coarse, and boorish with Darya. But was that the *real* Louis Nenda, or was it a pose?

"Well?" Hans Rebka was staring at her impatiently. Darya came back to the present with a jerk and realized that her thoughts had strayed off in a quite unexpected and inappropriate direction.

"I'm sorry," she said. "Point one: Nenda and Atvar H'sial were alive when the ship got here. Kallik is sure of that. Point two: There are no suits missing. Point Three: The air on the surface of this planetoid is breathable. Point four—not proved, but a good working assumption: This planetoid is hollow. Point five—another working hypothesis: The inside of Glister contains the same sort of air as there is on the surface. Put them together: if Louis Nenda and Atvar H'sial are still alive—or even if they're dead—we know where they can be found." She pointed at the floor.

"Inside Glister." Rebka was frowning. "That's what I decided, too, while you were sitting there daydreaming. I don't much like that idea."

"I never said you would."

"It gives us another problem."

"I know. To see if we're right, we have to get inside. And we haven't seen any sign of an opening or a hatch."

"On the descent, we certainly didn't." Rebka sat down in the control chair. "But that's not surprising—we had other things on our minds. There could be ways in just a hundred meters away, or there could be openings around the other side that we've never seen."

"And we won't find them sitting here." Darya stood up. She was full of an irrational energy. "You know what? I want to find Nenda and Atvar H'sial, and spit in their eye for trying to kill us on Quake. But even if they didn't exist, I'd want to find a way to the interior. And so would you. You pretend you're not interested in Builder artifacts, but you're the man who was all ready to risk a descent into Paradox, before you were sent to Dobelle. And this *is* an artifact. I've studied all twelve hundred and thirty-six of them, and I'm sure of it. Come on, let's take a look outside." Darya placed her hand on the control that would move her suit from full open to closed mode, then paused. "The air out there is supposed to be breathable. I might as well test it a little. Keep your eye on me."

She headed for the lock, expecting to hear Rebka's voice ordering her to stop. Instead he said in an amused tone, "I swear, if it isn't one of you wanting to run off and do something crazy, it's the other. Wait for me."

"And me," Kallik said.

"And don't worry about the air," Rebka added. "After the analysis was finished and came out positive I put my suit on partial transparency. Glister's atmosphere is fine."

"And you call *me* crazy." Darya stepped through into the lock.

In the time they had been inside Nenda's ship, Glister had made a quarter-turn on its axis. Gargantua was visible as a half-disk, while Mandel and Amaranth were hidden behind the planetoid. Darya emerged to an overhead dazzle of orbiting fragments and a cold, orange twilight. The air was odorless, tasteless, and chilly in her nose and lungs. Her breath showed as a puff of white fog when she exhaled.

What now?

Darya stared around at the featureless horizon. She began to walk forward, moving across Glister in the direction away from the *Dreamboat*. As she went she scanned the surface ahead. It had not occurred to her before, but without light from Mandel, visibility was going to be much reduced. Even using the image intensifiers in her suit she could not see details more than fifty meters away.

Darya slowed her pace. Kallik was a lightning calculator, but the Hymenopt was fifty meters behind and Darya would have to work it out for herself. A little more than a kilometer in radius. So the surface area of Glister was a bit less than seventeen square kilometers. And she could see things clearly for at most fifty meters in each direction. Assume that they split up and found an efficient way of covering the whole area. Then each of them would have to walk over fifty kilometers to be sure of finding whatever might be there.

Not good enough. And she should have thought it through before she left the ship. Darya waited for Rebka and Kallik to catch up with her.

"I've changed my mind." She outlined the problem. "It will take us too long. I think we ought to go back inside and use Nenda's ship; he doesn't need it at the moment. And we should do a low-orbit traverse of Glister, a few hundred meters up, and use every sensor on board to explore the surface. Anything odd that we find—cracks, openings, hatches, markings, whatever—we'll have the ship's computer make a note of it, and then later we take a closer look ourselves. On foot. Can you fly the *Have-It-All*, Hans? If not, we can go back and use the *Dreamboat*. Though I'm sure the equipment there isn't as good."

"It isn't. As you saw, Nenda travels first-class. I can fly his ship. And I bet that Kallik can fly it at least as well as me."

"I have flown it often, on both planetary and stellar missions," the Hymenopt concurred.

"So let's go back inside." Darya was turning toward the ship when she noticed an odd effect on the horizon behind Hans Rebka. It was as though she were suffering slight vertical double vision, with a thin brighter layer added above the sphere's original curved boundary. As she watched, the region thickened and solidified; faint sparkles appeared within it as random points of light. Part of Glister looked the way it had when she first saw it, from far out in space. Darya halted for a closer inspection.

Increased intensity added color. The cloud became a gauzy orange patch, lying close to Glister's uniform horizon, and extended over more than a quarter of the circle. As Darya watched the nimbus grew in size. The twinkle of interior lights became brighter.

"Hans!" She pointed. "Look there. Did you see anything like that before, when you were out on the surface?"

He stared, and at once took her arm to begin pulling her toward the *Have-It-All*.

"We sure didn't. Come on. And hurry."

"What is it?"

"Damned if I know. I've never seen anything like it in my life. I think maybe me and Kallik weren't too smart when we banged on the surface to learn more about the interior structure. Bit like knocking on the door to say, hey, we've arrived." He was still holding her arm. "Come on, both of you, get moving. I prefer to watch that thing, whatever it is, from inside the ship—with the shields up. Close your suit completely, just in case. And *don't look back*."

Darya at once felt an irresistible urge to look behind her. The orange shimmer was bigger, spreading more than a third of the way across the horizon and perceptibly closer. Kallik had not moved, but that did not mean she would be left behind. When she decided to travel, the Hymenopt's eight wiry legs could carry her a hundred meters in a couple of seconds.

"It has a discrete structure." Kallik's calm voice came through Darya's suit phone. "The points of light are reflections of incident radiation from Gargantua on individual small components, each no more than a few centimeters across. Their angles change constantly, which is why they sparkle like that. To appear as bright as they are, those components must be almost perfect reflectors. I can see no sort of connection between the parts."

The leading edge of the cloud was within twenty meters of the Hymenopt when Kallik finally turned. The thin black legs became a blur, and a second later she was by Darya's side. "I concur with Captain Rebka. This is a phenomenon outside my experience."

"Outside anyone's." The *Have-It-All* was only forty meters away. Darya could not resist looking back again. The cloud was not gaining. They could crowd inside the airlock and have it closed before the twinkling fog arrived. With the ship on standby, there was a good chance they could even take off from Glister before the leading edge touched the hull.

"Ahead!" Kallik spoke at the same moment as Hans Rebka began to swear.

Darya turned. A gauzy light was in front of them, rising like a sparkling vapor up through Glister's impervious surface. It thickened and spread as she watched, forming a tenuous barrier between them and the starship.

Rebka jerked to a halt, and they stared around them. The cloud behind was still moving forward. It had become opaque, and its edges were spreading wider. In a few more seconds its borders would meet with those of the fog ahead, to encircle the three completely.

Kallik was already moving forward. Rebka shouted at her. "Kallik! Come back. That is an order."

"Ck-ck." The Hymenopt kept moving. "With apologies,

Captain Rebka, it is an order I cannot obey. I must not risk the life of a human when perhaps that can be avoided. I will report my experiences for as long as I am able."

Kallik was entering the cloud. It swirled up around her thin legs and tubby body. She was quickly reduced to a sparkling outline of light.

"I am not able to see the structure of individual components." The voice was as calm as ever. "They appear to be unconnected, and each one is different and has independent mobility. They have a definite crystalline nature. In their appearance I am reminded of water-snowflakes—there is the same diversity of form and fractal structure. I feel them pressing against my suit, but there is no sensation beyond simple external pressure. And now . . . they are *within* my suit—despite the fact that it is set for full opacity! Apparently they penetrate our protective materials as easily as they move through the planetoid's surface. I question whether a ship's shields can offer any obstacle or protection.

"The flakes are now in contact with my thorax and abdomen. They are touching me, sensing me, as though in examination of my structure. They are *inside* me, I feel them. Their temperature is difficult to estimate, but it cannot be extreme. I feel no discomfort."

Kallik had vanished from sight. Her voice briefly faded, then came back to full strength. "Can you hear me, Captain Rebka? Please reply if you can."

"Loud and clear, Kallik. Keep talking."

"I will do so. I have now taken seven paces into the cloud, and it is tenuous but quite opaque. I can no longer see the sky or the surface of the planetoid. I also register a power drain from my suit, but so far I am able to compensate. *Eleven paces.* There is minor resistance to my forward progress, although not enough to impede my movements. The surface beneath my feet feels unchanged. I am having no trouble breathing, thinking, or moving my limbs.

"*Eighteen paces.* The resistance to my motion has lessened. Visibility is improving, and already I can see the outline of Master Nenda's ship ahead of me. *Twenty-two paces.* I can see the stars again. Most of the cloud is behind me. I am standing on the surface of the planetoid, and I appear to be physically unaffected by my passage through it. *Twenty-seven paces.* I am totally clear.

"Captain Rebka, I humbly suggest that both of you proceed through the cloud at once and join me here. I will prepare the *Have-It-All*'s lock for multiple entries and the controls for takeoff. Can you still hear me?"

"I hear you. We're on our way, we'll see you in a couple of minutes." Hans Rebka was pulling at Darya's arm again, but she needed no urging. Together they stepped into the sparkling orange glow. Darya began to count steps.

At seven paces the view around her faded. The stars overhead clouded and dissolved. She saw delicate crystals, hundreds of them, a handbreadth from her face. She heard Rebka's voice: "Seven paces, Kallik. We're almost a third of the way."

Eleven steps. Small points of pressure were being applied directly to her body, *within* her body. Like Kallik, Darya could not say if their touch was hot or cold. She felt that the crystals were touching her innermost self, measuring her, *evaluating* her. She found herself holding her breath, reluctant to inhale the cloud of crystals. She plowed on. There was a definite resistance to her forward motion, almost like walking underwater.

"Fourteen paces," said a gargling and distorted voice. That was Rebka, and he *sounded* as if he were underwater.

Eighteen steps. According to Kallik, she should start to see something more than the sparkling mist. Darya peered ahead of her. She could see only foggy points of light. Resistance to her progress was increasing.

It was not supposed to happen this way!

She struggled to force herself ahead, but the surface beneath her feet afforded less traction. She felt it becoming spongy, giving beneath her weight.

She wanted to sink to her knees, lean forward, and explore that insubstantial ground with her hands. But instead of releasing her, the sparkling points of light were holding her more and more tightly. She could barely move her arms and legs.

"Darya?" She heard Hans Rebka's voice faintly in her suit phone. It was the thinnest thread of sound, miles and miles away, the signal full of static.

She made a final effort to push herself forward. Her limbs would not move. She was fully conscious but fixed in position, as firmly as a fly in amber.

Keep your head! she told herself. Don't let yourself get panicky.

"Hans!" She tried to call to him, struggling to keep the fear from her voice. That concern was unnecessary, for no sound came from her throat. And now no sound was reaching her ears, not even the faint static that was always present with suit phones. The touch of the crystals on her body was fading, but still she could not move. The sparkling mist had given way to an absolute blackness.

"Hans!" It was a soundless scream. Fear had taken over. *"Hans!"*

She listened, and she waited.

Nothing. No sound, no sight, no touch. No sensations of any kind. Not even pain.

Was this the way that life was to end, in universal darkness? Had the death that she had escaped so closely on Quake followed her to claim her here?

Darya waited. And waited.

She had a sudden vision of a personal hell that lay beyond death itself: to be held fully conscious, for eternity, unable to move, see, speak, hear, or feel.

Kallik had walked unscathed through the crystal fog. She had no reason to think that Darya Lang and Hans Rebka would fare any differently.

She heard his voice say, "Seven paces, Kallik. We're almost a third of the way." That was satisfactory. She listened for the next progress report, at twelve or fourteen steps.

It did not come when she expected; but before there was time to be alarmed, the barrier of sparkling mist in front of her changed, to form a series of swirling vortices that were sucked back into the hard surface. She waited, eagerly watching for the other two to appear out of the wreaths of fog.

The mist thinned. No familiar human outlines emerged. In another few seconds the fog had vanished completely. The surface ahead of Kallik was bare.

She ran forward, at a speed that only those who threatened a Hymenopt with deadly violence would ever see. Two seconds and a hundred and fifty meters later she stopped. Given the snail's pace of human movement, there was no way that Hans Rebka and Darya Lang could have traveled so far in the time available.

Kallik reared up to her full height and employed every eye in her head.

She saw Gargantua, looming on the horizon. She saw Louis Nenda's ship, and beyond it the *Summer Dreamboat*, almost hidden by the tight curvature of the planetoid.

And that was all.

Kallik stood alone on the barren surface of Glister.

CHAPTER 9

The hierarchy was clear in J'merlia's mind: humans were
inferior to Cecropians, but they were well above Lo'tfians
and Hymenopts, who were in turn vastly superior to Varnians,
Ditrons, Bercia, and the dozens of other ragtag and marginally
intelligent species of the spiral arm.

That hierarchy also defined a command chain. In the
absence of Atvar H'sial or another Cecropian, J'merlia
would obey the orders of a human without question. He did
not have to *like* it, but he certainly had to do as he was told.

So J'merlia had not complained when he was ordered
to remain on Dreyfus-27 while the other three went off
to look for Louis Nenda and Atvar H'sial on the *Have-
It-All*. All the same, he was desperately envious of Kallik.
The Hymenopt was on her way to seek her master, perhaps
to help him, while J'merlia stayed here making Dreyfus-
27 a more habitable habitat. Suppose that Atvar H'sial
needed help? Who would provide it, if J'merlia was not
there? Who could even *communicate* with a Cecropian,
via pheromonal transfer? Not Darya Lang, or Hans Rebka,
or Kallik.

The cleanup operation had been given no particular
starting time, so J'merlia did not feel obliged to begin at
once to improve the living quarters of Dreyfus-27. Instead
he remained in his suit on the rocky surface, close to the
communications unit that Hans Rebka had removed from
the *Dreamboat*.

His experiences would have to be vicarious ones, gleaned from the verbal and occasional visual messages sent back to him. That was still better than nothing, and J'merlia possessed strong interspecies empathy. He had exulted when Kallik reported the first image of the *Have-It-All* on the *Dreamboat*'s sensors. He had waited in agony when all signals suddenly became garbled during the dive to the surface of Glister. He had rejoiced when the report came of their safe landing, and when he learned of the apparently undamaged condition of Louis Nenda's ship. He had puzzled over the anomalous physical parameters of the planetoid itself, and the presence of a swarm of energetic Phages surrounding it. And he had nodded agreement at Darya Lang's suggestion that Glister must itself be an artifact.

The *Dreamboat*'s final message for the record indicated that Darya Lang was placing the ship on remote-controlled status, while she went out onto the surface of Glister to join Hans Rebka and Kallik in their direct inspection of Louis Nenda's starship.

J'merlia shivered with excitement and anticipation. The next communication would be the crucial one. The *Have-It-All* seemed undamaged, and that was wonderful. But were Louis Nenda and Atvar H'sial alive or dead? J'merlia waited six hours for an answer, crouched unmoving by the com unit.

The long-awaited transmission came as a voice signal—from Kallik! "Report #11031," she began. "09:88:3101. Unit ID R-86945."

Louis Nenda's ID. So the *Have-It-All* was certainly in working order. But even before the real message began, J'merlia knew from the slow and strained speech that something had gone terribly wrong.

"This is Kallik. The whereabouts of Captain Rebka and Professor Lang are unknown to me. I am alone on the surface of Glister . . ."

The Hymenopt gave a concise and unhappy summary of events since Darya Lang's last message. She ended: "It is unclear whether Masters Nenda and Atvar H'sial are living or dead. The same is true of Professor Lang and Captain Rebka. Logic suggests that regardless of their condition they will be found, if anywhere near here, in the interior of Glister. I know of no way to achieve entry to the sphere. I propose to fly the *Have-It-All* on a low-altitude survey, seeking possible entry points. Such a discovery is a low-probability event, but I will try it before exploring more risky alternatives."

J'merlia looked at the message-source locator. Kallik was on a planetoid in a higher orbit than Dreyfus-27, so she was steadily falling behind. In another half hour Glister would be hidden behind the curved bulk of Gargantua. Messages would become impossible for a while. Already the signal was distorted by electronic noise, faded and broken.

J'merlia switched to his own transmission mode. "Kallik. What are we going to do? The masters are gone." His voice rose to a wail. "There is no one left to direct us!"

He waited impatiently through the three-second round-trip delay. Kallik was the smart one; she would have answers.

"I understand," a faint voice said, "and I have the same problem. All we can do is try to imagine what the masters would want, and function accordingly. For the moment, your position is clear. You were instructed to remain on Dreyfus-27. You should do so. My own position is more . . . difficult."

There was a long pause. J'merlia could guess at Kallik's suffering, and he sympathized strongly with it. The Hymenopt had disobeyed an order from Rebka when she walked forward into the fog, but that was not the problem. J'merlia would have done the same thing, to keep humans from risk. But Kallik had then been convinced by her own safe passage that Rebka and Lang could proceed unharmed through the shining mist. She had told them so—and she had been wrong. Her action may have led to their deaths. Kallik could not sit and wait, as J'merlia was waiting. She had to find a way to atone for her mistake.

"If my survey does not reveal an entry point," Kallik went on at last, "and I have little confidence that it will, then one other avenue is open to me. Our first attempts to penetrate the surface of Glister were unsuccessful. We could not cut into it or burn any mark in it. But the cloud that we saw came from *within* Glister. It emerged from an apparently solid surface. And yet when the cloud touched me, I feel sure that it possessed solid components. We tend to ascribe supernatural powers to the Builders, and therefore we ignore simple explanations. But it occurs to me that a gaseous or liquid form of surface, held to rigidity by an intense electromagnetic field, would be easy to achieve even with our technology. If that is the case, local cancellation of the field will permit entry to or exit from Glister. The instruments to explore that possibility are here, on the *Have-It-All* . . ." Her voice disappeared, then came back more weakly. ". . . prefer a more conventional mode of access, but . . . as last resort."

The signal was going, but Kallik sounded determined again, free of J'merlia's own sense of desolation and foreboding. Perhaps it was because she had the ships available to her, he thought. She could *do* something. If everyone on Glister was dead, Kallik could even fly home to seek a new master. J'merlia could not go anywhere, could not imagine any other master than Atvar H'sial. Maybe Kallik was less accustomed to slave status, with its freedom from difficult choices.

"Kallik, please call me. As soon as you can. I do not like to be alone."

After a too-long delay: "Certainly. I will contact you . . . line-of-sight communication . . . but . . . fading again. . . . six hours . . ."

The signal was almost gone. "If you do not hear . . . whatever you must . . . patient." The final word was a whisper against the hiss of interference.

J'merlia huddled over the communication set. Be patient. What else *could* he do?

First Atvar H'sial and Louis Nenda. Then Darya Lang and Hans Rebka. Everything and everyone, little by little, taken away from J'merlia.

Kallik was all he had left, the only remaining contact within hundreds of millions of kilometers. And now?

He listened and listened. She was gone.

By the standards of any normal inhabitant of Lo'tfi, J'merlia was already insane.

He had to be. Lo'tfians were communal animals. Only a crazy being could stand to be plucked out of the home environment to serve a Cecropian dominatrix as her interpreter. As far as the Cecropians were concerned, Lo'tfian slaves were selected for their ability to learn the Cecropian pheromonal form of speech; but from the Lo'tfian perspective, selection took care of itself through quite a different mechanism.

Any Lo'tfian could learn the Cecropian form of communication; with their talent for languages, that was easy. But only a few rare males, mentally off-balance to the point of madness, could bear to be yanked away from the society of the warrens.

Separation was worse than it could ever be for a human. When Lo'tfi was first discovered by the Cecropians, the dominant species roaming the surface of that planet possessed intelligence without technology. For millions of years, male Lo'tfians had lived most of their pleasant and peaceful lives out under the clear, cold skies of Lo'tfi. They had minimal intellectual curiosity. Any difficult decisions were made for them by the blind females, snuggled away in the burrows. The food-seeking males had seen the stars, but incuriously, as an element of the world that told them only when certain plants would be available to collect.

The arrival of the Cecropians, bearing the news that around those bright points of light circled other worlds populated by other beings, had been received with tolerant disinterest by the burrow females. They had little interest in the surface, and even less in what lay beyond. Communication had been established at a leisurely pace. The Cecropians, it transpired, had no interest in conquering the planet, or in living there. They hated those cold, clear skies.

And they did not want to exploit Lo'tfi. The Cecropian terms for peaceful coexistence were simple. All they sought were beings with the sense organs to understand human sonic and Cecropian pheromonal speech, and the intelligence to learn both forms of language.

The loss of a small number of surplus Lo'tfian males, as the only price for being left alone, was acceptable to the negotiators—and anyway, argued the burrow females making the deal, wasn't anyone crazy enough to go of bad breeding stock, even if he stayed?

J'merlia had left Lo'tfi, to become servant and interpreter to Atvar H'sial. In Lo'tfian terms he was therefore demented already. Now he was contemplating an action that would put his previous insanities into the shade.

Six hours. Twelve hours. Twenty. And never a signal from Kallik, or anyone else. Never a reply to his own, increasingly frantic, messages.

The orbits of Dreyfus-27 and Glister had passed and re-passed. At first J'merlia had been able to force himself to set the unit into recording mode while he did a little work on the interior of Dreyfus-27. As the hours passed, the urge to remain near the communicator became stronger and stronger.

At thirty hours he had waited as long as he could stand. Hans Rebka had told him to remain on Dreyfus-27. Kallik had told him the same thing. But they and Darya Lang were in *danger*.

The *Summer Dreamboat* was already in remote-controlled status. He used the communicator to bring it on a maximum-velocity trajectory to Dreyfus-27.

The ship ran the gauntlet of the Phage belt and arrived with another dent in the hull from a glancing blow. J'merlia gave it one moment's inspection to make sure the damage was superficial, then boarded the *Dreamboat* and set a least-time return course.

No messages came in during the flight back to Glister. In his preoccupation with the problem at hand, J'merlia did not think to send any record of his decision to abandon Dreyfus-27 in favor of a trip to the planetoid.

At two thousand kilometers Glister became visible. So did the matrix of pinpoint lights whirling in orbit around the little sphere. J'merlia gripped the controls himself, ready to override the collision avoidance system if he had to. The computer was ready for the free-fall trajectories of natural bodies, not the directed attack of energetic Phages; Kallik might have been able to devise alternative programs in the time available, but J'merlia certainly could not.

Two hundred kilometers. There was a jerk of violent acceleration. A close approach—near enough to stare down a Phage's dark pentagonal maw as it whizzed past only forty meters away. Eighty kilometers. Another, closer, miss, and a second violent thrust to the left. Fifty. The *Dreamboat* began decelerating so hard that J'merlia's front claws could not move on the controls. He sat rigid, staring out of the port as the ship corkscrewed its way through a sea of Phages. He counted scores of near misses.

When he was convinced that the ship was doomed, they were suddenly clear and in the final moments of descent. The whine of overstressed engines died to a high-pitched whisper. J'merlia, already in his suit, activated the display screens for an all-around look at the surface.

Nothing. No orange shimmer, no moving humans, no sign of the *Have-It-All*.

But from his position close to the surface he could see less than one percent of the surface of the planetoid, and during the flight down there had been no time for a visual search. Maybe Kallik and the other ship were just a few hundred meters away, hidden behind the curve of Glister. And Kallik had been wrong. That surface was not totally featureless. He could see something, a slate-gray mass peeping above the horizon.

According to Kallik and Hans Rebka, the atmosphere outside was breathable. But according to them, the whole place was safe. J'merlia put his suit to full opacity and stepped outside. He started to walk across the smooth surface toward the drab surface lumpiness.

Halfway there he paused. Was that thing what it seemed

to be? He stared for a long time, then turned his lemon-colored compound eyes upward. Was it imagination, or were they moving still lower and faster than Darya Lang's report had suggested?

He turned and went back to the *Dreamboat*, placing the ship into full self-protect mode.

On the surface once more, he again began to walk around the curve of Glister. That crumpled mass might have been there when the others arrived on the planetoid, hidden beyond the horizon. It might have been there for a million years. J'merlia certainly hoped so.

But it might be a very recent and ominous addition. Every few steps, he found himself pausing to scan the sky.

Was it? It certainly looked that way, although every Builder specialist swore one would never be found in a substantial gravity field.

The closer he came, the more the object he was approaching looked like the gray remnant of a shattered Phage.

CHAPTER 10

Where was she?

Darya's first thought when the shimmering mist faded was huge relief. Nothing was changed. She was standing exactly where she had been when the cloud swept over them. Ahead of her was the same convex, gray, faintly luminous plain, barren of features, stretching away from her feet to a near horizon. The light that shone down upon it was the same cold, orange gloom.

But there was no sign of the *Have-It-All*, or of Kallik. And the strange light did not cast shadows.

Darya raised her eyes. Gargantua had vanished. The pinpoint brilliance of stars and orbiting fragments was gone. In their place was a smooth overhead illumination, as featureless as the floor beneath her feet.

She felt a touch on her arm.

"All right? No aftereffects?" Hans Rebka sounded as unruffled as she had ever heard him.

What was the old saying? If you're calm *now* it means you just don't understand the problem. "What happened to us? Where are we? How long were we unconscious?"

"I'll pass on the first two. But I don't think we were unconscious at all. We were held for less than five minutes."

She grabbed his arm, needing the sheer *feel* of a human being. "It seemed like forever. How do you know how long it was?"

"I counted." He was staring hard at the curved horizon, measuring it with his eye. "It's something you learn on Teufel if you're trapped outside during the *Remouleur*— that's the dawn wind—and you have to go to earth. Count your heartbeats. It does two things: lets you estimate time intervals, and proves you're still alive. I just counted to two hundred and thirty. If you'll stand there for a minute, I think I'll be able to answer your second question. I know where we are."

He walked away fifty paces, turned, then called to Darya, "I"m going to hold my hand out and gradually lower it. Let me know when it goes below the horizon."

When she called to him. "Now!" he nodded in satisfaction and came hurrying back to her. "I thought so from my first look; now I'm sure. The surface we are on is still a sphere, or very close to it—but the radius is *less* than before. You can see it in the way the surface curves away on each side."

"So we're on another sphere, *inside* Glister."

"That's my best guess." He pointed up. "Kallik and the *Have-It-All* are right up there, through the ceiling. But there's no way to reach them, unless we can persuade that cloud to come back and carry us through."

"Don't say that!" Darya had been staring around her.

"Why not? Uh oh. Damnation. Is it listening to me? Here we go again."

As though responding to his words, an orange shimmer was flowing up and around them from the smooth gray surface. Darya resisted the urge to run. She was sure it would do no good. Instead she reached for Hans Rebka's hand and held it tightly. This time when the twinkling points cut off all light, sound, and mobility, the result was far less disturbing. She waited, sensing the faint throb of her own pulse and counting steadily.

One hundred and forty-one . . . two . . . three. The fog was dispersing. One hundred and fifty-eight . . . nine. It was gone. She was free, still gripping his hand hard enough to hurt.

At her side, Rebka grunted in surprise. "Well, it may be no better, but at least it's *different*."

They had sunk through to another level. The curvature of the surface was no longer noticeable, because there was no visible horizon against which to check it. They stood in a connected series of chambers. All around them structures ran in an eye-baffling zigzag of webs, pipes, nets, and partitions, from slate-gray floor to glowing ceiling. The "windows" between the chambers were set at random heights, and there were few openings at floor level. Whatever inhabited these chambers did not move like humans.

Nor did they walk through walls. Darya noticed that the retreating fog of orange lights did not penetrate the new structures. Instead it crawled around and over them, to wriggle its way through the small openings in nets and webs.

She glanced down to her feet. The outer layers of Glister had been unnaturally clean and totally dust-free, but here there were fragments of broken pipe and long lengths of cable. Everything had the neglected and disused look of a room that had not seen a cleanup in a million years. And yet the walls themselves seemed perfectly solid.

Rebka had been making his own inspection. He walked to one of the partitions, and as soon as the twinkling lights had left it he slapped his palm hard against the flat surface. He did the same thing to one of the fine-meshed webs and shook his head.

"Perfectly solid, and strong. We won't push those aside. If we want to go anywhere, we'll have to follow the holes in the walls—if we can climb up to them."

Since their arrival on Glister, Darya had felt increasingly useless. She just didn't know what to *do*. Whereas Hans was so used to trouble, he took it all in stride. She could contribute nothing. Unless it was information . . .

"Hans! What would you say the gravity field is here?"

He stopped his careful inspection of the walls and webs. "A standard gravity, give or take twenty percent. Why? Is it giving you trouble?"

"No. But it's *more* than it was, back on the surface. If Glister had a uniform density, or most of the mass was near the outside, then the field would *decrease* as you went closer to the center. So there has to be a big field source down near the middle. And it can't be a normal mass; nothing natural is that dense."

"So it's something new. Let's go and take a look below." Rebka began to walk slowly down one of the corridors, a hallway wide enough for the local vertical to change appreciably across its width.

Darya followed, pausing often to examine the wall materials and the complicated interlocking nets that covered most of the "windows." Her nervousness disappeared as she realized that this was truly a new Builder artifact—the first one discovered in more than four hundred years. And she was the first scientist ever to examine it. Even if she could escape, she should first give the place the most thorough examination of which she was capable. Otherwise she would never forgive herself—and neither would a thousand other Builder specialists.

So it was panic button off, observation hat on. What else could be said about their surroundings?

Many of the partitions slanted up all the way from floor to glowing ceiling. With their help she could judge the height of the chamber. It was *high*—maybe sixty meters. Nothing human needed that much space; but it was consistent with the enormous chambers found on other Builder artifacts.

She stepped to one wall and examined the material. Close up, it displayed a fine, grainy structure like baked brick. From the appearance it seemed brittle, as though one sharp blow would shatter it, but she knew from experience with Builder materials that that was an illusion. The structure would possess a material strength beyond anything else in the spiral arm. Left to stand for a million years in a corrosive atmosphere of oxygen, chlorine, or fluorine, it would not crumble. Bathed in boiling acids for centuries, it would not dissolve. Darya had no idea how long this chamber had been unoccupied, but the surfaces should have been as dust-free as if they were polished daily. And they were not. There was dust *everywhere*.

Maintenance on Glister was sloppily done, if it was done at all.

Darya took the knife from her suit belt and jabbed at the gray wall. The tip was a single crystal of dislocation-free carbon-iridium, the hardest and sharpest material that human technology could create. And yet the blade did not make even a nick. She moved to one of the tight-drawn nets and tried to cut through a thin strand. She could see no mark when she was done. Even the thinnest web would be an impossible barrier to anything that could not, like the cloud, dissolve to small individual components. It was hard to believe that the dust all around them had come from gradual flaking away from the walls. There had to be some other source. Somewhere on Glister there had to be other materials, not built to Builder standards of near-infinite permanence.

Hans Rebka had been waiting impatiently as she chipped at the wall and sawed at the net. "It'll take you a long time to cut your way out like that," he said. "Come on. We have to keep moving."

He did not say what Darya had already thought. The air here might be breathable—though why, and how? There was nothing to create or maintain an atmosphere acceptable to humans—but beyond air, they needed other things to stay alive. Twelve hours had passed since their last meal, and although she was too nervous to feel hungry, Darya's throat was painfully dry.

They walked on, side by side, taking any floor-level connection between chambers and slowly descending through a long succession of sloping corridors. At last they came to a room containing the first sign of working equipment inside Glister—a massive cylinder that began to hum as they approached. It took in air and blew it out through a series of small vents. Rebka placed his hand and then his face close to one of the apertures.

"It's an air unit," he said. "And I think we just started it going. Somehow it reacted to our presence. Here's something for you to think about: If units like this maintain a breathable atmosphere *inside* Glister, what does it *outside*?"

"Probably nothing. There's nothing up there to do anything, no machinery at all. The surface must be permeable, at least sometimes and somewhere. That's how we were carried in here. Right through the floor."

"So all we have to do is work out a way to make the ceilings permeable again, and out we go. Of course, we need a way to jump straight up about a hundred meters." He stared upward. "The hell with it. I'd still like to know how the unit knew the atmosphere is good enough for both humans and Hymenopts."

"Right. Or what kind of atmosphere Glister had, before the *Have-It-All* arrived. Why would it need one, until we got here? Maybe it didn't have one at all."

Rebka gave her a startled glance. "Now that's what I call *real* custom service. Air designed to order. Now you're making *me* nervous."

They walked on past the air unit and half a dozen other constructs whose purpose Darya could only guess at. She itched to stay and examine them, but Hans was urging her forward.

The eighth device was a waist-high cylinder with a surface like a honeycomb, riddled with hexagonal openings each big enough to accommodate a human fist. The outside of the panel was cold and beaded with drops of moisture. Rebka touched one, sniffed his finger, and touched it to his lips.

"Water. Drinkable, I think, but it tastes flat."

Darya followed his example. "Distilled. It's a hundred percent pure, with no salts and minerals. You're just not used to clean water. You can drink it."

"Just now I'll drink anything. But we won't get much from panel condensation." He peered into one of the openings. "I'm going to try something. Don't stand too close."

"Hans!"

But already he was reaching his arm deep into the aperture. He drew out a cupped handful of water and took a cautious sip. "It's all right. Come and take some. At least we won't die of thirst.

"And following up on your earlier line of thought," he added as they reached in to fill the bottles attached to their suits, "I wonder what liquid *that* was producing a week ago. Ethanol? Hydrochloric acid?"

"Or liquid methane. What do you think the *temperature* was on the surface of Glister, when Gargantua was a long way from Mandel?"

They moved on, to reach a point where the uniform curvature of the convex floor was broken by a descending ramp. Rebka stood on the brink and stared down.

"That's pretty steep. Looks slick, too. More like a chute than a corridor, and I can't see the bottom. Once we go down there, I'm not sure we'll be able to climb back up."

"We need food. We can't get back to the surface, and we can't stay here forever."

"Agreed." He sat down on the edge. "I'm going to slide. Wait until I call back and tell you it's all right."

"No!" Darya was surprised at the strength of her own reaction. She came forward and sat next to him. "You're not leaving me up here by myself. If you go, I go."

"Then hold tight." They eased side by side over the edge.

The chute was less steep than it looked. After a sheer start it curved into a gentle spiral. They skidded down and soon reached terminal velocity of no more than a fast walking pace. As they descended, the light changed. The cold orange that mimicked Gargantua's reflected glow was replaced by a bright yellow-white that came from ahead of them and reflected from the smooth walls of the chute. Finally the gradient became so shallow that they could no longer slide forward.

Rebka stood up. "The free ride's over. I wonder what this was intended for originally. Unless you think *it* wasn't here, either, until we came along and needed it."

They had emerged to stand at the edge of a domed chamber, a giant's serving dish fifty meters across. The floor ahead formed a shallow bowl, gently sloping all the way into the center, and above them stood an arched ceiling in the form of a perfect hemisphere. Hans and Darya stared around the chamber, adjusting to the white dazzle. To eyes accustomed for the last few hours to cold hues and dusty slate-gray, the new environment was sheer brilliance. The circular floor of the room was marked off like an archery target, in bright concentric rings of different colors. From the boundaries of those gaudy rings rose hemispheres, faintly visible, forming a nested set. Corridor entrances, or perhaps the delivery points of chutes like the one that they had just descended, stood at intervals around the outer perimeter of the chamber. A single dazzling globe at the room's apex provided illumination.

And in the middle of the chamber, at the central depression directly below the light . . .

Darya gasped. "Look, Hans. It's *them!*"

The smallest translucent dome stood around the bright blue bull's-eye of the innermost ring. At its center was a raised dais, a meter and a half tall; upon that, facing outward, stood a dozen transparent structures like great glass seats.

Side by side in two of those seats, held by some invisible support, sat Louis Nenda and Atvar H'sial.

Darya began to move forward, but she was restrained by Hans Rebka's hand on her arm.

"This is the time to be most careful. I think they're both unconscious. Look at them closely."

Darya stood and stared. Between them and the central dais rose the half-dozen translucent nested hemispheres. They interfered with her view of Nenda and Atvar H'sial, but Darya could still see enough detail to prompt new questions.

Louis Nenda's overall appearance was at first sight no different from the last time she had seen him. The arms of the short, swarthy body rippled with muscle, and the shirt was wide open at the neck to show a powerful and thickly haired chest.

Or *was* that hair? It looked wrong, discolored and uneven. She turned to Rebka.

"His chest—"

"I see it." Hans Rebka was blinking and squinting,

having the same problem with perspective as Darya. The hemisphere introduced a subtle distortion to the scene. "It's all covered with moles and pockmarks. Did you ever see his bare chest before?"

"No. He always kept it covered."

"Then I don't think it's a recent change. I bet he was like that when he arrived on Opal."

"But what is it?"

"A Zardalu-technology augment. The first records on Nenda when he requested access to Opal said he was augmented, but they didn't say how. Now we know. Those nodules and pits are pheromone generators and receptors. It's a rare and expensive operation—and it's painful, like all the Zardalu augments. But that's how he could work directly with Atvar H'sial. They can *talk* to each other, without needing J'merlia." Rebka studied the other man for a few seconds longer. "My guess is that he's physically unchanged, and just unconscious. It's a lot harder to tell about Atvar H'sial. What do you think?"

Darya moved her attention to the Cecropian. She had spent more time with Atvar H'sial, so her estimate of condition ought to be better. Except that the Cecropians were so alien, in every respect . . .

Even seated, with her six jointed legs tucked away underneath her, Atvar H'sial towered over the Karelian human Louis Nenda. A dark-red, segmented underside was surmounted by a short neck with scarlet-and-white ruffles, and above that stood a white, eyeless head. The thin proboscis that grew from the middle of the face could reach out and serve as a delicate sense organ, but at the moment it was curled down to tuck neatly away in a pouch on the bottom of the pleated chin.

Neither the Cecropian nor the Karelian human had the empty look of death. But was Atvar H'sial conscious?

"Atvar H'sial!" Darya called as loudly as she could.

If the alien was at all aware of her surroundings, that should produce a response. Originating on the clouded planet of a red dwarf star, the Cecropians had never developed sight. Instead they "saw" by echolocation, sending high-frequency sonic pulses from the pleated resonator in the chin. They received and interpreted incoming signals through yellow open horns set in the middle of the broad head. As one result Cecropians had incredibly sensitive hearing, all through and far beyond the human frequency range.

"H'sial! Atvar H'sial!" Darya shouted again.

There was no reaction. The yellow horns did not turn in her direction, and the pair of fernlike antennas above them, disproportionately long even for that great body, remained furled. With hearing usurped for vision, Cecropians "spoke" to each other chemically, with a full and rich language, through the emission and receipt of pheromones. The unfurled antennas could detect and identify single molecules of many thousands of different airborne odors. If Atvar H'sial were conscious, those delicate two-meter-long fans would surely have stretched out, sniffing the air, seeking pheromones from the source of the sound.

"She's unconscious, too. I feel sure of it." Darya was moving forward to the place where the outermost ring of color began on the floor. Before she reached the edge of that first annulus of vivid yellow, Hans Rebka again restrained her.

"We don't know *why* they are unconscious. It looks safe enough in there, but it may not be. You stay here, and I'll go in."

"No." Darya moved more quickly down the slope of the shallow bowl. "Why *you* again? It's time we started sharing the risks."

"I have more experience."

"Fine. That means you'll know how to get me out of trouble if I need you. I'll go in just a little way." Darya was already stepping gingerly through the haze of the first hemisphere. She put her feet down carefully, feeling the ground ahead.

"All right, I'"m through that one." She turned to look at Hans. He did not seem any different. She did not feel it. "No problem so far. Didn't notice anything, no resistance to motion. I'm going to cross the yellow zone."

She stared ahead. Yellow to green to purple. Five paces for each—it should be easy. Halfway between the second and third hemispheres she paused, confused for a moment about what she was doing.

"Are you all right?" She heard his call from behind her.

She turned. "Sure. I'm going to . . . the center."

And then she paused, oddly uncertain of her goal. She found it necessary to look around her before she knew what was happening.

There, in the middle, where Atvar H'sial and Louis Nenda are sitting, she reminded herself. In the chairs.

"I'm halfway there," she called. "Nearly done the green. Next stop, purple."

She was moving again. Bright lights, bright colors. Yellow to green to purple to red to blue. Five zones. Not following the usual order, though, red to orange to yellow to green to . . . the order in—what's that thing called? Hard to remember. The rainbow. Yeah, that's it.

These colors are not like the colors in the . . . whatever. Damn it, I've lost the word again. Keep moving. Only two more to go, and I'll reach what's-their-names. Yellow to green to purple to red . . . to—what was the name of that color— to yellow to . . . green . . .

Darya's eyes were wide open. She was lying on a hard, flat surface, staring up at a domed blue ceiling. Hans Rebka was bending over her, his face sweaty and pale.

She sat up slowly. In front of her was the great chamber, with its circular rings of color. At the center stood the dais with its two silent forms.

"What am I doing lying here? And why are you letting me sleep? We won't be able to help those two if we spend time loafing around."

"Are you all right?" At her impatient nod Hans said, "Take your time. Tell me the very last thing that you remember."

"Why, I was saying that I wanted to go into the rings,

to bring Louis Nenda and Atvar H'sial out, and you were trying to talk me out of it. And then I was all ready to put my foot—" she was suddenly puzzled. "I was at the edge of the yellow ring, and now we're ten steps outside it. What happened, did I pass out?"

"More than that." His face was anxious. "Don't you remember crossing the yellow ring, and then the green one, and starting in on the purple one?"

"I didn't. I couldn't have. I only started out a minute ago. I just put my foot onto the yellow zone, and then—" She stared at him. "Are you telling me . . ."

"You said it a minute ago. You passed out. But not here." He pointed. "Way over there. You were halfway to the dais when your voice went all confused and dreamy, then you sat down on the floor. And then you lay down and stopped talking. That was three hours ago, not one minute. You were unconscious in there for nearly all that time."

"And you came in after me? That was crazy. You could have passed out, too."

"I didn't go all the way in. I didn't dare. I've seen something like this before—and you've written about it in your artifact catalog. It was your suggestion that this is a Builder artifact that told me what the problem had to be."

"Unconsciousness? That's not a Builder effect."

"Not unconsciousness. Memory loss. It's the same thing that happens to people who try to explore Paradox, except that what it does there is far worse. You only lost a few hours. They come out with their memories wiped clean. I've seen victims who tried to enter and came out more helpless than newborn babies."

Excitement replaced alarm. Darya had studied the artifacts since childhood, but until Summertide she had only seen Sentinel firsthand. "You're saying that there's a Lotus field inside those hemispheres. That's absolutely *fascinating*."

She could see from Rebka's look that the word was not one he would have chosen. She hurried on. "But if it *is* a Lotus field, however were you able to get me out? If it affected me like that, it would do the same to you."

"It would have. It did, a little bit. You were all right in the yellow ring, you still knew what you were doing, so I was willing to risk that much. I went that far. But the field would have caught me, too, if I'd gone all the way in to get you. Then we'd have lain there helpless until we starved to death, or somebody else came along to kill us or get us out."

"But you got me out."

"I did. But I didn't go in for you. I stood in the yellow zone and I hauled you out from there, like a hooked fish. Why do you think you were in so long? I had to find something to use as a grapple. It wasn't easy. It took me hours to find something I could use, then another hour to fish for you."

Darya turned to face the center of the chamber. "Atvar H'sial and Louis Nenda are right in the middle of it. Do you think their memories are wiped clean?"

"I can't say, but if this is anything like Paradox the field may affect the approach route and not the middle. They could be fine—or they could be wiped. We won't know until we get them out."

"Can you do for them what you did for me—haul them clear?"

"Not with this." Rebka indicated the length of noosed cable that lay on the floor at Darya's side. "It's too short, and they look like they're tied somehow to those seats."

"So how do we get them out?"

"We don't. Not for the moment." Rebka helped her to her feet. "We have to find some other way to do it. Come on. At least I know a bit more about the layout of this place—I ran up and down half the corridors off this room, scavenging for something I could use as a rope. This is a wild place—some parts are spotless; others have a ten-million-year dust layer. But don't ask me what any of it is *for*—that's a total mystery."

Darya allowed him to lead her to a doorway, three entrances farther around the room's perimeter. "It's hard to see why Glister is here at all," she said. "But it's not the prize mystery."

"Plenty of choices for that." Rebka sounded weary, but Darya knew from experience that he would ignore fatigue until he actually collapsed. "I can list a bundle," he went on. "The fast Phages. The atmosphere on the surface. The way we got inside. The equipment that provides air and water. The Lotus field in the chamber we just left. They're all candidates. Take your pick."

"You haven't listed the one most on my mind." The path was spiraling down, heading in a gentle, curving ramp toward the middle of Glister. Darya was thirsty—and suddenly so hungry that it was hard to think of anything else.

How long since she had eaten? It felt like forever. Her mind might have been switched off for three hours, but her stomach had not been. It kept careful track of missed meals.

"The tough one is this," she said at last. "Why did the orange cloud on the surface let Kallik pass through untouched, but grab *us*, and Louis Nenda and Atvar H'sial, and bring us down here? There's something on Glister that *knows the difference* between humans, Cecropians, and Hymenopts. *That's* the biggest mystery of all."

ENTRY 19: HYMENOPT.

Distribution: The Hymenopt cladeworld is not definitely known, but it is believed to be one of the eighty worlds subjected to large-scale surface reshaping by the Zardalu, roughly twenty thousand years ago.

Hymenopt societies flourish today on eighteen of those worlds, having been transported there by the Zardalu and abandoned at the time of the Great Rising. Eight of these colonies subsequently became technologically advanced enough to achieve interplanetary travel. One Hymenopt world was an independent discoverer of the Bose Drive, but for cultural reasons it limited its use.

After the Great Rising the Hymenopt worlds were lost from spiral-arm communication, until finally they were rediscovered by the Decantil Survey and Census of territories of the Zardalu Communion.

Since then, slave Hymenopts have been taken to all worlds of the Communion, and also to dozens of planets of the Cecropia Federation. The total Hymenopt population is unknown, but certainly it is in the tens of billions.

Physical Characteristics: The Hymenopts in their own colonies contain six separate functional groups, designated as Regents, Recorders, Defenders, Feeders, Breeders, and Workers. There is a progression among these forms, in that Breeders following metamorphosis become Feeders, and finally Regents, while Defenders in the later stages of their lives become Recorders. Workers maintain the same form all their lives.

It should be noted that the only Hymenopts employed as slaves are the Workers. The others do not leave their colonies. Thus when another species of the spiral arm refers to "a Hymenopt," that is by implication a Hymenopt *Worker.* The following physical description applies to them alone.

Hymenopt Workers are sterile female eight-legged arthropods. The paws on all limbs are prehensile and capable of the manipulation of small objects; however, only the four forelimbs are normally used for delicate work. Despite the fancied resemblance of the Hymenopt Workers to the Earth Hymenoptera, which led to their naming by Decantil survey biologists, the physiological similarity is at best superficial. The Hymenopts do, however, possess a tough exoskeleton and a powerful sting at the end of the rounded abdomen. (This, combined with their speed of movement, suggests that the slavery of a Hymenopt Worker is a matter of choice and habit, rather than force.)

Hymenopts see with a ring of simple (i.e., not compound) eyes, circling a smooth head. The need for all-around vision encourages them to remain upright on most occasions, although for rapid movement they revert to a horizontal position. The Hymenopts' eyes are sensitive to a range of wavelengths from 0.3 to 1.0 micrometers, which more than spans the range of human optics. Their sensitivity to low light levels is superior to that of humans; this has led some exobiologists to offer an unconvincing identification of the Hymenopt cladeworld based on fainter sunlight and stellar spectral properties.

History: The earliest history of the Hymenopts has been lost, together with knowledge of their cladeworld. Today, the planet of Ker is generally considered to be the center of Hymenopt civilization, and it is certainly the principal storage point for Hymenopt records.

It was on Ker that the Bose Drive was discovered, seven thousand years ago. That invention led to a dominance of Ker among other Hymenopts which has never been challenged. According to the Ker archives, some form of Hymenopt oral history and race memory extends back sixty thousand generations. Since a breeding cycle lasts for seventy standard years, Hymenopts have therefore been intelligent, with a well-developed language, for over half a million years. By contrast, written records on Ker go back less than ten thousand.

Ker is the moving force, main market center, and principal beneficiary of the sale of Hymenopt slaves. Its inhabitants are eager to maintain that role, and they follow general Hymenopt practice by discouraging interaction and commerce with any other species, except for the purpose of Hymenopt slave trading.

Culture: In the Hymenopt worlds, societal control equals *breeding* control. Since the other five groups are sterile, the Breeders in principle possess unique power; however, each Breeder knows that she will one day undergo metamorphosis to Feeder (responsible for feeding the young) and then to Regent (responsible for all colony development decisions). These three groups therefore cooperate to constitute the "Superior Triad" of Hymenopt culture, with the Workers, Recorders, and Defenders forming the "Inferior Triad." It would be unthinkable for one member of the Superior Triad to sell another member for use as a slave.

Crossbreeding outside the colony is recognized as genetically beneficial, but travel is tightly controlled. It is approved in advance, and applies only to mating. No Hymenopt colony desires, or permits, uncontrolled transfers of individuals. This factor, more than any other, limits Hymenopt interest in interstellar, or even interplanetary, commerce. The slave trade of Ker is the single significant exception.

—From the *Universal Species Catalog* (Subclass: Sapients).

Clade Sterile

CHAPTER 11

The following facts were deemed too anecdotal for the formality of the *Universal Catalog* (Subclass: Sapients). Few beings of the spiral arm, however, would dispute them:

> AN ADULT HYMENOPT HAS REFLEXES TEN TIMES AS FAST AS ANY HUMANS.
>
> A HYMENOPT CAN RUN A HUNDRED METERS IN LESS THAN TWO SECONDS.
>
> USED IN CONCERT, A HYMENOPT'S EIGHT TRIPLE-JOINTED LEGS WILL PROPEL HER TEN METERS INTO THE AIR UNDER TWO STANDARD GRAVITIES.
>
> THE RETRACTED YELLOW STING IN THE END OF A HYMENOPT'S STUBBY ABDOMEN CAN BE READIED IN A FRACTION OF A SECOND TO DELIVER STIM-ULANTS, ANESTHETICS, HALLUCINOGENS, OR LETHAL NEUROTOXINS. THEY ARE EFFECTIVE ON ALL KNOWN INTELLIGENT ORGANISMS.
>
> WITH VOLUNTARILY REDUCED METABOLISM, A HYMENOPT CAN SURVIVE FOR FIVE MONTHS WITH-OUT FOOD OR WATER; ENCYSTED, SHE WILL ENDURE FOR FOUR TIMES AS LONG.
>
> A HYMENOPT IS AS INTELLIGENT AS A CECROPIAN OR A HUMAN, WITH MORE MENTAL STAMINA THAN EITHER.

Kallik, of course, knew all these things. And yet it never occurred to her that her own slave status was in any way unnatural. In fact, she thought it inevitable. Her race memory extended back well over ten thousand years, to the time when every Hymenopt had been a slave.

Hymenopt race memory lacked the precision of nerve-cell memory. The few billion bits available for its total storage reduced recollection to a mere caricature of the original direct experience. Yet the brain, insistent on offering race memories in the same format as other experiences, clothed the skeleton of recollection in a synthetic flesh of its own creation.

Thus, Kallik "remembered" the long enslavement of her species as a series of visual flashes; but no amount of effort would make those images detailed. If she made the attempt, the result was the product of her own imagination.

She could make a picture in her mind of the Zardalu, the land-cephalopod masters who had ruled the thousand worlds of the Zardalu Communion until the Great Rising. If she thought hard, she could make specific images: of stony beaks, big and strong enough to crush a Hymenopt's body . . . but she could not see how they fitted to the Zardalu body. Of huge, round eyes . . . but they were floating free and disembodied, high above her head. Of hulking bodies, girthed with supporting straps and slick with fatty secretions that allowed the Masters to survive on land . . . but the legs that carried those bodies were vague shadow legs, undefined in size, color, or number.

She had only the most confused memory of the disappearance of the Zardalu: her mind fed back a whirl of flying bodies, a green fire, a world turned black, a sun exploding. And then, great calm; an absence of all Zardalu images.

For Kallik's social class, the Great Rising and the vanishing of the tyrant Zardalu brought little change. She had been born a Worker; had she remained on the Homeworld she would have remained one. Her role would always have been Worker, rather than Regent, Recorder, Defender, Feeder, or Breeder. She had been bred for slavery, born for slavery, raised for slavery, and sold for slavery. Nothing made her so uncomfortable as a total absence of masters. She *needed* them—humans, Cecropians, or Hymenopts.

The disappearance of Lang and Rebka stimulated her to frantic activity. She moved at once to make a low-altitude survey of the surface of Glister, traversing the slowly rotating planetoid on a path that would allow a close inspection of every square meter.

The survey took over an hour. It was wasted time. Kallik remained convinced that Glister was hollow, but the sphere showed no trace of external structure. Nothing suggested a way to reach the hidden interior. If fact, if Kallik had not *seen*, with her own multiple pairs of black eyes, that sparkling cloud absorbed into the surface, she would have judged Glister's exterior totally impermeable.

When the futile ground survey was over Kallik raised her eyes again to scan the heavens far above the ship. She was no nearer finding Rebka and Lang, and—ominously—the Phages were no longer remaining at a safe distance. The presence of the *Have-It-All*, moving in its survey orbit around the planetoid, seemed to madden them. Three times Kallik had seen a Phage dropping in on a trajectory that carried it to within a couple of kilometers above the ship. Each approach came a little closer. Now she could see two more Phages, dropping in low.

She returned the *Have-It-All* to the surface of Glister, roughly where they had first found it, and went to her own quarters. The time for tentative measures was past. She selected equipment and carried it down from the ship to the surface. It would measure the E-M field associated with Glister and compute an external field to cancel it in magnitude and phase.

She sent a terse message to Opal, explaining what she was about to do. She could not signal to J'merlia, since Dreyfus-27 was still shielded by the mass of Gargantua.

Kallik dragged the field generator and inhibitor forty meters away from the *Have-It-All*. She had one more problem to solve. If she focused the field on the surface with a five- or ten-meter effective range, the device itself would sink through into Glister if the surface became fluid or gaseous. The only way to prevent that was to run a pair of lines attached to the generator right around the body of the sphere, one following a geodesic around the "equator" and the other a geodesic over the "poles." Downward forces would then be held by tension in the cables, and supported by the surface strength of the whole of Glister.

Kallik paused for thought.

The lines would be supported, unless of course the *local* field cancellation somehow caused a *global* cancellation. Then Glister would become a ball of gas or liquid, and Kallik, the *Have-It-All*, and the *Summer Dreamboat* would plunge together into the unknown interior.

A Hymenopt had no shoulders to shrug. Instead, Kallik clucked and chirped softly to herself while she made the final connections of the thin, dislocation-free cables to the field generator. She was a fatalist. So Glister might become liquid. Well, no one ever promised that life would be risk-free. She hurried back to the *Have-It-All* and left a message for J'merlia on the recorder of the ship, the equivalent of "So long, it's been nice knowing you." If she returned safely, she could erase it.

She turned on the power, stood back, and watched.

The result was at first disappointing. The generator was a compact device, operating with microwave energy beamed from the *Have-It-All*. There was nothing to show that it was in operation, and the equipment stood exactly as she had left it, with no sound or movement.

Then she heard it; a faint creaking of the thin, tight-strung cables, protesting as they took up the strain of the generator's weight. The unit itself stood on three solid legs, but now the bottom few centimeters of those legs were invisible. They had sunk through into the surface of Glister.

Kallik moved cautiously toward the field generator. Its position was stable, moving neither downward nor upward.

She touched one of the taut support lines, estimating the tension. From the feel of it, the generator would have dropped right on through without them. The surface looked subtly different for a radius of about five meters from the field's center, where the support lines bent downward and disappeared.

Kallik reached down. Her forelimb penetrated the gray surface, but she felt nothing.

She had brought with her from the ship half-a-dozen spent power canisters. She lobbed one to land by the field generator. The surface did not change in appearance, but the metal canister vanished at once and without a trace. The absence of ripples around the point of disappearance argued for a gaseous rather than a liquid region around the generator.

Kallik retreated a couple of steps. So it would swallow a power canister easily, and perhaps a Hymenopt with no more difficulty. But was the canceled field zone deep enough to provide true access to the interior? Or did it come to a solid bottom, a few meters down?

Kallik knew that she would not find answers by standing and thinking about it.

She went back to the ship and procured another length of cable, securing it first to a brace on the *Have-It-All*'s main hull and then cinching it around her own midriff. If someone came along and decided to fly the *Have-It-All* off on an interplanetary mission while Kallik was down inside Glister, she would be in deep trouble.

But she was in deep trouble anyway.

She moved to the edge of the zone of change. For a few seconds she paused there, hesitating. There was no guarantee that what she was doing would help Darya Lang and Hans Rebka—still less that it was the *best* way to help them. If there was a better solution, it was her duty to find it.

As she stood thinking there was a *whoosh!* of disturbed air not far overhead. It was a Phage, hurtling by no more than fifty meters from the surface. The dark maw was closed, but it could open in a few seconds.

Kallik whistled an invocation to Ressess-tress, the leading non-deity of the Hymenopts' official atheism. She blinked all her eyes, stepped forward, and dropped through into the impalpable surface of Glister.

CHAPTER 12

The *Incomparable*—incomparably rattly, rusty, cumbersome, and smelly—was approaching Gargantua. Birdie Kelly and Julius Graves focused their attention on the satellites and waited for a detailed view of Glister itself, while E. C. Tally stared steadily at a display of the giant planet. He had been sitting silently for fifteen hours, since the moment when the *Incomparable*'s sensors had provided their first good look at Gargantua.

That was fine with Birdie Kelly. Tally's designers had recognized that the embodied computer's body would need rest, but apparently his inorganic brain functioned continuously. Over the past three days, Birdie had been wakened from sound sleep a dozen times with a touch and a polite "May I speak?"

Eventually Birdie had lost it. "Damn it, Tally. *No more questions*. Why don't you go and ask Graves something for a change? Julius and Steven between 'em know ten times as much as I do."

"No, Commissioner Kelly, that is not true." E. C. Tally shook his head, practicing the accepted human gesture for dissent and the conventional human pause before offering a reply. "They know much more than ten times as much as you do. Perhaps one hundred times? Let me think about that."

The first sight of Gargantua had kept him quiet for a while. But now he was perking up and coming out of his reverie over by the display screens. To Birdie's relief, though, he was turning to Julius Graves.

"If I may speak: with respect to the communications that we have received from Darya Lang and from Kallik. Professor Lang suggests that Glister is a Builder artifact, and Kallik agrees. Does any other evidence suggest the presence of Builder activity in the vicinity of Gargantua?"

"No. The nearest artifact to Gargantua is the Umbilical, connecting Quake and Opal." The voice was Steven Graves's. "And it is the only one reported in the Mandel stellar system."

"Thank you. That is what my own data banks show, but I wondered if there might be inadequacies, as there have been in other areas." Tally reached out and tapped the screen, where Gargantua filled the screen. "Would you please examine this and offer your opinion?"

His index finger was squarely on an orange-and-umber spot below Gargantua's equator.

"The bright oval?" Graves asked. He looked for only a moment, then turned his attention to the other screen, where the sensors were set for analysis of a volume of space surrounding Glister. "I'm sorry. I have no information about that."

But to his own great amazement, Birdie did. He finally knew something that Graves did not! "It's called the Eye of Gargantua," he burst out. "It's a great big whirlpool of gases, a permanent hurricane about forty thousand kilometers across." He pointed to the screen. "You can even see the vortices on the image, trailing away from it on both sides."

"I can see them. Do you know for how long the Eye of Gargantua has existed?"

"Not really. But it's been around for as long as the Dobelle system has been colonized. Thousands of years. When people came out here exploring for minerals, ages ago, the survey teams all took pictures of it. Every kids' book talks about it and has a drawing of it. It's a famous bit of the stellar system, one of the 'natural wonders' you learn about in school."

"You are speaking metaphorically. I learned nothing in school, for I did not attend it." E. C. Tally frowned. He had been experimenting with that expression as a way of indicating a paradox or dichotomy of choice, and he felt the look had reached a satisfactory level of performance. "But knowledge is not the issue. The Eye of Gargantua should not be described to children as one of the natural wonders of the stellar system. For a good reason: it is not one."

"Not one *what*?" Birdie cursed himself. He should have known better than to have jumped into a conversation with Tally.

"The Eye of Gargantua is not a natural wonder of the stellar system. Because it is not *natural*."

"Then what the blazes is it?"

"I do not know." Tally attempted another human gesture, a shrug of the shoulders. "But I know what it is not. I have been calculating continuously for the past fifteen hours, with all plausible boundary conditions. The system that we see is not a stable solution of the time-dependent, three-dimensional Navier-Stokes equation for gaseous motion. It should have dissipated itself, in weeks or months. In order for the Eye of Gargantua to exist, some large additional source of atmospheric circulation must be present right there." He touched the screen. "At the center of the eye, where you can see the vortex—"

"Phages!" Julius Graves broke in excitedly. "They're there all right. We're getting an image of fragments around Glister, but it's not like the one that Rebka and Lang sent back from their first sighting. The cloud around it extends all the way down to the surface. If those are all Phages . . ."

"Can we fly down through them, as did Captain Rebka and Professor Lang?" Tally addressed Birdie Kelly, as the most experienced pilot. "They reached the surface safely."

"Fly down there—in this scumbucket?" Birdie glared around at the controls and fittings of the ore freighter. "We sure as hell can't. Take a look at us. The drive don't work at more than half power, there's no weapons to pop

Phages with, and we're about as mobile as a Dowser. If those are all Phages down there, and they're half as nippy as Captain Rebka says, we've got problems. Maybe if they get a good *sniff* of this ship before they start chewing, we'll have a chance. I know Phages are supposed to eat anything, but there have to be limits."

"A sniff—"

"I was *joking,* E.C. What I mean is, we'd better stay well out of the way."

"But we don't have to rely on the *Incomparable* to get us there," Julius Graves said. "We can use the *Summer Dreamboat.* It took the others safely past the Phages, and Professor Lang said in her last message that she left it on remote control. We can call it up to us, and fly it down."

"But what about Rebka and Lang and Kallik?" Birdie did not like the assumption that they were all going down to Glister, danger or no danger. "They'll need a ship if they want to get out of there in a hurry."

"They'll have one—the *Have-It-All.* It's still there if they need it. And we can surely borrow the *Dreamboat* for a few hours. We'll have it back to them before they even know it's gone. But it will take a while for the *Dreamboat* to get here. We ought to give the command at once. So if you will please proceed, Commissioner . . ."

It *was* a Phage on the surface of Glister.

Or maybe it was best to say that it was the devastated remains of one. J'merlia had approached as closely as he cared to and confirmed that the heap of slate-gray debris contained regular pentagonal elements. But he could see nothing of organs or an internal structure, and other factors made him question that this was a Phage as they were known in the rest of the spiral arm. For one thing, Phages were supposed to be just about indestructible. This one looked as though it had hurtled vertically and at high velocity into the surface of Glister. It should have smashed a giant hole. But the impact had left no mark, or else the mark had since vanished.

What could Glister be made of, to remain unscathed after such a blow?

J'merlia lifted lemon-yellow eyes on their short eyestalks to the heavens and looked for more Phages. They were there, whipping past overhead. Lower on every pass, if he was any judge.

He trotted on, scanning the surface of Glister for anything familiar. It was less than five minutes before he came across a taut cable running from horizon to horizon. He followed it and soon saw the *Have-It-All*. He hurried to the ship hoping to find Kallik or the missing humans, but a quick look inside showed that the cabins were deserted; the message from Kallik confirmed that. Forty meters away stood a piece of equipment, partially sunk into Glister's smooth gray surface. Four tight-stretched lines at ninety degrees to each other appeared to support the machine.

J'merlia decided that the lines probably ran all the way around the planetoid. There was no point in following them. He went closer to the machine and recognized it as a field monitor and inhibitor. If it was operating as Kallik had suggested, the surface around it might offer no resistance to weight. J'merlia went forward cautiously to the place where one of the lines vanished into Glister's interior. When he placed a forelimb on the surface at that point, it went down without resistance. The smooth gray appeared totally insubstantial.

He straightened up. Another cable ran from a stout stanchion on the *Have-It-All*'s hull all the way to the point where it plunged into the unblemished surface by the field inhibitor. Anyone might try to climb down that rope, into the unknown gray region—or, more likely, use it as a way to return to the outside of Glister.

J'merlia went back to the ship and gave it a more thorough inspection. As when Rebka and Lang had found it, everything was in working order. Given an hour or two to familiarize himself with the controls, he could make a fair shot at flying it anywhere in the spiral arm via the Bose Network Transition Points.

Which more and more felt like a good idea. Every few minutes now he heard the whistle of Phages overhead. Something was maddening them, and that something was probably the presence of newcomers on the surface of Glister. The place was not safe anymore; even as he watched, a Phage came sailing by with open maw, no more than a hundred meters above the *Have-It-All*.

It was only a matter of time before some furiously energized Phage, by accident or design, made a direct hit on him or on the ship. He had to get away from the planetoid, or he would soon be of no use to anyone.

J'merlia was feeling increasingly uncomfortable with his own actions. He had come to Glister with a poorly defined idea of saving Rebka, Lang, and Kallik, and perhaps Atvar H'sial and Louis Nenda. But having arrived here he had no idea what to do next. He lacked Kallik's initiative and decisiveness. It certainly seemed a poor idea to follow her to the interior of Glister. On the other hand it was no better to stay on the surface, because that option appeared more dangerous with every minute.

J'merlia sat in the cabin of the *Have-It-All* and dithered. He had had enough of this free-thinking misery; what he longed for was a master to give him directions.

His own orders had been to stay on Dreyfus-27. It was the one thing he had been told to do, and he had disobeyed. He did not want to go back to Dreyfus-27—it was too far from Glister—but maybe he should take a good intermediate step. He could fly the *Summer Dreamboat* far enough from Glister to be safe from the Phages, yet close enough to monitor everything that happened on the planetoid's surface. Then if Kallik or one of the others appeared, J'merlia could have the ship down to pick them up in a few minutes.

It was not a good solution, but it was a reasonable compromise. He hesitated for a few minutes more, until a Phage came whistling past almost close enough to grab him.

The *Summer Dreamboat* was no more than two minutes' travel at a rapid trot. J'merlia closed the cabin of the *Have-It-All* and set off for the other ship.

He was less than a hundred meters away when it rose smoothly from the surface of Glister. As J'merlia gaped up, it hurtled away at maximum acceleration into the glimmering void above his head.

CHAPTER 13

Seen from a distance with the great bulk of Gargantua as backdrop, Glister was an insignificant mote. Without the telltale signal from the *Have-It-All*'s beacon, the planetoid would have been too small to notice, lost amid a thousand larger fragments.

But viewed from the *inside* . . .

The floors, bulging walls, and arched ceilings of the lower levels were formed of broad interlocking hoops, each one pleated and rigid and glowing with its own faint phosphorescence. It was like walking through the curling alimentary canal of a giant alien beast. Some sections were filled with nets and cables, like those found on the higher levels, while others were totally empty; occasional areas were littered with pieces of equipment placed apparently at random.

Darya was muttering to herself as Hans Rebka led the way deeper and deeper, on through endless corridors.

"What's that?" he asked over his shoulder as she swore more loudly than usual.

"Calculations. Depressing ones. The radius of Glister is one-point-one-six kilometers. Even if each interior level is fifty meters high, that's a hundred and twenty square kilometers of floor. How long is it going to take us to look at it all?"

"Don't worry about it. You'll starve to death first."

Hans Rebka had to be hungry, too, but he was defiantly

cheerful. Starvation, or even the mention of it, did not make Darya cheerful. It made her grouchy. Back on Sentinel Gate she had not missed a meal in twenty years. That thought was no help at all. "We don't seem to be finding anything useful. Where do you think you're taking us?"

Hans did not answer. In spite of her grumbles, it was Darya who had insisted on stopping every few minutes to take a close look at some novel structure or machine. Every object in the interior of Glister was a product of the Builders' technology and therefore a source of fascination to the professor in her. She could recognize many of them, devices that occurred in some of the other 1236 known Builder artifacts scattered around the spiral arm, but a number were totally unfamiliar, and she wanted to inspect them closely and estimate their function. Rebka was the one who had to drag her away, every time, insisting that they must find the control center of Glister before they did anything else. Since the planetoid was artificial and habitable, *something* had to be keeping it in working order.

Rebka had not mentioned his own secret fear. Gravity was increasing steadily as they wound their way down toward the center of Glister. Now it was close to two gees. Beneath their feet must be some powerful field source. They could still walk easily enough—but what would they do if it rose higher yet? No one knew what gravity field the Builders had found natural. A central control room for Glister might occupy a high-gee environment that neither he nor Darya could tolerate.

From the curvature of the floor he estimated that they were still about six hundred meters from the center of Glister. Given a choice of paths, he had always descended. It was only an instinct, the belief that the most important regions of the planetoid ought to be near the center rather than on some upper level. If he was wrong, he would have doomed both of them.

In spite of all that, Rebka was quite enjoying himself. This was what life was all about. Exploring things that no human had ever seen before, with an interesting companion—what more could a man ask, unless it was for a little food?

"I think we're coming to something," he said. "The light ahead is different. It's getting fainter."

The answering growl behind Rebka sounded skeptical. He wondered if it was just Darya's stomach. As the illumination from walls and ceiling faded, he stepped forward more cautiously. Soon he could see nothing ahead, not even the floor, but his instincts told him they were approaching something new.

"Stay there." He kept his voice down to the softest whisper. "I don't know what's ahead, but I want to feel my way for a bit before we shine a light." Even those breathed words sounded strange, hollow and echoing.

He went down on hands and knees and felt his way forward. Five meters farther on, his left hand found itself groping into empty space. He reached out as far as he could on both sides. Nothing. The tunnel ended in a blind drop. There was no light below, or in any direction. He crawled back to join Darya and placed his mouth next to her ear.

"We'll have to use your flashlight," he whispered. "Take a look ahead. Be careful how you shine it—straight down on the floor first, then raise it up slowly." He moved aside to allow her to come level with him, then paced her carefully forward.

"No farther now!" He stopped her. "There's nothing ahead."

Darya nodded, unseen in the darkness. The light beam shone on the floor at her feet, then moved out over the lip in front of them. As it came higher its narrow beam reflected faintly off a distant wall. Darya inched forward, shining the light downward. One more step, and she would be over the edge.

The ledge she stood on was halfway up the wall of a great open room, with a sheer drop below that plunged twenty meters before it curved around to form the bowl-shaped empty floor of the chamber.

Darya stepped back a pace. In this gravity field, any fall could be fatal. She shone the beam higher. Above them was a vaulted ceiling, confirming the spherical shape of the chamber. The domed vault was featureless, without lights or support struts. The whole room had to be at least sixty meters across.

"Something's there." Hans kept his voice to a whisper, but the echoes came rolling in from across the room, reluctant to die. *There . . . there . . . there . . . there.*

"Right in the middle. Shine the light in the center."

Darya pointed the flashlight straight ahead. Hovering in the middle of the room without any visible support was a silvery sphere about ten meters across. She thought at once of the sphere that had risen from the broken surface of Quake at Summertide, but this one was hundreds of times smaller.

And it was more active. The ball had been hanging in a fixed position, but as the beam touched it the surface became a play of motion. The flashlight reflected an undulatory pattern, like slow waves on a ball of rippling mercury. The waves grew and steadied. The sphere began to deform and elongate.

There . . . there . . . there . . . there . . . A rusty, creaking voice filled the chamber, as deep and ancient as the sea. *There . . . there . . . there . . . there. Center . . . center . . . center . . . center.*

Darya was so excited that she could hardly hold the flashlight steady. The sphere had become a distorted ellipsoid. A frond of silver began to grow upward from the top, slowly evolving to a five-sided flower that turned to face Darya and Hans. Open pentagonal disks extruded from the front of the ball, pointing toward the flashlight beam. A long, thin tail grew down, extending to the floor of the chamber. In three minutes the featureless sphere became a horned and tailed devil-beast, with a flowerlike head that sought the source of the intrusion.

A flickering green light shone from an aperture in the body of the demon and illuminated Hans and Darya. The inside of the great chamber shimmered with its reflection. Darya turned off the flashlight.

Human form . . . human . . . human. Too soon . . .

soon . . . soon . . . The weary voice came echoing across to them. *Who . . . who . . . who . . . who . . .*

Hans and Darya turned to look at each other.

He shrugged. "What do we have to lose?" He faced into the chamber and spoke at normal volume. "Can you understand me? We are humans. We were brought against our will into this planetoid. We do not know how to leave it."

The flower head was nodding toward them. The light from the being's body modulated in color and intensity as it bobbed up and down in the middle of the chamber.

"It's no good," Darya said. "You can't expect it to understand a word." But while she was speaking the voice began again.

Brought inside . . . inside. Yes, we understand human . . . human . . . human . . . You were brought inside to be . . . others, in case others were needed . . . you may not be needed. You were to stay there . . . near the outside . . . not come here . . .

Darya stepped closer to the edge. "Who are you? Where did you come from? What is this place?"

"One question at a time," Rebka said softly, "or it won't have any idea what you're asking."

But the demon figure in front of them was already speaking again, and more fluently. *I am The-One-Who-Waits . . . The one who waited in the heart of the double world, in the Connection Zone . . . I came from the heart of that world, when it opened to the signal . . .*

"From inside Quake," Darya said. "At Summertide! It must have come in the big silver sphere, the one that grabbed the *Have-It-All.*"

. . . for which I had waited long. In human time, one fortieth of a galactic revolution. I waited . . .

"That's six million years! Are you a Builder?"

"Don't keep interrupting, Darya. Let it talk!"

—waited long for the Event. I am not a Builder, only a servant of the Builders. I am The-One-Who-Waits. Who seeks the Builders?

"I do!" Darya moved dangerously close to the edge. "All my life, ever since I was a child, I have studied the

Builders, wanted to know more about them. The Builders have been my life's work."

The Builders are not here. The ones who fly outside are not true Builders. This is the Connection Zone . . . the testing place, where we wait for the question to be answered. Wait.

The green light was extinguished and the chamber plunged again into darkness. Darya was teetering on the edge of the drop until Hans Rebka seized her arm and pulled her back to safety.

She shook herself loose; she did not feel even a twinge of nervousness. "Did you hear that, Hans? The *Connection* Zone! The Builders aren't here, but there's access to them from inside Glister. I knew it. They can be reached from here!"

"*Maybe* they can. Darya, calm down." Rebka grabbed her again, pulled her close, and spoke with his mouth next to her ear. "Did you hear me? Cool off, and think before you jump to conclusions. You've been in communication for about two minutes with something that says it's at least six million years old, and you're willing to take everything it says at face value. What makes you think you understand what it means, or it understands you? Lots of what it said makes no sense—'the ones who fly outside are not true Builders.' That's not information, it's gibberish. More than that, where did it learn to speak our language? How did it even recognize the human *shape*, if it's been locked away inside Quake for six million years? There were no humans *anywhere* that long ago."

But the green light was pulsing again, illuminating them and the whole of the domed chamber.

The testing proceeds. The rusty voice spoke again. *It comes close to completion . . . close enough to be sure that the modified one is a true human, and acceptable. It is not necessary for you to be here . . .*

"Then take us back to the surface," Rebka said.

"No!" Darya moved in front of him. "Hans, if we go back now we may as well never have come here at all. There are so many things we might be able to find out here about the Builders. We may never have as good an opportunity."

You seek the Builders, the creaking voice went on, as though neither human had spoken. *I am not a Builder, and I cannot guarantee the result. But if it is your desire to encounter the Builders—*

"It is!"

Then, GO.

"No. Darya, will you for God's sake wait a minute! We don't know—"

Rebka's shout was too late. They were standing on the brink of the tunnel as the edge turned suddenly to vapor.

Free-fall!

Rebka looked down to his feet. They were accelerating at a couple of gees along a featureless vertical shaft that ended half a kilometer below them in a darkness so total that the eye rejected its existence.

"What is it?" Rebka heard Darya's despairing cry beside him.

"It's Glister's gravity field—whatever creates it—maybe a . . ." He did not finish the phrase. If they were falling toward the event horizon of a black hole they would know about it soon enough—know it for maybe a millisecond, before tidal differential forces reduced their bodies to component elementary particles.

"Hans!" Darya screamed.

Two hundred meters to go, still accelerating, faster than ever. Maybe a second left. And now the darkness possessed a structure, like a roiling whirlpool of black oil, curling and tumbling onto itself. They were heading into the churning heart of that dark vortex.

Rebka's empty stomach was churning, too.

A fraction of a second to go.

Childhood on Teufel had taught him one thing above all others: there was always a way out of every fix—if you were smart enough.

You just had to *think.*

Think.

Apparently he was not smart enough. He was still thinking, unproductively, as he dropped into the depths of that writhing blackness.

CHAPTER 14

The unmanned *Summer Dreamboat* had arrived in one piece and in working order.

That was the good news. The bad news was that it had been touch and go.

Five grazing encounters with Phages had delivered hammer blows to the *Dreamboat*'s hull, one strong enough to dent and puncture the top of the cabin. The repair was not difficult, and Birdie Kelly was already half finished. But the significance of those five near misses was not the damage that they had done. It was what they revealed about the state of the Phages. Steven Graves and E. C. Tally had monitored the ascent of the *Dreamboat* and were agreed for once: the little ship's survival, even with all collision-avoidance systems active, had been mainly a matter of luck. The Phages were more active than ever, all the way down to the surface of Glister. A descent with accelerations that humans could stand had less than a one-percent chance of success.

The *Summer Dreamboat* had been moved for repairs into the capacious ore hold of the *Incomparable*. Graves and Tally were floating free in the air-filled interior, talking and talking.

And watching me work, Birdie thought. Same as usual. The other two were long on talk, but when anything calling for physical effort came along they managed to leave all the *doing* to him. And they lacked a decent sense of danger. Birdie hated to work with heroes. He had listened to Steven and E. C. Tally casually talk odds of a hundred to one against, and shuddered. Fortunately, Julius Graves seemed to have more rational views.

"Those odds are totally unacceptable," he was saying. "When you and Steven are in agreement, I am forced to listen. We cannot afford to take such a risk."

"May I speak?"

"Which means we have a real problem," Graves continued, ignoring Tally's request. "J'merlia is on Dreyfus-27. Probably deep inside it, since he does not answer our calls. So he can't help. And everyone else is on Glister. And we have no safe way of getting to them." He paused. "Did you say something, E.C.?"

"Steven and I agreed on the probability of survival if the *Summer Dreamboat* simply makes a direct descent to Glister. Or rather, we disagreed in the third significant digit of the calculated result. But there are other options. It depends on the probability level which one uses to define 'safe.' For example, there is a technique that would raise the probability of a successful landing of the *Summer Dreamboat* on the surface of Glister to a value in excess of zero-point-eight-four."

"A five-out-of-six chance of getting there in one piece?" Julius Graves glared at Tally. "Why didn't you mention it earlier?"

"For three reasons. First, it came to me only after a review of analogous situations, of other places and times. That review was completed only thirty seconds ago. Second, the technique should provide a safe landing, but the odds of a safe subsequent ascent are incalculable without additional data concerning the surface of Glister. And third, the procedure would probably lead to the loss of a valuable asset: the *Incomparable*."

"Commissioner Kelly." Graves turned to Birdie. "The *Incomparable* is the property of the government of Dobelle. As the representative of the government, how would you view its possible loss?"

Birdie had finished the patch on the *Dreamboat*'s hull

and burned his thumb doing it. He pushed himself off and glared around the *Incomparable*'s hold as he floated up to grab a support beam at Tally's side.

"It's a filthy barrel of rust and rot, it stinks like a dead ponker, and it should have been thrown on the scrap heap fifty years ago. If I never see it again, that's too soon."

Tally was frowning at him. "Am I to take it, then, that you would sanction the potential loss of the *Incomparable*?"

"In one word, matey, yes."

"Then if I may speak, I will outline the technique. It is something that can be found in the older parts of the data banks. In old times, when human individuals wished to accomplish an objective that certain other guarding entities sought to prevent, they often employed a method known as *creating a diversion* . . ."

Agreement in principle did not guarantee agreement in practice. E. C. Tally and Steven Graves had argued endlessly about the best method. Should the *Incomparable* be sent in well ahead of the *Dreamboat*, passing through the periphery of the cloud of orbiting Phages and seeking to draw them away from Glister? Or was it better to fly the old ore freighter on a trajectory that would impact Glister, and take the *Dreamboat* in not far behind, relying on its being ignored in the presence of the freighter's larger and more tempting target?

Tally and Steven Graves had finally agreed on one thing—that they had insufficient data.

"Since there is not enough information to make a reasoned choice," Tally said apologetically to Birdie Kelly, "the only thing I can suggest is that we resort to aleatoric procedure."

"What's 'aleatoric' mean, when it's at home?" Birdie was reaching into his jacket pocket.

"An aleatoric procedure is one that contains chance and random elements."

"Why, that's just the way I was thinking myself." Birdie produced a deck of cards and shuffled it expertly. He held it out to Tally. "Pick a card, E.C., any card. Red, and the ships fly a long way apart from each other. Black, and we tuck ourselves up the old *Incomparable*'s tailpipe."

Tally selected a card from the spread and turned it over. "It is black." He had stared in great curiosity when Birdie shuffled the deck. "What you did just then—it was difficult to see, but is it designed to randomize the sequence?"

"You might say that." Birdie gave E. C. Tally a thoughtful glance. "Didn't you ever play cards?"

"Never."

"If we get out of this alive, why don't I teach you?"

"Thank you. That would be informative."

"And don't you worry," Birdie patted Tally on the shoulder. "We won't be playing for high stakes. At first."

"That could have been us." Julius Graves was staring straight up. "Not a comforting thought."

They had finally decided that since the *Dreamboat* needed time and maneuvering space to land on Glister, it would be a mistake to have the *Incomparable* fly in all the way to the surface. Instead, the bigger ship had been programmed to zoom down to ten kilometers and then veer away from the planetoid, with luck luring the cloud of attacking Phages with it.

As the *Dreamboat* increased the power level of its drive for the last hundred-meter deceleration to the surface, the *Incomparable* could be seen skirting the northern horizon of Glister. The old ship was at the center of a dense cluster of marauding Phages. Already it had sustained a dozen direct hits. The drive was still flaring, but Phage maws had gouged great chunks from the body of the freighter. About twenty Phages clung to the flanks of the *Incomparable*, like dogs worrying an old bull.

"They'll be back," Julius Graves went on. "The way they're going, they'll have swallowed the freighter completely in another half hour. And Phages don't get indigestion, or lose their appetite, no matter what they ingest."

Birdie had chosen an approach trajectory to bring them no more than fifty meters from the *Have-It-All*, on the side of the ship away from Kallik's field inhibitor. There had been no time to examine that installation during their descent, and would not have been even if the *Dreamboat*'s evasive movements from a handful of isolated Phages had been smooth enough to permit it. Now they had to hurry over to the inhibitor and decide what to do before any Phages returned to harass them.

The two men and the embodied computer had their suits set to full opacity. Kallik, Darya Lang, and Hans Rebka had certainly been able to breathe the atmosphere; and just as certainly, they had disappeared from the surface of Glister. Their vanishing and failure to reappear was unlikely to be the result of Glister's air—but it could be. As E. C. Tally pointed out, quoting from the most ancient part of the data banks, "Taking a *calculated risk*, sir, does not oblige one to act *rashly*."

While Graves and Tally went on to the site of the field inhibitor, Birdie took a quick look inside the *Have-It-All*. He headed first for the control room. The ship was untouched, ready to fly within a few seconds of giving the command. That gave Birdie his first warm feeling for quite a while. He patted the control console and hurried back outside.

He had half expected to see the surface of Glister littered with crashed Phages, but there were only two crumpled remains in sight. Did they lose interest if no organic life-forms were present? That was a new thought—though not an encouraging one, to an organic life-form.

Birdie followed the stretched cable from the *Have-It-All*'s stanchion to the place where Graves and E. C. Tally were standing. Tally had his hand on the line, close to the point where it disappeared into the gray surface, and he was tugging on it vigorously. As Birdie came up to them Tally released the cable, reached down, and pushed his hand easily *into* the slate-colored plane.

"Observe," he said. "The field inhibitor is still operating, with near-perfect field cancellation. The surface offers negligible resistance to the penetration of my hand, and at this point it must, I think, be a weakly secured gaseous form. But the cable itself offers considerable resistance to its own withdrawal. We conclude that it must be secured at its lower end, within the interior of Glister."

"In other words," Graves said, "it's tied to something."

Now that he was close enough, Birdie could see that the surface for a radius of a few meters around the field inhibitor appeared slightly indistinct. And the legs of the inhibitor equipment stood not *on* Glister, but buried a few centimeters in that hazy gray.

"So who shall be first?" Graves asked.

"First for what?" But Birdie knew the answer to that question before he asked it. The one thing that made no sense was to come all the way here, run the gauntlet through that belt of aggressive Phages, and then sit and wait for the same Phages to come back and dive-bomb them. The only way to go was *down*, into that gray horridness.

Tally had taken hold of the cable without waiting for discussion. "It is possible that I will be unable to return messages to you through the suit communications system," he said calmly. "However, when I reach a point where it is appropriate for another to descend, I will strike the cable—thus." He hit it with the palm of his suited hand. "Feel for the vibration."

He pushed his feet over the edge and swung hand-over-hand down the cable. His body disappeared easily into a gray opacity. When only his head showed above the smoky surface he paused.

"It occurs to me that my words leave the required action for some possible future situation inadequately defined. A contingency may arise in which I become unable to strike the cable in the manner that I described. If I do not signal in a reasonable time, say, one thousand seconds, you should assume that contingency."

"Don't worry your head about that," Birdie said. "We'll assume it."

"That is satisfactory." E. C. Tally disappeared completely. A second later his head popped up again from the gray haze. "May I ask, if I do not signal in one thousand seconds, what action you propose to take?"

Birdie stared off to the horizon. The hulk of the *Incomparable* had vanished—devoured, or flown far away, he could not tell. There was a cloud of glittering motes visible in the same direction. The same Phages, probably, sensing motion on the surface of Glister and coming back for another go at it.

Except that these Phages were not interested in the surface of Glister. They wanted to have a go at humans. At *him*.

"I don't know what action we'll take, E.C.," Birdie said. "But don't be surprised if it happens before you count out your thousand seconds."

The cable went down ten meters through gray obscurity, then emerged into a spherical region with another gray floor and a ceiling above it that glowed with cold orange light.

Birdie clung to the line, high up near the ceiling, and peered downward.

It was a long drop—a horrid long drop, for somebody from a planet where the buildings were never more than a couple of stories high; and there was no sign of E. C. Tally down there. But the cable went on, straight downward, into the floor.

Birdie slightly relaxed the grip of his hands and knees and continued his controlled descent. When he came to the part of the second floor where the line ran through, that surface proved just as insubstantial as the first one. The field inhibitor had been focused downward, and for all Birdie knew, its effect went right through Glister and out the other side. He allowed himself to drop on through. Somewhere above him, Julius Graves was waiting for his signal, as he had waited for E. C Tally's. But this was no time to give it, suspended in midair.

The gray fog filled his nose and mouth, passing through his supposedly sealed suit as though it did not exist. The gas was thin, tasteless, and odorless, and it did not interfere with Birdie's breathing. In another ten meters he was through that and dropping again toward a spherical surface.

This level was more promising. There were structures and partitions and webs, dividing the space into giant, oddly-shaped rooms. Birdie was coming down into one of the bigger open areas. He released the line with his crossed legs, let go with his hands, and dropped the last few feet. The gravity was more than he had realized. He landed heavily and flopped backward to a sitting position. Before he stood up he took a quick look around.

Dull gray walls. A jumble of nets and unconnected support lines on the floor, right by his side. He was sitting on a length of flexible netting, springy enough to be a bed. The cable he had come down ran off to the right, to a descending ramp that became part of a brightly lit tunnel.

Off on that right side—he stopped, stared, and stared again. On that right side, close to the entry to the downward ramp, was E. C. Tally.

And crouched next to him, eight legs splayed, was J'merlia.

Birdie scrambled to his feet. The Lo'tfian was supposed to be hundreds of thousands of kilometers away, on Dreyfus-27. What was he doing here?

Birdie jerked at the line he was holding, to send a signal back to Graves that it was safe to descend, and hurried across to the other two.

"You were right about messages, E.C.," he said. "I assume you tried to send something through your suit communicator, but we didn't hear a thing."

"Nor I from you. The surface is presumably impervious to electromagnetic signals, though it permits material objects to pass through with no difficulty." E. C. Tally gestured to J'merlia. "It is not necessary for you to introduce the two of us, Commissioner Kelly. We have already done that. Although J'merlia and I never met before, I recognized the Lo'tfian form from stored records."

"That's as may be. But what's *he* doing *here*? Why aren't you over on Dreyfus, J'merlia, the way Captain Rebka's messages said you would be?"

"I beg forgiveness for that act. I came to Glister to seek the masters, Atvar H'sial and Louis Nenda, and also the Hymenopt Kallik. But when I was on the surface, I was forced to seek refuge in the interior from the attack of Phages. The ship that I had arrived in, the *Summer Dreamboat*, took off from the surface and left me helpless."

"Sorry, J'merlia, that was our doing—we needed it to come down in. But you were a bit ambitious, wouldn't you say, looking for Nenda and H'sial and Kallik? Seeing as how we've all no idea where any one of them is. You'd have been better off staying on Dreyfus, out of harm's way. Phages are bad news."

"With apologies, Commissioner Kelly. The Phages are, as you say, amazingly aggressive. It was unwise of me to come here. But there is good news also. I know where the masters are! And the Hymenopt Kallik. They are all three together, in a chamber closer to the center of Glister."

"I can't believe it." Birdie turned to E. C. Tally. "Is J'merlia telling the truth?"

"I have no direct evidence that supports his statement. But if you will accept indirect evidence, according to the central data banks the species that lead the spiral arm in deliberate falsehood are humans and Cecropians. Everyone else, including J'merlia and all Lo'tfians, is far behind."

"With respect, Commissioner Kelly, you may verify that I speak the truth. All you need to do is act as I did— follow the cable. It led me all the way from the surface, to where the masters and Kallik can be found."

"Which would certainly be direct evidence." E. C. Tally gestured to Birdie. "Go ahead, Commissioner, with J'merlia. When Councilor Graves joins me we will come after you. The cable provides an unambiguous trail for us to pursue."

Birdie found himself following the thin figure of J'merlia

down an angled and jointed tunnel, whose sudden changes
of direction made his head spin. The tunnel branched
occasionally, and parts were so dimly lit that the walls could
not be seen, but J'merlia followed the thin line wherever
it led. Birdie trailed along behind, his hand touching the
Lo'tfian's back. Their emergence into a giant domed
chamber came as a shock.

The downward-curving floor formed a shallow circular
bowl, marked off in concentric rings of pure color. Under
the brilliant overhead light their reflection hurt the eyes.
From the meeting place of each pair of rings rose
insubstantial hemispheres, arching up over the middle of
the chamber. The line that J'merlia had been following
led toward that center, straight as a spoke on a wheel.
Halfway in it stopped. Kallik was lying on the floor there,
a compact dark bundle on the boundary between a purple
and a red ring. In two front paws she held the spool for
the line, and the other end had been wrapped securely
around her body.

And *beyond* Kallik's unconscious form . . .

The innermost ring was blue, purest blue, a mono-
chromatic 0.47-micrometer blue. At its center stood a
raised dais of the same color, with a dozen glassy seats
upon it. In two of those seats lolled the unmistakable forms
of Louis Nenda and Atvar H'sial.

Birdie started forward. He was restrained by J'merlia's
grip on his sleeve.

"With respect, Commissioner, it may be unwise to
proceed farther."

"Why? They don't look dead, just unconscious. But they
could be in bad shape. We have to get 'em out and take
care of them, soon as we can."

"Assuredly. My first reaction was the same as yours,
that I must proceed at once and rescue the masters. But
then I thought to myself, the Hymenopt Kallik surely
operated with the same imperative. She saw the masters,
she went forward toward them—and she did not reach
them. When I realized that, I also realized that the worst
way for me to serve the masters would be to become

unconscious, as they are. I returned for safety to the second outer chamber. I had formulated no safe plan of action when the human, E. Crimson Tally, appeared."

"He's not a human. Tally's an embodied computer." Birdie did not go into details. He was too busy thinking about the other things that J'merlia had said.

"Why didn't you just grab hold of the line and pull Kallik out?" he went on. "She doesn't weigh much."

"I was unable to do so, Commissioner. Try it, if you wish."

Birdie seized the end of the line and heaved, as hard as he could. Kallik did not move a millimeter, and the line inside the pattern of rings did not even leave the floor. It was held there, fused to the surface or secured by some form of field. Birdie was still tugging and swearing when E. C. Tally and Julius Graves arrived.

There were five minutes of questions, suggestions, and counter-suggestions. At the end of it no one had bettered J'merlia's first proposal: that it was safe to do now what he had been reluctant to do before. He would enter the hemispheres and attempt to retrieve Kallik. If he failed, for any reason, the others would be on hand to help him. He would wear a line around him, so that if he became unconscious he could be pulled out.

"Which we know doesn't work for Kallik," Birdie said.

But he had no better ideas. They all watched in silence as J'merlia walked forward steadily, passing through the yellow and green rings and half of the purple one. At that point he hesitated. The thin head began to turn, and the pale yellow eyes on their short eyestalks moved dreamily from side to side.

"J'merlia!" Julius Graves shouted at him—loudly. The Lo'tfian stared around in a vague and puzzled way. He folded his thin hind legs and began to sit down.

"That's enough!" Graves was already pulling on the line. "Get him out, quick—while he can still stand."

J'merlia came reeling back from inside the pattern of rings. At the edge of the green annulus he jerked up to his full height and peered around him, but he allowed the others to haul him all the way out. On the edge of the yellow ring he sank down to his belly.

"What happened?" Tally asked. "You were progressing well, and then you halted."

"I don't remember." J'merlia crouched down on all his limbs and turned his eyestalks to stare back into the circle. "I was going in. Steadily, without difficulty. And then all at once I was going *out*, facing the other direction and being pulled clear."

"A Lotus field." Graves was nodding his head soberly. "Once Darya Lang pointed out that Glister is a Builder creation, we might have expected it. There are Lotus fields on many artifacts. The most famous one surrounds and protects Paradox. But J'merlia is lucky—he was exposed to only peripheral-field strength. Only the most recent of his memories were erased."

"Which may not be true of Kallik," E. C. Tally said. "And still less of Louis Nenda and Atvar H'sial. The Lotus field of Paradox erases all memories."

"From men," J'merlia said, "and from Lo'tfians and Hymenopts. But from machines? Or from computers?"

The others turned to look at E. C. Tally. He nodded. "According to the records, all memories are lost in Paradox, from Organics or Inorganics. However." He bent down to release the line from J'merlia and place it around his own body. "However, this is not Paradox. The Lotus field here may not be the same. An experiment is in order."

They watched in silence as he cautiously stepped into the yellow ring, then passed across the five-meter band that led to the green. In the middle of the green annulus he paused and looked back.

"I feel some slight disturbance of circuits." His voice was calm. "It is not enough to inhibit performance, nor to prevent my further progress. I will proceed."

He walked on, descending across the shallow bowl of the floor. Five paces short of the place where J'merlia had faltered, he paused again.

"I must return." His voice had become halting and slow. "I cannot retain information. It is being destroyed in both current and backup files . . . I record a loss of fourteen thousand sectors in the past three seconds." He turned and took one hesitant step away from the center. Then he seemed to freeze.

"Twenty-three thousand more sectors are gone," he said dreamily. "The rate is increasing."

"That's enough." Graves heaved on the line, and Tally came bobbing and weaving back to the periphery of the chamber. At the edge he halted and shook off Birdie Kelly's supporting hands.

"Do not worry, Commissioner Kelly. I have lost some data—all recent—but I am still fully functional. Most of my stored memory has not been affected."

"But we've answered the main question," Graves said. "The field is just as effective on organic or inorganic memories. So we can't get them out—any of them."

"We must." J'merlia stood up and made a movement as though he was ready to run back toward the middle of the chamber. "The masters are in there! Kallik is there! We cannot abandon them."

"I am sorry, J'merlia." Graves walked across to place himself between the Lo'tfian and the silent forms at the center of the room. "If we could do something to help Kallik and the others, we would—even though Atvar H'sial and Louis Nenda tried to kill us, back on Quake. But we can't do a thing to get them out."

"That statement is plausible, but not proven." E. C. Tally had been standing motionless. Now he raised his hands to touch the sides of his head. "I would like to question it. When I was receiving my original indoctrination, before I set out for Dobelle, there were calibration problems. To make the required adjustments, it was necessary to remove my brain."

Tally ignored Birdie Kelly's gasp of horror. He was feeling carefully around his temples. "I pointed out to the technicians at the time that my embodied design was intended for continuous sensory input. They employed a neural bundle connecting my brain to my spine. I lost sensory feeds and body control for a few seconds as the

attachment was being made, but I was otherwise unaffected. Now, my observations suggest that J'merlia is the
strongest and most agile of us. If he were to ascend the
cable all the way to the surface, enter the *Have-It-All*,
and return with a long high-capacity neural cable . . ."

Birdie Kelly had never seen anything so disgusting in
his whole life. And that was saying something.

E. C. Tally lay on his side on the gently curving floor,
eyes closed. A coil of high-capacity cable lay by him. His
head was supported on a folded blanket taken from the
Have-It-All, and he was giving calm directions to Julius
Graves and J'merlia.

"The skull is of course real bone, and the skin was
grown naturally. But for convenience of access the blood
vessels were terminated in the rear section, on a line one
centimeter above my ears. The blood supply to the upper
skull has been rerouted to veins and arteries in my
forehead. The upper cranium is hinged at the front and
secured with a line of pins at the back. You will see the
access line when the hair is lifted. If you raise the skin
at the back you should see the pressure points, marked
in blue on the bone."

Graves inserted a thin spatula into the horizontal gap
a few inches above E. C. Tally's rear hairline. As he levered
upward there was a gleam of white bone. Three blue dots
were revealed on the smooth rear of the skull.

"I see them. Three of them?"

"That is correct. Very good. When those pressure points
are simultaneously depressed, the rear pins release. You will
find that the whole upper cranium lifts forward about the
hinged line in the forehead. The skin, veins, and arteries
there should stretch, but they will remain intact above the
hinged region." When Graves hesitated, Tally added, "Do
not concern yourself about my sensations. Naturally, the
warning signals that you know as pain have been modified
in my case. I will feel nothing that you recognize as
discomfort."

Graves nodded, and while J'merlia held the spatula in

position he reached in and pressed the three marked places on the white bone. There was a sharp click. The rear part of the skull jerked upward a couple of millimeters, revealing a narrow dark slit.

"That looks like poor design," Graves said. "Isn't there a danger that the release could be triggered accidentally?"

"Not while I am functional. I must cooperate, or be incapable of internal state transitions, before the release can take place. Now—grasp the rear hair and lift the upper cranium, rotating it about the forward hinge."

The whole cap of the skull eased upward under Graves's gentle pressure. Birdie saw the inside of the hemisphere, with its intricate network of red blood vessels. Below it was a bulging gray ovoid, sitting in the skull case as snugly as an egg in an eggcup.

"Very good." Tally remained completely still. "You will now see what appear to be the meninges—the outer protective membranes of the human brain. In my case they are of course artificial. I was embodied with my own independent power supply, so there is no need for anything other than a neural body-brain interface. You will find the neural interface when you lift me out of the skull cavity. Lift me only a few centimeters, and proceed with caution. It would be undesirable to disable the interface prematurely. A strong pull would unseat the connection."

Graves was reaching into Tally's head and cautiously lifting out a roughly spherical object, small enough to hold comfortably in his two cupped hands. As the wrinkled ball was raised, a short coiled spiral was revealed. It ran between the bottom of the embodied computer and the lower hindbrain of E. C. Tally's body, above the end of the spinal column. Clear liquid dripped from the coil onto Graves's hands as the computer brain was lifted free of its body.

"Now," Tally continued. "The next phase should be simple, but I will not be able to guide you through it. Commissioner Kelly, you and J'merlia must make sure that my body does not move—there may be some reflex muscle activity. Councilor Graves, you must break the connection between me and the body, and then connect it again through the high-capacity cable. Do it as quickly as you can, consistent with care, but do not worry if it takes a minute or two. This body's own hindbrain will permit it to function normally for at least that long, while I am absent. Also, do not be afraid to touch the inside of the skull cavity. This body is well protected against infection. Carry on, please, as soon as you feel ready."

Graves nodded. There was another click as he reached in and delicately separated the body and the sphere of the embodied computer. E. C. Tally's limbs jerked against Birdie and J'merlia's restraining grasp; then the body slumped and steadied.

The ends of the neural cable had been placed close to hand. Julius Graves picked up the male connector. After a few seconds of effort he inserted it snugly into position at the upper end of the body's hindbrain.

"Half the job done." He was breathing loudly through his mouth. "But the other one doesn't want to go in. Hold him still." Graves's fingers were slippery with cerebrospinal fluid. He could not force home the connector attaching the computer brain to the neural cable.

"Hold on a minute." Birdie Kelly wiped his hands down his pants, then reached across to take both the brain and the connector from Graves. He pressed the plug home hard onto the multiple prongs of the computer's receptor.

"Gently!" Graves said. But the body of E. C. Tally was already sitting up and lifting free of J'merlia's grip.

"Hmm—kkh—khmmm." The torso shivered, and the eyes snapped open.

Graves bent close. "E. C. Tally! Can you hear me?"

"Very well." The topless head turned. "Excuse me, Councilor, but there is no need to shout like that. This body is equipped with excellent sensory apparatus."

The skull was still gaping wide, the empty cranium inverted and hanging upside down in front of Tally's bright blue eyes. Birdie Kelly stared at that empty skull, split open like a coconut, and at the neural cable that ran from the base of the brain to the little sphere in his right hand.

His torso wanted to shiver, too. Life on Opal was tough, but it had not prepared him for this sort of thing.

As Birdie watched, Tally reached up, took the open skull case in both hands, and casually rotated it back into position. "It won't quite close, I'm afraid," he said, "because the neural connector inhibits the seal. If possible we should tie it in place. It would be inconvenient to have the upper cranium detached and lost."

He turned to glance at the sphere that Birdie was holding. "Handle me with care if you please, Commissioner Kelly. What you have in your hands represents a substantial investment of Fourth Alliance property. I'm afraid that the body has already suffered minor damage, since it was not anticipated that we would need to perform brain removal in an unprepared facility." A thin trickle of blood was running down the left side of Tally's forehead. He wiped it away casually, stared around the chamber, and continued. "Also, my motor and sensory performance is somewhat impaired. The signal-carrying capacity of the neural cable is less than that of the original connection. I am able to see with rather less definition, colors are muted, and I sense that my muscular control is diminished. However, it should certainly be adequate for our purposes."

He rose to his feet, staggering a little before he caught his balance. At his direction J'merlia and Graves tied a makeshift bandage around his head, adding an extra wrapping to hold both the upper cranium and the external neural cable in position. Birdie Kelly was still holding the brain in nervous hands, doing his best to avoid jiggling it or putting any pressure on it.

"Are you sure you are ready?" Graves asked. "Don't you want to practice moving?"

But Tally was already stepping forward. "That would be pointless," he said. "My coordination would not improve. But as one precaution, let me do this." He picked up the strong line that he had used on his previous foray toward the center of the room and tied it around his waist. "You can always haul me back here. So now, if J'merlia will pay out the neural cable, Commissioner Kelly, as necessary . . ."

Tally took two staggering steps forward and began to weave his way down the gentle slope that led to the center of the chamber. He was soon into the first of the concentric rings. At the far edge of the yellow annulus he paused for a moment, while the others froze. Then he was off again, heading for the silent figure of Kallik. Birdie Kelly watched him, afraid even to blink, as J'merlia paid out cable from the reel that he was holding, at a pace just enough to prevent the line from tightening or drooping to touch the floor. There was something wholly unnatural about that human form, head bloody and bandaged, moving into the shallow and brightly lit cauldron of gaudy colors. He staggered as he walked, and the two cables trailing behind him swayed and jerked with a life and rhythm of their own.

"Come out at once if you feel you are losing memories," Graves called.

Tally waved an arm without slowing his progress. "Certainly. Though I do not expect that to happen. How can it, when *I* am with you in the hands of Commissioner Kelly?"

He was already past the green ring and moving on to the purple one. Two seconds more, and he was sinking slowly to sit on the floor beside Kallik, careful to keep his head upright. His fingers touched the Hymenopt's furry thorax. "She is alive. Unconscious, but not apparently injured. I cannot lift the line around her from the floor, but if I release her from it I see no difficulty in carrying her out."

Tally stood up and peered toward the center of the chamber. "But first, I think it is better if I proceed all the way in, and examine the situation there. I can retrieve Kallik as I return."

Not what I'd do, Birdie thought. A bird in the hand . . . He glanced at the sphere of the now-disembodied computer. It was strange that the only way to pass messages to the real E. C. Tally was to call them to the brainless body moving slowly toward the middle of the room, and have the sensory input fed back through the cable to the brain that Birdie was holding.

Tally was moving more slowly. The low central platform was only fifteen meters away, but he took twenty cautious seconds to reach it. Two steps from the silent figure of Louis Nenda he paused.

"There is something peculiar about the dais itself. As I have approached it, an interior structure has gradually become visible. It is a set of dodecahedra, invisible from fifteen meters. At ten I saw a hazy outline, like gray smoke. Now the pattern is apparently solid. Tendrils run from two of the dodecahedral faces and surround the heads of Louis Nenda and Atvar H'sial. That must be why the bodies can remain seated upright, although both are unconscious."

Birdie glanced at Graves, then peered toward the platform. From where he stood it looked empty except for the outward-facing seats, the Cecropian, and the human.

"I propose to try to remove Nenda from the platform first," Tally said. "I have no idea if there will be resistance, active or passive."

He took the final two steps, reached up, and grasped Louis Nenda by the shoulders. He began to lift. To the watchers it appeared that the two bodies moved to an unstable position, leaning back far from the vertical.

"There is definite resistance," Tally said. "But also there is progress. We are a few centimeters farther from the platform, and the connecting tendril has thinned. It is starting to turn in on itself, like a ring of blown smoke—" He lurched backward suddenly, and fell to the floor with Nenda on top of him. "—and now the tendril has gone completely. Be ready to reel in the line and the neural cable. We are coming out."

With Nenda's body set over his right shoulder in a fireman's lift, Tally began to walk slowly back from the center of the chamber. Another minute, and he was by the side of Julius Graves. Together they lowered Louis Nenda to the floor.

Birdie Kelly stared at the pitted and noduled chest, gray and disfigured. "Look at that. What did they do to him?"

Graves bent low, studying the roughened skin. "Nothing was done here, according to Steven. This is a Zardalu augment, designed to permit a human to speak to a Cecropian via pheromonal transfer. We thought this was a lost technology, and a banned one. There must be places in the Communion where the old slave races had mastered and retained parts of the Zardalu sciences."

Tally had already turned and was heading back toward the middle of the vaulted chamber. Cable was pulling through J'merlia's too-tight grip. He began to pay it out again just as Louis Nenda grunted and his lips twitched.

"Where the hell am I?" The eyes opened and glared around. The squat figure began trying to sit up.

"That's a good sign," Graves said. "He can speak, so at least he hasn't been wiped totally clean." He turned to Nenda. "You're inside a planetoid near Gargantua. Do you remember coming here?"

Nenda shook his dark head and struggled to his feet. "Not a glimmer." His speech was labored and swollen-tongued.

"So what's the last thing you do remember?"

Nenda ignored the question. He was too busy staring at the others. "How about that. Fancy you showing up. Julius Graves. And Birdie Kelly. And J'merlia. And all alive."

"All alive, and no thanks to you." Graves leaned close. "Come on, Nenda, this is important. What's the last thing you recall, before you went unconscious?"

Nenda rubbed his hand over his unshaven jaw. "Last thing I remember?" He gave Graves a cautious look. "Mmm. Last thing I remember, Atvar H'sial an' me were lifting off Quake in the *Have-It-All*. Summertide was nearly there. I guess it came, and I guess it went."

"You don't remember firing on another ship?"

"Firing? Me?" Nenda cleared his throat. "No way. I didn't fire on anything."

"Remember it or not, you'll have to answer for that

when we get back to Opal. You've already been formally charged with lethal assault."

"Won't be the first time someone's accused an innocent man." Nenda was recovering fast, the black eyes blinking furiously. "What happened to At? She was with me on the ship."

"Atvar H'sial?" Graves turned toward the middle of the great chamber. He nodded. "In there. Good. I see they're on the way out now."

J'merlia was squeaking with excitement. While Graves and Nenda were talking, E. C. Tally had returned to the dais, pulled Atvar H'sial clear, and was staggering back toward them. He was doubled over with the weight of the great Cecropian body. Nenda followed Graves's gesture, taking in the bandaged, tottering form, the cable leading from its head to where they stood, the recumbent figure of Kallik four paces behind, and the backdrop of the great, vaulted chamber.

"Hey, what's going on here? What'd you do to At?"

"We did nothing, and we're not sure what's going on. All we know is that you and Atvar H'sial were unconscious in the middle of the chamber, and we have been trying to rescue you."

"And Kallik? What did you do to my Hymenopt?"

"She became unconscious, trying to get you out."

J'merlia was jumping up and down with excitement as Tally emerged from the outermost ring. As the Lo'tfian helped to lower Atvar H'sial to the floor, Tally staggered a couple of paces farther and sat down suddenly. The blue eyes closed, and his hands went up to touch his bandaged head.

"This body is regrettably close to its physical limit." He spoke in a whisper. "I must rest for a few moments. However, we can be pleased with our progress. I am confident that the difficult part is all over. Kallik weighs little. I will take a brief pause to recuperate, and then I will carry her out of the chamber. She is ready to be moved."

"Hell, I can get her." Nenda was pushing forward. "You sit down, take it easy. She's mine, and she's my responsibility."

"No." Graves caught his arm. "Go in there and you'll be in the same condition as she is in—as *you* were in. The chamber contains a Lotus field. That is why it was necessary to disembody E. C. Tally before he entered." He pointed at the rough-surfaced sphere that Kelly was handing to J'merlia. "His brain remained here."

Nenda took another and more thoughtful look at the crouched body and the cable running from its bandaged head. "Good enough," he said after a few moments. "I'd better look after At, though—she'll be coming round in a minute, from the look of her, and she might get violent. Don't worry, I know how to handle her."

The Cecropian's black wing cases had opened to reveal four delicate vestigial wings marked by red and white elongated eyespots. The end of the proboscis was moving out from its home in the pleated chin, and the yellow trumpetlike horns on the head were lifting.

At the same time, the brain-empty body of E. C. Tally was struggling to its feet. His eyes opened slowly. "I must go now and recover Kallik."

"It's too soon." Graves moved to Tally's side.

"No. It must be soon. The interface is beginning to be affected by seepage of cerebrospinal fluid. The performance of the neural connect is diminishing, and I am receiving worsening sensory inputs. I will go to Kallik while I am still able to see her. Otherwise, we must begin all over again."

Tally did not wait for approval. The body gave a stuttering step forward, then leaned to one side. It began a crablike shuffle down the slope, heading for the unconscious Hymenopt. Tally's body had taken ten steps and had almost reached Kallik when Atvar H'sial gave a shrill, earsplitting scream, rose fully upright, and leapt toward Julius Graves.

In the next second Birdie Kelly saw everything and could do nothing.

The Cecropian ran into Graves first and sent him sprawling. Then the councilor and the Cecropian together collided with Birdie. One of her legs knocked him flying

and sent the reel of cable spinning away to the periphery
of the room. At the same time the brain of E. C. Tally,
too securely held by the Lo'tfian, jerked free of the cable
and rolled away with J'merlia inside the yellow ring and
toward the chamber's center. As the neural connect was
broken, Tally's body, moving toward Kallik, crumpled and
fell to the floor. Another of Atvar H'sial's legs came
sweeping across Birdie and knocked him flat on his back.

He lay staring up at the ceiling. He could not move.
All that he could see was a part of the chamber's domed
ceiling, Julius Graves's equally domed bald head, and part
of one of Atvar H'sial's wing cases. A big weight was sitting
on his chest. He was half-stunned from the bruising impact
of the back of his head on the floor, his nose was bleeding,
and half his teeth felt as though they had been jarred loose.

If E. C. Tally had not assured them that the difficult
part was all over, Birdie would never have guessed it.

CHAPTER 15

At the last moment the swirling void below turned blood-red. Darya felt herself stretched from head to toe, while forces of compression rippled their way along her body. Just as they became intolerable she flashed into the heart of the red glare. Before she could record any new sensation she was through, falling in open space.

Hans was at her side, still holding her arm. Straight ahead, rushing toward them, was the bloated sphere of Gargantua.

It filled half the sky. There was no way they could avoid collision with the planet. In one heartbeat it doubled in apparent size, and from the way that the gas-giant's appearance was changing Darya could determine their exact impact point. They were accelerating into the unwinking Eye of Gargantua. The Eye had become a huge spiraling swirl of orange and umber, with a point at its center as black and lifeless as intergalactic space.

What was that dark pupil? Darya could not guess, but she knew that she would never find out. They would not get that far. They would burn up in one flash of light, human meteors consumed by the outer atmosphere of the planet. As they came closer Darya saw that they were heading right into the empty pupil of the Eye, following the center line of another dark vortex that narrowed all the way in.

As Hans vanished from her side, Darya entered the

tunnel of the vortex. Within it she could feel nothing—
no air, no light, no forces. On all sides were the cloudy
orange swirls of the Eye, but she heard and felt no touch
of atmosphere.

The vortex was closing, a tightening spiral that shrank
until it became no wider than her body. Darya was
plunging along the centermost line, deep into the maelstrom of the Eye. Forces again racked her body, but now
they were *twisting*, from head to neck to chest to hips
to legs to feet. As they became unbearable there was a
final agonizing shear, and she found herself again in open
space.

She felt no acceleration, but she could see that she
was moving.

Faster and faster. As she watched, Mandel was in front
of her . . . was off to the left . . . was shining from behind
. . . was no bigger than a pinpoint of light when she turned
her head.

After half a minute of total confusion, the analytical part
of her brain asserted itself. She was seeing the universe as
a series of still images, but there was no force of acceleration
and there was no sign of an external gravity field. She must
be pausing at each location for a fraction of a second before
undergoing an instantaneous translation to another position.
It was the universe in stop-motion, experienced as a series
of freeze-frames. Although she was not traveling faster than
light through ordinary space-time, she was certainly reaching
each new location in less time than light would take. And
since there was no sign of Doppler shift in the starscape
around her, she must be sitting *at rest* between transitions,
until the next one transported her to a new place.

It was a series of Bose Transitions, but without the Bose
Network stations needed for all human interstellar travel.
Each jump must have been a least a few million kilometers—and increasing. Mandel was no brighter now than
any other star in the sky.

How fast was she moving in inertial space? She would
have to estimate her rate of change of position. Darya
looked around for a reference frame. She could see a blue

supergiant, off to her right. It was surely no closer than a hundred light-years. Yet it was changing its apparent position at maybe a degree a second. Which meant she was moving at close to two light-years a second.

And still accelerating, if that word could be applied to her series of instantaneous translations. As she watched, the constellations ahead were beginning to change, to melt, to reconfigure themselves into unfamiliar patterns.

The blue supergiant was already drifting away behind her. Darya stared all around, looking for some new reference point. She could find only one. The gauzy fabric of the Milky Way was a band of light, far away to her left. It had become the single constant of her new environment.

Darya fixed her eyes on that familiar sight—and realized, with a shiver, that it was beginning to move. She was plunging downward, out of the galactic plane. The globular clusters of the Magellanic Clouds were in front of her. They had emerged from the clutter of the spiral arm to form glittering spheres of stars.

How fast? How far?

She could not say. But in order for her motion relative to the whole Galaxy to be noticed, she had to be skipping hundreds of light-years in each transition. Another minute, and much of the Galaxy's matter lay below her. She was far below the spiral arm and catching a hint of a monstrous flattened disk. Below her feet she could see the sweeping curve of the spiral itself. Individual stars were disappearing, moment by moment, into a sea of spangles that glittered around dark dust clouds and lit the filaments of gaseous nebulas with multi-colored gemstones.

As she watched the stars faded again, merging to become the hazy light of distant millions. Far off to her left the disk had swelled up and thickened. She was far enough from the main plane to be clear of obscuring gas and dust clouds. She gazed in wonder at the glowing bulge of the galactic center. Hers were surely the first human eyes to see past the spiral arm to the densely packed galactic nucleus and to the massive black hole that formed the hub of the Galaxy.

How far? How fast?

She seemed to be moving straight away from the galactic disk, and now the blaze of the central hub was off at an angle of forty-five degrees to her direction of motion. With her lungs frozen and her heart stopped in her chest, Darya made her estimate. The Phemus Circle territories were about thirty thousand light-years from the center of the Galaxy, so she must be about that far from the galactic plane. And the angle of the hub was changing, at maybe ten degrees a minute. That gave her a speed of a hundred and seventy-five light-years a second.

Ten thousand light-years a minute. A million light-years in an hour and a half. The Andromeda Galaxy in twice that time.

Even as that thought came, the mad drive ended. The universe stopped its giddy rush and clicked into a fixed position.

Ahead of Darya in the open void sat a great space structure, agleam with internal lights, sprawling across half the sky, of a size impossible to estimate. Darya had the sense that it was huge, that those trailing pseudopods of antennas and twisting tubes of bright matter, spinning away into space from the central dodecahedron, were millions of kilometers long.

Before she could confirm that impression, there came a final transition. Stars, galaxies, and stellar clusters vanished. Darya found herself standing on a level plain. Overhead was nothing. At her feet, defining the level surface itself, were a billion twinkling orange lights.

And next to her, his suit open so that he could scratch his chin, stood Hans Rebka.

"Well," he said. "We-ell, that's one for the record books. Try and describe *that* in your trip report."

He was silent for a few moments, breathing deep and staring around him. "Maybe we ought to trade ideas," he said finally. "If either of us has any. For a start, where in the hell are we?"

"You opened your suit!"

"No." He shook his head. "I never had time to *close* it when we dropped—nor did you."

To Darya's astonishment she saw that he was right. Her own suit was fully transparent. "But we were out in open space—airless vacuum."

"I thought so, too. I don't remember needing to breathe, though."

"How long were we there? Did you count heartbeats?"

He smiled ruefully. "Sorry. I don't know if I even *had* heartbeats. I was too busy trying to figure out what was happening—where you had gone, where I was going."

"I think I know. Not what was happening, but where we went and where we are now."

"Then you're six steps ahead of me." He gestured out at the endless plain in front of them. "Limbo, didn't it used to be called? A nowhere place where lost souls went."

"We're not lost. We were brought here, deliberately. And it was my fault. I told The-One-Who-Waits how keen I was to meet the Builders. It took what I said at face value."

"Didn't work, though, did it? I don't see any sign of them."

"Give them time. We only just got here. Do you remember flying down into the Eye of Gargantua?"

"Until the day I die. Which I'd like to think is a fair way off, but I'm beginning to wonder."

"The eye is the entry point to a Builder transportation system. It must have been there as long as humans have been in the Mandel system, maybe long before that; but it's no surprise that no one ever discovered it. A ship's crew would have to be crazy to fly down into it."

"Explorer ships' crews *are* crazy. People did plenty of mad things when this system was first being colonized. I know that ships went down deep into Gargantua's atmosphere and came back out—some of them. But I don't think that would be enough to do what we did. We had to be given that first boost from Glister, to rifle us exactly down the middle of the vortex. When I was in there it seemed to just fit my shoulders. There wasn't room for another person, let alone a ship."

"I had the same feeling. I wondered where you'd gone, but I knew there wasn't room for both of us. All right. So we had a first boost from the gravity generator on Glister, then a second boost from a shearing field in the Eye of Gargantua. That put us square into the main transportation system, and then right out of the spiral arm. Thirty thousand light-years, I estimate."

"I wondered about that. I looked around, and I could see the whole damned galaxy, spread out like a dinner plate—though the way I'm feeling, I hate to even *mention* the word 'dinner.'"

"And then one final transition, to bring us in here." Darya gazed around, up to the segmented dark ceiling, and then across the glittering plain of the floor.

"Where we can stand and stare until we starve. Any more ideas, Professor?"

"Some." Now that the mind-numbing journey was over she was beginning to think again. "I don't believe we were brought all this way to starve. The-One-Who-Waits sent us, so something must know we're here. And although this is part of the Builders' own living place, I'll bet it has been *prepared* for us, or beings like us." Darya swung her hand around a ninety-degree arc of the level floor. "See the flat surface? That's not natural for a Builder structure."

"We don't know how Builders think. Nobody ever met one."

"True. But we know how they *build*. When you've studied Builder artifacts as long as I have, you begin to form ideas about the Builders themselves. You can't *prove* things, but you learn to trust your instincts. We don't know where the Builders evolved, or when, but I'm sure it was in an aerial or free-space environment. At the very least, it was a place where gravity doesn't mean the same thing as it does to us. The Builders work naturally in all three dimensions, every direction equal. Their artifacts don't provide any feel for 'up' or 'down.' A level plain like this is something that *humans* like. You don't encounter it in the artifacts. You don't expect a gravity field close to one gee in a structure like this, either—complete with a breathable atmosphere. And look at that." She pointed to the ceiling, apparently kilometers above them. "You can see it's built of pentagonal segments. That's common to many Builder structures. So I think we're inside a dodecahedron, a shape you find over and over in Builder artifacts, and I think they just added a flat floor and air and gravity for the benefit of beings like us. I'm not sure this plain is anything like as big as it looks, either. You know the Builders can play tricks with space that confuse our sense of distance."

"They can. But I think this place is really big, no matter what tricks are being performed."

Hans Rebka had not raised his voice, but Darya's stomach tightened at the sudden tension in it. Hans was not supposed to get nervous. That was her privilege.

"It's certainly big," he went on, "if *that* is anything to judge by."

He was pointing off to their left. Darya at first saw nothing. Then she realized that above the twinkling sea of orange spangles shone the steadier light of a bright sphere. It was tiny at first, no more than a shiny marble of silver, but as she watched it grew steadily. It was advancing across the level plain, apparently at a constant speed. There was no way to judge its distance, or to tell if it was rolling or traveling by some other method.

"Welcoming committee," Rebka said, almost under his breath. "Everybody smile."

It was not rolling. Darya was somehow sure of that, even though she could see no signs of surface marking. She had the feeling that it was flying or floating, its bottom only a fraction of a millimeter above the orange cloud of sequins.

And it was not small at all. It was sizable. It was growing. It was *huge*, three times the size of The-One-Who-Waits. It towered over them, and still it was not close.

Twenty paces away it halted. A steady series of ripples moved across the spherical surface, like waves on a ball of mercury. As they grew in amplitude the globular form bulged up to form a stem. On top of it a familiar pentagonal flowerlike head drooped to face them. Five-sided disks were extruded from the front of the sphere, while a silver tail stretched down to moor the object to the floor. A flickering green light shone from a newly formed aperture in the central belly.

There was a long silence.

"All right, sweetie," Rebka said in a gruff whisper. "What now?"

"If this is like The-One-Who-Waits, it needs to hear us speak a few words before it can key in to our language." Darya raised her voice. "My name is Darya Lang, originally from the planet Sentinel Gate. This is Hans Rebka, from the planet Teufel. We are human, and we arrived from the star Mandel and the planet Gargantua. Are you like The-One-Who-Waits?"

There was a ten-second silence.

"One—Who—Waits," a groaning voice said. Its tone was deeper than that of the sphere on Glister, and it sounded even more tired. "The One Who . . . Waits. Human . . . human . . . hu-u-man . . . hmmm."

"Needs a pep pill," Rebka said softly. "Are you a Builder?" he called to the horned and tailed nightmare floating in front of them.

The being drifted a few paces closer. "Human, human, human, . . . At last. You are here. But two are the same. Where is . . . the other?"

"The other," Rebka said. "What's it mean?"

Darya shook her head. "There is no other," she said loudly. "We do not understand. We are the only ones here. We ask again, are you like The-One-Who-Waits?"

The silver body was humming, with a low tone almost too deep for human ears. "There must be . . . another . . . or the arrival is not complete. We have two forms only . . . but the message said that the third one was on the way and would soon arrive . . ." There was another long silence. "I am not like The-One-Who-Waits, although we were created in the same way."

"Not a Builder," Darya said in a quick whisper. "I knew it. We're seeing things that the Builders *made*, just like The-One-Who-Waits. Maybe some kind of computers, incredibly old. And I don't think that they're—well, that they're *working* quite right."

That was a new thought for Darya, and one hard to accept. Usually Builder artifacts seemed to perform as well after five million years as the day they were made. But The-One-Who-Waits, and now this new being, gave Darya an odd feeling of disorganization and randomness. Perhaps not even the Builders could make machines last forever.

"I am not . . . a computer." The being's hearing must have been more sensitive than a human's, or it was directly reading their minds. "I am Inorganic, but a grown Inorganic. The-One-Who-Waits stayed always close to Old-Home, but I was grown here. I am . . . I am . . . a *Speaker-Between*. An Interlocutor. The one who must . . . interface with you and the others. The task of The-One-Who-Waits is done. But the task of Speaker-Between cannot start until the third one is here." The weary voice was slowing, fading. "The third one. Then . . . the task of Speaker-Between can begin. Until then . . ."

The surface of the great silver body began to ripple. The five-sided flower on top was shortening.

"Hey! Speaker-Between! You can't stop there." Rebka ran forward across the surface, his shoes kicking up sprays of glittering orange. "And you can't leave us here. We're humans. Humans need food, and water, and air."

"That is known." The body was swelling at the base and descending toward the flat surface, while the silver tail withdrew into it. "Do not worry. The place has been prepared for your kind. Since the third is already on the way, you will have no need for stasis. Enter . . . and eat, drink, rest."

The silver globe of Speaker-Between had deformed to a bulging hemisphere with a wide arched aperture at the center. "Enter," the fading voice said again. The opening moved around to face the two humans. "Enter . . . now."

Rebka swore and backed away. "Don't go near it."

"No." Darya was moving forward. "I don't know what's inside, but so far nothing here has tried to hurt us. If they wanted to kill us, they could have done it easily. Come on. What do we have to lose?"

"Other than our lives?" But he was following her.

The opening that they entered was filled with the green glow of hidden lights. From the outside it could have been of any depth. One step inside, and Darya realized that she was actually in a small entrance lock, three meters deep. When she went across to the inner door and pushed it aside, an open chamber with slate-gray, somber walls and a high ceiling was revealed.

Too high. She walked through and stared upward. Forty meters, to that arched, pentagonal center? It had to be at least that—which meant that she was in a room taller than the *outside* dimensions of Speaker-Between. And that was physically impossible. Before she could move there came a sighing, slithering noise. Sections of the chamber's level floor in front of her began to buckle and lift. Partitions and furniture grew upward, thrusting like strange plants though a soft, springy surface.

"A place prepared for *us*? I'm not so sure of that." Hans Rebka advanced cautiously past her, toward a cylindrical structure that was still emerging from the floor. It had a bulbous, rounded upper end, and it was supported on a cluster of splayed legs. "Now this is really interesting. It's a food-storage unit and food synthesizer. I've seen one like it, but not in use. It was in a *museum*."

"It's not typical Builder technology."

"I'm sure it's not." An oddly perplexed expression crept into Rebka's eyes. "If I didn't know better, I'd start wondering . . ."

The top of the cylinder was surrounded by a thin fog, and a layer of ice crystals covered its surface. Rebka touched it cautiously with one fingertip, then jerked away.

"Freezing cold." He turned up the opacity level of his suit to provide thermal insulation and reached out with a protected hand to pull a curved lever set into the upper part of the cylinder. It moved reluctantly to a new position. Part of the cylinder body turned, revealing the interior. Three shelves stood inside, loaded with sealed white packages.

"You're the biologist, Darya. Do you recognize any of these?" Rebka reached in and quickly lifted out a handful of flat packages and smooth ovoids, placing them on the saucerlike beveled top of the cylinder. "Don't touch them with your bare hand or you may get frostbite. They're really cold. We can't eat yet, but you can tell your stomach we may be getting close."

Darya set her suit gauntlet to full opacity and peeled open a rounded packet. It was a fruit, mottled green and yellow, with a thin rind and a fleshy stalk at one end. She turned it over, examining texture and density and scraping a thin sliver from the surface, then allowed the gauntlet to heat it. When it grew warm in her hand she sniffed it, tasted it, and shook her head.

"Fruit aren't my line, but I've never seen anything like this before. And I don't think I've ever read anything about it, either. It could be from an Alliance world, but it's not a popular fruit, because they tend to be grown everywhere. Do you really think it's edible?"

"If it's not, why would they have stored it here? I'm using your logic, Darya—if they want to kill us, they can find easier ways. I think we can eat this, and the other food. Speaker-Between didn't seem too happy to see the two of us, because it was expecting something else. But we're part of the show, too. We have to be fed and watered. And you don't bring somebody thirty thousand light-years and then let them accidentally poison themselves. My worry is a bit different." He rapped the bulging side of the cylinder. "I know construction methods in the Phemus Circle and the Fourth Alliance, and I've been exposed to the way they do things in the Cecropia Federation. But this isn't like any of them. It's—"

He was interrupted by the creaking sound of long-neglected hinges. Thirty meters away, the whole side of the room was sinking ponderously into the floor. Beyond it stood another chamber, even larger, with a long bank of objects like outsized coffins at its center.

Darya counted fourteen units, each one a pentagonal cylinder seven meters long, four wide, and four high.

"Now those *are* Builder technology," she said. "Very definitely. Remember Flambeau, near the boundary between the Alliance and the Cecropia Federation? That artifact is filled with units just like this, a lot of them even bigger. They're all empty, but they're in working order."

"What do they do? I've never seen anything like these before." Rebka was walking cautiously forward toward the nearest of the fourteen. Each of the monster coffins had a transparent port mounted in its pentagonal end. He put his face close to it, rubbed at the dusty surface with his gauntleted hand, and peered in.

"No one is sure what they were intended for *originally*." Darya rapped the side of the unit, and it produced a hollow booming sound. "But we know they can be used to preserve things pretty much indefinitely—objects, or organisms—and we assume that was their main purpose. There's a stasis field inside each unit, externally controlled. You can see the settings on the end there. Clock rates in the interior have been measured for the Flambeau units, and they run an average of sixty million times slower than outside. Spend a century in one of those stasis tanks, and if you remained conscious you'd feel as though one minute had passed."

Rebka did not seem to be listening. He was still poised with his face against the port.

She tapped his shoulder. "Hey, Hans. Come up for air. What's so fascinating in there? Let me take a peek."

She moved to his side. The stasis tank did not seem to be empty, but its inside was almost dark. Darya could see vague outlines, but for details she would have to wait a couple of minutes until her eyes had adjusted to the interior light level.

She took his arm and squeezed it. "Can you see what's in there? Come on, if it's interesting don't keep me in suspense."

Still he did not speak, but at Darya's words and touch he finally turned to face her.

She looked at his twitching face, and her grip on his arm slackened. Her hand dropped to her side.

Nothing shocked Hans Rebka. Nothing ever touched his iron self-control.

Except that now the control had gone. And behind his eyes lurked an unreasoning terror that Darya had never expected to see.

CHAPTER 16

After Atvar H'sial had knocked Julius Graves headlong into Birdie Kelly, broken the connection between E. C. Tally's brain and body, and sent J'merlia rolling and spinning into the pattern of concentric rings, Louis Nenda did not hesitate.

As the Cecropian went scuttling out of the chamber, wing cases wide open, Nenda followed at once.

Let the mess back there sort itself out!

He was cursing—silently. It was no use shouting. Atvar H'sial had astonishing hearing, but she did not understand human speech. And his own pheromonal augment was worthless when she was in full flight, because the necessary molecules had no chance to diffuse into her receptors.

The near-darkness of Glister's interior made no difference to Atvar H'sial. Her echolocation vision worked as well in pitch blackness as in bright sunlight; but it made things hellishly difficult for Louis Nenda. A Cecropian did not care where she moved, into chambers light or dark, just so long as there was air to carry sound waves. But *he* sure cared. He was bouncing off dark walls, tangling in nets, tripping over loose cables, diving down steep slopes without any idea what he would meet at the bottom. And all the time he had not the slightest idea where she was heading. He doubted that she knew it herself.

Enough of this, he thought.

He slowed down after a particularly bruising collision

with an invisible partition. It would be too easy to knock himself out, and he could not afford that.

The good news was that he could track her, infallibly. The Zardalu augment had been designed for pheromonal speech, with all its subtleties, so simply following another's scent through Glister's sterile interior was ridiculously easy. Even if she crossed and recrossed her own path, the strength of the trail would show him exactly where she had gone.

The corridors of Glister turned and twisted, apparently at random. He patiently followed the unmistakable airborne molecules of Cecropian physiology, turn by turn, wherever they led. The only thing he could be sure of was that they were descending, following a gravity gradient to regions of steadily increasing field. But the stronger field increased the danger of injury from a fall. He slowed his pace still further, confident that Atvar H'sial could not get away from him. As he walked he began to make plans.

One word with Graves had been enough to convince him that telling the truth to the councilor would be a terrible idea. He had fought back his own initial urge on awakening—violent flight—because Atvar H'sial was still trapped in the Lotus field. At that point it made sense to blame the field itself and "forget" anything that had happened back on Quake.

Of course, he remembered it all perfectly: the wild ascent from the planet's surface, the capture of the *Have-It-All* by the dark sphere, the giddy plunge through space, their arrival at Gargantua and the little planetoid that orbited it—and, finally, the release of the ship onto the surface, while the sphere that had captured and held them moved inside. He had been aware of events right up to the moment on the planetoid's surface when the orange cloud surged up around them. He even had a vague memory after that, of being carried down, down, down through multiple levels of the interior. Then came a blank, until he had wakened to find Julius Graves crouched over him.

Graves's mention of the Lotus field allowed him to piece

together most of the rest. He and Atvar H'sial had been locked in the field—but *why*, when it would have made more sense just to kill them—until the others had come along. And finally that crazy robot with the human body and the pop-top skull case had dredged them out.

Pity that Atvar H'sial had run wild before E. C. Tally had been able to get Kallik, too. Nenda missed his Hymenopt servant. No matter. There was plenty of time for Tally to pull Kallik free now—if ever they could stick Tally's popout brain back in his dumb head and connect it so it worked.

Louis Nenda paused. He was standing in an unlit passageway, but the pheromonal scent was increasing in strength. He concentrated and generated his own message, sending it diffusing out from his chest nodules. "Atvar H'sial? Where are you? I can't see you—you gotta steer me in."

As usual, he found it easiest to speak his message at the same time as it was generated chemically. It was not necessary to identify himself. If the Cecropian received any message at all, Nenda's individual molecular signature would be built into it.

"I am here. Wait." The messenger molecules drifted in through the darkness. A few seconds later, Atvar H'sial's hard claw took Nenda's hand. "Follow. Tell me if the thermal source ahead is also for you a source of seeing radiation."

"Why'd you take off like that?" Nenda allowed himself to be led through the darkness, until he saw a glimmer of light ahead. "Why didn't you wait until they got Kallik out? She's my Hymenopt—she shouldn't be doin' work for them."

"Just as J'merlia is mine, and he should not be serving humans. But he is." The Cecropian led them into a long rectangular room, warmed and dimly lit by a uniform ruddy glow from the walls. "The failure to recover J'merlia and Kallik is, I agree, regrettable, but I judged it necessary. As soon as I became conscious I smelled danger to you and me. Councilor Graves was dominant in that group.

He had a clear intention to restrict our freedom at once. I was not sure we could prevent that. With an imperfect understanding of events, it is always better to remain unimpeded in one's actions. Therefore, we had to escape."

"How'd you know I'd follow you?"

There was no explicit message of reply, but the chemical messengers of grim humor wafted to Nenda's chest receptors.

"All right, At. So I don't like the idea of being locked up, any more than you do. What now? We're not safe. Graves and the rest of them can come after us anytime. J'merlia can track you, easy as I could. We're still in deep stuff."

"I do not disagree." The Cecropian crouched in front of Nenda, lowering herself so that the blind white head was on a level with his. The open yellow trumpet horns quivered on either side of the eyeless face. "We must pool information, Louis Nenda, before we make a decision. I lack data items that you perhaps gained from Julius Graves. For example, where are we now? Why were we brought here? How much time did we spend unconscious? And where is our ship, the *Have-It-All*, and is it in working condition for our escape?"

"I can take a shot at answering some of those."

Nenda rubbed at his cheek and chin as he provided Atvar H'sial with a summary of his own experiences since waking from the Lotus field. There was a three-or four-day stubble there, but that did not tell him much; he had no idea how fast hair grew inside the field. Some of what he told Atvar H'sial had to be guesswork.

"So if you believe Graves," he concluded, "we're still inside a hollow planetoid, goin' round Gargantua. Same one as we were brought to after Summertide, for a bet. Graves says he's got no more idea than we have as to *why* we were dragged here, or why we were stuck in the middle of that room like two drugged flies. You can be damn sure it wasn't done for our benefit, though. I don't know how long we were held there. Enough for Graves and the rest of 'em to get their hands on a ship after Summertide and fly it out to Gargantua. Don't ask me where that computer with the strung-out brainbox came from. I never saw him before, or anything like him. Mebbe they brought him from Opal. I think they went back there before they started for here, because Birdie Kelly is with 'em, too."

"I registered Kelly's presence. Do not worry about him. Graves is the principal danger; also perhaps the embodied computer, but not Birdie Kelly."

"Yeah. And Graves told me he wants to take us back home and charge us with lethal assault. He'll do his best to keep us in one piece till then, otherwise he'd never have stopped me going back into the Lotus field for Kallik. Graves seems pretty sure he *can* take us back to trial, so there has to be at least one ship available: the one they came in, or the *Have-It-All*, or maybe both of 'em. We should be able to escape, if we can just find our way back to the surface."

The great blind head was nodding, a foot from Nenda's face. "Very good, Louis. So I have one more question: *When* should we choose to escape?"

"As soon as we can. It won't be more than a couple of hours before Graves is on our trail again. Why hang around?"

"For one excellent reason." Atvar H'sial swept a jointed forelimb in a long arc, covering the room they stood in. "Examine. I have not had time for a complete survey, but as I moved through the chambers of this planetoid I saw evidence of Builder technology unlike anything known to the spiral arm. This is a treasure house, a cornucopia of new equipment with a value too great to estimate. It can be ours, Louis."

Nenda reached out and patted the Cecropian's wrinkled proboscis. "Good old At. You never give up, do you? Ever. And people tell me I'm the greedy one. Got any ideas how we prevent interference from Graves?"

"Some. But first things first." Atvar H'sial unfolded her legs and rose to her full height. "If profit is to be maximized, this must be treated as a multistage endeavor. We will need great capital to exploit this planetoid, and we must plan to return here when we have suitable financing.

To obtain that, before we leave we must select a few items of machinery and equipment, small and light enough to take with us for trade to the richest worlds of the spiral arm. I could do that, but you are more experienced. And as soon as we have decided what to take, we must evade Julius Graves and his group, and leave."

"Then we'd better get a move on, before they come looking." Nenda reached out to grasp one of the Cecropian's forelimbs, hoisting himself to his feet. "You're right, I do like to price goodies. 'Specially when I know I won't be paying for 'em. Let's go to it, At, and pick 'em out."

After the first few minutes Louis Nenda was willing to admit Cecropian superiority for the exploration of Glister. He could see dead ends easily enough, when the light level permitted. But Atvar H'sial, with her sensitive sonar and echolocation, could "see" around bends in corridors, and know ahead of time when she was approaching a large open area. And she did so just as well in total darkness.

Nenda did not bother after a while to peer ahead. He focused on what he was best at, walking behind Atvar H'sial and making a mental catalog of novel equipment and artifacts as they came to them. There was plenty of choice. In less than half an hour he reached forward and tapped her carapace.

"I think we're done. I've tagged a dozen portable items, an' I don't think we can handle more than that."

Atvar H'sial halted and the white head turned. "You are the expert on salable commodities; but I would like to hear your list."

"All right. I'll give 'em in order, top choice first. That little water-maker in the second room we looked at. Remember it? No sign of a power source, no sign of a supply. But five hundred cubic meters a minute of clean water production. You could name your own price for a few of them on Xerarchos or Siccity, or any of the dust worlds."

"I agree. It was also a leading item on my own list. Do you know its mass?"

"I can lift it, that's all I care about. Then for number-two choice, I liked that cubical box on gimbals three chambers back, the one with the open top and a blue haze over it."

"Indeed? I observed that object. But I found nothing remarkable about it."

"That's because you don't see using light. When I looked down into the open top I could see stars. But when I turned the box on the gimbals, I was looking at Gargantua, right through the planetoid. It's an all-direction see-through—let's you look at distant objects and not be bothered by near ones. It'd be marvelous for ship navigation in dust clouds.

"My number-three choice is harder to justify. The sphere, the one that was floating, not attached to anything, in the room we just left."

"To my viewing it appeared entirely featureless."

"To me, too. But it was a lot cooler than everything around it."

"Which should be physically impossible."

"That's why we want it. Impossible gadgets are always the most valuable. I've no idea how it works, an' I don't care. But I can tell you a dozen places that would pay a lot for it, looking to maybe find a closed infinite heat sink. Number four—"

"Enough. I am persuaded. I accept your list. but there is one more thing that I would like to do, before we collect the items of choice and seek egress from the planetoid." Atvar H'sial motioned in front of her with one forelimb. The yellow horns faced ahead, open as wide as they would go and scanning slowly from side to side. "There is another chamber ahead; a huge, open one, possessing anomalous acoustical properties. At certain frequencies, it appears completely empty. At others, I detect a spherical object at its center."

"You think we might find something specially valuable? No point taking risks, just to be nosy."

"I cannot estimate the value. I will only say that an object transparent at certain acoustic frequencies is as potentially valuable to Cecropian society as glass, transparent to certain frequencies of light, is to humans. I know exactly where we could sell such a discovery. To me, it might be the most precious thing on this world."

Atvar H'sial was advancing slowly as she spoke, to a place where the tunnel ended in a blind drop. Nenda moved to her side and took a look down. After one startled glance he swore and stepped back. She had an indifference to heights that came from her remote flying ancestors, but he did not share it. They were on the brink of a twenty-meter drop, slowly curving away below to a bowl-shaped floor.

Atvar H'sial was pointing to the middle of the chamber. "There. Do you sense anything with your eyes?"

"Yeah. It's a silver sphere." Nenda took another step back. "I don't like this, At. We oughta get out of here."

"In one moment. To my senses, that sphere is *changing*. Do you observe it, also?"

Nenda, set to retreat, stood and stared in spite of himself.

Atvar H'sial was right. The sphere was changing while he watched. And in a way that tricked the eye. The whole surface began to ripple, like oscillations on a ball of mercury. Those vibrations became a pattern of standing waves, growing in amplitude until they changed the whole shape. A five-sided flowerlike head was sprouting above, while a slender barbed tail extended down toward the floor of the chamber.

Ahh. A sighing voice echoed through the whole chamber. *Ahhh. At last.*

A green light flickered from an aperture in the deformed sphere's center. It shone on Atvar H'sial, lighting up the crouched, insectile form and the great blind head. Louis hid away behind her.

At last, the voice said again. It sounded as old as time itself. A strange, pungent aroma came drifting across the room. *At last . . . we can begin. You are here. The testing is complete. The duties of The-One-Who-Waits are ending, and the selection process can begin. Are you ready?*

The creature poised in the center of the chamber was unlike anything that Louis Nenda had met in thirty years of travel around the spiral arm. But what was Atvar H'sial seeing? The Cecropian seemed frozen, her long antennas unfurled and bristling. The being in the middle of the chamber had been partially invisible to her sonar. Did she see it at all now, and recognize the danger?

"At!" Nenda sent the pheromonal signal with maximum urgency. "I don't know if you're getting the same message as I am from that thing, but believe me, we're in trouble. It wants us. Don't reply to me, just back up."

You are the form, the voice was saying, and the green light had focused on the Cecropian. *The third awaited form. Do not move*—Atvar H'sial had finally taken a step backward, bumping into Louis Nenda—*the transition is ready to begin.*

Louis Nenda reached forward, grabbing one of the Cecropian's forelimbs. "At! No messing about. Let's get out of here!" He turned and took one step.

Too late.

Before his second step the floor vanished. He was falling freely, plummeting down a vertical shaft. He looked down. Nothing, only darkness that baffled the eye. He looked up. Above him was Atvar H'sial, wing cases fully extended, vestigial wings wide open, all six legs tensed. She was poised for a hard landing—on top of Louis Nenda.

He looked down again, seeking the bottom of the shaft. He could not see a thing, but given the small size of the planetoid, the end of the fall had to be no more than a second or two away.

And then what? Nothing pleasant, that was for sure.

Nenda fell and swore. Hindsight was wonderful. They had been a little bit too greedy. He and Atvar H'sial should have left when they could, as soon as they had picked out all they needed.

He stared down into a rolling, viscous blackness and had time for a final thought: They would have been better off staying with Julius Graves. At the moment, a formal trial for lethal assault seemed positively inviting.

CHAPTER 17

When Louis Nenda and Atvar H'sial went scurrying into the darkness, Birdie Kelly was not at all sorry to see the back of them. Graves might want to arrest the pair, but the Karelian human Nenda had always struck Birdie as crude and violent, and the silent, winged Cecropian gave him the creeps.

Good riddance to both. Birdie pushed Julius Graves off him, struggled to his feet, and looked around.

Things were a mess. He was not sure where to begin.

Graves was winded and gasping for breath, but otherwise he seemed all right. Birdie ignored him. Kallik was unconscious, lying on the floor halfway to the center of the room, and Birdie could do nothing for her.

The body of E. C. Tally, a little closer, was in the worst shape. It lay motionless, with the cable trailing from the bleeding head and ending in a bare plug a few feet from where Birdie stood. There was nothing to be done for Tally, either, because his body was deep in the Lotus field.

Birdie looked for J'merlia. The Lo'tfian was lying on the curved floor, just inside the pattern of concentric rings, and he was still holding E. C. Tally's disconnected brain firmly in two of his forelimbs. If he had been knocked out, too, or affected by the Lotus field . . .

But as Birdie watched, J'merlia began to move, crawling out toward the perimeter of the outer circle. Birdie took the loose end of the neural connect cable and went around to meet him.

"Where is Atvar H'sial?" J'merlia asked as soon as he crossed the boundary of the yellow ring.

"Ran for it. With Louis Nenda. We'll worry about them later. Here." Birdie held out the connector. "Turn Tally's brain around this way, and let's see if we can plug him in again."

The connection was supposed to be handled delicately, but it had been yanked free with great force. Now the neural bundles refused to mesh easily into position. The plug slipped out of the socket when it was released. Birdie knew nothing about the care and maintenance of embodied computers, but he said a prayer, placed the connector into position again, and pushed—this time a lot harder.

Down on the curved bowl of the floor, the body of E. C. Tally jerked and spasmed. There was a grunt and a *whoosh* of lungs violently expelling air.

"Tally!" J'merlia called. "Can you hear me?"

The battered figure with its bloody head was on hands and knees, struggling to stand up. It failed on half a dozen tries, supporting itself on its bruised forearms each time it fell forward. At last the body stayed upright.

"I hee-ar . . . poo-erly." The speech was garbled. "It is diffigult . . . to speag. Some of my gonnegtor interfaces were des-troyed when they were pulled out. Others are . . . degraded. I am seeging to gompensate. Do not worry, I was designed with high-cirguit redundancy. I am . . . improving. I will be all right. I will be *fine*."

Birdie was not so sure. As Tally said those last words, he had fallen flat on his face again.

"Take it *slowly*, E.C. We have plenty of time."

"Brr-err," E.C. Tally replied. "Grarr-erff." But he was making progress. He was standing again, shaky but upright. As Birdie and J'merlia watched, he took two tentative steps—in exactly the wrong direction.

"No. E.C.!" Birdie shouted. "Wrong way. Come toward the outside. You're heading for the middle of the room."

"I am well . . . aware of that." The head turned slowly,

to look back at them. The voice was reproving. "Since it will be necessary at some point to retrieve the Hymenopt Gallig, surely it is more efficient to do so now, and thereby egonomize on both time and motion."

E. C. Tally was improving all right, Birdie thought—if a return to his usual wrongheadedness could be considered an improvement. But he carefully paid out neural cable while Tally limped forward until he reached Kallik. Blood streamed from the open skull as Tally bent down and laboriously cradled the little Hymenopt in his arms.

"We are goming out now. Prepare to restore me . . . to the granial gavity, as soon as I reach you. Sensory inputs via the gonnegt gable are degenerating. Please geep talging, so that I gan sense your diregtion. I gan no longer see."

"This way—this way—this way—" J'merlia called, but he did not wait. When Tally was still inside the yellow ring the Lo'tfian rushed forward, took part of Kallik's weight, and led the way back to Birdie Kelly. As Kallik was released, E. C. Tally groaned and sank to the floor beside her.

"Quickly." Julius Graves had finally recovered his wind enough to be helpful. He was removing the bandage from Tally's skull. "Steven says that there will be permanent damage if an impaired neural connector is used for more than a minute or two. We are close to that limit already."

As the bandage came off Birdie turned the cranium on its hinged flap. "All right, E.C., here we go. We'll have you back online in a few seconds.

"Now!" he said to J'merlia, who stood ready. The connector came free of the disembodied brain, at the same moment as Birdie pulled the cable out of the hindbrain socket. Tally's body slumped against Birdie. The blue eyes closed.

Julius Graves took the short connecting spiral of the computer's hindbrain connection and set it carefully into its usual position. There was a brief spasm of Tally's limbs, but before anyone had time to worry the eyes had flickered open.

"Very good," E. C. Tally said. "We suffered a loss of interface for only two-point-four seconds. All sensory and motor functions appear to be normal. Now, the closing of the cranial cavity is something that I prefer to do for myself. So if you do not mind—"

He reached up, pushed away Graves's supporting hands, and grasped the open top of the skull. He turned it backward on its hinge. Birdie, standing behind him, had another quick view of a red network of blood vessels in the skull's lining; then the cranium tilted to fit snugly over the protective membranes of Tally's spherical brain. Tally exerted vertical pressure. There was a faint click. The skull was again a battered but seamless whole.

As E. C. Tally calmly reached up a forearm to wipe blood from his eyes, the other three could begin to attend to other worries. Birdie realized that Kallik was conscious and silently watching.

"Are you feeling all right?"

The Hymenopt shook her head. "Physically, I am functioning normally. But mentally, I am very confused. Confused as to how I came to be here, but even more as to how *you* came to be here. The last thing I remember was going down there." She pointed toward the center of the chamber. "My master was at the center. Now he has vanished, and so has Atvar H'sial. Where are they?"

"Good question." Birdie was automatically coiling up the neural cable. Old habits of neatness died hard. "J'merlia, can you bring Kallik up to date, while the rest of us decide where we go from here?"

He turned to Julius Graves. "I'm not in charge, never have been. But I want to find Professor Lang and Captain Rebka as much as you do, and help them if they need help. And I know you want to get your hands on Nenda and that Cecropian, and give 'em what's due. But don't you think it's time we forgot all that and started acting rational? I mean, like getting out of here and going someplace where we know what's happening to us."

Listening to himself, Birdie was amazed at his own nerve. Here he was, a real nobody, telling a resentative of the central council what he ought to do. But Graves did not seem annoyed. The bald head was nodding slowly, and the radiation-scarred face wore a serious expression.

"Commissioner Kelly, I cannot argue with you. You, as well as J'merlia, Kallik, and E. C. Tally, have been drawn into a situation of great danger, for no better reason than my desire to bring Louis Nenda and Atvar H'sial to justice, and to satisfy my own curiosity. That is unfair, and it is also unreasonable. I intend to continue to explore Glister. I hope to find Nenda and H'sial, and also Hans Rebka and Darya Lang. But that is not your responsibility. As of this moment you are officially relieved. You, E. C. Tally, J'merlia, and Kallik are all free to return to the surface. Take the *Summer Dreamboat*, go back to Opal, and report. Leave the other ship for my use, and for the others if I can find and rescue them."

It was a better answer than Birdie dreamed of getting. He stood to attention. "Yes, *sir!* Kallik, J'merlia. E.C.? All ready to go?"

But the embodied computer was shaking his head. "Go, Birdie Kelly, as soon as you are prepared. However, I cannot accompany you. I was sent to the Dobelle system with a mission: Find out what happened at Summertide, and learn why Captain Rebka and the others elected to remain there afterwards. Full answers have not been provided, and my query registers remain unfulfilled. I must go with Councilor Graves."

Which left the two aliens. Even as Birdie turned to them, he suspected that he was going to be disappointed. Kallik was hopping up and down, emitting the chirps and whistles that told of high excitement.

"The masters are alive! The masters are alive! J'merlia says that they are conscious, and somewhere within Glister. Honored humans, please grant us permission to seek them and offer again our services."

"You still want to go after those two crooks?" Birdie did not have much hope after that speech, but he tried. "Kallik, they deserted you and J'merlia and left you to die on Quake. They ran away from you here, when you were still stuck in the Lotus field with no idea when or how you'd get out. They don't care what happens to you. You don't owe them anything."

"But they are the *Masters*! Our true and wonderful and only masters." Kallik turned to Graves. "Revered Councilor, please grant us permission to accompany you. We will obey any orders that you choose to give us. Let Commissioner Kelly go home—but please do not send us with him to Opal. Let us remain with you and seek the masters."

Hearing her, and looking at J'merlia and E. C. Tally, Birdie had his own moment of truth. They were all suggesting that he should try to fly—*alone*—through that blizzard of murderous Phages. Without Kallik to help as navigator, his survival chances were close to zero. And then if by some fluke he did make it, he would have to fly all the way to Opal facing the bitter fact of his own lack of courage.

What a choice: a fool, or a coward. And the coward had a near-certain chance of being killed as he tried to fly away from Glister. Birdie might be safer here.

He sighed. "I was just joking. I'd rather find out what happened to the others. Lead on, Councilor. We're all in this together."

"Wonderful. I am glad you will stay. You are a great asset." Graves gave him an admiring smile.

Birdie cringed. If there was one thing worse than being a coward, it was being mistaken for a hero.

Kallik's lonely wandering through the interior of Glister before the others arrived was paying off. As she moved the Hymenopt had mapped out in her head a rough plan of many of the chambers and corridors. She already knew that the lower levels were high-gee environments, unsuitable for human or Cecropian habitation. And she was also fairly sure that there was no way they could reach the surface, other than the one she had created with the field inhibitor. To reach that, Nenda and Atvar H'sial would have to pass again through the chamber with the Lotus field. Since they had not done so, they must still be somewhere in the lower levels of Glister's interior.

Julius Graves led the way, followed by the two aliens. Tally was next, still holding the reel of neural cable that Birdie had rewound. There might be no more Lotus fields in the interior—Kallik knew of none—but it was best to take precautions.

Birdie came last. The rear was no safer than anywhere else, but he wanted to be alone to think. He was still brooding over his decision to stay on Glister. He had blown it. It had occurred to him, too late, that he ought at least to have gone back to the surface and taken a *look* at what was going on there. For all he knew, the Phages had wandered away to seek other targets. He might have had a clear ride home. And even if they had not gone, he could have come back here and been no worse off than he was now.

They had been descending steadily, through a succession of corridors, sliding ramps, and chambers of all shapes and sizes. At this point Birdie was not sure he could find his own way back, but that did not matter too much because E. C. Tally would have every turn and twist recorded in his inorganic data banks.

Birdie bumped suddenly into the back of the embodied computer. Graves, in front of the others, had paused, and Birdie had not been paying attention.

The councilor turned. "Something is ahead." His deep, hollow voice was reduced to a hoarse whisper. "There are peculiar sounds. You wait here. J'merlia and I will proceed. We will return in five minutes or less. If we do not, Commissioner Kelly will be in charge of all subsequent actions."

He was gone before Birdie could object. *All subsequent actions.* He was being promoted from peon to president, with no idea what he ought to do. "How do I know when five minutes is up?" he asked E. C. Tally.

"I will keep you informed. My internal clock is accurate to the femtosecond." Tally held up one grimy finger. "Since Councilor Graves's final words to you it is exactly . . . forty-six seconds. Forty-seven. forty-eight. Forty-nine. Fifty."

"Stop that, E.C. I can't think when you keep on counting."

"Indeed? How strange. I have no such trouble. I offer condolences for your restriction to serial processing."

"Talking like that is just as bad. Keep quiet. Just tell me when it's every minute."

"Very well, Commissioner. But one minute has already passed."

"So tell me when it's two." Birdie turned to Kallik. "You have better ears than we do. Did you hear any sounds from in front of us?"

Kallik paused to reflect. "Sounds, yes," she said at last. "But nothing remotely human. Wheezing, and groaning. Like a venting Dowser."

"Now come on, Kallik. There can't possibly be a Dowser here—it would fill up the whole planetoid. Were there any *words*?"

"Possibly. Not in a language that I am able to comprehend. But J'merlia is a far better linguist than I am, perhaps you should ask him."

"He's not here—he's with Graves."

"When he returns."

"But if he returns, I won't need—"

"Two minutes," Tally said loudly. "May I speak?"

"My God, E.C., what now? I told you to keep quiet. Oh, go on then, spit it out."

"I am concerned by our immediate environment. As you may know, the functioning of my brain requires shielding from electromagnetic fields. As a result, the protective membranes contain sensitive field monitors. The corridor in which we are standing contains evidence of field inhibitors, and that evidence becomes stronger the farther that we go."

"So what? Don't you think we have more important things to worry about?"

"No. Assuming that the field inhibitors are functional, and that the interior structure of Glister relies upon the same methods as the surface for its stability, we would experience a significant change in environment were the field inhibitors to be turned on. As they could be, at any time."

"Change of environment. What do you mean, a change of environment?"

"In simple terms, we would fall through the floor. After that, I cannot say. I have no information as to what lies below. But let me observe that the outer parts of Glister average fifty meters between successive interior layers. A fifty-meter drop in this high a gravity field would render everyone of our party inoperative, with the possible exception of Kallik."

"Gawdy!" Birdie stepped sharply backward and stared down at his feet. "A fifty-meter fall? We'd all be mushed."

Before he could say more there was a patter of multiple feet in the tunnel ahead of them. J'merlia came scuttling back.

"It is all right," he said excitedly. "Councilor Graves says that it is safe to move forward to join him. He is in conversation with a being who dwells within Glister. It can converse in human speech—and it knows the present whereabouts of Atvar H'sial and Louis Nenda! It means us no harm, and we are in no danger. Please follow me."

"Now hold on a minute. And you, too, Kallik." Birdie grabbed the short fur on the back of the Hymenopt, restraining her—though if she had decided to go, nothing he or any human could have done would have stopped her. "You can tell us we're safe, J'merlia, but that's not what E.C. says—according to him, the tunnel floor could dissolve underneath us, any time. We'd all fall through and be killed. The farther we go the worse it gets. Can't whoever it is wait just a bit, while we check if we're safe?"

"I do not know." J'merlia stood thinking for a moment, his narrow head cocked to one side.

"I suppose it can," he said at last. "After all, it's been waiting for six million years. Maybe a few minutes more won't matter too much."

From the internal files of the embodied computer E. Crimson Tally: A note for the permanent and public record, concerning new anomalies of human behavior.

A recent experience leads me to suspect that the information banks employed in the briefing of embodied computers are so flawed in their representation of human reactions that their data are not merely useless but positively pernicious.

My observation is prompted by this recent experience:

After the removal and reinsertion of my brain, it was not clear to me that I would be able to perform at my previous level. Although my brain itself of course functioned as well as ever, the body's condition was obviously physically degraded. Moreover, I believed that my interface was impaired, although I knew that I was not the best judge of that.

Tests would easily have confirmed or denied the hypothesis of reduced function. However, without any procedures for performance evaluation, the humans of the group have treated me with noticeably *increased* respect following the event of brain removal and subsequent violent interruption of the interface.

Logic suggests only one explanation. Namely, the presence of a bloodied bandage around my head, which to any rational being warns of reduced function, has been taken instead as an *elevator* of status. Physical damage in humans demands increased respect. The more battered my skull, the greater the deference with which I am treated!

One wonders to what extremes this might be carried. If the top of my head were missing permanently, would all my actions be increasingly venerated?

Probably.

And if I were to be destroyed completely?

This matter demands introspection.

...

CHAPTER 18

Birdie had worked twenty-six and a half years—which felt like forever—for the government of Opal. Based on that, he had often said that humans were the most ornery, crackpot, cuss-headed critters in the universe.

But he would not say it anymore. There were others, he had just decided, who had humans beat for madness, from here to Doomsday.

They had been standing at the end of the tunnel, over a horrible sheer drop into nothing. And there was Julius Graves, with that big bald head of his, leaning out over the edge looking at a thing like a big silver teapot, with a flower for a spout, floating on nothing. And Julius, or maybe it was Steven, was *talking* to it, as if it were his long-lost brother.

"I do not follow your meaning, The-One-Who-Waits," he said. "This is our first visit. We have never been here before."

And the teapot had talked back!

Not at first, though. First it made a noise that sounded to Birdie like a set of bagpipes that needed pumping up. Then it wheezed. Then it screeched like a steam blower. Then it said, imitating Graves's accent, "Not you, the individuals. That was not my meaning. You, the *species.*"

Which seemed to make no more sense to Graves than it did to Birdie, because the councilor had wrinkled up his bulging bald head and said, "Our *species* has been here before?"

There was another groan, like the sound made by a dying dowser—Kallik had been right about that. Then: "The necessary members of your species came here. We had more than were needed. One would have been sufficient. But three humans came, including the one with the special additions."

At that Kallik gave a screech right in Birdie's ear, louder than anything the teapot-creature had produced. "Additions!" she said. "Augmentation. That must mean the master Nenda. He was here, and he is still alive."

The-One-Who-Waits must have understood her, because it went on, "One with augmentation, yes, alive, and there was also a necessary one of the *other* form, the great blind one with the secret speech. She, too, was passed along."

And that set J'merlia off, as bad as Kallik. "Oh, Atvar H'sial," he said, grabbing Birdie's arm and moaning the Cecropian name like a hymn. "Oh, Atvar H'sial. Alive. Commissioner Kelly, is that not wonderful news?"

Birdie chose not to answer. It seemed to him that the survival of any bug was no big deal, and especially one that had used J'merlia as a slave. But he was learning fast. Lo'tfians and Hymenopts had their own weird rules of what was important.

J'merlia's wails had not put The-One-Who-Waits off its stride for a minute. The teapot spout opened a bit more at the end, and the body quivered a little bit. Then it said, "So sufficient was already passed along. The three species are here. Your further presence is unnecessary. We will set in motion a safe passage for all of you to your homeworlds."

It seemed a bit early to start doing handstands and breaking out the liquor, but those words were still the best thing that Birdie had heard since they left Opal. Safe passage to their homeworlds—they were all going home! If The-One-Who-Waits had not been hanging five steps away in the middle of nothing, Birdie would have been tempted to hang around its neck and kiss it.

But then came the worst bit, the thing that Birdie could not believe. J'merlia and Kallik stepped forward and set up a wailing and a chittering and a whistling enough to deafen. "No, no, that cannot be. We must follow the masters. You must pass us along also. We cannot return without the masters."

That had finally seemed to put The-One-Who-Waits off a bit. It made a horrible throat, stomach, and bowel-clearing noise. "Is it your wish to be passed along also? Is that the meaning of your words?"

Birdie decided that sitting around waiting for six million years must leave one none too bright. But Kallik and J'merlia did not seem to agree. "It is, it is," they piped up. "Pass us along, it is our fondest desire. Pass us along."

"Such an action is possible," The-One-Who-Waits admitted. "It presents no difficulties, although the transit time cannot of course be exactly predicted. But for the others, the three humans, a safe passage to your home-worlds . . ."

This was it! "Yes!" Birdie said. "To our home—"

"No," Julius Graves said before Birdie could get out another word. "Not me. That would be totally inappropriate. My task is not complete. I must determine what happened to Professor Lang and Captain Rebka. And I must seek to arrest Louis Nenda and Atvar H'sial and return them to the Alliance for justice. Pass me along also, if you would be so kind."

It had to be one of the most stupid statements that Birdie had ever heard in his whole life. Atvar H'sial and Louis Nenda had been shipped off to nowhere, with any luck all the way to hell, and instead of saying bye-bye, good riddance, and let's all go home, Julius Graves wanted to chase after them!

"Then—" The-One-Who-Waits said. But it had waited a second too long. E. C. Tally jumped in.

"May I speak? I cannot possibly return to Sol with my own task so incomplete. I was charged to learn what happened at Summertide, and why. I am no nearer to an answer now than the day I left the tank on Persephone. Logic suggests that the answer must involve the actions of Atvar H'sial and Louis Nenda. It is appropriate that I also be 'given passage,' whatever that expression may signify, to join the others."

That confirmed Birdie's view that E. C. Tally was a robotic idiot. If the embodied computer was half as smart as he ought to be, he would have headed for home and made up some yarn about Summertide when he got there. Any six-year-old on Opal could have managed that. But Tally must have had bad training, so he only knew how to tell the truth.

When J'merlia and Kallik moved forward, Birdie had been left at the back of the group. Now he stepped to the front, too close to the edge for comfort. He knew just what he wanted—to be sent to Opal, home, and beauty, nice and safe, the way The-One-Who-Waits was promising.

"I'd like—" he began.

But still he had no chance to say it, because the teapot started vibrating like a struck gong. Birdie was convinced that it was getting ready to do something drastic, and he jumped smartly backward. While he was doing it, Graves hopped in and started talking again. From the tone of voice it was Steven.

"Before we are all passed along to join the others," he said, "I have questions. About this planetoid, and the Builders, and why they *need* humans and Cecropians. And where we will be going. And who you are, and what your own role is in all this. And what are the *three* species you mentioned. Those are questions that I feel sure you can answer, as perhaps no one else can. So if you would be so kind . . ."

Birdie was sure that Steven would be told to shut up. But instead The-One-Who-Waits gave another of those rude noises that would discourage Birdie from ever inviting it to parties. It stopped vibrating all over and hung in the air for a while. Finally it came drifting closer.

"Questions," it said. To Birdie it sounded exhausted, as though it had been planning to go off somewhere quiet and take another six-million-year nap, and Graves was interfering with the scheme. "That is perhaps . . . predictable. And not unreasonable."

The-One-Who-Waits kept moving forward until it was actually crowding them back on the ledge. No one touched it, but Birdie could tell that the silver surface was cold, cold enough to put a chill into the air all around it. Close up, he still could not see what the other was made of, but there were teeny little ripples running over the surface, no more than a millimeter or two high. The-One-Who-Waits had to be at least partly liquid. As it settled down on its tail, Birdie could see its shape sag, bulging out at the bottom.

"Very well," it said at last. "I will talk to you. It is best if I begin with my own history . . ."

Birdie groaned to himself. Wouldn't you just know it! Six million years old, and more alien than anything in the whole spiral arm—but no different in some ways from the rest of them.

Given a choice of subjects, The-One-Who-Waits was going to talk about *himself*.

CHAPTER 19

A flag buried deep in Rebka's brain told him what he was looking at in the tank. He had never seen anything like it before, but the skin of his arms tingled and hair stood up on the back of his neck.

"Hans?" Darya said again. "Move over. It's my turn."

She tugged at the sleeve of his suit. Then something in his rigid posture told her that this was nothing trivial, and he was not going to move. She crowded closer to him and again peered in through the tank's transparent port.

It took a while for her eyes to adapt to the reduced light level. But while she was still making that visual adjustment, her brain objected loud and clear: *Alert! This is a stasis tank!* There should be *no* light inside, none at all. Not while the tank was preserving the stasis condition. What was going on?

But by then she could see, and all rational thinking had stopped. No more than three feet from her face was a great, lidded eye, as big across as her stretched hand. That cerulean orb was almost closed. It sat in a broad, bulbous head of midnight blue, over a meter wide. Between the broad-spaced eyes was a cruel hooked beak, curving upward, easily big enough to seize and crack a human skull.

The rest of the body sprawled its length seven meters along the tank; but Darya needed to see no more.

"*Zardalu.*" The word came from her lips as a whisper, forced out against her will.

Hans Rebka stirred beside her. The soft-spoken word had broken his own trance.

"Yeah. Tell me I'm dreaming. There's no such thing. Not anymore."

"And it's *alive*—look, Hans, it's moving."

And with that remark, Darya's own sense of scientific curiosity came flooding back. The Zardalu had been exterminated in the spiral arm many thousands of years earlier. Although they were still the galactic bogeymen, everything about them was theory, myth, or legend. No one knew any details—not of their physiology, their evolution, or their habits. No one even knew how the cephalopods, originally a marine form, had been able to survive and breathe on land.

But Darya suddenly realized that she could answer that last question. She saw a sluggish ripple of peristalsis running along the length of the great body. The Zardalu must be breathing using a modification of the technique employed by ordinary marine cephalopods for propulsion—except that instead of drawing in and expelling *water* like a squid, the Zardalu employed that same muscular action to take in and expel *air*.

And for locomotion?

She stared at the body. The upper part was a round-topped cylinder, with bands of smooth muscle running down it. The eyes and beak were placed about one meter down. Below the beak sat a long vertical slit, surrounded by flexible muscular tissue. There was no difference in width between head and torso, but below that long gash of the mouth was a necklace of round-mouthed pouches, about six inches wide and circling the whole body. Darya could see pale blue ovals of different sizes nestled within the pouches. Stretched out along and beyond the main body was a loose tangle of thick tentacles, also pale blue. They were amply strong enough to walk on, though a set of broad straps wrapped around their thickest parts. Two of the tentacles ended in finely dividing ropy tips.

If those thin filaments were capable of independent control, Darya thought, a Zardalu would have manipulative powers beyond any human—beyond any other being in the spiral arm.

She felt an uncomfortable awe. The Zardalu might fill her with dread, but at the same time she knew that they were beautiful. It was a beauty that came from the perfect matching of form and function. The combination of muscular power with delicate touch could not be missed. The only anomaly was the webbing that girded the upper part of the tentacles.

"What are the straps for, Hans?" she whispered. "They can't be for physical support. Do you think they're for *carrying*—offspring, or supplies and weapons?"

But Rebka was still staring at the slow ripple of movement along the body. "Darya, this shouldn't be happening. It's impossible. Remember, this is a *stasis* unit. Everything's frozen, just like time has stopped. But that thing in there is *breathing*—slow, but enough to see. And look at that eye."

There was a flicker of movement in the heavy lid. While they watched, the tip of one thick tentacle twitched and curled a few centimeters.

Rebka stepped sharply away from the tank. "Darya, that Zardalu isn't in stasis. It may have been, a few hours ago. But now it's starting to wake up. I've no idea how long reanimation will take, but Speaker-Between must have started the process as soon as we arrived. He said that there were 'two forms only' here, and I assumed that he meant the two of us. But now it looks as though he meant two *species*, Human and Zardalu. We have to try to find him and warn him. He probably has no idea what the Zardalu were like."

He was already moving from one stasis tank to the next, peering in for only a moment at each.

"They're all the same. All starting to wake."

He hurried back to the food-supply unit, grabbing handfuls of still-frozen packets and stuffing them into his pockets. Darya marveled that at a time like this he could still think of food. She remembered how hungry she had been feeling, but at the moment she could not have eaten a thing.

He turned impatiently to her. "Come on."

She obeyed—reluctantly. It was against all her instincts, to leave something so novel, about which so many students and experts on the cultures of the spiral arm had expended so much speculative effort. Hans might be right when he said that Speaker-Between might have no idea what the Zardalu were like; but that was just as true of *human* knowledge of the Zardalu. There was speculation and theory, but no one *knew* anything. And here she was, with a perfect opportunity to determine a few facts.

Only one thing made her follow right after Rebka: the fear that had crept up her spine unbidden, like a capillary flow of ice water, when she first saw that dark-blue skin and bulky body. She did not *want* to be alone with a Zardalu, even an unconscious one.

According to all expert knowledge, humans had never encountered Zardalu. The Great Rising had happened before humanity moved into space. But there could be deeper wisdom than anything in the data banks. The submerged depths of Darya's brain told her that there *had* been encounters, back before human recorded history.

And they had been bloody and merciless meetings. Sometime, long before, the Zardalu scouts had taken a close look at Earth. They had been stopped before they could colonize. Not by any action of early humans, but by the Great Rising. Dozens of intelligent races and scores of planets had been annihilated in that rebellion. And Earth had benefitted, unknowing, from their sacrifice. The Zardalu had been exterminated.

Or almost exterminated.

Darya found herself shaking all over as she went after Hans. He was right. They had to find Speaker-Between and warn him, even if they were not sure what they were warning him *about*.

Reaching the Interlocutor should in principle be trivially

easy. They had entered the sphere of his body and never left it. Therefore they must still be inside Speaker-Between.

But Darya did not believe it. She did not trust the evidence of her senses anymore. The chambers containing the stasis tanks and the Zardalu were just too big to fit inside Speaker-Between. The Builders had a control of the geometry of space-time beyond anything dreamed of by the current inhabitants of the spiral arm. For all she knew, Speaker-Between could be very far away—thousands of light-years, as humans measured things.

She glanced behind her as she followed Hans Rebka to the two doors of the chamber—the same doors through which they had entered, less than an hour before. The great coffins still sat silent. But now that she knew their contents, that silence had become ominous, a calm that heralded coming activity. She was strangely uncomfortable about leaving that chamber, and even more uneasy about staying there.

As they passed through the first sliding door and then the second one, Darya knew at once that her instincts had been correct. The outside *had* changed. They were emerging not into the level and infinite plain where they had encountered Speaker-Between, but to a somber gray-walled room. And instead of high-ceilinged emptiness, or the webs, cables, nets, and partitions of Glister, Hans and Darya were standing before hundreds of ivory-white cubes, ranging in size from boxes small enough to tuck easily under one arm, to towering objects taller than a human. The cubes were scattered across the floor of the rectangular room, like dice cast by a giant.

Nothing moved. There was no sign of Speaker-Between.

To Darya's surprise, after Rebka's careful inspection of their surroundings he walked forward to look at a couple of boxes. They stood side by side and came about up to his knees. He sat down on one of them, reached into his pocket, and pulled out a packet. As she stared he opened it and started to peel the thin-skinned fruit that it contained.

"It's still a bit cold on the inside," he said after a few moments. "But we can't afford to be too picky."

"Hans! The Zardalu. We have to find Speaker-Between."

"You mean we'd like to." He bit off a small piece of the fruit, chewed it, and frowned. "Not too great, but it's better than nothing. Look, Darya, I want to find Speaker-Between and talk to him as much as you do. But how? I hoped we'd find that we were still inside him, so coming out would bring us back to talk to him. It didn't work. This place is stranger than anything I've ever seen in my life, and I doubt if you're any more at home than I am. You saw the size of this artifact when we were approaching it. We could spend the rest of our lives looking for somebody, but if he doesn't *want* to be found, we'd never get near him."

Darya visualized the monstrous space construct that they had seen on the final transition of their approach, its delicate filaments stretching out millions of kilometers. Rebka was right. Its size was too big to contemplate, let alone search. But the idea of *not* searching . . .

"You mean you're just going to sit there and do nothing?"

"No. I could make a case for that—when you don't know what to do, do nothing. I'm going to sit and *eat*. And you should do the same." He patted the box beside him. "Right here. You're the logical one, Darya. Think it through. We have no idea where Speaker-Between is, or how to go about looking for him. And we don't know our way around here—I mean, we don't even know this place's *topology*. But if you were to ask the most *likely* place for Speaker-Between to show up, I'd say it's right here where he left us. And if you were to ask me the best way for us to spend our time, I'd say we should do two things. We should eat and rest, and we should stay where we can easily keep an eye on what's happening back in that other room, with the Zardalu. We really ought to eat in there, too, but staring at those tanks I know I couldn't manage a bite."

Signs of human frailty in Hans Rebka? Darya did not

know if she approved of that or not. She sat down on a white box with a fine snowflake pattern on its sides. The top was slightly warm to the touch. It gave a fraction of an inch under her weight, just enough to make it comfortable.

Maybe it was not weakness in Rebka at all. *When you don't know what to do, do nothing.* One might think that would be her philosophy, the research worker who had lived in her study for twenty years. But instead she felt a huge urge to *do something*—anything. It was Rebka, the born troubleshooter who had lived through a hundred close scrapes, who could sit and relax.

Darya accepted a lump of cool yellow fruit. *Eat.* She ate. She found it slightly astringent, with a granular texture that encouraged hard chewing. No aftereffects. Rebka was right about that, too. They surely would not have been brought all this way only to be poisoned or left to starve. Except—what right did they have to make any assumptions about alien thought processes, when everything that had happened since they arrived at Gargantua had been a total mystery?

She accepted three more pieces of unfamiliar food. Still her stomach was making no objections, but she wished that what they were eating could be warmed. She felt chilled. Shivering, she set her suit at a higher level of opacity. She was ready to ask for more fruit when she noticed that Rebka was sitting up straighter on his seat and staring around him. She followed his look and saw nothing.

"What is it?"

He shook his head. "I don't know. Only . . ." He was focusing his attention on the far side of the room. "Feel it? It's not my imagination. A draft—and getting stronger."

A *cold* draft. Darya realized that she had been feeling it for a while, without knowing what it was. There were chilly breezes blowing past them, ruffling his hair and tugging gently at her suit.

"What's causing it?" But Darya knew the answer, even as Hans was shaking his head in bewilderment. She could

see a swirling pattern forming on the far side of the room.
A rotating cylinder of air had darkened there, streaked
horizontally like muddy water on glass. It formed a vortex
column that ran from floor to ceiling. She stood up and
grabbed Rebka's arm.

"Hans. We have to get out of here and back to the
other chamber—it's getting stronger."

The circulation pattern created by the vortex was
becoming powerful enough to generate a minor gale,
driving around the whole inside of the room. Who could
say how fierce it would get? If it continued to strengthen,
she and Hans would be swept off their feet.

He was nodding, not trying to speak over the scream
of wind. Holding on to each other, they fought their way
back to the shelter of the doorway. Rebka turned in the
entrance.

"Wait for a second before we go through." He had to
shout in her ear to be heard. "It's still getting stronger.
But it's *closing*—look."

The spinning cylinder of air was drawing in on itself .
From a width of five meters, it tightened as they watched
to become no wider than a man's outstretched arms. Its
heart became an oily, soft-edged black, so dark and dense
that the wall of the chamber could not be seen through
it. The scream of wind in the room grew to a new intensity,
hurting Darya's ears.

She backed farther into the doorway. The force of the
wind was terrifying. The vortex loomed darker, more and
more dangerous. She reached out to pull Rebka back—he
was leaning into the room, even while gusts tore at his hair
and buffeted his body. Her fingers grabbed the back of his
suit. The wail of rushing air rose higher and higher.

She tugged. Rebka fell off balance backward. She
bumped into the closed door.

In that same instant, everything stopped. The wind
dropped, the sounds faded.

There was a moment of total silence in the chamber;
and then, in that uncanny stillness, there came a soft
pop no louder than a cork being removed from a bottle.

The vortex changed in color to a blood-red, and began to fade.

Another moment, and the silence was broken more substantially. Out of the thinning heart of the spinning column staggered a form. A *human* form.

It was Louis Nenda. He was greenish yellow in complexion, stripped to the waist, and cursing loudly and horribly.

The little black satchel that he always carried with him flapped against his bare chest. Two steps behind him, creeping along miserably with all six limbs to the ground, came the giant blind figure of Atvar H'sial.

Back on Quake they had been enemies. Nenda and Atvar H'sial had tried to kill Darya Lang and Hans Rebka, and Rebka, at least, would have been happy to return the compliment.

Thirty thousand light-years made quite a difference. They greeted each other like long-lost brothers and sisters.

"But where in hell *are* we?" Nenda asked when his nausea had eased enough to allow any form of speech beyond swearing.

"A long way from home," Rebka said.

"Ratballs, I know *that*. But where?"

As they exchanged information—what little of it they had—Darya learned that her own journey here had been a pleasure trip compared with what had happened to the two new arrivals.

"Stop an' go," Nenda said. "Go an' stop, all the way." He belched loudly. "Jerkin' around, turned ass-over-teacup, right way up one minute and wrong way up the next. Went on forever. I'd've puked fifty times, if I'd had anything in my guts." He was silent for a few moments. "At says it was just as bad for her. And yet you come so easy. There must be more than one way to get here. We traveled steerage class and got the rough one."

"But the fast one, too," Rebka said. "By the look of it, you and Atvar H'sial left Glister days after us. We thought we were only on the way for a few minutes, but it could have been a lot more—we don't know how long we were stuck in nowhere, between transitions."

"Well, I thought we were on the way for *weeks*." Nenda belched again. "Gar. That's better. Thirty thousand light-years, you said? Long way from home. Let that be a lesson to you, At. Greed don't pay."

"Can she understand you?" Darya had been staring at the pitted and nodulated area of Nenda's bare chest, watching it quiver and pulse as Nenda spoke.

"Sure. At least, whenever I use the augment she can. I speak the words at the same time, usually, because that way it's easier to know what I want to say. But At picks it all up. Watch. You hear me, At?"

The blind white head nodded.

"See. You ought to have an augment put in, too, so you can chat with At an' the other Cecropians." He stared at Darya's chest. "Mind you, I'd hate to see them nice boobs messed up."

Any sympathy that Darya might have had for the Karelian human evaporated. "If I were you, Louis Nenda, I'd save my breath to plead with the judge. You have formal charges waiting for you, as soon as we get back to the spiral arm. Councilor Graves already filed them."

"Charges for what? I didn't do a thing."

"Your ship fired at us." Rebka said. "You tried to destroy the *Summer Dreamboat* after Summertide."

"I did?" Nenda's face was blandly innocent. "You sure it was me, Captain, and not three other guys? I never even heard of no *Summer Dreamboat*. I don't remember firing at anything. Doesn't sound like the sort of thing I'd do at all. Do you think we fired at a ship, At?" He paused. The Cecropian did not move. "No way. See, she agrees with me."

"She's as guilty as you are!"

"You mean as innocent."

Rebka's face had lost its usual pallor. "Damn you, I don't think I'll even wait until we get back home. I can file charges on you right here, just as well as Graves can." He took a step closer to Nenda.

The other man did not move. "So you're feeling mad. Big deal. Go on, try to arrest me—and tell me where you'll lock me up. Maybe you'll shut me away with your girlfriend here. I'd like that. So would she." He grinned admiringly at Darya. "How about it, sweetie? You'll have more fun with me than you've ever had with him."

"If you're trying to change the subject, it won't work." Rebka moved until he and Nenda were eyeball to eyeball. "Do you really want to see if I can arrest you? Try a few more cracks like that."

Nenda turned to Darya and gave her a wink. "See how mad he gets, when anybody else tries for a piece?"

He had been watching Rebka out of the corner of his eye, and he batted away the hand that grabbed for his wrist. Then the two men were standing with arms braced, glaring at each other.

Darya could not believe it. She had never seen Rebka lose his temper before—and Louis Nenda had never been anything but cool and cynical. What was doing it to them? Tension? Fatigue?

No. She could see their expressions. They were trying each other out, testing to see which rooster was top of the dunghill.

So that was how people behaved on the primitive outworlds. Everyone would think she was making this up if she told them all about it back on Sentinel Gate.

The two men were still standing with arms locked. Darya reached over and tugged at Rebka's right hand. "Stop it!" she shouted at them. "Both of you. You're acting like wild beasts."

They ignored her, but Atvar H'sial reached out with two jointed forelimbs, grabbed each man around the waist in one clawed paw, and lifted them high in the air. She pulled them effortlessly away from each other. After a second or two she allowed their feet to touch the ground, but she still held them far apart.

The blind head turned toward Darya, while the proboscis unfurled and produced a soft hissing sound.

"I know," Darya said. "They *are* like animals, aren't

they? Hold them for a minute or two longer." She spread her arms wide, as though pushing the men farther apart. Atvar H'sial might not understand her words, but she surely could take her meaning.

Darya went to stand between them. "Listen to me, you two. I don't know which of you is more stupid, but you can have your idiocy contest later. I want to say just one word to you." She paused, waiting until they turned their attention fully to her. "Zardalu! D'you hear me? *Zardalu.*"

"Huh?" Louis Nenda's hands had still been reaching out toward Rebka. They dropped to his sides. "What are you talking about?"

Darya gestured at the doorway behind her. "In there. Fourteen Zardalu."

"Crap! There's not been a Zardalu in the spiral arm for thousands of years. They're extinct."

"You're not in the spiral arm anymore, boy. You're thirty thousand light-years out of the plane of the galaxy. And back in that room there's fourteen stasis tanks, with a Zardalu in each one. *Alive.*"

"I don't believe it. Nobody's ever seen a Zardalu, not even a stuffed or a mummified one." Nenda turned to Hans Rebka. "You hear her? She trying to make a joke?"

"No joke." Rebka straightened his suit, where Nenda had pulled it half off his shoulders. "She's telling the truth. They're in stasis tanks, but I don't know how long that will last. The stasis was beginning to end when we saw them."

"You mean you stood there and picked a fight with me, when there's *Zardalu* waking up in there? And you call *me* dumb! You have to be crazy."

"What do you mean, *I* picked a fight!"

Darya stepped between them again. "You're *both* crazy, and you're both to blame. Are you going to start over? Because if you are, I hope Atvar H'sial understands enough to crack your heads together and knock some sense into you."

"She does. She will." Nenda stared at the closed door. Suddenly he was his old calm self. "Zardalu. I don't know what you're smoking, but maybe we better get in there. I'll tell At what's been happening. She's like me, though— she won't really believe it until she takes a peek for herself."

He turned to Atvar H'sial. "You're not gonna like this, At." The gray pheromone nodules on his chest pulsed in unison with his human speech. "These two jokers say there's *Zardalu* in there. You heard me. Fourteen of 'em, in stasis but alive and gettin' ready to trot. I know, I know."

The Cecropian had squatted back onto her hindmost limbs, furled the antennas above her head, and tucked her proboscis into its pleated holder.

"She don't like to hear that," Nenda said. "She says a Cecropian ain't afraid of anything in the universe, but Zardalu images are part of her race memory. A bad part. Nobody knows why."

Hans Rebka was sliding open the first of the two doors. "Let's hope she doesn't find out. I'd suggest that you and Atvar H'sial hang back a bit—just in case."

He opened the second door. Darya held her breath, then released it with a sigh of relief. The great pentagonal cylinders lay exactly as they had left them, silent and closed.

"All right." Hans Rebka moved forward. "You wanted proof, here it is. Take a look in there."

Rebka walked cautiously to the transparent port in the end of the stasis tank and peered in through it. After a few seconds he gave a long sigh.

"I know," Rebka said softly. "Impressive, eh? And scary, too. We have to find a way to turn that stasis field back on, before they wake up and try to get out."

But Louis Nenda was shaking his head. "I don't know what game you're playing, *Captain* Rebka and *Professor* Lang. I just know it's a stupid one."

He stepped away from the long casket.

"There's thirteen more to look at, but I'll bet money they're all like this one." He turned to face Darya. "It's *empty*, sweetheart. Empty as a Ditron's brainbox. What do you have to say about *that*?"

ENTRY 42: DITRON.

Distribution: Never having achieved an independent spaceflight capability, Ditrons are found in large numbers only on their native world (*Ditrona*, officially Luris III, Cecropia Federation, Sector Five). Transported Ditron colonies can also be found on the neighboring worlds of Prinal (Luris II) and Ivergne (Luris V). In the early days of the Cecropian expansion, Ditrons were taken to the other stellar systems, but generally they did not thrive there. Diet deficiencies were blamed at the time, but more recent analyses make it clear that psychological dependencies were as much a factor. Ditrons, at the third stage of their life cycle, fail to survive if the group size dwindles below twenty.

Physical Characteristics: It is necessary to consider separately the three stages of the Ditron life cycle, conventionally designated as S-1, S-2, and S-3. The Ditrons are unique among known intelligent species in that their highest mental levels are achieved not in their most mature form, but rather in their premature and premating (S-2) stage.

The larval form (S-1) is born live, in a litter of no less than five and no more than thirteen offspring. The newborn Ditron masses less than one kilogram, but it has full mobility and is able to eat at once. It is near-blind, possesses sevenfold radial symmetry, is asexual, herbivorous, and lacks measurable intelligence.

S-1 lasts for one Ditron summer season (three-fourths of a standard year) at the end of which time a body mass of twenty-five kilos has been achieved and metamorphosis begins. S-1 moves below ground, as a flat, pale-yellow disk about one meter in diameter. It emerges in the spring as S-2, a slender, dark-orange, many-legged carnivore with bilateral symmetry and a fierce appetite. An S-2 Ditron will prey on anything except its own S-1 and S-3 forms. It possesses no known language, but from its behavior patterns it is judged to be of undeniable intelligence. Consideration of the S-2 Ditron first led to that species' assignment as an intelligent form.

In this life stage the Ditron is solitary, energetic, and antisocial. Attempts to export S-2 Ditrons to other worlds have all failed, not because the organism dies but because it never ceases to feed voraciously, to attack its captors at every opportunity, and to try to escape. A confined S-2 will solve within minutes a maze that will hold most humans or Cecropians for an hour or more.

S-2 lasts for fourteen years, during all of which time the Ditron grows constantly. At the end of this period it masses twelve tons and is fifteen meters long. No more formidable predator exists in the spiral arm (archaeological workers on Luris II have discovered an ancestral form of the Ditron S-2 that was almost twice the S-2's present size, and apparently just as voracious; it probably, however, lacked intelligence).

The transition to S-3 arrives suddenly, and apparently without warning to the S-2 itself. It is conjectured that the first sign of a change to S-3 state is a substantial fall in Ditron S-2 intelligence, and a sudden urge for clustering. The formerly antisocial creature seeks out and protects the cocoon clusters of other changing S-2's. Up to a hundred Ditrons tunnel deep into sites by soft riverbanks, where each spins its own protective cocoon. New arrivals protect the site from predators, before themselves beginning to tunnel. Metamorphosis takes place over a two-year period. Emerging S-3's have dwindled to a body mass of less than one ton. The material of the residual cocoon is a valuable prize, for anyone able to thwart the guardianship offered by the protective S-2's.

The form of the S-3 is a large-headed upright biped, brownish-red in color, two-eyed, and with bilateral symmetry. Its alert appearance and large brainbox persuaded early explorers of Luris III that the S-3 must be a more intelligent and certainly more friendly form than its S-2 progenitor.

Unfortunately, the head of the S-3 is employed mainly as a resonance cavity. It enables the creature to produce mating calls that can be heard over large distances, but the skull contains mostly air. The brain itself is little more than the couple of hundred grams of material required to allow an S-3 to find a mate, to copulate, and to bring forth the S-1 larval form.

The attempt to use Ditrons as a slave species has been made many times, because the S-3 is undeniably docile and tractable and enjoys company; but the main result has been frustration to the Ditron owners. Only the Cecropians continue to cultivate S-3 slaves, either as pets or for purposes that remain obscure.

History: Ditrons possess no written or oral history. Paleontological research shows that these beings have changed little in form, though considerably in size, over the past three million years.

Culture: None. S-1 and S-3 Ditrons are mindless. S-2 Ditrons, undeniably intelligent, build no structures, use no tools, wear no clothing, and keep no records. All attempts at communication with S-2's have been ignored.

—From the *Universal Species Catalog* (Subclass: Sapients).

CHAPTER 20

The period before the coming of intelligence had been quiet, peaceful, and eons long. The final emergence was a miracle in itself; and like all miracles, nothing before it presaged its arrival.

The nutrients in the middle atmosphere of the gas-giant were rich and abundant; the climate was unvarying; a total absence of competition removed any stimulus to evolution.

The dominant life-form drifted idly in its buoyant sea of high-pressure hydrogen and helium, loose aggregations of cells that combined, dissociated, and recombined with endless variety. The results were sometimes simple, sometimes complex, and always without self-awareness. They had persisted unchanged for eight hundred million years.

When it came, the pressure was provided from without, and from far away. A supernova, nine light-years from the Mandel system, sent a sleet of hard radiation and superfast particles driving into the upper atmosphere of Gargantua. The dominant life-form, tens of thousands of kilometers down, was well protected; it drowsed on. But small and primitive multicelled creatures, eking out their own existence almost at the edge of space, felt the full force of the incident flux. They had been harmless, unable to compete with the loosely organized but more efficient assemblies of life below; now they mutated in the killing storm of radiation. The survivors grew voracious and

467

desperate, and expanded their biosphere—downward. Like vermin, they began to infest the deep habitats and to modify the food chains there.

The Sleepers below had to quicken—or die. At first their numbers dwindled. They mindlessly sought refuge in the depths, down in the unfathomable abyss near the rocky solid core, where living conditions were harsh and food less plentiful.

It was not enough. The vermin followed them, gnawing at their evanescent structures, interfering with their placid drift at the whim of currents and temperature gradients.

The Sleepers had a simple choice: adapt or die. Since permanence of form was essential to survival, they became unified structures. They formed tough skins to protect those structures, integuments hard enough to resist the vermin's attack. They developed mobility for escape. They learned to recognize and avoid the swarms of starving nibblers. They themselves became rapid and aggressive eaters.

And they developed *cunning*. Not long afterward came self-awareness. In a few million years, technology followed. The Sleepers pursued the vermin back to the upper edge of the atmosphere, for the first time claiming that domain as their own.

Now they found themselves familiar with and at home in environments ranging from million-atmosphere pressures at the interface with Gargantua's rocky central core, to the near-vacuum of the planet's ionosphere. They developed materials that could endure those extremes of pressure, and as great extremes of radiation and temperature. Finally they decided to move to a place where the still-annoying vermin could not follow: space itself.

The technology went with them. The Sleepers became the Builders. They spread with no haste from star to star in the spiral arm. Never again would they occupy a planet. Their homeworld became Homeworld, and finally Old-Home, abandoned but not forgotten. It remained the central nexus of the Builders' transportation system.

They were Sleepers no more; and yet in one essential way they were as they had always been. The active and aggressive behavior patterns forced upon them by the vermin were only a few millions years deep. They were overlaid like a thin veneer on a deeper behavior, one derived from that idyllic and near-infinite era of idle drifting.

The Builders made their great spaceborne artifacts, with a communication network that stretched across and beyond the spiral arm; but they did so almost absent-mindedly, with no more than a small part of their collective consciousness. They were Builders, certainly; but more than that they were *Thinkers*. For them, contemplation was the highest and the preferred activity. Action was a sometimes necessary but always unwelcome digression.

The new stability persisted for almost two hundred million years, while the Builders busied themselves in a leisurely analysis of the nature of the universe itself. Then came a new *Great Problem*, more troublesome even than the vermin. And further change was forced upon them . . .

The-One-Who-Waits fell silent. At some hidden command the lights in the great chamber dimmed further. The alien lifted a few centimeters above the surface of the tunnel, where in front of it sat Julius Graves, with J'merlia and Kallik on each side. E. C. Tally and Birdie Kelly were just behind, cross-legged on the hard tunnel floor and stiff-jointed from two hours of silent attention. When it had finally become fluent in human speech, the voice of The-One-Who-Waits had proved to be slow and hypnotic, forcing the listeners to ignore their surroundings and their own physical needs.

Birdie stirred and inspected each of the others in turn. E. C. Tally was in the worst shape of anyone. The embodied computer was leaning forward and supporting himself wearily on his hands and elbows. Apparently the need for rest and recuperation had not been sufficiently explained to him; before long, by the look of it, Tally would collapse from simple exhaustion.

At the front, Graves sat with his face invisible to Birdie. The two aliens by his side had expressions unreadable at the best of times. The only thing they seemed to care about was finding Louis Nenda and Atvar H'sial, so that they could grovel again to their old masters. They were sprawled on the floor, all jointed legs, staring up at the shining body a few feet away from them.

"And what was the new *Great Problem?*" Graves asked.

"That information was not considered useful to me." The weary voice sounded more tired than ever, as though it would welcome a rapid end to the conversation. "I, of course, was *created* by the Builders, long ago, so although my data sources here are large, they are limited to information judged necessary for my effective functioning. You will obtain more answers than I can give you when you reach Serenity—the main artifact, far from the main galactic plane."

"And we will find the Builders there?" Graves had become the official spokesman of the group.

"That information also is not available here." The-One-Who-Waits paused. "The present whereabouts of the Builders are unknown to me. But this I know, that you must work with Speaker-Between, the Interlocutor, one who wears my shape. When the Builders chose to move to Serenity, they also postponed certain other decisions until particular events occurred. Those events are now imminent, and involve Speaker-Between."

"When did the Builders leave the spiral arm?"

"I am not exactly sure." The-One-Who-Waits made a now-familiar soft bubbling noise, like water boiling over, and went on. "I myself waited for six million of your years, in the interior of that planet you call Quake. But of course, I was already old before that . . . I am not sure how old. Mmmm. Ten million of your years? Twelve?"

There was another substantial silence, during which Birdie wondered if Builder constructs could suffer from senility.

"I would be still waiting still," The-One-Who-Waits went on, "but a few weeks ago the signals were at last received. They indicated that every Builder structure in the spiral arm had finally been visited by a member of one of the chosen intelligent species.

"The plan could at last proceed. The tidal energies available at Quake during Summertide were harnessed to open the planet. They permitted me to be sent to the vicinity of Old-Home. I came to the gate of the transportation system, where we are now.

"Very soon you will enter that gate, at your own request. Unless you have a final question?

"If we may not meet the Builders, even on Serenity, can't you at least describe to us what they look like?" Graves said.

"It is not necessary for me to do so. You are already familiar with ones who wear the external appearance of the Builders: the Phages."

"There's a popular theory that says the Phages are artifacts," Steven Graves said. "Are you saying that the Phages were *constructed* by the Builders in their own image, to look like them?"

"No. The Phages *are* Builders—devolved forms, debased and degenerate. Their intelligence has been lost. They are able to propagate themselves, and to perform the most elementary acts of matter and energy absorption, and that is all. For all the time that I have known, they have been a nuisance to every free-space structure in the spiral arm. Planetary interiors, like the inside of Quake, are safe, and intense gravity fields discourage their presence."

"What happened, to turn Builders into Phages?" Graves asked.

"I cannot say." The-One-Who-Waits was stirring, lifting higher off the floor. "I know only that it was another consequence of the *Great Problem*, the one that led the Builders to leave the spiral arm and seek a long stasis in the Artifact.

"Now, no more questions. It is time for you to enter the gate."

Birdie looked all around him. All this talk about a gate. There was nothing in sight that resembled a gate, even vaguely.

"I don't know where your gate is," he began. "But about that safe passage that you promised us, back to our home planets—"

He was in midsentence when the floor evaporated beneath his feet. He heard a rushing sound all around him. Birdie took one look down. He was falling, dropping into nothingness.

He closed his eyes.

Looking back on what happened next, Birdie decided he must have kept his eyes squeezed tight shut until he felt firm ground again beneath his feet. Or then again, maybe he had just fainted. He was not willing to argue that point. He knew only two things for sure: First, when the others described the journey, he had no idea what they were talking about. He did not remember one thing about it.

Second, when he did finally open his eyes . . .

He was standing on a flat, endless plain, beneath a dull and featureless ceiling of glowing grayness.

And he was not alone. Surrounding him, looming over him, reaching out toward him with pale-blue tentacles, even before his eyes had finished opening, were—

—the stuff of nightmares.

He saw a dozen hulking bodies of midnight blue. They were closing in, sharp beaks gaping.

At that point Birdie felt more than ready to close his eyes and faint again.

ENTRY 16: ZARDALU.

Distribution: Like all information concerning the Zardalu, species-distribution data are based on fragmentary historical records and on incomplete race memory of other species. The great empire known as the *Zardalu Communion* is believed to have formed a roughly hemispherical region, over a thousand light-years across and centered on 1400 ly, 22 hours, 27° north (coordinates in galactic-plane angular measure, radial distances with respect to Sol; coordinate shifts to Cecropia reference frame are given in Appendix B). The face of the hemisphere comprising the Zardalu Communion is roughly tangent to the edge of Crawlspace (see *HUMAN* entry), and the lower part of the hemisphere itself overlaps the Cecropia Federation (see *CECROPIA* entry).

At its height, just before the Great Rising of approximately eleven thousand years ago, the Zardalu Communion ruled in excess of one thousand worlds. There is evidence that preliminary missions to worlds of the Fourth Alliance and of the Cecropia Federation took place just before the Rising, and that the Zardalu intended to expand into those regions.

Despite rumors today of hidden worlds inhabited by Zardalu—rumors that possess the force and persistence of multispecies legend—it should be noted that *no Zardalu has been encountered since the Great Rising*. It can be confidently stated that the Zardalu are extinct and have been extinct for eleven thousand years.

Physical Characteristics: No physical remains or pictures have been discovered. The Zardalu records were systematically destroyed, along with all evidence of Zardalu existence, at the time of the Great Rising. The following data represent a consensus derived from race memories, largely of the Hymenopts. They are undoubtedly subject to the distortion natural for a slave species remembering their former masters:

The Zardalu were land-cephalopods, possessing between six and twelve tentacles. Their size is not know with any precision, but it is certain that they were considerably larger than a Hymenopt (which seldom stands above one and a half meters, even with legs fully extended.) A suggested plausible height for a standing Zardalu would be three meters, although Hymenopt impressions record it as at least twice that.

Evidence suggests that the Zardalu possessed smooth, grease-coated skin ranging in color from pale powder-blue (tentacles) to deep blue-black (main torso). The head possessed large, lidded eyes, a formidable beak, and one main ingestion mouth.

Details of interior anatomy are not available. The existence of an endoskeleton, or the lack of one, is purely conjectural. Based upon their large size, and upon their ability to move and function well on land, it seems likely that the Zardalu possessed at least a rudimentary skeleton, or substantial interior sheaths and bands of semirigid cartilaginous material.

No information is available concerning Zardalu intelligence or culture level, and nothing is known about the Zardalu mating or family habits. They retain to this day the reputation of having been prodigious breeders, but that reputation is not based on scientific evidence.

History: Almost nothing can be said here with any authority, beyond this: Based on their wide distribution and integrated empire, the Zardalu must have developed space travel at least twenty thousand years before Cecropians or Humans, and possibly much longer ago than that.

The original homeworld of the Zardalu clade remains unknown, although its name, Genizee, is well established in legend. Quite likely it was one of the dozens of worlds cindered and sterilized in the bitter struggle of the Great Rising. Certainly any of the subject races able to find and annihilate the home of the Zardalu would have done so, without hesitation.

Culture: Five words summarize all recollections of Zardalu culture: imperialistic, powerful, determined, expansionist, and ruthless. It is a perverse testament to the Zardalu that they still evoke such strong images in the minds of intelligent beings everywhere, even though they have been gone for over ten millennia.

—From the *Universal Species Catalog* (Subclass: Sapients).

CHAPTER 21

Darya arrived back in the silent chamber a little bit
early, before the other three. In the past four hours
she had become convinced that the search was going
nowhere. She was also tired, and becoming hungry
again.

Even so, she could not sit down until she had taken a
look inside each of the big tanks. Logically she knew that
the coffins would be empty. It made no sense for the
Zardalu to have gone back into stasis, even assuming that
they knew how the tanks worked.

But logic had nothing to do with it. She had to see
for herself and make *sure*.

Atvar H'sial crept quietly into the room a few minutes
later, right on time. She and Darya nodded to each other.
That was about as far as they could go without Louis
Nenda as interpreter, but Darya was sure that the
Cecropian had also found nothing useful. She could read
that much from body language, just as Atvar H'sial must
be able to read her.

Rebka and Nenda came in together. They looked angry
and worried.

"Nothing?" Darya asked.

They shook their heads simultaneously.

"Washout," Nenda said. "No Builders, no Speaker-
Between, no Zardalu. Bugger 'em all. From the look of
it, we'd take ten thousand years searching this place

properly. Screw it." Just as Darya had done, he and Rebka went compulsively across to the tanks and peered inside to make sure that they were empty.

"It's worse than I thought," Nenda said when he came back. "At says she didn't catch one whiff of them, nowhere. And she can smell a gnat's armpit at a hundred kilometers. Stinkers like them ought to be a cinch. They've vanished, every one of them. What do we do *now*, boys and girls?"

It was smell that had persuaded Nenda, not any argument offered by Darya or Hans Rebka. When Atvar H'sial had risen high, poked her big white head inside one of the big tanks, pulled forth on one claw a trace of fatty smear, and assured them all that nothing smelled remotely like that anywhere in the spiral arm, Nenda had become an instant believer. The Cecropian knew scents better than any human knew sights. Darya had put her own head into one of the tanks and caught the faintest whiff of ammonia and rancid grease.

Rebka was sitting on top of one of the coffins, his chin cupped in his hands. "What do we do?" he repeated. "Well, I guess that we keep looking. Speaker-Between said the action would start when all three species were present. We didn't know what he was talking about then, but now we do."

"We're all here," Nenda said. "Humans, Cecropians, and Zardalu. Great—except we can't find the Zardalu."

"*We* can't. But I'll bet that Speaker-Between can. This is his home ground."

"Yeah—and *we* can't find Speaker-Between." Nenda walked forward to stand in front of the tank and stare up insultingly at Rebka. "Great work, Captain. If you're so convinced Speaker-Between will find us, I don't know why we bothered looking."

Rebka did not move. "Because I'd like to tell him about the Zardalu before *they* tell him," he said quietly. "Just in case he doesn't know their reputation. Got any ideas, smart guy? I'm ready to be amazed."

"That shouldn't take much."

"All right." Darya stepped between them. "That will do. Or I'll set Atvar H'sial on both of you. I thought we agreed, we can't afford to bicker and fight until we're out of this mess."

"I said I'd *cooperate*. I never said I'd bow down in front of him, or that I'd agree with him when he said something really dumb—"

Nenda was interrupted by Atvar H'sial, who came gliding through the air to land by his side. She grabbed him by the arm with one clawed forepaw and pulled him backward so that his head was in contact with the front of her carapace.

"Hey, At," he said. "Whose side are you on? Now just stop that!"

He had been drawn close to the Cecropian and turned bodily to face the chamber entrances. "*What!*" His chest nodules were pulsing. "Are you sure?"

He twisted and called back to Darya. "Behind the tanks. Get a move on! You, too, Captain."

"What's happening?" Rebka eased off the top of the stasis tank, but he came forward instead of moving into hiding.

"At says she's getting a whiff of Zardalu. From out there." Nenda nodded toward the entrance. "She's hearing sounds, too, faint ones. Somethin's coming this way."

"Tell Atvar H'sial to get behind the tanks with Darya. You, too. I'll stay here."

"We playing heroes, Captain?" Nenda rubbed at his bare and pitted chest. "That's fine with me." He turned his body. "Come on, At, let go of me."

The Cecropian did not move. She was crouched forward, her long antennas unfurled and extended as far as they would go. She pulled Nenda closer to her lower carapace.

"Go on," Rebka said. "What are you both waiting for?"

But Nenda had stopped pushing at Atvar H'sial's encircling forelimbs and was peering at the entrance. "I changed my mind. I got to stay here."

"Why, man?" Rebka advanced to stand at his side.

"We shouldn't all wait here if there's Zardalu on the way."

"Agreed. So you get back in there with the professor." Nenda turned his head and gave Rebka a curiously distant glance. "At says she smells Hymenopt. Not just any old Hymenopt, either—she smells *Kallik*. I stay."

The next minute was filled with tense inactivity. Nothing emerged from the chamber entrance. Atvar H'sial offered no further information or comment via Louis Nenda. No one else could hear, see, or smell anything unusual. Darya, feeling both foolish and cowardly, came from behind the tanks and moved forward to join the other three. Hans Rebka gave her a sharp look, but he did not suggest that she go back.

The smell came first, a faint and alien whiff that drifted in on the currents of air circulation. Darya did not recognize it. The sudden lump in her chest had to be pure nerves. But she craned forward, straining to see into the gloom beyond the tunnel's mouth, looking for something that loomed three times the height of a human.

"Almost here, according to At." Nenda's gruff voice was reduced to a whisper. "Coupla' seconds more. Hold your hats on."

A shape was moving out of the darkness, slowly, with an odd sideways motion. One moment it could hardly be seen, the next it was fully visible.

Darya heard a bark of laughter from Louis Nenda, standing to her left. She felt like echoing it. The menace had arrived. It was no seven-meter land-cephalopod, supporting itself on a massive sprawl of tentacled limbs. Instead she was looking at a human male, slightly below average height. He wore a bloody bandage around his head, and from his awkward movement he had something badly wrong with his legs or his central nervous system.

He shuffled forward to within a couple of paces of the group. "Some of you do not know me," he said. His voice was quite matter-of-fact. "But I know all of you. You are Darya Lang, Hans Rebka, Louis Nenda, and the Cecropian, Atvar H'sial. My name is E. C. Tally.

I am here to deliver a message, and to ask a question. But first, tell me who is the leader of this group."

Hans Rebka and Louis Nenda glared at each other until Nenda shrugged. "Go ahead. Be my guest."

Rebka turned to E. C. Tally. "I am. What's your question?"

"First, I must make a statement. I am here only as a messenger. The rest of the group that came here with me consists of the humans Julius Graves and Birdie Kelly, the Lo'tfian, J'merlia, and the Hymenopt, Kallik. They are now prisoners of that species known in the spiral arm as *Zardalu*. The others will be executed at once should you seek to free them by violence. I should add that my cooperation was forced by their threat to execute Councilor Graves on the spot if I did not function as requested. And now, the question. Are there members here of other intelligences of the spiral arm, or are you the only ones? Please give the answer loudly and clearly."

"I can't give a definite answer. All I can say is that we are the only ones here *that we know of*."

"Logic demands that no fuller answer can be justified. I am sure that will be satisfactory. In fact—"

Rebka and the others in the group were no longer listening. Moving out behind the embodied computer and overshadowing him completely came three huge forms. The one in the middle was carrying Kallik, holding her upside down with two tentacles wrapped firmly around the abdomen, so that the gleaming yellow sting could not be employed. That alone was enough to leave Rebka gasping. No organism in the spiral arm should have been able to restrain an adult Hymenopt, one-on-one. But Kallik was not struggling. Her eyes were open, and one of her hind limbs was twisted at a peculiar angle. The cruel blue beak hovered close to the back of Kallik's neck, ready to bite.

The other two Zardalu were carrying nothing but improvised clubs fashioned from the twisted exteriors of food containers. They were almost identical in appearance, except for the necklaces of round-mouthed pouches running around the body below the slitted mouths. In the Zardalu standing on the right, the pale-blue ovals within those pouches were far more prominent, bulging out far from the tight flesh.

The beak of the Zardalu in the center moved, to produce a high-pitched chittering sound. Kallik replied. There was another brief exchange of clicks and whistles.

"Hey, Kallik," Nenda called.

The Hymenopt did not look at him. "E. C. Tally's function as a messenger is now over," she said woodenly. "He cannot communicate with the Zardalu, and he is regarded as expendable. He was sent here first as a decoy, in case a killing trap had been set up around this chamber. I *can* communicate with you, and also with the Zardalu. I will therefore be the interpreter for all subsequent messages. The leader of the Zardalu is the one who is holding me. She is to be identified for message purposes as Holder."

"Son of a bitch," Nenda whispered, just loud enough for Rebka to hear. "What have they done to her? That's not my Kallik, the real Kallik."

"They came here prepared for a fight," Rebka said, just as softly. "Ten thousand years in stasis, and still they wake up ready to take on the universe. Watch what you do and say. We can't afford to make one wrong move."

"Tell me about it."

The Zardalu on the left stretched out two of the pale-blue midbody tentacles and pulled E. C. Tally effortlessly back toward it. At the same moment, Kallik was turned in midair by the Zardalu that held her and placed on the ground in front of Louis Nenda. She stood favoring her twisted hind limb. The ring of bright black eyes in the Hymenopt's round head stared up at him unblinking. Nenda nodded slowly. He did not speak.

"Holder knows that you are my former master," Kallik said. "She orders me to tell you that I now serve Holder and Holder alone."

Louis Nenda swallowed. Darya could see his jaw muscles clenching and unclenching. "I hear you," he said at last. "Tell Holder that I received the message, and I understand it."

"And ask Holder," Rebka added, "what they want from us. Tell her that we are recent arrivals. We do not know our way around here. We do not know how to reach Speaker-Between, or any other inhabitant of this artifact."

"Holder is aware of many of these things," Kallik said, after another brief exchange with the Zardalu who stood behind her. The Hymenopt's eyes flickered shut, one by one, in a curious pattern, before she continued. "She does not know Speaker-Between's wishes, and she does not care. She and her companions have a single objective. If you help them to achieve it, you and the hostage group will be allowed to live. If you do not cooperate, or if you attempt opposition or treachery, you and all your offspring will die."

"Nice terms. All right, we understand. What's their objective?"

"It is to be released from this place and given a ship for their use. They must be allowed to leave here, without pursuit, and go wherever they choose. For that to happen, Holder and the others know that they will need the cooperation of the beings, whoever they may be, who rule this place. She knows that you are not the rulers."

"That's all got nothing to do with us. What are we supposed to do?"

"Something very simple. Holder also knows that the rulers of this place wish to perform their own experiments using Zardalu, Humans, and Cecropians. Holder is willing to leave one Zardalu here for that purpose. She has already made the selection of that individual. When the ruler beings of this world come to meet with you again, you are to state that you will cooperate with them only after one condition has been fulfilled: namely, all the Zardalu, save one, must have been permitted to leave here in a fully equipped interstellar ship, to go to a destination of their choosing. After that event you Humans and Cecropians will be free to act as you choose, to cooperate with the rulers here or to resist them."

"Tell Holder, wait for one minute." Rebka turned to the other two humans. "You heard all that. I don't think we can do anything except agree, or say we do. But we ought to tell Atvar H'sial what's going on."

"She knows already," Nenda said. "Look at her." The Cecropian's blind white head was nodding. "I've been giving her pheromonal translations as we went. She agrees, we have no choice but to cooperate."

"Darya?"

"What else can we do, if we don't want Birdie Kelly or Councilor Graves killed?"

"Not a thing." Rebka turned again to Kallik. "You probably followed that, but here is our official response. Tell Holder that we agree to her terms. Tell her we have no idea when we will be contacted by Speaker-Between, or by any other of the beings who control this artifact. But when they do get in touch with us, we will tell them that the price for our cooperation is the release of all the Zardalu, except one. And we will refuse to cooperate until that has been done."

Kallik nodded and again began a clicking and whistling conversation with the Zardalu. A tentacle reached out, seized Kallik around the midsection, and drew her back.

"Holder orders me to tell you that you have made a wise decision," the Hymenopt said. "Naturally, the hostages will continue to be held. However, one of them is close to a terminal condition and is not worth keeping. Holder will use that being, and one other small thing, as examples. She wishes to prove to you the seriousness of Zardalu intention, and to point out to all of you the folly of possible treachery. Holder says, do not try to follow. She will return, at a time of her choosing."

As Kallik finished speaking, the Zardalu reached out with another tentacle and grabbed the Hymenopt's injured hind limb. Kallik gave a whistling scream of pain as her leg was twisted off at the upper joint and pulled free of her body. The leg was carried at once to the slitted mouth and swallowed whole.

At the same moment, the Zardalu who had been

holding E. C. Tally pushed him forward. The rough, sharp-edged club that it was holding swung sideways with frightful force, to contact Tally's head just above ear level. The whole top of the skull sheared off and flew away across the chamber.

The Zardalu retreated into the tunnel with Kallik. The body of E. C. Tally sprawled motionless in front of Darya Lang. Blood dribbled from the topless head.

The three humans did not move at once to pick up E. C. Tally. It was left to Atvar H'sial, less knowledgeable about human physiology and human survival needs, to move across to him and lift the ruined body to an upright position. She carried it to where the battered top of the skull was lying on the floor.

"What's she doing?" Darya Lang asked. Her voice was shaking. "He's dead."

Louis had been sitting slumped on the ground, muttering to himself. At Darya's words he looked up and hurried to his feet.

"She's doing what I should have been doing, if I had any sense. Tally *looks* like a human, but he isn't one. Graves says he's an embodied computer. Back on the planetoid he had his brain popped right out of his head, and it didn't worry him a bit. Come on. Maybe there's some way to get him functioning again."

At first sight it seemed a forlorn hope. The body was limp and lifeless, and the top of the skull had been ripped away to reveal the stark white of broken bone.

"First thing," Nenda said. "Gotta stop the bleeding."

"No." Hans Rebka was reaching into the brain cavity. "That looks bad, but it's not the worst problem. We've got to get his brain back in charge of his body, quickly, or he's done for. Tell Atvar H'sial to hold him. *Tightly.*" The arms and legs were beginning to jerk as Rebka felt under the brain. "See, here's the problem. That blow jarred the neural connection loose. I'm trying to reseat it. Anything happening?"

"Ye-e-s. Yes, indeed." It was E. C. Tally who answered,

in a slurred and gurgling voice. "Thank—you. It was apparent to me . . . at once, that the blow had severed the brain-body interface, but without . . . sensory inputs I had no idea what happened next. Nor could I . . . communicate the problem." The bright blue eyes opened and blinked away blood. Tally glanced around him. "I am now functional. Relatively speaking. I am operating with backup-mode interfaces, but for the time being they appear to be adequate. Where are the Zardalu?"

"Gone. For the moment." Darya had taken the loose top of the skull from Atvar H'sial and was gazing at it hopelessly. It was a mass of bloody, matted hair and sharp-edged bone. "They took Kallik with them."

"They will surely be back. Allow me." Tally reached out and removed the cap of skin, hair, and bone from Darya's hands. He studied it, his blue eyes intent. "The front hinges are gone, completely sheared away. But the rear pins appear intact. They may hold it in position, provided that I do not make sudden movements or allow my head to move far from the vertical."

He became silent again.

"Are you all right?" Rebka asked.

Tally waved a hand at him. "I have been running diagnostic programs. I had hoped that the only major problem would be the inevitable necrosis of the skull, deprived of its blood supply. But now I know that there are other more serious difficulties. This body is close to end-point failure. It cannot function for more than another few hours; twenty at the outside, in continuous operation. Perhaps twice that long if it is given adequate rest. After that I will become unable to move; then I will lose all sensory inputs. It is important that I transfer potentially useful information to you at once, before any of this happens."

As Tally spoke he was trying to maneuver the loose skull into position. It would not seat cleanly. After a few seconds he gave up the effort. "There is also more structural damage than I thought. We may as well bandage it as best we can and forget it. This is as good a result as

I am able to achieve." He sat on the floor with his hands to his head, while Hans Rebka carefully wound the bandage again around the bloodied hair and skin.

"Now," Tally went on. "May I speak? Prepare yourselves to receive information from me. It would be a tragedy if facts that I have already collected could not be passed to you because of my own motor systems malfunctions."

"You can start anytime. I'm listening." The episode with the Zardalu had left Louis Nenda pale, but not from fear. He was scowling, and his nostrils were dilated. "Any information you can give about those blue bastards, I want."

"There is one factor that Julius Graves says is of overwhelming importance. He instructed me to tell it to you, if any possible opportunity arose. Did you see the ring of pouches on each of the Zardalu?"

"Like a bead necklace, all the way around their bodies? Sure. Hard to miss 'em."

"But you probably do not know what they are. They are *reproductive* pouches. Young are developing within each of the swollen beads. The Zardalu appear to be hermaphroditic, and any one of them will produce multiple live offspring. We saw young ones, actually appearing. And they eat ravenously, as soon as they are born."

"There's plenty of food available around here."

"Adequate for us, and for the adult Zardalu forms. But the immature Zardalu are mainly *meat-eaters*. According to what Kallik heard, the Zardalu consider that inferior young will develop if feeding is restricted to what is available from the food suppliers here."

"What do you mean, *inferior*?" Nenda asked. "We're all eating it. Inferior how?"

"I do not know. But Julius Graves is convinced that unless the Zardalu are allowed to leave soon and go where they wish, you and the hostages will be seen as a necessary food supply for their young. Compliance with their demands is most urgent."

Darya was nauseated. But Rebka just shrugged, and Nenda said, "So we're all gonna be kiddie munchies. Great.

I don't see knowin' that does much for us. What else do you have?"

"I can take you at once to the chamber where the Zardalu are located, if that is your wish."

Rebka glanced at the others. "Not quite the top item on our agenda, is it? We don't know what we'd do with it if we had it. Maybe we'd like that later. What else?"

"Something whose value cannot be determined, though Steven Graves argues that it is significant. Kallik is the only one who can communicate with them. The Hymenopts were the slaves of the Zardalu in the distant past, and the Hymenopt language has not changed. Kallik said—"

"Hold on a minute, Tally," Hans Rebka interrupted. "You keep on telling us Kallik said this, Kallik said that. I don't think we can trust a single thing that Kallik tells us. The Zardalu have taken her over completely."

"Uh-uh." Nenda shook his head. "It looked that way, but it ain't so. Kallik and me, we've got codes we use when we can't speak. You couldn't read that flickering pattern of her eyes, when she was down groveling in front of the middle Zardalu. But I could. She was saying to me, over and over, '*Wait. Not yet.*' She knew I was ready to bust out, an' she was telling me it wasn't the time."

"Did she say anything else to you?" Rebka asked. "Any details of their weapons, or maybe their weak spots?"

"Hey, be reasonable. Those eye codes aren't a real *language*. But I'll tell you one thing Kallik told me, indirectly. The Zardalu are *strong*. Nothing should be able to hold an adult Hymenopt. We couldn't do it, if we all tried at once. That Zardalu did it easy. We'll need something special if we're gonna fight 'em."

"But Kallik was weakened," Darya said. "Even before they tore her leg off, she was injured. She might be dead by now."

"Naw." Nenda was turning back to Tally. "You lot just don't know your Hymenopts. Takes a lot more than that to worry Kallik—she's regrowing that leg right now, won't think twice about it. But it makes the point even stronger, and it's not such a nice one. See, if a Zardalu could hold *her*, and do that to her, it'd turn any of us into mincemeat. And talking of mincemeat, let's hear the rest from Tally before the baby Zardalu start squeakin' for dinner. What else did Kallik say?"

The embodied computer had sunk down to a sitting position and was holding the sides of his head. "She was listening to them when we were first captured, before they realized that she could understand Zardalu speech. By the way, Kallik does not hold a high opinion of their intelligence. They did not worry themselves with what they had *already* said in front of her, even *after* they learned that she could understand them. She heard much of their conversation. Apparently they were captured by The-One-Who-Waits, or something like him, during the very last days of the Great Rising. They were transported here already in stasis. At that time, planet after planet ruled by the Zardalu Communion had joined the revolution. Zardalu were being systematically exterminated, and their last few outposts overrun and wiped out. These fourteen individuals had fled to space to escape. They were the last ones left. Kallik says *they think that they are the only surviving members of their species*."

"I hope they're right," Rebka said. "Be thankful if they are."

"But that's why they are so absolutely determined to escape from here, and to lie low while they recuperate. Their strength has always been their breeding powers. Given a quiet planet and a century or two, there will be hundreds of millions of Zardalu. They will again be organized, and ready to start over."

The tall form of Atvar H'sial had crouched silent through all the talk. Now she stirred and turned the open yellow trumpets on each side of her head toward Louis Nenda.

"I agree with that," he said. He turned back to the others. "I've been filling At in as we went along on what Tally's been saying. She makes a good point. If the Zardalu were captured and put in stasis back near one of their home planets, and they only just came out of it, it's possible they don't have any idea where they are now. Me and At never spoke to Speaker-Between, but I get the idea he's a bit obscure. And the Zardalu must be confused as hell, just coming out of stasis. Maybe they think they can jump into a ship and take off, and find a place to hide within a few light-years. That ain't' so, but let's make sure that *we're* not the ones who tell 'em. At says the smart thing to do is let 'em have a ship, help 'em take off out of here—and *then* let the blue bastards find they're thirty thousand light-years from anywhere, and screw 'em six ways from Tuesday."

"That's fine," Rebka said. "Assuming that Speaker-Between goes along with it. But I don't see why he would. If he hasn't told them already where they are, he'll probably tell them next time he meets them."

"We can't stop that. But we can make sure it doesn't come from *us*. And maybe steer the conversation in other directions if we get the chance. Might not be hard, if these Zardalu aren't the brightest specimens." Louis Nenda stared at E. C. Tally, whose head was drooping forward onto his chest. "Go on. What else?"

Tally did not speak.

"Leave him alone," Darya said. "He's on his last legs."

"How do you know?"

"Just look at him. He's swaying."

"He may be worse later." Nenda bent down and peered at Tally's drooping eyelids. "The body's resting, but he's not asleep. And this could be our last chance. Give him a jab, Professor, get him going."

"No." This time it was Hans Rebka who spoke. "You're not an expert on embodied computers, Nenda. Neither am I. Tally knows the condition of that body better than any human ever could. If he thinks he has to have rest, he rests. We don't argue."

"So what are the rest of us supposed to do? Sit around here, and wait till the Zardalu ring the dinner bell?"

"More or less." Rebka moved forward and dragged E. C. Tally along the smooth floor, until he could prop him up against a wall.

"We've been on the go for days. Every one of us looks ready to drop. We need rest. I'm going to follow Tally's example and take a short nap. If you have any sense you'll do the same. We can take turns to keep watch. And if you all want to be ready for action when the Zardalu come back, better make sure you're not exhausted."

He sat down by Tally's side. "Otherwise . . . Well, otherwise when that bell rings, you may find you're the first course on the menu."

CHAPTER 22

Two hours later Darya Lang was alone and prowling the space behind the stasis tanks. Hans Rebka and Louis Nenda had eaten; then Rebka had said with no sign of emotion, "Nice and quiet now. Better get some sleep."

He and Nenda lay down next to Atvar H'sial. All three dropped off at once, apparently without a care in the world.

Sleep. Darya could no more sleep than she could have breathed fluorine.

She glared at the snoring Hans Rebka. She had been having an affair with a robot, a being who lacked all normal fears and feelings. And Nenda was just as bad, if not worse, lying there flat on his back with his mouth open.

E. C. Tally had remained in an upright position, but the embodied computer was also silent. Darya did not dare to try to talk to him. His brain might be engaged in computation, but his body was resting as best it could. Tally was too far gone for rest to extend to restoration.

The bad thing was that Rebka was quite right, and she knew it. It *was* important to rest and keep up one's strength. She had managed to force down a little food, so that was a success. But whenever she closed her eyes the memory of those towering blue-black forms came rushing back, along with a jumble of frightening thoughts. Where were the Zardalu, right now? What was happening to Graves, Birdie Kelly, Kallik, and J'merlia? Were they all still alive?

Finally she gave up any attempt to relax. She left the chamber and went wandering into the surrounding labyrinth of corridors. Even with an imagined Zardalu behind every partition, walking around was better than sitting and watching the others sleep. Her earlier search for Speaker-Between had produced no clear sense of place, and that made her feel uncomfortable. She was a person who needed a sense of spatial context, and now she had a chance to establish one.

It took a couple of hours of systematic search to build up an architectural sense of location. The three-dimensional picture that finally formed in her brain was disconcerting. Darya found that she would reach the end of a corridor, or come out into a broad open chamber, and find viewports set into the walls. They looked out onto vast, open-space structures, long cylinders and spirals and graceful cantilevers of unguessable purpose, arching out beyond the limits of vision. As Nenda said, it would take thousands of years to explore all that complexity— and even longer to understand its function.

But as she walked, the possibility of real exploration also became less and less likely. She could certainly *see* hundreds of thousands, maybe millions, of kilometers of the Builder artifact known as Serenity. But she could not *reach* them. When she plotted out in her mind the places that she had been able to visit before she came to some kind of blind end, the accessible region shrank to modest proportions. She had been able to move only a couple of kilometers in any direction. Maybe *that* was the reason Speaker-Between was so confident that their little group could easily be contacted whenever the alien chose to do so.

The other side of that thought was more disturbing: if their movements were so constrained, escape from the Zardalu also became impossible. For if she and her companions could not move freely through the whole of Serenity, no matter where they hid they would be discovered by any determined pursuer.

Darya tried to bury that thought and keep on walking. Another point had been nagging at her subconscious, but for a while she had trouble pinning it down. It came to her only when she began to move back toward the chamber where she had left the others sleeping.

Gravity. The chamber with the stasis tanks had a field of maybe three-quarters of a standard gravity; but now that she was walking "downhill" she realized that for the past half hour she had been traveling through a region of weaker gravitational force. Carry that thought a little further, and it suggested that there had to be some source of gravitational field in the direction that she was now headed.

When Darya came back to the chamber with the stasis tanks she did not stop. Instead she went straight on through, heading toward the region of strongest gravity field.

She squashed another disquieting thought: This is the direction taken by the departing Zardalu. She wished that Tally had told them just where the Zardalu had set up their camp, but she forced herself to keep moving. In less than a kilometer, the field strengthened substantially. The tunnel she walked in branched a couple of times. Each time she followed the "downward" track. The tunnel began to spiral lower in a tightening helix.

Darya paused. The air within all the chambers remained fresh, through a gentle circulation from unknown sources. But now she could feel a stronger breeze blowing. She licked the back of each hand and held them out in front of her, palms facing and a couple of feet apart. The back of her left hand felt noticeably colder. The light wind was coming from that direction.

Darya went forward more cautiously than before. The moving air was strong enough to ruffle her exposed hair. Already she had a suspicion of what she would find. As she followed the curve of the tunnel, she caught a glimpse of movement ahead.

It was a relief to find something familiar—and yet it was still frightening. The dark, swirling vortex ahead of her, no more than thirty or so steps down the sloping path, was a close relative of the one into which she and Hans Rebka had fallen on Glister. It had the same eye-frustrating property as the circulation pattern that had, while she watched, bodied forth Louis Nenda and Atvar H'sial and then vanished.

Darya was convinced that she was staring into one end of a space transportation system. But she had no idea where she would be taken if she allowed herself to drop into it, or even if there was any way that she could survive the transition. It did *not* represent what she now realized she had been hoping to find when she began her wanderings: an escape route from the Zardalu.

The whirling vortex had a hypnotic quality, tempting her to move closer. Darya resisted and backed away. The slope became rapidly steeper, the gravity field stronger and stronger. Half a dozen more steps, and she would be sucked in, no matter how hard she tried to drag herself away.

Would it *really* take a traveler back to the spiral arm? Or did it lead on to somewhere unknown, and still farther afield? Perhaps at its end lay a true space-time singularity, a maelstrom that would reduce the doomed voyager to independent subnuclear components.

Darya was not willing to find out. But that dark vortex might be a possible last resort, a preferred final alternative to dismemberment by a Zardalu beak. She headed for the chamber where the others lay sleeping.

She went cautiously. The Zardalu were firmly in her mind, to the point where she could think of little else.

No one had said it, but Darya was quite sure that the Zardalu would not leave peacefully, even if they got what they asked for. They would want to be sure that no one could follow them—that no one knew any Zardalu still *existed*; the safest way to make sure of that was to get rid of anyone who had met them.

A sudden deep chuckle from behind her made her muscles tense and her heart leap in her chest. She spun around as something gripped her arm.

"Hey, there," a soft voice said.

It was Louis Nenda. She had heard nothing of his silent approach.

"Don't you ever do that again!"

"Nervous?" He chuckled again. "Calm down, Professor. I won't eat you."

"What are you doing here? Couldn't you sleep, either?"

He shrugged. "Little bit. Then I woke up. Too mad to get much rest."

"Too *mad*?"

"Mad. Angry. Pissed. As I've ever been. You saw what that Zardalu did to Kallik."

"I did. But I'm surprised *you* feel that way. She was your faithful slave, and you left her to die, down on Quake; and you fired at a ship with her in it, at Summertide."

"I told Graves and the others, I don't remember firing on no ship." He grinned. "Anyway, even if that happened, I didn't know Kallik was on board, did I?"

"But you admit that you left her to die on Quake."

"Hell, no. I'd have picked her up before things got too hot. Anyway, that's not the point. Kallik is *my* Hymenopt; she belongs to *me*. What I do with her, that's one thing. What that blue bastard did to her, that's something else. It had no right to touch her." He frowned. "What was its name?"

"Holder."

"Right. Well, let me tell you, when we have it out with 'em, nobody else touches Holder. That one's *mine*. And it's dead meat. I'm gonna have Holder's guts fried up and eat 'em for breakfast, even if they make me puke for a week after."

"You talk big when they're not here. You were as quiet as the rest of us when they were."

"I was. And so was Atvar H'sial. Me and her, and Rebka, too, we know how you play this game. You don't rush in, you don't act hasty. You watch, and you wait, and you pick your time. Don't confuse caution with cowardice, Professor."

Darya looked down at the squat, glowering figure. "You talk a good line, Nenda, but it won't help when the Zardalu come. They're three times the size of you, and ten times as strong. And they probably have weapons, and you have none."

Nenda was turning, getting ready to move on. He gave her a pitying smile. "Sweetie, you may be a smart professor, but you don't know much about the real world. You think I don't have weapons? That'll be the first time, then, since I was a little kid." He reached down to his calf, and pulled out a long, thin-bladed knife. "This is just for starters. But it'll do pretty good to make sausage skin out of Zardalu guts. And if you think that *I'm* carrying weapons, go take a look at what Atvar H'sial carries around under her wing cases. She's a real believer in self-preservation. She's smart, though. She knows you use it at the right time, and not before."

He winked at her. "Gotta go. Sleep well, now, and sweet dreams. Remember, me and At are here to look after you."

Darya glared at him as he went on, around a bend in the corridor.

"Watch where you're going," she called after him. "There's a vortex and maybe a field singularity, a few hundred meters that way. I'd be really heartbroken if you fell into it."

He did not answer. Darya continued to the chamber, oddly comforted by the encounter. Louis Nenda and Hans Rebka had at least one thing in common: so many awful things had happened to them already in their lives, nothing broke their spirit.

E. C. Tally had not moved. But Hans Rebka was awake and sitting up—and Atvar H'sial had disappeared.

"No idea," Rebka said in answer to her question. "Don't know about her, or Nenda either. Or you, until you just appeared."

"I saw Nenda." Darya gave him a quick recap of her meeting with Louis Nenda, and of her own travels. "But it's not a safe way out," she said, when she came to the vortex, and her conviction that it was the entry point to a transportation system. "It's not useful at all, until we know if it's meant to take living objects. And it can't be used even then, until we discover its termination points."

"I'm not so sure of that. Things are what people think they are. Don't rule out that vortex."

He refused to explain. And he said nothing more on the subject, except to add thoughtfully, when Darya complained that Speaker-Between had talked with them just once and then deserted them completely, "Speaker-Between and your vortex have one thing in common, and it's something we'd better not forget. They are *alien*, both of them. One of the worst mistakes we can make is to think we understand alien thought patterns—even when it's a *familiar* alien. We think it's hard to know what motivates Atvar H'sial or Kallik or one of the Zardalu; but it's a thousand times as difficult to know what a Builder or its constructs is trying to achieve."

"Do you think we and Speaker-Between are misunderstanding each other?"

"I'm sure we are. Let me give you just one example. We're all feeling angry because we've been left here alone, with no idea what comes next from Speaker-Between. We're upset because we know no way to reach him. But he has been in existence, sitting and waiting, for millions of years! From his point of view, a day—or even a year—is like the blink of an eye. He probably has no idea we're chafing over his absence."

He put his arm around her, leading the way to where Tally was sitting silent and with closed eyes.

"Darya, we have no idea when or if Speaker-Between is likely to return. If you didn't sleep at all, you ought to try again. I caught a couple of hours, and you can't imagine how much better I feel." He saw her looking around. "Don't worry, I won't leave you sleeping if the Zardalu come back. And I won't leave. I'll keep watch right here."

At his insistence, Darya lay down and closed her eyes. Given their situation, she did not expect to catch even a second of rest. She thought again of the Zardalu, of Kallik's whistle of pain as her leg was twisted from her body, of the top of Tally's skull flying across the chamber. Then she recalled Hans Rebka's calm, pale face, and Louis Nenda's anger at what had happened to Kallik, and his irrational self-confidence.

We might be as good as dead, she thought, but those two will never for a second admit it.

She opened her eyes and saw Hans Rebka watching over her. He nodded. She closed her eyes again and was asleep within thirty seconds.

Louis Nenda had not gone far after his encounter with Darya Lang. Less than three hundred meters from where she was sleeping, he was sitting cross-legged on the floor of a small, poorly lit room. Crouched across from him, her carapace close enough for him to reach out and touch, was Atvar H'sial.

"All right." Nenda's pheromonal speech pattern diffused across to the waiting Cecropian. "What did you get from the sonics?"

"Less than you hope. In fact, I think it may be wise to share this information with Captain Rebka and Professor Lang. It has no conceivable commercial value."

"Let me hear it, though, before we decide that."

"What I saw through low-frequency sonic imaging is probably exactly what you received through your own vision. The external form of the Zardalu is impressively powerful."

"Nothing new there. One of 'em was enough to hold Kallik."

"Easily so. The more interesting information came from the whole-body ultrasonic imaging. The necklace of pouches that circles each Zardalu below the main ingestion organ contains, as E. C. Tally reported, young Zardalu in various stages of development. The broad bands of webbing around the upper part of the tentacles conceal no weapons, as I am sure you also suspected, but food and personal belongings. I do not see that as a threat. More important: the Zardalu have twin circulation centers for their body fluids. The main one, that which carries hematic oxygen, was readily accessible to ultrasonic imaging. It lies deep within the center of the main trunk, half a meter below the necklace, and half a meter below the surface."

Atvar H'sial produced simultaneously the pheromonal equivalents of a curse, a sigh, and a mocking laugh. "Regrettably, the heart is not so easily accessible to your knives as to my sonar. It lies deep. The same is true for their brain center, and for the main conduits of their central nervous system. The brain is below the heart, and the nerve column runs down from there, in the centermost line of the body. It is an efficient design for protection from harm, far better than yours or mine."

"Damnation."

"I know. I am sorry, Louis Nenda. I was able to read your emotions when Kallik's leg was torn off, and I share your ambitions. But their realization will call for more than simple violence."

"What about *your* weapons? Don't you have anything that can take 'em out of action?"

"Not permanently. It was difficult to bring effective weapons through the Bose Transition Points."

"I told Darya Lang you'd blow the Zardalu away."

"That is, unfortunately, wishful thinking. I have knives, but too short to reach the Zardalu brain or heart. I also have three flash electrostatic devices. Not intended as weapons, but they will inflict a painful surface burn. On something the size and strength of a Zardalu, however, they would be no more than irritants."

"Forget it. You might as well try and tickle 'em to death. Is that all?"

"I have one device which was not seen as a weapon in the Bose Network. It could serve me well—but at your expense, as well as that of the Zardalu."

Atvar H'sial reached back under her wing cases and produced a small black ovoid. Nenda stared at it curiously.

"Doesn't look like much. What's it do?"

"It's known as a Starburst. I have two of them. They each produce an intense flash of light in the wavelength range from oh-point-four to one-point-two micrometers. Any creature which sees by means of such radiation will be temporarily or permanently blinded, depending on ocular sensitivity and directness of exposure. I believe that Zardalu eyes operate in that wavelength region. So, unfortunately, do humans', Lo'tfians', and Hymenopts'. I, of course, will be unaffected."

"Better tell me when to shut my eyes, then. It's nice, but it don't solve any problems. How and where could you ever use it? We gotta *think*, At."

"We do; and I am obliged to point out to you that we do not have a monopoly on that process. Distasteful as it will be to you, Louis, we must work with Captain Rebka and Professor Lang. At least until such time as the Zardalu are no longer a problem. After that . . ." The great blind head swung around, as though taking in the whole of the million kilometers of Serenity that surrounded them. "After that, and only after that, can we again begin to operate in rational terms. Which is to say, *commercial* terms; for which, I suggest, there is more than tempting potential here."

"You had the same impression as I did. If we could once get the run of this place, there's things that will have the whole spiral arm drooling."

"And there is far more than we have so far been permitted to see. Somewhere in this artifact lies the technology that *built* the being that Rebka and Lang identify as Speaker-Between, and created an inter*galactic* transportation system. If those secrets can be ours—"

The Cecropian paused. The great antennas on top of the blind head suddenly unfurled like sails, two meters long and a meter wide. They turned to face back toward the chamber where she and Louis Nenda had left Tally and Rebka.

Nenda turned with her. "What's wrong, At? More Zardalu?"

"No. But I am receiving faint new aromatics, like those from The-One-Who-Waits, diffusing in from far away. Unless I am gravely mistaken, the one known as Speaker-Between is entering the stasis-tank chamber containing Rebka, Lang, and Tally. It is, I suspect, a meeting that we would be wise to attend."

CHAPTER 23

Free movement around the interior of Serenity might be denied to humans, but there were others for whom that restriction did not apply.

Darya had new proof of that when Speaker-Between appeared. The alien construct drifted up like a silver ghost through the impervious floor of the chamber. Halfway through he stopped and began decreasing steadily in size. When Louis Nenda and Atvar H'sial came hurrying into the room and had their first sight of the Interlocutor, they were confronted by a bulging hemisphere apparently immovably embedded in the solid floor. Speaker-Between looked just like the upper half of The-One-Who-Waits.

The flower-shaped head craned forward briefly to face the new arrivals, then turned back to Rebka, Lang, and the newly awakened E. C. Tally. The embodied computer was pale and shaky, but fully alert.

"We've been waiting for you since the last meeting," Rebka said. "There are big problems. Do you know who the Zardalu are?"

"Of course." The flower head drooped and nodded. "Since their arrival they have been my responsibility. It was I who turned off the stasis tanks to permit their reanimation. What is the purpose of your question?"

"They are awake now."

"As they should be."

"And they are dangerous. They have harmed two of

501

our group already, and they are threatening the rest of us. I'm sure you didn't bring our group all this way just to let the Zardalu destroy us."

Speaker-Between did not reply at once. He began to intone in a low mumble: "*Human, Cecropian, Zardalu . . . Human, Cecropian, Zardalu . . .*" Then, after a few moments of silence, he said, "All are present and available. That is as it should be. The process can begin—"

"Not if it involves any of us, it can't." Rebka stepped forward, close enough to touch the shining surface of Speaker-Between. "Until you listen to us, and we get answers to a few major questions, we don't do one thing."

"That cannot be. Your involvement is . . . required."

"Well, just you try to get it, without talking to us first. We won't do it. Not a human, or a Cecropian. There's a transportation-system entry point not far from here. We'll use it if we have to."

Rebka had taken a random shot, fishing for information. But Speaker-Between's answer confirmed Darya's guess.

"That would be most unwise," the Interlocutor said. "Without suitable keys prior to use, no safe endpoint of travel is guaranteed. A transition would surely be fatal."

"We'll risk that. We won't cooperate unless we have some answers from you."

"I say to you, cooperation is *required*." Speaker-Between was silent for a few seconds. "But I will listen, and talk if necessary, at least briefly."

"How briefly?"

"For no more than eight of your hours."

"We don't have that long anyway. Let me tell you about the Zardalu, and what they're doing."

"I am hearing." The flower head sighed. "Speak, if you must."

Speaker-Between had listened to Hans Rebka's explanation in total silence. The others interrupted only once, with Louis Nenda's mutter of rage when Rebka came to the Zardalu treatment of Kallik.

"Very good," the Interlocutor said when Rebka came

at last to the Zardalu recent threats. "That is all very good. It has begun."

"What has?"

"The process of *selection*." Speaker-Between lifted himself through the floor, until the whole body and the horned tail were revealed to Nenda and Atvar H'sial for the first time. "The Zardalu, it seems, understand what is needed without explanation. But for the rest of you . . . listen carefully."

To the Builders, it was simply *The Problem*. Compared with that, everything from the transformation of planets to the creation of stars was trivial. And like all problems that demanded their full concentration, this one was purely abstract.

What is the long-term future of the universe?

And tagged onto that central question, as a disturbing corollary, came the other, more personal one:

What is the purpose of the Builders, and what role will they play in the evolution of the universe?

The Builders could not answer, but they were enormously long-lived and endlessly patient. They pondered those questions for two hundred million years and at last came up with a conclusion that was worse than a question: it was a *paradox*.

They concluded that chaotic elements made the long-term future of the universe *undecidable*, in the Gödelian sense of a question that could not be answered from within the framework of the universe itself; but at the same time, undecidable or not, the future of the universe *would happen*. Thus, with or without the Builders, the undecidable question would finally be answered.

Faced with paradox, the Builders made a typical Builder decision. They moved inward, burrowing deep into the nature of their own consciousness. They examined mental processes and thinking structures. They discovered individual quirks of thought and habit, but still they were unable to decide: Were those individual attributes basic to *The Problem*, or irrelevances to it?

Again, the Builders were at an impasse. Worse than that, their inability to deal with *The Problem* began to produce disastrous effects on the Builders themselves. Instead of the pattern of slow evolution and development that had marked hundreds of millions of years, a rapid process of Builder *devolution* began. Debased forms of Builder appeared: the Phages.

It was a way to escape from an intolerable mental problem. Mindless, forgetting their own individual history, ignorant of the accomplishments of their kind, the Phages were as long-lived as their intelligent brothers. Soon they became a nuisance through the whole of the spiral arm. Wherever Builders could live, so could the omnivorous Phages. With their lack of intelligence and their sluggish reflexes, they were rarely dangerous; but they became a great irritation to the equally slow-moving Builders.

Again, the Builders took refuge in their own approach to a new difficulty.

They were no closer to a solution of *The Problem*, but they did not have to hurry. They would *wait*, moving themselves into long-term stasis and leaving their servants and constructs behind to waken them when the right time came and circumstances changed. Then they would address *The Problem* again, in a different epoch.

There was logic in that decision to wait; for although the Builders had been unable to solve *The Problem* alone, in the future they knew they might have help.

In the course of their development of the spiral arm, the Builders had seen nothing remotely like themselves; but they had noted in passing the development of other life-forms, creatures of the "little worlds," high in heavy elements, whose genesis bore little resemblance to the Builders' own gas-giant origins. The new ones were different . . .

"Different *how*?" That was Louis Nenda, posing a question asked of him by Atvar H'sial. It was the first interruption to the slow words of Speaker-Between.

"Short-lived." Speaker-Between answered without a pause. "Incredibly ephemeral, yet filled with violence, irrational lusts, illogical hopes. Far from ready to be useful, and yet . . ."

The Builders had no difficulty with *short-term* projections of the future, up to ten or twenty million years. Their analytical tools were adequate to estimate rates of species development, and to predict with high accuracy that certain life-forms were on an evolutionary path leading inevitably to self-awareness, intelligence, and technology.

It was far harder to predict where such forms would arrive *philosophically*. Would they develop their own perspective on the purpose of the universe? Would they, one day, despite their strange origins, become suitable collaborators for the Builders themselves?

No forecasting techniques of the Builders could answer that question definitively. It was again related to *The Problem*, and on that question they had already broken the edge of their intelligence.

The Builders saw clearly the emergence of three particular little-world intelligences in the spiral arm. They predicted that each might have a major impact on the future. One of those species, surely, would add the new dimension to Builder thought necessary for a reexamination of *The Problem*. One species. But which one?

That question could not be answered until the species emergence was completed and their civilizations and philosophical underpinnings were established. Only one thing seemed clear: although all three species were very different from the Builders, the one most likely to be useful in adding new insight to *The Problem* would be *the one who differed most from the Builders themselves*.

"You still keep saying we're so *different* from the Builders," Darya said. "I can see that we have far shorter lives. And we are not yet anywhere near so advanced technologically. But those don't seem like *profound* differences—time could change both of them."

"It could, and it will." The silver flower head was nodding, gleaming with internal lights. "But time cannot change certain elements common to you, the Zardalu, the Cecropians. Common to the Lo'tfians and the Hymenopts also, it appears, although those species came later and their influence on the spiral arm has been less. The element possessed by all your species is difficult to capture in a single word. I will call it *prodigality*."

"You'd better call it something different if you want me to understand it," Louis Nenda said. "What do you mean, *prodigality*?"

"Fertility. Abundance. *Wastefulness*." Speaker-Between hesitated, struggling with words. He had been doing a good job so far, despite a tendency to long, inscrutable pauses. Darya wondered how much was being subtly distorted by language difficulties. She itched to have her hands on one of the omnilingual translation units so common on far-off Sentinel Gate—and so rare on a poor world like Opal.

Far-off Sentinel Gate.

She realized that seen from Serenity, Opal and Sentinel Gate were next-door neighbors. Eight hundred light-years was nothing, when one was sitting thirty thousand light-years outside the Galaxy.

"Maybe it is best to offer an example," Speaker-Between went on at last. "I have functioned for many millions of years. It is likely that I will function for millions more. If I were to suffer injury, I would repair myself. If I need to do so, I can modify and improve my own operations and organization.

"I am a constructed entity, but the Builders themselves, my creators, developed naturally in the same way. They live forever, by your standards, and they are capable of *individual* self-improvement and transformation.

"Compare that with the beings of your worlds. You are short-lived, every one of you, knowing that each one of you will die, and die very soon, yet you are not obsessed by thoughts of death, or of a future without your presence. By the standards of the Builders, you are incredibly rapid breeders, and your species changes equally rapidly. Yet you are not capable of *self*-improvement, as individuals. That does not matter, for—most astonishing of all—*the survival of an individual is to you of no importance.*"

Louis Nenda gave Darya a little nudge with his elbow. "Hear that? You could sure as hell have fooled me."

"Shhh!"

"The Builders found, on many of the little worlds, wonderfully designed organisms," Speaker-Between continued. "They were highly specialized to run, or fly, or hover in the air, or hunt other creatures with great skill. But the Builders found something even more amazing. Once an individual organism fell in any way from perfect functioning, because of age or minor injury, it was *expendable*. It was allowed to die. That wonderful mechanism was thrown away, while another just as exquisite was created to take its place. That approach to life, that *prodigality*, and the idea that it could ever lead to *intelligent* life—was so alien to the Builders as to be incomprehensible. For if intelligence is any one thing, it is surely *the accumulation of experience.*

"But, the Builders argued, in that incomprehensibility lay the possibility of progress with *The Problem*. They had exhausted the familiar. Therefore, strangeness was absolutely essential to any possible advance. The Builders did not know which of the emerging intelligent life-forms was likely to prove most different from them, but they knew this: *The most alien was the one they would need.* And so they took steps to set up the necessary selection procedure.

"And it was simple. When those three species were sufficiently developed technologically to reach out from the little-worlds and explore the Builder artifacts that populate the spiral arm, they would be ready. Individuals of the three species would be taken as the opportunity occurred. They would be brought here. And here they would meet for the selection process. Stasis might be needed, to assure that representatives were available at the same time, but that was not a problem. Stasis technology has been available for 150 million years. In any case, the Builders predicted emergence close to the same time for each species.

"What was never anticipated was that the individuals of two *different* species might arrive here *together*, as happened with you two." The flower head dipped toward Nenda and Atvar H'sial. "However, that presents no problem. In fact, it simplifies matters, since I do not need to repeat an explanation. Thus, no further wait is needed."

The Interlocutor's voice began to grow deeper and softer. The silvery shape drifted slowly downward. Soon the tail disappeared into the floor, and then the bulging round of the lower body.

"For now you are here, all three species, exactly as required," Speaker-Between said dreamily. "The conditions are met. My initial task has been carried out. The selection procedure can begin.

"In fact, the actions of the Zardalu show that it has *already* begun . . ."

"Wait" Darya cried. The flower head was all that remained above the smooth floor. "The Builders—tell us where are they located *now*."

The slow descent halted for a second. "I know many things." The torpor of the voice had been replaced by a curious agony. "But that, *I do not know*."

The blind head nodded. The silver pentagon drifted downward out of sight.

Hans Rebka, Louis Nenda, and Atvar H'sial had understood immediately. It was Darya Lang, the unworldly professor, and E. C. Tally, the even less worldly embodied computer, who had to have it explained to them—and still had difficulty believing the answers.

After Speaker-Between had left they asked the same questions over and over again of their companions.

"Darya, how many times do you need to be told?" Hans Rebka said at last. "Remember, we're dealing with *alien* thought processes. From *their* point of view, what they're doing is perfectly logical. They have convinced themselves that the beings who may be able to help them with their problem should have the maximum amount of what they think of as 'little world' characteristics—violence and energy and strangeness. The Builders don't want to work with more than one species at a time, so they're going to pick one out. Or rather, they'll let one species pick itself. The 'selection procedure' is designed with that in mind."

"May I speak?"

"No," Nenda said. "You may listen. I'll give it to you in words of one syllable, Tally. That's what the two of you seem to need. The Builders have set us up in a three-way knockout contest. Humans against Cecropians against Zardalu. Winner gets the big prize—survival, and a chance to work with the Builders. Losers get you-know-what."

"But that's absolutely—" Darya checked herself. She had been about to say *inhuman*, which was a ridiculous comment. Instead she changed it to, "That's absolutely barbaric. *You*—Louis Nenda. You wouldn't go into a fight to the death with your friend Atvar H'sial, would you?"

"Course not." Nenda stared across at the hulking Cecropian. "Least, not till I was sure I'd *win*. Look, Professor, what I'd choose to do and not do ain't the issue. We were just told the rules. We didn't pick 'em. I think there's only one way for us to operate—and At agrees with me, she's been trackin' our talk. First, we gotta take care of the Zardalu and bust their asses. *After* that we decide how we'll squabble between humans and Cecropians."

"There are fourteen of them," Tally said quietly. "And nine of us—four of whom are already Zardalu hostages."

Nenda snorted. "What do you want to do, go and explain *arithmetic* to Speaker-Between and say it's not fair? By the time he shows up again we could all be dead."

"Nenda's right, E.C." Rebka took over again. "It doesn't matter how we got into the position we're in, or how little we like it. We have to accept it and work out how we'll survive. If we sit here and wait for the Zardalu to come back, that takes us nowhere. They'll find out we didn't reach any deal with Speaker-Between for them, and they'll blame us."

"But what can we *do*?" Darya felt she was not getting her urgency across to Rebka. He was as cool and thoughtful as if they were having a round-table discussion of landing permits on Opal. "The Zardalu could be here any minute."

"Could, and probably will." Rebka glanced around, assessing each member of the group. "So let's find out what we've got between us, information and possessions."

"Right!" Nenda said. "Then we better do a little reconnoiter, see where they are and what they're doing. I've had experience in that, and so has At. Tally can tell us where to find 'em."

"But they're so big, and so strong . . ." Darya found it hard to say what she was really thinking, that the thought of the Zardalu gave her the shivers. And she did not like the look in Nenda's eyes, either, an odd blend of pleasure and anger.

"What can *observing* them do?" she continued. "It won't make them weaker, or us stronger."

"*Wrong.*" Nenda glared at her. "Information is strength, sweetheart. We take a peek at 'em. Then we come back here, pool all we've got and all we know. And then we *hit 'em*, quick. Zardalu, here we come! I'll bet that's the *last* thing they're expecting."

It was the last thing that Darya was expecting, too. Pool *what*? They didn't have a thing—not even information. The Zardalu held all the cards: strength, numbers, ruthlessness, hostages.

But looking at the determination on the faces of Hans Rebka and Louis Nenda, Darya did not think her views were going to count for much.

CHAPTER 24

"Have you ever seen a human birth—a normal one, I mean, not in a tank or with an animal surrogate?" Birdie Kelly was speaking in a whisper.

Julius Graves avoided a spoken answer altogether, relying on his head shake being visible even in the low-level light.

"Well, *I* have," Birdie went on softly. "A dozen times, back on Opal. And let me tell you, it's a terrific effort for the mother, even when everything goes fine. You see it once, it makes you glad you're male. The women get pleasure out of it later, you see it on their faces when they hold their baby. But that don't make it less painful, or less hard work. But these critters . . ." He shook his head.

The two men were sitting in a corner of the room. J'merlia was a few meters away with Kallik. Occasionally they whistled and clicked gently to each other, but most of Kallik's attention was on the Zardalu.

The fourteen massive bodies lay sprawled between them and the only entrance. Now and again a great lidded eye would turn and blink toward Graves and Kelly; otherwise the land-cephalopods seemed scarcely aware of human presence. Certainly they were not worried that any of the group might escape.

The Zardalu talked to each other in their own language, which to Birdie sounded just like the speech Kallik used. Steven Graves had assured him that was an illusion. The

Zardalu vocal chords merely produced a range of frequencies and vocal fricatives similar to a Hymenopt's; or, just as likely, the Hymenopts had many centuries earlier been trained to speak so that their masters would understand.

But it was not their speech that held Birdie Kelly's attention. As they spoke, or ate, or simply lay and rested, the Zardalu were giving birth. They performed the act quickly, easily, and casually.

Birdie and Julius Graves had watched the whole process, while Steven Graves recorded it in his capacious memory, against the time—the unlikely time, Birdie thought—when he would be able to add it to the central data banks of the Fourth Alliance. Steven had also noted his opinion that the Zardalu had evolved in and preferred a low illumination level. He based that on the fact that they had sought out the least well lit chamber they could find that contained a food supply.

Steven had not tried to check his ideas against Kallik's spotty flashes of race memory of the Zardalu. She was unreliable. The others had all seen her when the giant land-cephalopods had first appeared. What she had done then, and was doing now, went well beyond cooperation for possible future gain. At the first sight of the ancient masters Kallik had dropped flat and groveled on her belly, unwilling to look up with any of her ring of black eyes.

The Zardalu accepted her servitude as natural. The injury to her leg had been done to confirm Holder's dominance when Kallik was lying helpless, not because she was resisting. Like Louis Nenda, the Zardalu must know that the loss of a limb was not a major trauma to a Hymenopt.

As Graves and Kelly watched, another four Zardalu were giving birth. The first sign was a rhythmic pulse in one of the swollen locations on the necklace of pouches. That was followed, in less than five minutes, by the appearance from that pouch of a rounded cone, like the tip of a shell. It was pale blue in color and quickly swelled to protrude six inches from the opening of the pouch.

At first Birdie had thought that cone-tip to be the head of the newborn. He realized his mistake when the pointed tip began to bulge farther and split open. From it emerged a smooth, rounded egg shape of pale apricot. That surprised Birdie more than he was ready to admit. He had grown to expect everything about the Zardalu, from eyes to torso to tentacle tips, to be some shade of blue.

The egg shape was the cerebral sac of a live infant, born head first. It arrived as a miniature version of the parent, except for its rudimentary tentacles. It wriggled completely free of the pouch in a couple more minutes, took a first, rippling breath, then slithered down the adult's body to a haven under the canopy of tentacles. Birdie caught a last glimpse of pale orange, then saw nothing for another few minutes. But soon the beak and mouth appeared from between the bases of two of the parent's tentacles. There was a faint whistling sound. Fragments of food selected from the containers in the center of the chamber were fed in by the parent to the complaining offspring.

From the reaction of the young Zardalu, that was not what they wanted. Within another few minutes they were pushing farther out, biting hungrily with their sharp-edged beaks at the parent's flesh.

And meanwhile, a second pouch on the necklace was steadily beginning to swell . . .

"I'm afraid they won't settle for that for very long," Graves said. "It's meat they want."

"Kallik said that they can survive on other food—if they have to." Birdie hoped he sounded more optimistic than he felt.

Graves nodded. "But they don't see any reason why they *should*. We have to change that, if we can." He began to ease his way quietly over to Kallik. The site of the Hymenopt's lost limb had already sealed, and the bud of new growth was peeping through.

"We've been waiting for over five hours now," Graves said as soon as he was close enough for her to hear his whisper. "How long before they do something new?"

As he spoke, Graves saw Birdie Kelly's reproachful look. For the past few hours there had been unspoken agreement that they would not rely on the Hymenopt for *anything*. Graves shrugged in reply. What other options did they have? They could not understand the Zardalu, even if their captors were willing to talk to them.

Kallik whistled softly to J'merlia, then said. "I do not know. They are not discussing their plans in my hearing. However, I see new signs of impatience. There are already more young ones than mature Zardalu, and they are under pressure to find a more suitable habitat. They wish to leave this place."

"Will they permit you to ask them a question, or transmit a suggestion?"

"It would not be appropriate for a slave to do so."

"But suppose that a human were to *order* you to do it?"

Kallik stared up at Julius Graves with bright, inscrutable eyes. "If the Zardalu were told that the human concerned was my former master, they *might* understand if I were to ask a question on his behalf. Or—" She paused.

"Yes?"

"Or they might be violently enraged, thinking that I offer less than total obedience to them. They might choose to kill me, as a being of divided loyalty."

Julius Graves shook his head. "Then let's forget it."

"However," Kallik went on, "I do not think that is the most probable outcome. They know that I am their only avenue of communication with you, and with the other humans. They will not want to lose that channel. What is your message?"

"I would like to propose that I be used as an emissary to Captain Rebka and the others. Tell the Zardalu that I can explain the need for rapid action by the other group, and I can point out to them why the Zardalu must leave this place as soon as possible. I would like you to emphasize that my role in human affairs has always been that of an intermediary between species. Ask them if I may serve in that role now."

Kallik held another brief, whistling conversation with J'merlia. "Wait here," she said at last. "I will try." She crawled away toward the tight cluster of Zardalu, keeping her stubby body always close to the floor and her yellow sting fully sheathed.

"And I thought *one* traitor was bad enough," Birdie Kelly said softly, as soon as Kallik was out of earshot. "You're worse than she is. At least she was *raised* to be a slave."

"You know me better than that, Commissioner. Or you ought to. I've spent my life working on interspecies problems. That's what this is, you know. I can't just sit back now and *watch*."

"So you want to sell out to them, be another slave."

"Of course I don't. But at the moment we're just bargaining chips as far as the Zardalu are concerned. That's not good enough. We have to establish some form of direct communication with them. They need to think of us as *people*—reasoning, intelligent beings, the same as they are."

"*Them*, think of us that way. Fat chance! What makes you think they respond to reason?"

Graves nodded to where a group of midnight-blue bodies had moved to cluster around Kallik. "Improbable, perhaps. But look over there. Maybe it is working."

One of the forms had towered up onto its powerful tentacles and was moving toward them, followed by the little Hymenopt.

In front of J'merlia it stopped and bent down to stare at him with cool, pale-blue eyes, each as big as the Lo'tfian's head. Then it turned to offer the same inspection of Graves and Birdie Kelly.

A soft fluting and a series of clicks came from the cruel, sky-blue beak. Finally the Zardalu rose to its full height and stalked away across the chamber, back to its companions.

"Well?" Graves asked. "What did it say to us? Did they agree?"

Kallik was shaking her head. "With all respect, I think that perhaps it was a mistake to rouse them by asking your question. They say that I am quite adequate to provide all the communication that is needed with humans, and that if necessary J'merlia can communicate with his master, the Cecropian Atvar H'sial. Further, they say that the other group will be permitted just one more hour, to hold a meeting with the beings who control this place and arrange for the Zardalu to leave for a destination of their own choosing. If nothing is done in that time, actions will be taken."

Birdie Kelly glared at Graves. "I told you. A washout! So why did that thing even bother to come over here? What did it say to us, Kallik?"

"Not one word *to* you, I fear. But certainly words *about* you. It told me that a decision had been made. In one hour, the Zardalu will again contact the other group. If at that time no satisfactory arrangement has been made for the Zardalu to leave this place, another hostage will be sacrificed." The Hymenopt gazed at Birdie with dark, unblinking eyes. "With great regrets, Commissioner, the decision was made that you should be that sacrifice."

Birdie stared at Kallik, unable to speak. It was Julius Graves who jumped to his feet. "You go right back there, and tell them we'll *all* fight them to the death, before we let something like that happen." Graves's radiation-scarred face became pale with rage. "Commissioner Kelly is as valuable as any of us! He has as many talents as I do! We won't let them think of *any* of us as expendable."

"With respect, Councilor Graves." Kallik's ring of eyes had turned away to avoid Birdie completely. "The issue was not talents, or who is expendable. You and the commissioner appear to have been judged equal in that regard."

"So what the devil was it?"

Kallik's eyes moved to Julius Graves, still avoiding Birdie. "It was something much simpler, Councilor. The Zardalu young are growing and becoming more demanding.

"You are very thin. Commissioner Kelly is undeniably *better fleshed*."

CHAPTER 25

Birdie Kelly had never thought of himself as a hero. Quite the opposite. When other men went looking for trouble, Birdie was already looking for cover.

But this time it was different. He was the target, and there *was* no cover. He had to do *something*.

Birdie's minor shift toward bravery began as a horrified inspection of the Zardalu, particularly their hungry young. They seemed to be forever peeking out from under the protective umbrellas of tentacles, begging for food. They light-orange beaks were small, only half an inch across, but there was no doubt about their sharpness. They cut easily through any food fragment, even the hardest shells or rinds, and they made the adult Zardalu jump when the infants, dissatisfied with what was offered to them, nicked the tough flesh at the base of their parents' bodies.

After the first morbid fascination of that sight wore off, Birdie shuffled quietly over to Julius Graves. "Councilor, what are we going to do? You heard Kallik—another hour and we're done for. Me first, then all of us."

Graves was nodding, the great bald head furrowed with worry. "I know, I know. We won't let them take you, Commissioner. They'll have to fight all of us before that happens. But what can we do? They refuse to listen to me, or allow me to act as an intermediary with the others. If only they would sit down, and *talk* . . ."

Talk was not what Birdie had in mind. In his experience,

people who wanted to sit down and talk were the ones who were going to lose the argument. What he would have preferred was more along the lines of a nice 88-gauge automatic cannon.

He nodded and crawled back to his place. Julius Graves was full of talk, but he was not going to do one damned thing. Certainly he would not be able to stop the Zardalu from using Birdie as baby-chow any time they felt like it.

Birdie stared again at their captors. His inspection moved from a horrified stare at the young ones to a general survey of all the land-cephalopods.

They certainly had that *look* of invulnerability. But he knew it was an illusion. Eleven thousand years earlier, species who had been trained from birth to believe in Zardalu superiority had risen to fight their tyrant masters— and won. They had exterminated the Zardalu, except for these last few remaining specimens.

There had to be some chink in the armor, some flaw that had been exploited at the time of the Great Rising . . .

It was certainly not easy to see one. Birdie had watched earlier, when two of the Zardalu picked up empty food containers and squeezed them to form rough clubs. Now he wandered over to a food container himself, and put all his weight on it. It did not budge a millimeter. Birdie sat down again with a new respect for the power of those three-meter ropy tentacles. They could pulverize him without putting one of their nonexistent hairs out of place.

So. They were as strong as they looked.

How well did they see and hear? None of the Zardalu was turned his way at the moment. Birdie drummed lightly on the side of the empty food box with his fingertips, producing a light *pa-pa-pa-pam*. No result. A few harder blows with the flat of his hand produced no reaction from the Zardalu.

Birdie stood up, slowly and quietly, went across to the side of the chamber, and began to edge his way around it. The Zardalu were close to the single exit, but on one side there was space for a human to slide along the wall without coming within tentacle range of any of them.

Birdie sidled along until he was no more than a few paces from the nearest Zardalu. He soon reached a point where he could see out of the chamber. The exit led to an open corridor. One mad dash would take him out there and on his way through the unknown interior. He rose onto the balls of his feet. At that very moment the biggest one, the one identified as Holder, fluted a few liquid sounds to where Graves, Kallik, and J'merlia were lying.

"With respect, Commissioner Kelly," Kallik called. "The Zardalu do not want you in your present location. You are commanded to return at once to join the rest of us. And when you do so, the Zardalu order you to refrain from hammering on the food containers. The noise creates unrest in the young."

Birdie nodded. The scariest thing of all was that the Zardalu did not bother to *threaten* him with consequences if he did not obey. *They* knew *he* knew. He was turning to inch his way back along the same smooth gray wall when he caught sight of movement in the outside corridor. He forced himself to keep turning, resisting the urge to stop and stare. His split-second glance had not been enough to identify the individual person. But it *was* a person, and not a Zardalu, Cecropian, or other alien. Someone human was out there, crouched low in the angle of the corridor, peeping out now and again to observe what was going on inside the chamber. And far behind, almost indistinguishable from the darker shadows, Birdie thought he had caught a glimpse of another, less familiar form.

Birdie slid steadily back along the wall and returned to sit by Julius Graves. A few minutes earlier he had been convinced that the Zardalu were hard of hearing; now he was not so sure. For all he knew they could hear the slightest whisper. And even if they could not, certainly Kallik could, and the traitorous Hymenopt would tell the Zardalu anything that she heard.

He leaned forward to put his mouth right next to

Graves's ear. "Don't say anything or do anything," he breathed. "But help may be on the way."

"What?" Graves said, loud enough to be heard twenty yards off. "You'll have to speak up, Commissioner. My hearing isn't too good."

"Nothing," Birdie said hurriedly. "I didn't say a thing."

Several of the Zardalu turned to stare at them with those huge, heavy-lidded eyes of cerulean blue. Before Birdie had time to feel guilty at rousing them to attention, another land-cephalopod, closer to the door, started up onto his powerful splayed tentacles. There was a pipe-organ whistle from the ingestion organ, and the Zardalu headed out of the chamber.

Birdie had never seen anything that big move so fast and so silently. The Zardalu flashed out of the room like a silent specter of midnight blue, one moment there, the next vanished. Birdie heard the sound of rapid movement outside and a startled cry. He knew that the sound had not come from the vanished Zardalu. Those were human vocal cords, the same ones that now produced a hoarse roar of pain.

"What was that?" Graves asked. "What happened?"

Birdie did not need to answer. The vanished Zardalu was coming back into the room. It was not alone. Dangling two meters from the ground, suspended by one brawny tentacle wrapped around his neck to carry his weight and cut off his breathing, hung the kicking, purple-faced figure of Louis Nenda.

"Not to spy." Louis Nenda rubbed at his bruised throat. Released from the killing grip of the tentacle but with another sinewy extensor wrapped snugly about his chest and arms, he was reluctant to meet the gaze of either humans or aliens. He kept his eyes downcast, and he spoke in a low voice.

"Not to spy," he said again. "Or to turn against my fellow humans. I came here to—to try to—*negotiate*."

Kallik was crouched in front of him, half her ring of eyes fixed on his expression, the others attentive to her masters. The leader of the Zardalu whistled and fluted, and its companion's grip on Nenda tightened.

"You were told in the last meeting that you were not to take the initiative," Kallik translated. "You were told to stay and arrange with the being called Speaker-Between for the Zardalu's immediate departure from this place. Are humans too stupid to understand direct command?"

"No." Nenda was struggling for breath. The ropy arm around his chest was gradually tightening. "We held that meeting, just like we said we would. But it was no good! Speaker-Between wouldn't agree they could leave. We can't control him!"

There was a louder series of clicks from Holder as those words were passed on.

"But you suggested that you could. You must be taught a lesson," Kallik translated.

Another tentacle came forward and wrapped its ropy end section around Nenda's left leg. It began to pull. As the limb was slowly twisted and stretched downward, Nenda roared in agony.

"Let him go! Right now." Julius Graves rashly ran forward to stretch up and beat at the Zardalu's lower body. Another tentacle came up and batted him contemptuously away. At the same time, Kallik produced a rapid series of chirps and whistles.

The twisting and pulling ended, and Nenda sagged in the Zardalu's grasp.

"I have explained," Kallik said to Graves, lying winded on the floor, "that humans are quite different from Hymenopts. The removal of any limb would be far more serious in Louis Nenda's case than in mine. It would probably result in death."

Graves nodded. But as Nenda's leg was released, Holder spoke again to Kallik.

"Holder asks," the Hymenopt said to Nenda, "why should your death matter? You were once my master, and perhaps I am trying to serve you, even now. I said that is not so. But Holder points out that the young ones are in need of proper food, and the value of your continued existence is not clear. Holder is sure that you were attempting to spy, even though you deny it. and Finder, the Zardalu who captured you, thought that it saw another stranger, far along the corridor, one that fled when you were taken. Another spy, perhaps, who escaped when you could not? But that is not the issue here. Can you suggest one reason why you should be allowed to live? If so, give it quickly."

Nenda glanced at Julius Graves and Birdie Kelly, then looked away. His face and neck were covered in sweat. "I can give Holder a reason," he said huskily. "That is why I came here. I can be very valuable to you, if you will promise that my life will be spared. And if you don't hurt me any more. I am not able to—to stand more pain."

"Holder is amused by your ignorance and presumption," Kallik replied after another brief exchange with the Zardalu leader. "A Zardalu makes no promise. But it will listen to you, rather than killing you at once. What do you possibly have that is of value?"

Nenda licked his lips. "Tell Holder this. They want to escape from here and get back to a planet in the old Zardalu Communion. Well, I can show them how to do it. Right now."

Another whistled exchange. "Holder does not believe you."

"Tell Holder that I can prove it. In her travels through this artifact, one of our party found the entry point to a Builder transportation system. She told the rest of us about it—explained exactly where it is, how to use it. It's in working order. Tell Holder I can take her there, and they can be on their way to where they want to go. They'll be gone before Speaker-Between even knows they found the entry point."

"Nenda! You can't do this." Julius Graves had dragged himself back to his feet. "God knows, I don't want you or anyone else killed. But think of what you'll be doing if you show them how to make a transition. You'll be putting Zardalu *back into the spiral arm*, letting them run free to start their—"

A muscular tentacle reached out and swatted Graves

across his upper arm and shoulder. Graves cried out in pain and collapsed to the floor.

Birdie Kelly hurried across to his side. While the Zardalu held a longer conversation among themselves, he examined Graves.

"Not broken," he said softly. "A deep bruise. Maybe a cracked collarbone, though I don't think so. Hold still. Don't try to move your arm. I'll tie it against your chest." He glared across at Louis Nenda and raised his voice. "And you, you bag of slime. You're worse than Kallik. You'd better hope we don't get out of this alive. Or your name and Kallik's will be a curse everywhere in the spiral arm."

"Silence." Kallik gestured to J'merlia, who had all the time been crouched close to the floor, his pale-lemon eyes jittering nervously on their stalks from one speaker to the next. The Lo'tfian crept forward to stand next to Julius Graves.

"Help him to walk, J'merlia, if he needs it," Kallik said. "Holder has decided. We are going with Nenda—all of us. The Zardalu will inspect the transportation system. And it had better function as Nenda promises, or you will all suffer." She pointed one wiry limb at the Zardalu standing next to her, where a pale-orange oval was just visible behind the fringe of tentacles. "Holder says we should not try to escape as we travel. The young ones are hungry. They do not mind how their food is provided to them—dead, or alive."

The journey through the darker tunnels of the Builder artifact took a long time. The Zardalu were willing to investigate Louis Nenda's claim, but they were not naive enough to believe that there was no trickery or traps. They went slowly, using hostages to probe suspect areas and inspecting every corridor closely before they went into it.

Julius Graves and J'merlia were made to walk in front, as triggers for possible booby traps. They were closely followed by six Zardalu. Birdie Kelly, next in line, was amazed to see that the newly born were still emerging, even while the blue towers in front of him were gliding forward. As he watched, the bright apricot of two more miniature Zardalu emerged from their birth sacs in the necklace of pouches. As soon as they were completely born they slithered down the rubbery, oil-coated trunk to take refuge beneath the main body, sheltered by surrounding tentacles. Minutes later the little beaks appeared, begging for food. The parents fed them as they walked with scraps taken from the broad webbing satchels circling the base of their torsos.

Louis Nenda was at Kelly's side. Birdie rebuffed the other man's attempt to talk to him. After a couple of tries Nenda turned around to Kallik, who walked at the rear in the middle of the remaining eight Zardalu.

"Ask Holder somethin', will you?" he said. "Ask what happens when we get to the transportation system. Remind her how much I'm doing to help 'em. Say it's only fair that I should be set free."

There was a fluting whistle from the giant Zardalu as the message was translated.

"Holder agrees, at least in part," Kallik said. "*If* everything is as you promised, you will not be killed. If everything is *not* as you say, you should be trembling."

Birdie turned his head. "*You* ought to be eaten, Nenda, you lousy traitor. That'd save the rest of us—because your stinking carcass would poison every Zardalu that touched it. If there's any justice, you'll be the first to go."

"Justice? Ah, but there ain't no justice, Commissioner." Nenda was staring all around him, eyes bloodshot and intense. "Not here, and not anywhere in the spiral arm. You've been around long enough to know that. There's only people like you and me, and blue bastards like the Zardalu."

Birdie glared at him. The damnable thing was that Nenda was right. There *was* no justice. There never had been, and there never would be. If there were, he would not be here at all. He would be back home on Opal, safe in bed.

Birdie made his own gloomy inspection of their surroundings as they walked on through dark corridors and big, open chambers. Even this tiny piece of the artifact was huge and eerily alien. Since arriving here and being captured by the Zardalu, he had been dragged from one place to the next, never having an opportunity to know quite where he was going or why. Now, examining the objects that they passed, Birdie realized that he could not guess the purpose of *any* of them. *Something* certainly kept the place ticking; there was fresh air in the corridors, food in the lockers, and functioning waste disposal units for beings with needs as different as those of humans and Lo'tfians and Zardalu. But it was a wholly *hidden* something. There was no sign of *mechanisms*, no pumps or supply lines or ducting. Birdie had no idea how the artifact functioned. It was depressing to reflect that he was never likely to know.

He was pulled out of his musings when he bumped into the massive back of one of the Zardalu. Ahead of them, J'merlia and Julius Graves had suddenly stopped and turned around. They had reached the edge of a slope that spiraled gently down into darkness.

"What is wrong?" Kallik called from behind.

"It gets really steep down there," Graves said. "The tunnel is narrowing, and past this point it's no more than three or four meters wide. The gravity field is increasing, too. Once I take another ten steps I'm not sure I'll be able to pull back."

"That's all right." Nenda pushed forward through the solid rank of the Zardalu. "Stop where you are. Feel that stronger air current? It comes from the vortex itself. We're nearly there, at the ramp that leads to the transportation system."

He moved forward again, to stand at the very brink of the descending spiral. The breeze from the rotating singularity at the end of the tunnel blew his perspiration-drenched dark hair back from his face. "Kallik, tell Holder we are here. Explain that using the system is easy. All they have to do is walk down and enter the vortex itself."

He turned, trying to move back to join Birdie Kelly. But the Zardalu would not let him through. Instead, Birdie and Kallik were pushed *forward*, so that within a few seconds all the Zardalu stood to the rear of the group.

Holder fluted and whistled.

"They say we must go first," Kallik said. "All of us. Before they enter the system, we must do so. We're going with them, back to the spiral arm."

Nenda glanced over his shoulder, down the curved slope that led to the vortex, then looked back to Kallik. "But I'm the one who brought them here! Tell 'em that, Kallik. Tell 'em they promised I'd have my freedom."

Julius Graves laughed, wincing at the pain it produced in his injured arm and shoulder. "No, Louis Nenda, they didn't promise. No Zardalu said anything like that. You heard what you wanted to hear. They never intended to allow any of us to go free. When we arrive at their destination, and they have no more use for us, you'll learn what their plans for us really are. I am not a vindictive man—a councilor cannot afford to be—but in this case I agree with Birdie Kelly. If there is justice in the universe, you will be the first to go."

"And if there is risk," Kallik said, "then Holder says you will share it. If there is danger down at the vortex, speak of it now. For perhaps with that warning your life will be spared."

Nenda turned to face the Hymenopt. He opened his mouth as though to reply, but instead he placed two fingers between his teeth and produced a high-pitched whistle followed by a loud cry: "Close your eyes! Cover them with your hands."

As he shouted, a small black ellipsoid came curving up in a smooth arc from the dark depths of the tunnel.

Nenda shot a glance at the others. He cursed. Kallik and J'merlia had at once obeyed his shouted command and tucked their heads down toward the protection of their multiple legs. But Julius Graves and Birdie Kelly were doing the worst thing possible: they were staring straight at the ovoid as it passed over their heads.

He could do nothing about Graves, but Birdie Kelly was within reach. Nenda thrust his arm out, a fraction of an inch from Birdie's face, so that the other man reflexively blinked. Nenda held his arm there and at the same moment squeezed his own eyes tight shut. He threw his other arm up to shield his face. The last thing he saw before his eyes closed was a Zardalu tentacle, reaching up toward the oval shape to smash it back where it had come.

The Zardalu was a split second too late. With his eyes closed and one forearm jammed hard across them, Louis Nenda saw the world turn bright red.

He felt his skin tingling in the flood of radiation. He stood and waited, for what felt like forever and could have been no more than half a second. The light level in the tunnel had to be just incredible if so much could bleed its way in past his arm and through his eyelids.

When everything went black he uncovered his eyes. He grabbed Birdie Kelly in both arms and pushed him over to drop to the floor of the tunnel. He landed on top of Birdie, curling into a ball as he did so.

His precautions were unnecessary. The Starburst must have triggered just a meter or two in front of the assembled Zardalu. When the brightness of a supernova flashed into being, they had all been staring at it. Now every Zardalu eye was covered by tentacles, and fluid was beginning to seep past the fine tendrils at the ends. Disorganized whistles, clicks, and moans filled the tunnel.

Nenda's own world was a maze of flickering images, with the red network of veins in his eyelids superimposed on them. But he could see. Well enough to know that their problems were just beginning.

Sightless Zardalu blocked the way out of the tunnel. They were thrashing around with their tentacles, grabbing blindly at anything above waist height. The way back along the tunnel was closed by a mass of writhing, muscular snakes.

For the moment Nenda was far enough away to be safe. Birdie Kelly had pulled free and was crawling toward a niche where the wall met the floor. Nenda was tempted to follow, but there was barely room for one person. If Birdie could

remain tucked into the narrow space and survive the groping
tentacles, fine. If not . . .

Nenda turned to the others. J'merlia and Kallik had
dropped instinctively to the ground in a splay of thin limbs.
The big problem was Julius Graves. The Councilor had
been blinded. He was groping his way farther along the
tunnel, to the place where it steepened rapidly. A couple
more steps and he would fall forward, pulled by the
increasing gravity field past the point of no return and
into the vortex.

Nenda dared not shout a warning. The Zardalu would
home in on his call. He launched himself toward the
councilor, grabbed him around the knees, and heaved
backward.

Graves was caught with one leg in the air, ready to take
another blind step. He fell sideways and to the left, crying
out with pain as he landed on his injured arm.

That was all the clue that the Zardalu needed. Half a
dozen long tentacles converged at once on the place. They
reached for Graves. But they found Louis Nenda.

Before he saw them he felt their touch on his leg, like
oiled silk over solid rubber. He tried to escape by crawling
farther down the tunnel, toward the vortex. He was too
late. One sinewy arm circled his legs; another coiled
around his waist. They tightened and lifted him high in
the air. His head hit the tunnel roof. Then he was being
dragged toward the Zardalu. Even before the pain began,
he knew what was going to happen. The tentacles around
his body and his legs belonged to two different aliens.
One of Holder's long arms had him at the waist, but
another Zardalu at the front of the group held his knees.
They were both blinded, unaware of what the other was
doing. And each was intent on pulling Louis Nenda within
reach of its own beak.

Held high above the heads of the Zardalu, Nenda saw
Darya Lang, Hans Rebka, and E. C. Tally appear in the
tunnel behind them. They each held a flashburn unit. They
began using them to sting and burn the Zardalu from the
rear, forcing them to spin around so that they would lose

their sense of direction, then driving them forward along the corridor in reflexive jerks.

But that would not help Nenda. The two holding him were in the front of the group, shielded from the humans by the Zardalu behind them.

The tentacles began to tighten on his body, pulling in opposite directions. He could not breathe. His lower back felt as if it were breaking. He was stretched, pulled apart by terrible forces. He knew what was going to happen. In another second he would be torn in two. He could do nothing to prevent it.

In his agony Nenda could not see clearly. When something black flashed past him, flying through the air toward the Zardalu, he did not know what it was. He made a great effort and turned his head.

As he did so, the tearing forces on him slackened for a moment. He realized that the flying object he had seen was Kallik.

The Hymenopt had leapt straight out of a crouched position with all the power of her wiry legs. Her spring carried her high in the air, to the top of the head of one of the Zardalu holding Nenda. Kallik's clawed paws dug into the Zardalu's tough hide and held there. She clutched the rounded head above the blinded eyes and the wicked beak.

The Zardalu was reaching up with two of its tentacles, but Kallik did not flinch. The yellow sting appeared from its sheath at the bottom of her stubby abdomen. The furred Hymenopt body moved sideways an inch or two, seeking an exact position. The abdomen tilted. The sting sank with surgical precision into the Zardalu's head, at a point exactly between the great lidded eyes. The abdomen pulsed with a full poison discharge. The sting withdrew. A moment later Kallik dropped free and scuttled back, away from the forest of threshing arms.

The stung Zardalu made no noise, but the killing pressure around Nenda's legs slackened at once. The uplifted tentacles wilted. the great body shuddered, then froze into position. A moment later, the paralyzed Zardalu

convulsed and toppled forward. It narrowly missed J'merlia
and Julius Graves and lay motionless, poised on the very
brink of the steep tunnel that led to the vortex.

And crawling above it, clinging upside down to the
ceiling of the tunnel, came the great winged form of Atvar
H'sial.

The Cecropian remained hanging on the ceiling until
she was past the recumbent body of the Zardalu. Then
she dropped down, clear of the still-motionless tentacles,
and pushed with all her strength at the hulking body. The
Zardalu hung poised for a moment at the edge, then
started away down the slope. Nenda heard it rolling and
slithering toward the vortex at the bottom. It made no
sound.

He was glad to see it go, but that did not solve his
own problem. Although he was no longer being pulled
apart, Holder's tentacle still crushed his midsection and
he was being drawn steadily toward the gaping sharp-
edged beak.

He lacked the breath to cry out for help. Kallik, her
sting sac temporarily emptied, had leapt at the second
Zardalu, but she found herself gripped by a pair of
tentacles. Then she and Nenda were being pulled together
toward Holder's beak.

Atvar H'sial had turned from the vanished Zardalu and
was watching the wild confusion in the tunnel. The yellow
trumpet horns on each side of her head pointed toward
Louis Nenda and Kallik as the two were pulled closer and
closer to the Zardalu beak.

Atvar H'sial crouched silent, apparently inactive.

Only at the last moment, when Nenda was close enough
to reach out and touch Holder's blinded eyes and opening
maw, did the Cecropian act.

She took a glassy ovoid from within her wing cases.
As Nenda was moved into position and the Zardalu's maw
gaped at its widest, Atvar H'sial jumped.

Two hind limbs stabbed at Holder's blinded eyes. That
was merely a distraction, while a forelimb thrust the oval
object deep into Holder's ingestion slit. A split second

after the Cecropian withdrew her arm, the maw snapped shut.

The Zardalu emitted a strange, quivering scream. The great body jerked full upright. The tentacles holding Nenda and Kallik went limp. And as he dropped to the tunnel floor, Louis Nenda saw what no sighted organism in the universe had ever seen before: a Zardalu interior, as it must appear to a Cecropian's ultrasonic imaging.

The Starburst had triggered deep inside Holder. The light it provided was so intense that the body of the Zardalu became translucent, lit from within to reveal the interior organs. A diffuse blue glow shone from the maw, from the beak, from the eyes, even from the lower part of the canopy of tentacles. Nenda could see the dark ellipsoid of the brain, nestled in the center above the long cord of the central nerve conduit. Above that he could make out the shape of the eight-chambered heart, pumping its copper-based blood through the massive body. The Starburst itself was at the back of the maw, a dazzling point of blue.

As Nenda watched, that point of light vanished. Holder became again a tall cylinder of midnight blue, supported on powerful tentacles.

Except that those tentacles would no longer support the body. They splayed wider and wider, to spread across the whole width of the corridor. The torso slumped down at their center, lower and lower, until Holder stretched full-length along the floor, head toward her companions.

Louis Nenda moved out of reach. Atvar H'sial had insisted that the Starburst was not really a weapon. It would not *explode* inside a Zardalu, and it would not kill one. But even without that, the strength of the internal illumination was enough to put the Zardalu out of action, at least in the short term.

Nenda intended to handle the longer term himself. He had promised to take care of Holder *personally*, at the moment when the Zardalu had pulled Kallik's leg off.

He drew the long knife from its holder on his calf. Maybe he could not *stab* the Zardalu's heart, because it sat too deep; but he could sure as hell *carve a way down* to it. And now he knew exactly where it lay in the body.

Nenda started forward. And then he hesitated.

Twelve Zardalu were still active. The burns that Hans Rebka, Darya Lang, and E. C. Tally had inflicted from behind were having the desired effect, spinning the Zardalu round and round, driving the pain-maddened aliens steadily forward toward the steep ramp that led down to the transportation vortex.

But that created a new problem. Birdie Kelly lay immobile in his narrow niche by the tunnel wall. Either he knew that his only hope was in remaining still, or he had fainted. But Nenda, Kallik, Graves, J'merlia and Atvar H'sial were all *in front* of the Zardalu. And even though their adversaries were blinded, those tentacles and beaks had undiminished killing power. There was no way to drive them down the ramp, without the whole group being forced along with them.

And the Zardalu were adapting to their blindness. Even as Nenda watched, E. C. Tally came within inches of being swept up by a thrashing, powerful arm.

The embodied computer was in awful physical shape, and he should not have been in the battle at all. He was weaving and staggering, one leg dragging useless as he moved. He stepped close to one of the Zardalu, giving it a maximum intensity burn and forcing it to move, then tottering backwards. But a sweeping arm missed him by only a split-second.

Nenda swore and put away his knife.

Pleasure deferred, not pleasure denied. He'd get Holder later.

It was not safe to speak, but he stood up, braving the forest of waving tentacles. He gestured to Hans Rebka. When the other finally noticed him, he pointed at Graves and the others in his group, and then to the tunnel behind them.

Rebka nodded. He understood the problem. Nenda and the rest were penned in by the Zardalu. He patted the flashburn unit he was holding. Should they stop driving the Zardalu forward?

But they might begin to recover their sight at any time. Rebka and the others had to keep harassing them, to drive them over the brink before they knew of the danger.

Nenda shook his head. He made the gesture of firing a flashburn unit, and shrugged. *Keep on burning them. We'll have to find the solution here for ourselves.*

Rebka nodded again. He raised a clenched fist in encouragement, stepped closer to one of the turning Zardalu, and burned its eye.

Sound thinking. Make sure they stay blind. But Nenda did not have time to watch.

He made a split-second inventory of the rest of his group. Atvar H'sial could take care of herself, better than anyone. Kallik was missing a limb, but the wound was already sealed. To a Hymenopt it was no more than a minor inconvenience. She'd be all right. No time to worry about J'merlia, either, he'd follow Atvar H'sial's lead. Birdie Kelly was as safe as anyone, provided that he did not move.

Which left Julius Graves: blinded, battered, and bloody useless.

Nenda cursed. Typical of a councilor, to jump in and do something stupid when he did not know what was really going on. And to hand out orders into the bargain. Nenda had felt like kicking him for sticking his nose in, back in the other chamber when he was trying to lure the Zardalu to the transportation vortex and Graves had insisted on becoming involved.

He resisted the urge to roll the feebly moving Graves down the steep tunnel and be rid of him. There was always the chance that Rebka or Darya Lang might see him do it.

What was the answer?

Nenda felt the touch of a tentacle on his back. He jumped clear and looked around. In the moment he had been wondering what to do, the Zardalu had been driven a foot closer by Rebka and the others. Four feet more, and escape from those killing arms would be impossible.

He ran to J'merlia and Kallik's side, pointing up to the tunnel ceiling and waving them on. Without waiting to see the results he moved to Atvar H'sial, placing himself right under the dark-red carapace.

"Graves." He pointed, though it was unnecessary with a pheromonal message. "The ceiling. Can you?"

Atvar H'sial nodded. "I can. If he is unconscious."

Which he was not. Not yet. Nenda moved over to Julius Graves and delivered a rabbit punch to the back of the councilor's neck, knocking him cold.

Atvar H'sial picked up the body easily in two mid-limbs and began to climb up the wall to the corridor ceiling. Nenda saw that J'merlia and Kallik were already there. They were hanging upside down, waiting for a good moment to hurry over the heads of the maddened Zardalu.

Which left only one problem. How was *he* going to get away? The Zardalu completely blocked the corridor, higher than his head. Crawling along ceilings was easy enough for bugs, impossible for him.

He could see only one answer. It was one that did not appeal at all.

Better do it now before you decide you can't face it, he told himself.

Nenda moved to the prostrate body of Holder. As the other Zardalu groped for him he forced his way headfirst into the thick tangle of Holder's limbs. The space between the base of the tentacles was scarcely as wide as his body. There was a throat-clutching smell of musk and ammonia. Nenda shivered at the greasy touch of Zardalu flesh on his face. He could not do it this way; he would choke before he was halfway. He clumsily turned around to move in feet first.

Push. A bit farther. Do it. Don't think of where you're going.

He forced himself on until he was completely hidden. His legs were cramped against the bottom of Holder's torso. The lower body sac felt soft and unprotected. Maybe that was the point of vulnerability for the Zardalu, something that had been known in the Great Rising and then forgotten.

Nenda dismissed the thought. He could not use the information, while if Holder were to become conscious now . . .

Don't think of that, either. There was plenty else to worry about. The pain of his twisted limbs and bruised middle made him gasp when he moved—although ten seconds earlier he had been too busy to notice it.

Think *positive*. Think we're *winning*.

Maybe they were. The sounds of the fight above and about him continued. He heard the sizzle of flashburn units on Zardalu flesh, whistles and clicks of pain, the pounding of enraged tentacles against walls and floor. Powerful tentacles slapped against Holder's body.

And then he heard a new sound. It was a human being in final agony.

He risked pressing his face to the space between two tentacles and peered out.

E. C. Tally's failing body had been too slow. A Zardalu had him in four of its python arms. Hans Rebka and Darya were there, running in dangerously close to burn the eyes and the maw.

To no effect. The Zardalu was filled with its own rage and blood lust. It was slowly pulling Tally apart. As Nenda watched both arms were plucked free, then the legs, one by one. They went into the body pouch—even in the middle of battle, food for ravenous Zardalu young would not be wasted. Finally the bloody stump of torso was hurled away, to smash against the corridor wall. The top of the skull flew loose, to be cracked like an eggshell a moment later by a threshing Zardalu tentacle.

Nenda pulled his head back. There was nothing to be done for Tally. At least Atvar H'sial and the others must have made it across the ceiling to the relative safety of the higher corridor level, for there was no sign of them. He had to lie low a while longer, as Lang and Rebka tried to push the disoriented Zardalu the final few meters. He looked out along the line of Holder's tentacles. Just three steps more, and they would be on the ramp to the vortex, right on the point of no return.

The stab of agony in his right thumb was so unexpected that for a moment Nenda had no idea what was happening. The half-muffled cry squeezed out of him was shock more than pain.

He lifted his hand. Clinging to it, its beak firmly set in the bleeding flesh, was a young Zardalu. As Nenda watched it swallowed a piece from the base of his thumb. In the same motion it snapped for another bite.

He smacked the creature away with his other hand and stared around him. Now that he could see better in the shade of the sheltering tentacles, he could make out four small rounded shapes, pale apricot against the blue of the unconscious parent.

The Starburst had been enough to knock out Holder, but the offspring were far from quiet. All the other infants were crawling single-mindedly toward him.

"Not today, Junior. Try a bit of this." Nenda grabbed them as they came and held them one after another to the underside of the adult Zardalu's tentacles. After a moment's hesitation they attacked the tough flesh with their sharp beaks. Holder's body began to twitch.

Nenda cursed his own stupidity. How dumb could you get? He ought to have let them keep on at him, rather than risk waking the unconscious adult.

He groped for the black satchel at his side, opened it, and pulled out random bits of food. It was his reserve supply, but if Holder woke up now Louis Nenda would never need food again.

The young Zardalu grabbed the fragments eagerly. Cannibalism was not apparently their first preference.

Holder's body rolled suddenly to the left. Nenda froze in horror. Then he realized that none of the tentacles was moving. Something was rolling the great body from *outside*, pushing it closer to the ramp. The sizzle of flashburn units was louder.

He took another look along the line of Holder's tentacles. The Zardalu were past him! He could see a confusion of stumbling bodies. While he had been preoccupied with the young ones, the adults had been herded forward. He watched them stagger one by one onto the beginning of the ramp, then overbalance and start away down the incline. Once they were on the steepest section the blind Zardalu were unable to stop. They could have no idea what was happening to them.

Going, going . . . *gone*.

The last Zardalu vanished, to cries of triumph from Rebka and the others. Nenda joined in, then realized that Holder's body was still moving toward the tunnel that led to the vortex. A couple more meters and it, too, would be rolling on its way.

"Hey!" He forced himself up from the sheltering tentacles, pushing with his legs and not worrying about arousing Holder. As his head poked free he found he was staring at the startled face of Darya Lang. She was leaning her weight against Holder's body. Birdie Kelly was by her side.

"Nenda!" she said. "You're alive."

"You've got a talent for the obvious, Professor."

"You disappeared. We felt sure they'd got you—torn you to bits, or one of them took you in whole."

"Yeah. Ass first. I just took a rest in there."

"No time to chat, Nenda." That was Hans Rebka, straining on the upper part of Holder's torso. "It's starting to come round—eyes opening. Get out here and help."

Nenda forced his way free to add his weight to the others. Everyone was there except Julius Graves and E. C. Tally. Nenda put his shoulder to the Zardalu body, standing between Atvar H'sial and Birdie Kelly. Kelly nodded at him in an embarrassed way. Nenda nodded back and put his weight into the effort to move Holder.

Four strong pushes from everyone, then Rebka was shouting: "Stand back! She's going."

Nenda had one glimpse of a bleary eye, huge and heavy-lidded, opening less than a foot from his face. Then the last Zardalu was rolling and sliding and skidding its way faster and faster toward the dark whirlpool of the vortex. Holder vanished, the great body twisting around on itself as it entered the spinning singularity.

"*It is done.*" That was a jubilant pheromonal comment from Atvar H'sial, straightening up. "Exactly as we planned it. And yet you appear less than content."

Nenda bent over, rubbing his sore hand at his sore legs, his sore back, sore midriff—sore *everything*. "We did all right. But I promised myself Holder's guts—personally. Didn't get the chance."

"I think perhaps you saw as much of Holder as a wise being would wish to." The Cecropian version of humor came flooding in on Nenda. Atvar H'sial was feeling extra good. "Upon consideration, we were very lucky. My respect for the Zardalu as fighting machines is considerable. If we had met them under other circumstances, when they were not disoriented by their stay in the stasis tanks and confused as to their location . . . I confess, I am happy to see the last of them. The tearing power of those tentacles is close to unbelievable."

"Tearing power! They got Tally! Where is he?"

Atvar H'sial gestured. What was left of the body of E. C. Tally was slumped against a wall, twenty meters away. Darya Lang and Hans Rebka were hurrying back along the corridor toward it. Birdie Kelly was already there.

"He's gone," Kelly said.

But Darya Lang went down on her knees, lifting Tally's shattered skull gently in her hands and saying, "Tally. Tally, can you hear me?"

The limbless torso shivered. The head nodded a millimeter, and one bruised eye slitted open to reveal a blue iris.

"I hear." The words were a whisper from purple lips. "May I speak?"

"For God's sake, yes." Darya leaned close. "But Tally, listen. *We did it.* The Zardalu have gone, all of them, down the vortex. But we can't help you. I'm sorry. We don't have medical equipment."

"I know. Don't worry. *Other* body, back on Persephone. Waiting. Few more seconds, this body done." The slitted eye opened wide, scanned. The stump of torso tried to sit up. "Darya Lang. Hans Rebka. Birdie Kelly. Last request. *Turn me off.* Understand? One week with no sensory input . . . like trillion years for human. Understand? Please. *Turn me off.*"

"I will." Birdie Kelly knelt at his side. "How?"

"Switch. Base of brain."

"I'll find it. I promise. And when you're turned back on it will be in your new body. I'll see to it myself."

A trace of a smile appeared on Tally's guileless face. The first technicians had never gotten it right. The effect was ghastly.

"Thank you. Good-bye." The battered head lifted. "It is a strange thought to me, but I will—*miss* you. Every one of you."

The body of E. C. Tally shuddered, sighed, and died. Birdie Kelly reached down into the skull cavity, lifted the brain out, and unplugged it, then knelt with face downcast. It was illogical—this was only the temporary loss of a piece of computing equipment—but . . .

I will miss you.

The humans around Tally fell into a respectful silence.

That was broken by Julius Graves, staggering toward them from higher up the corridor where Atvar H'sial had put him down and abandoned him. For the past few minutes he had been blundering blindly into walls, futilely calling out the names of the others. They had been otherwise engaged. Now he was following the sounds of their voices. And just when he seemed to be getting close, they had all stopped talking.

Louis Nenda finally went over to him. "Come on, Councilor. The baddies are gone. It's all over. You're safe to join the party."

Graves peered at him, seeing nothing. "Louis Nenda? I think I owe you an apology. We all do. You *planned* this, didn't you?"

"Not just me. Me an' At an' Lang an' Rebka. We were all in it."

"But you had the most dangerous role—you had to lure them to the trap. That story you gave the Zardalu, about leading them to a safe escape. It was all nonsense, wasn't it?"

Mention of the Zardalu made Nenda rub again at his sore back and middle. "I don't know it was *nonsense*, exactly. Main thing is, they went into the vortex an' the hell out of here. Mebbe they had a happy landing."

"And maybe?"

"Mebbe they're all frying in hell. Hope so. Hold still." Nenda reached out and lifted Graves's eyelids. He studied the misty blue eyes for a few seconds. "Don't like the look of that. I tried to warn you about the Starburst. But I daren't give too much warning, in case the Zardalu cottoned. You must have been staring straight at it when it popped. I don't think you'll get your sight back."

Graves made an impatient gesture. "That is a detail. Back on Miranda, I'll have a new pair of eyes in less than a day. Tell me *important* things. Was anyone of our party killed?"

"E. C. Tally. We've saved his brain. Nobody else is dead. We were lucky."

"Good. That simplifies things. We won't have to waste time on medical matters." Graves gripped Nenda's arm. "We must act quickly. We have an assignment of the highest priority. Since I cannot see, the rest of you must— as soon as possible—arrange a meeting for me."

Nenda stared at him in irritation. The Zardalu were gone for two minutes, and Graves became as bossy as ever.

He felt a repeat of his earlier urge to roll the councilor down the slope and into the vortex. It would make life a lot simpler. "Meeting? With who?"

"Who else?" Graves tightened his grip and started walking Nenda forward, straight at one of the tunnel walls. "Who else, but Speaker-Between?"

CHAPTER 26

In the next twenty-four hours Julius Graves learned what Hans Rebka and Darya Lang had long understood: Speaker-Between had his own agenda, with its own timetable. He did not choose to appear simply because a human wished to talk to him. They had to await his convenience, and the logic of that convenience could not be predicted.

With certain exceptions, the other survivors accepted that constraint. They concentrated on food, drink, and rest, and they needed all three. But Louis Nenda, muttering that being called a *hero* by everybody was worse than being called a villain, wandered off by himself; and a blind and insomniac Graves chose to follow, prowling the interior of the artifact with J'merlia as his eyes and guide. They rapidly confirmed Darya Lang's theory that the artifact of Serenity was gigantic, equal in volume and living space to the biospheres of a dozen worlds; but only a tiny fraction of that could be attained, unless the traveler learned Speaker-Between's knack of gliding through walls and floors.

Graves lacked that ability. As the hours wore on his agitation grew. He finally came back to the main chamber and joined the others, still restless.

"What's the big deal?" Birdie Kelly asked. He had become Graves's confidant, as well as the official custodian of E. C. Tally's brain, which he carried with the distracted air of a man holding an unexploded bomb. "Tally isn't suffering. Actually, he's not doing anything at all. Must be nice to be able to switch yourself off when things get nasty." Birdie became aware of Graves's sightless glare. "Anyway, with the Zardalu gone, this place is safe enough. Come on, Councilor. Lighten up."

"I'm not worrying about *Tally*. And I'm not worrying about *us*." Graves flopped moodily down by one of the big Zardalu stasis tanks. "I'm worried about *these*." He rapped the side of the tank. "And what was in them."

"The Zardalu? They're all dead."

"Are they? Can you *prove* that to me?" Graves closed his blind eyes and slumped there breathing through his mouth. As usual when he spoke to Birdie, all his questions seemed to be rhetorical.

"I know they went down the vortex," he continued, just when Kelly wondered if the councilor was falling asleep. "But who is to say that they are dead? Professor Lang is sure that the vortex is part of a *transportation system*. She says that Speaker-Between confirmed that, or at least didn't deny it. Transportation systems are not designed to kill their passengers. Suppose that the Zardalu were transported *safely*—and have finished up somewhere in the spiral arm?"

"Suppose they were?" Birdie sniffed. "Big deal! They've been gone for God knows how long, eleven thousand years or something like that, and there's only a few of them left. I'm not afraid of the Zardalu." Not when they're all dead, or thirty thousand light-years away, he added to himself. "I can't see 'em doing much damage in a couple of days."

"That's not what I'm worried about!" Graves's tone provided the "you idiot," though he did not say the words. "I'm worried about *tracing* them. If this vortex is anything like a Bose Network Transition Point, the transition trail decays exponentially with time. Today we may be able to say just where they went. Tomorrow it becomes a bit more difficult. A week from now it's a major task, and in a month it's impossible no matter what technology you have available. The Zardalu could be tucked away where no one can find them. What do you say to *that*?"

Birdie was saved from saying anything by the return of Louis Nenda. That reluctant hero nodded coldly at Graves and Kelly and went over to the food-supply cabinets. He had a second satchel slung at his side, far bigger than his usual black one. He had made it, and a crude jacket, from webbing left behind by the Zardalu. He was packing the satchel and the jacket pockets with enough food for a week.

"Wish we had a way to *heat* this," he grunted. "Cold food is lousy." He turned to Graves. "Your buddy's back, you know. Over in the next room but one."

"Buddy?"

"Old moan-'n'-groan. Speaker-Between."

Graves was on his feet at once. "What is he doing there?" But he did not wait for an answer. He was blundering out of the chamber, shouting to Lang and Rebka, who were deep in private conversation. "Professor! Captain! He is here. Now is our chance."

"Chance for what?" Hans Rebka had been busy telling age-old lies to Darya Lang, with her thorough approval. But again Graves did not wait for an answer. He allowed Nenda to lead him through the nearest chambers, while the rest of the group followed at their own pace.

Nenda's statement had been partly true. The Builder construct was *half*-visible, just the tail and lower part of the silver body. The upper part was presumably there, but it was hidden by the ceiling of the room, fifteen meters above their heads.

Graves listened to Nenda's description in total frustration. "But if he's stuck up there, how the devil am I supposed to—"

"Easy." Nenda nodded to Kallik, who had entered with Atvar H'sial and J'merlia. "Go get 'em."

The Hymenopt crouched on seven limbs—the lost eighth was regrowing fast, and nearly a foot long—and sprang straight up. She grabbed and swung on Speaker-

Between's barbed tail. After a few seconds, they both began to descend.

"The Zardalu are gone." Graves started to speak even before Speaker-Between's flower-petal head was fully in view. "But it is of paramount importance that we follow them—at once!"

"If you would kindly release my tail . . ." The silver pentagon turned slowly to face Graves. "Your request cannot be fulfilled. The Zardalu indeed are gone. I therefore judge that they are losers. You were able to defeat and banish them. But the evaluation is not yet over. Is it necessary to remind you that there can be only one species judged fit to work with the Builders? I would be derelict in my own duties should I halt this evaluation before it is complete."

"You do not understand. Can you guarantee that the Zardalu were all killed when they entered the vortex?"

"One moment." Speaker-Between coalesced to a sphere, then just as rapidly rippled back to form the horned and tailed chimera. "That question is not easy to answer," he said when he was fully reconstructed. "The Zardalu suffered an unstructured transition. It is not one that is highly forbidden, and therefore it is not inevitably fatal. The Zardalu *could* have survived it. They *may* be alive. They *may* be all dead. What is the relevance of the question?"

"To you, perhaps very little. To us, and to all intelligences of the spiral arm, it is very great. If there is a chance that the Zardalu survive, it is imperative that we return to alert our fellows."

"Imperative to whom? It is not imperative to me, or to my masters." Speaker-Between floated toward Julius Graves, settling close enough for the councilor to reach out and touch him. "You do not appear to understand. There is no technical difficulty in returning you to your homes, or to any location in the spiral arm or out of it; and it may be possible to determine where the Zardalu went, though that is less sure. But those issues are academic. I say again, *the selection procedure is not complete.* There remain both humans and Cecropians. Until only one remains, it is not permitted for you to leave."

"Hopeless." Graves turned to the others. "Totally hopeless. I have worked with a score of intelligences, through the whole of the spiral arm, but with this—this silver *bubble-brain* there can be no meeting of minds, no basis for negotiation."

"Mebbe. And mebbe not." Louis Nenda glanced around at the others. "D'you agree with the councilor? Nothin' to lose, nothin' to gain? 'Cause if you do, mind if I take a shot?"

"Go ahead." Hans Rebka had a little grin on his face. "Try your thing."

"All right." Nenda walked over to stand right in front of Speaker-Between. "The selection procedure isn't over, you say. I'll buy that. But the Zardalu are out of it, so it's just between two species. Cecropians, and humans. Right?"

"That is a correct conclusion."

"And it doesn't matter *how many* humans and Cecropians fight it out, does it? You were quite happy to leave us to tackle fourteen Zardalu, even though there were only a handful of humans, and a couple of aliens."

"In our experience, the number of entities is rarely the deciding factor."

"Fair enough. So the selection could be done just as well if there was only *one of each*—one human, and one Cecropian?"

"That is wholly reasonable."

"All right, then. So what's the point of keeping this whole crazy roster? Let the rest go—and *keep just two of us*. Me and Atvar H'sial. We'll fight it out between us."

"*No.*" Graves was shaking his head violently. "That is a sacrifice that I will not ask of anyone. To leave you here, while the rest of us return to safety, it would be—"

"Hey, what do you mean, *safety*? Goin' back is different for me and At than for the rest of you. Look what happens to us when we get there. We're charged with serious crimes the minute we hit civilization, and next thing you know we're jailed or brain-wiped. Not much fun in that."

"I am the person who brought those charges." Graves's skeletal face bore an expression of anguish. "I will petition to have them dropped. After what you and Atvar H'sial did, to save us from the Zardalu—"

"You can *petition*, sure you can. Maybe that'll get us off the hook. But maybe it won't. Seems to me, At and yours truly ain't much worse off *here* than we are *there*. For the rest of you, it's a different story. You get to go back home, and write your nice little reports on everything that happened. Chase the Zardalu, too, if there's time left over and they didn't fly ass-over-tentacle up their own wazoo. But *me*." He shrugged.

The flower head was nodding. "Your internal disputes are not germane to my decision. However, the proposal you make is acceptable. If one human and one Cecropian remain to complete the selection process, the rest may return to the spiral arm. It can be to your most recent departure point, or to any other place of your choosing. If you wish it, and if I can ascertain it, your destination can even be the final arrival point of the Zardalu— assuming that location is able to support life."

"No, thanks." Rebka cut off discussion, just as Graves was about to start up again. "We have to warn other people before we start chasing. We'll go back to somewhere safe."

He turned to Louis Nenda. "As for you . . . I don't usually find it hard to know what to say. But you've got me this time. All I can think of is, thanks—from all of us. And pass that thank-you on to Atvar H'sial."

Nenda grinned. "I will, in a minute. First I've got to explain to At what she just volunteered for."

Graves stared at him pop-eyed. "You *are* joking, aren't you? Atvar H'sial already gave her approval for your proposal."

"Sure. Sure I'm joking." Nenda was turning casually away. "Don't worry about it. No problem."

But Kallik was stepping forward. "So it is settled, then. The rest will return. And Atvar H'sial, Louis Nenda, and their loyal servants, Kallik and J'merlia, will remain."

"Whoa, now." Nenda held up his hand. "I never said *that*." He looked at Speaker-Between and Hans Rebka.

"If you don't mind, At and I and J'merlia and Kallik need a few words in private. Five minutes?"

He ushered the other three out of the chamber at once, not waiting for a nod of assent.

"You see, Kallik." His voice was oddly gentle as they came to a smaller room, out of earshot of the others. "You have to understand the situation. Things are different now. Not like what they was, back in the good old days before we went to Quake. They've changed. And *you've* changed, you and J'merlia. I've been translating for Atvar H'sial as we go, and she agrees with me completely. It wouldn't be *right* for you to be slaves anymore—either of you."

"But Master Nenda, that is what we *want*! J'merlia and I, we followed you from Opal, only that we might be with you and serve you again."

"I know. Don't think we don't appreciate that, me and At." Nenda had tears in his eyes. "But it wouldn't work out, Kallik. Not now. You've been deciding your own actions ever since we left you behind on Quake. You've been thinking for yourselves, *doing* for yourselves. You've tasted independence. You've *earned* independence."

"But we do not *want* independence!" J'merlia's voice rose to a mournful wail. "Even though Atvar H'sial agrees with you, this should not be. It *must* not be."

"See? That makes my argument exactly." Nenda reached out to pat J'merlia's narrow thorax. "Listen to yourself! Atvar H'sial says what she wants you to do— an' you start *arguing* with her. Would you have done that two months ago?"

"Never!" J'merlia held up a claw to cover his compound eyes, appalled at his own temerity. "Argue with Atvar H'sial? Never. Master Nenda, with my most humble apologies and sincere regrets—"

"Stow it, J'merlia. You've proved the point. You and Kallik go on back, and start helping to run the spiral arm. You're as qualified as any species. I've known that for a long time."

"But we don't *want* to help to run the spiral arm!"

"Who does? That's what humans call the *Smart Bugs'
Burden*. You gotta go back there and carry it, even though
you don't want to. Otherwise, it will be the Ditrons who'll
have to organize things."

"Master Nenda, please say that you are joking! The Ditrons,
why they have less brains than—than some of the—"

"Before you put your foot in it real bad, J'merlia, I'll
say yeah, I was joking. But *not* about the fact that you
and Kallik have to go back. For one thing, Kallik's the
only intelligent being in the spiral arm who's actually *talked*
to Zardalu. That might be important."

J'merlia crawled forward and placed his head close to
Atvar H'sial's hind limbs. "Master Nenda, I hear you. But
I do not want to leave. Atvar H'sial is my dominatrix, and
has been since I was first postlarval."

"Don't gimme that—"

"Allow me, Louis, if you will." The pheromonal message
from Atvar H'sial carried a glint of dry humor. "With all
respect, violent action is your forte, not reasoned per-
suasion." The towering Cecropian crouched low to the
floor and brought her smooth blind head close to
J'merlia. "Let us reason together, my J'merlia. Would
you agree with me when I say that any intelligent being
either *is* a slave, or is *not* a slave? That those two
conditions are the only two logical possibilities?"

"Of course." J'merlia, once the slave-translator for Atvar
H'sial, caught every nuance of meaning in her chemical
message. He shivered without knowing why, sensing
already that his cause was lost.

"Now you and Kallik," Atvar H'sial continued. "You are
both intelligent beings, are you not?"

"Yes."

"Therefore either you are slaves, or you are not slaves.
Agreed?"

"That is true."

"And if you are *not* slaves, then it is inappropriate for
you to *pretend* that you are, by stating that you must
remain here to serve me and Louis Nenda. You should
go back to the spiral arm with the others and begin to

live the life of free beings. A nonslave should not mimic a slave. True?"

"True."

"But suppose now that you *are* slaves, both you and Kallik; then you have no choice but to *obey the orders of your masters*. And those orders are quite explicit: Louis Nenda and I order you to return to the spiral arm and assist in finding the Zardalu if they are still alive. Thus in either case, slave or nonslave, you cannot remain here with us."

"Thanks, At." Nenda stepped forward and nodded to the Cecropian. "Couldn't have put it better myself." He turned to J'merlia and Kallik. "So that's the deal. We all go back in there now. You tell Speaker-Between and the others that you're ready to go. Right?"

Kallik and J'merlia exchanged a brief flurry of clicks and whistles.

"Yes, Mas—" Kallik caught herself before the word was fully out. "Yes, Louis Nenda. We are ready. J'merlia and I agree that we must return to the spiral arm with the others. We have no choice. We want to add only one thing. If ever you and Atvar H'sial need us, then you have to send only one word, *Come*, and we will hasten to your side."

The Hymenopt touched her black round head to the floor for a fraction of a second, then stood fully upright. She and J'merlia began to walk, without permission, from the chamber.

"And we will come *joyfully*," she added.

"Joyfully," J'merlia repeated. "A human or a Cecropian may find this hard to understand—but there is no pleasure in *enforced* freedom."

CHAPTER 27

All set.

But Birdie Kelly was going mad with frustration.

Everything had been ready for hours. The descending ramp to a new transportation vortex sat waiting in the next chamber, close enough for the airflow around the spinning singularity to be felt on skin and exoskeletons. Speaker-Between had assured the group that the system was prepared to receive them, with an assured safe destination. It would transfer to Midway Station, halfway between the planets of Quake and Opal; a perfect location from Birdie's point of view, since it was the last place in the spiral arm where the Zardalu were likely to have arrived.

But now, at the very last moment, everyone seemed to be having second thoughts about going at all.

"If I had one more opportunity to *reason* with Speaker-Between, I feel sure I could persuade him of the unsound basis for the Builders' plan." That was Steven Graves, talking with Hans Rebka. Julius, unable to handle the idea of leaving Louis Nenda and Atvar H'sial to their uncertain fate, had abandoned the field to his interior mnemonic twin. Steven had been making the most of his opportunity.

"It stands to reason," he went on, "that many races working *cooperatively* would have more chance of helping the Builders to solve *The Problem* than any species working *alone*. Humans and Cecropians should be engaged in a joint effort, not fighting each other to decide who will assist the Builders."

"It stands to *your* reason," Rebka countered. Like Birdie he was itching to be on his way, though for different reasons. He was still seeing nightmares in midnight blue returning to dominate the spiral arm. He wanted to follow the trail before it was too cold. "You know that the Builders have a completely different worldview from any species we have ever met. And Speaker-Between is a Builder construct. You could argue with him for a million years— he has that much time—and you'd never persuade him to abandon two hundred million years of Builder prejudice. Give up, Steven, and tackle a problem we may be able to solve. Ask yourself where the Zardalu went, and what they are doing."

On that crucial question, Speaker-Between had been too vague for comfort. The best after-the-fact analysis showed that the Zardalu transition had been completed to an end point on a Builder artifact, probably in the old Zardalu Communion territories. It did not indicate which one, or offer any idea of what might have happened next.

Darya Lang was proving just as reluctant to leave.

"I know *someone* has to go back home and worry about the Zardalu." She was examining a series of incomprehensible structures that lined the chamber, an array of fluted glass columns with turbulent green liquid running through them. "But if I leave, who is going to study things like *this*? I've spent my whole working life seeking the Builders. Now that I've run them down, it makes no sense to leave. Once I go I may never have an opportunity to come back."

"Of course you will." Louis Nenda seemed as keen as anyone to speed the others' departure. He took her by the arm and began to lead her in the direction of the vortex ramp. Ahead of him, Atvar H'sial was shepherding J'merlia and Kallik in the same direction.

"You heard what Speaker-Between says," Nenda continued. "The transport-system entry point on Glister won't be closed. You can go there and return here whenever you like. And when you go to Glister next time you'll be a lot better prepared. *And* you can have a good look at the wild Phages, too."

He reached his arm around Darya and deliberately stroked her hip. "Better go, sweetie, before I change my mind about lettin' you run off with Rebka."

She quietly removed herself from his arm and stared down at him from her six-inch height advantage. "Louis Nenda, I swore when I first met you that if you ever laid a lecherous finger on me, I'd bat your brains out. Now you've done it, and I can't bring myself to flatten you. You've changed, haven't you? Since you went to Glister? You touched my hip just to annoy me."

"Naw." The bloodshot eyes flicked up to meet her face, then went straight back to stare at her midriff. "I didn't do it *just* to annoy you. And it isn't a change just since Glister." His hoarse voice became even gruffer than usual, and he reached out to take her hand. "It happened before that. On Opal, when we first met."

He seemed ready to say more, but Speaker-Between appeared again, drifting up the tunnel that led to the vortex. He seemed oblivious to the strong gravity field, and to the swirling air around his silver body.

"The time is right," the creaky voice said. "The system is ready for planned transitions. However, the trip is much easier on individuals if they pass through singly. Who will be first?"

Everyone stared at each other, until Hans Rebka stepped forward. "I guess I will. I'm ready."

One by one, the others formed into single file behind him. Birdie Kelly, followed by J'merlia, Kallik, and Julius Graves. Darya Lang came last of all, still staring around her at the mysterious works of the Builders. Beside the line, awkwardly, as though unsure of their own role in the others' departure, stood Atvar H'sial and Louis Nenda.

"You may proceed." Speaker-Between drifted to the back of the group.

"Thanks." Rebka turned to look at the others, one by one. "I don't think this is a time for speeches, so I'll just say, see you there, and I know we're lucky to be on our way home." His eye caught Louis Nenda's. "And I wish you were coming with us. Tell Atvar H'sial, we owe both of you our special thanks. Tell her I don't know what you two did back on Quake, but so far as I'm concerned, what you did *here*, to get rid of the Zardalu, and the sacrifice you are making now, by staying, more than cancels that out. I hope I'll see you again, back in the spiral arm."

Nenda waved his hand dismissively. "Ah, we don't need thanks. Me and At, we'll manage. You go ahead, Captain. And good luck."

Rebka nodded and stepped onto the descending ramp of the tunnel. The others watched him walk forward, leaning far back to keep his balance. His hair and clothes began to blow wildly about him, and his pace slowed. Twenty meters along he paused. They heard his voice echoing through to them, oddly distorted.

"This is the point of no return. A couple more meters and I'll have no choice but to go." He turned and waved. *"Meet you at the other end. Safe trip everybody, and bon voyage."*

He took two slow steps, and then a new force gripped him. He tumbled forward down the ramp. There was an audible gasp, a *whomp* of displaced air, and a shiver in the outline of the tunnel walls.

The others peered down toward the spinning singularity. Rebka was gone.

"You may proceed," Speaker-Between said.

"Yeah," Birdie Kelly said softly. "I may. But I may not." He was clutching the rough sphere of E. C. Tally's brain to his chest like a holy relic. "Come on, Birdie. You've been saying for weeks that you want to go home. So let's do it. Feet, get moving."

As Louis Nenda patted him on the shoulder Birdie took a first hesitant step along the tunnel. The whole line followed, like a slow processional.

"One by one," Speaker Between cautioned.

Birdie was muttering to himself as he walked forward. Halfway along the tunnel he reached some decision and started to run. He shouted as he hit the transition zone, and again there was the rush of displaced air.

J'merlia and Kallik tried to pause by Louis Nenda and Atvar H'sial, but the Cecropian waved them on.

"That's right," Nenda said. "Keep moving, Kallik, don't hold up the line. And don't worry about us. We'll fight things out here between us. Get on back to the spiral arm."

"As you command. Farewell, beloved Master." The rear-facing eyes in the Hymenopt's dark head watched Nenda all the way, to the point where she was taken by the vortex field. Kallik vanished in silence, followed a few seconds later by a shivering J'merlia.

Julius Graves refused to be hurried. He paused in front of Louis Nenda and shook his hand. "Good luck. If you do succeed in returning, you can be sure of one thing. Whatever you did at Summertide on Quake, the charges against you and Atvar H'sial will be dropped. Please make sure that she knows, too."

"Appreciate it, Councilor." Nenda shook Graves's hand vigorously. "I'll tell her. And don't worry about us. We'll get by."

"You are a very brave man." The misty-blue eyes stared sightless into Nenda's dark ones. "You make me proud to be a human. And if I were a Cecropian, I would be just as proud." Graves touched his hand to Atvar H'sial's foreclaw and stepped onto the ramp.

In seconds he was gone. Darya Lang stood alone with Louis Nenda and Atvar H'sial.

She took Nenda by the hand. "I agree with Julius Graves. I don't care if you *were* a criminal before you came to Opal, it's what you are like *now* that counts. People *do* change, don't they?"

He shrugged. "I guess they do—when they have a reason to. And mebbe I had a good reason."

"The Zardalu?"

"Naw." He refused to meet her eyes, and his voice was gentle. "Nothin' so exotic. A simple reason. You know what they say, the love of a good woman, an' all that stuff . . .

but you should be going, and I shouldn't be talking this way."

"Why not?"

"Because I'm nothin'. You've got a good thing going with Captain Rebka, and you're a lot righter for him than you ever could be for somebody like me. I come up the hard way. I'm loud, an' I'm coarse, an' I don't know how to talk to women, never did."

"I'd say you're doing just fine."

"Well, this isn't the time an' place for it. Go now. But maybe if I ever get back to the spiral arm—"

"You'll come right to Sentinel Gate, and look for me." Darya turned to nod to Atvar H'sial. "I want to say good luck to her, too, but that's stupid. I know only one of you can win, and I hope it's you, Louis. I have to go now—before I make a complete fool of myself. The rest of them will be waiting at the other end. I mustn't stay longer."

She reached out to take his face between her hands, leaned down, and kissed him on the lips. "Thanks, for everything. And don't think of this as good-bye. We'll meet again, I just know we will."

"Hope so." Nenda reached out and patted her again on the curve of her hip. He grinned. "This sure feels like unfinished business. Take care of yourself, Darya. And stay sassy."

She walked away from him along the ramp, turning to smile and wave as she went. There was a moment when she stood motionless, with the vortex blowing her hair into a cloudy chaos around her head. Then she took one more step and spun away down to the singularity. There was the usual explosion of displaced air. She did not cry out.

Nenda and Atvar H'sial stood staring after her.

"It is finished," Speaker-Between said from behind them. "I will receive confirmation when they reach their destination. And now—for you it begins. You must continue, human and Cecropian, until the selection process is complete."

"Sure thing. You're just gonna leave us to it, then?"

"I am. I see no need for my presence. I will check periodically to ascertain the situation, just as I did when your group expelled the Zardalu."

Speaker-Between was sinking steadily into the floor. The tail and lower part of his body had already vanished.

"Hold on a minute." Nenda reached out to grab the flowerlike head. "Suppose that *we* want to contact *you*?"

"Until one of you triumphs over the other, there can be no reason for me to talk to you. A warning: Do not seek to escape using the transportation system. You will not be accepted by it. In case of need, however, I will tell you a way to reach me. Activate one of the stasis tanks. That fact will be drawn to my attention . . ." The stem was sinking, until only the head itself was left. It nodded, at floor level. "This is farewell—to *one* of you. I do not expect to see both of you again."

Speaker-Between disappeared. Atvar H'sial and Louis Nenda stared at each other for a full minute.

"Has he gone?" The pheromonal message diffused across to Nenda.

"I think so. Give it a few more seconds, though." And then, when another half minute had passed, he said, "We oughta start right now, but we haven't had a chance to talk for a while. What do you think?"

"I think that something new and unprecedented has happened to the iconoclastic Louis Nenda." The pheromones were full of mockery. "I did not understand your spoken interaction with the female, but I could monitor your body chemistry. There was *emotion* there—and genuine sentiment. A grave weakness, and one that may prove your undoing."

"No way." Nenda snorted "You were reading me wrong, dead wrong. It's an old human saying: Always leave 'em hot, someday it may pay off. That's all I was doing."

"I was *not* reading you wrong, Louis Nenda. and I remain unpersuaded."

"Hey, you didn't hear *her*. She was all ready to change her mind and stay—I could see it in her eyes. I couldn't have that, her stickin' around and poking her nose in. I *had* to make her realize how noble I was, see, remainin' here like this, because then she couldn't stay, too, without making me look less like Mr. Wonderful. Anyway I don't want to talk about that. Let's drop it an' get right to the real stuff."

"One moment more. I may accept that you were not deceiving me concerning your feelings for the woman, Darya Lang—accept it *someday*, if not yet. But I know you were seeking to deceive me, and everyone else, on another matter."

"Deceive you? What are you talkin' about?"

"Please, Louis. I am not a larval form, or a human innocent. If I inspected the Zardalu and their equipment with ultrasonic signals, is it likely I would do less for you? Let us discuss the contents of your satchel—the small one. Open it, if you please."

"Hey, I was goin' to show you anyway, soon as the rest was gone. You don't think I'd try an' keep it from you, do you? We both know that wouldn't work for more than a minute."

"I knew that you could not *succeed* in doing so. It is good to hear that you did not intend to try." Atvar H'sial turned the yellow trumpets of her hearing organs to Nenda as he crouched down to open the little satchel that accompanied him everywhere.

After a few moments a pale-apricot head peeped out.

Atvar H'sial released the chemical equivalent of a sigh. "Louis Nenda, I *knew* of this, minutes after the last adult Zardalu vanished into the vortex. Where did you get it?"

"Little bugger bit me, when I was hiding inside Holder." Nenda peered into the satchel, careful to keep clear of the young Zardalu's questing beak. "Greedy little devil, that's for sure—eaten every last scrap of food I stuck in there."

"But you did not have to take and hide it. What act of folly is this, to keep in your possession a member of the spiral arm's most dangerous life-form? It can be of no use to you in the struggle here."

"Well, you don't seem too upset. Look at it this way. If the other Zardalu are all *alive*, then one more won't make a bit of difference. An' if the others are all *dead*, one surviving specimen would be absolutely priceless to anybody who got back home. Think of it, At."

"I did think of it—long since." The Cecropian reached out a forelimb and picked up the infant Zardalu. It wriggled furiously in her grasp. "And I agreed with you; otherwise I would have made my own thoughts known." She watched the writhing orange form. "It is alive, and obviously healthy. Apparently the Zardalu idea that their young need meat in order to thrive has no validity."

"Or maybe with no meat they grown up less vicious. That'd be nice. So you agree—I should keep it?"

"At least for a while." Atvar H'sial placed the little Zardalu down on the ground, close to Nenda's feet. "But let me give you a solemn warning. The Zardalu were the galaxy's most feared species. There must have been good reason for that, and our small victory over a few bewildered and desperate specimens does nothing to gainsay it. Remember, in a couple of years this infant will be big enough to tear you apart and eat you."

"Mebbe. I'm not worried. Hell, if I can't control a *baby*, I oughta be ashamed of myself."

"It will not *remain* a baby. And perhaps you *will* be ashamed of yourself—if you live so long. But now . . ." Atvar H'sial crouched close to Louis Nenda. Her emotional intensity had heightened, in subtle waves of chemicals. "Now the time for conversation has ended, and the time for action is here. There is a battle to be fought. Are you ready to put your new plaything to one side and begin the conflict?"

CHAPTER 28

"I must reiterate to you the *great importance* of this matter." The speaker paused, and his eyes glared out of the screen. "And although it pains me to add this, I must remind you of your failure to honor your *commitment* and *promises.*"

Darya Lang wriggled in her wicker chair and stared at Professor Merada's recorded image with a mixture of disbelief and irritation. The video signal had been sent skipping across the Bose Communications Network, bearing its MOST URGENT—IMMEDIATE ACTION insignia and her full name and title. Within minutes of her final descent from Midway Station and her arrival at the surface of Opal, the video in her room had been flashing for attention.

"Forty standard days," the speaker went on. "The fifth edition of the *Universal Artifact Catalog* is due for final compilation in just forty standard days! It cannot be completed without your assistance. As you well know, I told you of my great concern and worry when you announced your intention to travel to the Phemus Circle and observe the event you described as *Summertide.* If my cautionary words at the time were less strong than they should have been, it was only that I had your reassurance and *personal promise* that the journey would not affect your schedule for delivery of materials. It is imperative that the Catalog appear on time." The full mouth pursed in disapproval. "And if your material does

not reach me in twenty days, at the very latest, it will be *too late*. The consequences of that will be most severe. I intend to—"

Darya turned off the sound.

Hans Rebka had entered the room as the words *personal promise* were spoken. He was carrying a sheaf of messages. He shook his head, sighed, and dropped into a chair at Darya's side.

"Half an hour we've been back on Opal," he said, "and look at these. Dozens of 'em. From Shipping Control: 'Please explain the failure of the Zardalu Communion ship, the *Have-It-All*, to file a flight plan before leaving the Dobelle system.' From Port Authority: 'Define current location and status of the freighter *Incomparable*.' From Transient Control and Emigration: 'Provide the present location of the Cecropian, Atvar H'sial'—hell, I just wish I *could* provide that."

Darya gestured at the screen in front of her. "I have the same sort of problem. Look at him! What are you gong to do?"

"Dump the lot on poor old Birdie. You know the worst thing about all this? Everything has changed, yet I'm supposed to take all this bureaucratic nonsense *seriously*."

"No, it hasn't." Darya pointed at the screen again, where Professor Merada was still in full spate and shaking his finger out at her. "Hasn't changed, I mean. Three months ago, that message would have had me weeping. I'd have been totally *appalled* at the idea that I was missing a publication date. Now?" She shrugged. "So I miss a deadline by a couple of weeks. I'll get the work done, and we'll still publish on time. You see things differently after you've traveled sixty thousand light-years and had a fight with the Zardalu. *Everything* hasn't changed, Hans. Everything else is just the same—*we've* changed."

"Well, everything *will* change, unless people start taking us more seriously." Rebka slapped the sheaf of papers onto the low table in front of him. "Julius Graves sent a message straight to the Alliance Council from Midway Station, telling what happened to us and warning about the Zardalu. He just received a reply. Know what they did? Ordered him back to Miranda, for psychological examination. And he's a councilor!"

"Is he going?"

"He is. He has to. But he's madder than hell. He's taking Tally's brain to be reembodied, and I'm going with them. Between the three of us, maybe the Alliance will start to believe what we say."

"The *four* of us. I know." Darya held up her hand. "I told you I had to get back to Sentinel Gate and catch up on my work. But I'm going with you anyway. All that"—she jerked her thumb at the irate face of Professor Merada—"is like a shadow world. *Studying* the Builders was all right, when there was no alternative. But we've been beyond the shadows. The-One-Who-Waits and Speaker-Between are real. The Builders are real. The Zardalu are real. We have to make other people *believe* that. And then I have to go back to Glister—and try again."

"Try again, and bring some *proof*. When you go to Glister, I go, too. The whole spiral arm has to know what we know." Rebka shook his head in frustration. "All that effort, and we came back completely empty-handed. No Builder technology, no proof that we went anywhere, nothing but our word about the Zardalu—even the tip of one tentacle would have made all the difference. We went farther than anyone has ever been, and we came back with *nothing*."

"That's not true." Darya stood up, moved behind him, and started to massage the tight muscles of his shoulders. "We came out of it with *us*. You and me."

Rebka sighed and leaned back in his chair. "You're right. We're here. That's the only good piece. You know, I remember looking across at you when the Zardalu came along the tunnel leading to the vortex, and thinking that it was probably the last sight of Darya I'd ever have. I didn't like that idea at all. And thank God it wasn't true. We were unbelievably lucky, all of us."

"*Most* of us" Darya said quietly. "Not everyone."

The mood changed. They both went silent.

It was dusk on Opal, and the clouds had briefly opened. Without speaking, the two of them turned in unison to look up. They knew the direction. Out *that* way, thirty thousand light-years distant, floated the invisible enormity of Serenity. And somewhere within that great structure, lonelier and farther from home than any human or Cecropian had ever been, Louis Nenda and Atvar H'sial were locked in a final life-and-death struggle. No matter what happened, the logic of the Builders decreed that only one of them would win.

I can't help hoping that the one is Louis, Darya said to herself. And I know that Hans would be outraged if he ever found out I feel this way, but I pray that someday Louis will find a way to return.

Do you hear me, Louis Nenda? She stared upward, projecting her thought beyond the stars, beyond the galaxy. *Listen now. Come back. Come back safe.*

She felt it so strongly—surely he would read her emotions. Unless . . . The idea crept in like a wave of cold: unless Louis was dead already.

But that suggestion was . . . intolerable.

Darya brought her eyes down to the screen, to lose herself in the comforting warmth of Professor Merada's indignation.

EPILOGUE

"Tell me, Louis Nenda." The pheromonal message was
filled with quiet satisfaction. Outside the port, the
convoluted structure of Serenity stretched away in endless
arching spirals.

"Tell me this. Do humans have a word to describe the
actions of two beings who are convinced that between
them they can oppose and defeat an entire civilization,
one that is hundreds of millions of years old and of huge
technological powers?

"Sure. We wouldn't be humans if we didn't. In fact,
we have lots of 'em, with all shades of meaning. Fancy
words, like *hubris*, or plain ones like *chutzpah* and *balls*."

"I am delighted to hear that. Cecropians are the same.
We have more than one expression for what we are
proposing to do, but the most commonly used is *Fore-
ordained by the Great Creator*. Shall we proceed?"

"Just one second." Nenda reached down to his feet.
The infant Zardalu had bitten a chunk off the leather toe
of his boot, spat it out, and was ready for another go. He
pulled a lump of hard cheesy material from his pouch
and placed it where the hard bill could bite into it. "There.
Try that, little feller."

The Zardalu began to eat. Nenda stood up again and
stared out of the port at the alien abundance of the artifact.

"It's not just *a* fortune out there, At. It's *the* fortune.
The biggest one ever. And there's millions more cubic

kilometers of stuff we can't even see from here. Once we work it so the Builders and Speaker-Between do what *we* want *them* to do, an' not the other way round, we'll be sittin' on the ultimate jackpot."

"Indeed we will. And potentially, it is all ours."

"Hell, you can drop that *potentially*." Nenda glared at Atvar H'sial. "I don't like to hear no negative thinking. I'm tellin' you, we're a ravin' shoo-in certainty. Like Graves said when he left, it makes you proud to be a human or a Cecropian. You have to feel kind of sorry for The-One-who-Waits an' Speaker-Between an' all the rest of the Builders."

"With reason. Against us, they do not stand a chance."

"Not a prayer. They'll never even know what hit 'em."

Louis Nenda brushed his greasy hair away from his forehead, wiped his dirty hands on his pants, and stood tall.

"All right, let's go get 'em. Poor devils. Supposed to be smart, been around five hundred million years—and *still* don't know that guys like you and me always win."

THE WORLDS OF
CHARLES SHEFFIELD

Reigning master of real Science fiction

"He has the scientific grounding of a Clarke, the story-telling skills of a Heinlein, the dry wit of a Pohl or a Kornbluth, and the universe-building prowess of a Niven."
—Spider Robinson

A scientist of internationally recognized stature, Charles Sheffield is equally renowned as an award-winning author and a master of real SF. Explore his dazzling future worlds in these exciting volumes from Baen.

Proteus Combined   87603-1 ♦ $5.99 ☐

Proteus in the Underworld   87659-7 ♦ $5.99 ☐

In the 22nd century, technology gives man the power to alter his shape at will. Behrooz Wolf invented the form change process—now he will have to tame it.... "Earmarked with intriguing technology, intricately plotted, full of suspense..."   **—Publishers Weekly**

The Mind Pool   72165-8 ♦ $5.99 ☐

A revised and expanded version of the author's 1986 novel *The Nimrod Hunt*. "A considerable feat of both imagination and storytelling."   **—Chicago Sun-Times**

Brother to Dragons 72141-0 ◆ $4.99 ☐
Sometimes one man can make a difference. The John
Campbell Award winner for best novel of the year.
"...memorable characters and a detailed world that
recalls Charles Dickens." —*Chicago Sun-Times*
"It's a compulsive read...a page turner...riveting... Sheffield has constructed a background that is absolutely
convincing, and set against it a walloping good story."
—Baird Searles, *Asimov's*

Convergence 87774-7 ◆ $5.99 ☐
Convergent Series 87791-7 ◆ $5.99 ☐
Heritage Universe novels. "...thrilling and almost reli-
gious descriptions of galactic phenomena, both natural and artificial...if anyone can do a better job of this
sort, I'd like to know about him." —*Washington Post*

Between the Strokes of Night 55977-X ◆ $4.99 ☐
The Immortals seem to live forever and can travel light
years in days—and control the galaxy. On the planet
Pentecost, a small group challenges that control. "...this
is hard SF at its best." —*Kliatt*

If not available through your local bookstore, send this coupon and
a check or money order for the cover price(s) to Baen Books, Dept. BA,
P.O. Box 1403, Riverdale, NY 10471. Delivery can take up to ten weeks.

NAME: _____

ADDRESS: _____

_____

I have enclosed a check or money order in the amount of $ _____

" SPACE OPERA IS ALIVE AND WELL! "

And DAVID WEBER is the
New Reigning King of the Spaceways!

The Honor Harrington series:

On Basilisk Station
"...an outstanding blend of military/technical writing balanced by superb character development and an excellent degree of human drama.... very highly recommended...." —*Wilson Library Bulletin*

"Old fashioned space opera is alive and well."
—*Starlog*

Honor of the Queen
"Honor fights her way with fists, brains, and tactical genius through a tangle of politics, battles and cultural differences. Although battered she ends this book with her honor, and the Queen's honor, intact."
—*Kliatt*

The Short Victorious War
The families who rule the People's Republic of Haven are in trouble and they think a short victorious war will solve all their problems—only this time they're up against Captain Honor Harrington and a Royal Manticoran Navy that's prepared to give them a war that's far from short...and anything but victorious.

continued 🐾

DAVID WEBER

continued ☞

DAVID WEBER

On Basilisk Station
0-671-72163-1 ◆ $5.99 ☐

Honor of the Queen
0-671-72172-0 ◆ $6.99 ☐

The Short Victorious War
0-671-87596-5 ◆ $5.99 ☐

Field of Dishonor
0-671-87624-4 ◆ $5.99 ☐

Flag in Exile
0-671-87681-3 ◆ $5.99 ☐

Honor Among Enemies (HC)
0-671-87723-2 ◆ $21.00 ☐

Honor Among Enemies (PB)
0-671-87783-6 ◆ $6.99 ☐

In Enemy Hands (HC)
0-671-87793-3 ◆ $22.00 ☐

In Enemy Hands (PB)
0-671-57770-0 ◆ $6.99 ☐

For more books by David Weber,
ask for a copy of our free catalog.

If not available through your local bookstore send this coupon
and a check or money order for the cover price(s) + $1.50 s/h to
Baen Books, Dept. BA, P.O. Box 1403, Riverdale, NY 10471.
Delivery can take up to 8 weeks.

NAME: _____

ADDRESS: _____

_____

I have enclosed a check or money order in the amount of $ _____

EXPLORE OUR WEB SITE

BAEN.COM

*VISIT THE BAEN BOOKS
WEB SITE AT:*

http://www.baen.com
or just search for baen.com

Get information on the latest releases,
sample chapters of upcoming novels,
read about your favorite authors,
enter contests, and much more! ;)